FRANZ KAFKA

The Diaries

Translated by
ROSS BENJAMIN

PENGUIN BOOKS

PENGUIN CLASSICS

UK | USA | Canada | Ireland | Australia
India | New Zealand | South Africa

Penguin Classics is part of the Penguin Random House group of companies whose addresses can be found at global.penguinrandomhouse.com.

Penguin Random House UK
One Embassy Gardens, 8 Viaduct Gardens, London SW11 7BW

penguin.co.uk

Penguin Random House UK

Originally published in Germany in two volumes as *Tagebücher in der Fassung der Handschrift* by S. Fischer Verlag, Frankfurt am Main 1990
This translation first published in the United States of America by Schocken Books 2022
First published in Great Britain in Penguin Classics 2024
This edition published in 2025
001

Typeset by Six Red Marbles UK, Thetford, Norfolk
Printed and bound in Great Britain by Clays Ltd, Elcograf S.p.A.

The authorized representative in the EEA is Penguin Random House Ireland, Morrison Chambers, 32 Nassau Street, Dublin D02 YH68

A CIP catalogue record for this book is available from the British Library

ISBN: 978-0-241-69575-3

Penguin Random House is committed to a sustainable future for our business, our readers and our planet. This book is made from Forest Stewardship Council® certified paper.

MIX
Paper | Supporting responsible forestry
FSC® C018179
FSC www.fsc.org

PENGUIN CLASSICS

THE DIARIES OF FRANZ KAFKA

FRANZ KAFKA, one of the most important, groundbreaking writers of the twentieth century, was born in Prague in 1883 to German-speaking Jewish parents. He earned a doctorate in law, and in 1908 he entered the Workers' Accident Insurance Institute for the Kingdom of Bohemia, where he was employed until his early retirement in 1922. From 1917 until his death, at the age of forty, in 1924, he suffered from tuberculosis. While alive, he published the story collections *Contemplation* and *A Country Doctor*. The volume *A Hunger Artist*, which he had been preparing for publication in his final days, appeared shortly after his death. Despite his testamentary instructions to burn unread all the 'diaries, manuscripts, letters . . . sketches, and so on' he left behind, over the next several decades his friend and literary executor, Max Brod, brought nearly all of his unpublished writing – now familiar to us as some of the most influential novels and short stories of the twentieth century – into print. This included three unfinished novels, *The Trial*, *The Castle* and *Amerika*, which, along with *Metamorphosis and Other Stories*, are all available in Penguin Classics.

ROSS BENJAMIN's translations include Friedrich Hölderlin's *Hyperion*, Joseph Roth's *Job* and Daniel Kehlmann's *You Should Have Left*, *Tyll* and *The Director*. He was awarded the Helen and Kurt Wolff Translator's Prize for his rendering of Michael Maar's *Speak, Nabokov*, and he received a Guggenheim Fellowship for his work on Franz Kafka's diaries.

PRAISE FOR THIS EDITION

'Definitive . . . In Benjamin's historic edition, the shape of Kafka's days can be seen for the first time'
New Statesman

'The new volume, in a sensitive and briskly idiomatic translation by Ross Benjamin, offers revelation upon revelation. An invaluable addition to Kafka's oeuvre' *The New York Times*

'One of the finest translating achievements in recent history'
Literary Review

Contents

TRAVEL DIARIES

Translator's Preface: Glimpses into Kafka's Workshop

Franz Kafka (1883–1924) so enthralled the twentieth-century literary imagination that he came to be seen as the representative genius of the modern age. To this day an ever-expanding cosmos of secondary literature swirls around his work. At the same time, scholars have widely acknowledged that this work is too singular and elusive to be subject to any reductive interpretation. After all, how far can analytical methods be applied to fiction that borrows its logic from the liminal space between waking and dreaming? Often writing deep into the night, Kafka explored this unstable and destabilizing terrain in stories that have long been enshrined in the pantheon of modern literature. Yet his vision, idiom, and sensibility did not appear fully formed from the outset. Rather they were wrought and wrestled into being in the same arena where many writers enact the drama of linguistic self-creation—in his notebooks.

Between 1909 and 1923, Kafka kept various notebooks that he called his *Tagebücher*, or "diaries." In the pages of these notebooks, he interspersed many different kinds of writing: entries recording daily events, reflections, and observations; literary sketches; drafts of letters, reviews, and other texts; accounts of dreams; autobiographical recollections; impressions, synopses, and critical considerations of books, plays, and other cultural events and phenomena; descriptions of people with whom he was acquainted or crossed paths, particularly their physical appearances, gestures, clothing, habits of speech and communication; examinations of his own bodily states and symptoms, moods and perceptions, inner conflicts and predicaments; outbursts of anguish and bouts of self-torment; outlines for planned works; excerpts from his reading material; snapshots of his urban environment, his family and office spheres, and the social and cultural milieus in which he moved; sporadic jottings; enigmatic aphorisms; and all-but-finished prose pieces and stories.

In these disparate writings the line between life and literature cannot be sharply drawn. Often it cannot be determined in a given passage whether Kafka is registering a private experience, crafting fiction, or transforming the one into the other. He worked on his diary entries with unvarying literary intensity, revising, adding, cutting, correcting. His impulse to give artistic shape to what he wrote apparently made no distinctions. Kafka's diaries therefore have far more than biographical value. While they illuminate a great deal about his world as a German-speaking Jewish writer in Prague—and as a son, a brother, a friend, a lover, an employee, a reader, a patron of theatrical and other cultural venues, a frequenter of coffeehouses and other establishments, an observer of and participant in contemporary trends and movements, an occasional traveler—they also go beyond our interest in the man and his time: On every page they reveal the writer at work.

My translation of Kafka's diaries offers English-speaking readers for the first time the complete text on the basis of the German critical edition published in 1990 by S. Fischer Verlag and edited by Hans-Gerd Koch. The sole previous English version, first published in 1948–49, is based on an outdated, bowdlerized German edition prepared by Kafka's literary executor Max Brod, who had been Kafka's closest friend, had recognized and encouraged his gifts early on, and—since Brod was the more prolific, better-known, and better-connected writer of the two—had been instrumental in the publication and promotion of Kafka's work during his lifetime. The critical edition not only restores the unexpurgated text of the diaries but also redresses other significant inadequacies, inaccuracies, and distortions of the Brod edition.

Besides omitting or altering the names of and details about people still living at the time of the book's publication, Brod excised texts that could be considered literary works and indiscriminately suppressed passages of a sexual nature. In particular, he removed anything with a tinge of homoeroticism. He also manipulated the diaries in several places that presumably seemed to him to reflect unfavorably on himself or Kafka. Recent scholarship, such as Saul Friedländer's *Franz Kafka: The Poet of Shame and Guilt,* has drawn on the deleted passages to explore new avenues of interpretation. The emergence of fresh, provocative research on writings nowhere to be found in English suggests that the translation of the uncensored diaries is overdue.

By following the critical edition, my translation not only provides substantial new content but also reproduces the form in which Kafka wrote the diary entries. Unlike the Brod edition, which imposed an artificial chronology on the entries, the critical edition retains the sequence as it appears in the notebooks, because Kafka went back and forth between several of them at the same time, without dating every piece of writing. With this translation, English-speaking readers thus have at their disposal a faithful reconstruction in printed form of Kafka's handwritten diary entries, giving them insight into his praxis.

This sense of getting a glimpse into Kafka's workshop is enhanced by certain rough edges in the original manuscripts that the critical edition deliberately refrains from smoothing out, including fragments, however truncated, cryptic, or seemingly marginal; nonstandard and omitted punctuation; orthographic errors, unorthodoxies, and inconsistencies; occasionally awkward, convoluted, and even mangled syntax; repetitions; abbreviations; contractions; regionalisms; slips of the pen; and other linguistic idiosyncrasies and departures from conventional High German. I have attempted to preserve such elements wherever possible in my translation in an effort to give English-speaking readers a feel for Kafka's writing as he set it down on the page.

The Brod edition and its translation shied from this degree of linguistic fidelity for the sake of a more polished impression that might seem less unfamiliar or even jarring in places. Brod's editorial interventions reflect his commitment to minimizing the fragmentary nature of the diaries and effacing the peculiarities of Kafka's language in favor of a more formal, perfected, and supposedly pure High German. This was consistent with Brod's understanding of Kafka's anonymous, impersonal style in his published works. By depersonalizing and delocalizing Kafka's use of German in the diaries, stripping it of Austrian, Jewish, Czech, and Prague German inflections, correcting his ostensible mistakes, and expunging other traces of the immediacy and contingency of the text, Brod refashioned the open-ended, exploratory creative process inscribed in the notebooks into something more closely resembling a finished literary product. To use the terms first applied by Gerhard Neumann to two opposing conceptions of Kafka's posthumous writings, Brod presented the diaries to the extent possible in the guise of a *Werk,* a cohesive and fixed work, rather than *Schrift,* writing as a fluid, ongoing, goalless activity.

By seeking to do justice to the more spontaneous, provisional, and unpolished aspects of Kafka's diary writing that the critical edition brings to the fore, my translation approach diverges considerably from that of the 1948–49 English translation. The former translation appeared in two volumes, the first translated by Joseph Kresh and the second by Martin Greenberg in cooperation with Hannah Arendt. Although the translators—overseen by Arendt in her capacity as editorial director of Schocken Books—drew from copies of Kafka's manuscripts to make a number of modifications and additions to the text Brod had provided—notably, reinstating some twenty entries he had excluded—on the whole they followed Brod's version. The contrast between their approach and mine is apparent from the very first entries in the earliest notebook, a series of fragments, each one separated from the next by a horizontal stroke of the pen. In my translation:

> The spectators stiffen when the train passes.
>
> ———
>
> "Whenever he ahsks me" the ah broken free from the sentence flew away like a ball in the meadow.
>
> ———
>
> His seriousness is killing me. His head in his collar, his hair arranged immovably around his skull, the muscles at the bottom of his cheeks tensed in place
>
> ———
>
> Are the woods still there? The woods were still more or less there. But scarcely had my gaze gone ten paces when I gave up ensnared again by the boring conversation.
>
> ———
>
> In the dark woods in the sodden ground I found my way only by the white of his collar.
>
> ———
>
> In a dream I asked the dancer Eduardova to dance the czardas one more time. She had a broad streak of shadow or light in the middle of her face between the lower edge of her forehead and the center of

her chin. Just then came someone with the disgusting movements of an unconscious intriguer to tell her the train was about to depart. The way she listened to the message made it terribly clear to me that she would no longer dance. "I'm a bad awful woman am I not?" she said. Oh no I said not that and turned in no particular direction to leave.

The Brod edition, translated by Joseph Kresh, renders these entries as follows:

> The onlookers go rigid when the train goes past.
>
> "If he should forever ahsk me." The *ah*, released from the sentence, flew off like a ball on the meadow.
>
> His gravity is the death of me. His head in its collar, his hair arranged immovably on his skull, the muscles of his jowls below, tensed in their places——
>
> Are the woods still there? The woods were still almost there. But hardly had my glance gone ten steps farther when I left off, again caught up in the tedious conversation.
>
> In the dark woods, on the sodden ground, I found my way only by the whiteness of his collar.
>
> In a dream I asked the dancer Eduardova to dance the Czardas one time more. She had a broad streak of shadow or light across the middle of her face between the lower part of her forehead and the cleft of her chin. Just then someone with the loathsome gestures of an unconscious intriguer approached to tell her the train was leaving immediately. The manner in which she listened to this announcement made it terribly clear to me that she would not dance again. "I am a wicked, evil woman, am I not?" she said. "Oh no," I said, "not that," and turned away aimlessly.

At first glance, what might be most striking in both versions, regardless of the choices made by editors and translators, is how disconcertingly unrecognizable as diary entries these notes seem. There are neither dates nor contextual markers (until the mention of the dancer Eduardova, who performed with the Imperial Russian Ballet of St. Petersburg in Prague in 1909, though Kafka doesn't himself provide the points of reference). There's nothing that can be said with certainty to be a record of daily life, no clear signposts as to whether a given entry is fictional or autobiographical, figurative or observational. Nonetheless, the former translation, in accordance with Brod's editorial principles, neutralizes the disjointedness of the text in several ways: leaving out the dividing lines between the entries, indenting each one like a paragraph, adding standard punctuation where it was missing in Kafka's manuscript, and even inserting the long dash at the end of the third fragment so that instead of giving the impression of a broken-off piece of writing, it appears as if the sentence has been deliberately suspended in order to be interrupted by the one that follows. These changes lend the writing at least a facade of continuity, however elliptical the prose may be. In my translation, by contrast, the notes remain as Kafka wrote them, formally discrete entries, partitioned off from each other, not indented, and scarcely punctuated, giving them much more the appearance of stabs in the dark, a succession of aborted writing attempts.

The misleading presentation of the text in the previous translation has further consequences. Take, for example, the sentence translated there as "I am a wicked, evil woman, am I not?" This rendering presupposes that Kafka intended to use the two adjectives in a redundant fashion. In Kafka's handwriting, however, as the apparatus of the critical edition indicates, the adjective *schlechtes* was inserted above the adjective *böses*. By hewing more closely to the manuscript and placing the synonyms side by side without additional punctuation, *ein böses schlechtes Weib,* which I've translated as "a bad awful woman," maintains the possibility that one adjective was meant as a substitute for the other. The reader can as easily imagine Kafka striking the one or the other word as joining them by a comma. Leaving the text open and perceptibly unfinished thus makes it hospitable to all the potential texts Kafka might have written if he hadn't abandoned it, rather than diminishing this multiplicity by producing a final draft on his behalf. While, as a single case, this choice regarding one comma might seem microscopic, the strategy that it exemplifies informs so many similar moments throughout the diaries that the cumulative effect is a radically different version.

In the previous translation, the absence of contractions in the same line—"I am a wicked, evil woman, am I not?"—also belongs to an overall strategy: that of formalization of the language, which is as characteristic of the use of English throughout the previous translation as it is of Brod's editing of Kafka's German. For example, in Kafka's hand, as transcribed by the critical edition, the last word of the quoted passage is *Gehn,* a monosyllabic shortening of the two-syllable infinitive *Gehen.* In his notebooks, Kafka often shortened infinitives in this way, which—like his dropping of punctuation—probably had to do with the natural, somewhat spoken rhythm of his diary writing. This is among the linguistic quirks that Brod erased in his effort to reinforce the notion of Kafka's impeccably proper written High German. Since there is of course no direct equivalent for these shortened infinitives in English, I have instead taken their frequency in the diaries as a cue to use contractions throughout my translation wherever it has felt natural, in opposition to the artificial formality of the previous translation's general avoidance of contractions. Hence my translation of that line reads: "I'm a bad awful woman am I not?"

Another difference between my translation and the former English version is the treatment of the literary texts Kafka wrote in the diaries. Kafka famously penned his short story "Das Urteil" ("The Judgment") in his diary in a single overnight sitting, and then expressed in the following entry the next day his elation about the creative breakthrough this represented for him. In the Brod edition, the text of "The Judgment" itself is missing, and the subsequent entry refers readers to an endnote informing them that this entry was preceded by Kafka's draft of "The Judgment." In the critical edition, "The Judgment" is restored to its rightful place in the diary itself, and even though it is almost word for word the story Kafka later published, there are a handful of variants, and more importantly, the inspired act of composition itself in which Kafka was swept along can be witnessed in, for example, Kafka's shedding of quotation marks in the dialogue as the narrative momentum propelled him forward and the pace of his pen's movement across the page presumably quickened.

The story Kafka published in May 1913 under the title "Der Heizer" ("The Stoker"), which is also the first chapter of his unfinished novel *Der Verschollene* (*The Missing Person*), likewise had its genesis in the diaries, shortly after he finished "The Judgment." It is followed there by the beginning of the novel's second chapter, which Kafka broke off and resumed outside the diaries. Here too Brod substituted an endnote, whereas the critical edition includes the text, even keeping it in two parts in two separate notebooks out of chronological order, since Kafka set down the later part of the text in a notebook that he had begun earlier than the one in which he started writing it.

By translating this (still untitled) draft of "The Stoker" within the context of the freely flowing writing of the diaries, I have been able to highlight its status as a work in progress. For example, I've retained Kafka's varying spellings of New York in this text as elsewhere in the diaries, including "Newyork," "Newyorck," and even "Newyort." At one point, Kafka inadvertently wrote "Georg" instead of "Karl," confusing the first name of the story's protagonist with that of "The Judgment," which he had just completed in the same notebook. Only the inclusion of both texts in their original written proximity makes this intriguing slip visible in the English version of the diaries. Another inconsistency in the diary text of "Der Heizer" is the initial political title given to Karl's politician uncle living in America, *Staatsrat,* which I translate as "state councilor," a term that undoubtedly occurred more automatically to Kafka from his Austro-Hungarian context than *Senator,* which would have been proper to the American setting of the story. But as he continued the story, Kafka realized that the character's title should be *Senator* and switched to *Senator* from that point on. In the clean copy of "The Stoker" he prepared for publication, of course, he went back and replaced all the earlier uses of *Staatsrat* with *Senator,* but in my translation of the diaries as in the notebook, we can see him have the realization and make the switch. This is a prime example of the effect I hope to have achieved in my translation: that of catching Kafka in the act of writing.

To that end, I've replicated the intermittent linguistic stutters and stumbles that distinguish the diary versions of Kafka's literary texts as rough drafts. In dashing off the following line in "The Stoker," for example, Kafka left out the word "of" between "thought" and "him": "And so the cook had also thought him and informed his uncle of his arrival." Since the corresponding missing German preposition (*an*) was inserted in the published version of the story, its absence is part of the distinct texture of the diary draft. By reproducing this absence, my translation differs in the same way from English translations of the story in its final form.

Besides works that Kafka published in his lifetime—including a number of prose miniatures that began as diary entries, appeared in Prague literary journals, and were later collected in his first book, *Betrachtung* (*Contemplation*)—the diaries are filled with literary attempts, incomplete drafts, and false starts. Some fragments, such as several that begin with the words *Du sagte ich* ("You I said") and those surrounding them (see pp. 56–72), seem most likely interrelated despite being strewn among the diary pages in no particular order and with intervening entries. Brod assembled these discontinuous pieces into a single narrative, fabricating an integrated whole and thereby necessarily excluding successive rewrites that contained repetitions while at the same time veering off in alternative directions. In my translation, as in Kafka's notebooks and the critical edition, all the ways that these pieces might fit together into a story with a beginning, middle, and end remain entirely hypothetical. By giving us only one composite narrative, Brod's edition limited the richness, variety, and potentiality of Kafka's diaries.

In my translation, I have sought to convey a sense of the diaries' character as a laboratory for Kafka's literary production. In keeping with this character, I have consistently resisted tidying up his prose in places where it is jumbled in the original German. Among other things, this enables the reader to follow Kafka's own backtracking and fixing in subsequent reworkings of earlier drafts. For example, the first notebook contains six fragments beginning *Wenn ich es bedenke* ("When I think about it"), *Oft überlege ich es* ("Often I reflect on it"), and *Ich überlege es oft* ("I often reflect on it") (see pp. 7–13). The second of these fragments breaks off after a sentence that becomes garbled in the middle:

> I will hear no contradiction to this reproach, since I've already heard too many and since in most of the contradictions I've also been refuted, I include these contradictions in my reproach and now declare my education and this refutation have in a number of respects done me great harm.

Only in the third fragment does Kafka sort out this mishmash of formulations:

> And I voice my reproach to all of them, introduce them to each other in this way, but tolerate no contradiction. For I have truly endured enough contradictions already and since in most of them I have been

> refuted, I have no choice but to include these refutations too in my reproach and to say that besides my education these refutations too have in some ways done me great harm.

While the initially muddled sentence is likely to trip up the reader, its very muddledness also invites the reader to bear witness to Kafka's writing process: Here is the writer in the midst of writing one sentence when he decides that he has actually already begun a second sentence, but having hastily set down his ideas without proper structure or punctuation, instead of making corrections to what he's written, he goes on to start the whole piece over, recasting the passage more conscientiously and clearly in the new version. If as translator I had taken it upon myself to make the first version less cumbersome, the evolution of this particular piece of writing would have been less traceable to readers. So too in the diaries as a whole, rather than giving Kafka's writing a uniformly well-crafted veneer from start to finish, I have opted to let emerge a portrait of the writer making his way—at times gropingly—toward the writer he would become.

Hence my fidelity even to Kafka's outright mistakes, uncorrected by him and retained by the critical edition:

> Besonders die Beziehung *zwischen* einer auseinandergezogenen ringsherum fast in gleicher Breite über den Kopf vorragenden Frisur *zu* der meist zu lang erscheinenden geraden Nase verwirrte. [My emphasis.]

> Especially the relationship *between* a spread-out hairstyle protruding almost at an equal breadth all around her head *to* the straight nose that mostly appeared too long was confusing. [My emphasis.]

Brod considered the prepositional confusion in this passage a mere error to be invisibly corrected. But a sentence that in midflow forgets the grammatical form with which it began testifies to its origin as a direct transposition of the writer's thoughts to the page. The effect of such an unamended text is perhaps akin to that of a previously unreleased musical recording, an outtake or a demo: when the mediation of the sterilizing studio production is stripped away, bungles and random background noise become audible, re-embedding listeners in the original soundscape in which the music was made. The intrusions of such incidental elements, peripheral to a final work but intrinsic to a work in progress, bring us closer to the scene of creation.

In preserving the rawness of Kafka's writing in his diary notebooks, I have aimed to contribute to an ongoing reconsideration of his legacy. After his untimely death at the age of forty in 1924, Brod famously defied his testamentary instructions to burn unread all the "diaries, manuscripts, letters . . . sketches, and so on" he left behind. Instead, as steward of his literary estate, Brod set out on what would become a decades-long undertaking of bringing Kafka's unpublished work into print. To prepare this complex, disordered mass of material for publication, Brod applied a heavy editorial hand. Only in the wake of Brod's death in 1968 did a new generation of Kafka scholars, having gained access to the posthumous papers, uncover the full extent of the interventions by which he had transformed Kafka's fragmentary, unpolished manuscripts into more structurally coherent, smoothly readable editions. Brod's more unified, accessible adaptation of Kafka's literary bequest—particularly his editions of Kafka's three unfinished novels, *The Trial, The Castle,* and *The Missing Person* (which Brod titled *Amerika*)—secured the deceased writer an international reputation far beyond his limited, if enthusiastic, readership during his lifetime. At the same time, Kafka's worldwide reception was shaped by a misrepresentation of what he had actually written.

Perhaps Brod felt compelled to proceed in this way by his decision to expose to public scrutiny materials Kafka had wanted destroyed. All too aware of the perfectionism underlying Kafka's dissatisfaction with much of his work, yet determined to include the posthumous writings as important parts of Kafka's literary corpus, Brod may have viewed it as his task as editor to subordinate them to the standards—as he perceived them—of the published works. Since Kafka's own standards, however, prohibited publication in the first place, Brod was caught in a double bind. Perhaps he sought to compensate for his betrayal of his friend's last wishes by convincing himself that through his revisions he was being true to a higher ideal of Kafka and his writing.

On occasion, to be sure, Brod was also simply concerned with his own reputation. In the diaries, the most flagrant example of this may be his omission of some unflattering and embarrassing lines about himself. In a December 1911 entry, Kafka recounts how Brod returned to Prague from Berlin, where he had given a reading of his own writing and a few poems by Franz Werfel. He notes that a Berlin reviewer called Werfel "far more significant" than Brod himself, and that Brod "had to strike out this sentence before he brought the review to the *Prager Tagblatt* [a Prague daily newspaper] to have it reprinted." None of this appears in Brod's edition of the diaries. Decades after censoring a review of his reading by having the review republished without the part disparaging him, Brod censored Kafka's diary passage about the censorship, simultaneously re-censoring the original disparagement.

Leaving aside such self-interested tampering, however, Brod's editions of Kafka's unpublished writings above all promoted a certain pious myth of Kafka that Brod also fostered in his interpretive works and memoirs: that of the saintly, prophetic genius, whose purity places him at an elevated remove from the world. The later publication of more reliable German editions and new translations based on them has helped debunk this myth, opening the way for the rediscovery of a less sanctified Kafka. The critical edition of the diaries has furthered this steady dismantling of the Kafka myth, bringing to light facets of the writer formerly obscured, skewed, or neglected.

These include a more complicated sense of Kafka's sexuality. Perhaps Brod's elision of passages that could be read as homoerotic has ultimately drawn more attention to them than they otherwise would have received—still, this very elision suggests that these passages threatened the image of Kafka that Brod was striving to construct. In Kafka's description of a fellow train passenger, for example, Brod deleted the line "His apparently sizable member makes a large bulge in his pants." An entry written during Kafka's stay at a nudist sanatorium that in my translation reads "2 beautiful Swedish boys with long legs, which are so formed and taut that one could really only run one's tongue along them" Brod condensed to "Two handsome Swedish boys with long legs." At the sanatorium Kafka stood out among the naked men in keeping on his swimming trunks ("I'm known as the man with the swimming trunks") but finally allowed a new acquaintance to sketch him fully unclothed, as he recorded in his notebook: "Served as a model for Dr. Schiller. Without swimming trunks. Exhibitionistic experience." Brod's version reads only: "Posed for Dr. Sch." In an entry on Kafka and Brod's visit to a collector named Pachinger—in which Brod also cut Kafka's detailed notes on Pachinger's pornography collection and the man's tales of sexual escapades, which seem to display a lewd fascination on the diarist's part—Brod censored the following passage: "On women: The stories about his potency make one think about how he must slowly stuff his large member into the women. His trick in earlier days was to exhaust women until they couldn't go on. Then they were without a soul, animals. Yes this submissiveness I can imagine."

References to visits to prostitutes were also disguised in the Brod edition. At the same time, Brod let some such passages stand. One can only speculate on what struck him as too unseemly in those he camouflaged. Perhaps the single line he excised from the following description of a Milan brothel is telling. In my translation:

> The girl whose belly while she was sitting was without doubt unshapely over and between her outspread legs under her translucent dress, whereas when she stood up it dissipated like theater scenery behind veils and formed an ultimately tolerable girl's belly. The French girl whose sweetness showed itself to the concluding glance above all in her round and yet detailed, chatty and affectionate knees.—An imperious monumental figure, pushing the money just earned into her stocking.—The old man laying one hand over the other on his knee.—The girl by the door, whose scowling face is Spanish, whose putting her hands on her hips is Spanish and who stretches in a bodice-like dress of prophylactic silk. Hair runs thickly from her navel to her private parts.

It was only the very last line that Brod did not see fit to include. Did he judge the passage up to that point as appropriately distanced, observational, and literary, and the offending sentence as too crudely carnal and lascivious?

Brod's alteration of another entry on a brothel visit has broader ramifications, influencing—in connection with the entry preceding it—the reader's understanding of the nature of Kafka's self-reflection in these diary pages. The two entries are from October 1911. The first is a description of the atmosphere in Prague's Altneusynagoge (Old New Synagogue) on the eve of Yom Kippur, in which Kafka is looking somewhat askance at his fellow congregants and finally remarks on the presence of "the family of the brothel owner." He then begins a new entry describing some impressions from his visit to the aforementioned brothel a few days earlier. In that entry—which begins "In the Suha b. [brothel] three days ago"—Brod deletes the name of the establishment and Kafka's abbreviation "B." for *Bordell* or brothel. Nothing else in the entry signals unequivocally where it takes place. Consequently, the mention of "the family of the brothel owner" in the previous entry has been deprived of this retroactive context. Since it is no longer evident that this note refers to the family of the specific owner of the specific brothel Kafka himself recently visited, the previous English translator even replaced the definite article with an indefinite article: "the family of *a* brothel owner." Hence a few seemingly minor adjustments distort the substance of these diary entries. Whereas Kafka unflinchingly implicated himself in the impurity and false piety he found in the synagogue, the retouched text portrays Kafka as judging the other congregants from a loftier, less compromised position. This example is typical of how Brod's editorial choices served to tailor what Kafka revealed of himself to how Brod preferred for him to be seen.

There's a parallelism in Brod's covering up of occasional lapses in Kafka's generally positive and open-minded attitudes toward Eastern European Jews—the same lapses that the diarist himself was quick to register in his own self-examination. Between 1911 and 1912, the diary is full of Kafka's enthusiastic admiration for a traveling Yiddish theater troupe from Lemberg that gave a series of guest performances in Prague. Kafka attended more than twenty of these performances and wrote extensively about a number of them. He also developed relationships with members of the troupe, growing enamored of certain actresses and forming particularly close ties with the actor Jizchak Löwy, for whom he organized a recitation evening (see pp. 195–197 and notes 471–494) and whose stories of Jewish life in Warsaw he reproduced (see pp. 101–102 and note 231). For Löwy's recitation evening, Kafka even wrote and delivered an introductory lecture on Yiddish (see p. 195 and note 471). In his sympathetic support for the actors, he was sensitive to widespread antipathies among Prague's assimilated German-speaking Jewish bourgeoisie toward their fellow Jews from the East, who spoke Yiddish and came from an impoverished shtetl milieu often disdained in the West for its putative narrowness and backwardness. Indeed Kafka's father infuriated him by making contemptuous comments about Löwy, which included classic anti-Semitic comparisons to animals and insects: "Löwy—My father about him: He who lies down in bed with dogs gets up with bugs." (Incidentally, here it's unclear whether Kafka's father or the writer himself is responsible for the unconventional phrasing of the usual idiom about dogs and fleas.) Scholars have suggested that such tropes, prevalent as they were in the anti-Semitic culture in which Kafka reckoned with his own Jewishness, influenced the themes of his fiction, such as Gregor Samsa waking up as a monstrous insect or Josef K.'s last words at his execution: "Like a dog!" And yet, for all Kafka's protectiveness of Löwy in the face of his father's denigration, he records the following moment from an evening with his friend at the theater: "Moreover, L. confessed his gonorrhea to me; then my hair touched his when I leaned toward his head, I grew frightened due to at least the possibility of lice." Here Kafka confronts his own Western European Jewish anxiety about the hygiene of his Eastern European Jewish companion. Brod's unwillingness to publish these lines in his edition of the diaries runs directly counter to Kafka's recognition that whatever high-mindedness he elsewhere exhibited did not necessarily exempt him from reflexive, even visceral prejudices. Brod's edition thus does a disservice to Kafka's inclination to probe these very corners of himself.

Indeed, Brod's downplaying of Kafka's complex sexuality and all-too-human impulses, ambivalences, and shortcomings goes hand in hand with his ironing out of the technical imperfections in Kafka's manuscripts. Brod sought to uphold his conception of Kafka's pure, disembodied mode of writing at the expense of all the ways the language of the diaries is contaminated by vocal habits, by the manual act of writing, by the unruly body. The picture of Kafka that emerges from the uncensored diaries as a more multifaceted, less exalted figure is inseparable from the re-embodiment of his writing.

As an unabridged, faithful transcription of Kafka's notebooks, the critical edition of the diaries represents a decisive break with Brod's methods. And yet I would stop short of asserting that the purpose of my translation is to unveil to English-speaking readers the "authentic Kafka" retrieved by the critical edition. No level of fidelity can completely close the gap between edition and original manuscript, and of course an English translation of an edition based on a manuscript is at an even further remove. Far from reifying the "real Kafka," my effort to capture the provisionality, materiality, and mutability of Kafka's handwritten notebooks relies on drawing readers' attention to the text as an artifact rather than a vehicle for determinate meaning.

This approach is exemplified by my translation of a diary entry from February 15, 1914:

> How long this Saturday and Sunday seem to me in retrospect. Yesterday afternoon I had my hair cut, then wrote the letter to Bl., then visited Max for a moment in the new apartment, then parents' evening next to L. W., then Baum (met Krätzig in the tram "emergency puncture"), then on the way back Max's complaints about my silence, then the desire for suicide, then my sister returned from the parents' evening, incapable of reporting the slightest detail.

The word in the original German that I've translated as "emergency puncture" is *Notstich*. Contextually, there is no telling what, if anything, in the surrounding passage *Notstich* is related to. Within a list of Kafka's doings that weekend, it appears in parentheses following the reference to a fleeting encounter with Krätzig, a colleague of Kafka's, and it is set off by quotation marks. *Notstich* is a compound made up of *Not*, which designates a situation of necessity, emergency, distress, or adversity, and *Stich*, which means a stab, sting, stitch, prick, or pang. *Notstich* calls to my mind something like a tracheotomy, the lancing of a boil, the need to pierce a hole in something—an obstructed pipe, say, or bloated livestock—to relieve a blockage, an overaccumulation, or the like.

But what the word indicates at this point in Kafka's diaries and why he jotted it down is probably unknowable. External research has so far yielded no clues. "Emergency puncture" might well be an inaccurate translation of whatever Kafka meant when he wrote *Notstich*. What I've mirrored in my version is its textual function: "emergency puncture" is intended to be as baffling to readers as *Notstich* is, while pointing to a perhaps at least proximate semantic field. Brod simply left out the word in his edition. An empty signifier—but presumably it was not empty for Kafka. In making a note of something in one's diary, one is not necessarily concerned with its comprehensibility to any other reader. In my view, attempting to match the German with an equally indefinite and open placeholder is less of an evasion than merely omitting the word. Indeed, the term "emergency puncture" in my translation can be thought of as an emergency puncture itself, a necessary perforation in the legibility of the text.

Its very indecipherability reminds us that it belongs to a writer's notebooks: a repository of stray thoughts and paratactic associations, forming a heterogeneous assemblage that may make sense only to its maker. The way Kafka exploited the elasticity and hybridity of the diary form was particularly far-reaching. Therefore, in the absence of any hint as to their significance, I've nonetheless found it essential to include in my translation even inscrutable bits and pieces, however seemingly haphazard, erratic, or disconnected. *Notstich* as an opaque but insistently present written word—a stand-in, perhaps, for the written word itself or for the diaristic act of writing for the sake of writing—is thus emblematic of this undertaking.

A century has passed since Kafka kept these diaries. Their afterlife has consisted of a long, complex, and fraught reckoning with the question of what the principle of fidelity to the original means in this special case. If merely to transfer the contents of the surviving diaries—twelve quarto notebooks and two bundles of loose paper filled with dense handwriting, crossings-out, corrections and insertions squeezed in wherever possible, between the lines, in the margins, drawings here and there—to the typescript pages of a bound book, linear and uniform in format, is to depart from the character of the original, by what guidelines shall editors and translators make the many subsequent decisions that determine their renditions? There's no definitive answer to this question, of course, but having attempted to justify some of my choices in this preface, in the end I must let my translation itself serve as my response.

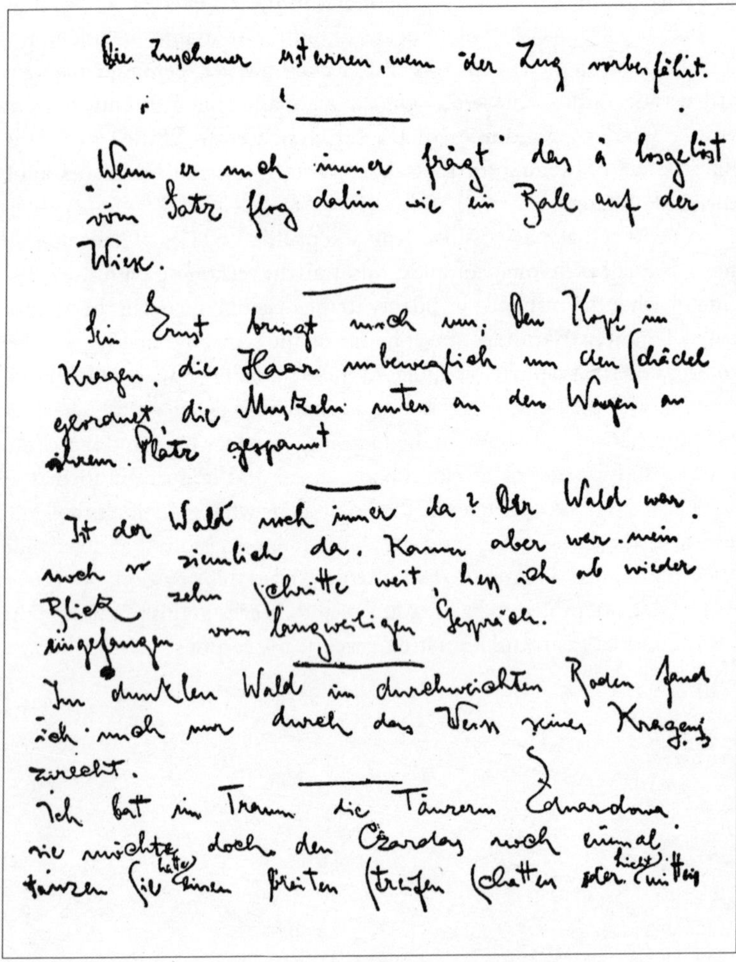
Die Zuschauer erstarren, wenn der Zug vorbeifährt.

„Wenn er mich immer frägt“ das ä losgelöst vom Satz flog dahin wie ein Ball auf der Wiese.

Sein Ernst bringt mich um. Den Kopf im Kragen, die Haare unbeweglich um den Schädel geordnet, die Muskeln unten an den Wangen an ihrem Platz gespannt

Ist der Wald noch immer da? Der Wald war noch so ziemlich da. Kaum aber war mein Blick zehn Schritte weit, ließ ich ab wieder eingefangen vom langweiligen Gespräch.

Im dunklen Wald im durchweichten Boden fand ich mich nur durch das Weiß seines Kragens zurecht.

Ich bat im Traum die Tänzerin Eduardowa sie möchte doch den Czardas noch einmal tanzen. Sie hatte einen breiten Streifen Schatten oder Licht mitten

Manuscript of the first page of the *Diaries*

DIARIES

First Notebook

The spectators stiffen when the train passes.

"Whenever he ahsks me" the ah broken free from the sentence flew away like a ball in the meadow.

His seriousness is killing me. His head in his collar, his hair arranged immovably around his skull, the muscles at the bottom of his cheeks tensed in place

---

Are the woods still there? The woods were still more or less there. But scarcely had my gaze gone ten paces when I gave up ensnared again by the boring conversation.

In the dark woods in the sodden ground I found my way only by the white of his collar.

In a dream I asked the dancer Eduardova to dance the czardas one more time.[1] She had a broad streak of shadow or light in the middle of her face between the lower edge of her forehead and the center of her chin. Just then came someone with the disgusting movements of an unconscious intriguer to tell her the train was about to depart. The way she listened to the message made it terribly clear to me that she would no longer dance. "I'm a bad awful woman am I not?" she said. Oh no I said not that and turned in no particular direction to leave.

Beforehand I questioned her about the many flowers stuck in her belt. "They're from all the princes of Europe" she said. I wondered what it meant that those flowers stuck fresh in her belt had been given to the dancer Eduardova by all the princes of Europe.

The dancer Eduardova, a lover of music, travels on the tram as everywhere else in the company of two violinists, whom she often has play. For it's not prohibited to play on the tram if the playing is good, is pleasant for the fellow passengers and costs nothing, that is, if afterward there's no collection. At first it's a bit surprising, to be sure, and for a little while everyone finds it inappropriate. But at full speed, in a strong breeze and on a quiet street it sounds pretty.

In the open air the dancer Eduardova is not as pretty as on stage. Her pallor, those cheekbones of hers, which stretch her skin so taut that scarcely more than a faint movement appears in her face, her big nose—which rises as if from a hollow—with which one can't make jokes like testing the hardness of the tip or lightly grasping it by the bridge and pulling it back and forth while saying "come along now," her broad high-waisted figure in overly pleated skirts, who can find that appealing—she almost resembles one of my aunts an elderly lady, many aging aunts of many people resemble her. But in the open air Eduardova reveals, apart from her very good feet, no compensation for these disadvantages, there's really nothing that would give rise to enthusiasm astonishment or even respect. And so quite often I've seen Eduardova treated with an indifference that even gentlemen who were usually very adroit, very correct, couldn't conceal, although naturally they took pains to do so in the presence of a dancer as famous as Eduardova was all the same.

My ear felt fresh rough cool juicy to the touch like a leaf.

I write this most definitely out of despair over my body and over the future with this body

When despair presents itself so definitely, is so closely bound to its object so firmly held back, as if by a soldier who covers the retreat and for this purpose lets himself be torn to pieces, then it is not real despair. Real despair has immediately and always overtaken its goal, (At this comma it became apparent that only the first sentence was correct)

Are you in despair?
Yes? you are in despair?
Run away? Want to hide?

I walked past the brothel as if past the house of a beloved.

Writers speak stench[2]

The seamstresses in the downpours.[3]

From the train compartment window[4]

At last after five months of my life in which nothing I wrote could satisfy me and for which no power will compensate me, though all would be obligated to do so, it occurs to me to speak to myself once again. When I really asked myself a question, I still responded, here there was still something to be wrested from me, from this heap of straw that I have been for five months and whose fate, it seems, is to be set alight in the summer and to burn away before the spectator can blink. If only that would happen to me! And it should happen to me ten times over, for I don't even regret the unhappy time. My condition is not unhappiness, but it's not happiness either, not indifference not weakness, not fatigue, not interest in anything else, so what is it then? The fact that I don't know is probably connected with my inability to write. And this is something I think I understand without knowing its cause. For whatever things occur to me occur not from the root, but beginning somewhere toward their middle. Just let someone try to hold them, let someone try to hold and cling to a blade of grass that only starts growing from the middle. Perhaps some can, Japanese acrobats, for example, who climb a ladder that isn't resting on the ground but on the upturned soles of a partner lying on his back and isn't leaning against a wall but goes straight up into the air.[5] This is more than I can manage, not to mention the fact that my ladder doesn't have even those soles at its disposal. That's not all, of course, and such a question still isn't enough to make me speak. But each day at least one line should be pointed at me as people are now pointing telescopes at the comet.[6] And if I would then appear once before that sentence, lured by that sentence, as I was last Christmas, for example, when I had gone so far that I could only barely contain myself and when I really seemed to be on the last rung of my ladder, which, however, stood steadily on the ground and against the wall. But what a ground! what a wall! And yet that ladder didn't fall, so firmly did my feet press it against the ground, so firmly did my feet raise it against the wall.

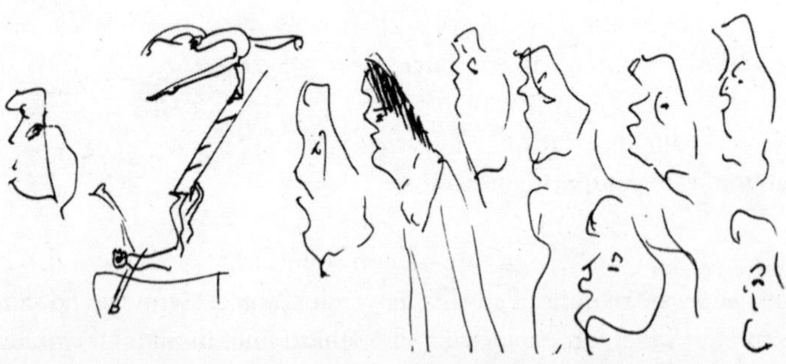

Today, for example, I committed three impertinences, toward a conductor, toward a superior of mine, well there were only 2, but they're plaguing me like stomach pains. Coming from anyone they would have been impertinences, all the more so coming from me. Thus I went outside myself, fought in the air in the mist and worst of all no one noticed that I committed, had to commit, the impertinence as an impertinence toward my companions too, had to bear the right expression, the responsibility; but the most awful thing was when one of my acquaintances took this impertinence not as a sign of a certain character but as the character itself, called my attention to my impertinence and admired it. Why don't I stay within myself? To be sure, I now tell myself: look, the world lets you strike it, the conductor and your superior remained calm as you left, the latter even said goodbye. But that means nothing. You can attain nothing when you abandon yourself, but what do you miss anyhow in your circle. To this speech I respond only: I too would rather receive a beating within the circle than myself give a beating outside it, but where the devil is this circle? For a while I did see it lying on the earth, as if sprayed there with lime, but now it just hovers around me, indeed doesn't even hover.

17/18 *(18/19)* May *(1910)*
Comet Night

Was together with Blei, his wife & his child,[7] at times heard myself in myself, roughly like the whimpering of a young cat, but still.

How many days have again gone by in silence; today is the 29th of May. Do I lack even the resolve to take this penholder, this piece of wood, in my hand every day. I suppose I do lack it. I row, ride, swim, lie in the sun.[8] Therefore my calves are good, my thighs not bad, my belly is passable, but my chest is very shabby and when my head on my neck

---

Sunday, 19 June $\overline{10}$ slept woke up, slept, woke up, miserable life

---

When I think about it, I must say that my education has in some respects done me great harm. I certainly wasn't educated in some remote place, say, in a ruin in the mountains, against that I couldn't utter so much as a word of reproach. At the risk of being misunderstood by every last one of my former teachers, I would gladly and preferably have been that little ruin dweller, burnt by the sun, which there in the midst of the rubble would have shone for me from all sides on the lukewarm ivy, even if at first I would have been weak under the pressure of my good qualities, which would have shot up in me with the power of weeds[9]

When I think about it, I must say that my education has in some respects done me great harm. This reproach applies to many people namely my parents, some relatives, several visitors to our house, various writers, one cook in particular who took me to school for a year,[10] a crowd of teachers, (whom I have to press close together in my memory, or else one will escape me here and there but since I've packed them so tightly together, the whole again crumbles away in places) a school inspector slowly walking passersby in short this reproach winds its way like a dagger through society. I will hear no contradiction to this reproach, since I've already heard too many and since in most of the contradictions I've also been refuted, I include these contradictions in my reproach and now declare my education and this refutation have in a number of respects done me great harm.

Often I reflect on it and then I always must say that my education has in some ways done me great harm. This reproach is directed against many people, indeed they stand here together, as in old group pictures they don't know what to do with each other, at the moment it doesn't occur to them to lower their eyes and in their anticipation they don't dare to smile. My parents are there, some relatives some teachers, one cook in particular, some girls from dancing lessons, some visitors to our house from earlier days, some writers, a swimming master, an usher, a school inspector, then some people whom I met only once on the street and others whom I can't remember at the moment and those whom I will never again remember and finally those whose instruction I being somehow distracted at the time didn't notice at all, in short there are so many that one must take care not to mention anyone twice. And I voice my reproach to all of them, introduce them to each other in this way, but tolerate no contradiction. For I have truly endured enough contradictions already and since in most of them I have been refuted, I have no choice but to include these refutations too in my reproach and to say that besides my education these refutations too have in some ways done me great harm.

Does one expect perhaps that I was educated in some remote place? No, in the middle of the city, I was educated in the middle of the city. Not, for example, in a ruin in the mountains or by a lake. My parents and their followers were until now covered with my reproach and gray; now they easily brush it aside and smile, because I have withdrawn my hands from them and brought them to my forehead and am thinking: I should have been the little ruin dweller, hearkening to the cries of the jackdaws, flown over by their shadows, cooling off under the moon, burnt by the sun, which, streaming through the rubble, would have shone for me from all sides on my bed of ivy, even if at first I would have been a little weak under the pressure of my good qualities which would have had to grow in me with the power of weeds.

Often I reflect on it and let my thoughts take their course without interfering and always, whichever way I look at it, I come to the conclusion that my education has in some ways done me terrible harm. This realization contains a reproach that is directed against many people. There are my parents, with my relatives, one cook in particular, my teachers, some writers, families friendly with mine, a swimming master, natives of summer resorts, some ladies in the city park though to look at them one wouldn't at all think so, a hairdresser a beggar woman, a helmsman my family doctor and many others and there would be even more if I were inclined and able to name them all in short there are so many that one must take care not to mention anyone in this crowd twice. Now one might think that such multitudes would be enough to make a reproach lose firmness, that it would simply have to lose firmness, for a reproach is not a commander, it only goes straight ahead and doesn't know how to spread out. Especially in this case, when it is directed against persons in the past. These persons may be held fast in memory with a forgotten energy, they will hardly have a floor left under them and even their legs will by now be smoke. And some benefit is now supposed to be derived from reproaching people in such a condition for mistakes they made once upon a time in the education of a boy who is now as incomprehensible to them as they are to us. But one cannot even make them remember that time, they can remember nothing and if one presses them, they brush one silently aside, no one can force them to do it, but obviously one cannot even speak of forcing, for most likely they don't so much as hear the words. They stand there like tired dogs because they use up all their strength to remain upright in one's memory. But if one truly managed to make them hear and speak, one's ears would simply buzz with counter-reproaches, for people take with them into the beyond their belief in the venerability of the dead and from there espouse it with tenfold conviction. And if this opinion were perhaps incorrect and the dead stood in especially great awe of the living, then they would be all the more committed to their own lived past, which is closest to them, after all, and again our ears would buzz. And if this opinion too were incorrect, and the dead were particularly impartial, even then they could never consent to being disturbed with unprovable reproaches. For even from person to person such reproaches are unprovable. The mere existence of past mistakes in education cannot be proven, much less their authorship. And now show me the reproach that in such a situation wouldn't turn into a sigh.

That is the reproach I have to level. Its core is sound, it has theoretical support. What has really been spoiled in me, however, I forget for the time being or forgive and don't yet make any fuss about it. On the other hand I can prove at any moment that my education wanted to make me into a different person than the one I have become. It is thus for the harm that my educators could have inflicted on me in accordance with their intentions that I reproach them, I demand from their hands the person I now am and since they cannot give him to me I make for them out of reproach and laughter a drumbeat into the world beyond. Yet all this only serves another purpose. The reproach that they have spoiled a part of me have spoiled a good beautiful part—in dreams it sometimes appears to me the way a dead bride appears to others—this reproach that is always on the verge of becoming a sigh, above all it should make its way across unharmed as an honest reproach which it also is. Thus it happens, the large reproach to which nothing can happen takes the small one by the hand, if the large one walks the small one hops, but once the small one has arrived on the other side, it distinguishes itself, as we've always expected and to accompany the drum it blows the trumpet.

Often I reflect on it and let my thoughts take their course, without interfering, but I always come to the conclusion that my education has spoiled me more than I can understand. In my external appearance I'm a person like others, for my physical education kept as much to the ordinary as my body too was ordinary, and even if I'm rather short and somewhat fat, I'm still appealing to many people, even girls. About that there's nothing to say. Just recently one of them said something very reasonable "Oh, if only I could see you naked one day then you must be especially pretty and kissable" she said. But if I were missing my upper lip here, an ear there, a rib here, a finger there, if I had hairless spots on my head and pockmarks on my face, it still wouldn't be an adequate counterpart to my inner imperfection. This imperfection is not innate and is therefore all the more painful to bear. For like everyone I too have in me from birth my center of gravity, which not even the most foolish education could displace. This good center of gravity I still have but to some extent I no longer have the body that goes with it. And a center of gravity that has no work to do turns into lead and lodges in the body like a bullet. But that imperfection is not deserved either, I have suffered its emergence through no fault of my own. That is why I can find remorse nowhere inside me, however much I search for it. For remorse would be good for me, it weeps itself out within itself; it takes the pain aside and settles everything alone like an affair of honor; we remain upright because it relieves us.

My imperfection is, as I said not innate, not deserved, nonetheless I endure it better than others who with great work of their imagination and selected aids endure much smaller misfortune an abhorrent wife, for example, impoverished circumstances, miserable professions and am at the same time not at all black in the face with despair, but white and red

I wouldn't be so if my education had penetrated me as deeply as it wanted to. Perhaps my youth was too brief for that, in that case I praise its brevity even now in my forties at the top of my voice. That alone made it possible for me to have powers left to become aware of the losses of my youth, further, to get over those losses, further, to reproach the past in all directions and finally a remnant of power for myself. But all these powers are themselves only a remnant of those I possessed as a child, which exposed me more than others to the corrupters of youth, indeed, a good racing car is the first to be pursued and overtaken by dust and wind and the obstacles fly toward its wheels so swiftly that one should almost believe in love.

What I still am now becomes clearest to me in the power with which the reproaches want out of me. There were times when I had in me nothing but reproaches driven by rage, so that despite my physical well-being I held on to strangers in the street, because the reproaches inside me threw themselves from one side to the other, like water in a basin being carried quickly.

Those times are over. The reproaches lie around in me like strange tools that I hardly have the courage to seize and lift anymore. At the same time the corruption by my old education seems more and more to be at work in me anew, the craving to remember, perhaps a general quality of bachelors of my age opens my heart again to those people my reproaches should strike and an event like yesterday's once as frequent as eating is now so rare that I make a note of it.

But even beyond that I myself I who have now put down the pen to open the window am perhaps my attackers' best helper. For I underestimate myself and this by itself means an overestimation of others but I overestimate them even apart from that and besides I also do myself harm directly. When the urge to reproach overcomes me, I look out the window. Who can deny that the fishermen are sitting there in their boats like students who have been carried out of school onto the river; true, their stillness is often incomprehensible like that of the flies on the windowpanes. And naturally the trams cross the bridge as always with a coarsened rush of wind and ring like damaged clocks, no doubt that the policeman black from bottom to top with the yellow light of the medal on his chest is reminiscent of nothing but hell and with thoughts similar to mine now contemplates a fisherman who suddenly, is he weeping is he having a vision or is the cork jerking, bends down to the edge of the boat.[11] All that is right but in its time now only the reproaches are right.

They are directed against many people, this can be frightening and not only I but also everyone else would rather look out the open window at the river. There are my parents and relatives, the fact that they have done me harm out of love makes their guilt still greater, for how much good they could have done me out of love, then families friendly with mine with an evil eye out of a sense of guilt they make themselves heavy and refuse to rise into memory, then the crowds of nursemaids, teachers and writers and one cook in particular among them, then all blending together in punishment a family doctor, a hairdresser, a helmsman, a beggar woman, a paper salesman, a park watchman, a swimming master then unknown ladies from the city park though to look at them one wouldn't at all think so, natives of summer resorts as a mockery of innocent nature and many others; but there would be even more if I were inclined and able to mention them all by name, in short there are so many that one must take care not to mention anyone twice.

I often reflect on it and let my thoughts take their course without interfering, but I always come to the same conclusion, that my education has spoiled me more than everyone I know and more than I comprehend. Yet I can speak about this only once in a while, for if someone asks me: "Really? Is that possible? Is one supposed to believe that" then out of nervous fear I immediately try to qualify it.

Externally I look like everyone else; have legs torso and head, pants, coat and hat; I was made to do plenty of gymnastics and if I have nonetheless remained rather short and weak it was simply not to be avoided. Besides, I am appealing to many people, even young girls, and those to whom I am not appealing still find me tolerable.

It is reported and we are disposed to believe that men in danger have no regard for even beautiful unknown women; they push them against the wall, push them with head and hands, knees and elbows, if they are ever hindered by these women from fleeing the burning theater. Then our chatty women fall silent, their endless talking gets a last word and period, their eyebrows rise from their resting position, the breathing movement of their thighs and hips ceases, their mouths, closed only loosely in fear, take in more air than usual and their cheeks seem a little puffed out.[12]

Sand: The French are all actors; but only the weakest among them act in the theater[13]

Claqueurs in the French theaters: commanders in the orchestra. Ha-ha for the next rows, dropping of newspaper for the men on the gallery

---

Wooden mallet signals the beginning[14]

19 / II 11
When I tried to get out of bed today I simply collapsed.[15] There's a very simple reason for it, I am completely overworked. Not by the office[16] but by my other work. The office plays an innocent part in it only insofar as, if I didn't have to go there, I could live in peace for my work and wouldn't have to spend those 6 hours a day there, which have so tormented me that you cannot imagine it, especially on Friday and Saturday, because I was full of my concerns. In the end as I am well aware this is only chatter, it's my fault and the office has the clearest and most justified claims on me. But for me it is a horrible double life from which insanity is probably the only way out. I am writing this in the good morning light and would certainly not be writing it if it weren't so true and if I didn't love you as a son does.
Incidentally I will certainly have recovered by tomorrow and will come to the office, where the first thing I will hear will be that you want me out of your department.

19 II 11
The special nature of my inspiration in which I the happiest and unhappiest of men am now going to bed at 2 o'clock at night [perhaps, if I can only bear the thought of it, it will remain, for it is higher than all before] is that I can do anything, not only with regard to a particular work. When I write down a sentence at random, for example, He looked out the window it is already perfect.

"Will you be staying here long?" I asked. With this sudden burst of speech some saliva flew out of my mouth as a bad omen.

Is it disturbing you? If it's disturbing you or perhaps keeping you from going up I'll leave immediately, but otherwise I'd like to stay, because I'm tired.[17]

---

28 III 11[18] Painter Pollak-Karlin, his wife[19] two large wide upper front teeth, which sharpen the large rather flat face, Frau Hofrat Bittner, mother of the composer,[20] whose old age pushes out her strong skeleton

so that at least while sitting she looks like a man:—Dr. Steiner's absent disciples make such heavy demands on him—During the lecture the dead press so closely toward him. Thirst for knowledge? But are they actually in need of it? Apparently so.—Sleeps 2 hours. Ever since his electric light was cut off once, he always has a candle with him.—He was very close to Christ.—He produced his play in Munich.[21] ("You can study it for a year and won't understand it") he designed the costumes, wrote the music.—He instructed a chemist.—Löwy Simon silk merchant in Paris Quai Moncey got the best business advice from him. He translated his works into French. The Hofrat's wife therefore had in her notebook "How Does One Attain Knowledge of Higher Worlds? at S. Löwy's in Paris."[22]—In the Vienna lodge there's a theosophist 65 years old, tremendously strong, previously a big drinker with a thick head, who constantly believes and constantly has doubts. It is supposed to have been very funny how during a congress in Budapest at a dinner on the Blocksberg one moonlit evening, when Dr. Steiner unexpectedly joined the gathering, he hid in fear with his mug behind a beer barrel (although Dr. Steiner would not have been angry about it)—He might not be the greatest contemporary spiritual researcher, but he alone has been given the task of uniting theosophy with science. And that's why he knows everything.—

Once a botanist, a great occult master, came to his native village. He enlightened him.[23]—That I'm going to call on Dr. Steiner was interpreted for me by the lady as a dawning recollection.—The lady's doctor, when she showed the first signs of influenza, asked Dr. Steiner for a remedy, prescribed this to the lady and thereby immediately restored her to health.—A French woman said goodbye to him with "Au revoir." He shook his hand behind her. Two months later she died. A similar Munich case.—A Munich doctor cures his patients with colors determined by Dr. Steiner.[24] He also sends them to the Pinakothek with the instruction to concentrate for half an hour or longer in front of a particular painting.—Downfall of the Atlantean world, Lemurian downfall and now the one through egoism.—We are living in a decisive time. Dr. Steiner's effort will succeed if only the Ahrimanic forces don't prevail.—He eats 2 liters of almond milk and fruits that grow high up.—He communicates with his absent disciples by means of thought-forms that he sends out to them without occupying himself further with them after their production. But they soon wear out and he has to reconstitute them—Frau Fanta: I have a bad memory. Dr. St. Don't eat eggs.

My visit to Dr. Steiner.[25]
A woman is already waiting (upstairs on the 3rd floor of the Viktoria Hotel on Jungmannsstrasse)[26] but implores me to go in before her. We wait. The secretary comes and holds out hope to us. Glancing down a corridor, I see him. A moment later he comes toward us with arms half spread. The woman declares that I was here first. Now I walk behind him as he leads me into his room. His black frock coat,[27] which on lecture evenings appears polished, (not polished, but only shiny due to its pure black) is now in the light of day (3 o'clock in the afternoon) dusty and even stained especially on the back and shoulders. In his room I try to show my humility, which I cannot feel, by looking for a ridiculous place for my hat; I put it on a small wooden stand for lacing boots. Table in the middle, I sit facing the window, he on the left side of the table. On the table some papers with a few drawings, which recall those from the lectures on occult physiology.[28] A magazine Annalen für Naturphilosophie covers a small pile of books, which seem to be lying around elsewhere too.[29] Only you can't look around, because he keeps trying to hold you with his gaze. But whenever he doesn't do so, you have to watch out for the return of the gaze. He begins with a few loose sentences: So you're Dr. Kafka? Have you been interested in theosophy long? But I press forward with my prepared speech: I feel a large part of my being striving toward theosophy, but at the same time I have the utmost fear of it. I'm afraid, namely, that it will bring about a new confusion, which would be very bad for me since my present unhappiness itself consists of nothing but confusion. This confusion lies in the following: My happiness, my abilities and any possibility of being in some way useful have always resided in the literary realm. And here I have, to be sure, experienced states (not many) that are in my opinion very close to the clairvoyant states described by you Herr Doktor,[30] in which I dwelled completely in every idea, but also filled every idea and in which I felt myself not only at my own limits, but at the limits of the human in general. Only the calm of enthusiasm, which is probably peculiar to the clairvoyant, was still missing from those states, even if not entirely. I conclude this from the fact that I have not written the best of my works in those states.—I cannot now devote myself fully to this literary realm, as would be necessary, and indeed for various reasons. Leaving aside my family circumstances, I couldn't live off literature if for no other reason than the slow emer-

gence of my works and their special character; moreover, my health and my character also hinder me from devoting myself to what is in the most favorable case an uncertain life. I have therefore become an official in a social insurance institute. Now these two professions could never tolerate each other and permit a shared happiness. The least happiness in one becomes a great unhappiness in the other. If I have written something good one evening, I am aflame the next day in the office and can accomplish nothing. This back-and-forth keeps getting worse. In the office I outwardly live up to my duties, but not my inner duties and every unfulfilled inner duty turns into an unhappiness that never leaves me. And to these two never-to-be-balanced endeavors am I now to add theosophy as a third? Won't it disturb both sides and itself be disturbed by both? Will I, already at present such an unhappy person be able to bring the 3 to a conclusion? I have come Herr Doktor to ask you this, for I sense that, if you consider me capable of it, I could actually take it on.

He listened very attentively, without appearing to observe me at all, completely devoted to my words. He nodded from time to time, which he seems to consider an aid to strong concentration. At first a quiet head cold bothered him, his nose was running, he kept working the handkerchief deep into his nose, one finger at each nostril

---

Since in contemporary Western European Jewish stories the reader has grown accustomed to immediately seeking and finding under or over the story the solution to the Jewish question too, but in "Jüdinnen" such a solution is not shown or even presumed, it is possible that the reader will without further ado recognize in this a deficiency of "Jüdinnen," and will look on only reluctantly if Jews are supposed to be walking around in the light of day without political encouragement from past or future. Here he must tell himself that, especially since the rise of Zionism, the possibilities for a solution are so clearly arrayed around the Jewish problem that in the end a turn of the writer's body is all that's required to find a particular solution appropriate to the part of the problem under consideration.[31]

I sensed at the sight of him what pains he had taken for my sake, which now—perhaps only because he was weary—gave him this certainty.

Wouldn't another little exertion have sufficed and the deception would have worked, perhaps worked even now. Did I defend myself, then? I did stand stubbornly here outside the house, but just as stubbornly I hesitated to go up. Was I waiting until the guests would come, singing, to fetch me?[32]

---

15 August 1911 The time that has now gone by, in which I haven't written a word, has been important for me because at the swimming schools in Prague,[33] Königssaal and Czernoschitz[34] I have stopped being ashamed of my body. How late I catch up on my education now at the age of 28, it would be called a delayed start in a race. And perhaps the harm of such a misfortune consists not in the fact that you don't win; that is actually only the still visible, clear, sound kernel of the misfortune, which goes on to blur and become boundless, driving you, who should run around the circle, into the interior of the circle. Aside from that I have also noticed many other things about myself in this time, which has to a small extent also been happy, and will try to write them down in the next few days.

---

20 VIII 11

I have the unhappy belief that I don't have time for the slightest good work, for I really don't have time to spread myself out in all directions for a story, as I would have to. But then I believe again that my trip[35] will turn out better, that I will take things in better, if I'm loosened up by a little writing and so I try again.

I sensed at the sight of him what pains he had taken for my sake, which now, perhaps only because he was weary, gave him this certainty. Wouldn't another little exertion have sufficed and the deception would have worked, perhaps worked even now. Did I defend myself, then? I did stand stubbornly here outside the house, but just as stubbornly I hesitated to go up. Was I waiting until the guests came, singing, to fetch me?[36]

I have been reading about Dickens. Is it so hard and can an outsider comprehend that one experiences a story in oneself from its beginning from the distant point to the approaching locomotive of steel, coal and steam, even now does not abandon it but wants to be chased by it and, having time for this, is chased by it and runs in front of it by one's own impetus wherever it thrusts and wherever one lures it.

I can't understand and can't even believe it. I live only here and there in a little word, in whose vowel ("thrusts" above), for example, I lose my useless head for a moment. First and last letter are beginning and end of my fishlike feeling.

24 August 1911
Sitting with acquaintances outdoors at a coffeehouse table and looking at a woman at the next table who has just arrived, breathes heavily under large breasts and with a heated shiny brownish face sits down. She leans her head back, a heavy down becomes visible, she turns her eyes upward, almost in the way she might sometimes look at her husband, who is now reading an illustrated paper next to her. If only one could persuade her that next to one's wife in a coffeehouse one is permitted to read at most a newspaper but never a magazine. A moment makes her aware of her corpulence and she moves away from the table a little.

---

26 Aug. *(1911)*[37] Tomorrow I'm supposed to leave for Italy.[38] This evening my father was so agitated that he couldn't fall asleep, because he was completely stricken with worry about the shop and with his thereby awakened illness. A wet cloth on his heart, nausea, shortness of breath, sighing while walking back and forth. My mother in her fear finds new consolation.[39] He has always been so energetic, he has always gotten over everything and now—I say that the misery with the shop could last only another ¼ year, then everything should be all right. He walks up and down sighing and shaking his head. It's clear that from his point of view his worries are not taken off his shoulders or so much as lightened by us, but even from our point of view they are not, even in our best intentions there's some conviction, however sad, that he must provide for his family.—Later I thought, he is lying beside my mother, let him press himself against her, close kindred flesh must be soothing.—With

his frequent yawning or his incidentally not unappetizing reaching into his nose, my father produces a slight scarcely perceptible reassurance about his condition, although when he is well he in general doesn't do this. Ottla[40] has confirmed this for me.—My poor mother wants to go to the landlord[41] tomorrow to beg.

26 Sept. 1911 The artist Kubin[42] recommends Regulin as a laxative, a crushed seaweed that swells in the intestine makes it tremble, thus acts mechanically in contrast to the unhealthy chemical effect of other laxatives, which merely tear through the feces thus leave them clinging to the intestinal walls.—He met Hamsun at Langen's.[43] He smirks for no reason. During the conversation, without interrupting it, he lifted his foot onto his knee, took a large pair of paper scissors from the table and cut off the fringes of his pants all around.[44] Shabbily dressed with some more valuable detail such as a tie.—Stories of an artists' boardinghouse in Munich where painters and veterinarians lived (the school for the latter was nearby) and where things were so dissolute that the windows of the house across the street, from where there was a good view were rented out. To satisfy these spectators, a boarder would sometimes jump onto the windowsill and spoon up his soup pot in a monkey posture.—A maker of false antiques who made them look weathered by riddling them with shot and who said of a table: Now we have to drink coffee on it three more times, then it can be sent off to the Innsbruck museum.—Kubin himself: very strong, but somewhat uniform movement of his face, with the same muscle tension he describes the most varied things. Looks different in age, size and strength depending on whether he is sitting, standing up, has on just a suit or an overcoat

Thurs 27 IX 11 Yesterday on Wenzelsplatz encountered 2 girls, kept my eyes too long on one of them, while it was the other who, as became apparent too late, was wearing a wide brown pleated coat as soft as household attire and a little open in front, had a delicate neck and delicate nose. Her hair was in an already forgotten way beautiful.—Old man with loosely hanging pants on the Belvedere.[45] He whistles; when I look at him, he stops; if I look away, he begins again; finally he whistles even when I look at him.—The beautiful large button beautifully attached at the bottom of the sleeve of a girl's dress. The dress worn beautifully too floating over American boots. How rarely I achieve something beautiful and this unnoticed button and its unknowing dressmaker achieve it.—The storyteller on the way to the Belvedere, whose lively eyes independent of the words she was saying at the moment contentedly surveyed her story to its end—Powerful half turn of the neck of a strong girl,

29 IX 11 Goethe's diaries: A person who has no diary is in a false position in the face of a diary. When, for example, he reads in Goethe's diaries "11 I 1797 busy at home all day with various arrangements" it seems to him as if he himself had never done so little in a day.[46]—Goethe's travel observations different from today's, because made from a mail coach with the slow changes of the terrain they develop more simply and can be followed much more easily even by someone who doesn't know those regions. A calm positively scenic thinking sets in. Since the region presents itself unharmed in its native character to the passenger in the carriage and the country roads too cut through the country much more naturally than the railroad tracks, to which they perhaps stand in the same relation as rivers to canals, no violence is required from the viewer either and without great effort he can see systematically. Hence there are few momentary observations, mostly only indoors where certain people immediately surge up boundlessly before one's eyes, such as Austrian officers in Heidelberg,[47] on the other hand the passage about the men in Wiesenheim is closer to the landscape "they wear blue coats and white vests adorned with woven flowers"[48] (quoted from memory). Wrote down a lot about the Rhine Falls near Schaffhausen in the middle in larger letters "Excited ideas"[49]

Cabaret Lucerna.[50] Lucie König[51] displays photographs with old hairstyles. Worn face. Sometimes she achieves something with her nose thrust high, with her arm upraised and a turn of all her fingers. Flabby face.—Longhen (painter Pittermann)[52] comic facial expressions. A performance that is obviously without enthusiasm and yet cannot be thought so listless, because then it couldn't be carried out every evening, especially since even when it was invented it was so listless that no satisfactory schema arose that would make the quite frequent appearance of the whole person unnecessary. Pretty clown-jump over a chair into the emptiness of the wings. The whole thing is reminiscent of a presentation in private company where one applauds an arduous insignificant performance with particular vigor out of social necessity, to ensure that the minus of the performance is evenly rounded off by the plus of the applause.—Singer Vašata.[53] So bad that one loses oneself in the sight of him. But because he is a strong person, he still keeps the audience's attention halfway concentrated with an animal power undoubtedly perceived only by me.—Grünbaum[54] is effective with the supposedly only apparent hopelessness of his existence.—Odys dancer.[55] Stiff hips. Real fleshlessness. To me red knees suit the dance "Frühlingsstimmung."

30 IX 1911

The girl in the next room the day before yesterday (Helli Haas).[56] I was lying on the sofa and on the brink of half-sleep heard her voice. I had the impression that she was especially heavily dressed, not only in her clothes, but also in the whole next room, with only her formed, naked round, strong dark shoulder, which I had seen in the bathhouse,[57] prevailing against her clothes. For a moment she seemed to me to be steaming and to be filling the whole next room with her vapors. Then she stood in a bodice of an ash-gray color, which stuck out so far from her body at the bottom that one could sit down on it and so, in a way, ride.

More Kubin: The habit of repeating the other person's last words in an approving tone under any circumstances even if one's own elaboration of them reveals that one doesn't at all agree with the other person. Annoying.—Listening to his many stories, one can forget what he is worth. Suddenly one is reminded of it and is frightened. There was talk of an establishment we wanted to visit being dangerous; he said he wouldn't go there; I asked him whether he was afraid he replied and moreover still had his arm linked in mine: Of course, I'm young and still have a lot ahead of me.—All evening he spoke often and in my opinion completely seriously about my constipation and his own. Toward midnight when I let my hand hang over the edge of the table he saw part of my arm and cried: But you're really sick. From then on treated me even more indulgently and later also fended off the others who wanted to talk me into going to the b.[58] with them. When we had already said goodbye, he called to me from a distance "Regulin!"

Tucholski and Safranski.[59] The aspirated Berlin dialect in which the voice needs pauses for rest, which are formed by "nich." The former a completely consistent person of 21. From the measured and strong swing of his walking stick, which gives his shoulder a youthful lift, to his considered pleasure in and disdain for his own literary works. Wants to become a defense lawyer, sees only a few obstacles—at the same time as the possibility of their removal: his high voice that after the manly sound of the first half-hour of speaking supposedly becomes girlish—doubts about his own ability to pose, which, however, he hopes to acquire from greater world experience—finally fear of a turn to world-weariness, as he has noticed among older Berlin Jews of his bent, although for the time being he senses no trace of this. He will soon get married.

Safranski, a student of Bernhard,[60] makes faces while drawing and observing that are connected with what is drawn. Reminds me that I myself have a strong capacity for transformation, which no one notices. How often I have had to imitate Max.[61] Yesterday evening on the way home, had I been a spectator, I could have mistaken myself for Tucholski. The foreign nature must be in me then as clearly and invisibly as one of those pictures that is hidden in another, where one would also never find anything if one didn't know that it's there. During these transformations I would especially like to believe in a dulling of my own eyes.

1 October Mon *(Sunday 1911)* Altneu Synagogue[62] yesterday. Kolnidre.[63] Muffled stock exchange murmur. In the anteroom a box with the inscription: "Secret donations appease indignation." Churchlike interior. Three pious apparently Eastern Jews. In socks. Bent over their prayer books, their prayer shawls pulled over their heads, making themselves as small as possible. Two of them are weeping, moved only by the holiday? One of them might only have sore eyes, to which he briefly brings the still-folded handkerchief, only to hold his face close to the text again a

moment later. The word is not actually or mainly sung, but in the wake of the word arabesques are drawn from the word, which is spun out as fine as a hair. The little boy who without the slightest conception of the whole and without any possibility of orientation, the noise in his ears, pushes his way and is pushed through the dense crowd. The apparent clerk who shakes rapidly while praying, which is to be understood only as an attempt to give the strongest possible, even if perhaps uncomprehending, emphasis to every word while sparing the voice, which wouldn't achieve a great clear emphasis in the noise anyhow. The family of the brothel owner. In the Pinkas Synagogue[64] I was seized incomparably more powerfully by Judaism.

In the Suha b. three days ago.[65] The one Jewess with a narrow face, or rather that tapers to a narrow chin but is shaken wide by her hair worn in voluminous waves. The three small doors that lead from the inside of the building into the salon. The guests as in a police station on the stage, drinks on the table, scarcely touched, of course. The flat-faced girl in the angular dress that begins to move only far down in a hem. Some of them here and previously dressed like the marionettes for children's theaters that are sold at the Christmas market, that is, with ruffles and gold stuck on and loosely sewn on so that one can tear them off with a single pull and they then fall apart in one's fingers. The landlady with the dull blond hair pulled tight over undoubtedly disgusting pads, with the sharply descending nose, the direction of which stands in some geometric relation to the hanging breasts and the stiffly held belly, complains of headaches, which are caused by the fact that today Saturday there is such a great commotion and nothing in it.

---

on Kubin: The story about Hamsun is suspect. From his works one could tell such stories by the thousands as firsthand accounts.

---

on Goethe: "Excited ideas" are merely the ideas that the Rhine Falls excite. One sees this from a letter to Schiller.[66]—The isolated momentary observation "Castanet rhythm of the children in wooden shoes"[67] has had such an influence, has been so universally accepted that it's unthinkable that someone, even if he had never read this remark, could feel this observation to be his own original idea.

---

2 October *(1911)* Sleepless night. The third in a row. I fall asleep easily, but after an hour I wake up as if I had laid my head in a false hole. I'm completely awake, have the feeling of having slept not at all or only under a thin skin, have the work of falling asleep ahead of me anew and feel rejected by sleep. And the rest of the night until toward 5 it goes on in such a way that I do sleep but at the same time intense dreams keep me awake. I am practically sleeping next to myself, while I myself must grapple with dreams. Toward 5 the last trace of sleep is used up, I only dream, which is a greater strain than being awake. In short I spend the whole night in the state in which a healthy person finds himself for a little while before actually falling asleep. When I wake up all the dreams are gathered around me but I take care not to think them through. Toward morning I sigh into the pillow, because for this night all hope is gone. I think of those nights at the end of which I was raised out of deep sleep and awoke as if I had been confined in a nut. A horrible apparition last night was a blind child apparently the daughter of my Leitmeritz aunt[68] who, however, has no daughter but only sons, one of whom once broke his foot. On the other hand, there were connections between this child and Dr. Marschner's daughter,[69] who, as I have recently seen, is on the way to turning from a pretty child into a fat stiffly dressed little girl. This blind or weak-sighted child had both eyes covered with a pair of glasses, the left under the rather distant lens was milky gray and roundly protuberant, the other receded and was concealed by a lens lying against it. For this lens to be inserted in an optically correct fashion, it was necessary instead of the usual holder going back over the ear to use a lever, the head of which could not be fastened otherwise than to the cheekbone, so that from this lens a little rod went down to the cheek, disappeared there in the pierced flesh and ended at the bone, while a new little wire rod came out and went back over the ear.—I believe this sleeplessness stems only from the fact that I write. For as little and as badly as I write, these small shocks make me sensitive, I feel especially toward evening and even more in the morning the wafting, the imminent possibility of great states that would tear me open and could make me capable of anything, and then the general noise that is in me and that I have no time to

command grants me no rest. In the end this noise is only a suppressed, restrained harmony, which if set free would completely fill me, indeed would expand me and even then fill me. But now, aside from raising faint hopes, this state only does me harm, since my nature doesn't have enough capacity to bear the present mixture, during the day the visible world helps me, at night all this cuts me up unhindered. This always makes me think of Paris, where at the time of the siege and later until the Commune the population of the northern and eastern suburbs, until then foreign to the Parisian, advanced in a period of months practically hour by hour through the connecting streets, moving haltingly like clock hands, into the center of Paris.

My consolation—and with it I now go to bed—is that I haven't written for so long, that therefore this writing could not yet fit into my present circumstances, that this, however, with some manliness must succeed, at least provisionally.

I was so weak today that I even told my boss the story of the child.—Now I remembered that the pair of glasses in the dream comes from my mother, who sits next to me in the evening and looks over at me during the card game[70] not very pleasantly from under her pince-nez. Her pince-nez even has, which I don't remember having noticed before the right lens closer to the eye than the left.

3 October *(1911)* The same sort of night, only fell asleep with even more difficulty. While falling asleep a vertically moving pain in my head over the root of my nose, as if from a forehead wrinkle pressed too sharply. To be as heavy as possible, which I consider good for falling asleep, I had crossed my arms and put my hands on my shoulders, so that I lay there like a soldier bearing his load. Again it was the power of my dreams which radiate even into the waking state before I fall asleep, that didn't let me sleep. In the evening and the morning the consciousness of my literary abilities is immense. I feel loosened to the bottom of my being and can draw up out of myself whatever I want. This luring forth of such powers that one then doesn't allow to work reminds me of my relationship to B.[71] Here too there are outpourings that are not released but in recoiling must annihilate themselves, except that here—

this is the difference—it is a matter of more mysterious powers and of my utmost.

On Josefsplatz[72] a large touring automobile with a family sitting tightly together drove by me. Behind the automobile, with the gasoline smell, a Paris breeze blew across my face.

Dictating a fairly long report to a district administration[73] in the office.[74] At the conclusion, which was supposed to rise to a climax, I got stuck and could do nothing but look at the typist Kaiser,[75] who, as is her habit, became especially lively, shifted her chair coughed, tapped around on the table and so drew the attention of the whole room to my misfortune.[76] The idea I've been searching for now takes on the added value that it will calm her down, and the more valuable it becomes the harder it is to find. At last I have the word "stigmatize" and the sentence that goes with it, but still hold everything in my mouth with a feeling of disgust and shame as if it were raw meat, cut out of my own flesh (so much effort has it cost me). At last I say it, but retain the great horror that everything in me is ready for a literary work and such a work would be a heavenly dissolution and a real coming alive for me, while here in the office for the sake of so wretched a document I must rob a body capable of such happiness of a piece of its flesh

---

4 *(October 1911)* I'm restless and poisonous. Yesterday before falling asleep I had in my head at the top left a flickering cool little flame. Over my left eye a tension has already taken root. When I think about it it seems to me that I couldn't stand it in the office even if I were told that in a month I would be free. And yet in the office I usually do my duty, am quite calm when I can be sure of my boss's satisfaction and don't experience my condition as horrible. Yesterday evening, moreover, I intentionally dulled myself, went for a walk, read Dickens, was then somewhat healthier and had lost the strength for sadness, which I regarded as justified even if it seemed to me to have receded somewhat, giving me hope for a better sleep. It was a little deeper too, but not enough and often interrupted. I told myself as consolation that even though I had

again suppressed the great movement that had been in me, I wouldn't let myself slip away, as I had always done in the past after such times, but rather I would remain clearly aware of the afterpains of that movement, which I had never done before. Perhaps in this way I could find a hidden steadfastness in myself.

Toward evening in the darkness of my room on the sofa. Why does one take quite some time to recognize a color but then after the decisive bend of the understanding quickly become ever more convinced of the color. When the light from the hall and the light from the kitchen affect the glass door from outside at the same time, greenish or rather not to depreciate the certainty of the impression, green light pours almost all the way down the panes. When the light in the hall is turned off and only the kitchen light remains, the pane closer to the kitchen turns deep blue, the other whitish blue so whitish that the whole drawing on the frosted glass (stylized poppy heads, tendrils, various four-sided figures and leaves) dissolves.—The lights and shadows cast on the walls and the ceiling by the electric light on the street and bridge[77] down below are disordered partly marred overlapping and hard to scrutinize. When the electric arc lamps down below were erected and when this room was furnished, there was simply no housewifely consideration for how my room would look from the sofa at this hour without its own lighting.—The glow cast up to the ceiling by the tram passing down below runs whitish, hazy and mechanically halting along the one wall and ceiling, broken at the line where they meet.—On the linen cabinet, which is bathed on top in a greenish pure light, the globe stands in the first fresh full reflection of the street lighting, has a luminous spot on its curve and looks as if the brightness were too strong for it, even though the light passes over its smoothness and leaves it behind rather brownish, like a russet apple.—On the wall over the bed the light from the hall brings forth a broad glow, which is bounded in a curved line from the head of the bed, appears to press down the bed, widens the dark bedposts, raises the ceiling over the bed

---

5 *(October 1911)* For the first time in several days restlessness again even before this writing. Rage at my sister,[78] who comes into the room and sits

down at the table with a book; waiting for the next little opportunity for the explosion of this rage. Finally she takes a visiting card from the case and picks her teeth with it. With departing rage, of which only a sharp steam remains behind in my head, and dawning relief and confidence I begin to write.

Yesterday evening Cafe Savoy. Jewish company[79]—Frau Klug "male impersonator." In a caftan short black pants, white stockings, a white shirt of thin wool that rises out of a black vest, is held in front at the neck by a thread button and then folds over into a broad, loose, flaring collar. On her head, enclosing her woman's hair but necessary anyhow and worn by her husband too, a small dark brimless cap, over it a large soft black hat with an upturned brim.[80]—I actually don't know what sort of people these are whom she and her husband portray. If I wanted to explain them to someone without confessing my ignorance, I would find that I take them for community servants, for employees of the temple, notorious idlers with whom the community has come to terms, schnorrers favored for some religious reasons, people who due to their separate status are particularly close to the center of the community's life, who due to their useless wandering and spying know many songs, clearly penetrate the circumstances of all the members of the community but due to their lack of connection to professional life don't know what to do with this knowledge, people who are Jews in an especially pure form, because they live only in the religion but live in it without effort, understanding or misery. They seem to make a fool of everyone, laugh immediately after the murder of a noble Jew, sell themselves to an apostate, dance with their hands on their sidelocks in delight when the unmasked murderer poisons himself and calls upon God, and yet all this only because they are so feather-light, lie on the floor under any pressure are sensitive, weep immediately with dry faces (they weep themselves out in grimaces), but as soon as the pressure is gone summon not the least weight of their own but must immediately spring into the air. Therefore they should actually cause a play as serious as "Der Meschumed"[81] by Lateiner[82] a lot of trouble, since they are always at the front of the stage at full height and often on tiptoe or with both legs in the air and don't unravel but rather cut up the agitation of the play. But now the seriousness of the play is unreeled in words so solid, weighed even when possibly improvised, taut with unified feeling that even when the plot happens only in the background of the stage, it always keeps its meaning. It is rather the 2 in caftans who are suppressed now and then, which befits their nature and despite their outspread arms and snapping fingers one sees only the murderer behind them, with the poison in him, his hand on his actually too-wide collar, staggering to the door.—The melodies are long, the body gladly entrusts itself to them. Due to their straight-running length, they are best met with the swaying of the hips, outspread arms raised and lowered in calm breathing, moving of the palms toward the temples and careful avoidance of touching. Somewhat reminiscent of the šlapak[83]—Some songs, the pronunciation "jüdische Kinderloch,"[84] some glimpses of this woman, who on the stage, because she's a Jew draws us listeners to her because we're Jews, without longing for or curiosity about Christians, sent a tremor over my cheeks. The government representative,[85] with the possible exception of a waiter and two maids standing to the left of the stage the only Christian in the hall is a pitiful person afflicted with a facial tic that especially in the left half of his face and also breaking forcefully into the right, contracts and leaves his face with the almost merciful speed I mean fleetingness of the second hand but also its regularity. When it passes over the left eye, it almost obliterates it. For this contraction new small fresh muscles have developed in the otherwise quite emaciated face.—The Talmudic melody of precise questions, entreaties or explanations: Into a pipe flows the air and takes the pipe along, while from small distant beginnings a large screw proud on the whole humble in its bends twists toward the questioned one.

6 *(October 1911)* The two old men in front at the long table by the stage. One of them rests both arms on the table and has only his face, whose false bloated redness with an irregularly four-sided, matted beard under it sadly conceals his old age, turned up to the right toward the stage, while the other directly opposite the stage holds his face, which old age has made really dry, back away from the table, on which he leans only with his left arm, and holds his right arm bent in the air to better enjoy the melody, which his toes follow and to which the short pipe in his right hand weakly yields. "Tateleben,[86] just sing along" cries the woman now to the one now to the other, bending down a little and thrusting out her arms encouragingly.

—The melodies are suited to catching every person who jumps up and embracing his whole enthusiasm without breaking apart, even if one won't believe that they give it to him. For especially the 2 in caftans hurry to the singing, as if it were stretching their body toward its truest need and the clapping of hands during the singing clearly indicates the best wellbeing of the person in the actor.—The proprietor's children in a corner remain children in their relationship with Frau Klug on the stage and sing along, their mouths between their pursed lips full of the melody.

The play: Seidemann, a rich Jew, apparently concentrating all his criminal instincts toward that goal, was baptized twenty years ago and at that time poisoned his wife, who refused to be forced into baptism. Since then he has taken pains to forget the jargon,[87] which, to be sure, unintentionally resonates under the surface in his speech, and especially in the beginning so that the listeners notice it and because the approaching events leave time for it he constantly expresses a great disgust for all things Jewish. He intends his daughter for the officer Dragomirow, while she, who loves her cousin young Edelmann, declares to her father in a great scene straightening up in an unusual stony posture broken only at the waist that she adheres to Judaism and ends a whole act with a contemptuous laugh at the constraint imposed on her. [The Christians in the play are: a good Polish servant of Seidemann's who later contributes to his unmasking, good above all because contrasts must be gathered around Seidemann, the officer, with whom the play scarcely concerns itself apart from the portrayal of his indebtedness, because as a noble Christian he interests no one, just like a presiding judge who appears later and finally a court usher, whose maliciousness does not exceed the requirements of his position and of the merriness of the 2 caftan people, although Max calls him a pogromist.] But for whatever reasons Dragomirow can marry only if his bills of exchange, which old Edelmann possesses, are redeemed, but the latter, although he is about to depart for Palestine and although Seidemann wants to pay them in cash, will not hand them over. The daughter is haughty toward the enamored officer and boasts of her Judaism even though she is baptized, the officer doesn't know what to do and, his arms limp his hands loosely clasped below, looks at the father, seeking help. The daughter flees to Edelmann, she wants to marry her beloved, even if for the time being in secret, since according to worldly law a Jewish man is not permitted to marry a Christian woman and she obviously cannot be converted to Judaism without her father's consent. The father comes, realizes that without trickery all would be lost and outwardly gives his blessing to this marriage. All forgive him, indeed begin to love him as if they had been in the wrong, even old Edelmann and especially he, although he knows that Seidemann poisoned his sister. (This gap might have resulted from an abridgement, or from the fact that the play is mainly spread orally from one acting troupe to another) Through this reconciliation Seidemann acquires above all Dragomirov's bills of exchange, for "you know" he says "I don't want this Dragomiriv to speak ill of the Jews" and Edelmann gives them to him for nothing, then Seidemann calls him to the portiere in the background, supposedly to show him something, and from behind stabs him fatally in the back with a knife through his dressing gown. (Between the reconciliation and the murder Seidemann was offstage for a while to think up the plan and buy the knife) In this way he intends to bring young Edelmann to the gallows, for the suspicion must fall on him, and his daughter will be free for Dragomirov. He runs away, Edelmann lies behind the portiere. The daughter appears wearing the bridal veil, on the arm of young Edelmann who has put on the prayer shawl. Her father as they see is unfortunately not yet there. Seidemann arrives and seems happy at the sight of the bridal couple. Then a man appears, perhaps Dragomirov

8 x *(1911)*

himself perhaps just the actor who plays him and actually a detective unknown to us and declares that he has to search the house "for one's life isn't safe in this house." Seidemann: Children. Don't worry, this is of course a mistake, obviously. Everything will be cleared up. Edelmann's corpse is found, young Edelmann torn from his beloved and arrested. For a whole act Seidemann with great patience and very well stressed little interjections (Yes, yes. Very good. Well that's wrong. Yes that's better. Certainly certainly.) instructs the two in caftans how to testify in court to the supposed years of enmity between old and young Edelmann. They get going with difficulty, there are many misunderstandings, thus they come forward in an improvised rehearsal of the court scene and declare that Seidemann has told them to portray the matter in the following way, until finally they have settled into that enmity so much that they even—Seidemann can no longer stop them—are capable of showing how the murder itself took place and the man stabs the woman to death with the help of a croissant. That is of course again more than will be necessary. Nonetheless Seidemann is sufficiently satisfied with the two of them and hopes with their help for a good outcome to the trial. Here, for the religious member of the audience, without its having been stated in any way, because it's self-evident, God himself intervenes in place of the retreating writer and strikes the villain blind. In the final act the presiding judge is again the eternal Dragomirow actor (in this too the contempt for Christianity is apparent one Jewish actor can play three Christian roles well and even if he plays them badly it doesn't matter) and beside him as defense lawyer with extravagant hair and mustache, quickly recognized, Seidemann's daughter. One recognizes her quickly, but in light of Dragomirow believes for a long time that she is a substitute actor, until one realizes toward the middle of the act that she has disguised herself to save her beloved. The two in caftans are each supposed to testify individually, but they find that quite difficult since they have practiced it together. They also don't understand the judge's High German, although the defense lawyer helps him out when it gets too bad, as he has to prompt him at other times too. Then comes Seidemann, who has already tried before to direct the two in caftans by tugging at their clothing, and with his fluent firm speech, with his reasonable attitude, with his correct manner of addressing the presiding judge as opposed to the earlier witnesses he makes a good impression, which is in terrible contrast to what we know of him. His testimony is rather empty, he unfortunately knows very little about the whole case. But now comes the last witness, the servant, who, without being entirely aware of it, is Seidemann's actual accuser. He observed Seidemann's purchase of the knife, he knows that Seidemann was at Edelmann's at the decisive time, he knows finally that Seidemann hated the Jews and especially Edelmann and wanted his bills of exchange. The 2 in caftans jump up and are happy to be able to confirm all this. Seidemann defends himself as a somewhat confused man of honor. Then the talk turns to his daughter. Where is she? At home of course and will bear him out. No, that she won't do, the defense lawyer asserts and will prove it, faces the wall, takes off the wig and turns to the horrified Seidemann as his daughter. The pure white of her upper lip looks reproachful when she removes the mustache too. Seidemann has taken poison to escape earthly justice, confesses his evil deeds but hardly to the people anymore, rather to the Jewish God, in whom he now professes his faith. Meanwhile the piano player has struck up a tune, the 2 in caftans feel seized by it and must start dancing. In the background stands the united bridal couple, they sing along, especially the serious groom in accordance with old temple custom.

First appearance of the two in caftans. They enter Seidemann's room with collection boxes on behalf of the temple. Look around, feel ill at ease, look at each other. Run their hands along the doorposts, find no mezuzahs.[88] Not by the other doors either. They refuse to believe it and jump into the air at various doors and, as if catching flies, keep hitting the tops of the doorposts with a slapping sound as they rise and fall. Unfortunately all in vain. Up to now they haven't spoken a word.

Resemblance between Frau Klug and last year's Frau Weinberg.[89] Frau Klug perhaps has a slightly weaker and more monotonous temperament, on the other hand she's prettier and more respectable. The Weinberg woman was always making the joke of bumping her fellow actors with her large behind. Moreover, she had a worse singer next to her and was completely new to us.

Male impersonator is actually a false term. Because she's clad in her caftan, her body is completely forgotten. Only by shrugging her shoulders and twisting her back as if she were being bitten by fleas does she remind us of her body. The sleeves, even though they are short, must be pulled up a bit all the time, which the spectator hopes will bring great relief to the woman, who has so much to sing out and also to explain in Talmudic fashion, and he even watches for it to happen.

Desire to see a large Yiddish theater, since the performance might well suffer from the small cast and imperfect rehearsal. Also the desire to know Yiddish literature, which apparently is allotted an uninterrupted stance of national struggle that determines every work. A stance, that is, which no literature not even that of the most oppressed people has in this pervasive fashion. Perhaps it happens among other peoples in times of struggle that the literature of national struggle rises to prominence and the enthusiasm of the audience makes other more remote works appear national in this sense, as with the Bartered Bride,[90] but here only the works of the first sort seem to exist and indeed continuously.

The sight of the simple stage, which awaits the actors as silently as we do. Since with its 3 walls, the chair and the table it will have to suffice for all events, we expect nothing from it, rather await the actors with all our strength and are therefore unresistingly attracted by the singing behind the bare walls, which introduces the performance.

9 X 11

If I should reach the age of 40, I will probably marry an old maid with protruding upper teeth somewhat exposed by the upper lip. The upper front teeth of Frl. Kaufmann,[91] who was in Paris & London, are shifted against each other like legs crossed hastily at the knees. But I'll hardly live to be forty years old, against that prospect speaks, for example, the tension that often lies over the left half of my skull, which feels like an inner leprosy and which, when I disregard the unpleasantness and try only to contemplate it, makes the same impression on me as the sight of the skull cross sections in textbooks or as an almost painless dissection while alive, where the knife a little bit cooling, careful, often stopping and turning back, sometimes lying at rest slices paper-thin coverings into even finer divisions very close to working brain parts.

Dream from last night, which even in the morning I did not yet consider beautiful apart from a small funny scene consisting of two counter-remarks, which resulted in that tremendous dream satisfaction, but which I have forgotten. I was walking—whether Max was there right at the start I don't know—through a long row of houses at the level of the second to 3rd floor, just as one walks in corridor trains from one carriage to another. I was walking very quickly perhaps also because sometimes the house was so fragile that one hurried for that reason alone. I didn't even notice the doors between the houses, it was just a huge suite of rooms and yet not only the differences between the individual apartments but also between the houses could be discerned. They were perhaps all rooms with beds through which I passed. A typical bed has remained in my memory, standing at my left side against the dark or dirty wall, which perhaps slants as in an attic, with a low mound of bedclothes on it and a blanket, actually only a coarse sheet, bunched up by the feet of the person who has slept here, hanging down in a corner. I felt ashamed to be walking through people's rooms at a time when many of them were still lying in their beds, therefore walked on tiptoe with large strides, by which I somehow hoped to show that I was walking through only under compulsion, was treating everything with as much care as possible and stepping lightly so that my walking through practically didn't even count. For the same reason I never turned my head in any one room and saw only either what was on the right toward the street or on the left toward the back wall. The row of apartments was often interrupted by brothels, through which, however, even though I was apparently taking this journey for their sake, I walked especially quickly, so that I remembered nothing but their being there. The last room of all the apartments, however, was again a brothel and here I remained. The wall opposite the door through which I entered, thus the last wall of the row of houses was either made of glass or broken through altogether and if I had walked on I would have fallen. It's even more likely that it was broken through, for the whores were lying toward the edge of the floor, two of them were clear to me, on the ground, the head of one hung down a little over the edge out into the open air. To the left was a solid wall, whereas the wall on the right was not complete, one saw down into the courtyard even if not to the bottom of it and a ramshackle gray staircase led down in several sections. Judging by the light in the room, the ceiling was the same as in the other rooms. I had to do mainly with the whore whose head hung down, Max with the one lying next to her on the left. I felt her legs and then kept pressing her thighs at regular intervals. My pleasure in this was so great that I was surprised that for this entertainment, which was indeed the most wonderful of all, one did not yet have to pay anything. I was convinced that I and I alone was cheating the world. Without moving her legs the whore then raised her upper body and turned her back to me, which to my horror was covered with large sealing-wax-red circles with paling edges and red splashes scattered between them. Now I noticed that her whole body was full of them, that I was holding my thumb on her thighs in such spots and that these little red particles as if from a shattered seal were on my fingers too. I stepped back among a number of men who seemed to be waiting against the wall near the entrance to the staircase, on which a little intercourse was taking place. They were waiting the way men in the country stand together on Sunday morning at the market. Therefore it was also Sunday. Here the funny scene happened, when a man, whom I and Max had reason to fear, walked away, then came up the stairs, approached me and while I and Max were anxiously expecting some terrible threat from him, asked me a ridiculously simpleminded question. Then I stood there and watched worriedly as Max sat on the ground somewhere to the left without fear in this establishment and ate a thick potato soup, out of which the potatoes peeked in the form of large balls, mainly one of them. He pushed it with the spoon, perhaps with 2 spoons into the soup or merely rolled it.

---

10 X 11 Wrote a sophistic article for and against the institute in the Tetschner-Bodenbacher newspaper.[92]

Yesterday evening on the Graben.[93] Three actresses coming toward me from rehearsal. It's so hard to quickly become familiar with the beauty of 3 women when you also want to look at 2 actors approaching behind them with their all too swinging and also springy actors' gait. The two, of whom the one on the left with his youthfully fat face, his open overcoat flapping around his strong figure is characteristic enough for both, overtake the ladies, the one on the left on the sidewalk, the one on the right in the road down below. The one on the left grabs his hat high up, reaches in with all 5 fingers, lifts it up and calls (only now does the one on the right remember): Goodbye! Good night! But while this overtaking and greeting have separated the gentlemen, the greeted women, as if led by the one closest to the road, who seems to be the weakest and tallest, but also youngest and prettiest, continue quite unswervingly on their way with a light greeting that barely interrupts their harmonious conversation. All this seemed to me at the moment to be strong evidence that the theater relationships here are orderly and well conducted.

The day before yesterday with the Jews in Cafe Savoy. "Die Sejdernacht" by Feimann.[94] At times (at the moment the consciousness of this shot through me) we didn't intervene in the plot only because we were too excited, not because we were mere spectators.

---

12 X 11 Yesterday at Max's[95] wrote in the Paris diary.[96] In the semidarkness of Rittergasse, fat and warm in her autumn outfit, Rehberger,[97] whom we have known only in her summer blouse and thin little blue summer jacket in which a girl with a not entirely flawless appearance is ultimately worse than naked. Then one had seen all the more her prominent nose in her bloodless face with cheeks into which one could have pressed one's hands for a long time before any redness would have appeared, the heavy blond down accumulating on her cheek and upper lip, the stray railroad dust that had flown between nose and cheek and the sickly white in the neckline of her blouse. But today we ran after her respectfully and when I had to take my leave at the entrance to a passage[98] to Ferdinandstrasse because of unshavenness and an otherwise shabby appearance (Max was very beautiful at the moment with a black overcoat, white face and gleaming glasses) I felt afterward several little jolts of affection toward her. And when I thought about why, I kept returning to the fact that she was so warmly dressed.

---

13 X 11 Artless transition from the taut skin of my boss's bald head to the delicate wrinkles of his forehead. An obvious, quite easily imitated failing of nature, bank notes should not be made in such a way.

I didn't consider the description of Rehberger successful, but it must have actually been better than I thought or my impression of Rehberger the day before yesterday must have been so incomplete that the description corresponded to it or even surpassed it. For, when I went home yesterday evening, the description came to my mind for a moment, imperceptibly replaced the original impression and I believed I had seen Rehberger only yesterday and indeed without Max, so that I prepared to tell him about her just as I have described her for myself here.

Yesterday evening on the Schützeninsel, didn't find my colleagues and left immediately. I caused quite a stir in my short coat with the crushed soft hat in my hand, for outside it was cold, but here hot from the breath of the beer drinkers, smokers and wind players of the military band. This band was not raised very high, nor could it be, because the hall is rather low and it filled one end of the hall to the side walls. As if installed, this crowd of musicians was pushed into this end of the hall. This impression of compactness was then lost a little in the hall, for the seats near the band were rather empty and the hall filled up only toward the middle.[99]

Talkativeness of Dr. Kafka.[100] Walked around with him for two hours behind the Franz Josef railroad station, asked him from time to time to let me leave, had interlaced my hands with impatience and listened as little as possible. It seemed to me that a person who does well in his profession, when he has talked his way into professional stories, must no longer be accountable; he becomes conscious of his proficiency, every story yields connections and indeed several, he surveys them all, because he has experienced them, must in haste and out of consideration for me withhold many, some I also destroy for him by asking questions, but thereby remind him of others, thereby show him that he also reigns deep into my own thinking, in most of the stories he himself has a great role, which he only hints at, whereby what is withheld seems to him even more significant, but now he is already so certain of my admiration that he can also complain, for even in his misfortune, his trouble, his doubt he is admirable, his opponents are also capable people and worth talking about, in a law firm that has 4 clerks and 2 bosses a dispute in which he alone opposed this firm was for weeks the daily topic of conversation among these 6 lawyers. Their best orator, a sharp lawyer, opposed him, this leads to the supreme court, the judgments of which are supposedly bad, contradictory, in a tone of leave-taking I say something in faint defense of this court, now he provides evidence that this court cannot be defended and again we must walk up and down the street, I am immediately astonished at the badness of this court, thereupon he explains why it must be so the court is overburdened, why and how, all right I have to leave, but now the court of cassation is better and the administrative court much better still and why and how, finally I can no longer be stopped, now he tries bringing up my own affairs, which are the reason I have come to him (establishment of the factory)[101] and which we have long since talked over, he hopes unconsciously to catch me in this way and to be able to lure me back to his stories. Now I say something but while speaking hold my hand out explicitly in parting and so am set free. Incidentally, he tells stories very well, in his storytelling the detailed expansiveness of briefs is mixed with the lively speech one often finds among such fat, black Jews, healthy for the time being, of medium height, excited by constant cigarette smoking. Legal expressions give the speech support. Paragraphs are cited the high number of which seems to banish them into the distance. Every story is developed from the beginning, statement and counter-statement are presented and positively shaken by personal interjections, unimportant things of which no one would think are first mentioned, then called unimportant and brushed aside, ("a man, his name is not important"—) the listener is personally consulted, questioned, while the story thickens nearby, sometimes even before a story that cannot interest him at all the listener is questioned, to no avail, of course, in order to create some provisional connection, the listener's interjected remarks are inserted not immediately, which would be annoying (Kubin)[102] but, though soon, nonetheless only at the right point in the course of the story, which, flattering the listener in an objective fashion, draws him into the story, because it gives him a very special right to be a listener here.

14 X 11 Yesterday evening at the Savoy. Sulamit by A. Goldfaden.[103] Actually an opera, but every sung play is called an operetta, it seems to me that this trifle alone points to a stubborn, overhasty artistic endeavor, also impassioned for the wrong reasons, cutting through European art in a partly chance direction. The story: A hero saves a girl, who—"I pray to you great mighty God"—has lost her way in the desert and, tormented by thirst, has thrown herself into a cistern. They swear to be faithful to each other (my dear, my love, my diamond found in the desert), invoking the well and a red-eyed desert cat as witnesses. The girl, Sulamith (Fr. Tschissik),[104] is brought back to Bethlehem to her father Monoach (Tschissik)[105] by Cingitang, Absolon's savage servant (Pipes),[106] while Absolon (Klug)[107] takes another journey to Jerusalem; but there he falls in love with Awigail a rich girl from Jerusalem (Klug),[108] forgets Sulamit and marries. Sulamit waits for her beloved at home in Bethlehem. "Many people go to Yerusholayim and come back beshulim."[109] "He the fine man means to be unfaithful to me!" Through desperate outbursts she acquires an all-embracing confidence and decides to pretend to be mad so that she will not have to marry and will be able to wait. "My will is of iron, my heart I make into a fortress." And even in the madness that she now feigns for years she enjoys the memory of her beloved sadly and

loudly, with the compelled permission of everyone, for her madness has to do with only the desert, the well and the cat. With her madness she immediately drives away her 3 suitors, with whom Manoach was able to get along in peace only by organizing a lottery: Joef Gedoni (Urich)[110] "I am the strongest Jewish hero," Avidanov, the landowner (R. Pipes) and the potbellied priest Nathan (Löwy)[111] who feels himself above everyone "Give her to me, I'm dying for her." Absolon has suffered misfortune one of his children was bitten to death by a desert cat, the other falls into a well. He remembers his guilt, confesses everything to Awigail, "Restrain your tears." "Stop splitting my heart with your words." "Alas, all I say is emes."[112] Some circles of thoughts form around the two of them and die away. Is Absolon to return to Sulamith and abandon Awigail? Sulamit too deserves rachmones.[113] Finally Awigail releases him. In Bethlehem Manoach laments over his daughter "Woe o my old years." Absolon cures her with his voice. "The rest Father I will tell you later." Awigail sinks away down there in the Jerusalem vineyard, as justification Absolon has only his heroism.

At the end of the performance we are still waiting for the actor Löwy, whom I would admire in the dust. He is to "announce" as usual. "Dear guests, I thank you in all our names for attending and cordially invite you to tomorrow's performance, in which the world-famous masterpiece—by—will be presented. Until we meet again!" Off with waving of hats. Instead we see the curtain first being held tightly shut, then tentatively pulled apart a bit again. This lasts a rather long time. Finally it is pulled far apart, in the middle a button holds it together, behind it we see Löwy take his step toward the front of the stage and, his face turned to us the audience, defend himself with only his hands against someone attacking him from below, until suddenly the whole curtain with its wire fastening on top is torn down by Löwy in his effort to hold on to something, and Löwy his knees buckling before our eyes is clasped by Pipes who played the savage and who is still stooped as if the curtain were drawn, and pushed off the stage sideways practically with his head. People run together in the side wing of the hall. Draw the curtain! they shout on the almost completely exposed stage, where Frau Tschissik is standing so pitifully with her pale Sulamit face, short waiters on tables and chairs put the curtain in decent order, the proprietor attempts to calm down the government representative, whose only wish is to get away and who is held back by this attempt to calm him down, behind the curtain Frau Tschissik can be heard: "And we want to preach morality to the audience from the stage. . . ."; because of this incident the assoc. of Jewish office assistants "Zukunft" which has taken charge of tomorrow evening and before today's performance held an ordinary general meeting[114] decides within half an hour to call an extraordinary meeting, a Czech member of the association prophesies complete ruin for the actors as a result of their scandalous behavior. Then one suddenly sees Löwy, who seemed to have vanished, being pushed toward a door by the headwaiter Roubitschek with his hands, perhaps also with his knees. He is simply to be thrown out. This headwaiter, who earlier and later stands there in front of every guest also in front of us like a dog, with a doglike snout which descends over a large mouth closed by humble side-wrinkles, has his

16 X 11 Strenuous Sunday yesterday. The whole staff gave my father notice.[115] With good speeches, cordiality, the effect of his illness, of his size and of his former strength, of his experience, of his cleverness, he wins almost all of them back in group and individual discussions. An important clerk Franz wants time to think, until Monday, because he gave his word to our manager who is resigning and would like to bring the whole staff into his newly to be established business. On Sunday the bookkeeper[116] writes he can't stay after all, Roubitschek is holding him to his word. I go to see him in Zižkov.[117] His young wife with round cheeks longish face and a small coarse nose of the sort that never spoils Czech faces. Too-long very loose, flowered and stained housecoat. It becomes especially long and loose because she makes especially hasty movements to greet me, to place the album on the table correctly in a final beautification and to disappear to have her husband fetched. The man with similar hasty movements perhaps imitated by his very dependent wife, swinging vigorously while his upper body is bent forward and his lower body stays strikingly behind. Impression of a person known for 10 years, often seen, rarely paid attention to, with whom one suddenly comes into closer contact. The less success I have with my Czech coaxing (indeed he already had a signed contract with Roubitschek, only he had been so flustered by my father on Saturday evening that he had not spoken of the contract) the more catlike his face becomes. Toward the end I act a little with a very comfortable feeling, thus I look around the room silently

with a somewhat elongated face and narrowed eyes as if I were following something hinted at into the inexpressible. But am not unhappy when I see that it has little effect, and instead of being spoken to by him in a new tone, I must begin anew to persuade him. The conversation was introduced with the fact that another Tullach[118] lives on the other side of the street, it was concluded at the door with his astonishment at my light suit in the cold. Characteristic of my initial hopes and ultimate failure. But I made him promise to come to see my father in the afternoon. My argumentation in places too abstract and formal. Mistake not to have called the wife into the room.

Afternoon to Radotin[119] to keep the clerk. As a result miss the meeting with Löwy, whom I think about constantly. In the train carriage: Tip of the old woman's nose with almost-still-youthfully taut skin. Does youth thus end at the tip of the nose and does death begin there? The swallowing of the passengers that slides down their throats, the widening of their mouths as a sign that they judge the railroad journey, the composition of the other passengers, their seating arrangement, the temperature in the carriage, even the issue of Pan[120] that I have on my knee and that some of them look at from time to time (since it is at least something they could not possibly have foreseen in the compartment) to be unobjectionable, natural, unsuspicious, while they still believe that everything could also have been much worse. Up and down in Herr Haman's yard, a dog puts a paw on the tip of my foot, which I rock. Children, chickens, here and there adults. A nursemaid occasionally leaning down from the balcony[121] or hiding behind a door is interested in me. Under her glances I don't know what I am at the moment, whether indifferent, ashamed, young or old, impertinent or devoted, holding my hands behind or in front, freezing or hot, animal lover or businessman, friend of Haman or petitioner, superior to the participants in the meeting, who sometimes go out of the establishment to the pissoir and back in an unbroken loop or ridiculous to them due to my light suit, whether Jew or Christian, etc. The walking around, wiping my nose, now and then reading Pan, fearfully avoiding the balcony with my eyes, only to suddenly realize that it's empty, watching the poultry, being greeted by a man, seeing through the tavern window the flatly and crookedly juxtaposed faces of the men, who are turned toward a speaker, all this contributes to it. Hr. Haman, who comes out of the meeting from time to time and whom I ask to use for us his influence on the clerk, whom he brought into our shop. Blackish brown beard, growing around cheeks and chin, black eyes, between eyes and beard the dark shades of the cheeks. He is a friend of my father, I knew him as a child and the idea that he was a coffee roaster always made him even darker and manlier to me than he was.

17 X 11 I finish nothing, because I have no time and there's so much pressure in me. If the whole day were free and this morning restlessness could rise in me by noon and tire itself out by evening then I could sleep. As it is, however, there remains for this restlessness only a twilight hour at most, it grows somewhat stronger, is then suppressed and uselessly and harmfully digs up the night for me. Will I be able to bear it for long? And is there any purpose in bearing it, will I then gain time?

When I think of this anecdote: Napoleon recounts at the court table in Erfurt: When I was still a mere lieutenant in the 5th regiment . . (the royal highnesses look at each other in embarrassment, Napoleon notices it and corrects himself) when I still had the honor of being a mere lieutenant . . . ; my neck veins swell with easily imagined pride artificially penetrating me.[122]

---

more in Radotin: I then walked around alone freezing in the meadow garden, then spotted in an open window the nursemaid, who had wandered with me to this side of the house—

<u>20</u> *(October 1911)* The 18th at Max's, wrote about Paris.[123] Wrote badly without actually entering the open space of actual description, which detaches one's foot from the experience. I was also dulled after the great exaltation of the previous day, which had ended with Löwy's reading.[124] During the day I had not yet been in an unusual state, went with Max to fetch his mother who had arrived from Gablonz, was with them in the coffeehouse and then at Max's, who played for me a gypsy dance from the "Maid of Perth."[125] A dance in which for pages only the hips sway with a monotonous ticking and the face has a slow warm expres-

sion. Until toward the end briefly and late the lured inner wildness then comes, shakes the body, overpowers it, compresses the melody so that it shoots into the heights and depths, (one hears especially bitter dull notes in it) and then comes to an unnoticed close. In the beginning and never lost through it all a strong closeness to gypsy life, perhaps because a people so wild in dance shows itself calm only to a friend. Impression of great truth of the first dance. Then leafed through "Aussprüche Napoleons."[126] How easily one becomes for a moment a tiny part of one's own tremendous conception of Napoleon! Then I went home already boiling, I could withstand none of my ideas, disordered, pregnant, disheveled, swollen, in the midst of my furniture rolling around me, flown over by my sorrows and worries, taking up as much space as possible, for despite my size I was very nervous, I entered the lecture hall.[127] From the way I sat, for example, and very truly sat, had I been a spectator, I would have recognized my state immediately. Löwy read humorous sketches by Scholem aleichem,[128] then a story by Perez,[129] a poem by Bialik[130] (only here did the poet in order to popularize his poem exploiting the Kishinev pogrom for the Jewish future, lower himself from the Hebrew into the jargon and translate his originally Hebrew poem into jargon himself), the "Lichtverkäuferin" by Rosenfeld.[131] A recurrent widening of the eyes, natural to the actor, which are now left like that for a little while framed by the raised eyebrows. Complete truth of the whole reading; the weak lifting of the right arm initiated from the shoulder; the adjusting of the pince-nez, which seems borrowed so badly does it fit on the nose; the position of the leg under the table, which is so stretched out that especially the weak connecting bones between upper and lower leg are active; the curve of the back, which looks weak and miserable, for at the sight of a unified uniform back the observer cannot be deceived in his judgment as he can at the sight of the face by the eyes, the hollows and protrusions of the cheeks but also by any trifle and be it beard stubble. After the reading while still on the way home I felt all my abilities concentrated and complained for that reason to my sisters,[132] at home even to my mother.

---

on the 19th at Dr. Kafka's regarding the factory.[133] The slight theoretical hostility that must arise between the parties during contract completions. How I searched with my eyes Karl's[134] face, which was turned toward the Doktor. This hostility must arise all the more between 2 people who are otherwise not used to thinking through their mutual relationship and therefore take exception to every trifle.—Dr. Kafka's habit of walking diagonally through the room, swaying his upper body forward tensely as if in a salon, at the same time telling stories and often at the end of a diagonal shaking off the ash of his cigarette into one of the 3 ashtrays distributed around the room.

---

this morning at Löwy & Winterberg.[135] How the boss braces himself with his back sideways in his armchair to gain space and support for his Eastern Jewish hand movements. The interplay and mutual reinforcement of the hand gestures and facial expressions. Sometimes he connects the two, either by looking at his hands or holding them close to his face for the convenience of the listener. Temple melodies in the intonation of his speech, especially while enumerating several points he leads the melody from finger to finger as if through various registers. Then met my father at the Graben with a Hr. Preissler, he even raises his hand so that the sleeve falls back a bit, (he doesn't want to pull the sleeve back himself) and in the middle of the Graben makes the powerful screwing movements with his hand slipping open and fingers spreading.

I'm probably sick, my body has been itching all over since yesterday. In the afternoon my face was so hot and multicolored that during my haircut I was afraid the assistant, who could see me and my mirror image the whole time, would recognize a serious illness in me. The connection between stomach and mouth is partly disturbed too, a gulden-sized lid either rises and falls or lies down below and radiates upward with a spreading effect of light pressure that covers the surface of my chest.

---

more in Radotin: invited her to come down. The first response was serious, although until then, with the girl entrusted to her, she had giggled and flirted in my direction in a way she would never have dared from the moment we became acquainted. We then laughed a lot together, although I was freezing down below and she up above at the open window. She pressed her breasts against her crossed arms and everything with apparently bent knees against the window balustrade. She was 17 years old and was under the impression that I was 15–16, of which she was not disabused through our whole conversation. Her small nose went a little awry and hence cast an unusual shadow on her cheek, which, to be sure, wouldn't be enough to help me recognize her. She was not from Radotin, but from Chuchle (the next station toward Prague),[136] which she wouldn't let me forget. Then a walk with the clerk, who would have stayed in our shop even without my journey, in the dark on the country road out of Radotin and back to the railroad station. On one side desolate hills used by a cement factory for its lime-sand needs. Old mills. Story of a poplar whirled out of the earth by a tornado together with its roots that had first gone steeply into the earth then spread out. Face of the clerk: dough-like reddish flesh on strong bones, looks weary, but robust within his limits. Shows no astonishment even in his tone of voice that we are going for a walk here together. On a large field bought by a factory as a precaution left unused for the time being, located in the middle of the town, surrounded by factory buildings that are illuminated strongly but only in places by electr. light. Clear moon, light-filled, therefore cloudy smoke from a chimney. Train signals. Rustle of rats beside the long path crossing the field, trodden by the population against the will of the factory.

Examples of the strengthening that I owe to this writing, trivial as it is on the whole:

Monday the 16th I was with Löwy at the National Theater to see "Dubrovnická trilogie."[137] Play and performance were dreary. All that remains in my memory from the first act is the beautiful sound of a mantel clock; the singing of the Marseillaise by Frenchmen marching into the city outside the window, the fading song is repeatedly taken up by the newcomers and rises; a girl dressed in black draws her shadow through the streak of light that the setting sun casts on the parquet floor. All that remains from the 2nd act is the delicate neck of a girl, which is stretched and tensed from shoulders clad in reddish brown between puffy sleeves to the small head. From the 3rd act the crushed frock coat, the dark fancy vest with a golden watch chain pulled across it worn by an old stooped descendant of the former gospars.[138] So it's not much. Moreover, L.[139] confessed his gonorrhea to me; then my hair touched his when I leaned toward his head, I grew frightened due to at least the possibility of lice; the seats were expensive, as a bad benefactor I had thrown out money here, while he was in need; finally he was even somewhat more bored than I. In short I had again proven the misfortune of all undertakings that I begin by myself. But while I usually unite myself inseparably with this misfortune, draw all earlier cases of misfortune up to me, all later ones down to me, this time I was almost completely independent, bore everything quite lightly as something occurring only once, and for the first time in the theater I even felt my head, as the head of a spectator, raised out of the amassed darkness of the armchairs and bodies into a special light, independent of the bad occasion of this play and this performance.

A second example: Yesterday evening on Mariengasse I held out both my hands to both my sisters-in-law[140] at the same time with an adroitness as if they were two right hands and I a double person.

---

21 *(October 1911)* A counterexample: When my boss discusses office matters with me (today the card-filing system), I can't look him in the eyes for long without my gaze against all my will taking on a slight bitterness, which forces either my gaze or his away. His gaze more fleetingly but more often, since he isn't conscious of the reason and yields to every impulse to look away but immediately lets his gaze return, since he takes the whole thing for only a momentary fatigue of his eyes. I resist more strongly, hence accelerate the zigzagging of my gaze, prefer to keep looking along his nose and into the shadows toward his cheeks, often hold my face in his direction only with the help of the teeth and tongue in my closed mouth, if necessary I do lower my eyes but never farther than to his tie, but immediately get the most complete look when he turns his eyes away and I follow him closely and without consideration.

The Jewish actors: Frau Tschissik has protrusions on her cheeks near her mouth. Resulting in part from sunken cheeks due to the woes of hunger, childbirth, travels and acting in part from unusual resting muscles that had to develop for the dramatic movements of her large originally surely ponderous mouth. As Sulamith[141] she had mostly let down her hair, which covered her cheeks so that her face sometimes looked like a girl's face from earlier days. She has a large, bony, moderately robust body and is tightly laced. Her gait easily takes on a solemn quality, since she has the habit of raising, stretching and slowly moving her long arms.

Especially when she sang the Jewish national anthem,[142] slightly rocked her large hips and moved her arms, bent parallel to her hips, up and down with cupped hands as if she were playing with a slowly flying ball.

22 *(October 1911)* Yesterday with the Jews "Kol-Nidre" by Scharkansky[143] rather bad play with a good witty letter-writing scene, a prayer by the lovers standing upright side by side with folded hands, the leaning of the converted Grand Inquisitor against the curtain of the Ark of the Covenant, he climbs the step and remains standing there his head bowed his lips on the curtain, holds the prayer book before his chattering teeth. For the first time on this fourth evening[144] my distinct inability to get a pure impression. Our large group and the visits at my sister's[145] table were also to blame for it. Still, I shouldn't have been so weak. With my love for Frau Tschissik, who sat next to me only thanks to Max, I behaved miserably.[146] But I will recover, even now it's better.

Frau Tschissik (I so enjoy writing the name) likes to bow her head at the table even while eating roast goose, one believes that one will get under her eyelids with one's gaze if one first looks carefully along the cheeks and then making oneself small slips in, without even having to raise the lids, for they are raised and indeed let a bluish gleam through, which lures one to this attempt. Out of the abundance of her true acting there now and then come thrusts of her fist, turns of her arm, which draws invisible trains into folds around her body pressing of her spread fingers to her breast because the artless scream doesn't suffice. Her acting is not varied: the frightened look at her antagonist, the searching for a way out on the small stage, the gentle voice that becomes heroic in a straight brief ascent aided only by a greater inner echo without growing louder, the joy that penetrates her through her face as it opens and expands across her high forehead to her hair, the self-sufficiency while singing a solo without the addition of new methods, the straightening up in resistance that forces the spectator to pay attention to her whole body; and not much more. But there is the truth of the whole and hence the conviction that not the least of her effects can be taken from her.

The sympathy we have for these actors, who are so good and earn nothing and in other ways too get far from enough gratitude and fame, is actually only sympathy over the sad fate of many noble endeavors and above all our own. That's why it is also so disproportionately strong, because it outwardly clings to strangers and in reality belongs to us. All the same, however, it is nonetheless so closely bound to the actors that I can't detach it from them even now. Because I recognize it, it binds itself still more closely to them in defiance.

The striking smoothness of Frau Tschissik's cheeks next to her muscular mouth. Her somewhat shapeless little girl[147]

Walking with Löwy and my sister[148] for 3 hours.

---

23 *(October 1911)* Through their presence the actors repeatedly convince me to my horror that most of what I have written about them until now is false. It is false because I write about them with unchanging love (only now when I write it down does this too become false) but varying strength and this varying strength doesn't strike the real actors loudly and correctly but dies away dully in this love, which will never be satisfied with the strength and therefore believes that, by hindering it, it is protecting the actors.

Quarrel between Tschissik and Löwy. T.: Edelstatt is the greatest Jewish writer. He is sublime. Rosenfeld is of course also a great writer but not the foremost. Löwy: Tsch. is a socialist and because Edelstatt writes social. poems, he's editor of a soc. Jewish newspaper in London, that's why Tsch. considers him the greatest. But who is Edelstatt, his party knows him, no one else, but Rosenfeld is known by the world.—Tsch.: It's not a matter of recognition. Everything by Edelstatt is sublime.—L.: I know him well too, of course. The Selbstmörder, for example, is very good.—Tsch.: What's the use of quarreling? We won't agree. I will assert my opinion until tomorrow and you too.—L.: I until the day after tomorrow.[149]

Goldfaden,[150] married, squanderer, also in great straits. About 100 plays. Made stolen liturg. melodies popular. The whole people sings them. The tailor at his work (is imitated) the maid etc.

With so little space for dressing one can't help as Tschissik says getting into quarrels. One comes excited from the scene, each regards himself as the greatest actor, steps on someone else's foot, for example, which is not to be avoided, thus not only a quarrel is prepared, but a great battle. Well in Warsaw, there were 75 small individual dressing rooms, each lit

---

At 6 o'clock I met the actors in their coffeehouse sitting around two tables, arranged according to the 2 hostile groups. On the table of the Tsch. group was a book by Perez.[151] L. had just closed it and stood up to leave with me.

Until the age of 20 L. was a bocher[152] who studied and spent his wealthy father's money. There was a group of young people of the same age who met on Saturday of all days in a locked establishment and smoked in their caftans and sinned in other ways against the holiday commandments.

"The great Adler" the most famous Yiddish actor from New York,[153] who is a millionaire, for whom Gordon wrote "Der wilde Mensch"[154] and whom L. in Karlsbad asked not to come to the performance, for he didn't have the courage to act in front of him on their poorly equipped stage.—Just sets, not this wretched stage on which one can't move. How will we perform Der wilde Mensch! One needs a divan there. At the Krystallspalast in Leipzig[155] it was great. Windows one could open, the sun shone in, one needed a throne in the play, very well there was a throne, I walked through the crowd toward it and was really a king. There it's much easier to act. Here everything flusters one.

---

24 *(October 1911)* My mother works all day, is merry and sad, as the case may be, without making the slightest fuss about her own states her voice is bright, too loud for ordinary speaking, but beneficial when one is sad and after some time suddenly hears it. For a long time I've been complaining that I am always ill but never have a particular illness that would force me to lie down in bed. This wish surely goes back for the most part to the fact that I know how comforting my mother can be when, for example, she comes from the illuminated living room into the dimness of the sickroom or in the evening, when the day begins to turn uniformly into night returns from the shop and with her worries and rapid instructions makes the already-so-late day begin again and encourages the sick one to help her with this. I would wish for this again because then I would be weak, therefore convinced by everything my mother would do and with age's more distinct ability to enjoy could have childlike pleasures. Yesterday it occurred to me that I have not always loved my mother as much as she deserved and as I could only because the German language hindered me from doing so. The Jewish mother is no "Mutter," the designation Mutter makes her a little odd (not itself, because we are in Germany) we give a Jewish woman the name German Mutter, but forget the contradiction that sinks all the more heavily into the feeling, "Mutter" is particularly German for the Jew, it unconsciously contains, besides the Christian splendor, Christian coldness too, the Jewish woman who is called Mutter therefore becomes not only odd but also foreign. Mama would be a better name, if only one didn't imagine "Mutter" behind it. I believe that only memories of the ghetto preserve the Jewish family, for the word Vater too is far from meaning the Jewish father.

Today I stood in front of Councilor Lederer,[156] who inquired unexpectedly, unbidden, childishly, mendaciously ridiculously and to the point of impatience about my illness. We hadn't spoken so intimately in a long time or perhaps ever at all, then I felt my face, never before viewed so closely by him, open for him into false, poorly comprehended parts, which, however, certainly surprised him. To myself I was unrecognizable. I know him quite well.

Second Notebook

When it had already become unbearable[157]—once toward evening in November—and I ran along the narrow carpet of my room as on a race track, frightened by the sight of the illuminated street turned around again and found a new goal far inside the room in the depths of the mirror and cried out, to hear only the cry, which nothing answers and from which nothing takes the power of the crying, which thus ascends without counterbalance and cannot stop, even when it goes silent, then the door opened out of the wall, so hastily because haste was necessary and even the carriage horses down below on the pavement rose like crazed horses in battle somewhere on their spread hind legs their throats exposed.

As a small ghost a child emerged from the completely dark corridor, where the lamp was not yet burning and stood still on tiptoe like a ballet girl, on an imperceptibly rocking floor beam. Immediately blinded by the dim light of the room, it was about to bury its face quickly in its hands, but calmed down unexpectedly with a glance at the window, outside whose cross the haze of the low street lighting, drifting upward, finally came to rest under the darkness. With its right elbow the child held itself upright against the wall of the room in front of the open door and let the draft from outside stroke its ankles also its neck, also its temples.

I looked briefly, then I said "H'lo" and took my coat from the fire screen, because I didn't want to stand there so half-naked. For a little while I kept my mouth open so that the agitation would leave me through my mouth. I had bad saliva in me, my eyelashes trembled in my face, in the l. corner of my forehead I felt a tension as from a painless gunshot, in short this visit, though expected, was the last thing I needed.

The child was still standing against the wall in the same spot, it had pressed its right hand against the masonry and very red-cheeked couldn't get enough of the fact that the whitewashed wall was coarse-grained and chafed its fingertips, which it kept looking at.

I said: Did you really mean to come to me? Isn't it a mistake? Nothing easier than a mistake in this big house. My name is so-and-so, I live on the fourth floor in room number 11. So am I the person you meant to visit?

"Hush, hush said the child over its shoulder it's all quite right."

"Then come farther into the room, I'd like to close the door."

"I've just now closed the door, don't trouble yourself, calm down altogether."

It's no trouble. But a lot of people live on this corridor, all of them are my acquaintances, of course; most of them are now returning from work; if they hear talking in a room, they simply believe they have the right to open the door and see what's going on. That's just the way it is. These people have their daily work behind them, to whom would they submit in their provisional evening freedom. Besides, you know this well too. So let me close the door

Well what's wrong? What's the matter with you? As far as I'm concerned, the whole house can come in. And once again, I've already closed the door, do you think only you can close the door? I've even locked it with the key.

All right then. That's all I want. You didn't even have to lock it with the key. And just make yourself comfortable, now that you're here. You're my guest, trust me completely. Don't be afraid to make yourself at home. I will force you neither to stay here nor to leave. Do I even have to say this? Don't you know me better than that?

No, you really didn't have to say it. What's more, you shouldn't have said it at all. I'm a child why make so much fuss about me?

It's not as bad as all that. A child, of course, but you're not so young at all. You're already quite grown up. Don't take it amiss, you're already at an age that is unpleasant to me. If you were a girl, you shouldn't so simply lock yourself in a room with me. Unless you liked me

We don't have to worry about that. I just wanted to say, the fact that I know you well doesn't protect me much, it only relieves you of the effort of telling me lies. But nonetheless you pay me compliments, stop it, I implore you, stop it. Moreover, I don't know you everywhere and all the time, especially in this darkness. It would be much better if you would have the room lit. No perhaps not. In any case I will keep in mind that you've threatened me.

What? I've threatened you? You can't mean that. Indeed I'm so glad that you're here at last. I say at last because it's already so late. It's incomprehensible to me why you've come so late. It's possible that in my pleasure I spoke in such a muddled way and that you understood it in that very way. I'll admit ten times over that I spoke in that way, indeed I threatened you with whatever you like.—Anything but a quarrel with a guest.—But how could you think it's true, how could you hurt me so, why are you trying with all your might to spoil this little while of your being here. A stranger would be more willing to meet me halfway than you.

I should think so, that was no wise insight, as close as a stranger can come to you I am already by nature. You know that too, so why the melancholy? If you say that you want to playact, I'll leave immediately

Really you dare to say even that to me? You're a little too bold. In the end you're in my room, after all. You're rubbing your fingers like mad against my wall. My room, my wall. And besides, what you say is ridiculous not just impertinent. You say your nature forces you to speak to me in this way. Really? Your nature forces you? That's nice of your nature. But then what is your nature? Your nature is my nature and if I act friendly to you by nature, you are not permitted to do otherwise

Is that friendly?

I'm talking about earlier.

Do you know how I will be later?

I know nothing.

And I went to the bedside table, where I lit the candle. (At that time I had neither gas—nor electric light in my room.) Then I sat for a while at the table until I grew tired of that too, put on my overcoat, took my hat from the sofa and blew out the candle. On my way out I got caught on a chair leg. On the stairs I met a tenant from the same floor. You're going out again you scoundrel? he said resting on his legs that were spread over two steps. "What am I supposed to do I said I've just had a ghost in my room." You say that with the same dissatisfaction as if you had found a hair in your soup.—You're joking, but keep in mind, a ghost is a ghost.—Quite true. But what if one doesn't believe in ghosts at all.—Well do you think I believe in ghosts?

The Little Ruin Dweller[158]

You I said and gave him a little push with my knee (with this sudden burst of speech some saliva flew out of my mouth as a bad omen) don't fall asleep.[159]

I want to leave, want to go up the stairs, if necessary with somersaults. From the social gathering I'm hoping for everything I lack, the organization of my powers above all, which are not satisfied by the sort of intensification that constitutes the sole possibility for this bachelor on the street. He is content just to hold his ground with his admittedly shabby but firm corporeality, protect his few meals, avoid influences of other people, in short hold on to as much as is possible in the dissolving world. What he loses, however, he seeks to regain by force, be it changed, weakened, indeed be it even only apparently his former property (and this it usually is). His is thus a suicidal nature it has only teeth for his own flesh and flesh only for his own teeth. For without a center, without a profession, a love, a family, an income, that is, without just holding out, tentatively of course, on a large scale against the world without thus astonishing it to some extent with a great complex of possessions one cannot protect oneself from momentarily destructive losses. This bachelor with his thin clothes, his art of prayer, his untiring legs, his feared rental apartment, the rest of his patchwork nature that has been called forth again this time after a long period holds all this together with both arms and must always lose two of his belongings when he catches some trifle at random. Naturally, this is where the truth lies, the truth that can nowhere be shown so purely. For he who really appears as a complete citizen, that is, travels on the sea in a ship with foam before him and with wake behind him, that is, with much effect all around entirely unlike the man on his few little pieces of wood in the waves, which even bump into each other and push each other under, he this lord and citizen is in no lesser danger. For he and his property are not one but two and whoever shatters the connection shatters him with it. Indeed we and our acquaintances are unrecognizable in this regard because we are completely concealed, I, for example, am now concealed by my profession, by my imagined or real woes, by literary inclinations, etc. But I of all people feel my depths far too often and far too strongly to be able to be even halfway content. And I need only feel these depths uninterruptedly for fifteen minutes, the poisonous world will flow into my mouth like water into the drowning man.

Between me and the bachelor there is at the moment scarcely any difference, only that I can still think of my youth in the village and perhaps, when I want perhaps even when my situation alone demands it, can cast myself back there. The bachelor, however, has nothing before him and therefore also behind him nothing. At the moment there's no difference, but the bachelor has only the moment. At that time, which today no one can know because nothing can be as annihilated as that time, at that time he missed the mark when he felt his depths continuously, just as one suddenly notices on one's body an ulcer that until now has been the least thing on our body, indeed not even the least, for it seemed not to exist yet, and now is more than everything we have possessed bodily since our birth. If until now we have been directed with our whole self at the work of our hands at what our eyes have seen, at what our ears have heard, at the steps of our feet, suddenly we turn completely toward the opposite, like a weather vane in the mountains. Now, instead of running away at that time, be it even in this last direction for only running away could keep him on the tips of his toes and only the tips of his toes could keep him in the world, instead of that he lay down, as children now and then lie down in the snow in winter to freeze to death.

He and these children, they know well that it's their fault that they lay down or otherwise yielded, they know that they should not have done it at any price, but they cannot know that after the change that is now happening to them on the fields or in the city they will forget every former guilt and every compulsion and that they will move in the new element as if it were their first.

I'm not falling asleep he replied and shook his head while opening his eyes. If I fell asleep, then how could I guard you? And don't I have to do that? Isn't that why you held on to me when we were in front of the church? Yes it was a long time ago, we know it, just leave your watch in your pocket.

As a matter of fact, it's gotten very late I said. I couldn't help smiling a little and to conceal it I looked intently into the house.

Do you really find it so appealing? So you'd like to go up, very much? Then just say so, I won't bite you. Look, if you believe that it will be better for you up there than down here, then just go up, immediately, without thinking of me. The fact that it's my view, that is, the view of some chance passerby that you will soon come down again and that it will then be very good if in some way someone is standing here whose face you will not even look at but who takes you under the arm strengthens you with wine in a nearby tavern and then leads you to his room, which as wretched as it is, still has a few panes between it and the night, for the time being you don't have to care a whit about this view. It is true, I can repeat it before whomever you want, down here we're doing badly, indeed we're even doing miserably, but I'm beyond help now whether I lie here in the gutter and dam the rainwater or drink champagne up there with the same lips it makes no difference to me. Besides, I don't even have the choice between these two things, indeed something of the sort which makes people pay attention never happens to me, and how could it happen under the structure of the ceremonies necessary for me under which I can only creep onward no better than an insect. You, to be sure, who knows all that may be in you, you have courage, at least you believe you have it, just try it, what do you risk, often one already recognizes oneself, when one pays attention in the face of the servant at the door.

If only I knew definitely that you are being honest with me. I would have long since been up there. But how could I draw out whether you are being honest with me. You're looking at me now as if I were a small child, that's no help to me, indeed that makes it even worse. But perhaps you want to make it worse. At the same time I can no longer tolerate the air on the street, so I belong up there in the social gathering by now, when I pay attention there's a scratching in my throat, and there you have it I'm coughing do you have an inkling, then, how it will be for me up there. And the foot with which I step into the hall will be transformed even before I draw the other after it.

You're right, I'm not being honest with you

But forgetting isn't the right word here. This man's memory has suffered as little as his imagination. But they just cannot move mountains; the man simply stands outside our people, outside our humanity, he is constantly starved, only the moment belongs to him, the perpetually continued moment of torment, which is followed by no glimmer of a moment of elevation, he always has only one thing: his pain but in the whole circumference of the world no second thing that could play the part of medicine, he has only as much ground as his two feet need, only as much hold as his two hands cover, thus that much less than the trapeze artist in a variety show, for whom they have even hung a safety net below. We others, we are held by our past and future, we spend almost all our idleness and how much of our profession letting them float up and down in balance. Whatever advantage the future has in size, the past makes up for in weight and at their end the two are indeed no longer distinguishable earliest youth later becomes bright as the future is and with all our sighs the end of the future is actually already experienced and past. Thus this circle, along the boundary of which we move, almost closes. Now, this circle certainly belongs to us, but belongs to us only as long as we hold it, if we move just once to the side, in some absentmindedness, in distraction fright, astonishment, fatigue, we've already lost it into space, until now we had our nose stuck in the stream of times, now we step back, former swimmers, present walkers and are lost. We are outside the law, no one knows it and yet everyone treats us accordingly.

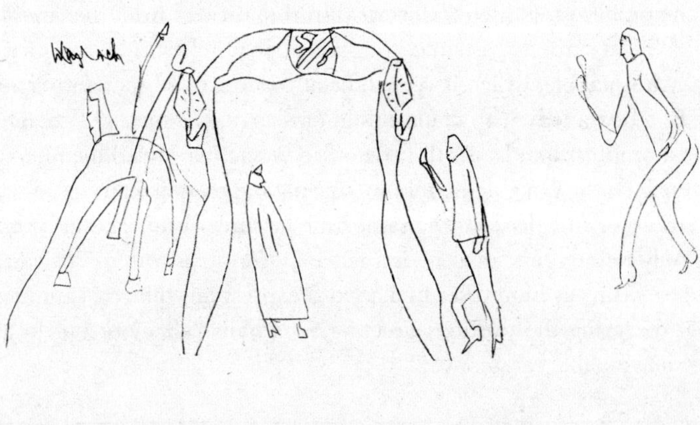

6/XI 10 Which, besides, I easily get over, for neither the one nor the other is permitted me and therefore it's not right for me to compare myself with you. And you! How long have you actually been in the city? How long have you been in the city I ask.

Five months. But I already know it well. You, I have given myself no rest. When I look back like this, I can't tell at all whether there have been nights, everything seems to me can you imagine, like one day and there were no times of day, not even differences of light

---

6 XI 10

Lecture by a Madame Chenu on Musset.[160] Jewish women's habit of lip-smacking, understanding of the French through all the preliminaries and difficulties of the anecdote, until, just before the closing words, which are supposed to live on in the heart on the ruins of the whole anecdote, the French is extinguished before our eyes, perhaps we have strained ourselves too much up to that point, the people who understand French leave before the end, because they have already heard enough, the others have heard far from enough, acoustics of the hall, which favor the coughing in the boxes more than the lecturer's words; Supper at Rachel's[161] she reads Racine: Phaedra with Musset, the book lies between them on the table, amid all sorts of other things. Consul Claudel, gleam in his eyes, which his broad face takes up and reflects, he keeps trying to say goodbye, he succeeds in part too, but not on the whole, for when he sends off one person, a new person is standing there, whom the already-sent-off one joins again. Over the lecture stage is a gallery for the orchestra. Noise of all sorts disturbs. Waiters from the corridor, guests in their rooms, a piano, a distant string orchestra, a hammering finally a squabble, which is very difficult to locate and therefore irritating. In a box a lady with diamonds in her earrings, their light changing almost uninterruptedly. At the box office young black-clad members of a French circle. One of them bows sharply in greeting, causing his eyes to dart across the floor. At the same time he smiles broadly. But he does this only before girls, men he immediately proceeds to look straight in the face with his mouth set in a serious expression, thereby simultaneously declaring the previous greeting a perhaps ridiculous but in any case unavoidable ceremony.

---

7 XI 10

Lecture Wiegler on Hebbel.[162] Sits on the stage in the set of a modern room, as if his beloved were going to leap in through a door to finally begin the play. No, he lectures. Hebbel's hunger. Complicated relationship with Elisa Lensing. In school he has an old maid as a teacher, who smokes takes snuff gives beatings and rewards the good ones with raisins. He travels everywhere [Heidelberg, Munich, Paris] with no really apparent intention. Is at first a servant to a parish magistrate, sleeps in a bed with the coachman under the stairs.

Now it perhaps seems to you as if I wanted to complain about this? But no, why complain about it, after all neither the one nor the other is permitted me. I just have to take my walks and that is supposed to be enough, but on the other hand there's no place in the world where I couldn't take my walks. But now it again seems as if I were vain about it[163]

So I have an easy time of it. I wouldn't have to stop here outside the house.

So don't compare yourself with me in this and don't let me make you uncertain. You are a grown man after all, are moreover as it seems, rather forsaken here in the city

---

Well don't you feel in light of your courage that you can't compare yourself with me in these matters. I don't understand that. How long have you been here in the city?

"Five months" I said so carefully that afterward I kept my mouth open. Yes, five months. That was right. I let the gate

---

In the end you will feel it, when you pay attention, in light of your

---

In this you simply can't compare yourself with me. But do I have to tell you that, in the end you will certainly feel it when you pay attention in light of your courage alone. How long have you actually been in the city.

Five months I said so carefully that afterward I kept my mouth open.

In this you simply can't compare yourself with me. That I even have to tell you that! Don't you feel it, when you pay attention, in light of your courage alone? How long have you actually been in the city?

And these mornings, one looks out the window, pulls the chair away from the bed and sits down to coffee. And these evenings one props up one's arm and holds one's ear with one's hand. Yes if only that weren't all! If only one acquired at least a few new habits, such as can be seen here in the streets every day

---

Julius Schnorr von Karolsfeld aft drawing by Friedrich Olivier, he is drawing on a hillside how beautiful and serious he is there (a tall hat like a flattened clown cap with a stiff narrow brim going into his face, wavy long hair, eyes only for his picture, calm hands, the board on his knees, one foot has slipped a little lower on the slope.)
but no that is Friedrich Olivier drawn by Schnorr[164]

So you mustn't think of me now.[165] And how do you want to compare yourself with me. I've been here in the city for over 20 years now. Can you even really imagine what that is. Twenty times I have spent every season here—

Now he shook his loose fist over our heads.

The trees here have been growing upward for twenty years, how small should one become under them. And these many nights, you know, in all the apartments. Now you lie against this wall, now against that one, thus the window wanders around you. And these mornings,

---

I am indeed close to it. Even now my protective being seemed to be dissolving here in the city, I was beautiful in the first days for this dissolution happens as an apotheosis, where everything that keeps us alive flies away from us, but even in flying away shines on us with its human light for the last time. So I stand before my bachelor and most likely he loves me for this reason, but without realizing why. Occasionally his speeches seem to indicate that he is well acquainted, that he knows whom he has before him and that he may therefore permit himself everything. No, it isn't so, however. Rather, he would confront everyone in this way, for he can live only as a hermit or a parasite. He is only a hermit out of compulsion, once this compulsion is overcome by forces unknown to him as in this case, he is a parasite who attaches himself impertinently however he can. He can be saved, to be sure, by nothing more in the world and so with regard to his behavior one can think of the corpse of a drowned man, which driven to the surface by some current bumps into a weary swimmer, lays its hands on him and would like to hold on. The corpse will not come to life indeed will not even be salvaged but it can pull the man under

---

So you mustn't think of me now. In a strange city it's pleasant, I know, to equate oneself once and for all with a man whom one regards as experienced

---

So you mustn't think of me now.

---

10 o'clock 15 November 1910 I won't let myself get tired. I will jump into my novella even if it should cut up my face.[166]

16 Nov. *(1910)* 12 o'clock I'm reading Iphigenie auf Tauris.[167] In it apart from individual overtly flawed passages the dried-out German language in the mouth of a pure boy is truly to be positively marveled at. Before the reader's eyes at the moment of reading, each word is borne by the verse into the heights, where it stands in a perhaps meager but penetrating light.

27 *(November 1910)* Bernhard Kellermann gave a reading:[168] some unpublished pieces from my pen, thus he began. Apparently a kind person, almost gray stiff hair, painstakingly clean-shaven, sharp nose, the flesh over his cheekbones often goes up and down like a wave. He's a mediocre writer with good passages (a man goes out into the corridor, coughs and

looks around to see whether anyone is there) also an honest person who wants to read what he promised, but the audience wouldn't let him, out of horror at the first mental institution story,[169] out of boredom with his way of reading, despite the story's bad suspense the people kept leaving one by one with a zeal as if a reading were being given next door. When he drank a little mineral water after ⅓ of the story, quite a number of people left. He was startled. It's almost finished, he simply lied. When he was finished, everyone stood up, there was some applause that sounded as if in the midst of all the standing people one had remained seated and was clapping by himself. But now Kellermann still wanted to read on, another story perhaps even several. Against the departure he only opened his mouth. Finally after he had been advised he said: I would still like to read a little fairy tale[170] that will take only 15 minutes. I'll pause for 5 minutes. Some people still remained, whereupon he read a fairy tale containing passages that would have entitled anyone to run from the farthest point of the hall straight through and over all the listeners.

Owe	Rudle[171]	1	K
	Kars[172]	20	h

You I said and gave him a little push with my knee (with this sudden burst of speech some saliva flew out of my mouth as a bad omen) don't fall asleep[173]

"I'm not falling asleep" he said quickly and shook his head while opening his eyes. If I fell asleep, then how could I guard you? And don't I have to do that? Isn't that why you held on to me when we were in front of the church? Yes it was a long time ago, we know it, just leave your watch in your pocket.

As a matter of fact, it's gotten very late I said and shrugged, thereby simultaneously apologizing for my impatience and reproaching him for keeping me so long.

"You" I said and gave him a little push with my knee (with this sudden burst of speech some saliva flew out of my mouth as a bad omen).

I haven't forgotten about you he said and shook his head even while opening his eyes.

Nor was I afraid of that I said. I ignored his smile and looked at the pavement. "I just wanted to tell you that I'm now definitely going up. Yes. For as you know I've been invited up there, it's gotten late and the guests are waiting for me. Perhaps some events are being postponed until I arrive. I don't want to claim it's so but it's still possible. You will now ask me whether I couldn't perhaps forgo the social gathering altogether.

I won't ask that, for first of all you're burning to tell me and secondly I don't care at all, because down here and up there are all the same to me. Whether I lie down here in the gutter and dam the rainwater or drink champagne up there with the same lips it makes no difference to me, not even in the taste

---

15 XII $\overline{10}$ I simply don't believe the conclusions I've drawn from my present condition, which has now lasted almost a year, my condition is too serious for that. Indeed I don't even know whether I can say that it's not a new condition. My actual opinion, to be sure, is: this condition is new, I've had similar ones, but never before one like this. It's as if I were made of stone, as if I were my own tombstone, there's no crevice for doubt or for faith, for love or repugnance, for courage or fear in particular or in general, only a vague hope lives, but no better than the inscriptions on tombstones. Almost no word I write fits with the next, I hear the consonants rubbing tinnily against each other and the vowels singing along like exhibition Negroes. My doubts stand in a circle around every word, I see them before I see the word, but what! I don't see the word at all, I invent it. That would certainly not yet be the greatest misfortune, only I would then have to be able to invent words capable of blowing the corpse smell in a direction other than straight into my own and the reader's face. When I sit down at the desk I feel no better than someone who falls in the middle of the traffic of the place de l'Opera and breaks both legs. Despite their noise all the carriages make their way silently from all sides to all sides, but the pain of that man establishes better order than the police, it closes his eyes and empties the square and the streets, without the carriages having to turn around. All the bustle is painful to him, for he is a traffic obstruction, but the emptiness is no less awful, for it sets his actual pain loose.

16 *(December 1910)* I will no longer abandon the diary. Here I must hold on, for only here can I.

I would like to explain the feeling of happiness that I have within me from time to time as I do right now. It's really something effervescent that fills me completely with a slight pleasant tremor and that persuades me of abilities of whose nonexistence I can convince myself with absolute certainty at any moment even now.

Hebbel praises Justinus Kerner "Reiseschatten"
"And a book like this scarcely exists, no one knows it"[174]

Die Strasse der Verlassenheit by W. Fred.[175] How are such books written? A man who on a small scale achieves something capable here stretches his talent into the large scale of a novel in so pitiful a way that one becomes ill even if one doesn't forget to admire the energy in the mistreatment of his own talent.[176]

This pursuit of secondary characters I read about in novels, plays, etc. This sense of belonging together I then have! In the "Jungfern von Bischofsberg" (is that what it's called?) there's mention of two seamstresses who make the linen for the one bride in the play. How are these 2 girls doing? Where do they live? What have they done that they are not permitted to come along into the play but veritably drowning in the downpours outside Noah's Ark are permitted only to press their faces one last time against a cabin window so that the patron in the orchestra sees something dark there for a moment.[177]

---

17 *(December 1910)* Zeno answered an urgent question as to whether nothing ever rests: Yes the flying arrow rests[178]

If the French by their nature were Germans, how much more they would then be admired by the Germans.[179]

That I've put aside and crossed out so much, indeed almost everything I've written this year, that definitely also hinders me a great deal from writing. Indeed it's a mountain, it's 5 times as much as I have ever written and by its mass alone it pulls everything I write away from under my pen to itself

---

18 *(December 1910)* If it weren't beyond doubt that the reason I leave letters (even those expected to contain nothing of significance, like one right now) unopened for a while is only weakness and cowardice, which hesitate to open a letter just as they would hesitate to open the door of a room in which a person, perhaps impatient by now, is waiting for me, then one could explain this leaving unopened of letters much better still by thoroughness. That is, assuming I am a thorough person, then I must try to prolong as far as possible everything concerning the letter, thus open it slowly, read it slowly and many times, think about it for a long time, prepare the clean copy with many drafts and finally hesitate even to send it off. All this lies in my power, only the sudden receipt of the letter itself cannot be avoided. Well I slow down even that in an artificial way, I don't open it for a long time, it lies on the table in front of me, it constantly offers itself to me, I constantly receive it, but don't take it.

Aesthete

---

evening ½ past 11. That I, as long as I am not freed from my office, am simply lost, that is clear to me above all, it's only a matter of holding my head as long as possible high enough that I don't drown. How hard that will be, what powers it will have to draw out of me is apparent in the mere fact that today I didn't adhere to my new schedule, to be at my desk from 8–11 in the evening, that at present I don't even regard this as such a great misfortune, that I have only hastily jotted down these few lines in order to get into bed.

19 *(December 1910)* Began to work in the office. Afternoon at Max's.

Read Goethe's diaries a little. The distance captures this life already calmed, these diaries set fire to it. The clarity of all the events makes them mysterious, just as a park fence gives the eye rest in contemplation of vast fields of grass and yet inspires our inferior respect.

Just now my married sister is coming to visit us for the first time.[180]

<u>20</u> *(December 1910)* What excuse do I have for yesterday's remark on Goethe (which is almost as untrue as the feeling described by it, for the real one was driven away by my sister)? None. What excuse do I have for having written nothing yet today? None. Especially since my disposition isn't the worst. I constantly have an invocation in my ear: "If you would come, invisible tribunal!"

So that these false passages, which won't leave the story at any price, finally give me peace I write two here:[181]

"His breaths were loud like sighs over a dream in which unhappiness is easier to bear than in our world, so that simple breaths are already sufficient sighing."

"Now I surveyed him as unhindered as one surveys a small puzzle game about which one says to oneself: "What does it matter that I can't get the little balls into their hollows, everything belongs to me, after all, the glass, the frame, the little balls and whatever else there is; this whole contrivance I can simply stick in my pocket."

<u>21</u> *(December 1910)* Oddities from "The Exploits of Alexander the Great" by Mikhail Kuzmin:[182]

"Child whose upper half was dead, lower alive," "child's corpse with moving little red legs"[183]

"the impure kings Gog and Magog, who fed on worms and flies, he drove into cracked cliffs and sealed them in until the end of the world with the seal of Solomon"[184]

"stone rivers, where instead of water stones rolled with a roar, past the sand brooks that flow for 3 days toward the south and for 3 days toward the north"[185]

Amazons, women with burnt-off right breasts, short hair, men's footgear[186]

Crocodiles that burned down trees with their urine[187]

Was at Baum's, heard such beautiful things.[188] I frail as before and always. To have the feeling of being bound and at the same time the other, that if one were unbound it would be even worse.

22 *(December 1910)* Today I don't even dare reproach myself. Shouted into this empty day it would have a disgusting echo.

---

24 *(December 1910)* Now I have taken a closer look at my desk and realized that nothing good can be done on it. There's so much lying around here, forming a disorder without regularity and without any compatibility of the disordered things, which otherwise makes every disorder bearable. Let there be whatever disorder there may on the green cloth, the same was allowed in the orchestra of old theaters. But the fact that from the standing room

25 *(December 1910)* from the open compartment under the upper part of the desk there are brochures, old newspapers, catalogues picture postcards, letters, all partly torn, partly opened coming out in the form of a staircase, this undignified state spoils everything. Individual relatively huge things in the orchestra appear in the greatest possible activity, as if it were permitted in the auditorium of the theater for the merchant to put his account books in order, the carpenter to hammer, the officer to brandish his saber, the priest to speak to the heart, the scholar to the intellect, the politician to the public spirit, for lovers not to restrain themselves, etc. Only on my desk the shaving mirror stands upright, the way one needs it for shaving, the clothes brush lies with its bristle surface on the cloth, the wallet lies open in case I want to pay, from the key ring a key sticks out ready for work and the tie is still partly looped around the taken-off collar. The next higher open compartment, already hemmed in by the small closed side drawers, is nothing but a junk room, as if the low balcony of the auditorium, basically the most visible part of the theater were reserved for the most vulgar people for old bon vivants, among whom the filth gradually comes from the inside to the outside, coarse

fellows who let their feet hang down over the balcony railing, families with so many children that one takes only a brief glance without being able to count them introduce here the filth of poor nurseries (indeed there's already a trickling in the orchestra) in the dark background sit incurably sick people, fortunately one sees them only when one shines a light in, etc. In this compartment lie old papers I would have long since thrown away if I had a wastepaper basket, pencils with broken points, an empty matchbox, a paperweight from Karlsbad, a ruler with an edge the bumpiness of which would be too awful for a country road, many collar buttons, dull razorblades (for them there is no place in the world), tie clips and another heavy iron paperweight. In the compartment above—

Wretched, wretched and yet well meant. Yes, it's midnight, but since I've slept very well, that is an excuse only insofar as during the day I would have written nothing at all. The burning electric light, the silent apartment, the darkness outside, the last waking moments they give me the right to write and be it even the most wretched things. And this right I use hastily. So that's who I am.

---

26 *(December 1910)* two ½ days I was—though not completely—alone and already I am, if not transformed, nonetheless on the way. Being alone has a power over me that never fails. My interior loosens (for the time being only superficially) and is ready to let something deeper emerge. A slight order of my interior begins to establish itself and I need nothing more, for disorder in the case of small abilities is the worst.

27 *(December 1910)* I don't have enough strength for another sentence. Yes, if it were a matter of words, if it sufficed to set down a word and one could turn away in the calm consciousness of having filled this word completely with oneself.

I slept part of the afternoon away, while I was awake I lay on the sofa, thought about some love experiences from my youth, lingered with annoyance over a missed opportunity (at the time I was lying in bed with a slight cold and my governess[189] read me "The Kreuzer Sonata,"[190] knowing how to enjoy my excitement), imagined the vegetarian supper, was satisfied with my digestion and worried about whether my eyesight would suffice for my whole life.

---

28 *(December 1910)* When I have behaved humanly for a few hours, as today with Max and later at Baum's, it's enough to make me haughty before bedtime

3 I 11

"You" I said and then gave him a little push with my knee. "I want to say goodbye." With this sudden burst of speech some saliva flew out of my mouth as a bad omen.

"But you've been considering that for a long time" he said stepped away from the wall and stretched.

No. I haven't been considering it at all.

Then what have you been thinking about?

I've been preparing myself for the last time for the social gathering. However hard you try, you won't understand it. I, just some man from the provinces, whom one can exchange at any moment for one of those people standing together by the hundreds in front of railroad stations after particular trains[191]

4 I 11 "Glaube und Heimat" by Schönherr.[192]
The wet fingers of the gallery patrons below me, who wipe their eyes.

6 I 11

"You" I said, aimed and gave him a little push with my knee, but now I'm going. If you want to see it happen, open your eyes

So you're going after all? he asked, looking at me with wide-open eyes, his gaze direct but nonetheless so weak that I could have fended it off with a wave of my arm. So you are. What am I supposed to do? I can't stop you. And even if I could, I don't want to. By which I only want to set you straight about your feeling that you could still be held back by me. And immediately he put on the face of low servants with which they are permitted in an otherwise regulated state to make the master's children obedient or afraid[193]

7 I 11 Max's sister, who is so in love with her groom that she tries to arrange things so as to speak with each visitor individually, since one can better express and repeat oneself about one's love to an individual[194]

7 I 11 As if by magic, for neither external nor internal circumstances, which are now more congenial than they have been for a year hindered me, I was kept from writing all through the free day, it's a Sunday.[195]—Some new insights into the creature of unhappiness that I am have consolingly dawned on me.

You I said, aimed and gave him a little push with my knee, open your eyes, I want to say goodbye. With this sudden burst of speech some saliva flew out of my mouth as a bad omen.

So you're going after all he said and looked at me with a gaze that ran over my face several times but seemed to meet me only by chance, since I could have fended it off with a wave of my arm.[196]

12 I 11 I haven't written much about myself in recent days, partly out of laziness (I now sleep so much and so soundly during the day, I have a greater weight while asleep) but also partly out of fear of betraying my self-knowledge. This fear is justified, for one's self-knowledge should be fixed once and for all in writing only when this could be done in the greatest completeness extending to all incidental consequences as well as with total truthfulness. For if this is not done—and I'm certainly not capable of it—then what has been written down, in accordance with its own intention and with the superior power of what has been fixed, replaces what has been merely generally felt only in such a way that the real feeling fades, while the worthlessness of what has been noted down is recognized too late.

A few days ago Leonie Frippon cabareteuse Stadt Wien.[197] Hairstyle a bound heap of curls. Bad bodice, very old dress (courtly lady), but very pretty with tragic movements, exertions of the eyelids, lunges of the long legs, well-understood stretching of the arms along the body, significance of the stiff neck at ambiguous points. Sang: Knopfsammlung im Louvre.

Schiller drawn by Schadow in 1804 in Berlin, where he had been highly revered. One cannot grasp a face more firmly than by this nose. The partition of the nose is pulled down a little due to the habit of tugging at the nose while working. A friendly somewhat hollow-cheeked person, whom the shaven face has probably given an aged appearance.[198]

---

14 I 11
Novel "Eheleute" by Beradt.[199] A lot of bad Jewishness. A sudden monotonous mischievous appearance of the author, for example, all were merry, but one man was there, he wasn't merry, or here comes a Herr Stern (whom we already know to the marrow of his novelistic bones). In Hamsun too there's something similar, but there it's as natural as the knots in wood, whereas here it drips into the plot like a fashionable medicine onto sugar.—Strange phrases are clung to without reason, for example, he attended to her hair, attended and again attended.—Individual people, without being brought into a new light, are brought out well, so well that even flaws in places do no harm. Minor characters mostly dismal.

17 I 11 Max read me the first act of "Abschied von der Jugend."[200] How can I, as I am today, measure up to this; I would have to search for a year before finding a true feeling within me and in the face of so great a work I'm supposed to be somehow entitled to remain seated in my chair in a coffeehouse late in the evening plagued by stray winds of a digestion that is bad despite everything.

19 I 11
Every day, since I seem to be utterly done for—in the past year I have woken up for no more than 5 minutes—I will either have to wish myself off the earth or else, without being permitted to see even the most moderate hope in it, begin anew as a small child. This will be outwardly easier for me than at the time. For in those days I still strove with scarcely a faint suspicion for a depiction that would be connected with my life from word to word, that I would draw to my breast and that would carry me away from where I was. With what misery (incomparable, certainly, to the present one) I began! What coldness pursued me for days from what I had written! How great the danger was and how almost uninterruptedly it was at work, so that I didn't feel that coldness at all, which, to be sure, didn't diminish my unhappiness much on the whole.

Once I planned a novel in which two brothers fought each other, one of whom went to America, while the other remained in a European prison. I began to write lines only now and then, for it tired me immediately. Thus, one Sunday afternoon, when we were visiting my grandparents[201] and had eaten the especially soft bread spread with butter that was always customary there, I wrote down something about my prison. It's quite possible that I did this for the most part out of vanity and by shifting the paper on the tablecloth, tapping with the pencil, looking around in the group under the lamp I wanted to tempt someone to take from me what I had written, look at it and admire me. The few lines described mainly the corridor of the prison, above all its silence and coldness; a sympathetic word was also said about the brother who stayed behind, because he was the good brother. Perhaps I had a momentary feeling of the worthlessness of my description, only before that afternoon I never paid much attention to such feelings when I sat among relatives to whom I was accustomed (my anxiousness was so great that the accustomed was enough to make me halfway happy) around the round table in the familiar room and could not forget that I was young and called out of this present tranquility to great things. An uncle who liked to laugh at people finally took from me the sheet of paper, which I was holding only weakly, looked at it briefly, handed it back to me without even laughing and said only to the others, who followed him with their eyes "The usual stuff," to me he said nothing. Though I remained seated and bent as before over my thus unusable sheet of paper, I had actually been driven out of the social sphere with one push, my uncle's judgment repeated itself in me with now almost real significance and even within the family feeling I got an insight into the cold space of our world, which I had to warm with a fire that I first wanted to seek

20 II 11
Mella Mars in the "Lucerna."[202] A witty tragedienne, who, as it were, appears on a reversed stage in the way tragediennes sometimes show themselves behind the scenes. When she appears she has a tired, indeed even flat empty old face, which is a natural start for all conscious actors. She speaks very sharply her movements are the same beginning with the bent-back thumb, which instead of bones seems to have hard sinews. Particular mutability of her nose through the changing lights and hollows of the muscles playing around it. Despite the endless flashes of her movements and words she emphasizes gently.

Small cities also have small areas for the walker.[203]

The young clean well-dressed boys next to me on the promenoir reminded me of my youth and therefore made an unappetizing impression on me.[204]

Kleist youthful letters 22 years old. Gives up the military profession. At home they ask: So which breadwinning field, for they thought that went without saying. You have a choice between jurisprudence & cameralism. But do you also have connections at court? "I said no at first in some embarrassment, but then declared all the more proudly that even if I had connections, according to my current notions I should be ashamed of counting on them. They smiled, I felt that I had been overhasty. One must beware of speaking such truths"[205]

21 II 11 My life here is as if I were quite certain of a second life, just as, for example, I got over the failed stay in Paris[206] by bearing in mind that

I would strive to go there again soon. With this the sight of the sharply divided patches of light and shadow on the street pavement.

For a moment I felt encased in armor.

How far from me, for example, my arm muscles are.

Marc Henry—Delvard.[207] The tragic feeling engendered in the spectator by the empty hall is favorable to the effect of serious songs, harmful to the funny ones.—Henry presents the prologue, while Delvard, behind a curtain she doesn't know is translucent arranges her hair.—At poorly attended events Wetzler[208] the organizer seems to wear his Assyrian beard, which is otherwise deep black, flecked with gray.—Good to let such a temperament blow on you, it lasts for 24 hours, no not so long.—Very extravagant clothing, Breton costumes, the undermost underskirt is the longest, so that one can count the wealth from a distance.—First Delvard accompanies, because they wanted to save an accompanist, in a wide low-cut green dress and freezes.—Parisian street cries. Paperboys are left out.—Someone speaks to me, before I take a breath I've been dismissed.—Delvard is ridiculous, she has the smile of old maids, an old maid of the German cabaret, with a red shawl that she fetches behind the curtain she makes revolution,[209] poems by Dauthendey with the same tough voice that cannot be chopped up. Only when she sat in a womanly way at the piano in the beginning was she endearing.—During the song "a Batignolles"[210] I felt Paris in my throat. Batignolles is supposed to have a pensioner character, even its Apaches.[211] Bruant[212] has given every quarter its song.

The Urban World[213]

Oskar M. an older student—if one looked at him closely, one was frightened by his eyes—stopped on a winter afternoon in the middle of the snowfall on an empty square in his winter clothes with his winter coat over them a shawl around his neck and a fur cap on his head. He blinked his eyes in reflection. He was so lost in thought that at one point he took off his cap and stroked his face with its curly fur. Finally he seemed to have come to a conclusion and set off with a dancing turn for home. When he opened the door of his parents' living room, he saw his father a clean-shaven man with a heavy fleshy face sitting at an empty table facing the door. "Finally" said the latter when Oskar had hardly set foot in the room, stay at the door I beg you, for I'm so angry with you that I don't trust myself. But Father said Oskar and realized only as he spoke how he had been running. Silence shouted his father and stood up, thereby covering a window. I command silence. And keep your buts to yourself, do you understand. At the same time he took the table with both hands and carried it a step closer to Oskar. I simply cannot bear your dissolute life any longer. I'm an old man. In you I thought I had a consolation of old age, instead you're worse for me than all my illnesses. Shame on such a son, who by laziness, wastefulness, malice, and stupidity is driving his old father into the grave. Here his father fell silent, but moved his face as if he were still speaking. Dear Father said Oskar, cautiously approaching the table, calm down, everything will be all right. Today I had an idea that will make me into as active a person as you can wish me to be. How's that? asked his father, looking into a corner of the room. Just trust me, I'll explain everything to you at dinner. Inwardly I was always a good son, but the fact that I couldn't show it outwardly so embittered me that I preferred to make you angry if I couldn't make you happy. But now let me go for another short walk so that my thoughts develop more clearly. His father, who becoming attentive at first had sat down on the edge of the table, stood up: I don't believe that what you've just said makes much sense, I think it's more likely chatter. But after all you're my son—Come on time we'll have supper at home and you can present your case then. This small confidence is enough for me, I'm grateful to you from my heart for it. But can't it be seen in my eyes alone that I'm completely occupied with a serious matter? For the time being I see nothing said his father. But it might be my fault, for I'm out of practice in looking at you at all. All the while, as was his habit, he called attention to how time was passing by regularly tapping the tabletop. The main thing, however, is that I have no more confidence in you at all Oskar. If I ever shout at you—when you came I did shout at you? didn't I?—I do so not in the hope that it could better you, I do so only for the sake of your poor good mother, who now perhaps doesn't yet feel any immediate sorrow over you, but under the sheer strain of fending off such sorrow, for she believes that by doing so she is in some way helping you, is gradually going to ruin. But in the end these are certainly things you know very well, and out of consideration for myself alone I wouldn't have mentioned them again if you hadn't provoked me to do so with your promises. During these last words the maid entered to tend the fire in the stove. No sooner had she left the room than Oskar cried out: But Father! I wouldn't have expected that. If I'd had only a little idea, let's say, an idea for my dissertation, which has been lying in my cabinet for 10 years now and needs ideas like salt then it's possible even if not probable that as happened today, I would have run home from my walk and said: Father happily I have such and such an idea. If in response to that you had said the reproaches from just now to my face with your venerable voice, then my idea would simply have been blown away and I would have immediately had to march off with some apology or without any. Now on the other hand! Everything you say against me helps my ideas, they don't stop, growing strong they fill my head. I will go because I can put them in order only in solitude. He swallowed his breath in the warm room. It might also be a paltry scheme that you have in your head said his father with wide eyes in that case I really believe that it holds you in its grip. But if something industrious has strayed into you, it will escape you overnight. I know you. Oskar turned his head as if he were being held by the neck. Let me be now. You're boring into me unnecessarily. The mere possibility that you can correctly predict my end should really not tempt you to disturb me in my careful reflection. Perhaps my past gives you the right to do so, but you shouldn't take advantage of it. There you see best how great your uncertainty must be when it forces you to speak against me like that. Nothing forces me said Oskar, his neck twitching. He also stepped up very close to the table, so that one no longer knew to whom it belonged. What I said, I said with reverence and even out of love for you, as you'll see later, for in my decisions consideration for you and Mama plays the greatest part. Then I must thank you now at once said his father since it's certainly very unlikely that your mother and I will still be capable of it at the right moment. Please Father just let the future go on sleeping, as it deserves. For if one wakes it before its time, then one gets a sleepy present. But that your son even has to tell you this. I didn't want to convince you yet anyhow, but only to announce the news to you. And in that at least, as you yourself must admit I've succeeded. Now Oskar there's actually one more thing that surprises me: why you haven't come to me often before with such a matter as you have today. It so befits your nature up to now. No really, I'm being serious.

Certainly you would have beaten me then instead of listening to me. I ran here, God knows, to quickly make you happy. But I can't reveal anything to you as long as my plan isn't completely finished. So why do you punish me for my good intentions and want explanations from me that now could still harm the carrying out of my plan.

Be quiet I don't want to know anything at all. But I have to answer you very quickly because you are retreating toward the door and apparently have something very urgent to do: You assuaged my initial anger with your trick, only now I feel even sadder than before and therefore I beg you—if you insist I can even fold my hands—at least tell your mother nothing of your ideas. Be content with me.

This is surely not my father who speaks to me like this cried Oskar, who had already put his arm on the door handle. Something has happened to you since noon or you're a stranger I'm now encountering for the first time in my father's room. My real father—Oskar was silent for a moment with his mouth open—he would have had to embrace me, he would have called my mother in. What's the matter Father?

You should have supper with your real father instead, I think. It would be more enjoyable.

He'll certainly come. In the end he can't stay away. And my mother must be there. And Franz whom I'm fetching now. Everyone. Thereupon Oskar pushed with his shoulder against the easily opening door as if he had intended to smash it down.

Having arrived in Franz's apartment he bowed to the little landlady with the words: The Herr Engineer is asleep I know, it doesn't matter, and without paying attention to the woman, who out of displeasure with the visit walked up and down to no purpose in the hall, he opened the glass door, which trembled in his hand as if it had been grasped in a sensitive place and shouted without concern for the inside of the room, which he could still scarcely see: Franz, get up. I need your expert advice. But I can't stand it here in the room, we have to go for a brief walk. You also have to have supper with us. So hurry. Gladly said the engineer from his leather sofa but which first get up have supper go for a walk, give advice? There must be some things I've missed too. Above all don't make jokes Franz. That's the most important thing, I forgot that.

I'll do you that favor immediately. But getting up—I'd rather have supper for you twice than get up once. Up now, I say! Don't argue. Oskar grasped the weak man by the front of his dressing gown and sat him up. You're brutal you know. With all due respect. He wiped his closed eyes with both little fingers. Say. Have I ever yanked you off the sofa like this. But Franz said Oskar with a grimace get dressed already. After all, I'm no fool, to have woken you for no reason.—Just as I wasn't sleeping for no reason either. I had the night shift yesterday, then today I've already been deprived of my midday sleep, also because of you—Why? Now look here, it really does annoy me how little consideration you have for me. It's not the first time. Of course, you're a free student and can do what you want. Not everyone is so fortunate. So one just has to have some consideration, darn it. True, I'm your friend, but they haven't taken my profession away from me yet because of that.—He showed this by shaking his flat hands back and forth. But judging by your present gabbing don't I have to believe that you've had more than enough sleep said Oskar who had pulled himself up onto a bedpost from where he looked at the engineer as if he now had somewhat more time than before. Well what do you want from me anyway? or rather why have you woken me asked the engineer, rubbing his neck vigorously under his goatee in the closer connection one has to one's body after sleep. What I want from you Oskar said softly, giving the bed a push with his heel. Very little. I told you already from the hall: that you get dressed. If you mean to imply by that Oskar that your news interests me very little, then you're completely correct. That's all right, in that case the fire it will kindle in you will burn entirely on its own account, without our friendship having interfered. The information will be clearer too, I need clear information, keep that in mind. But if you are perhaps looking for collar and tie, they're lying there on the chair. Thanks said the engineer, beginning to fasten collar & tie one can rely on you after all.

---

26 III 11

Theosophical lectures by Dr. Rudolf Steiner Berlin.[214] Rhetorical effect: Comfortable discussion of the objections of opponents, the listener is astonished at this strong opposition, further elaboration and praise of these objections, the listener begins to worry, complete immersion in these objections as if there were nothing else, the listener now considers a refutation altogether impossible and is more than satisfied with a cursory description of the possibility of a defense.

This rhetorical effect is consistent, moreover, with the rule of the devotional mood.—Constant looking at the palm of the held-out hand.—Omission of the period. In general the spoken sentence begins with its initial capital letter from the orator, bends in its course as far as it can out to the listeners and returns with the period to the orator. But if the period is omitted, then the sentence, no longer held back, blows directly on the listener with full breath.

---

previously lecture Loos and Kraus.[215]

In Western European stories, as soon as they want to include even a few groups of Jews, we are now almost accustomed to immediately seeking and finding under or over the depiction the solution to the Jewish question too. Yet in Jüdinnen such a solution is not shown indeed not even presumed, for those very characters who occupy themselves with such questions stand farther away from the center of the story, at a point where events are already spinning more rapidly, so that, even though we can still observe them closely, we no longer find an opportunity to receive from them calm information about their efforts. Without further ado we recognize in this a deficiency of the story and feel all the more entitled to such a criticism as today since the existence of Zionism the possibilities for a solution are so clearly arrayed around the Jewish problem that in the end the writer would have had to take only a few steps to find the possibility for a solution appropriate to his story.

But this deficiency arises from still another one. Jüdinnen lacks the non-Jewish spectators, the respectable opposing people, who in other stories lure the Jewishness out so that it advances against them, is astonished, afflicted with doubt, envy horror and finally, finally inspired with self-confidence, but in any case can draw itself up to its full height only opposite them. We demand just that, we don't accept any other dissolution of Jewish masses. And we invoke this feeling not only in this case, it is general in at least one respect. So too do lizards starting at our steps on a footpath in Italy delight us immensely we keep wanting to bend down, but if we see them at a dealer's crawling in disorder by the hundreds in the large jars otherwise used for pickling cucumbers, then we don't know how to orient ourselves

Both deficiencies unite into a third. "Jüdinnen" can do without that young man at the forefront who within his story usually seizes the best and leads them in a beautiful radial direction to the boundaries of the Jewish circle. That is just what we cannot grasp, that the story can do without this young man, here we sense a flaw more than we see it.[216]

Today is your birthday, but I'm not even sending you the usual book, for it would be nothing but pretense; at bottom I'm not even capable of giving you a book. I'm writing only because I so need to be close to you for a moment today and be it only with this card, and I've begun with the complaint so that you recognize me immediately.[217]

In Western European stories, as soon as they want to include even a few groups of Jews, we are now almost accustomed to immediately seeking and finding somewhere under or over the depiction the solution to the Jewish question too. In "Jüdinnen," however, such a solution is not shown, indeed not even presumed, for those very characters who concern themselves with such questions stand farther away from the center of the story, at a point where events are already spinning more rapidly, so that, even though we can still observe them closely, we no longer find an opportunity to receive from them calm information about their efforts. Without further ado we recognize in this a deficiency of the story and feel all the more entitled to such a criticism as today since the existence of Zionism the possibilities for a solution stand so clearly arrayed around the Jewish problem that in the end the writer would have had to take only a few steps to find the possibility for a solution appropriate to his story.

On closer examination this deficiency arises from a prior one. Jüdinnen lacks

It had by now become a habit of the four friends Robert Samuel, Max and Franz to use their short vacation every summer or autumn for a trip together. During the rest of the year their friendship consisted mostly in the fact that all four of them liked to meet one evening a week usually at Samuel's who as the wealthiest had a spacious room, to tell each other various things while drinking a moderate amount of beer. At midnight when they parted they were never finished with the telling, for Robert was secretary of an association, Samuel an employee of a commercial office, Max a civil servant and Franz an official in a bank, so that almost everything one of them had experienced in his profession during the week was unknown to the other three and told to them quickly but also incomprehensible to them without elaborate explanation. But above all the diversity of these professions meant that each of them was forced to describe his profession to the others again and again, for the others being only weak people after all didn't understand these descriptions thoroughly enough but for that very reason and also out of good friendship demanded them again and again. Stories about women, on the other hand, were rarely related, for even if Samuel personally would have enjoyed them, he took care not to demand that the conversation adapt itself to his needs, while the old maid who fetched the beer often appeared to him as an admonition. But they laughed so much on these evenings that Max said on the way home that this perpetual laughter was actually regrettable, because it made one forget all the serious matters of which, after all, everyone had enough to bear at the moment. While one was laughing one thought there would still be time enough for seriousness. But that wasn't correct, for seriousness naturally made greater demands on a person and it was clear, after all, that in the company of friends one was also capable of satisfying greater demands than alone. One should laugh in the office, because there one wouldn't achieve anything more. This opinion was directed at Robert, who worked a great deal in his in the old art association that he was rejuvenating and at the same time noticed the funniest things with which he entertained his friends. As soon as he began his friends left their seats, stood around him or sat down on the table and laughed especially Max and Franz with such abandon that Samuel carried all the glasses over to a little side table. When they were tired of telling stories Max sat down at the piano with suddenly renewed strength and played, while Robert and Samuel sat beside him on the little bench, Franz on the other hand who understood nothing of music, remained alone at the table looking through Samuel's picture postcard collection or reading the newspaper. When the evenings grew warmer and the window could be left open, all four might come to the window and with their hands behind their backs look down into the street without letting the traffic, light though it was, divert them from their conversation. Only now and then one of them went back to the table to take a sip or pointed at the curly hair of two girls sitting down below in front of their wine tavern or at the moon, which easily surprised them or Max described what he was telling with outspread fingers out in the air, reaching over his neighbor's shoulder, until finally Franz said it was cool, they should close the window. In summer they sometimes met in a public garden, sat down at a table at the very edge, where it was darker, drank to each other and with their heads together in conversation hardly noticed the distant brass band. Arm in arm, in step with each other, they then walked home through the park. The two at the ends twirled their canes or struck the bushes, Robert [One thinks one describes him correctly, but it is only approximated and is corrected by the diary.] invited them to sing, but then sang by himself well enough for four, making the other in the middle feel especially safe and secure. One such evening Franz, pressing his two neighbors more closely to him, said it was so nice to be together that he couldn't understand why they met only once a week, when it would certainly be easy to arrange to see each other, if not often, then at least twice a week why not twice instead. All were in favor of it, even the fourth one who from the outside had understood Franz's soft speaking only indistinctly. Such a pleasure would certainly be worth the slight trouble it would now and then cause one of them. It seemed to Franz as if, in punishment for speaking unbidden for all of them, his voice had grown hollow. But he didn't desist. And if one of them ever really couldn't come, then it would simply be his loss and he could be consoled the next time, but was that any reason for the others to have to forgo each other, weren't three enough for each other and if necessary even two. Of course, of course said everyone. Samuel detached himself from the end and walked just ahead of the 3 others, because in that way they were closer to each other. But then, on second thought, this seemed to him not to be the case and he preferred to link arms with them. Robert made a proposal: We meet every week and study Italian. We're determined to learn Italian for last year already we saw in the little piece of Italy where we were that our Italian suffices only to ask the way when we got lost you remember among the vineyard walls of the Campagna. And even for that it sufficed only with great effort on the part of those we asked. So we must study if we want to go to Italy again this year. There's no way around it. And isn't it best, then, to study together? No said Max we won't learn anything together. I'm just as certain of that as you Sam are in favor of studying together. Indeed I am said Samuel. We'll definitely learn very well together, I always regret only that we weren't together already in school. Do you realize that we've known each other for only 2 years. He leaned forward to see all 3. They had slowed their pace and loosened their arms. But we haven't learned anything together yet said Franz. I like it very much that way. I don't want to study anything at all. But if we must learn Italian, then it's better for each of us to learn it for himself. I don't understand that said Samuel. First you want us to meet every week, then you don't want it. "Nonsense said Max, Franz and I just don't want our togetherness to be disturbed by studying or our studying by togetherness nothing else." Quite right said Franz. There isn't much time left anyhow said Max it's June now and in September we want to leave. That's exactly why I want us to study together said Robert, looking wide-eyed at the two who were against him. His neck in particular grew limber when someone contradicted him.[218]

It probably lies in the nature of friendship and follows it like a shadow—one will welcome it, the other regret it, the third not even notice it

(Continuation of the text from page 256)

Schubal could be reproached for anything, it was for having been unable to break the stoker's recalcitrant spirit sufficiently in the course of time to prevent him from daring to appear before the captain today.[219]

Well one could perhaps still assume that the confrontation of the stoker and Schubal wouldn't fail to have the same effect before human beings as was its due before a higher forum, for even if Schubal could dissemble well, he would by no means necessarily be able to keep it up to the end. A brief flash of his wickedness should suffice to make it visible to the gentlemen, Karl would make sure of that. He was already roughly familiar with the acuity, the weaknesses, the moods of the individual gentlemen, and from that point of view the time spent here up to now had not been wasted. If only the stoker had been in better shape, but he seemed completely unfit for battle. If someone had held Schubal out to him, he probably could have cracked open his hated skull with his fists, like a thin-shelled nut. But even to take the few steps to him was probably more than he could manage. Why, then, hadn't Karl foreseen what could have been foreseen so easily, that in the end Schubal was bound to come, if not of his own accord, then summoned by the captain. Why hadn't he discussed a precise plan of attack on the way here with the stoker, instead of simply entering hopelessly unprepared where there was a door as they had done in reality? Could the stoker still speak at all, say yes and no, as would be necessary during the cross-examination, which, to be sure, lay ahead only in the most favorable case. He stood there, his legs apart, his knees slightly bent, his head somewhat raised and the air flowed through his open mouth as if there were no longer any lungs within to deal with it

Karl, on the other hand, felt stronger and more clearheaded than he had perhaps ever been at home. If only his parents could see him, fighting for a good cause before respected figures in a foreign land and even if he had not yet achieved victory, standing fully prepared for the final conquest. Would they revise their opinion of him? Sit him down between them and praise him? Look him just once just once in the eyes that were so devoted to them? Uncertain questions and the most unsuitable moment to ask them!

"I've come because I believe that the stoker has been accusing me of some sort of dishonesty. A girl from the kitchen told me she had seen him on his way here. Herr Captain and all you gentlemen, I'm prepared to refute every accusation with the help of my papers, if necessary with statements of unprejudiced and uninfluenced witnesses, who are standing outside the door." Thus spoke Schubal. That was certainly the clear speech of a man and judging by the change in the listeners' expressions one might have thought they were hearing human sounds for the first time in a long while. They didn't notice, to be sure, that even this fine speech had holes in it. Why was the first relevant word that occurred to him "dishonesty"? Should the accusation perhaps have begun here, instead of with his national prejudices? A girl from the kitchen had seen the stoker on his way to the office and Schubal had comprehended at once? Wasn't it his sense of guilt that sharpened his understanding? And he had immediately brought along witnesses and moreover called them unprejudiced and uninfluenced? Trickery nothing but trickery and the gentlemen tolerated it and even recognized it as proper behavior? Why had he undoubtedly allowed so much time to elapse between the kitchenmaid's report and his arrival here, if not for the sole purpose of letting the stoker so weary the gentlemen that they gradually lost their power of clear judgment, which was what Schubal had to fear most of all? Hadn't he surely after standing behind the door for a long time knocked only at the moment when the one gentleman's casual question gave him reason to hope the stoker was done for?

It was all clear and indeed that was how Schubal had presented it in spite of himself, but one had to tell it to the gentlemen in a different, still more palpable way. They needed shaking up. And so hurry, Karl, at least take advantage of the time before the witnesses appear and swamp everything.

But just then the captain waved Schubal away, whereupon the latter at once stepped aside—for his affair seemed to have been postponed for a little while—and began a soft conversation with the servant, who had immediately attached himself to him, during which there was no lack of side glances at the stoker and Karl as well as hand movements of the greatest conviction. Schubal seemed to be rehearsing his next great speech.

"Didn't you want to ask the young man here something, Herr Jakob?" the captain said amid general silence to the gentleman with the bamboo cane.

"Indeed" said the latter thanking him for the attention with a slight bow. And then asked Karl again: "What's your name anyway?"

Karl, believing it would be in the interest of the most important matter for this incident of the stubborn questioner to be settled quickly, answered briefly, without introducing himself as was his habit by presenting his passport, which he would have first had to search for: "Karl Rossmann."

"Well" said the man who had been addressed as Jakob, initially stepping back with an almost incredulous smile. The captain too, the chief purser, the ship's officer, indeed even the servant clearly showed excessive astonishment at Karl's name. Only the gentlemen from the harbor authority and Schubal remained indifferent.

"Well" repeated Herr Jakob, approaching Karl with somewhat stiff steps, then I am your Uncle Jakob and you are my dear nephew. Just as I suspected all along he said to the captain before hugging and kissing Karl, who silently submitted to everything.

What's your name? Karl asked after feeling himself released very politely but entirely unmoved and made an effort to predict the consequences this new event might have for the stoker. For the time being nothing indic. that Schubal could derive any benefit from this situation.

Don't you realize how lucky you are young man said the captain, believing the question injured the personal dignity of Herr Jakob, who had gone to the window, apparently to keep from having to show the others his agitated face, which, moreover, he was dabbing with a handkerchief. It is State Councilor Edward Jakob who has revealed himself to you as your uncle. No doubt quite contrary to your previous expectations, a brilliant career now awaits you. Try to recognize this as well as you can at this first moment and pull yourself together.

I do indeed have an Uncle Jakob in America said Karl facing the captain, but if I understood correctly, only the surname of the Herr State Councilor is Jakob"

That's true the captain said expectantly.

Well my Uncle Jakob, who is my mother's brother, has Jakob as his Christian name while his surname would of course have to be the same as my mother's, whose maiden name was Bendelmayer.

"Gentlemen!" cried the state councilor in response to Karl's explanation, returning cheerfully from his recovery post by the window. Everyone with the exception of the harbor officials burst out laughing, some as if moved, others impenetrably.

But what I said wasn't so ridiculous at all thought Karl.

"Gentlemen" repeated the state councilor you are taking part against my will and yours in a little family scene and therefore I cannot avoid giving you an explanation, since I believe only the Herr Captain (this mention led to an exchange of bows) is fully informed.

Now I really must pay attention to every word Karl said to himself and was pleased to notice with a sideways glance that life was beginning to return to the figure of the stoker.

For all the long years of my stay in America—though the word stay is poorly suited to the American citizen that I am with my whole soul—for all these long years I've been living completely cut off from my European relatives, for reasons that are first of all not pertinent here and secondly would really take too much out of me to tell. I even fear the moment I will be forced to tell them to my dear nephew, at which point some frank words about his parents and their circle will unfortunately be unavoidable.

"He is my uncle no doubt about it" Karl said to himself, listening intently. "He probably had his name changed."

Now my dear nephew has simply been—let's just say the word that really describes the situation—cast aside by his parents, just as one throws a cat out when it annoys one. I certainly don't want to gloss over what my nephew has done to be thus punished—glossing over is not the American way—but his guilt is such that the mere naming of it contains enough of an excuse.

"That sounds good" thought Karl "but I don't want him to tell everyone the story. Besides, it's not as if he could know it. How, then? But we'll see, he does seem to know everything."

"He was, namely" his uncle went on, leaning with slight bows on the bamboo cane planted in front of him whereby he actually managed to deprive the matter of some of the unnecessary solemnity it would otherwise definitely have had—he was, namely, seduced by a maid Johanna Brummer, a person of about 35 years of age. With the word seduced I by no means want to hurt my nephew, but it's just hard to find another equally fitting word.

Karl who by now had moved quite close to his uncle, here turned around to read from the faces of those present the impression the story had made on them. No one was laughing, everyone was listening patiently and seriously. After all, one doesn't laugh at the nephew of a state councilor at the first opportunity that presents itself. If anything, one might have said that the stoker was smiling at Karl albeit only very faintly, which, however, was first of all gratifying as a new sign of life and secondly excusable, since in the cabin Karl had tried to make a special secret of this matter, which was now becoming so public.

Well this Brummer his uncle went on had a child by my nephew, a healthy boy, who was christened Jakob, undoubtedly with my humble self in mind, because even my nephew's surely only quite casual mentions of me must have made a great impression on the girl. Fortunately I might add. For since his parents to avoid paying child support or being touched by any other scandal—I must emphasize that I'm acquainted neither with the laws there nor with his parents' other circumstances, but am aware only of two begging letters sent by his parents some time ago, which I left unanswered but kept and which constitute the only and, moreover, one-sided written contact I've had with them the whole time—since, as I was saying, to avoid the child support payments and the scandal his parents shipped off their son my dear nephew to America, irresponsibly ill-equipped, as one can see—the boy, were it not for the signs and wonders that are alive in America if nowhere else, left to fend for himself, would probably have immediately gone to ruin in an alley in the harbor of Newyork, if that maid hadn't sent me a letter, which after long wanderings came into my possession the day before yesterday, notifying me of my nephew's arrival the whole story together with a personal description of my nephew and, sensibly enough, the name of the ship. If I were aiming to entertain you, gentlemen, there are some passages from that letter—he pulled two huge closely written sheets of paper out of his pocket and waved them around—I might read aloud here. It would certainly have an effect, written as it is with a somewhat simple though always well-meant shrewdness and with much love for the father of her child. But I want neither to entertain you more than is necessary for the sake of clarification nor perhaps, at the very moment of welcoming my nephew, to hurt any feelings possibly retained by him, who can read the letter, if he likes, for his own instruction in the quiet of the room that is already waiting for him.

But Karl had no feelings for that girl. In the throng of a past pushed back ever farther she sat in her kitchen next to the kitchen cupboard, resting her elbow on top of it. She looked at him when he came into the kitchen now and then to fetch a glass of water for his father or to deliver instructions from his mother. Sometimes she was writing a letter in that awkward position by the side of the kitchen cupboard and drew inspiration from Karl's face. Sometimes she kept her eyes covered with her hand, then no word penetrated to her. Sometimes she was kneeling in her narrow little room next to the kitchen and praying to a wooden cross, Karl then observed her shyly through the crack of the slightly open door as he passed. Sometimes she was rushing around in the kitchen and recoiled laughing like a witch when Karl got in her way. Sometimes she closed the kitchen door when Karl had entered and kept holding the handle until he demanded to leave. Sometimes she fetched things he didn't want at all and pressed them silently into his hands. One time, however, she said "Karl!" and, while he was still astonished at the unexpected way she had addressed him, led him with grimaces and sighs into her little room, locking the door. She put her arms around his neck, choking him, and while she asked him to undress her, she actually undressed him and laid him in her bed as if from now on she would let no one else have him and would stroke him and care for him until the end of the world. "Karl, o my Karl" she cried as if she could see him and were confirming her possession of him, while he couldn't see the slightest thing and felt uncomfortable in all the warm bedclothes, which she seemed to have heaped up specially for him. Then she lay down with him and wanted him to reveal some secrets, but he couldn't tell her any and she grew annoyed in jest or in earnest, shook him, listened to his heart, offered her breast for him to listen to hers, but couldn't get Karl to do so, pressed her naked belly against his body, searched with her hand, so disgustingly that Karl shook his head and neck out of the pillows, between his legs, then thrust her belly against him several times, he felt as if she were part of him and perhaps for that reason a terrible helplessness had seized him. Weeping, after many entreaties on her part to meet again, he at last reached his bed. That had been all and yet his uncle had managed to make so much of it. And so the cook had also thought him and informed his uncle of his arrival. That had been nicely done by her and he might well repay her for it one day.

"And now" cried the senator I want you to tell me frankly whether I'm your uncle or not.

"You are my uncle" Karl said and kissed his hand and was kissed on the forehead in return. "I'm very glad to have met you, but you're mistaken if you believe that my parents only speak ill of you. But even leaving that aside, your speech contained several errors, that is, I don't think everything happened like that in reality. But you also really can't judge things so well from here and besides, I don't believe it will do any particular harm if the gentlemen have been somewhat misinformed about the details of a matter that really can't mean much to them."

"Well put" said the senator, leading Karl to the visibly sympathetic captain and saying "Don't I have a splendid nephew?"

"I'm happy" the captain said with a bow such as only people with military training can achieve "to have become acquainted with your nephew, Herr Senator. It's a special honor for my ship to have been able provide the setting for such a meeting. But the voyage in the steerage was probably awful, who can really know who is being carried there. Once, for example, the firstborn son of the highest Hungarian magnate, the name and the reason for the journey have slipped my mind, traveled in our steerage. I found out about it only much later. Now, we do everything we can to make the voyage as easy as possible for the people in the steerage, far more, for example, than the American lines, but to turn such a voyage into a pleasure is certainly more than we've been able to manage as yet."

"It did me no harm" said Karl.

"It did him no harm!" the senator repeated with a loud laugh.

There's just the matter of my suitcase, which I'm afraid I've— And with that he remembered everything that had happened and still remained to be done looked around and saw all those present silent with respect and astonishment in their previous spots their eyes on him. Only the harbor officials, insofar as their stern self-satisfied faces granted any insight, showed regret at having come at such an inopportune time and the pocket watch they now had lying in front of them was probably more important to them than anything that was going on or might still happen in the room.

The first person after the captain to express his sympathy was, strangely enough, the stoker. "I sincerely congratulate you" he said and shook Karl's hand, thereby trying to convey something like appreciation too. When he was about to address the senator with the same words, the latter, however, stepped back as if the stoker were exceeding his rights; the stoker then immediately desisted.

But the others now realized what was to be done and at once formed a jumble around Karl and the senator. So it happened that Karl even received congratulations from Schubal, which he accepted with thanks.

The last to come up, once things had calmed down again, were the harbor officials, who said two English words, making a ridiculous impression.

The senator was entirely in the mood to fully savor the pleasure by reminding himself and the others of more incidental details, which was of course not only tolerated, but also greeted with interest by everyone. Thus he drew attention to the fact that he had entered in his notebook Karl's most prominent distinguishing features mentioned in the cook's letter, in case it became necessary to use them at a moment's notice. Now during the stoker's unbearable chatter he had pulled out the notebook for no other purpose than to distract himself and had playfully tried to connect the cook's observations, which of course did not quite have a detective's accuracy, with Karl's appearance. "And that's how one finds one's nephew" he concluded in a tone as if he wanted to be congratulated once again.

"What will happen to the stoker now?" asked Karl, passing over his uncle's last story. In his new position he believed he could say whatever he thought.

"The stoker will get what he deserves" said the senator "and what the Herr Captain deems. I believe we've had enough and more than enough of the stoker, as all the gentlemen present will surely agree."

"But that's not the point when it's a matter of justice" said Karl. He was standing between his uncle and the captain and perhaps influenced by this position believed the decision lay in his hands.

And yet the stoker seemed to have lost all hope for himself. His hands were stuck halfway into his belt, which his agitated movements had revealed along with stripes of a patterned shirt. This didn't trouble him in the least, he had poured out all his woes, now let them also see the few rags he wore on his body and then let them carry him off. He imagined that the servant and Schubal as the two lowest-ranking people here should show him this last kindness. Schubal would then have his peace and would no longer be driven to despair, as the chief purser had put it. The captain would be able to hire no one but Romanians, everywhere Romanian would be spoken and perhaps then everything really would go better. There would no longer be a stoker chattering in the main purser's office, only his last chatter would be remembered quite fondly, since, as the senator had explicitly declared, it had indirectly given rise to his recognition of his nephew. That nephew had, besides, often sought to be of use to him before and had therefore long since thanked him more than sufficiently for his service in this recognition; it did not even occur to the stoker to demand anything further from him now. Besides, even if he was the senator's nephew, he was far from being a captain, but in the end it was from the captain's mouth that the harsh verdict would fall.—In accordance with his opinion the stoker also tried not to look at Karl, but unfortunately in this room full of enemies there was no other resting place for his eyes.

"Don't misunderstand the situation" the senator said to Karl "it might be a matter of justice, but at the same time it's a matter of discipline. Both and most especially the latter are subject here to the Herr Captain's judgment."

"That's true" murmured the stoker. Those who noticed and understood this smiled disconcertedly.

"But we have, moreover, already hindered the Herr Captain so much in his official duties, which, especially on arrival in Newyork, must be piling up incredibly, that it's high time for us to leave the ship, lest, to crown it all, we turn this minor squabble between two engineers into an event by interfering in some extremely unnecessary way. By the way, I understand your conduct perfectly dear nephew, but that is just what gives me the right to lead you away from here in a hurry."

"I'll have a boat launched for you immediately" said the captain, without, to Karl's astonishment, raising even the slightest objection to his uncle's words, though these undoubtedly could have been regarded as self-abasement on his uncle's part. The chief purser rushed headlong to his desk and telephoned the captain's order to the boatswain.

"Time is pressing" Karl said to himself, "but without offending everyone there's nothing I can do. I certainly can't abandon my uncle now, when he has only just found me again. The captain is polite, but that's all. Discipline is where his politeness ends, and my uncle was surely saying exactly what the captain thinks. I don't want to talk to Schubal, I'm even sorry that I shook hands with him. And the rest of the people here are chaff."

And absorbed in such thoughts he slowly went to the stoker, pulled the latter's right hand out of his belt and held it playfully in his own. "Why aren't you saying anything, my dear friend?" he asked. "Why are you putting up with everything?"

The stoker only furrowed his brow as if searching for a way to express what he had to say. Meanwhile he looked down at his hand and Karl's.

"Injustice has been done to you more than anyone on the ship, I'm quite certain of that." And Karl drew his fingers back and forth between the fingers of the stoker, who looked all around with shining eyes, as if he were experiencing a bliss that no one should begrudge him.

"But you must defend yourself, say yes and no, otherwise these people will certainly have no inkling of the truth. You must promise me you'll do as I say, for I have good reason to fear that I myself will no longer be able to help you at all." And now Karl wept as he kissed the stoker's hand and took the cracked, almost lifeless hand and pressed it against his cheeks, like a treasure that one must give up.—But then his uncle the senator was already at his side and pulled him, though with only the lightest pressure, away. "The stoker seems to have enchanted you" he said, and looked knowingly over Karl's head at the captain "You felt forsaken, then you found the stoker and are now grateful to him, that's certainly quite praiseworthy. But don't push it too far, if only for my sake, and learn to understand your position."

Outside the door a commotion arose, shouts could be heard and it even seemed as if someone were being brutally pushed against the door. A sailor entered, somewhat disheveled, with a girl's apron tied around his waist. "There are people outside" he cried, thrusting around once with his elbows as if he were still in the throng. Finally he came to his senses and was about to salute the captain when he noticed the girl's apron, tore it off threw it on the floor and cried: "That's disgusting, they tied a girl's apron around me." But then he clicked his heels and saluted. Someone tried to laugh, but the captain said sternly: "That's what I call a good mood. Who is outside, then?" "They're my witnesses" Schubal said, stepping forward "I humbly beg your pardon for their improper behavior. When these people have the voyage behind them, they sometimes go almost mad."—"Call them in at once" the captain commanded and immediately turning around to the senator said courteously but quickly: "Now be so kind, my esteemed Herr Senator to take your Herr Nephew and follow this sailor, who will bring you to the boat. I need hardly say what a pleasure and what an honor it has been for me to become personally acquainted with you, Herr Senator. I can only hope to soon have an opportunity to resume with you, Herr Senator our interrupted conversation about the circumstances of the American fleet and then perhaps to be interrupted once again in as pleasant a way as today." "For the time being, this one nephew is enough for me" Karl's uncle said with a laugh. "And now accept my many thanks for your kindness, and farewell. By the way, it would by no means be altogether impossible that on our next journey to Europe"—he pressed Karl affectionately to him—"we might spend more time together." "I'd be delighted" said the captain. The two gentlemen shook hands, Karl could extend his hand only silently and hastily to the captain, for the latter was already preoccupied with the 15 or so people who, led by Schubal, entered with some trepidation but still very loudly. The sailor asked the senator's permission to lead the way and then parted the crowd for him and Karl, who passed easily between the bowing people. It seemed that these generally good-natured people regarded Schubal's quarrel with the stoker as a joke, which didn't cease to be ridiculous even in the presence of the captain. Among them Karl noticed the kitchen girl Line, who, winking merrily at him, tied around her waist the apron that had been thrown away by the sailor, for it was hers.

Still following the sailor they left the office, turned into a small corridor, which brought them after a few paces to a little door from which a short flight of steps led down into the boat that had been prepared for them. The sailors in the boat, into which their guide immediately leaped with a single bound, rose and saluted. The senator was just admonishing Karl to be careful climbing down when Karl, still on the top step, burst into violent tears. The senator put his right hand under Karl's chin, held him pressed tightly against him and stroked him with his left hand. Thus they went down slowly, one step at a time, and, bound closely together, they got into the boat, where the senator picked out a good seat for Karl directly opposite him. At a sign from the senator, the sailors pushed off from the ship and were immediately hard at work. Scarcely had they gone a few meters from the ship when Karl made the unexpected discovery that they were on the side of the ship faced by the windows of the main purser's office. All 3 windows were occupied by Schubal's witnesses, who were saluting and waving amiably, even his uncle waved back and one of the sailors performed the feat of blowing a kiss up to them without actually interrupting the even rhythm of his rowing. It was truly as if the stoker no longer existed. Karl took a closer look at his uncle, whose knees were almost touching his own, and he began to doubt whether this man would ever be able to replace the stoker for him. And his uncle avoided his eyes and looked out at the waves heaving around their boat.

In his uncle's house Karl soon grew accustomed to his new circumstances. But his uncle also kindly obliged him in every trifle, and Karl never had to learn from bad experiences, such as usually so embitter the first days of one's life in a foreign country.

Karl's room was on the sixth floor of a building whose 5 lower floors, followed farther down by another 3 underground ones, were taken up by his uncle's business operations. The light penetrating his room through 2 windows and a balcony door astonished Karl whenever he entered here in the morning from his little bedroom. Where might he have had to live if he had come ashore as a poor little immigrant? Indeed, as his uncle, according to his knowledge of the immigration laws, even considered very likely, he might not have been let into the United States at all but rather sent home without concern for the fact that he no longer had a home. For one couldn't hope for sympathy here, and what Karl had read about America in this regard was quite correct; only the fortunate seemed to truly enjoy their good fortune here among the untroubled faces surrounding them.

Outside the room a narrow balcony extended across its full length. But what might well have been the highest vantage point in Karl's hometown here granted little more than a view over one street, which ran straight between two rows of positively choppy buildings and therefore seemed to be fleeing into the distance, where the forms of a cathedral rose tremendous out of a dense haze. And in the morning as in the evening and in the dreams of night this street was filled with constantly surging traffic, which, seen from above, presented itself as a mixture, strewn together out of ever new beginnings, of distorted human figures and of roofs of carriages of all sorts, from which a new multiplied wilder mixture of noise, dust and smells rose, and all this was seized and permeated by a powerful light, which was perpetually scattered, carried away and eagerly brought back by the multitude of objects and which appeared to the beguiled eye as corporeal as if over this street a glass pane covering everything were at every moment being smashed again and again with full force.

Cautious as his uncle was in all things, he advised Karl not to become seriously involved in anything at all for the time being. He should certainly examine and observe everything, but not let himself be taken captive. Indeed, a European's first days in America might be compared to a birth, and even if, lest Karl be unnecessarily afraid, one did accustom oneself here more quickly than when one entered the human world from the beyond, one should still keep in mind that one's first judgment always stood on shaky ground and that one should not let it perhaps muddle all one's future judgments, which would help one go on living here. He himself had known newcomers who, for example, instead of behaving in accordance with these sound principles, stood for days on their balcony and gazed down at the street like lost sheep. That was bound to confuse them! That solitary inactivity, which falls under the spell of a work-filled Newyork day, could be granted and perhaps recommended, even if not unreservedly, to someone traveling for pleasure, for one who would stay here it was ruin, one could in this case safely use this word, even if it was an exagger–

Third Notebook

26 XI *(October)* 1911 Thursday.

All afternoon yesterday Löwy read aloud from "Gott Mensch & Teufel" by Gordon[220] and then from his own Paris diaries. The day before yesterday I was at the performance of Der wilde Mensch by Gordon.[221]—Gordon is better than Lateiner, Scharkansky, Feimann,[222] etc. because he has more details, more order and more logic in this order, on the other hand what's no longer quite here is the immediate Judaism of the other plays that is improvised positively once and for all, the noise of this Judaism sounds duller and therefore for its part less detailed. Concessions are certainly made to the audience and sometimes one believes that one must stretch to see the play over the heads of the Newyorck Jewish theater audience, (the character of the wild man, the whole story of Frau Selde) but worse is the fact that palpable concessions are made to some vaguely perceived art too, that, for example, in Der wilde Mensch the plot flutters for an entire act due to doubts, that the wild man makes speeches that are humanly unclear but literarily so crude that one would rather close one's eyes, the older girl in G. M. und Teufel[223] is just the same. The plot of "D. w. M."[224] is in part very brave. A young widow marries an old man who has four children, and immediately brings her lover Wladimir Worobeitschik along into the marriage. The two of them then ruin the whole family, Schmut Leiblich (Pipes) must hand over all his money and becomes ill, the oldest son Simon (Klug) a student leaves the house, Alexander becomes a gambler and drunkard, Lise (Tschisik) becomes a whore and Lemech (Löwy), the idiot is driven to idiotic madness by hatred toward Frau Selde because she takes the place of his mother and by love because she is the first young woman close to him. Having gone this far, the plot is unraveled with the murder of Selde by Lemech. All the others remain incompletely and helplessly in the spectator's memory. The invention of this woman and her lover, an invention that asks no one's opinion gave me unclear varied self-confidence.

The discreet impression of the playbill.[225] One learns not only the names, but also something more, and yet only as much as must be made known to the public and even the most well-disposed and coolest public about a family exposed to their judgment. Schmut Leiblich is "a rich merchant" but it isn't said that he's old and sickly, a ridiculous ladies' man a bad father and an impious widower, who gets married on the anniversary of his wife's death. And yet all these descriptions would be more correct than that of the playbill, for at the end of the play he's no longer rich, because Selde has robbed him, he's also scarcely a merchant any longer, since he has neglected his business. On the playbill Simon is "a student" so something very vague, which to our knowledge many sons of our most distant acquaintances are. Alexander, this young man without character is only "Alexander," about "Lise" the domestic girl one also knows only that she is "Lise." Lemech is unfortunately "an idiot" for that is something that cannot be concealed. Wladimir Worobejtschik is only "Selde's lover," but not the corrupter of a family, not a drunkard, gambler, debauchee, do-nothing, parasite. With the description "Selde's lover" much has been revealed, but in light of his behavior it's the least one can say. Moreover, the setting of the action is Russia, the scarcely assembled characters are scattered over an enormous area or assembled at a small unrevealed point in this area, in short the play has become impossible, there will be nothing for the spectator to see / Nonetheless the play begins, the obviously great powers of the writer are at work, things come to light that are not to be expected of the characters on the playbill but which are conferred on them with the greatest certainty and if one only would believe the whipping, snatching, beating, shoulder-slapping, fainting, throat-cutting, limping, dancing in Russian top boots, dancing with lifted skirts rolling on the sofa because these are things, after all, where contradiction does no good. However, not even the climax of the spectator's excitement, experienced in retrospect, is necessary to recognize that the discreet impression of the playbill is a false impression, which can be formed only after the performance, but even now is incorrect, indeed impossible, and can arise only in a weary outsider, since for someone judging honestly after the performance there's nothing legitimate to be seen any longer between playbill and performance.

From the line onward[226] written in despair, because today the card playing is especially noisy,[227] I have to sit at the common table, O.[228] laughs with her mouth full, stands up, sits down, reaches across the table, speaks to me and I, to complete my unhappiness, write so badly and can't help thinking of Löwy's good Paris recollections,[229] written with uninterrupted feeling, which come from independent fire, while I, at least now, undoubtedly mainly because I have so little time, am almost entirely under Max's influence, which sometimes, to crown it all, even spoils my pleasure in his work. Because it consoles me, I'm writing down an autobiographical remark by Shaw, although it actually contains the opposite of consolation: As a boy he was an apprentice in the office of a land agent in Dublin. He soon gave up this position and traveled to London and became a writer. In the first 9 years from 1876–1885 he earned 140 K in all. "But although I was a strong young man and my family was in straitened circumstances, I did not throw myself into the struggle for life; I threw my mother into it and let her provide for me. I was no support for my old father, on the contrary, I hung on to his coattails."[230] In the end this doesn't console me much. The years he spent free in London have already gone by for me, the possible happiness passes more and more into the impossible, I lead a horrible substitute life and am cowardly and miserable enough to follow Shaw only to the point that I read the passage to my parents. How this possible life flashes before my open eyes with steel colors, with taut steel bars and airy darkness between them!

---

27 X 11 Löwy's stories and diaries:[231]
how Notre Dame frightens him, how the tiger in the Jardin de Plantes moves him as a representation of one who despairs and hopes, who satiates despair and hope with food, how his pious father in his fancy questions him as to whether he can now go for walks on Saturday, whether he now has time to read modern books, whether he is permitted to eat on the fast days, while he actually has to work on Saturday, has no time at all and fasts more than any religion has prescribed. When he strolls through the streets chewing on his black bread, it looks from a distance as if he were eating chocolate. The work in the cap factory and his friend, the

socialist, who considers everyone a bourgeois who doesn't work exactly the way he does, such as Löwy with his fine hands, who is bored on Sunday, who disdains reading as something luxurious, can't read himself and asks Löwy with irony to read him a letter he has received.

The Jewish purifying water every Jewish community in Russia has, which I imagine as a cabin with a pool of precisely determined outlines, with facilities arranged and supervised by the rabbi, which has to wash only the earthly dirt from the soul, the external condition of which therefore doesn't matter, which being a symbol therefore can be and also is dirty and stinking but still fulfills its purpose. The woman comes here to purify herself of her period, the Torah scribe to purify himself of all sinful thoughts before writing the last sentence of a Torah portion.

Custom of dipping the fingers three times in water immediately after waking, since the evil spirits settle at night on the second and third finger bone. Rationalist explanation: To prevent the fingers from immediately going to the face, because uncontrolled in sleep and dream they could, after all, have touched all sorts of places on the body the armpits, the bottom, the genitals.

The dressing room behind their stage is so narrow that if someone happens to be standing in front of the mirror behind the door curtain on the set and someone else wants to pass by, he must raise that curtain and momentarily show himself to the audience against his will.[232]

Superstition: If one drinks from an imperfect glass, the evil spirits gain entry into the person.

How raw the actors appeared to me after the performance, how I was afraid to dab them with a word. How I preferred to leave quickly after a hasty handshake, as if I were angry and dissatisfied because the truth of my impression was so impossible to express. Everyone seemed false to me except Max who calmly said some empty things. But false was the one who inquired about a shameless detail, false the one who gave a joking reply to a remark by the actor, false the ironic one, false the one who began to break down his manifold impression, all the rabble that, rightly pressed into the depths of the auditorium, now stood up late at night and again realized its value. (Very far from correct)

---

28 IX *(October 1911)* I did have a similar feeling, but neither acting nor play seemed to me anywhere near perfect that evening.[233] But this was just what obligated me to be especially in awe of the actors. When there are small even if many gaps in an impression, who knows who is to blame for them. At one point Frau Tschissik stepped on the hem of her dress and staggered for a moment in her princess-style whore's dress, like a massive pillar, at one point she made a mistake in her lines and to calm her tongue turned with great intensity to the back wall, although this didn't correspond to the words just then; it disconcerted me, but it didn't prevent the faint shivers at the top of my cheekbones that I feel whenever I hear her voice. But because my other acquaintances had a far more impure impression than I, they seemed to me obligated to be in even greater awe than I, also because in my opinion their awe would have been far more effective than mine, so that I had a double reason to curse their behavior.

"Axioms on Drama" by Max in the Schaubühne.[234] Has very much the character of a dream truth, to which the term "axioms" is also suited. The more dreamlike it becomes as it inflates itself, the more coolly one must treat it. The following principles are asserted:
The essence of drama lies in a lack is the thesis.

The drama (on the stage) is more exhaustive than the novel, because we see everything, about which we otherwise only read.

That only seems to be so, for in the novel the writer can show us only what's important whereas in the drama we see everything, the actor, the sets, hence not only what's important, therefore less. From the perspective of the novel, the best drama would therefore be completely without stimulation, for example, a philosophical drama that would be read by sitting actors in any set of a room.

And yet the best drama is one that offers the most stimulation in time and space, frees itself from all the demands of life, limits itself only to the speeches, to the thoughts in monologues, to the main points of what happens, manages everything else through stimulation and raised onto a sign borne by actors, painters, directors follows only its extreme inspirations.

Error of this argumentation: It changes its position without indicating it, at times sees things from the writer's room, at other times from the audience. Granted that the audience doesn't see everything from the perspective of the writer, that even he is surprised by the performance

29 IX *(October)* 11 Sun.

thus he did indeed have the play with all its details within him, moved along from detail to detail and only because he gathers all the details in the speeches has he given them dramatic weight and power. As a result, the drama in its highest development attains an unbearable humanization, which it is the task of the actor to pull down, to make bearable, wearing his prescribed role loosened frayed, flapping around him. The drama thus hovers in the air, but not as a roof borne by the storm, rather as a whole building, the foundation walls of which have been torn up out of the earth with a force that today is indeed very close to madness.

Sometimes it seems that the play rests up in the borders,[235] the actors have pulled off strips from them, the ends of which they hold in their hands or have wrapped around their bodies for the performance and that only now and then, to the horror of the audience, a strip that is hard to detach pulls an actor up into the air.

I dreamed today of a greyhound-like donkey, which was very restrained in its movements. I observed it closely because I was aware of the rarity of the phenomenon, but retained only the memory that its narrow human feet were unappealing to me because of their length and uniformity. I offered it fresh, dark-green cypress bunches, which I had just received from an old Zurich lady (the whole thing took place in Zurich), it didn't want them, only sniffed a little at them; but when I left them on a table, it devoured them so completely that only a scarcely recognizable kernel resembling a chestnut remained. Later there was talk that this donkey had never before walked on all fours, but had always held itself upright like a human being and had shown its silvery shining breast and its little belly. But this was actually not correct.

I also dreamed of an Englishman, whom I met at a gathering similar to that of the Salvation Army in Zurich.[236] There were seats there as in school, for under the writing surface there was even an open compartment; when I reached in at one point to arrange something, I marveled at how easily one makes friends while traveling. This was apparently in reference to the Englishman, who shortly thereafter approached me. He had light-colored loose clothes, which were in very good condition, only on the back of the upper arms instead of the clothing material or at least sewn on over it there was a gray, wrinkled material, hanging a little, torn into strips, dotted as if by spiders, which was reminiscent of the leather reinforcements in riding breeches as well as the sleeve protectors of seamstresses, shopgirls, female office clerks. His face too was covered with a gray material, which had very skillfully cut-out openings for mouth, eyes, probably also for the nose. But this material was new, napped rather flannel-like, very supple and soft, of excellent English manufacture. All this was so appealing to me that I was eager to become acquainted with the man. He wanted to invite me to his apartment too; but since I had to depart the day after tomorrow, that fell through. Before he left the gathering, he put on several more apparently very practical articles of clothing, which after he had buttoned them up made him quite inconspicuous. Even though he couldn't invite me to his home, he still asked me to go with him onto the street. I followed him, we stopped at the curb across from the meeting place, I below, he above, and found again after some conversation that nothing could come of the invitation.

Then I dreamed that Max Otto and I had the habit of packing our suitcases only when we were in the railroad station.[237] We carried our shirts, for example, through the main hall to our distant suitcases. Even though this seemed to be a common custom, it didn't turn out well for us, especially because we began to pack only just before the arrival of the train. Then we were naturally agitated and had little hope of catching the train, let alone getting good seats.

Even though the regular guests and employees of the coffeehouse[238] are fond of the actors, they can't maintain their respect amid the dispiriting impressions, and disdain the actors as starvelings, vagabonds, fellow Jews just as in historical times. Thus the headwaiter wanted to throw Löwy out of the hall, the doorman a former brothel employee and current pimp shouted little Tschissik down when she in the excitement of her sympathy during "Der wilde Mensch"[239] wanted to pass something to the actors and the day before yesterday, when I accompanied Löwy back to the coffeehouse after he had read me the first act of "Elieser ben Schevia" by Gordon[240] in Kaffee City,[241] that fellow called to him (he's cross-eyed and between his crooked pointy nose and his mouth he has a hollow out of which a small mustache bristles): "Come on, idiot. (Allusion to the role in Der wilde Mensch) They're waiting. There's a crowd here today you really don't deserve. There's even an artillery volunteer here, look." And he points to one of the curtained coffeehouse windows, behind which that volunteer is supposedly sitting. Löwy runs his hand over his forehead: "From Elieser ben Schevia to this."

The sight of stairs moves me so much today. Early in the morning and several times since I've taken pleasure in the triangular section visible from my window of the stone railing of the staircase that leads down on the right from the Čechbrücke to the quay plateau.[242] Very inclined, as if it were giving only a quick hint. And now I see on the other side of the river a ladder on the slope leading to the water. It has always been there, but is revealed only in autumn and winter by removal, of the swimming school lying in front of it the rest of the year and lies there in the dark grass under the brown trees in the play of perspective.

Löwy: Four friends became great Talmud scholars in their old age. But each had a special fate. One went insane, one died, rabbi Elieser became a freethinker at the age of 40 and only the oldest of them, Akiba, who hadn't begun to study until the age of 40, attained complete knowledge. Elieser's disciple was reb Maier, a pious man, whose piety was so great that the freethinker's instruction did him no harm. He ate, as he said the kernel of the nut, the shell he threw away. One Saturday Elieser went for a ride, reb Maier followed on foot, the Talmud in his hand, walking only 2000 paces, to be sure, for any farther is not permitted on Saturday. And this walk gave rise to a symbolic dialogue. Come back to your people said reb M. Reb El. refused with a play on words.[243]

---

30 IX *(October 1911)* This longing I almost always have, once I feel my stomach is healthy, to heap up in myself fantasies of taking terrible risks with food. I satisfy this longing especially in front of smokehouses. If I see a sausage labeled as an old hard Hauswurst, I bite into it in my imagination with all my teeth and swallow quickly, regularly and heedlessly like a machine. The despair that this act even in the imagination has as an immediate result increases my haste. I shove the long rinds of rib meat unbitten into my mouth and then pull them out again from behind tearing through my stomach and intestines. I eat dirty grocery stores completely empty. Fill myself with herrings, pickles and all the bad old sharp foods. Candies are poured into me like hail from their tin pots. In this way I enjoy not only my healthy condition, but also a suffering that is without pain and can pass immediately.

It is my old habit not to let pure impressions, whether they are painful or pleasurable, once they have reached their highest purity, spread beneficially through my whole being, but rather to cloud and dispel them with new unforeseen, weak impressions. It is not ill intent to harm myself but weakness in enduring the purity of that impression, though this weakness is not acknowledged, but rather tries to fend for itself amid inner quiet by evoking with seeming arbitrariness the new impression, instead of doing the only right thing by revealing itself and calling other powers to its support. On Saturday evening,[244] for example, after listening to the good novella by Fräul. T., which actually belongs more to Max, at least belongs to him to a greater extent with more attached to it than one of his own,[245] then after listening to the excellent play "Conkurrenz" by Baum,[246] in which dramatic force can be seen in the work and in the effect just as uninterruptedly as in the product of a living craftsman, after listening to these two literary pieces I was so downcast and, having been quite empty inside for several days, was quite unpreparedly filled with such heavy sorrow that I declared to Max on the way home that nothing could come of Robert & Samuel. For this declaration not even the slightest courage was necessary at the time in the face of either myself or Max. The conversation that followed confused me a little, since R. & S. was at the time far from my main concern and I therefore didn't find the right answers to Max's objections.[247] But later, when I was alone and not only the disturbance of my sorrow by the conversation but also the almost always effective consolation of Max's presence had disappeared, my hopelessness grew so much that it began to dissolve my thinking (here, while I pause for dinner Löwy comes to the apartment and disturbs me and delights me from 7 o'clock to 10) But instead of waiting at home for what would happen next, I carelessly read 2 issues of Aktion[248] a little of Die Missgeschickten,[249] finally some of my Paris notes[250] too and went to bed actually more content than earlier but obdurate. It was similar several days ago when I returned from a walk in unrestrained imitation of Löwy with the external force of his enthusiasm turned toward my goal. Then too I read and talked a great deal in confusion at home and wasted away.

31 XI *(October 1911)* Although today I've read this and that in the Fischer catalogue in the Inselalmanach in the Rundschau,[251] I'm now quite aware of having taken everything in either lastingly or fleetingly, but while fending off any damage. And for this evening I would believe myself capable of enough if I didn't have to go out with Löwy again.

For several muddled reasons I felt an embarrassment that pushed down my eyes in the presence of a marriage broker who visited us today at noon for one of my sisters. The woman had a dress that age, shabbiness and dirt gave a light-gray shimmer. When she stood up, she kept her hands in her lap. She was cross-eyed, which seemed to increase the difficulty of disregarding her when I had to look at my father, who asked me some questions about the young man on offer. On the other hand, my embarrassment decreased again because I had my lunch in front of me and even without embarrassment would have been sufficiently occupied with making mixtures from my 3 plates. In her face, as I at first saw only partially she had such deep wrinkles that I thought of the uncomprehending astonishment with which animals would surely look at such human faces. Her small nose, angular especially in its somewhat upturned end, stuck out of her face in a strikingly corporeal way.

When, on Sunday afternoon, just overtaking three women I stepped into Max's house[252] I thought: There are still one or two houses in which I have something to do, women walking behind me can still see me turn to enter a front door on a Sunday afternoon for work, conversation, purposefully, hastily, appreciating it from this point of view only as an exception. This need not remain so for long.

I read Wilhelm Schäfer's novellas, especially when reading aloud, with the same attentive pleasure with which I would run a piece of string over my tongue. Yesterday afternoon I didn't like Valli[253] much at first, but when I had lent her "Die Missgeschickten," she had read it for a little while and by then must have been well under the influence of the story, I loved her because of this influence and stroked her.

Lest I forget it, in case my father should call me a bad son once again, I'm writing down that in the presence of several relatives, for no special reason whether simply to oppress me or supposedly to save me he called Max a "meshuggener ritoch"[254] and that yesterday when Löwy was in my room he ironically shook his body and twisted his mouth while speaking of strange people being let into the apartment, what could interest one in a strange person, why one formed such useless relationships, etc.—I shouldn't have written it down after all, for I've positively written myself into hatred of my father, for which he has actually given no cause today and which at least with regard to Löwy is disproportionately great in comparison to my father's words as I have written them down and which even increases because I can't remember what was truly malicious in my father's behavior yesterday.

I XI II Today greedily and happily began to read Geschichte des Judentums by Grätz.[255] Because my longing for it had far overtaken the reading, it was at first stranger to me than I thought and I had to stop now and then to let my Judaism collect itself in peace. Toward the end, however, I was indeed moved by the imperfection of the first settlements in the newly conquered Canaan and the faithful handing down of the imperfection of the popular leaders (Joshua, the judges, Eli)

Yesterday evening goodbye to Frau Klug.[256] We (I & Löwy) ran along the train and saw Frau Klug looking out in the dark behind a closed window of the last carriage. She quickly stretched her arm toward us while still inside the compartment, stood up, opened the window, standing broadly in it for a moment with her outer garment open, until opposite her rose the dark Herr Klug, who can open his mouth only wide and bitterly and close it only curtly as if forever. In the course of the 15 minutes I spoke to Hr. Klug only a little and looked at him for perhaps only two moments, otherwise during the weak, intermittent conversation I couldn't avert my eyes from Frau Klug. She was completely dominated by my presence, but more in her imagination than in reality. When she addressed Löwy with the repeated introductory phrase "You, Löwy," she was speaking for my benefit, when she pressed herself against her husband, who sometimes left her with only her right shoulder at the window, squashing her dress and the puffy overcoat, she was taking pains in that way to give me an empty sign. The first impression I had at the performances, that she didn't find me particularly pleasant, must have been correct, she rarely invited me to sing along, when she did it was without feeling, when she asked me something I unfortunately answered incorrectly ("do you understand that?" I said "yes" but she wanted "no" in order to reply "neither do I") she didn't offer me her picture postcards[257] a second time, I showed a preference for Frau Tschissik, to whom I wanted to give flowers to Fr. Klug's detriment. But this aversion was joined by respect for my doctorate, which was unhindered by my childlike appearance, indeed was even increased by it. This respect was so great that her frequent but not at all particularly emphasized way of addressing me, "You know Herr Doktor," so rang with it that I half unconsciously regretted deserving it far too little and wondered whether I wouldn't be entitled to be addressed in exactly the same way by everyone. But since I was so respected by her as a person, I was even more so as a member of the audience. I shone when she sang, I laughed and looked at her the whole time she was on stage, I sang the melodies with her, later the words, I thanked her after several performances; for this she naturally liked me again. But when she spoke to me out of that feeling, I was embarrassed, had nothing to say and made her embarrassed, so that she must have returned in her heart to her initial aversion and stayed with it. She had to make all the more effort to reward me as a member of the audience and she was glad to do so, for she's a vain actress and a good-natured woman. Especially when she was silent up there in the compartment window, she looked at me with a mouth enraptured by embarrassment and cunning and with blinking eyes that swam on the wrinkles coming from her mouth. She had to believe I loved her, as was also true, and with those glances gave me the only fulfillment she as an experienced but young woman, good wife and mother could give a doctor of her imagination. Those glances were so urgent and supported by phrases like "there were such nice guests here, especially some of them" that I defended myself, and those were the moments I looked at her husband. When I compared the two of them I was groundlessly amazed that they would depart from us together and yet concerned themselves only with us and had no glance for each other. Löwy asked whether they had good seats; yes if it stays this empty Fr. Klug answered, looking briefly into the compartment, the warm air of which her husband will spoil with his smoking. We spoke of their children for whose sake they were leaving; they have 4 children, 3 of them boys, the oldest is 9 years old, they haven't seen them for 18 months now. When a gentleman quickly got on nearby, the train seemed about to depart, we said goodbye in haste, shook each other's hands, I lifted my hat and then held it against my chest, we stepped back as one does when trains depart, by which one means to show that all is over and one has reconciled oneself to it. But the train didn't leave yet, we stepped up close again, I was really happy about it, she asked after my sisters. Surprisingly the train began to move slowly, Fr. Klug prepared her handkerchief for waving, I should write to her, she called, did I know her address, she was already too far away for me to be able to answer her with words, I pointed to Löwy from whom I could get the address, that's good, she quickly nodded to me and him and let the handkerchief flutter, I lifted my hat, at first awkwardly, then the farther she was, the more freely. Later I remembered that I'd had the impression the train was not actually departing but only traveling the short distance of the railroad station to perform a play for us and then sinking away. In half-sleep that same evening Frau Klug appeared to me unnaturally small almost without legs and wrung her hands with her face contorted as if a great misfortune had befallen her.

This afternoon the pain over my forsakenness came into me so piercingly and forcefully that I realized that the strength I gain through this writing and have truly not intended for this goal is expended in this way

---

As soon as Hr. Klug enters a new city one notices how his and his wife's jewels disappear into the pawnshop. As their departure approaches he gradually redeems them again

---

Favorite sentence of the wife of the philosopher Mendelssohn: How sick I am of tout l'univers![258]

One of the most important impressions during the goodbye to Fr. Klug was that I always had to believe that as a simple middle-class woman she was holding herself by force below the level of her true human destiny and required only a leap, a flinging open of the door, a turned-on light to be an actress and subjugate me. She really did stand above, after all, and I below as in the theater.—She got married at the age of 16, is 26 years old.

---

2 XI 11 This morning for the first time in a long while the pleasure again in imagining a knife twisted in my heart.

In the newspapers, in conversation, in the office the vehemence of the language often seduces one, then the hope, born of a present weakness, for sudden all-the-stronger illumination at the very next moment, or strong self-confidence by itself or mere negligence or a great present impression that one wants to shift into the future at any price or the opinion that present true enthusiasm justifies any confusion in the future or the pleasure in sentences that are elevated in the middle by one or two jolts and open the mouth gradually to its full size, even if they let it close far too quickly and tortuously or the trace of the possibility of a decisive judgment aimed at clarity or the effort to keep the actually concluded speech flowing or the desire to abandon the subject in haste if necessary on one's belly or despair that seeks a way out for its heavy breath or the longing for a light without shadow—all these can seduce one to sentences like: "The book that I've just finished is the most beautiful I've ever read or is more beautiful than any I've read before."

To prove that everything I write and think about them is false, the actors (apart from Hr. and Fr. Klug) have stayed here again, as Löwy, whom I met yesterday evening, told me; who knows whether they haven't departed again today for the same reason, for Löwy hasn't called at the shop, even though he promised to. Yesterday the son of the café owner Hermann left too[259]—

3 XI 11 to prove that both things I had written down were false, a proof that seems almost impossible, Löwy came yesterday evening himself and interrupted me in my writing

---

Karl's[260] habit of repeating everything in the same tone of voice. He tells someone a story from his business admittedly not with so many details that they would in themselves finish off the story, but nonetheless in a slow manner, thorough only due to that, as a communication that isn't trying to be anything else and is therefore also done with upon its completion. A little while passes with another matter, he unexpectedly finds a transition to his story and pulls it out again in its old form, almost without any addition but also almost without any omission, with the harmlessness of a person who carries around the room a ribbon attached treacherously to his back. Now my parents are especially fond of him, hence feel his habits more strongly than they notice them—and so it happens that they, particularly my mother, unconsciously give him the opportunity for repetitions. If one evening the moment for the repetition of a story won't quite come, then my mother is there, she asks and indeed with a curiosity that doesn't cease even after the question has been asked, as one would expect. And even after several evenings my mother positively chases with her questions after stories that have already been repeated and could no longer come by themselves. But Karl's habit reigns so powerfully that it often has the strength to justify itself completely. No one ends up with such regular frequency in a position to tell individual family members a story that basically concerns all of them. The family circle, which in such cases grows slowly at intervals always only by one person, must then be told the story almost as often as people are there. And because I'm the only one who has recognized Karl's habit, I'm also usually the one who hears the story first and whom the repetitions give only the slight pleasure of confirming an observation.

Envy of a supposed success of Baum's[261] whom I'm actually so fond of. Here the feeling of having in the middle of my body a ball of yarn, which quickly winds itself up with countless threads that it stretches from the edge of my body to itself.

Löwy—My father about him: He who lies down in bed with dogs gets up with bugs. I couldn't contain myself and said something disordered. My father's especially calm reply (though after a long pause that was otherwise filled): "You know that I must not get agitated and must be treated with care. Such talk from you is the last thing I need. I have enough agitation right now, quite enough. So don't bother me with such things." I say: "I'm trying hard to restrain myself" and feel in my father as always at such extreme moments the existence of a wisdom of which I can grasp only a breath.

Death of Löwy's grandfather, a man who had an open hand, knew several languages, had taken long journeys deep into Russia and who once refused to eat on a Saturday at the home of a wonder rabbi[262] in Yekaterinoslav because the long hair and a colorful neckerchief of that rabbi's son made the piety of the house suspicious to him.—The bed was set up in the middle of the room, the candleholders of friends and relatives were borrowed, the room thus full of light and smoke of the candles. About 40 men stood around his bed all day to take heart from the dying of a pious man. He was conscious until his end and at the right moment with his hand on his breast began to recite the prayers meant for this time. During his suffering and after his death the grandmother, who was with the women gathered in the next room wept incessantly but during the dying she was completely calm because it is a commandment to ease the dying man's death to the best of one's ability. With his own prayers he departed. For this death after so pious a life he was much envied.

Pesach festival.[263] An association of rich Jews rents a bakery, its members take over all the tasks of producing the so-called 18 minute-matzos[264] for the heads of the families: the fetching of water, the koshering, the kneading, the cutting, the perforating.

5 XI 11 Yesterday slept after Bar-Kochba.[265]
from 7 on with Löwy, read aloud a letter from his father. Evening at Baum's.[266]

I want to write, with a constant trembling on my forehead. I'm sitting in my room in the headquarters of the noise of the whole apartment. I hear all the doors banging, their noise spares me only the footsteps of those running between them, I hear even the slam of the oven door in the kitchen. My father bursts through the doors of my room and passes through in his dragging dressing gown, the ashes are being scraped out of the stove in the next room, Valli asks shouting into the indefinite through the hall as if through a Paris street whether Father's hat has been cleaned yet, a hiss that wants to be my friend raises the cry of an answering voice. The apartment door is unlatched and makes a noise as if from a catarrhal throat, then continues to open with the brief singing of a woman's voice and closes with a dull manly jerk that sounds the most inconsiderate of all. My father is gone, now begins the gentler more scattered more hopeless noise, led by the voices of the two canaries. I thought of it before, but with the canaries it occurs to me anew, whether I shouldn't open the door a little crack, crawl like a snake into the next room and thus on the floor ask my sisters and their governess for quiet.[267]

The bitterness I felt yesterday evening when Max read aloud my little automobile story[268] at Baum's. I was isolated from everyone and in the face of the story I positively kept my chin pressed to my chest. The disordered sentences of this story with gaps through which one could stick both hands; one sentence sounds high, one sentence sounds low as the case may be; one sentence rubs against the next like the tongue against a hollow or false tooth; one sentence comes marching up with so rough a beginning that the whole story falls into morose astonishment; a sleepy imitation of Max (reproaches dulled – – spurred on) sways in, sometimes it looks like a dancing course in its first fifteen minutes. I explain it to myself by saying that I don't have enough time and peace to bring up from my depths the possibilities of my talent in their entirety. Therefore it's always only broken-off beginnings that come to the surface, broken-off beginnings, for example, through the whole automobile story. If I were ever able to write a larger whole well formed from beginning to end, then the story would never be able to detach itself from me definitively and I might listen calmly and with open eyes as a blood relative of a healthy story to a reading of it, but as it is every little piece of the story wanders homelessly and drives me in the opposite direction.—At the same time I can still be glad if this explanation is correct.

Performance of Bar-Kochba by Goldfaden.[269]
False judgment of the play in the whole hall and on the stage. I had brought along a bouquet for Frau Tschissik with an attached visiting card inscribed with gratitude and was waiting for the moment when I could have it presented to her. Now the performance had begun late, Frau Tschissik's main scene had been promised me only for the 4 act, in impatience and fear the flowers could wilt I had the waiter unwrap the flowers during the 3rd act (it was 11 o'clock), now they lay sideways on a table, the kitchen staff and several dirty regular guests handed them to each other and sniffed them, I could only watch worriedly and angrily nothing else, during her main scene in the prison I loved Fr. Tschissik and yet inwardly pressed her to finish, finally the act unnoticed by me in my distraction had come to an end, the headwaiter held out the flowers, Fr. T. took them between the closing curtains, she bowed in a small crack of the curtain and didn't come back again. No one noticed my love and I had wanted to show it to everyone and in that way make it valuable to Fr. T., they'd hardly even noticed the bouquet. Meanwhile it was already past 12 everyone was tired, several spectators had left early, I'd had the urge to throw my glass at them.—With me was the controller Pokorny from our institute[270] a Christian. He, whom I usually like, bothered me. My concern was the flowers, not his affairs. At the same time I knew that he understood the play poorly, while I had no time, desire or ability to impose on him help he didn't think he needed. Finally I felt ashamed before him that I myself was paying such poor attention. He also bothered me in intercourse with Max and even by the memory that I liked

him before, would like him again afterward and that he could take my behavior today amiss.—But I wasn't the only one bothered in this way. Max felt responsible because of his laudatory article in the newspaper.[271] It was too late for the Jews accompanied by Bergmann. The members of the Bar-Kochba Association had come because of the name of the play and were bound to be disappointed.[272] Since I'm acquainted with Bar-Kochba only from this play, I wouldn't have given any association that name. Two shopgirls in their whores' evening dresses were in the back of the hall with their lovers and had to be silenced by loud shouts during death scenes. Finally people on the street banged on the large windows in annoyance that they saw so little of the stage.

On the stage the Klugs were missing.[273] Ridiculous extras. "Coarse Jews" as Löwy said. Traveling salesmen who weren't even paid. Most of the time they were concerned only with concealing or enjoying their laughter, even if they otherwise meant well. A round-cheeked man with a blond beard, at the sight of whom one could hardly contain one's laughter, looked especially funny when he laughed due to the unnaturalness of the stuck-on shaking full beard which during his certainly unintended laughter bordered his cheeks incorrectly. Another man laughed only when he wanted to, but then a lot. When Löwy died singing, writhed in the arms of these two elders, was supposed to slide slowly to earth with the fading song, they put their heads together behind his back to at last be able to laugh their fill unseen by the audience (as they believed). Even yesterday when I remembered this at lunch I couldn't help laughing.—In prison Fr. Tschissik has to take the helmet off the drunken Roman governor (the young Pipes) visiting her and put it on herself. When she takes it off, a crumpled towel falls out, which Pipes apparently stuffed in because the helmet pinched him too much. Yet even though he must have known that the helmet would be taken off him on stage, he looks reproachfully at Frau Tschissik forgetting his drunkenness.—Beautiful things: how Frau T. writhed under the hands of the Roman soldiers (though she first had to pull them to her, for they were apparently afraid to touch her), while due to her care and art the movements of the three people almost only almost followed the rhythm of the singing; the song in which she heralds the appearance of the Messiah and manages only due to her power not to spoil the effect when she represents harp playing by movements of violin bowing; in the prison, where at the frequent approach of footsteps she breaks off her song of mourning, hurries to the treadmill and turns it while singing a work song, then runs off again to her song and again to the mill, how she sings in her sleep when Papus visits her, and her mouth is open like a squinting eye, how in general the corners of her mouth when opening are reminiscent of the corners of the eyes.—In the white veil, as in the black she was beautiful.—Newly recognized movements of hers: Pressing her hand deep into her not very good bodice, brief jerk of her shoulders and hips in scorn, especially when turning her back to the one scorned.—She led the whole performance like the mother of a family. She prompted everyone, but never faltered herself; she instructed the extras, implored them finally pushed them if necessary; when she wasn't on stage, her clear voice mingled with the weak choral singing on stage; she held the folding screen (which in the last act was supposed to represent a citadel), which the extras would have knocked over ten times.—I had hoped to satisfy my love for her a little with the bouquet, it was completely useless. It's possible only through literature or through sleeping together. I write this not because I didn't know it, but because it's perhaps good to write down warnings often.

---

7 XI 11 Tuesday Yesterday the actors together with Fr. Tschissik left once and for all.[274] I accompanied Löwy to the coffeehouse in the evening, but waited outside, didn't want to go in, didn't want to see Fr. Tschissik. But as I was walking up and down, I saw her open the door and come out with Löwy, I approached them with a greeting and met them in the middle of the road. Fr. Tsch. thanked me with the great but natural vowels of her pronunciation for my bouquet, only now had she learned that it was from me. So that liar Löwy hadn't said anything to her. I was worried about her, because she was wearing only a lightweight dark blouse with short sleeves and I asked her—I was on the verge of touching her to drive her—to go into the establishment lest she catch a cold. No she said, she wouldn't catch a cold, she had a shawl, after all, and she lifted it a little to show it and then drew it tighter around her chest. I couldn't tell her that I wasn't actually worried about her but was only glad to have found a feeling in which I could enjoy my love and therefore I told her again that I was worried. In the meantime her husband, her little girl and Hr. Pipes had come out too and it became apparent that it was not at all decided that they would travel to Brünn,

as Löwy had convinced me, rather Pipes was even determined to go to Nuremberg. That would be best, he said, a hall would be easy to get, the Jewish community was large, furthermore the journey to Leipzig and Berlin very comfortable. Besides, they had discussed it all day and Löwy, who had slept until 4, had simply kept them waiting and made them miss the ½ past 7 train to Brünn. In the midst of these arguments we entered the establishment and sat down at a table, I opposite Frau Tsch. I would have liked so much to distinguish myself, in itself it wasn't hard, I would only have to know some train connections, tell the railroad stations apart, bring about the decision between Nuremberg or Brünn, but above all shout down Pipes, who was behaving like his Bar-Kochba and whose shouting Löwy very reasonably even if unintentionally countered with a very rapid, moderately loud chatter that was not to be interrupted and, at least for me, rather incomprehensible at the time. Now instead of distinguishing myself, I sat slumped in my chair looked from Pipes to Löwy and only now and then met the eyes of Fr. Tsch. on the way; but when she answered me with a glance (all she had to do, for example, was smile at me because of Pipes's excitement) I looked away. This wasn't senseless. Between us there could be no smiling at Pipes's excitement. Facing her I was too serious for that and quite tired of this seriousness. If I wanted to laugh at something, I could look over her shoulder at the fat woman who had played the governor's wife in Bar-Kochba. But I actually couldn't look at her seriously either. For that would have meant that I love her. Even the y. Pipes behind me in all his innocence would have had to recognize that. And that would have been really unheard of. I a young man who is commonly taken to be 18 years old, declares before the evening guests of Café Savoy, in the circle of surrounding waiters, before the table of actors to a 30-year-old woman, whom hardly anyone even considers pretty, who has 2 children of 10 & 8 years of age, whose husband is sitting next to her, who is a model of respectability and frugality—declares to this woman his love, to which he has completely fallen victim, and—now comes the actually stranger part, which, to be sure, no one else would have noticed—immediately renounces the woman, just as he would renounce her even if she were young and single. Should I be grateful or should I curse that despite all unhappiness I can still feel love, an unearthly one though for earthly objects. Fr. Tschissik was beautiful yesterday. The actually normal beauty of the small hands, the light fingers, the rounded forearms, which are so perfect in themselves that even the unaccustomed sight of this nakedness doesn't make one think of the rest of the body. The hair parted into 2 waves and brightly illuminated by the gaslight. The slightly blemished skin around the right corner of the mouth. As if in childlike complaint her mouth opens, running above and below into delicately shaped indentations, one thinks that this beautiful word formation, which spreads the light of the vowels in the words and with the tip of the tongue preserves the pure contour of the words, can succeed only once and marvels at its everlastingness. Low white forehead. The powder I've seen used up to now I hate, but if this white color, this veil of somewhat clouded milk color hovering low over the skin comes from powder, then let everyone powder. She likes to have two fingers at the right corner of her mouth, perhaps she also stuck the fingertips into her mouth, yes perhaps she even put a toothpick into her mouth; I didn't look closely at these fingers, but it appeared almost as if she had put a toothpick into a hollow tooth and let it rest there for 15 minutes.

---

8 XI 11 all afternoon at the Doktor's regarding the factory.[275]

The girl who, only because she was walking arm in arm with her beloved, looked around calmly.

The clerk at Karl's reminded me of the actress who played Manette Salomon at the Odeon in Paris 1 ½ years ago.[276] At least when she was sitting. A soft bosom broader than it was high squeezed by woolly material. A face broad down to the mouth, but then quickly narrowing. Natural curls neglected in a straight hairstyle. Zeal and calm in a strong body. The memory was strengthened as I now realize by the fact that she was working diligently [on her typewriter the little bars (Oliver system) flew like old-time knitting needles] also walked back and forth, but spoke barely a few words in half an hour, as if she were holding Manette Salomon within her.

When I was waiting at the Doktor's[277] I looked at the one typist and thought about how hard it was to make out her face even while viewing it. Especially the relationship between a spread-out hairstyle protruding almost at an equal breadth all around her head to the straight nose that mostly appeared too long was confusing. When the girl, who was reading a document, made a more striking turn, I was almost taken aback by the observation that due to my thinking I had remained stranger to the girl than if I had brushed her skirt with my little finger.

When the Doktor, reading the contract aloud, came to a passage that dealt with my possible future wife and possible children I noticed opposite me a table with two large chairs and a smaller one around it. At the thought that I would never be capable of filling these or any 3 chairs with me, my wife and my child, I was overcome by a longing for this happiness so desperate from the very start that in this agitated state I asked the Doktor my only remaining question during the long reading, which immediately exposed my complete misunderstanding of an extensive section of the contract that had just been read.

---

continuation of the goodbye: About Pipes, because I felt oppressed by him, I noticed above all the notched and darkly dotted ends of his teeth. Finally I had half an idea. "Why go as far as Nuremberg at one stretch?" I asked, "why not give one or two performances at a smaller way station?" Do you know one? asked Fr. Tsch.[278] far from as sharply as I write it, thereby forcing me to look at her. The whole of her body visible above the table the whole roundness of shoulders, back and breast was soft, despite her bony almost coarse build in European dress on stage. Ridiculously I mentioned Pilsen. Regular guests at the next table very reasonably mentioned Teplitz.[279] Hr. Tsch. would have supported any way station, he only has confidence in small undertakings, Fr. Tsch. too without their having communicated much, she also asks all around about the fares, several times they said: it would be enough if one earned parnussa.[280] Her little girl rubs her cheek against her arm; she surely doesn't feel it, but for the adult the childlike conviction arises that nothing can happen to a child with its parents, even if they're wandering actors, and that the real troubles aren't found so close to the earth but rather only at the adults' eye level. I was very much in favor of Teplitz, because I could give them a recommendation letter for Dr. Polaček[281] and so lend my support to Fr. Tschissik. With opposition from Pipes, who himself made the lots for the 3 possible cities and directed the drawing of lots with liveliness, Teplitz was drawn for the third time. I went to the next table and excitedly wrote the recommendation letter. With the excuse that I had to go home to get Dr. P.'s exact address, which was not actually necessary and which no one at home knew either, I took my leave. In embarrassment, while Löwy got ready to accompany me, I played with the woman's hand and her little girl's chin.

---

9 XI 11 dreamed the day before yesterday: nothing but theater, I now up on the gallery, now on the stage, a girl of whom I'd been fond a few months ago played a part, tensed her supple body when she held on to the back of a chair in terror; from the gallery I pointed to the girl, who was playing a breeches part, my companion didn't like her. In one act the set was so large that nothing else could be seen, no stage, no auditorium, no darkness, no footlights; instead all the spectators were in great crowds on the set, which represented the Altstädter Ring,[282] probably seen from the entrance to Niklasstrasse. Even though one consequently should not actually have seen the square in front of the town hall clock and the Kleiner Ring, short rotations and slow oscillations of the stage floor nonetheless made it possible, for example, to look out over the Kleiner Ring from Kinsky Palace. This had no purpose but to show the whole set whenever possible, since it was simply there in such perfection and since it would have been a crying shame to overlook any of this set, which, as I was well aware, was the most beautiful set on the whole earth and of all time. The lighting was characterized by dark, autumn clouds. The light of the gloomy sun shone diffusely in this or that stained-glass window of the southeast side of the square. Since everything was executed in life size and without betraying itself in the smallest detail, it made a moving impression that some of the casements were blown open and shut by the moderate wind without a sound because of the great height of the houses. The square sloped steeply, the pavement was almost black, the Tein Church was in its place but in front of it was a small imperial castle, in whose forecourt all the other monuments that stood on the square were assembled in great order: the Marian Column, the old fountain in front of the town hall, which I myself have never seen, the fountain in front of the Niklas Church and a board fence that has now been put up around the excavation for the Hus memorial. The performance—one

often forgets in the auditorium that it's only a performance, all the more so on the stage and in this scenery—portrayed an imperial celebration and a revolution. The revolution, with huge crowds sent up and down the square, was probably greater than had ever taken place in Prague; it had apparently been transposed to Prague only because of the set, while it actually belonged in Paris. Of the celebration one at first saw nothing, the court had in any case left for a celebration, in the meantime the revolution had broken out, the people had penetrated the castle, I myself ran into the open straight over the ledges of the fountains in the forecourt, but the return to the castle was supposed to be impossible for the court. Then the court carriages came from Eisengasse at such furious speed that they had to apply the brakes far from the castle entrance and scraped across the pavement with locked wheels. They were the sort of carriages one sees at festivals and parades, on which tableaux vivants are exhibited, thus they were flat, surrounded by a garland of flowers and from the bottom of the carriage a colorful cloth hung down all around, covering the wheels. One became all the more aware of the terror signified by their haste. The horses, which reared before the entrance, dragged them as if unconsciously in a curve from Eisengasse to the castle. Many people were streaming past me out onto the square, mostly spectators whom I knew from the street and who had perhaps just now arrived. Among them was also a girl of my acquaintance, but I don't know which; beside her walked a young elegant man with a yellowish brown small-checkered ulster, his right hand deep in his pocket. They were walking toward Niklasstrasse. From that moment on I saw nothing more.

Schiller somewhere: The main thing is (or something like that) "to transform affect into character"[283]

II XI II Saturday. Yesterday at Max's all afternoon. Decided the sequence of the essays for "Die Schönheit hässlicher Bilder." Without good feeling. But that's just when Max loves me most or does it only seem so to me because I am then so clearly conscious of my scant merit. No he really loves me more. He wants to include my Brescia in the book too.[284] All that is good in me resists it. I was supposed to go with him to

Brünn today.[285] All that is bad and weak in me held me back. For the prospect that I should really write something good tomorrow I can't believe.

The girls tightly embraced by their work aprons especially in the back. One at Löwy and Winterberg[286] this morning whose apron flaps, closed only on her behind, didn't join together in the usual fashion but rather passed over each other, so that she was wrapped up like a swaddled baby. Sensual impression of this as I've also unconsciously always had of swaddled babies, who are so squeezed into their wrappings and beds and laced up with ribbons, quite as if to satisfy a desire.

Edison said in an American interview about his journey through Bohemia that in his opinion the relatively higher development of Bohemia (in the suburbs there are wide streets, little gardens in front of the houses, when traveling through the country one sees factories being built) rests on the fact that the emigration of Czechs to America is so great and that those returning one by one from there bring new ambition with them from there.[287]

As soon as I recognize in some way that I let ills rest that I would actually be meant to remedy (for example, the extremely content, from my point of view desolate life of my married sister),[288] I lose for a moment the feeling in my arm muscles.

I will try to gradually compile everything indubitable about me, later the credible, then the possible, etc. Indubitable in me is the greed for books. Not so much to own or to read them as to see them, to convince myself in a bookseller's display of their continued existence. When there are several copies of the same book somewhere every single one gives me pleasure. It's as if this greed came from my stomach, as if it were a misdirected appetite. Books I own give me less pleasure, whereas my sisters' books do give me pleasure. The longing to own them is incomparably smaller, it's almost absent.

---

12 XI 11 Sunday. Yesterday lecture Richepin "La legende de Napoleon" in the Rudolphinum.[289] Rather empty. As if to test the manners of the lecturer a large piano is placed on the way from the small entrance door to the lecturer's table. The lecturer comes in, with his eyes on the audience he wants to reach his table by the shortest path, therefore comes too close to the piano, is startled, steps back and walks gently around it, no longer looking at the audience. In the enthusiasm at the end of his speech and in the great applause he has naturally long forgotten the piano, since it didn't make itself conspicuous during the lecture, with his hands on his chest he wants to turn his back to the audience as late as possible, therefore takes several elegant steps sideways, naturally bumps into the piano a little and must arch his back a little on tiptoe before making his way into open terrain again. At least that's how Richepin did it.—A tall strong fifty-year-old with a waistline. The stiffly whirling hairstyle of Daudet, for example, is pressed rather tightly against his head without being destroyed. As with all old southerners who have a thick nose and the broad wrinkled face proper to it, from whose nostrils a strong wind can blow as through horses' muzzles and at the sight of whom one knows well that this is the final state of their face, no longer to be overtaken but still long-lasting, his face too reminded me of the face of an old Italian woman behind an admittedly very naturally grown beard.—The newly painted light gray color of the concert podium rising behind him was disconcerting at first. His white hair positively stuck to this color and granted no contour. When he bent his head back the color began to move, his head almost sinking in it. Only toward the middle of the lecture when one's attention became completely concentrated did the disturbance cease, especially when he stood up during the recitation with his tall black-clad body and guided the verses and dispelled the gray color with waving hands.—In the beginning he was embarrassing, so much did he pay compliments in every direction. In telling of a Napoleonic soldier whom he had known and who had had 57 wounds, he remarked that the variety of colors on this man's upper body could have been imitated only by a great colorist like his friend Mucha,[290] who was present.—I noticed in myself a progress in being moved by people on the podium. I didn't think of my pains and worries. I was squeezed into the left corner of my armchair but actually into the lecture, my hands folded between my knees. I felt an effect of Richepin on me such

as Solomon must have felt when he took young girls to bed. I even had a slight vision of Napoleon, who in a systematic fantasy also stepped out of the small entrance door, even though he might just as well have stepped out of the wood of the podium or out of the organ. He weighed down the whole hall, which at those moments was densely filled. As close as I actually was to him, I never had and even in reality never would have had doubts about his effect. Perhaps I would have noticed any ridiculousness of his attire, as in Richepin's case, but noticing this would not have disturbed me. How cool I was, in contrast, as a child! I often wished to be confronted with the Kaiser to show him his lack of effect. And that wasn't courage, only coolness.—He recited poems like speeches in the chamber. He pounded on the table as an impotent onlooker at battles, with swinging outstretched arms he cleared a path for the guards through the middle of the hall, empereur he shouted with only his upraised arm that had become a flag and in a repetition made it positively echo back from an army shouting down in the plain. During the description of a battle a little foot tapped on the floor somewhere, one looked, it was his foot that hadn't had enough confidence in itself. But it didn't disturb him.—For Die Grenadiere, which he read in a translation by Gerard de Nerval[291] and especially revered there was the least applause.—In his youth Napoleon's tomb was opened once a year and the invalids being led past in a procession were shown the embalmed face, more a sight of terror than of admiration, because the face was bloated and greenish; therefore they later abolished this opening of the tomb. But Richepin saw the face while being carried in the arms of his great uncle, who had served in Africa and for whom the commandant had the tomb specially opened.—A poem he intends to recite (he has an infallible memory, which a strong temperament must actually always have) he announces long before, discusses it, the coming verses already causing a slight earthquake under these words, in the case of the first poem he even said he would present it with all his fire. He did.—In the case of the last poem, he could then heighten the effect by proceeding unnoticed into the verses (by Viktor Hugo) standing up slowly, not sitting down again even after the verses, taking up and maintaining the great movements of the recitation with the last force of his prose. He concluded with the vow that even after 1000 years every dust speck of his corpse, if it had consciousness, would be ready to answer Napoleon's call.—The French short-winded with its rapid succession of valves with-

stood even the most simpleminded improvisations, didn't break even when he spoke several times of the poets who beautify everyday life, of his own imagination (eyes closed) as that of a poet, of his hallucinations (eyes reluctantly opened wide into the distance) as those of a poet, etc. Here he also sometimes covered his eyes and slowly uncovered them taking away one finger after the other.—He has served, his uncle in Africa, his grandfather under Napoleon, he even sang 2 lines of a war song.—
13 XI 11 And this man is as I learned today, 62 years old

14 XI 11 Tuesday. Yesterday at Max's, who returned from his reading in Brünn.[292]
Afternoon while falling asleep. As if the solid skullcap embracing the painless cranium had moved more deeply inward and left part of the brain outside in the free play of lights and muscles.

To wake up on a cold autumn morning with yellowish light. To force one's way through the almost closed window and just outside the panes, before one falls, to hover, arms outspread belly arched legs bent backward like the figures on the bows of old-time ships.

Before falling asleep. It seems so awful to be a bachelor, to struggle to preserve one's dignity as an old man asking to be received when one wants to spend an evening with people, to carry one's meal home in one's hand, to be able to expect no one lazily with calm confidence, to give a gift to someone only with difficulty or annoyance, to say goodbye outside the front door, never to be able to push one's way up the stairs with one's wife, to be ill and have only the consolation of the view out one's window when one can sit up, to have in one's room only side doors leading into strange apartments, to feel the strangeness of one's relatives, with whom one can remain friendly only by means of marriage, first the marriage of one's parents, then when its effect fades one's own, to have to marvel at strange children and not be permitted to keep repeating: I have none, to have an unchanging sense of one's age since no family grows with one, to model oneself in appearance and behavior on the one or two bachelors of our youthful memories. All this is true, only one easily makes the mistake of spreading out future woes so much before oneself that one's gaze must go far beyond them and never again returns, while today and later one will stand there oneself in reality, with a real body and a real head thus also a forehead to slap with one's hand.[293]

Now to attempt a sketch for the introduction to Richard and Samuel.[294]

---

15 XI 11 Yesterday evening already with a presentiment pulled the cover off the bed, lay down and again became aware of all my abilities, as if I were holding them in my hand; they tightened my chest, they inflamed my head, for a little while, to console myself for not getting up to work, I repeated: That can't be healthy, that can't be healthy and with almost visible intent tried to pull sleep over my head. I kept thinking of a cap with a visor that to protect myself, I pushed down over my forehead with a strong hand. How much I lost yesterday, how the blood was pressed in my cramped head, capable of anything, and only held by forces that are indispensable for my mere life and are being wasted here.

There's no doubt that everything I've invented in advance even in a good feeling word for word or just roughly but in explicit words, on the desk in the attempt to write it down, appears dry, wrong, immobile, obstructive to all that surrounds it, anxious, but above all full of gaps, even though nothing of the original invention has been forgotten. This is naturally due in large part to the fact that I invent good things free of paper only in the time of exaltation, which I fear more than I yearn for it, however much I do yearn for it, but that then the fullness is so great that I have to refrain, thus blindly take only what I grab at random out of the stream, so that in the considered act of writing it down this acquisition is nothing in comparison to the fullness in which it lived, is incapable of bringing back this fullness and therefore is bad and disturbing, because it tempts uselessly.

---

16 IX *(November)* 11 At noon today before falling asleep—but I never fell asleep—the upper body of a woman made of wax lay on me. Her face was bent back over mine, her left forearm pressed my chest.

Haven't slept for three nights, in the slightest attempt to do something immediately at the bottom of my strength.

---

from an old notebook: "This evening after having studied from 6 o'clock in the morning on, I noticed how my left hand had for a little while been clasping the right by the fingers out of sympathy."[295]

18 XI 11 Yesterday at the factory. Rode back on the tram, sat in a corner with legs stretched out, saw people outside, shop lamps alight, walls of viaducts while passing through, backs and faces again and again, a country road leading out of the main street of the suburb with nothing human on it except people going home, the glaring electric lights of the railroad station that were burned into the darkness, low sharply tapering chimneys of a gasworks, a poster about the guest performance of a singer de Treville,[296] which gropes its way along the walls into a street near the cemeteries, from where it then returned with me out of the cold of the fields into the cozy warmth of the city. One accepts strange cities as a fact, the residents there live without penetrating our way of life, just as we cannot penetrate theirs, one must compare, one can't resist, but one knows well that this has no moral or even psychological value in the end one can often even refrain from comparing, since the all-too-great difference of the living conditions relieves us of the task. The suburbs of our native city, however, are also strange to us, but here comparisons have value, a half-hour walk can prove it to us again and again, here people live partly within our city partly on the poor dark edge rutted like a great sunken lane, even though they all have a circle of common interests greater than any other group of people outside the city. Therefore I always enter the suburb with a mixed feeling of fear, of forsakenness, of sympathy, of curiosity, of haughtiness, of pleasure in travel, of manliness and come back with contentment, seriousness and calm; especially from Žižkov.[297]

---

19 XI 11 Sun.

Dream: In the theater. Performance "das weite Land" by Schnitzler[298] adapted by Utitz.[299] I sit at the very front on a bench, believe I'm sitting in the first row until it eventually becomes apparent that it's the second. The back of the bench is facing the stage, so that one can see the auditorium comfortably, the stage only after turning. The author is somewhere nearby, I can't hold back my unfavorable judgment of the play, with which I'm apparently already familiar, but to make up for it I add that the third act is supposed to be witty. With this "supposed to be," on the other hand, I want to say that, when the good parts are spoken of, I am not familiar with the play and must rely on hearsay; therefore I repeat this remark once again not only for myself, but nonetheless disregarded by the others. Around me there's a great crowd, all seem to have come in their winter clothes and hence overfill the seats. People next to me, behind me whom I don't see talk to me insistently, show me new arrivals, mention their names, my attention is called especially to a married couple pushing their way through a row of seats, since the woman has a dark-yellow, manly, long-nosed face and moreover as far as one can see in the crowd out of which her head rises, is wearing men's clothing; standing beside me strangely free is the actor Löwy, but quite unlike the real one and he's making excited speeches in which the term "principium" is repeated, I keep expecting the term "tertium comparationis," it doesn't come. In a box of the second tier actually only in a corner of the gallery, on the right when seen from the stage, which there adjoins the boxes, some third son of the Kisch family[300] is standing behind his sitting mother and speaking into the theater, dressed in a beautiful frock coat with its flaps spread out. Löwy's speeches have a connection to these speeches. Among other things, Kisch points high up to part of the curtain and says, there sits the German Kisch,[301] by which he means my schoolmate who studied German literature. When the curtain rises the theater begins to darken and Kisch would disappear anyhow, he moves, to make this clearer, with his mother up the gallery and away, again all arms coats and legs very spread out. The stage is somewhat lower than the auditorium, one looks down, one's chin on the back of the seat. The set consists mainly of two low thick columns in the middle of the stage. A banquet is being portrayed, in which girls and young men participate.

I see little, for even though when the play began many people left from the first benches in particular apparently to go backstage, the girls staying behind block the view with large flat, mostly blue hats moving back and forth over the whole length of the bench. A small 10–15 year-old boy, however, I see especially clearly on the stage. He has dry, parted, straight-cut hair. He doesn't even know how to place the napkin properly on his thighs, must look down attentively for this purpose and is supposed to be playing a bon vivant in this play. As a result of this observation I no longer have great confidence in this theater. The company on the stage is now awaiting various arrivals who climb down onto the stage from the first rows of the audience. But the play isn't well rehearsed either. Thus an actress Hackelberg[302] has just arrived, an actor leaning urbanely in his armchair addresses her as "Hackel-," then realizes his mistake and corrects himself. Now a girl arrives whom I know (her name is Frankel I think), she climbs over the back of my very seat, her back when she climbs over is completely naked, the skin quite blemished there's even a scratched, bruised spot, the size of a doorknob, over the right hip. But then she acts, when she turns around on the stage and stands there with an unblemished face, very well. Now a singing rider is supposed to be approaching from a distance at a gallop, a piano simulates the clopping of hoofs one hears the approaching stormy song, finally I also see the singer who to give the singing the natural swelling of something rapidly coming closer, is running along the gallery up above toward the stage. He is not yet at the stage or finished with the song and yet he has given the utmost in haste and in shouting song, the piano too can no longer imitate more distinctly the hoofs striking stones. Therefore both cease and the singer approaches with quiet singing, only he makes himself so small that only his head rises above the gallery railing, so that one can't see him so clearly. With that the first act is over, but the curtain doesn't go down, and the theater remains dark. On the stage 2 critics are sitting on the floor and writing with their backs leaning against a piece of scenery. A dramaturge or director with a blond pointed beard comes leaping onto the stage, still in flight he extends a hand to give an instruction; in the other hand he is holding a bunch of grapes, which earlier was in a fruit bowl of the banquet and eating from it. Again facing the auditorium I see that it is lit with simple kerosene lamps, which are mounted on simple candelabra as on streets and are now of course burning only very faintly. Suddenly, impure kerosene or a defective wick must be the cause, the light sprays out of one of these lamps and sparks shower down in a broad burst on the spectators who cannot be disentangled by one's gaze and form a mass black as earth. Then a gentleman stands up out of this mass, positively walks on it toward the lamp, apparently wants to rectify the situation, but first looks up at the lamp, remains standing beside it like that for a little while and when nothing happens, he goes calmly back to his seat, in which he sinks away. (I confuse myself with him and bow my face into the blackness.)

I and Max must be fundamentally different. As much as I admire his writings when they lie before me as a whole, inaccessible to my intervention or anyone else's, even today a number of short book reviews,[303] every sentence he writes for Richard and Samuel involves a reluctant concession on my part, which I feel painfully to my depths. At least today.[304]

This evening I was again full of anxiously restrained ability.

---

20 XI 11 Dream of a picture, supposedly by Ingres. The Girls in the Woods in a Thousand Mirrors or actually: The Virgins etc. To the right in the picture, grouped and airily drawn in the style of pictures on theater curtains, a group was closer together, toward the left they were sitting and lying on a huge branch or a flying ribbon or floating by themselves in a chain gradually rising toward the sky. And now they were reflected not only toward the viewer but also away from him, growing more indistinct and manifold, what the eye lost in detail it gained in fullness. But in front stood a naked girl unaffected by the reflections, propped up on one leg with her hip protruding. Here Ingres's draftsmanship was admirable, only I was actually pleased to find that too much real nakedness had remained in this girl even for the sense of touch. From a place concealed by her came a shimmer of yellowishly pale light.[305]

My repugnance for antitheses is certain. They do come unexpectedly but don't surprise, for they have always been very close at hand; if they were unconscious, it was only at the outermost edge. They do produce thoroughness, fullness, unbrokenness but only like a figure on a magic disk; we've chased our little idea around in a circle. As different as they can be, they are just as devoid of nuance, they grow under one's hand as if bloated by water, with the initial prospect of boundlessness and with a final medium never-changing size. They roll themselves up, cannot be stretched out, give no clues, are holes in wood, are an onslaught at a standstill, draw antitheses down upon themselves as I've shown. If only they would draw them all down upon themselves and forever.

---

for the drama:[306] English teacher Weiss,[307] how one evening on Wenzelsplatz, his shoulders straight, his hands deep in his pockets, his yellowish overcoat in tight folds, he hastened across the road with powerful strides just past the still stopped but already ringing tram. Away from us.

E. Anna!
A. (looking up) Yes.
E. Come here.
A. (long calm steps) What do you want?
E. I wanted to tell you that I've been dissatisfied with you for some time.
A. Well!
E. It's true.
A. Then you simply have to give me notice, Emil.
E. So quickly? And you don't even ask the reason?
A. I know it.
E. Really?
A. You don't like the food.
E. (stands up quickly, loud) Do you know that Karl is leaving this evening or don't you?
A. (inwardly unperturbed) Why, yes, unfortunately he is leaving, you didn't have to call me here for that.

---

21 XI 11 My former governess, the one who was black and yellow in the face, with an angular nose and a wart somewhere on her cheek that was so dear to me in those days was at our apartment today for the second

time in a short period to see me. The first time I wasn't home, this time I wanted to be left in peace and to sleep and gave instructions to say I wasn't there. Why did she educate me so badly, I was obedient, after all, she is saying it now herself in the hall to the cook and the housekeeper,[308] I had a quiet disposition and was good. Why didn't she take advantage of that and prepare a better future for me. She's a wife or widow, has children, has a lively way of speaking that doesn't let me sleep, thinks that I'm a tall, healthy gentleman at the fine age of 28, that I think back fondly to my youth and in general know what to do with myself. But now I'm lying here on the sofa, kicked out of the world, waiting intently for the sleep that refuses to come and when it comes will only graze me, my joints are sore with fatigue, my scrawny body is trembling to its ruin in agitations, of which it must not become clearly aware, my head is throbbing to an astonishing degree. And here are the 3 women standing outside my door, one praising me as I was, two as I am. The cook says I will go straight, she means without any detour to heaven. So it will be.

Löwy: A rabbi in the Talmud had the principle, in this case very pleasing to God, to accept nothing, not even a glass of water from anyone. But now it happened that the greatest rabbi of his time wanted to meet him and so invited him to a meal. To decline the invitation of such a man, that wasn't possible. The first rabbi therefore set off sadly. But because his principle was so strong, a mountain thrust itself between the two rabbis.

Anna (sits at the table, reading the newspaper.)

Karl (walks around the room, as soon as he comes to the window he stops and looks out, at one point he even opens the inner window.)

Anna Please leave the window closed, it's freezing

Karl (closes the window) We simply have different concerns.

22 XI 11

Anna. But you've acquired a new habit Emil, a quite abhorrent one. You can start from any trifle and with its help find a bad quality in me.

Karl (rubs his fingers) Because you have no consideration, because you're altogether incomprehensible.[309]

There's no doubt that a main obstacle to my progress is my physical condition. With such a body nothing can be achieved. I will have to get used to its perpetual failure. From the last few wildly dreamed-through but barely even snatchily slept-through nights I was so incoherent this morning, felt nothing but my forehead, saw a halfway bearable condition only far beyond the present one and in sheer readiness for death at one point would have liked to curl up with the documents in my hand on the cement tiles of the corridor. My body is too long for its weakness, it has not the least fat to generate a blessed warmth, to preserve inner fire, no fat on which the spirit might at some point nourish itself beyond its daily need without damage to the whole. How is the weak heart, which recently has often stabbed me, supposed to push the blood down the whole length of these legs. To the knee would be enough work, but then it is washed with only decrepit strength into the cold lower legs. But now it is already needed again up above, one waits for it while it dissipates down below. Due to the length of the body everything is pulled apart. What can it accomplish then, when perhaps even if it were compressed, it wouldn't have enough strength for what I want to achieve.

---

from a letter of Löwy's to his father: When I come to Warsaw, I will walk around among you in my European clothes like "a spider before your eyes, like a mourner among bridegrooms"

L. tells of a married friend who lives in Postin a small city near Warsaw and in his progressive interests feels lonely and therefore unhappy. "Postin, is that a big city?" "This big" he holds out the palm of his hand to me. It is clad in a napped yellowish-brown glove and presents a wasteland.

---

23 XI 11 on the 21st the 100th anniversary of Kleist's death the Kleist family had a wreath placed on his grave with the inscription: "To the best of their house"[310]

What conditions I'm dependent on due to my way of life! Last night I slept somewhat better than during the past week, this afternoon even quite well, I even have that sleepiness which follows moderately good sleep, as a result I'm afraid I won't be able to write as well, feel individual abilities turning more deeply inward and am prepared for all surprises, that is, see them already.

---

24 XI 11 Schhite (he who learns the art of ritual slaughter.) Play by Gordyn.[311] In it Talmud quotations, for example, When a great scholar commits a sin in the evening or at night, one is no longer permitted to reproach him for it in the morning, for in his learnedness he has undoubtedly already repented it himself—If one steals an ox, then one must give back 2, if one slaughters the stolen ox, then one must give back 4, but if one slaughters a stolen calf, then one must give back only 3, because it is assumed that one had to carry the calf away, thus has done hard work. This assumption determines the punishment even if one has led the calf away easily.

Honorableness of bad thoughts. Yesterday evening I felt especially miserable. My stomach was upset again, I had written with difficulty, I had strained to listen to Löwy's reading in the coffeehouse (which was at first quiet and had to be spared by us, but which then came to life and didn't leave us in peace), my sad immediate future appeared to me not worth stepping into, forsakenly I walked down Ferdinandstrasse. Then at the entrance to Bergstein[312] thoughts of the more distant future came to me again. How would I bear it with this body pulled out of a junk room? Even the Talmud says: A man without a wife is no person. In the face of such thoughts nothing could help me but to say to myself: "Now you bad thoughts come, now because I am weak and have an upset stomach. Now of all times you want to be thought through. You're only after what does you good. Shame on you. Come another time, when I'm stronger. Don't take advantage of my condition in this way." And indeed, without even waiting for other evidence, they retreated, gradually dispersed and didn't disturb me again for the rest of my walk, which naturally was not overly happy. But they apparently forgot that if they want to respect all my bad conditions, they will rarely have their turn.

The gasoline smell of an automobile coming from the theater drew my attention to how visibly the theatergoers approaching me while making final adjustments to their coats and hanging opera glasses are awaited by a beautiful domesticity (and be it even lit only by one candle, that's appropriate, after all, before bedtime) but also how they appear as if they are being sent home from the theater, as subordinates before whom the curtain has gone down for the last time and behind whom the doors have opened through which, before the beginning of or during the first act, they entered haughtily because of some ridiculous concern.

Fourth Notebook

28 XI 11 Have written nothing for 3 days.

25 XI *(1911)* spent all afternoon in Cafe City[313] persuading Miška[314] to sign a statement that he was only a clerk with us, thus not subject to compulsory insurance and my father would not be obligated to make the large additional payment for his insurance.[315] He promises me to do so, I speak a fluent Czech, in particular I apologize elegantly for my mistakes, he promises to send the statement to the shop on Monday, I feel, if not liked, then at least respected by him, but on Monday he sends nothing, is not even in Prague any longer, but has left.

Evening dull at Baum's without Max.

Reading of "Die Hässlichen,"[316] a still-too-disordered story, the first chapter is more the storage area of a story.

26 XI *(1911)* Sun. R. & S. with Max[317] in the morning & afternoon until 5. Then to A. M. Pachinger.[318] Collector from Linz, recommended by Kubin, 50 years old, huge, with tower-like movements, when he is silent for some time one bows one's head, for he is entirely silent, whereas when speaking he does not entirely speak, his life consists of collecting and copulating. Collecting: He began

with a collection of postage stamps, then moved on to graphic art, then collected everything, then saw the uselessness of this collection that would never be rounded off and limited himself to amulets, later to pilgrimage medals and pilgrimage leaflets from Lower Austria and South Bavaria. These are m. and l. that are reissued separately for each pilgrimage, are mostly worthless in their material and also artistically, but often contain pleasing depictions. He now also began to publish industriously on them, and indeed for the first time on this subject, for the systematization of which he first established the points of view. Naturally, the previous collectors of these things, who had neglected to publish, were indignant, but then had to resign themselves to it. Now he's a recognized expert on these pilgrimage medals, from all over come requests for identification and appraisal of these medals, his voice carries weight.[319] Moreover, he collects everything else too, his pride is a chastity belt (scapular?), which together with all his amulets was exhibited at the Dresden Hygiene Exhibition.[320] (He was just there and had everything packed for transport.) Then a beautiful knight's sword of a Falkensteiner. His relationship to art has a bad clarity attainable only through collecting. From the coffeehouse in the Hotel Graf[321] he leads us up to his overheated room, sits down on the bed, we on 2 chairs around him, so that we form a quiet assembly. His first question "Are you collectors?" "No only poor enthusiasts." "That doesn't matter." He pulls out his portfolio and fairly pelts us with bookplates, his own and others',[322] mixed in with a prospectus for his next book "Zauberei und Aberglaube im Steinreich."[323] He has already written a great deal, especially on "motherhood in art,"[324] he considers the pregnant body the most beautiful, for him it's also the most pleasant to screw. He has written about amulets too. He was also in the employ of the Vienna Court Museums, was in charge of excavations in Braila at the mouth of the Danube, invented a process named after him for binding excavated vases, is a 13fold member of learned societies and museums, his collection is bequeathed to the Germanic Museum in Nuremberg, he often sits at his desk at night until 1 or 2 o'clock and again at 8 in the morning. We have to write something in a female friend's album that he has taken with him on the trip to fill up. Those who produce things themselves come first. Max inscribes a complicated verse, which Hr. P. tries to translate with the saying "After a storm comes a calm." Beforehand he read it aloud with a wooden voice. I write:

Little soul
you leap in dance etc.[325]

he again reads aloud, I help, finally he says: "A Persian rhythm? What's that called again? Ghazal? Right?" We can't agree with that and can't guess what he means either. Finally he quotes a ritornello by Rückert.[326] Well then he meant ritornello. It's not that either, though. All right, but it has a certain melodiousness. While leaving he throws apart the bed so that it fully adjusts to the warmth of the room, he also gives instructions for further heating.—He's a friend of Halbe.[327] He would like to talk about him. We'd much rather talk about Blei.[328] But there's not much to say about him, he's disdained in the Munich literary societies because of lit. obscenities, he's divorced from his wife, who as a dentist had a well-visited studio and supported him, his daughter 16 years old blond with blue eyes is the wildest girl in Munich.[329] In Sternheim's "Hose"[330]—Pachinger was with Halbe in the theater—Blei played an aging bon vivant. When Pachinger met him the next day, he said "Herr Dr., yesterday you played Dr. Blei." How so? how so? he said in embarrassment, but I played so-and-so."—Kubin's married life is bad. His wife is a morphinist. P. is convinced that Kubin is one too. One need only observe him when from the greatest liveliness he suddenly declines with sharp nose and hanging cheeks, must be woken, rouses himself to find his way back into the conversation, after an interval grows quiet again, which is then repeated at ever shorter intervals. He is also often at a loss for words.—On women: The stories about his potency make one think about how he must slowly stuff his large member into the women. His trick in earlier days was to exhaust women until they couldn't go on. Then they were without a soul, animals. Yes this submissiveness I can imagine. He loves Rubens women as he says, but means those with large breasts bulging on top and flat and hanging baggily below. He explains this preference by saying that his first love was such a woman, a friend of his mother and mother of a schoolmate

29 XI *(1911)*

who seduced him at the age of 15. He was better in languages, his schoolmate in mathematics, so they studied together in the schoolmate's apartment, that's where it happened. He shows photographs of his favorites. His present one is an older woman sitting on a chair with her legs spread, arms raised, face wrinkled with fat, thus showing her masses of flesh. In a picture of her in bed the breasts, spread out and swollen so that they look positively congealed, and the belly raised toward the navel are equivalent mountains. Another favorite is young, her picture is only a picture of the long breasts pulled out of the unbuttoned blouse and a face looking away and tapering into a beautiful mouth. During his time in Braila he was very popular with the fat, long-suffering wives of businessmen who were starved by their husbands and staying there for their summer holiday. Very fruitful carnival in Munich. According to the registration office, during carnival over 6000 women come unaccompanied to Munich apparently only to be copulated with. They're married women, girls, widows from all over Bavaria, but also from the bordering lands.

From the Talmud: If a scholar goes looking for a bride, he should take an amhorez[331] with him, since he would be too absorbed in his scholarliness to notice what's necessary.—Through bribes the telephone and telegraph wires around Warsaw have been supplemented to form a complete circle, which in accordance with the Talmud makes the city into a bounded area, a courtyard, as it were, so that it's possible for even the most pious man to move, to carry trifles (like handkerchiefs) on his person, within this circle on Saturday.—The gatherings of the Chassidim,[332] at which they converse cheerfully about Talmudic questions. If the conversation falters or if someone doesn't participate, they make up for it with singing. Melodies are invented, if one succeeds family members are called in and it's repeated and rehearsed with them. During one such conversation a wonder rabbi, who often had hallucinations, suddenly buried his face in his arms, which were resting on the table, and remained in that position amid general silence for 3 hours. When he awoke he wept and performed a completely new merry military march. This was the melody with which angels of death had just escorted to heaven the soul of a wonder rabbi who had died at that time in a faraway Russian city.—According to the Kabbalah,[333] on Friday the pious get a new perfectly heavenly, more tender soul, which stays with them until Saturday evening.—On Friday evening two angels escort each pious man home from the temple; the master of the house stands as he greets them in the dining room; they stay for only a short time.

"Love for an Actress" "A Theater"[334]

The education of girls, their adulthood, their adjustment to the laws of the world has always had special value for me. Then they no longer run so hopelessly out of the way of one who is only casually acquainted with them and would like to speak casually with them, they stop for a little while and even if it be not exactly in the part of the room where one wants them, one no longer has to hold them with gazes, threats or the power of love, when they turn away, they do it slowly and don't intend to wound by it, then their back has become broader too. What one says to them doesn't get lost, they listen to the whole question without one's having to hurry, and they answer, if jokingly, nonetheless precisely the question asked. Indeed they even ask questions themselves with their face raised, and a brief conversation isn't unbearable to them. They hardly let a spectator disturb them anymore in the work they have just been doing, thus take him less into consideration, yet he is also permitted to look at them longer. Only to get dressed do they withdraw. It's the only time during which one can be uncertain. The rest of the time, however, one no longer has to run down streets, head off at front doors and wait again and again for a fortunate coincidence, even though one has certainly learned by now that one doesn't possess the ability to force it. But despite this great change they have undergone, it's no rarity that in an unexpected encounter they come up to us with a mournful expression, lay their hand flat in ours and with slow movements invite us like a business associate to enter the apartment. They walk heavily up and down in the next room, but when we penetrate there too in lust and defiance they sit in a window niche and read the newspaper without a glance for us.

---

3 XII 11 I have now read a bit of Schäfer's Karl Stauffers Lebensgang. Eine Chronik der Leidenschaft[335] and am so seized and held captive by this great impression penetrating to my depths, which are hearkened to only at moments, but at the same time am driven so far by the fasting forced on me by my upset stomach and by the usual excitement of the free Sunday that I must write, just as in the face of external excitement imposed by external circumstances all one can do is flail one's arms.

The unhappiness of the bachelor, whether apparent or real, is so easy for the surrounding world to divine that, at least if he has become a bachelor out of pleasure in secrecy, he will curse his decision. True, he walks around with his coat buttoned his hands in his high coat pockets, his elbows sharp, his hat low over his face, a false already native smile is supposed to protect his mouth as the pince-nez his eyes, his pants are narrower than looks good on thin legs. But everyone knows how he's doing, can enumerate his sufferings to him. Coolness wafts on him from his core, into which he looks with the even sadder other half of his double face. He moves from place to place positively without cease, but with expected regularity. The farther he recedes from the living, for whom he still, and this is the worst mockery, must work, like a conscious slave who must not express his consciousness, the smaller the space that is deemed sufficient for him. While the others, even if they have been lying in a sickbed all their life, nonetheless must be struck down by death, for even though in their own weakness they would have long since fallen by themselves, they still hold on to their loving strong healthy relatives by marriage, he, this bachelor even in the middle of his life apparently of his own volition contents himself with an ever smaller space and when he dies, the coffin is just right for him.

How I recently read Mörike's autobiography[336] to my sisters, began well but continued even better and finally, my fingertips together, overcame inner obstacles with my persistently calm voice, provided my voice a constantly expanding vista, and finally the whole room around me could receive nothing but my voice. Until my parents, returning from the shop, rang the bell.

Before falling asleep felt on my body the weight of the fists on my light arms.

---

8 Dec. *(1911)* Friday, haven't written in a long time, only this time it was actually to some extent out of satisfaction, for I've finished the first chapter of R. & S. myself and regard especially the initial description of

the sleep in the train compartment as successful.[337] Even more, I believe something is happening in me that is very close to Schiller's transformation of affect into character.[338] Over all my inner resistance I must write this down

---

A walk with Löwy to the governor's castle, which I called the fortress of Zion.[339] The tracery of the entrance gates and the sky color went very clearly together.—Another walk to the Hetzinsel.[340] Story about Frau Tschissik how they took her into the company[341] in Berlin out of pity, an initially worthless duettist in an old-fashioned dress and hat. Reading of a letter from Warsaw, in which a young Warsaw Jew complains about the decline of the Jewish theater and writes that he'd rather go to the "Nowosti" the Polish operetta theater than to the Jewish one, for those miserable sets and costumes, the indecencies, the "moldy" couplets etc. are unbearable. Just think of the main effect of a Jewish operetta, which consists in the prima donna marching with a procession of small children behind her through the audience onto the stage. All are carrying small Torah scrolls and singing: toire is die beste schoire—the Torah is the best commodity.

Beautiful solitary walk after those successful passages in R. & S. over the Hradschin and the Belvedere. On Nerudagasse a plaque: Anna Křižová dressmaker, trained in France by the Dowager Duchess Ahrenberg née Princess Ahrenberg.—In the middle of the first castle courtyard I stood and watched a calling out of the castle guard.[342]

Max wasn't pleased with the last parts I wrote,[343] at least because he regards them as unsuitable for the whole, but possibly also finds them bad in themselves. This is very probable, because he warned me against writing such long passages and regards the effect of such writing as something jelly-like.

To be able to speak with young girls, I need older people close by. The slight disturbance emanating from them enlivens the conversation for me, the demands on me immediately seem to me lowered, whatever I utter without considering my words can still, if it doesn't apply to the girl, be appropriate for the older person, out of whom I can also if it becomes necessary, coax a great deal of help.

Frl. Haas.[344] She reminds me of Frau Blei,[345] only her nose in its length, slight double bend and relative narrowness looks like the ruined nose of Frau Blei. But apart from that she has in her face a blackness with scarcely any external grounds, which can be driven into the skin only by a strong character. Broad back, a far advanced tendency toward a woman's swelling back; heavy body, which then becomes thin in the well-cut jacket and for which even this narrow jacket is loose. After embarrassments in the conversation a free raising of the head means that a way out has been found. I certainly wasn't lying on the ground in this conversation, had not abandoned myself inwardly either, but if I had seen myself only from outside, I wouldn't have been able to explain my behavior in any other way. In the past I couldn't manage to express myself freely with new acquaintances because the presence of sexual desires unconsciously hindered me, now I'm hindered by their conscious absence.

Encounter with Herr and Frau Tschissik on the Graben. She was wearing her whore's dress from "Der wilde Mensch."[346] When I break down her appearance as I saw it at that time on the Graben into its details, she becomes improbable. (I saw her only fleetingly, for I was frightened at the sight of her, didn't greet them, wasn't seen either and didn't immediately dare to turn around.) She was much smaller than usual, her left hip was not momentarily but constantly protruding, her right leg was bent, the movement of her neck and head, which she brought closer to her husband, was very hasty, with her bent right arm extended to the side she sought to link arms with her husband. He was wearing his little summer hat with the brim pushed down in front. When I turned around they were gone. I guessed that they had entered Kafe Central,[347] waited a little on the other side of the Graben and after a long while was lucky enough to see her come to the window. When she sat down at the table, one saw only the edge of her cardboard hat covered with blue velvet.—In a dream I was then in a very narrow also not particularly high-ceilinged, glass-vaulted passage,[348] similar to the impassable communications in primitive Italian paintings, from a distance also similar to a passage we saw in Paris branching off from the rue des Petits Champs. Only the one in Paris was certainly wider and filled with shops, but this one ran along between bare walls, appearing scarcely to leave space for two people walking side by side, but when one really walked in it, as I did with Frau Tschissik then there was a surprising amount of space, though this didn't surprise us. While I walked with Frau T. toward the one exit, in the direction of a possible observer of the whole thing, and Fr. Tschissik at the same time apologized for some transgression (it seemed to be addiction to drink) and implored me not to believe her slanderers, at the other end of the passage Herr T. was whipping a shaggy blond St. Bernard, which stood opposite him on its hind legs. It wasn't quite clear whether T. was only playing with the dog and neglecting his wife because of it or whether he had himself been seriously attacked by the dog or whether he ultimately wanted to keep the dog away from us.

With L.[349] on the quay.[350] I had a slight fainting spell that suppressed my whole being, got over it and after a little while remembered it like something long forgotten.

Even leaving aside all other obstacles (physical condition, parents, character), I find a very good excuse for not limiting myself to literature despite everything in the following dichotomy: I can venture nothing for myself as long as I have achieved no greater work that satisfies me fully. That is certainly irrefutable.

I have now and already had in the afternoon a great longing to write my whole anxious condition wholly out of me and just as it comes out of the depths to write it into the depths of the paper or to write it down in such a way that I can incorporate what I've written fully into me. This is no artistic longing. When Löwy spoke today of his dissatisfaction and of his indifference to everything the troupe does, I attributed his condition to homesickness, but didn't hand this explanation over to him, as it were, even though I had voiced it, instead keeping it for myself and enjoying it temporarily for my own sadness.

9 Dec. *(1911)* Stauffer-Bern:[351] "The sweetness of production obscures its absolute value."[352]

If one submits to a book of letters or memoirs, no matter by whom in this case by Karl Stauffer-Bern, doesn't draw him into oneself by one's own power, for that requires art, and art gratifies itself, but rather in self-abandonment—he who does not resist soon undergoes this—lets the collected stranger draw one away and make one into his relative, then it is no longer anything special when, brought back to oneself by closing the book, after this excursion and this recuperation one feels better again in one's own newly recognized, newly shaken being, having contemplated it for a moment from a distance, and one stays behind in it with a freer head.

---

10 Dec. *(1911)* Sun. I must go visit my sister and her little boy.[353] When my mother returned from my sister the day before yesterday at 1 o'clock at night with the news of the boy's birth, my father moved through the apartment in his nightshirt, opened all the doors, woke me the maid and my sisters and announced the birth in such a way as if the baby had not only been born but had also already led an honorable life and had its funeral.

Only later can it surprise us that these circumstances of a stranger's life,[354] despite their liveliness, are described immutably in the book, even though we believe we know firsthand that nothing is more remote from an experience like, for example, grief over the death of a friend[355] than the description of that experience. But what is right for us isn't so for the stranger. For if with our letters we can't do justice to our own feeling—here, naturally, there are a multitude of gradations blurring on both sides—if even in our best condition we must rely again and again on expressions like "indescribable," "inexpressible" or a "so sad" or so beautiful followed by a rapidly crumbling "that"-clause, then as if in compensation for this we are given the ability to comprehend strangers' accounts with the calm precision we lack at least to that extent with regard to our own letter writing. The ignorance in which we find ourselves about those feelings that have at one time or another smoothed or crumpled the letter before us, this very ignorance becomes understanding, since we are forced to keep to the letter lying here, to believe only what is written in it, thus to find this perfectly expressed and from a perfect expression, as is only just, to see the open road into the most human. Thus Karl Stauffer's letters, for example, contain only the account of the short life of an artist

---

13 XII 11 Out of fatigue haven't written and have been lying alternately on the sofa in the warm and in the cold room with sick legs and disgusting dreams. A dog lay on my body, a paw close to my face, I woke up from this, but was still afraid for a little while to open my eyes and look at it.

Biberpelz.[356] A patchy play dwindling away without rising to a climax. False scenes with the head official. Delicate acting by Lehmann from the Lessing Theater. Tucking of her skirt between her thighs when she bends down. The thoughtful look of the common people, raising of both palms, which are placed one under the other on the left in front of her face, as if to weaken voluntarily the power of her denying or protesting voice. Unadvised coarse acting of the others. Impertinences of the comedian toward the play (draws his old saber, mixes up the hats) My cold aversion. Went home, but even while still there sat with the admiring notion that so many people take on so much excitement for an evening (they scream, steal, are stolen from, harassed, applauded, neglected) and that in this play, if one only looks at it with squinting eyes, so many disordered human voices and exclamations are thrown together. Beautiful girls. One with a smooth face, uninterrupted surfaces of skin, round cheeks, hair beginning high up, eyes abandoned and somewhat bulging in this smoothness.—Beautiful passages of the play in which the Wulffen woman reveals herself to be at the same time a thief and an honest friend of the clever, progressive, democratic people. A Wehrhahn in the audience should actually feel vindicated.—Sad parallelism of the 4 acts.

In the first act there's stealing, in the second is the court, the same in the 3rd and 4th act—

"Der Schneider als Gemeinderat" with the Jews. Without the Tschissiks, but with two new, terrible people, Herr and Frau Liebegold.[357] Bad play by Richter.[358] The beginning Molierian the ostentatious councilman bedecked with watches.—The Liebgold woman can't read, her husband has to rehearse with her.—It's almost customary for a comedian to marry a serious actress and a serious actor a comic actress and in general for only married or related women to be taken along.—How once at midnight the piano player probably a bachelor, slipped out the door with his sheet music.

Brahms concert by the Singverein.[359] The essence of my unmusicality is that I can't enjoy music cohesively, an effect arises in me only now and then and how rarely it's a musical one. The heard music naturally draws a wall around me and the only enduring musical influence on me is that, confined in this way, I'm different than when free.—There is no such reverence in the audience for literature as there is for music. The singing girls. The mouths of many of them were held open only by the melody. Neck and head of one with a ponderous body flew while she sang.—Three priests in a box. The middle one with a little red cap listens with calm and dignity, untouched and heavy, but not stiff; the one on the right slumps with a pointy, rigid wrinkled face; the one on the left fat rests his face at an angle on his half-opened fist.—Played. Tragische Ouverture. (I hear only slow solemn steps performed now here now there. It's instructive to observe the music passing from one group of players to another and to verify it with the ear. The destruction in the conductor's hair.)
Beherzigung by Goethe, Nänie by Schiller Gesang der Parzen, Triumphlied—The singing women who stood up above at the low balustrade as if on a piece of early Italian architecture.

There's no doubt that, although I have stood for quite some time in literature, which has often engulfed me, for three days aside from a general longing for happiness I've felt no genuine longing for literature. In the same way, last week I regarded Löwy as my indispensable friend and have now dispensed with him easily for three days.

When I begin to write after a long time, I pull the words as if out of the empty air. If one is attained, then it's only this one here and all the work begins anew

---

14 XII *(1911)* My father reproached me at noon because I don't concern myself with the factory. I explained that I had participated because I expected profit, but I can't be involved in the work as long as I'm in the office. My father went on scolding, I stood at the window and was silent.[360] In the evening, however, I caught myself thinking, as a result of that midday conversation, that I could be very content with my present position and only had to beware of having all my time free for literature. Scarcely had I subjected this thought to closer scrutiny when it was no longer astonishing and already seemed familiar to me. I denied my ability to take advantage of all my time for literature. This conviction came only from a momentary state, to be sure, but was stronger than it. I also thought of Max as of a stranger, even though this evening he has an exciting reading and performance in Berlin;[361] now it occurs to me that I thought of him only as I was approaching Frl. Taussig's[362] apartment on my evening walk

---

A walk with Löwy down by the river. The one pillar of the arch ascending on the Elisabethbrücke,[363] illuminated on the inside by an electr. lamp, as a dark mass between light streaming out on the sides, looked like a factory chimney and the dark wedge of shadow stretching above it toward the sky was like rising smoke. The sharply bounded green areas of light by the side of the bridge.

How while reading aloud Beethoven und das Liebespaar by W. Schäfer[364] various thoughts (about supper, about Löwy, who was waiting) not at all connected with the story I was reading went through my head with great clarity without disturbing my reading, which especially today was very pure.

---

16 *(17)* XII *(1911)* Sun.[365] 12 o'clock noon. Idled away the morning with sleeping and newspaper reading. Fear of finishing a review for the Prager Tagblatt.[366] Such fear of writing always expresses itself in my occasionally without being at my desk, making up introductory sentences of what I'm supposed to write, which immediately prove to be unusable, dry, broken off long before the end and which point with their protruding breaks into a sad future.

The old arts at the Christmas market. Two cockatoos on a crossbar draw fortunes. Mistakes. A girl gets an inamorata prophesied.—A man offers artificial flowers for sale with verses: To jest růže udělaná z kůže.[367]

The young Pipes while singing. As the only gesticulation the r. forearm is rolled back and forth at the joint, the half-opened hand opens a little more and then contracts again. Sweat covers his face, especially the upper lip as if with splinters of glass.[368] A buttonless ascot is hastily stuck behind the vest of the frock coat.—The warm shadow in the soft red of the mouth cavity of the singing Frau Klug.[369]

Jewish streets in Paris rue Rosier branching off from rue de Rivoli[370]

If a disordered education, which in itself has only the most meager coherence indispensable to mere, uncertain existence, is suddenly called upon to work within a limited time, therefore by necessity vigorously, to develop, to speak, then there ensues only a bitter response, containing a mixture of arrogance about what has been achieved and can be tolerated only with all one's unpracticed powers, a brief look back at the knowledge escaping in surprise, which is especially agile because it was more sensed than settled and finally hatred and admiration for one's surroundings.[371]

Before falling asleep yesterday I imagined a drawing of a group of people isolated like a mountain in the air, which in its drawing technique seemed to me completely new and once invented easy to execute. Around a table was a gathering, the ground extended somewhat farther than the circle of people, but for the time being, looking with great intensity, I saw of all the people only a young man in antiquated dress. He had rested his left arm on the table, his hand hung loosely over his face, which was looking up playfully at someone bending over him worriedly or questioningly. His body especially his right leg was stretched in careless youthfulness, he was lying more than sitting. The two distinct pairs of lines that bounded the legs crossed and connected lightly to the borderlines of the body. With faint corporeality the palely colored clothes bulged between these lines. In astonishment at this beautiful drawing which produced a tension in my head that I was convinced was the same and indeed enduring tension by which, when I wanted, the pencil in my hand could be guided, I forced myself out of my twilight state to be better able to think the drawing through. Then it soon turned out, to be sure, that I had imagined nothing but a small group made of gray-white porcelain.

In periods of transition, as the past week has been for me and at least this moment still is, I'm often seized by a sad but calm astonishment at my emotionlessness. I am separated from all things by a hollow space, to the boundary of which I don't even push myself.

Now, in the evening, when my thoughts begin to become freer and I would perhaps be capable of some things, I must go to "Hippodamie" at the National Theater, premiere by Vrchlicky.[372]

There's no doubt that a Sunday can never be of more use to me than a weekday, since its special schedule jumbles up all my habits and I need the extra free time to adjust myself halfway to this special day.

At the moment that freed me from the office, I would undoubtedly immediately fulfill my longing to write an autobiography. I would need such a drastic change before me as a temporary goal at the beginning of writing in order to steer the mass of events. I cannot foresee, however, an elevating change other than this one, which itself is so terribly improbable. But then the writing of the autobiography would be a great joy, since it would happen as easily as the writing down of dreams and yet would have a completely different, great result that would influence me forever while also being accessible to the understanding and feeling of everyone else.

---

18 XII 11 Hippodamie the day before yesterday.[373] Wretched play. A wandering around in Greek mythology without rhyme or reason. Kvapil's essay[374] on the playbill, which expresses between the lines the view, visible all through the performance, that a good production (which here, however, was nothing but an imitation of Reinhardt[375]) can make a bad piece of writing into a great theatrical work. All this must be sad for a Czech who has seen only a little of the world.—The governor,[376] who during the intermission got some fresh air from the corridor through the little open door of his box.—The apparition of the dead Axiocha, invoked as a silhouette, who soon disappears because, only recently deceased, at the sight of the world she feels her old human suffering again too deeply.

Max arrived yesterday from Berlin. In the Berliner Tagblatt he was called selfless, by a Fackel man, to be sure,[377] because he had read the "far more significant Werfel." Max had to strike out this sentence before he brought the review to the Prager Tagblatt to have it reprinted.[378] I hate W.,[379] not because I envy him, but I envy him too. He's healthy, young and rich, unlike me in all respects. Besides, he has written very good things early and easily with a musical sense, he has the happiest life behind him and ahead of him, I work with weights I can't get rid of, and I'm completely cut off from music.

I'm unpunctual, because I don't feel the pains of waiting. I wait like a cow. For when I feel a purpose, even if a very uncertain one, of my momentary existence, I'm so vain in my weakness that, once this purpose has been set before me, I will gladly tolerate anything for its sake. If I were in love, what I could do then. How long I waited years ago under the arcades on the Ring until M.[380] came by and even if she only passed by with her lover. I've missed the time of arranged meetings partly out of negligence, partly out of ignorance of the pains of waiting, but also partly in order to attain new more complicated purposes in the renewed uncertain seeking-out of those people whom I had arranged to meet, thus also the possibility of long uncertain waiting. From the mere fact that as a child I had a great nervous fear of waiting, one could conclude that I was destined for something better, but that I had a presentiment of my future.

My good states don't have time or permission to live themselves out naturally; my bad ones, on the other hand, have more of it than they require. I've now been suffering from such a state, as I can calculate from the diary, since the 9th, for almost 10 days. Yesterday I lay down in bed with a fiery head once again and was about to rejoice that the bad time was over and to fear that I would sleep badly. But it passed, I slept fairly well and wake badly.

---

19 XII *(1911)* Yesterday "Dawids Geige" by Lateiner.[381] The disowned brother, an artistic violinist, returns a rich man as in the dreams of my early Gymnasium days,[382] but first, dressed as a beggar, his feet bound in rags like a snow shoveler, he tests his relatives who have never left home: His honest poor daughter, his rich brother, who won't give his son in marriage to his poor cousin and who despite his age wants to take a young wife for himself. Only later does he reveal himself by tearing open a frock coat, under which the decorations of all the princes of Europe hang on a sash tied across his chest. With violin playing and singing he turns all the relatives and their circle into good people and puts their affairs in order.

Frau Tschissik acted again. Yesterday her body was more beautiful than her face, which seemed narrower than usual so that her forehead, which wrinkled at the first word, was too striking. The beautifully rounded moderately strong large body didn't belong to her face yesterday, and she reminded me vaguely of hybrid creatures like mermaids, sirens, centaurs. When she stood before me later with a contorted face, a blemished complexion marred by the makeup, a stain on her dark blue, short-sleeved blouse I felt as if I were supposed to speak to a statue in a circle of merciless spectators. Frau Klug was standing beside her and observing me. Fräulein Weltsch[383] was observing me from the left. I said as many stupid things as possible. Thus I didn't desist from asking Frau T.[384] why she had gone to Dresden, even though I knew that she had quarreled with the others and had left for that reason and that this subject was therefore painful to her. Ultimately it was even more painful to me only nothing else occurred to me. When Frau Tschisik joined us while I was speaking with Frau Klug, I turned to Frau T., saying "Pardon!" to Frau Klug as if I intended to spend my life with Frau T. from now on. Then, as I was speaking with Frau T., I realized that my love had not actually seized her, but only flew around her, now closer, now farther. Indeed it cannot find peace.—Frau Liebgold played a young man in a costume that tightly embraced her pregnant body. Because she doesn't obey her father (Löwy), he pushes her upper body down onto a chair and strikes her on the behind, over which the pants are stretched extremely taut. Löwy later said he touched her with the same repugnance as he would a mouse. But seen from the front she's pretty, only in profile does her nose descend too long, too pointed and cruel.

I got there only at 10 o'clock, took a walk beforehand and savored the slight nervousness of having a seat in the theater and going for a walk during the performance, that is, while the soloists are attempting to sing me there. I missed Fr. Klug too, listening to whose always lively singing means nothing other than testing the world for its firmness, which I actually need.

Today at breakfast I spoke with my mother by chance about children and marriage, only a few words, but during this talk I realized clearly for the first time how untrue and childlike my mother's conception of me is. She regards me as a healthy young man who suffers a little from fancying himself ill. This fancy will fade by itself with time, though a marriage and having children would eliminate it most thoroughly. Then the interest in literature too would diminish to the degree that is perhaps necessary for educated people. The interest in my profession or in the factory or in whatever comes into my hands at the moment will take hold with natural undisturbed intensity. Hence there is not the slightest, remotely tangible reason for permanent despair over my future, for temporary despair, which, however, is not profound either, there is cause when I believe I've upset my stomach once again or when I can't sleep because I write too much. There are thousands of possible solutions. The most probable is that I suddenly fall in love with a girl and will no longer be able to be without her. Then I'll see how good everyone's intentions toward me are and how no one wants to hinder me. But if I become a bachelor, like my uncle in Madrid,[385] it won't be a misfortune either because in my cleverness I'll know how to adapt myself.

23 XII 11 Sat. If, in view of my whole way of life, which is leading in a direction foreign and false to all my relatives and acquaintances, the fear arises and if it's expressed by my father, that I will become a second Uncle Rudolf,[386] that is, the fool of the new generation of the family, the fool somewhat altered for the needs of a different time, then I will from now on be able to feel how in my mother, whose opposition to this opinion dwindles over the years, everything is concentrated and strengthened that speaks for me and against Uncle Rudolf and is driven like a wedge between the conceptions of the two of us.

The day before yesterday at the factory. At Max's in the evening, where the painter Novak was spreading out the lithographs of Max. I didn't know how to compose myself in the face of them, how to say yes or no. Max presented several views he had already formed, whereupon my thinking rolled around them to no avail. Finally I grew accustomed to the individual sheets of paper, cast off at least the surprise of the unpracticed eye, found a chin round, a face compressed, an upper body armor-like, but he looked more as if he were wearing a huge dress shirt under his street suit. The painter presented several arguments against this that were not understandable at the first or at the second attempt, weakening their significance only by making them to us of all people, who, if his words were inwardly proven, had spoken the cheapest nonsense. He asserted that it was the felt and even conscious task of the artist to incorporate the portrait subject into his own art form. To achieve this he had first prepared a portrait sketch in color, which also lay before us, showed in dark colors an actually too-sharp dry likeness (this too-great sharpness I can only now acknowledge) and was declared by Max the best portrait, since besides its likeness around the eyes and mouth it bore noble, composed features, which were strengthened to the right degree by the dark colors. Asked about this, one couldn't deny it. From this sketch the painter now worked at home on his lithographs, striving, by altering lithograph after lithograph, to distance himself more and more from the natural phenomenon, but at the same time not only not to violate his own art form but also, stroke by stroke, to move closer to it. Thus, for example, the ear lost its human convolutions and the detailed edge and became a deepened semicircular whorl around a small dark opening. Max's bony chin, beginning to form from the ear, lost its simple boundary, as indispensable as it seems and as little as the removal of an old truth turned into a new one for the viewer. The hair dissolved in sure, understandable outlines and remained human hair, however much the painter denied it. While the painter had demanded from us understanding of these transformations, he then indicated only hastily but with pride that everything on these sheets had significance and that even the accidental was necessary because its effect influenced everything that followed. Thus, next to one head a narrow, pale coffee stain went down almost the whole picture, it was integrated, calculated and no longer to be removed without damage to all the proportions. In the left corner of another sheet was a large scarcely noticeable blue stain made up of scattered dots; now this stain had even been made intentionally, for the sake of the slight illumination passing over the picture from it, in which the painter had then continued to work. His next goal was now to include first and foremost the mouth, to which some things but not enough had already been done, and then the nose in the transformation, about which, in response to Max's complaint that in this way the lithograph would distance itself more and more from the beautiful color sketch, he remarked that it was not at all out of the question that it would approach it again. In any case one could not overlook the certainty with which the painter at every moment of the conversation trusted in the unforeseen of his inspiration and that only this trust made his artistic work with the best justification into an almost scientific one.—Bought two lithographs "Apple Salesgirl" and "Walk"[387]

An advantage of keeping a diary consists in the fact that one becomes aware with reassuring clarity of the transformations one incessantly undergoes, which one naturally believes, senses and admits in general too, but which one unconsciously denies whenever it's a matter of gaining hope or peace from such an admission. In the diary one finds proof that, even in conditions that today seem unbearable, one lived, looked around and wrote down observations, that this right hand thus moved as it does today, when the possibility of surveying our condition at that time does make us wiser, but we therefore must recognize all the more the undauntedness of our striving at that time, which in sheer ignorance nonetheless sustained itself.

From Werfel's poems[388] my head was as if filled with steam all yesterday morning. For a moment I feared the enthusiasm would sweep me away without stopping into nonsense.

Agonizing conversation the evening before last with Weltsch.[389] My glances ran startled back and forth on his face and neck for an hour. At one point, in the midst of a facial contortion caused by agitation weakness and thoughtlessness, I didn't know for sure whether I would get out of the room without permanent injury to our relationship. Outside in the rainy weather meant for silent walking I heaved a sigh and then waited contentedly for an hour in front of the "Orient"[390] for M.[391] Such waiting with slow glances at my watch and indifferent walking back and forth is for me almost just as pleasant as lying on the sofa with legs stretched and hands in my pants pockets. (In half-sleep one then believes one's hands are no longer in one's pants pockets at all, but rather they seem to lie as fists at the top of one's thighs)

---

24 XII *(1911)* Sun. Yesterday it was merry at Baum's. I was there with Weltsch. Max is in Breslau. I felt free, could carry out every movement to its completion, I replied and listened as is proper, made the most noise and if at some point I said something stupid, it didn't become the main thing, but was immediately washed away. The walk home with Weltsch

in the rain was the same, despite puddles, wind and cold it went by for us as quickly as if we had taken the tram. We were both sorry to say goodbye.

As a child I was afraid and if not afraid then uneasy when my father, as he being a businessman often did, spoke of the last or the ultimo. Since I wasn't curious and even if I asked at some point, my slow thinking made me unable to digest the answer quickly enough and because often a weakly active curiosity once arisen was satisfied by question and answer alone without demanding a meaning too, the expression the last remained for me a tormenting mystery which, as a result of more attentive listening, was joined by the expression ultimo even if never with such strong significance. It was also bad that the last, feared for so long, could never be purely overcome, for when it had at some point gone by without special signs indeed without special attention, for the fact that it always came after roughly 30 days was something I noticed only much later, and when the first had thus happily arrived, one began, not with special horror, to be sure, but this was added without examination to the other incomprehensible things, to speak again of the last.

When I arrived at W.'s[392] yesterday at noon, I heard the voice of his sister[393] greeting me, but I didn't see her herself until her weak figure detached itself from the rocking chair standing in front of me.

My nephew's[394] circumcision this morning. A short man with crooked legs, Austerlitz[395] who has 2800 circumcisions behind him, carried the thing out very skillfully. It's an operation made more difficult by the fact that the boy, instead of lying on a table, is lying on his grandfather's lap and that the surgeon, instead of paying close attention, must murmur prayers. First the boy is immobilized by wrapping him up, leaving only the member free, then the area to be cut is precisely defined by putting a perforated metal disk on it, then with an almost ordinary knife a sort of fish knife the cut is made. Now one sees blood and raw flesh, the moule[396] busies himself in it briefly with his long-nailed trembling fingers and pulls skin obtained somewhere like the finger of a glove over the wound. Immediately everything is all right, the baby has hardly cried. Now comes just one more little prayer, during which the moule drinks wine, and with his not yet completely blood-free fingers brings some wine to the baby's lips. Those present pray: "As he has now entered into the covenant, so shall he enter into knowledge of the Torah, into a happy marriage and into the performance of good deeds."

When I heard the man who accompanied the moule say the prayer after the meal today and those present apart from the two grandfathers spent the time in dreams or boredom with a complete lack of understanding of the prayer, I saw before me Western European Judaism in a clear unforeseeable transition, about which the first to be affected are not worried, but rather as true transitional people bear what is imposed on them. These religious forms, having arrived at their final end, had even in their present practice such an undisputed merely historical character that only the passage of a very short time within this morning seemed necessary to arouse historical interest among those present by telling them about the outdated former custom of circumcision and its half-sung prayers

---

Löwy, whom I keep waiting ½ an hour almost every evening, said to me yesterday: For several days I've been looking up at your window while waiting. First I see light there, when I've come as usual before the arranged time, so I assume you're still working. Then the light is put out, the next room remains lit, so you're having supper; then your room is lit again, so you're brushing your teeth; then the light is put out, so you're already on the stairs, but then it's burning again—

---

25 XII *(1911)* What I discern of contemporary Jewish literature in Warsaw through Löwy and of contemporary Czech literature through partial insight of my own suggests that many advantages of literary work, the movement of spirits, the unified coherence of a national consciousness that in outward life is often inactive and always splintering, the pride and the support the nation receives through a literature for itself and in the face of the hostile surrounding world, this diary keeping of

a nation, which is something completely different from historiography and as a result of this, a more rapid and yet always widely examined development, the detailed spiritualization of the extensive public life, the binding of dissatisfied elements, which here, where only indolence can do harm, are immediately of use, the configuration of the people formed by the bustle of the magazines and always dependent on the whole, the restriction of the nation's attention to its own circle and admission of the foreign only in reflection, the emergence of respect for those active in literature, the awakening of higher striving among the youth, which is temporary but has a lasting effect, the absorption of literary events into political concerns, the refinement of the opposition between fathers and sons and the possibility of its discussion, the presentation of the national flaws in a manner that is especially painful, it is true, but forgivable and liberating, the emergence of a lively and therefore self-confident book trade and the greed for books—all these effects can be produced even by a literature that has developed in an actually not unusual breadth, but due to the lack of significant talents has that appearance. The liveliness of such a literature is even greater than that of one rich in talent, for since there are no writers here before whose gift at least the majority of doubters would have to be silent, literary conflict on the greatest scale gains a true justification. Literature broken through by no talent therefore also displays no gaps through which the indifferent could slip. The claim of literature to attention thereby becomes more compelling. The independence of the individual writer, naturally only within the national borders, is better preserved. The lack of irresistible national models keeps the completely incapable away from literature. But even weak abilities don't suffice to be influenced by the indistinct character traits of the currently prevailing writers or to introduce the results of foreign literatures or to imitate the already introduced foreign literature, something one can discern from the mere fact that, for example, within a literature rich in great talents like the German one the worst writers keep to their own country with their imitation. The creative and gratifying force, in the above directions, of a literature bad in its particulars proves to be especially effective when deceased writers begin to be entered into the literary historical record. Their undeniable past and present effects become something so actual that it's interchangeable with their writings. One speaks of the latter and means the former, indeed one even reads the latter and sees nothing but the former. But since those effects cannot be forgotten and the writings don't influence memory by themselves, there's also no forgetting and no remembering. Literary history presents an immutable trustworthy block, to which the taste of the day can do little damage. The memory of a small nation is no smaller than the memory of a large one, hence it digests the available material more thoroughly. Fewer experts in literary history are employed, it is true, but literature is less an affair of literary history than an affair of the people and therefore it is preserved if not purely nonetheless securely. For the demands that the national consciousness within a small people makes on the individual mean that everyone must always be prepared to know, to bear to defend the part of the literature that falls to him and at least to defend it, even if he doesn't know or bear it.

Circumcision in Russia.[397] In the whole apartment, wherever doors are found, palm-sized plaques printed with Kabbalistic signs are hung up to protect the mother from evil spirits in the time between the birth and the circumcision, when they can become especially dangerous to her and the baby, perhaps because her body was opened so much and thus offers easy entrance to everything evil and because the baby too as long as it has not been brought into the covenant can put up no resistance to evil. That's also why, so that the mother doesn't remain alone for one moment, a female attendant is taken in. Also serving to ward off the evil spirits is that for 7 days after the birth with the exception of Friday 10–15 children, always different ones, led by the belfer (assistant teacher), are admitted toward evening to the bed of the mother there recite the Shema Israel[398] and are then given sweets. These innocent 5-8-year-old children are supposed to be especially effective in keeping away the evil spirits, who press the most heavily toward evening. On Friday a special celebration is held, as in general during this week several banquets come one after another. Before the day of the circumcision the evil ones grow wildest, therefore the last night is a vigil and one spends it watching over the mother until toward morning. The circumcision usually takes place in the presence of relatives and friends, often over 100 of them. The most respected person present is permitted to carry the baby. The circumciser, who officiates without payment, is usually a drunkard, since busy as he is he cannot participate in the various feasts and therefore only tosses down some schnapps. All these circumcisers thus have red noses and bad breath. It's therefore also not appetizing when, after the cut has been performed, they suck the bloody member with this mouth as prescribed. The member is then covered with sawdust and is healed in roughly 3 days.

For the Jews and naturally especially those in Russia a strict family life seems not so much to be common and characteristic, for family life is found among Christians too, after all, and it's actually disruptive to the family life of the Jews that the woman is excluded from Talmud study, so that when the man wants to converse with guests about learned Talmudic matters, that is, the center of his life, the women withdraw if not have to withdraw to the next room, thus it's even more peculiar to them that they come together so often at every possible opportunity, whether for prayer, or for study or for discussion of divine matters or for mostly religiously based feasts, at which alcohol is drunk only very moderately. They positively flee to each other.

By the power of his works Goethe probably holds back the development of the German language. Even if prose has in the meantime often moved away from him, in the end as at present it has still returned to him with strengthened yearning and has appropriated even old expressions found in Goethe but otherwise not connected with him, in order to rejoice in the completed sight of its boundless dependence.

My name in Hebrew is Anschel like my mother's maternal grandfather,[399] whom my mother, who was 6 years old when he died, remembers as a very pious and learned man with a long white beard. She remembers how she had to hold on to the toes of the corpse and at the same time ask forgiveness for possible trespasses committed against her grandfather. She also remembers her grandfather's many books filling the walls. He bathed every day in the river, even in winter, then he chopped a hole in the ice to bathe. My mother's mother[400] died young of typhus. From this death onward her grandmother[401] grew gloomy, refused to eat, spoke with no one, one day, a year after the death of her daughter, she went for a walk and never returned, her corpse was pulled out of the Elbe. An even more learned man than her grandfather was my mother's great-grandfather, Christians and Jews held him in equally high esteem, during a conflagration his piety brought about the miracle that the fire leaped over and spared his house, while the houses around it burned down. He had 4 sons, one was converted to Christianity and became a doctor. All of them except my mother's grandfather died early. The latter had a son, my mother knew him as mad Uncle Nathan,[402] and a daughter, my mother's mother.

---

to run against the window and weak after exerting all one's strength step through the splintered wood and glass and over the window balustrade.

---

26 XII *(1911)* Slept badly again, the 3rd night now. Thus I've spent the 3 holidays, during which I hoped to write things that would help me through the whole year, in a state of need. A walk on Christmas Eve with Löwy toward Stern.[403] Yesterday "Blümale oder die Perle von Warschau."[404] For her steadfast love and faithfulness Blümale is distinguished by the author in the title with the honorific "Pearl of Warsaw." Only the exposed long delicate neck of Fr. Tschissik explains the shape of her face. The gleam of tears in Frau Klug's eyes while she sings a regularly undulating melody, into which the listeners hang their heads, seemed to me in its significance to go far beyond the song, beyond the theater, beyond the cares of the whole audience indeed beyond my powers of imagination. View through the rear portiere into the dressing room straight to Frau Klug, who is standing there in a white underskirt and short-sleeved shirt. My uncertainty about the feelings of the audience and therefore strenuous inner incitement of its enthusiasm. My skillful amiable manner of speaking with Fräul. T.[405] and her companion yesterday. It was part of this freedom of my good disposition, which I felt yesterday and even as early as Saturday, that, although I didn't even remotely need to, out of a certain yieldingness to the world and an exuberant modesty I used a few outwardly embarrassed words and movements. I was alone with my mother and that too I took lightly and beautifully; looked at everyone with firmness.

Continuation[406]

The old writings get many interpretations, which proceed in the face of the weak material with an energy that is only dulled by the fear that one could advance too easily to the end and by the awe on which people have agreed. Everything is done in the most honest way, except that the work is undertaken within a bias that is never unraveled, brooks no fatigue and is spread for miles by the raising of a skillful hand. In the end, however, bias obstructs not only a clear view but also insight, thereby drawing a line through all these remarks.

Because there's a lack of cohesive people, there's an absence of cohesive literary actions. [An individual matter is pushed down low in order to be able to observe it from up high, or it is raised up high so that one can claim one's place above by its side. False.] Even if the individual matter is often thought through with calm, one still doesn't arrive at its boundaries, where it is connected with similar matters, one reaches soonest the boundary with politics, indeed one even strives to see this boundary before it's there and often to find this contracting boundary everywhere. The narrowness of the space, furthermore the regard for simplicity and regularity, and finally the consideration that due to the internal independence of literature the external connection with politics is harmless, lead to the spread of literature in the country by its clinging to political slogans.

There's a general pleasure in the literary treatment of small themes, which are permitted to be only so large that a small enthusiasm can be expended on them and which have polemical prospects and supports. Now and then literarily considered insults roll, around stronger temperaments they fly. What within great literatures takes place down below and forms a not indispensable cellar of the edifice, here happens in full light, what there gives rise to a momentary convergence, here brings about nothing less than the decision on life and death of all.

List of things that today are easy to imagine as antiquated: the begging cripples on the way to promenades and excursion spots, the unilluminated atmosphere at night, the bridge toll[407]

A list of those passages from "Dichtung & Wahrheit" that, by an indeterminable peculiarity, make an especially strong impression of liveliness not fundamentally connected with what is actually depicted, for example, evoke the image of the boy Goethe, curious, richly dressed, well-liked and lively as he penetrates the homes of all his acquaintances just to see and hear all that is to be seen and heard. Leafing through the book now I can't find such passages, all seem clear to me and contain a liveliness unsurpassable by any accident. I must wait until I'm reading innocently one day and then stop myself at the right passages.[408]

It's unpleasant to listen when my father, with incessant sideswipes at the happy situation of people today and above all of his children, tells of the sufferings he had to endure in his youth. No one denies that for years, due to insufficient winter clothing, he had open sores on his legs, that he often went hungry, that when he was only ten years old he had to push a cart through the villages even in winter and very early in the morning—only, as he won't understand, these correct facts in comparison with the further correct fact that I haven't suffered all this permit not the slightest conclusion that I have been happier than he, that those sores on his legs entitle him to be arrogant, that from the very beginning he assumes and claims that I can't appreciate his sufferings in those days and that in the end, precisely because I haven't had the same sufferings, I must be boundlessly grateful to him. How gladly I would listen if he would tell uninterruptedly of his youth and his parents, but to hear all this in a boastful and scolding tone is torment. Again and again he slaps his hands together: "Who knows that today! What do the children know! No one has suffered that! Does a child understand that today!" Today there was again similar talk with Aunt Julie[409] who visited us. She also has the huge face of all the relatives on Father's side. Her eyes are, by a tiny disturbing nuance, wrongly embedded or colored. At the age of 10 she was hired out as a cook. In great cold she had to run out for something in a wet little skirt, the skin on her legs cracked, the little skirt froze and didn't dry until that evening in bed.

27 XII 11 An unhappy person who is to have no child is terribly confined in his unhappiness. Nowhere a hope for renewal, for help from

happier stars. He must make his way afflicted with unhappiness when his circle is finished, content himself and no longer take up the thread to test whether on a longer path, under different circumstances of body and time, this unhappiness he has suffered could disappear or even bring forth something good[410]

This feeling of falseness I have when writing could be represented by the image of a man waiting in front of two holes in the ground for an apparition that can come only out of the one on the right. But while this very hole remains under a faintly visible lid, one apparition after another rises out of the one on the left, seeks to draw his eyes to itself and in the end achieves this effortlessly by its growing size, which finally, however much he tries to ward it off, covers even the correct opening. But now, if the man doesn't want to leave this place—and he doesn't want that at any price—he is reliant on these apparitions, which, however, due to their fleetingness—their strength is used up in the mere appearing—cannot satisfy him, but which, when they falter out of weakness, he dispels upward and in all directions, only to bring up others, since the continuous sight of one is unbearable and since the hope also remains that after exhaustion of the false apparitions the true ones will finally ascend.

Schema for the characterization of small literatures:[411]
Effect in a good sense here as there in any case.
Here the effects in the particulars are even better.

1 Liveliness
  a Conflict   b. Schools   c Magazines
2 Relief
  a Lack of principles   b Small themes   c Easy symbol formation   d Falling away of the incapable
3 Popularity
  a Connection with politics   b Literary history   c Faith in literature, its legislation is left to it,

It's hard to change one's mind when one has felt this useful joyful life in all one's limbs

How little power the above image has. Between actual feeling and comparative description an incoherent premise has been inserted like a board.

---

28 XII 11 The torment that the factory causes me. Why did I let it pass when they obligated me to work there in the afternoon.[412] Now no one compels me by force, but my father does so with reproaches, Karl with silence and my sense of guilt. I know nothing about the factory and during the commission's inspection[413] this morning I stood around uselessly and as if battered. I deny that it's possible for me to figure out all the details of the factory's operation. And if this were accomplished by endlessly questioning and pestering all involved, what would be achieved? I wouldn't know how to really do anything with this knowledge, I'm suited only to illusory tasks, to which the upstanding sense of my boss adds the salt and the appearance of an actual good performance.[414] But by this negligible effort expended on the factory I would, on the other hand, deprive myself of the possibility of expending a few afternoon hours on myself, necessarily leading to the complete annihilation of my existence, which is growing more and more restricted anyhow.

This afternoon on a walk I saw for a few paces nothing but imagined members of the commission that had so frightened me in the morning coming toward me or crossing my path.

---

29 XII 11
those lively passages in Goethe. P. 265 "I therefore drew my friend into the woods"[415]

The growth of powers by extensive strong memories. An independent wake is turned toward our ship and with the heightened effect the consciousness of our powers increases, as do they themselves.

Goethe: 307 "Now during these hours I heard no other conversation than about medicine or natural history and my imagination was drawn over into a completely different field."

The difficulties of finishing even a short essay lie not in the fact that our feeling demands a fire for the end of the piece that the actual previous content has been unable to generate out of itself, they arise rather from the fact that even the shortest essay demands from the author a self-satisfaction and a lostness in himself out of which it is difficult to step into the air of the ordinary day without strong determination and external incentive, so that before the essay is roundly closed and one is permitted to slide quietly away, one runs away driven by restlessness and then the conclusion must practically be finished from outside with hands that must not only work but also hold on.

---

30 XII 11 My propensity to imitate has nothing theatrical about it, above all it lacks unity. The coarse, strikingly characteristic in its entirety I can't imitate at all, my attempts of that sort have always failed they're against my nature. I have a decided propensity, on the other hand, to imitate details of the coarse, I have the urge to imitate certain people's manipulations of walking sticks, the position of their hands, the movement of their fingers and I can do it without effort. But this very effortlessness, this thirst for imitation distances me from the actor, because this effortlessness is countered by the fact that no one notices my imitating. Only my own satisfied or more often reluctant recognition indicates to me that I've succeeded. Far beyond this external imitation, however, goes the internal, which is often so convincing and strong that no room at all remains within me to observe and verify this imitation, but rather I first find it in memory. But here the imitation is also so perfect, replacing me myself with a leap and fall, that on the stage, provided that it could even be made visible, it would be unbearable. More than the extreme limit of acting cannot be imposed on the spectator. If an actor who is directed to beat another, in the excitement, in the excessive onrush of the senses, really beats him and the other screams in pain, then the spectator must become a human being and intervene. But what rarely happens in this way happens in minor ways countless times. The essence of the bad actor consists not in the fact that he imitates weakly, but in the fact that, due to deficiencies of his education, experience and talent he imitates the wrong models. But his most essential flaw remains that he doesn't preserve the boundary of the play and imitates too strongly. His dim

conception of the demands of the stage drives him to it and even if the spectator believes that this or that actor is bad because he stands around stiffly, plays with his fingertips at the edge of his pocket, bends his hands improperly on his hips, listens for the prompter, maintains an anxious seriousness at any price, regardless of whether times change completely, this actor who has dropped from nowhere onto the stage is bad only because he imitates too strongly, even if he does so only in

31 XII 11

his opinion. Precisely because his abilities are so limited, he is afraid to do less than everything. Even if his ability should not be downright indivisibly small, he still doesn't want to reveal that under certain circumstances and with the involvement of his will less than all his art can be at his disposal. Happening without regard for the watchers in the orchestra, steered according to the purely felt needs of the portrayal, the free

In the morning I felt so fresh for writing, but now the idea that I'm supposed to read to Max in the afternoon hinders me completely.[416] This also shows how incapable I am of friendship, provided that friendship in this sense is even possible. For since a friendship is not conceivable without the interruptions of daily life, even if its core remains unharmed, many of its expressions are blown away again and again. From the unharmed core they form anew, to be sure, but since every such formation requires time and not every expected one succeeds, it's never possible, even leaving aside the changing of personal moods, to take up the thread where it was broken off last time. In deep-rooted friendships this must give rise to an unease before every new encounter, which need not be so great that it is felt in itself, but which can disturb the conversation and behavior to such a degree that one is consciously astonished, especially since one doesn't recognize or can't believe the reason. How, then, am I supposed to read to M. or even think while writing down what follows that I will read it to him.

I'm also disturbed by having leafed through the diary this morning to see what I could read to M. Now I've found in this examination neither that what I've written up to now is especially valuable nor that it simply must be thrown away. My judgment lies between the two and closer to the first opinion, yet it is not such that according to the value of what I've written, despite my weakness, I would have to regard myself as exhausted. Nonetheless, the sight of the many things I've written has diverted me almost irretrievably from the wellspring of my own writing for the next few hours, because my attention has, as it were, lost itself downstream in the same river's course.

While I sometimes believe that all through the time I was in Gymnasium and even earlier I was able to think especially sharply and can no longer judge this fairly today only due to the later weakening of my memory, at other times I again realize that my bad memory only wants to flatter me and that, at least in matters insignificant in themselves but heavy with consequences, I behaved with great mental laziness. Thus I remember, to be sure, that during my Gymnasium days I often debated—even if not at great length, I probably tired easily even then—with Bergmann in a Talmudic way either found within or imitated from him about God and his possibility. At the time I liked to take up the theme found in a Christian magazine—I think "Die christliche Welt"[417]—in which a watch and the world and the watchmaker and God were compared with each other and the existence of the watchmaker was supposed to prove that of God. In my opinion I was able to refute that very well against Bergmann even if this refutation wasn't firmly rooted in me and I first had to put it together like a puzzle for my use. Such a refutation once took place as we were walking around the town hall tower. I remember it well because we reminded each other of it once years ago.[418]—But while I believed I distinguished myself in this—nothing but the longing to distinguish myself and the pleasure in having an effect and in the effect motivated me—it was only due to insufficiently strong thought that I tolerated always going around in bad clothes,[419] which my parents had made for me by one customer after another, for the longest time by a tailor in Nusle.[420] Naturally I realized, which was very easy, that I was especially badly dressed and I even had an eye for when others were well dressed, only for years my thinking didn't manage to find the cause of my miserable appearance in my clothes. Since even then I was on the way more in presentiments than in reality to having a low opinion of myself, I was convinced that the clothes took on this appearance, first stiff as boards then hanging in wrinkles, only on me. I didn't want new clothes at all, for if I was going to look ugly, I wanted at least to be comfortable and also to avoid presenting to the world, which had grown accustomed to the old clothes, the ugliness of the new ones. These always long-lasting refusals toward my mother, who often wanted to have new clothes of this sort made for me, since with the eyes of an adult she could still find differences between these new clothes and old ones, recoiled on me insofar as I had to imagine with my parents' confirmation that my appearance didn't matter to me at all.

2 I II *(1912)* Hence I yielded to the bad clothes even in my posture, went around with a bent back, slanted shoulders, awkward arms and hands; was afraid of mirrors, because they showed me in an ugliness that was in my opinion unavoidable and moreover couldn't be reflected entirely truthfully, for if I had really looked like that, I surely would have caused a greater stir, endured gentle pushes in the back from my mother on Sunday walks and far too abstract admonitions and prophecies, which I couldn't connect with my then present worries. On the whole I lacked mainly the ability to make even the slightest provision for the actual future. In my thinking I kept to present things and their present conditions not out of thoroughness or too firmly held interest, but rather, to the extent that it wasn't caused by weakness of thinking, out of sadness and fear, out of sadness because since the present was so sad for me, I believed I couldn't leave it before it resolved itself into happiness, out of fear because just as I was afraid of taking the smallest present step, I considered myself with my contemptible childish demeanor unworthy of judging seriously and responsibly the great manly future, which also usually seemed to me so impossible that every small step forward appeared to me fraudulent and the next unreachable. I admitted miracles more easily than true progress, but was too cool not to leave the miracles in their sphere and true progress in its own. I could therefore spend a long time before falling asleep imagining that I would one day ride into the Jewish quarter as a rich man in a four-horse carriage liberate with a command an unjustly battered beautiful girl and take her away in my carriage; but untouched by this playful belief, which probably fed on nothing but an already unhealthy sexuality, remained the conviction that I wouldn't pass that year's final exams and if that were accomplished, that I wouldn't progress in the next class and even if that too were avoided by swindle, that I would surely fail once and for all in

the Matura and that I would moreover most certainly, no matter at what moment, suddenly surprise my parents, who had been lulled to sleep by my outwardly regular advancement, as well as the rest of the world by revealing an unheard-of ineptitude. But since I always regarded only my ineptitude—only rarely my weak literary work—as a signpost pointing to the future, thinking over the future never benefited me; it was only a further elaboration of the present sorrow. When I wanted to, I could actually walk upright, but it made me tired and I also couldn't understand what harm a stooped posture could do me in the future. If I should have a future, then my feeling was that everything would sort itself out. Such a principle was chosen not because it contained confidence in a future that was, to be sure, not believed to exist, rather its only purpose was to make my life easier. To walk, to dress to wash, to read, above all to confine myself at home in a way that caused me the least difficulty and demanded the least courage. If I went beyond that, I came up with only ridiculous ways out. At one point it seemed impossible to continue to do without a black dress suit, especially since I was also faced with the decision of whether I wanted to participate in a dancing class. That tailor from Nusle was summoned and the cut of the suit discussed. I was indecisive as always in such cases, for they made me afraid of being swept away by a clear answer not only into an unpleasant immediate future but also beyond that into an even worse one. Thus I didn't want a black suit at first, but when I was shamed in front of the stranger by the reference to my not having a dress suit, I put up with a tailcoat even being proposed; but since I regarded a tailcoat as a terrible upheaval, which one could ultimately speak about but never decide on, we agreed on a tuxedo, which due to its resemblance to the ordinary suit jacket seemed to me at least bearable. But when I heard that the suit vest was necessarily cut low and I would thus have to wear a starched shirt too, I became, since something of the sort was to be fended off, resolute almost beyond my strength. I didn't want a tuxedo of that sort but rather if I had to have one a tuxedo lined and trimmed with silk but closed high. Such a tuxedo was unknown to the tailor, but he remarked that whatever sort of jacket I was imagining, it couldn't be a dancing suit. All right, then it wasn't a dancing suit, I didn't even want to dance, that was still far from decided, but I wanted the described jacket made for me. The tailor had all the more difficulty understanding as I had up to then always allowed myself to be measured and fitted for new clothes with ashamed haste, without comments or requests. Therefore, also because my mother was pressing, I had no choice but to go with him, painful as it was, across the Altstädter Ring to the display of a seller of old clothes, in whose display I had for quite some time seen an unobjectionable tuxedo of that sort spread out and recognized it as usable for me. Unfortunately, however, it had already been removed from the display, it couldn't be made out inside the shop even by straining one's eyes, I didn't dare enter the shop just to see the tuxedo so that we returned in the earlier disagreement. But I felt as if the future tuxedo had already been cursed by the uselessness of this journey, at least I used the irksomeness of all the arguing as a pretext to send away the tailor with some small order and an empty promise about the tuxedo and remained wearily behind under my mother's reproaches, forever—everything happened to me forever—kept from girls, an elegant demeanor and dances. The cheerfulness I simultaneously felt about this made me miserable and moreover I was afraid I'd made a fool of myself in front of the tailor as none of his customers had before.

---

3 I 12 Read a lot in the Neue Rundschau. Beginning of the novel "Der nackte Mann," somewhat too-thin clarity on the whole, infallible in the details. "Gabriel Schillings Flucht" by Hauptmann. Education of people. Instructive in the bad and the good.[421]

New Year's Eve. I had planned to read to Max from the diaries in the afternoon I had been looking forward to it and didn't manage to do it.[422] We didn't feel in harmony, I sensed in him that afternoon a calculating pettiness and haste, he was almost not my friend, but still dominated me to the extent that I saw myself through his eyes leafing uselessly through the notebooks again and again and found this leafing back and forth, which showed the same pages flying by again and again, abhorrent. To work together in this mutual tension was naturally impossible and the one page of R. & S.[423] that we managed to produce amid mutual resistance is only proof of Max's energy, but otherwise bad. New Year's Eve at Čada's.[424] Not so bad, because Weltsch, Kisch[425] and someone else added fresh blood, so that in the end, though only within the limits of that group I found my way back to Max. In the crowd on the Graben

I then squeezed his hand without even looking at him and with my 3 notebooks pressed against me, as it seems to me in memory, proudly went straight home

---

The flames that shot upward in the forms of ferns surrounding a crucible on the street in front of a new building.[426]

In me a concentration on writing can be recognized quite easily. When it had become clear in my organism that writing was the most productive direction of my being, everything thronged there and left empty all the abilities that were directed toward the pleasures of sex, eating, drinking, philosophical reflection music first and foremost. I wasted away in all these directions. This was necessary because my powers in their entirety were so slight that only gathered could they halfway serve the purpose of writing. Naturally I didn't find this purpose independently and consciously, it found itself and is now hindered only by the office, but here thoroughly so. In any case, however, I must not bemoan the fact that I can't bear a beloved, that I understand of love almost exactly as much as I do of music and have to content myself with the most superficial chance effects, that on New Year's Eve I had black salsify with spinach for dinner and drank with it ¼ liter of Ceres[427] and that on Sunday I couldn't participate in Max's reading of his philosophical work;[428] the compensation for all this is perfectly clear. Thus I only have to throw the office work out of this community in order, since my development is now completed and as far as I can see I have nothing more to sacrifice, to begin my real life, in which my face will at last be able to age in a natural way with the progress of my works.

The turnabout a conversation takes when there's first detailed discussion of concerns of our innermost existence and hereupon not exactly breaking it off but naturally not developing out of it either the subject comes up of when and where we will see each other next and what circumstances must be considered in this regard. If this conversation also ends with a handshake, then we part in the momentary faith in a pure and firm structure of our life and with respect for it.

In an autobiography it is unavoidable that quite frequently in the place where "once" should truthfully be written, "often" is written. For one always remains conscious that memory draws out of the darkness, which the word "once" blows to pieces, the word "often" admittedly does not fully spare either but preserves at least in the opinion of the writer, carrying him over parts that might not have been found in his life at all but give him a substitute for those he no longer even faintly touches in his memory.[429]

Fifth Notebook

4 I II *(1912)* Only as a result of my vanity do I enjoy reading to my sisters so much (that today, for example, it got too late for writing) Not that I'm convinced I'll achieve something significant in the reading, rather I'm dominated only by the craving to press so close to the good works I read that I merge with them, not through my own merit but only in the attention of my listening sisters, which is excited by what is read and dulled for the inessential, and under the concealing effect of the vanity I therefore also participate as a cause in all the influence the work itself has exerted. That's why I actually read admirably to my sisters too, imbuing many stresses with what feels to me to be an extreme precision, because afterward I am rewarded in excess not only by myself but also by my sisters. But if I read to Brod or Baum or others, my reading must seem horribly bad to everyone due to my claims to praise alone, even if they know nothing of the quality of my other reading, for here I see that the listener maintains the separation between me and what is read, I'm not permitted to connect completely with what is read without, according to my feeling, which can expect no support from the listener, becoming ridiculous, with my voice I fly around what is to be read, try to penetrate here and there, because one wants this, but don't intend it seriously, because one doesn't expect it from me at all; but what one actually wants, to read calmly and distantly without vanity and to become passionate only when my passion demands it, that's more than I can manage; although I believe that I've reconciled myself to this and thus content myself with reading badly to everyone except my sisters, my vanity, which this time should have no right, still shows itself in that

I feel hurt when someone finds fault with something in what is read, I turn red and want to read on quickly, just as I strive in general, once I've begun reading, to read endlessly in the unconscious yearning that in the course of the long reading the vain false feeling of unity with what is read will be generated at least in me, forgetting that I will never have sufficient momentary strength to have an effect through my feeling on the clear general view of the listener and that at home it's always my sisters who begin the desired mix-up

---

5 I II *(1912)* For 2 days I've been detecting in myself coolness and indifference when I want to. Yesterday evening during a walk every little street noise, every glance directed at me, every photograph in a display case was more important to me than I was.

Uniformity: A Story[430]

When one seems to have made a final decision to stay home in the evening, has put on one's dressing gown, is sitting after dinner at the illuminated table and has undertaken that work or play after the completion of which one habitually goes to bed, when outside there's inclement weather, which makes staying home natural, when one has also kept still for so long at the table by now that going out would be bound to cause not only paternal anger but also general astonishment, when, besides, the staircase is now dark and the front door locked and when despite all this one stands up in sudden unease, changes one's coat, immediately appears dressed for the street, declares that one must go out and does so after a brief goodbye, believes that one leaves behind either more or less anger depending on the speed with which one slams the apartment door and thereby cuts off the general discussion of the departure, when one finds oneself on the street with limbs that reward this quite unexpected freedom one has provided them by moving with special agility, when one feels all decisiveness excited in oneself by this single decision, when one recognizes with greater significance than usual that one has more strength than one has need to easily bring about and endure the swiftest changes, that left alone with oneself one grows in understanding and calm and in the enjoyment of them, then for this evening one has stepped out of one's family so completely that one couldn't achieve this more thoroughly by taking the most distant journeys and one has had an experience that, because one's solitude is extreme for Europe, one can only call Russian. It becomes even stronger when one calls on a friend at this late evening hour to see how he is doing.[431]

Invited Weltsch to come to Frau Klug's benefit.[432] Löwy with his severe headaches, which probably indicate a serious head ailment, leaned against the wall of a house down on the street where he was waiting for me, his right hand on his forehead in despair. I pointed him out to Weltsch, who leaned out the window from the sofa. I believed it was the first time in my life I'd observed from the window in this easy way an incident closely concerning me down on the street. In itself such observation is familiar to me from Sherlock Holmes.

6 I 12 "Vicekönig" by Feimann yesterday.[433] My susceptibility to the Jewishness in these plays abandons me, because they are too monotonous and degenerate into a wailing that is proud of isolated stronger outbursts. At the first plays I could think I had come upon a Judaism in which the beginnings of my own would rest and would develop toward me and thereby enlighten me and bring me farther in my ponderous Judaism, instead the more I hear, the more they recede from me. The people remain, of course, and I cling to them.—Frau Klug had a benefit and therefore sang some new songs and made a few new jokes. But only during her opening song was I completely under her spell, then I have the strongest connection to every little part of her appearance, to her arms, outstretched while she sings, and her snapping fingers, to her tightly twisted sidelocks, to her thin shirt going flatly and innocently under her vest, to her lower lip that she purses at one point, enjoying the effect of a joke (you see, I know all languages, but in Yiddish), to her fat little feet, which, in the thick white stockings, are pressed down by her shoes to behind her toes. But since she sang new songs yesterday, she damaged her main effect on me, which consisted in the fact that here a person exhibits herself who has discovered a few jokes and songs that present her temperament and all her powers to the utmost perfection.

Since this presentation succeeds, everything has succeeded and if it gives us pleasure to let this person affect us often, then we will naturally—and in this all the listeners might agree with me—not be deterred by the constant repetition of the ever same songs, rather we will approve of it as an aid to concentration just like the darkening of the hall, for example, and from the woman's point of view recognize in it the very undauntedness and self-confidence that we are seeking. Therefore, when the new songs came, which could show nothing new about Frau Klug, because the earlier ones had so perfectly done their duty, and when these songs made a claim on our attention as songs, though there was no reason at all to give it to them and when they in this way distracted from Frau Kl., but at the same time showed that she herself didn't feel at ease in these songs either and made partly failed partly exaggerated faces and movements, one couldn't help growing morose and remained consoled only by the fact that the memory of her perfect performance in the past, due to its unshakable truthfulness, was too firm to be disturbed by the present sight.

---

7 I 12

Unfortunately Frau T.[434] always has roles that show only the essence of her own character, she always plays women and girls who at a single blow become unhappy, derided, dishonored, aggrieved, but who are not granted time to develop their character in a natural sequence. In the erupting natural power with which she plays these roles, which are high points only in the performance but, due to the richness they demand, are mere hints in the written play, one recognizes what she would be capable of achieving.—One of her important movements comes as a shiver from her somewhat stiffly held, twitching hips. Her little daughter seems to have one hip completely stiff.—When the actors embrace each other, they hold each other's wigs down.—Recently, as I was going with Löwy up to his room, where he wanted to read me the letter he had written to the Warsaw writer Nombert,[435] we met Herr and Frau T.[436] on the landing. They were carrying their costumes for Kol-Nidre,[437] which were packed in tissue paper like matzos,[438] up to their room. We stopped for a little while. I had the railing for support of my hands and sentence stresses. Her large mouth moved so close in front of me in surprising but natural shapes. The conversation threatened to end in hopelessness because of me, for in my striving to express in haste all my love and devotion I got only as far as the observation that the troupe's affairs were going miserably, that their repertoire was exhausted that they thus couldn't stay much longer and that the lack of interest in them among the Prague Jews was incomprehensible. On Monday I should—she asked me—come to Sejdernacht, even though I'd already seen it.[439] Then I will hear her sing that song (bore Isroel)[440] of which, as she remembered from an old remark, I'm especially fond.

The nocturnal appearance that I and Max, Weltsch not so much, had yesterday at noon on the Graben, because we so rarely go for a walk during the day.

Yeshivas[441] are Talmudic colleges supported by many communities in Poland and Russia. The costs aren't very great, because these schools are usually housed in an old unusable building containing, besides the classrooms and bedrooms of the pupils, the apartment of the Rosh-Yeshiva,[442] who also performs other community duties, and of his assistant. The pupils pay no tuition and get their meals in rotation at the homes of the community members. Although these schools are based on the most orthodox principles, it is here, of all places, that apostate progress begins, for because young people come together here from afar, and particularly the poor, the energetic, who strive to get away from home, since the supervision isn't very strict here and the young people here are completely reliant on each other and the most essential part of their education consists in studying together and explaining difficult passages to each other, since the piety in the various hometowns of the students is of the same kind, which doesn't give them much to tell each other, while the suppressed progress rises or falls in the most diverse ways depending on the various local circumstances, so that in this case there's always a lot to talk about, since furthermore there's always only one or another of the forbidden progressive writings in the hands of an individual, while in the Yeshiva they are brought together from all sides and can be especially effective here, because every possessor spreads not only the text but also his own fervor, for all these reasons and their immediate consequences, in recent times all progressive writers, politicians, journalists and scholars have come out of these schools. On the one hand this has caused the reputation of these schools among the orthodox to decline steeply, on the other hand progressively minded young people are flocking to them more than previously.—One famous Yeshiva is that of Ostro, a small town 8 hours by train from Warsaw. All Ostro is actually only the area bordering a very short stretch of the country road. Löwy claims it's as long as his cane. When a count stopped in Ostro once with his four-horse traveling carriage, the front 2 horses and the rear of the carriage were already standing outside the town.[443]—Löwy decided at about the age of 14, when the constraint of life at home seemed to him unbearable to go to Ostro. His father had just slapped him on the shoulder as he was leaving the close[444] toward evening and casually told him to come to him later, he had to speak with him. Because once again there was obviously nothing to be expected here but reproaches, L. went directly from the close without luggage, in a somewhat better caftan because it was Saturday evening, and with all his money, which he always carried with him, to the railroad station and took the 10 o'clock train to Ostro, where he arrived at 7 o'clock in the morning. He went straight to the Yeshiva, where he didn't cause much of a stir, because anyone can enter a Yeshiva and there are no particular terms of admission. It was remarkable only that he wanted to enter now of all times—it was summer—which wasn't customary, and because he had a good caftan. But they soon reconciled themselves to this too, because such very young people, bound together by their Judaism to a degree unknown to us, get to know each other easily. He excelled in his studies, since he had brought a great store of knowledge with him from home. He liked talking with the strange boys, especially since, when they found out about his money, they all crowded around him with offers. One of them, who wanted to sell him "days," especially astonished him. "Days" were what free meals were called. They were a salable object because the community members, who sought to do a deed pleasing to God by providing the free meals to all without distinction, didn't care who sat at their table. If a student was especially clever, he could manage to fill one day with twice the free meals. He could bear these double meals all the better as they weren't very substantial and after the first one could still gobble down the second with great pleasure and because it also happened that while one day was doubly filled, other days were empty. Nonetheless, everyone was glad, of course, to find an opportunity to sell such surplus free meals at a profit. Now if someone came in summer as Löwy did, that is, at a time when the free meals had long since been distributed, then the only way to get them at all was by buying them, for the originally surplus free meals were all reserved by speculators.—Night in the Yeshiva was unbearable. Even though all the windows were open because the night was warm, the stench and the heat wouldn't stir from the rooms, because the students, who had no actual beds, lay down to sleep without undressing, in their sweaty clothes, wherever they were last sitting. Everything was full of fleas. In the morning everyone wet his hands and face only hastily with water and resumed his studies. Most of the time they studied together, usually two from one book. Often debates bound several into a circle. The Rosh-Yeshiva explained only now and then the most difficult passages. Although L. later—he stayed in Ostro for 10 days, but slept and ate at the inn—found 2 like-minded friends (it wasn't so easy to find each other, because one always first had to carefully test the sentiments and trustworthiness of the other) he was very happy to return home, since he was used to an orderly life and couldn't stand the homesickness.

In the large room was the noise of the card playing and later of the usual conversation that my father, when he's healthy as he is today, carries on loudly if not coherently. The words constituted only slight tensions of a formless noise. Little Felix[445] slept in the girls' room, the door of which was wide open. I slept on the other side in my room. Out of consideration for my age, the door of this room was closed. Besides, the open door implied that they still wanted to lure F. to the family, while I was already cut off.

Yesterday at Baum's. Strobl[446] was supposed to come, but was at the theater. B. read aloud a feuilleton "on the folk song"; bad. Then a chapter from "Des Schicksals Spiele und Ernst";[447] very good. I was indifferent, in a bad mood, got no pure impression of the whole. On the way home in the rain Max told me the present plan of "Irma Polak."[448] I couldn't acknowledge my state, since M. never quite recognizes it. I therefore had to be insincere, which in the end spoiled everything for me. I was so full of self-pity that I preferred to speak to Max when his face was in the dark, even though mine could then betray itself more easily in the brightness. But then the mysterious end of the novel moved me despite all obstacles. On the way home after saying goodbye remorse over my falseness and pain over its unavoidability. Intention to start a special notebook on my relationship with Max. What is not written down flickers before one's eyes and optical accidents determine the overall judgment.

When I was lying on the sofa and there was loud talking in the rooms on both sides of me, on the left only by women, on the right more by men, I had the impression that they are crude Negro-like unappeasable beings, who don't know what they're saying and only talk to make the air move, who lift their faces while talking and gaze after the words they speak.

Thus the rainy, quiet Sunday goes by for me, I sit in my bedroom and have peace but instead of deciding to do some writing, into which, the day before yesterday, for example, I would have wanted to pour myself with all that I am, I've now been staring for quite a while at my fingers. I believe that this week I have been utterly influenced by Goethe, have just exhausted the strength of this influence and have therefore become useless.

From a poem by Rosenfeld depicting a sea storm: "The souls flutter, the bodies tremble."[449] While reciting Löwy clenches the skin of his forehead and of the root of his nose as one believes only hands can be clenched. At the most moving passages, which he wants to bring home to us, he comes closer to us himself or rather he enlarges himself by making his appearance clearer. He steps forward only a little, keeps his eyes open wide, tugs with his absent left hand on his frock coat and holds the right out to us open and large. And, even if we're not moved, we're supposed to recognize how moved he is and explain to him the possibility of the described misfortune.

For the painter Ascher[450] I'm supposed to serve as a nude model for a Saint Sebastian.

If I return to my relatives now in the evening, I will, since I have written nothing that would make me happy, seem to them no more foreign more contemptible, more useless than to myself. All this naturally only according to my feeling (which cannot be deceived by any observation, however precise) for actually they all have respect for me and love me too.

---

24 I 12 Wed. Haven't written for so long for the following reasons: I was angry with my boss and cleared it up only through a good letter; was at the factory several times; read Pinez "L'histoire de la litterature judeo-allemande"[451] 500 pgs. and indeed greedily, as I've never done before with such thoroughness, haste and pleasure in the case of similar books; now I'm reading Fromer "Organismus des Judentums";[452] finally I had a lot to do with the Jewish actors, wrote letters for them, prevailed on the Zionist association to ask the Z. associations of Bohemia whether they want to have guest performances by the troupe, I wrote the necessary circular and had it copied;[453] saw Sulamit once again and Herzele Meliches by Richter once, was at the folk song evening of the Bar Kochba Association and the day before yesterday at "Graf von Gleichen" by Schmidtbonn.[454]

Folk song evening: Dr. Nathan Birnbaum gives the lecture. Eastern Jewish habit, when the speech falters, of inserting "my dear ladies and gentlemen" or just "my dears." Is repeated at the beginning of Birnbaum's speech to the point of ridiculousness. But as far as I know Löwy I believe that these constant phrases, which often occur in ordinary Eastern Jewish conversation too such as "Weh ist mir!" or "S'ist nischt" or "S'ist viel zu reden" are not meant to conceal embarrassment, but rather, as ever new wellsprings, to churn the stream of speech still lying there too heavily for the Eastern Jewish temperament. But not in Birnbaum's case.

26. I 12

—The back of Herr Weltsch[455] and the silence of the whole hall while listening to the bad poems.—Birnbaum: His hair, worn longish, stops sharply at the neck, which due to this sudden exposure or due to itself is very erect. Large crooked nose, not too narrow and yet broad on the sides, which looks beautiful mainly as a result of the good proportionality to the large beard.—Singer Gollanin. Peaceful, saccharine, heavenly, condescending smile, held for a long time with the face leaning sideways and downward, the lips somewhat pursed with the wrinkled nose, but it's also possible that this is merely part of the mouth technique.[456]—

Pinès: Histoire de la Litterature Judéo-Allemande. Paris 1911[457]
[. . .]
connection with their brothers in Holland through the jargon.
First book 1507 Venice, Bovomaisse, translation of an Engl. novel.

Tsena-Urena de Jakob ben Isack de Janow (d. Prague 1628) Legends, women's book, very beautiful
Folk songs: (Evreiskia narodnia piesni w Rassia Ginsbourg & Marek 1901)
[. . .]
the mother of the righteous one

Soldier's song:

They cut our beard and sidelocks
And they forbid us to celebrate Saturday and the holidays.

or

At the age of 5 I entered the "Cheder" and now I'm supposed
to ride horses!

Wos mir seinen, seinen mir
Ober jueden seinen mir

Haskala, movement introduced by Mendelssohn at the beginning of the 19th century, adherents are called Maskilim, hostile to the folk jargon in favor of Hebrew and the European sciences. Before the pogroms of 1881 it wasn't nationalistic, later strongly Zionist. Principle formulated by Gordon: "At home be a Jew, outside a human being." To spread its ideas the Haskala must use the jargon and however much it hates the latter it founds its literature
One of the most popular books "Kolumbus" by Chaikel Hurwiz de Ouman. Translation of a German book.

Further endeavors of the Haskala "la lutte contre le chassidisme, l'exaltation de l'instruction et des travaux manuels. Levinsohn, Aksenfeld, Ettinger

Badchen the sad folk and wedding singers (Eliakum Zunser) Talmudic trains of thought

Le Roman populaire: Aisik Meier Dick 1808–1894 didactic, Haskalic, Schomer, even worse

Titles, for example, Der podriatschik (l'entrepreneur) ein höchst interessanter Roman. Ein richtiger fact vun leben or "Die eiserne Frau oder das verkaufte Kind. Ein wunderschöner roman"

furthermore in America serial novels "Zwischen menschenfresser" 26 volumes

S. J. Ambramowitsch (Mendele Mocher Sforim) lyrical, funny in a subdued way, hazy compositions "Fischke der krumer" (Eastern Jewish habit of biting the lips)

J. J. Linetzki Dos polnische juengel

End of the Haskala 1881. New nationalism and democratism. Rise of jargon literature

S. Frug poet, country life at any price

Délicieux est le sommeil du seigneur dans sa chamber
Sur des oreillers doux, blancs comme la neige
Mais plus délicieux encore est le repos dans
le champ sur du foin frais
A l'heure du soir, après le travail

Talmud: He who interrupts his studies to say, how pretty this tree is, deserves death

---

Laments at the western wall of the temple

Poem: La fille du Schamesch

The beloved rabbi is on his deathbed. The burial of a shroud the size of the rabbi and other mystical means no longer help. The community elders therefore go from house to house at night with a list and collect from the community members waivers of days and weeks of their lives in favor of the rabbi. Deborah la fille du Schamesch gives her whole life. She dies, the rabbi recovers. At night when he is studying alone in the synagogue, he hears the voices of the whole suppressed course of Deborah's life. The singing at her wedding, the screams of childbirth, the lullabies, the voice of her son studying the Torah, the music at her daughter's wedding. At the same time as the dirges sound over her corpse, the rabbi too dies.

Perez né 1851 bad Heine lyricism and social poems

Rosenfeld the poor jargon public ensured his livelihood by taking up a collection

M. Spektor: better than Dick, social & national interests

Destruction of the mikwe destroys the community Jakob Dienesohn: His villains are better rewarded. Sentimental	} Treatment of higher themes

S. Rabinowitsch (Scholem-Aleichem)

né 1859. Custom of large anniversary celebrations in jargon literature Kassriliwke, Menachem Mendel, who left home and brought his whole fortune with him; although he has until now only studied Talmud, in the big city he begins to speculate on the stock exchange, makes different decisions every day and always informs his wife of them with great self-satisfaction; until he finally must ask for traveling money

Purim, the ghetto quarter full of masks

Perez

The figure of the batlen, frequent in the ghettos, averse to work and grown clever through idling, lives in the circles of the pious and learned. Many signs of unhappiness in them, since they are young people who despite the pleasure of inactivity also languish in it, live in dreams, live under the released power of unquenched desires.

mithat nechiko death by a kiss: reserved only for the most pious

Baalschem, before he was a rabbi in Miečeboz, he lived in the Carpathians as a vegetable gardener later he was his brother-in-law's coachman. The illuminations came to him on solitary walks. Zohar "Bible of the Kabbalists"

Jewish theater 1708 Frankfurt Purim plays

Ein schoen neu Achaschwerosch-spiel

Abraham Goldfaden, 1876/77 Russo-Turkish war, Russian and Galician army suppliers had gathered in Bucharest, Goldf. had also strayed here in search of earnings heard the public in the cafés singing jargon songs and was encouraged to found a theater. He was not yet able to put women on the stage here. In 1883 jargon perfor. were forbidden in Russia. In 1884 they began in London and New York (Lateiner Horowitz)

J. Gordin in 1897 in an anniversary publication of the Jew. theater in New York: The jargon theater has an audience of hundreds of thousands, but it cannot hope for the emergence of a writer with powerful talent as long as the majority of its authors are people like me, who have become dramatic authors only by chance, who write plays only because they are forced to do so by the circumstances of their lives and who, like me, remain isolated and see all around them only ignorance, envy, enmity and spite.

Beckermann (Sch.) Gitil die kremerke, sehr a interessanter Roman, wos die Leser wellen sein zufrieden. Vilna 1898

Missionary book: Beweise aus den alten Propheten, dos der Messias schon gekommen 1819 London

31 I 12. Wrote nothing. Weltsch brings me books about Goethe, which cause me a distracted, nowhere usable excitement.[458] Plan for an essay "Goethe's Horrible Nature." Fear of the 2-hour evening walk I've now introduced for myself.

4 II 12 3 days ago Wedekind: Erdgeist.
Wedekind and his wife Tilly act in it.[459] Clear well-defined voice of the woman. Narrow crescent-shaped face. The lower leg branching off sideways when she stands calmly. Clarity of the play even in retrospect, so that one goes home calmly and self-confidently. Contradictory impression of what is quite firmly established and yet remains strange.

On my way to the theater, I felt well. I tasted my depths like honey. Drank them in an uninterrupted gulp. In the theater this passed immediately. It was incidentally the previous theater evening: "Orpheus in der Unterwelt" with Pallenberg.[460] The performance was so bad, applause and laughter around me in the standing room so great, that I didn't know what else to do but to run away after the 2nd act and thereby silence all this.

The day before yesterday wrote a good letter to Trautenau about a guest performance by Löwy.[461] Every reading of the letter calmed and strengthened me, so much was unspoken reference made in it to everything good in me.

The zeal with which I read about Goethe (Goethe's Conversations, Student Years, Hours with Goethe, A Stay of Goethe's in Frankfurt),[462] which permeates me and keeps me from doing any writing.

Schmerler,[463] merchant, 32 years old, religiously unaffiliated, philosophically educated, interested in fine literature mainly only to the extent that it pertains to his writing. Round head, black eyes, small vigorous mustache, firm cheek flesh, squat figure. Has studied for years from 9 o'clock to 1 o'clock at night. Born in Stanislau, knows Hebrew and jargon. Married to a woman who makes an impression of being limited only due to the completely round shape of her face.

Coolness toward Löwy for two days. He asks me about it. I deny it.

Calm, withdrawn conversation with Fräulein T. on the gallery between the acts of Erdgeist.[464] To achieve a good conversation one must positively slide one's hand more deeply, more lightly, more sleepily under the subject to be dealt with, then one lifts it astonishingly. Otherwise one bends back one's fingers and thinks of nothing but the pain.

Story: The Evening Walks. (Invention of quick walking) Introductory beautiful dark room.

Frl. T. described a scene in her new story, in which a girl with a bad reputation enters the sewing school one day.[465] The impression on the other girls. I remark that those who feel clearly in themselves the capacity and desire to acquire a bad reputation and thereby can at the same time immediately imagine what it means to plunge into such a misfortune will be sorry for her.

Lecture Dr. Theilhaber a week ago in the banquet room of the Jewish Town Hall on the decline of the German Jews.[466] It is inexorable, for 1.) if the Jews gather in the cities, the rural Jewish communities disappear. The striving for profit consumes them. Marriages are made only for the sake of providing for the bride. 2 child system

2. Mixed marriages 3.) Baptism

Funny scenes when Prof. Ehrenfels,[467] who grows more and more beautiful and whose bald head is bounded on top by a hazy contour in the light, his hands placed together and pressing each other, with his full voice modulated like a musical instrument, smiling with confidence at the meeting, stands up for mixed races

---

5 II 12 Mon. Wearily even gave up reading "Dichtung und Wahrheit." I'm hard on the outside, cold on the inside. When I came to Dr. Fleischmann[468] today, although we came together slowly and deliberately, it was as if we had collided like balls, which drive each other back and, themselves out of control, get lost. I asked him whether he was tired. He wasn't tired. Why did I ask? I'm tired I replied and sat down.

To lift oneself out of such a state should actually be easy even with forced energy. I tear myself away from the chair, run around the table with great strides, limber up my head and neck, make my eyes blaze, tense the muscles around them. Work against every feeling, welcome Löwy enthusiastically if he comes, kindly tolerate my sister in the room while I'm writing, draw into myself all that is said at Max's in long drafts despite the pain and effort. Now it's possible, to be sure, that I would succeed almost completely in some of this, but with every clear flaw—and they are unavoidable—the whole, the easy and the difficult, will falter and I will have to turn back in a circle. Therefore the best advice remains to accept everything as calmly as possible, to behave like a heavy mass and if one feels oneself blown away, not to be lured into any unnecessary step, to look at the other with an animal gaze, to feel no remorse, to abandon oneself to the unconsciousness that one believes to be distant even though one is presently being burned by it, to let one's angular unchangeable limbs lie as they please, in short to press down with one's own hand whatever ghost of life is left, that is, to increase even more the final gravelike peace and let nothing else continue to exist. A characteristic movement of such a state is to run one's little finger over one's eyebrows.[469]

Short fainting spell yesterday in Kafé City with Löwy. The attempt to conceal it by bending down over a newspaper

---

Goethe's beautiful silhouette in full figure. Secondary impression of the disgusting at the sight of this perfect human body, since to surpass this level is unimaginable and yet this level looks only pieced together and accidental. The erect posture, the hanging arms, the narrow neck, the bend of the knees.

The impatience and grief because of my weariness are nourished especially by the prospect, never let out of sight, of the future that is thereby prepared for me. What evenings, walks, despair in bed and on the sofa,

7 II 12 still lie ahead of me, worse than those already endured!

Yesterday at the factory. The girls in their clothes that are in themselves unbearably dirty and ragged, with their hair disheveled as if they had just woken up, with their facial expression fixed by the incessant noise of the transmissions and by the individual machine, which, though automatic, halts unpredictably, are not human beings, one doesn't greet them, one doesn't apologize when one jostles them, if one summons them for a small task, then they carry it out but immediately return to the machine, with a head movement one shows them where they are needed, they stand there in underskirts, they're at the mercy of the slightest power and don't even have enough calm understanding to recognize and propitiate this power with glances and bows. But when it's six o'clock and they shout it to each other, when they untie the scarves from their necks and hair, when they dust themselves off with a brush that is passed around the hall and is shouted for by impatient ones, when they pull the skirts over their heads and when they clean their hands as well as possible, then they are, in the end, women after all, can smile despite pallor and bad teeth, shake their stiffened bodies, one can no longer jostle them, stare at them or overlook them, one squeezes oneself against the greasy crates to clear the way for them, keeps one's hat in one's hand when they say good evening and doesn't know how to take it when one of them holds our winter coat for us to put on.

---

8 II 12 Goethe: My pleasure in production was boundless.[470]

I have grown more nervous, weaker and have lost a large part of the calm in which I took pride years ago. When I got the card from Baum today saying he cannot give the lecture for the Eastern Jewish evening after all and I therefore had to believe that I would have to take it over,[471] I was overcome by completely uncontrollable twitches, the throbbing of my veins leaped along my body like little fires; when I sat, my knees trembled under the table and I had to press my hands together. Yes, I will give a good talk, that's certain, and on that evening the unease itself, heightened to an extreme, will pull me together so tight that there won't be space even for unease and the speech will come straight out of me as if out of a gun barrel. But it's possible that afterward I will fall down and in any case won't be able to get over it for a long time. So little physical strength! Even these few words are written under the influence of weakness.

Yesterday evening at Baum's with Löwy. My liveliness. Recently Löwy translated a bad Hebrew story "The Eye" at Baum's.

---

13 II 12 I'm beginning to write the lecture for Löwy's recitations. It's on Sunday the 18th. I won't have much time to prepare and am here actually striking up a recitative as in an opera. Only because I've been beset

by an uninterrupted agitation for days and, withdrawn to some extent before the actual beginning, I want to write a few words only for myself, in order to get going a little before I stand in front of the public. Cold and heat alternate in me with the alternating words within the sentence, I dream melodic rise and fall, I read sentences by Goethe as if I were running along the stresses with my whole body.

25 II 12 Hold fast to the diary from today on! Write regularly! Don't give up! Even if no salvation comes, I want to be worthy of it at every moment. This evening I spent in complete indifference at the family table, my right hand on the back of the chair in which my sister was playing cards next to me, my left weak in my lap. From time to time I tried to become aware of my unhappiness, I barely succeeded.—

I have written nothing for so long because I organized a recitation evening by Löwy in the banquet room of the Jewish Town Hall on 18 II 12, at which I gave a short introductory lecture on jargon.[472] For two weeks I lived in worries, because I couldn't manage to write the lecture. The evening before the lecture I suddenly succeeded. Preparations for the lecture: Meetings with the Bar-Kochba Association,[473] putting together the program, tickets, hall, numbering the seats, key to the piano (Toynbee Hall),[474] elevated stage, piano player, costumes, selling tickets, newspaper notices,[475] censorship by the police and the religious community. Places where I was and people with whom I spoke or to whom I wrote: In general: with Max, with Schmerler,[476] who visited me, with Baum, who had at first taken on the lecture, then declined it, whose mind I changed again in the course of an evening devoted to that purpose and who the next day canceled again by pneumatic postcard,[477] with Dr. Hugo Hermann and Leo Hermann[478] at Kafé Arco,[479] often with Robert Weltsch[480] in his apartment, with Dr. Bloch about selling tickets[481] (in vain) Dr. Hanzal,[482] Dr. Fleischmann,[483] visit to Frl. Taussig,[484] lecture at Afike Jehuda (Rabb. Ehrentreu on Jeremiah and his time[485] at the social gathering afterward short failed talk about Löwy), at the teacher Weiss's[486] (then in the café, then on a walk, from 12 to 1 he stood as lively as an animal outside my front door and wouldn't let me in[487]) At Dr. Karl Bendiener's about the hall, in the corridor of the Town Hall with old

Dr. Bendiener, twice in Liebers's apartment on Heuwagsplatz,[488] several visits to Otto Pick at the bank,[489] at the Toynbee presentation[490] with Hr. Roubitschek and the teacher Stiassny about the piano key, then fetching the key at the latter's apartment and bringing it back, with the caretaker and servant of the Town Hall about the stage, at the Town Hall office about the payment (twice), visit to Frau Freund at the exhibition "Der gedeckte Tisch" about the sale[491]
Wrote: to Frl. Taussig, to an Otto Klein (to no avail) for the Tagblatt[492] (to no avail) to Löwy ("I won't be able to give the lecture, save me!")
Agitations: because of the lecture a night twisted up in bed, hot and sleepless, hatred of Dr. Bloch, horror of Weltsch (he won't be able to sell anything) Afike Jehuda, in the newspapers the notices don't appear the way one expects, distractedness in the office, the stage doesn't come, little is sold, the color of the tickets upsets me, the presentation must be interrupted because the piano player has forgotten the sheet music at home in Košíř,[493] frequent indifference toward Löwy, almost abhorrence.
Benefits: Pleasure in L.[494] and confidence in him, proud, supernatural consciousness during my lecture (coldness toward the audience, only the lack of practice hinders me in the freedom of enthusiastic movement) strong voice, effortless memory, recognition, but above all the power with which I loudly, firmly, decisively, flawlessly, unrelentingly, with clear eyes, almost in passing, quell the impertinence of the three town hall servants and give them instead of the demanded 12K only 6K and these even like a great master. Here powers show themselves to which I would gladly entrust myself if they would remain. (My parents weren't there.)

---

also: Academy of the Herder Association[495] on the Sophieninsel.[496] At the beginning of the lecture Bie shoves his hand into his pants pocket. This face, satisfied under all the deception, of people who work as they please. Hoffmannstal reads with a false tone in his voice. Collected figure, beginning with the ears pressed against the head. Wiesental. The beautiful parts of the dance, for example, when in sinking back to the ground the natural heaviness of the body shows itself.

Impression of the Toynbee Hall.[497]

Zionist meeting. Blumenfeld. Secretary of the World Zionist Organization[498]

In my self-reflection a new consolidating force has recently emerged, which I can recognize at this moment and only now, since in the past week I have been positively dissolving in sadness and uselessness.

Changing feeling in the midst of the young people in Café Arco.

---

26 II 12 Better self-confidence. Heartbeat closer to my wishes. The hiss of the gas light over me.

I opened the front door to see whether the weather would tempt me to take a walk. The blue sky couldn't be denied, but large blue-suffused gray clouds with flap-shaped bent edges were hovering low, as one could gauge by the nearby wooded hills. Nonetheless, the street was full of people out for walks. Baby carriages were steered by the firm hands of mothers. Here and there a wagon came to a stop in the crowd and waited until the people parted for the horses stepping up and down. Meanwhile the driver, calmly holding the trembling reins, stared ahead, didn't overlook a single detail, examined everything several times and at the right moment gave the wagon the final impetus. Children could run, as little space as there was. Girls in light clothes with hats as distinctly colored as postage stamps walked on the arm of young people and a melody, suppressed in their throats, revealed itself in the dancing step of their legs. Families kept together well and even if at some point they were scattered in a long row there were arms stretched slightly backward, waving hands, shouts of pet names to link the lost ones. Solitary men sought to close themselves off even more by putting their hands in their pockets. That was petty foolishness. First I stood in the front door, then I leaned against it to watch more calmly. Clothes grazed me, at one point I seized a ribbon adorning the back of a girl's skirt and let it be drawn out of my hand by the departing girl; when I stroked a girl's shoulder at one point just to flatter her, the passerby who followed gave me a slap on the fingers. But I pulled him behind the one bolted leaf of the front door, my reproaches were raised hands, looks out of the corners of my eyes, a step toward him a step away from him, he was happy when I released him with a push. From now on, naturally, I often called people over to me, a beckoning with the finger sufficed or a quick, nowhere hesitating glance.

In what an effortless sleepiness I wrote this useless, unfinished thing.

Today I'm writing to Löwy. I'm writing the letters to him here, because I hope to achieve something with them:

Dear friend

27 II 12 I have no time to write letters twice.

At 10 o'clock yesterday evening I was walking with my sad gait down Zeltnergassse.[499] In the vicinity of the Hess hat shop[500] a young man stops three paces diagonally in front of me, thereby bringing me to a halt too, takes off his hat and then runs toward me. In my initial fright I step back, think at first that someone wants to know the way to the train, but why in this manner, then believe, since he is coming intimately close to me and looking me in the face from below, because I'm taller, that he might want money or something even worse. My confused listening and his confused talking intermingle. "You're a lawyer aren't you? Doctor? Please couldn't you give me some advice? I have a matter for which I need an attorney." Out of caution, general suspicion, and worry that I could make a fool of myself, I deny being a lawyer, but am prepared to give him some advice, what is it? He begins to tell me, it interests me, to strengthen the trust I ask him to tell me while walking, he wants to accompany me, no I'd rather walk with him, I'm not going anywhere in particular.

He is a good reciter, in the past he wasn't nearly as good as now, now he can even imitate Kainz[501] so that no one can tell the difference.

People will say he only imitates him, but he actually adds a lot of his own. True, he's small, but he has facial expressions, memory, demeanor, everything, everything. In his military days in the camp out in Milowitz he recited, a comrade sang, they really amused themselves very well. It was a beautiful time. He likes best to recite Dehmel, the passionate suggestive poems, for example, about the bride imagining her wedding night,[502] when he recites that, it makes a huge impression especially on the girls. Well that goes without saying. He has Dehmel very beautifully bound, in red leather. (With descending hands he describes it) But the binding isn't what matters, of course. He also likes very much to recite Rideamus.[503] No they don't contradict each other at all, he mediates, speaks between them, whatever occurs to him, makes a fool of the audience. Then Prometheus is on his program too. Here he wasn't afraid of anyone, not even Moissi,[504] Moissi drinks, he doesn't. Finally he likes very much to read from Swet Marten; that's a new Nordic writer. Very good. It's sort of epigrams and short sayings. Especially the ones about Napoleon are excellent, but also all the others about other great men.[505] No, he can't recite anything from it yet, he hasn't rehearsed it yet, hasn't even read all of it, but his aunt read it to him recently and he liked it so much

So he wanted to appear in public with this program and so offered himself to the "Women's Progress"[506] for a presentation evening. Actually, at first he wanted to present "Eine Gutsgeschichte" by Lagerlöf and even lent this story to the chairwoman of the Women's Progress, Frau Durège-Wodnanski,[507] for her consideration. She said that the story was beautiful but too long to be presented. He understood, it was really too long, especially since on the intended presentation evening his brother was also supposed to play piano. This brother, 21 years old, a very nice boy, is a virtuoso, he was at the music academy in Berlin for two years (4 years ago now). But came back completely corrupted. Not actually corrupted, but his boardinghouse landlady fell in love with him. He later said that he was often too tired to play, because he constantly had to ride around on this boardinghouse bag.

Since the Gutsgeschichte wasn't suitable, they agreed on the other program Dehmel, Rideamus, Prometheus and Swet Marten. But now, to show Frau Durège from the outset what sort of person he actually is, he brought her the manuscript of an essay "Joy of Life" that he had written this summer. He had written it on summer holiday, writing in shorthand during the day, making a clean copy in the evening, polishing, crossing out, but it actually hadn't been much work, since it had been successful immediately. He'll lend it to me, if I want, admittedly it's written in a popular style, intentionally, but there are good ideas in it and it's betamt as they say. (Sharp laugh with raised chin.) I can leaf through it here under the electric light. (It's an appeal to the youth not to be sad, for after all there's nature, freedom, Goethe, Schiller Shakespeare, flowers, insects, etc.) The Durege woman said she didn't have time to read it just now, but he could lend it to her, she would give it back to him in a few days. Even then he was suspicious and didn't want to leave it there, resisted, said, for example, Look Frau Durege why should I leave it here, it's only banalities, after all, yes it's well written, but—Nothing helped, he had to leave it there. That was Friday.

28 II 12 On Sunday morning while washing it occurs to him that he hasn't read the Tagblatt yet. He opens it, by chance straight to the first page of the entertainment supplement. The title of the first essay "The Child as Creator" strikes him,[508] he reads the first lines—and begins to weep with joy. It's his essay, word for word his essay. So something has been printed for the first time, he runs to his mother and tells her. The joy! The old woman, she's diabetic and divorced from his father, who, incidentally, is in the right, is so proud. One son is already a virtuoso, now the other is becoming a writer!

After the initial excitement he now considers the matter. How did the essay get into the newspaper? Without his consent? Without the name of the author? Without his receiving a fee? It's actually a betrayal of trust, a fraud. This Frau Durege is a devil. And women have no soul says Mohamet (repeated often) One can easily imagine how this plagiarism came about. Here was a beautiful essay, where is one going to find another like it anytime soon. So Frau D. went to the Tagblatt, sat down with an editor, both overjoyed, and now they began the revision. It had to be revised, of course, for first of all one shouldn't recognize the plagiarism at first glance and secondly the 32-page essay was too long for the newspaper.

In response to my question of whether he wouldn't show me passages that correspond, since this would especially interest me and since only then can I give him advice on how to proceed, he begins to read his essay, opens to another passage, turns pages without finding and finally says that everything was copied. For example, the newspaper said: The soul of the child was a blank sheet of paper and "blank sheet of paper" also appeared in his essay. Or the expression "moniker," how else would anyone have come up with "moniker." But he can't compare individual passages. Everything was indeed copied, but simply disguised, in a different sequence, abridged and with small extraneous additions.

I read aloud several of the more striking passages from the newspaper. Is this in the essay? No. This? No. This? No. Yes but those are simply the added passages. At the core everything everything is copied. But proving it, I'm afraid, will be difficult. He'll certainly prove it with the help of a skilled lawyer, that's what lawyers are for, after all. (He looks forward to this proof like an entirely new task completely separate from this matter and is proud of his belief in his ability to accomplish it)

That it's his essay one sees moreover from the mere fact that it was printed in 2 days. Usually it takes at least 6 weeks before an accepted piece goes to press. But naturally haste was necessary here, lest he interfere. That's why 2 days sufficed.—Besides, the newspaper essay is called "The Child as Creator." That has a clear connection to him and besides it's a taunt. "Child" refers to him, for he used to be regarded as a "child" as "stupid" (he really was only during his military days, he served 1½ years) and the title now implies that he a child has achieved something as good as this essay, that he has thus proven himself as a creator, but at the same time has remained stupid and a child by letting himself be cheated in this way.—The child mentioned in the first part refers to a female cousin from the country, who is presently living with his mother.—But the plagiarism is proven especially convincingly by a circumstance that he realized, to be sure, only after extended consideration: "The Child as Creator" is on the first page of the entertainment supplement, but on the third is a short story by a certain "Feldstein."[509] The name is obviously a pseudonym. Now one needn't read this whole story, it's enough to skim the first lines and one knows immediately that Lagerlöf is here being shamelessly imitated. The whole story makes it even clearer. What does this mean? It means that this Feldstein or whatever her name is is a creature of Durege, that she read at her home the "Gutsgeschichte," which he brought to her, that she used this reading to write this story and that both women are thus taking advantage of him one on the 1st) the other on the 3rd page of the entertainment supplement. Naturally anyone can read and imitate Lagerlöf of his own accord, but here his influence is just too obvious. (He keeps flipping the one page back and forth)

Monday at noon, immediately after the bank closed, he naturally went to Frau D.'s. She opens the apartment door only a crack, she is quite anxious: "But, Herr Reichmann why are you coming at noon. My husband is asleep. I can't let you in now." "Frau D. you absolutely must let me in. It's about an important matter." She sees I'm serious and lets me in. Of course, her husband definitely wasn't at home. In the next room I see my manuscript on the table and immediately start thinking. "Frau D. what have you done with my manuscript. You gave it to the Tagblatt without my consent. How much were you paid?" She trembles, she knows nothing, has no idea how it could have gotten into the newspaper. J'accuse Frau D. I say, half jokingly but still in such a way that she notices how I truly feel and I repeat this j'accuse Frau D. the whole time I'm there, so that she remembers it and even say it several times in parting at the door. I understand her fear well, of course. If I make it public or sue her, she'll be discredited, after all, must leave the Women's Progress, etc.

From her apartment I go directly to the office of the Tagblatt and have the editor Löw[510] called out. Naturally, he comes out completely pale, can hardly walk. Nonetheless, I don't want to go into my matter immediately and also want to test him first. So I ask him "Herr Löw, are you a Zionist?" (For I know that he was a Zionist) "No" he says. I know enough, it's clear he must dissemble in front of me. Now I ask about the essay. Again uncertain talk. He knows nothing, has nothing to do with the entertainment supplement, will if I'd like fetch the appropriate editor. Herr Wittmann come here, he calls and is glad that he can leave. Wittmann comes, again completely pale. I ask: "Are you the editor of the entertainment supplement." He: Yes. I say only "j'accuse" and leave.

At the bank I immediately telephone the "Bohemia." I want to give them the story for publication. But it's impossible to get a good connection. Do you know why? The Tagblatt office is close to the main post office,[511] from the Tagblatt they can easily control, block and make the connections as they please. And indeed on the telephone I keep hearing indistinct whispering voices obviously of Tagblatt editors. They have a great interest, after all, in not allowing this telephone connection. Then I hear (naturally quite indistinctly) some of them persuading the operator not to make the connection, while the others are already connected with the Bohemia and are trying to keep them from accepting my story. "Operator" I shout into the telephone "if you don't make the connection immediately, I'll complain to the post office management." My colleagues all around me at the bank laugh when they hear me talking so forcefully with the telephone operator. Finally I have the connection. "Call the editor Kisch.[512] I have an extremely important piece of news for the Bohemia. If it doesn't take it, I'll immediately give it to another newspaper. It's high time." But since Kisch isn't there, I hang up without revealing anything.

In the evening I go to the Bohemia and have the editor Kisch called out. I tell him the story, but he doesn't want to publish it. "The Bohemia, he says, can't do something like that, it would be a scandal and we can't risk that, because we're dependent. Give it to a lawyer, that would be best."

Coming from the Bohemia I met you and so I'm asking your advice.

"I advise you to settle the matter amicably."

Indeed I thought that would be better. She's a woman, after all. Women have no soul says Mohamet with good reason. To forgive would also be more human, more Goethean.

"Certainly. And then you also won't have to give up the recitation evening, which would otherwise be lost, after all."

"But what should I do now"

"Go there tomorrow and say that this one time you're willing to assume unconscious influence."

"That's very good. That's really how I'll do it"

"You needn't forgo revenge because of this. Simply have the essay printed elsewhere and then send it to Frau D. with a nice dedication."

"That will be the best punishment. I'll have it printed in the Deutsches Abendblatt.[513] They'll take it from me; I'm not worried about that. I'll simply demand no payment."

Then we speak about his acting talent. I say he should have training. "Yes you're right about that. But where? Do you perhaps know where it can be studied?" I say: That's difficult. I don't know very much about it. He: It doesn't matter. I'll ask Kisch. He's a journalist and has a lot of connections. He'll definitely give me good advice. I'll simply telephone him, spare him and myself the journey and find out everything.

And with Frau D. you'll do as I advised you?

"Yes, only I've forgotten; what did you advise me to do?" I repeat my advice.

"All right that's how I'll do it." He goes into Kafe Corso I go home with the experience of how refreshing it is to speak with a perfect fool. I barely laughed, but was only wide awake.

The melancholy "formerly" common only on company plaques

---

2 III 12 Who will confirm for me the truth or probability of the notion that it's only due to my literary calling that I am otherwise uninterested and hence heartless.

---

3 III 12. The 28th II at Moissi's performance.[514] Unnatural sight. He sits with apparent calm, whenever possible has his folded hands between his knees, his eyes in the book lying freely in front of him and lets his voice come over us with the breathing of someone running.—Good acoustics of the hall. Not a word gets lost or comes back only in a breath, rather everything grows gradually larger as if the voice, long since otherwise occupied, continued to have an immediate aftereffect, it grows stronger in accordance with the tendency given to it and encompasses us.—The possibilities of one's own voice that one sees here. Just as the hall works for Moissi's voice, his voice works for ours. Shameless tricks and surprises, during which one has to look at the floor and which one would never do oneself: Singing of individual verses at the very beginning, for example, Schlaf Mirjam mein Kind, a wandering around of the voice in the melody; rapid utterance of the May Song, seemingly only the tip of the tongue is stuck between the words; division of the phrase November wind in order to let the "wind" blow down and whistle upward.—If one looks at the ceiling of the hall, one is lifted by the verses.—Goethe's poems unattainable for the reciter, but one can't easily find fault with this recitation for that reason, because each one works toward the goal.—Great effect later when, during the encore "Rain Song" by Shakespeare,[515] he stood upright, was free of the text, stretched and crumpled his handkerchief in his hands and his eyes shone.—Round cheeks and yet angular face. Soft hair stroked again and again with soft hand movements.—The enthusiastic reviews one has read about him benefit him in our opinion only until the first listening, then he becomes entangled in them and can produce no pure impression.—This manner of sit-

ting recitation with the book in front of one is somewhat reminiscent of ventriloquism. The artist seems uninvolved, sitting just like us, in his lowered face we hardly see the movements of his mouth now and then and he lets the verses speak in his place over his head.—Although so many melodies could be heard, the voice seemingly being steered like a light boat in the water, the melody of the verses could not actually be heard.—Some words were dissolved by the voice, they were touched so gently that they leaped up and had nothing more to do with the human voice, until the voice then of necessity named some sharp consonant, brought the word down to earth and concluded it.

A walk afterward with Ottla, Frl. Taussig, Herr and Frau Baum and Pick, Elisabethbrücke, quay, Kleinseite, Radetzkykaffee,[516] Steinerne Brücke, Karlsgasse. I only just had the prospect of a good mood, so that not that much fault could be found with me.

---

5 III 12 These infuriating doctors![517] Determined in a businesslike way and so ignorant of healing that, if this businesslike determination left them, they would stand like schoolboys before the sickbeds. If only I had the strength to found a naturopathic association. By scratching around in my sister's ear Dr. Kral turns an inflammation of the eardrum into an inflammation of the middle ear; the maid falls down while tending the fire, with that speed of diagnosis he has when dealing with maids the doctor declares it an upset stomach and resulting congestion of blood, the next day she lies down again, has a high fever, the doctor turns her to the right and left, determines it's angina and quickly runs away lest the next moment refute him. Even dares to speak of the "basely strong reactions of this girl," in which the truth is that he's accustomed to people whose physical condition is worthy of his medical treatment and produced by it and that, more than he knows, he feels offended by the strong nature of this girl from the country.

Yesterday at Baum's. Read aloud "Der Dämon."[518] Unfriendly impression on the whole. Good precise mood on the way up to Baum's, immediate waning upstairs, embarrassment toward the child.[519]

Sunday: In the Kontinental among the card players.[520] "Journalisten" with Kramer beforehand 1 ½ acts. Much forced merriness is visible in Bolz, which, to be sure, also gives rise to a little that is real and delicate.[521] Met Frl. Taussig outside the theater, during the intermission after the 2nd act. Ran into the cloakroom, came back with coat flying and escorted her home.

---

8 III *(1912)* Was reproached the day before yesterday because of the factory. Then for an hour on the sofa thought about jumping-out-the-window.

Yesterday Harden lecture on "theater."[522] Apparently improvised in its entirety, I was in a fairly good mood and therefore didn't find it as empty as others. Good beginning: "At this hour, in which we have come together here for a discussion of the theater, the curtain is parting in all the playhouses of Europe and the other continents and revealing the scene to the audience." With an electric light attached movably to a stand at chest height in front of him, he illuminates his shirtfront, as in the display of a linen shop, and in the course of the lecture varies the illumination by moving this light. Toe dancing to make himself taller as well as to exert his improvisational ability. Pants tight even in the groin area. A short tailcoat like one nailed onto a doll. Face serious in an almost strained way, now resembling an old lady, now Napoleon. Paling hue of the forehead as with a wig. Probably corseted.

Read through some old papers. It takes all one's strength to bear it. The unhappiness one must endure when one interrupts oneself in a task that can only ever succeed at one stretch and this has always happened to me up to now, in reading through things one must go through this unhappiness, even if not with the old intensity, in a more compressed way.

Today while swimming I thought I felt old powers, as if they had been untouched by the long intervening period

---

10 III 12 Sun.

He seduced a girl in a small town in the Isergebirge,[523] where he stayed for a summer to restore his weakened lungs. Incomprehensibly, the way lung patients sometimes behave, after a brief attempt at persuasion he threw the girl his landlord's daughter, who liked to take a walk with him in the evening after work, into the grass on the riverbank and, while she lay there unconscious with terror, took possession of her. Later he had to fetch water from the river in his cupped hands and pour it over the girl's face just to bring her to life. "Julchen, but Julchen," he said, bending over her, countless times. He was prepared to take all responsibility for his transgression and only strained to make himself understand how serious his situation was. Without reflection he couldn't have realized it. The simple girl who lay before him, now breathing regularly again and keeping her eyes closed only out of fear and embarrassment, couldn't worry him; big strong person that he was, he could push the girl aside with his toe. She was weak and plain, could what happened to her have any significance that would last even until tomorrow? Didn't anyone comparing the two of them have to come to the same conclusion? The river stretched calmly between the meadows and fields toward the more distant mountains. There was still sunshine only on the slope of the opposite bank. The last clouds were drifting away under the clear evening sky.

Nothing, nothing. In this way I make ghosts for myself. I was involved, even if only slightly, solely in the passage "Later he had to . . ." above all in the "pour." For a moment I thought I saw something real in the description of the landscape.

So forsaken by myself, by everything. Noise in the next room.

---

11 III 12 Yesterday unbearable. Why doesn't everyone take part in the evening meal. It would just be so nice.

The day after our conversation the reciter Reichmann ended up in the madhouse.[524]

Today burned many old disgusting papers.

W. Freiherr von Biedermann Gespräche mit Goethe[525]
how the daughters of the Leipzig copperplate engraver Stock comb his hair in 1767

How in 1772 Kestner found him lying in the grass in Garbenheim and how he was "conversing with some people standing around him, an epicurean philosopher (v. Goué, great genius) a stoic philosopher (v. Kielmansegg) and something between the two (Dr. König) and he was quite content."

---

with Seidel in 1783 5–7 II "Once he rang in the middle of the night and when I enter his room, he has rolled his iron rolling bed from the lowest end of the room up to the window and is observing the sky. "Have you seen nothing in the sky?" he asked me and when I answered no "then run to the guardroom and ask the sentry whether he has seen nothing." I ran there; but the sentry had seen nothing, which I reported to my master, who was still lying in the same position and observing the sky with a fixed gaze. Listen he then said to me "this is a significant moment: either we're having an earthquake at this instant or we're going to have one." And now I had to sit down on his bed and he demonstrated to me from what signs he had gathered this." (Messina earthquake)

---

with von Trebra (1783 Sept.) a geological walk through underbrush and rocks. Goethe ahead

---

To Herder's wife in 1788. Among other things he also said that for 14 days before the departure from Rome he had wept like a child daily

---

How Herder's wife observes him in order to write everything to her husband in Italy.

In the presence of Herder's wife Goethe interests himself a great deal in Herder

---

Visit to Kagliostro's family

1794 14 Sept. spent from ½ past 11, when Schiller was dressed to 11 o'clock without interruption in literary consultations with Schiller in his room and often so

David Veit 19 Oct. 1794 always Jewish observation therefore as easy to take in as if it had happened yesterday.

"That evening in Weimar "Der Diener zweier Herrn" was performed quite nicely, to my astonishment. Goethe was also in the theater and indeed as always in the section of the nobility. In the middle of the play he leaves this section—which he is said to do very rarely—sits down, as long as he couldn't talk to me, behind me—as the women sitting near me told me—and as soon as the act is over, he comes forward, gives an extremely friendly bow and begins in a quite intimate tone———brief dialogue about the play——Hereupon he falls silent for a moment; meanwhile I forget that he is the theater manager and say: "They're performing it quite nicely too." He keeps looking straight ahead, and so in my stupidity—but really in a feeling that I don't yet know how to analyze—I say once again: "They're performing quite nicely." At that moment he gives me a bow, which, however, really was as friendly as the first one and he's gone! Have I offended him or not? . . . You won't believe how anxious I still am, even though I've already been assured by Humboldt, who now knows him well, that he often leaves so quickly and Humboldt has taken it on himself to speak with him about me once again"[526]

---

another time, they're talking about Maimon "I kept interrupting and often came to his aid; for he generally cannot remember many words and constantly makes faces"

1795 With Schiller. from 5 o'clock in the evening to 12, even 1 o'clock at night we sit together and chatter.

1796 first ½ of Sept. While reading aloud Hermann's conversation with his mother at the pear tree. He wept. "Thus one melts over one's own coals" he said, drying his tears

---

"The wide wooden balustrade of the old gentleman's box." Goethe liked to have a supply of cold food and wine on hand in his box at times, more for others—residents and visitors of significance—whom he not infrequently received there.

Performance of Schlegel's Alarcos in 1802
"in the middle of the orchestra Goethe, seriously and solemnly enthroned in his tall armchair"
people grow restless, finally at one passage uproarious laughter, the whole house shakes. "But only for a moment. In an instant Goethe jumped up, shouted with a booming voice and a threatening movement Silence Silence and that worked like a magic spell. Immediately the tumult died down and without further disturbance but also without the slightest sign of applause the unhappy Alarcos drew to an end"

Stael: What seems to French people to be the wit of foreigners is often only ignorance of French
Goethe called an idea of Schiller's neuve et courageuse, that was admirable, but it turned out that he had meant to say hardie.

Was lockst Du meine Brut hinauf in Todesglut. Stael translated aïr brulant. Goethe said he had meant the glow of coals. She found that extremely maussade and tasteless. German poets lacked the fine sense of the seemly.

1804 Fondness for Heinrich Voss.—Goethe read Luise with the Sunday gathering.
"It fell to Goethe to read the passage about the wedding which he did with the deepest feeling. But his voice grew subdued, he wept and gave the book to his neighbor. A holy passage he cried out with a fervor that shook us all"

"We were sitting at lunch and had just consumed the last bit when Goethe ordered a cake "because Voss still looked so hungry"

"But he is never kinder and more pleasant than in the evening in his room when he is undressed or sitting on the sofa."

"When I visited him I found it quite comfortable at his home. He had lit the fire, had undressed down to a woolen vest, in which the man looks quite magnificent."

Books Stilling, Goethe Jahrbuch

Correspondence between Rahel and D. Veit.

---

12 III 12

In the rapidly passing tram a young man sat in a corner, his open overcoat billowing around him, his cheek against the window his left arm stretched along the back of the seat and looked over the long empty bench with observant glances. He had become engaged today and thought of nothing else. He felt at home in the state of a bridegroom and in this feeling he sometimes looked fleetingly up at the ceiling of the car. When the conductor came to give him the ticket, with some jingling he easily found the right coin, placed it briskly in the conductor's hand and seized the ticket with two fingers spread in the form of scissors. There was no real connection between him and the tram and it would have been no surprise if without using platform or steps he had appeared on the street and had gone his way on foot with the same glances.

Only the billowing overcoat endures, everything else is contrived.

---

16 III 12 Saturday Again encouragement. Again I take hold of myself, like the balls that fall and that one catches in falling. Tomorrow, today I begin a larger work that is to conform in an unforced way to my abilities. I will not abandon it, as long as I can. Better to be sleepless than to go on living like this.

Kabaret Lucerna.[527] Several young people each sing a song. If we are fresh and listen, we are reminded by such a performance of the conclusions that the lyrics permit for our life more than this can be done by the performance of practiced singers. For the force of the verses is not increased at all by the singer, they maintain their independence and tyrannize us with the singer who doesn't even have patent leather boots, whose hand at one point won't leave his knee and when it must, still displays its reluctance, who throws himself as quickly as possibly onto the bench in order to show as little as possible the many small awkward movements he has to muster for it.—Love scene in spring in the manner of photographic postcards. Faithful portrayal that moves and shames the audience.—Fatinizza, Viennese singer. Sweet meaningful laugh. Memory of Hansi.[528] A face with insignificant, mostly also too-sharp details held together and balanced by laughter. Ineffective superiority over the audience, which one must ascribe to her when she stands on the front of the stage and laughs into the indifferent audience.—Stupid dance by Degen[529] with flying will o' the wisps, twigs, butterflies, paper fires, death's head.—4 Roking Girls. One of them very beautiful. No playbill mentions her name. She was the one on the extreme right from the auditorium. How she busily threw her arms, how her thin long legs with delicate playing little bones were in especially tangibly silent motion, how she didn't keep time but how she didn't let any fright disturb her in her busyness, what a gentle smile she had in contrast to the contorted one of the others, how her face and hair were almost voluptuous in comparison to the thinness of her body, how she called "slowly" to the musicians also for her sisters. Their dancing master, a young strikingly dressed thin person stood behind the musicians and rhythmically waved one hand regarded neither by musicians nor by the dancers and with his own eyes on the auditorium.—Warnebold, fiery nervousness of a strong person. In movements sometimes a joke, the power of which is uplifting. How after the announcement of the number he hurries to the piano with long strides.

Read "aus dem Leben eines Schlachtenmalers"[530]
Read Flaubert aloud with satisfaction.

The man in top boots in the rain

Wishes.

Necessity of speaking about dancers with exclamation points. Because in that way one imitates their movement, because one remains in the rhythm and then the thinking doesn't disturb in the enjoyment, because then the activity always remains at the end of the sentence and has a more lasting effect.

17 III *(1912)* In these days read "Morgenrot" by Stössl.[531]

Max's concert on Sunday.[532] My almost unconscious listening. From now on I can no longer be bored by music. I no longer try, as I used to do in vain, to penetrate this impenetrable circle that soon forms around me with music, I also take care not to jump over it, which I might well be capable of doing, rather remain calmly with my thoughts, which develop and flow away in this constriction without intrusive self-observation being able to enter this slow throng.—The beautiful "Der magische Kreis" (by Max) that in places seems to open the singer's breast.—Goethe "Trost im Schmerz." Alles geben die unendlichen Götter Ihren Lieblingen ganz, die Freuden die unendlichen, die Schmerzen die unendlichen ganz.—My ineptitude in the face of my mother, in the face of Frl. T.[533] and in the face of everyone later in the Kontinental and then on the street.

Mam'zelle Nitouche on Monday.[534] The good effect of a French word within a sad German performance.—Boarding school girls in light-colored dresses run with outstretched arms into the garden behind a fence.—Barrack yard of the dragoon regiment at night. Officers are celebrating a farewell party in a hall of the rear barrack building that is reached by a few stairs. Mam'zelle Nitouche comes and is induced by love and recklessness to participate in the celebration. What can happen to girls! In the morning at the convent, in the evening appearing for a canceling operetta singer and at night in the dragoon barrack.

Today spent the afternoon with painful fatigue on the sofa.

18 III 12[535] I was wise, if you will, because I was prepared to die at any moment, but this was not because I had taken care of everything I was required to do, but rather because I had done none of it and also couldn't hope ever to do any of it.

---

22 III *(1912)* (the last few days I've written wrong dates) Baum's reading in the Lesehalle.[536] Grete Fischer, 19 years old, getting married next week.[537] Dark flawless thin face. Arched nostrils. She has always worn hunter-style hats and clothes. Also that dark green gleam on her face. The strands of hair running along her cheeks seem to unite with fresh ones growing along her cheeks, as in general the appearance of a light down lies over her whole face, which is bowed into the darkness. Points of her elbows propped weakly on the back of the chair. Then on Wenzelsplatz a brisk bow turn and straightening up of her poorly and roughly dressed thin body, carried out to completion with little strength. I looked at her much less often than I wanted to.

---

24 III *(1912)* Sun. yesterday. "Die Sternenbraut" by Christian von Ehrenfels.[538]—Lost in viewing, confronted with a confusing rough context, well connected with myself in the presence of the 3 married couples of my acquaintance.—The sick officer in the play. The sick body in the tight uniform that makes health and resoluteness a duty.

In the morning in a pure mood for ½ an hour at Max's.

In the next room my mother is conversing with Herr and Frau Lebenhart.[539] They're speaking about vermin and corns. (Hr. Lebenhart has 6 corns on each finger.) It's easy to see that no actual progress is made by such conversations. They're exchanges of information that will be forgotten again by both parties and that even now proceed obliviously with no sense of responsibility. For that very reason, however, because such conversations are unthinkable without absentmindedness, they show empty spaces that if one wants to keep at it, can be filled only with thinking or better with dreaming.

---

25 III 12 The broom sweeping the rug in the next room sounds like the jerkily moving train of a dress

---

26 III 12 Just don't overestimate what I've written, in that way I make what is to be written unattainable.

27 III *(1912)* On the street on Monday I grabbed a boy who, with others, was throwing a large ball at a servant girl walking defenselessly in front of them, just as the ball was flying toward the girl's behind, by the neck, choked him in great rage, pushed him aside and ranted. Then walked on and didn't even look at the girl. One forgets completely one's earthly existence, because one is so completely filled with rage and is permitted to believe that on some occasion one will fill oneself to the brim in the same way with even more beautiful feelings

---

28 III *(1912)* From Fr. Fanta's lecture "Berlin Impressions":[540] Grillparzer once didn't want to go to a gathering, because he knew that Hebbel, with whom he was friendly, would be there too. "He will question me again about my opinion on God and when I won't know what to say, he will become rude."– My stubborn behavior.

---

29 III 12

The pleasure in the bathroom.—Gradual recognition. The afternoons I spent with my hair.

I IV 12 For the first time in a week an almost complete failure in writing. Why? Last week too I went through various moods and protected the writing from their influence; but I'm afraid to write about it.

---

3 IV *(1912)* —Thus a day has passed—In the morning office, in the afternoon factory, now in the evening shouting in the apartment from the right and left, later fetching my sister from Hamlet[541]—and I haven't known what to do with a single moment

---

8 *(6)* IV 12 Holy Saturday.[542]

Complete recognition of oneself. To be able to clasp the circumference of one's abilities like a little ball. To accept the greatest decline as something known and thus remain elastic in it.

Longing for a deeper sleep that dissolves more. Metaphysical need is only death need

---

How I spoke affectedly today in front of Haas,[543] because he praised Max's and my travel account, so that at least in this way I could make myself worthy of the praise, which does not apply to the account, or so that I could continue the effect, attained by swindling or lying, of the travel account in this swindle or in Haas's kind lie, which I sought to make easier for him

Sixth Notebook

<u>6 May 1912</u> 11 o'clock for the first time in quite a while complete failure with writing. The feeling of a tested man.

Dream recently: I was riding with my father in the tram through Berlin. The big-city character was represented by countless toll barriers regularly standing upright painted in two colors, smoothed off blunt at the end. Otherwise everything was almost empty, but the throng of these toll barriers was great. We came to a gate, got off without feeling it, stepped through the gate. Behind the gate rose a very steep wall, which my father climbed almost dancing, his legs flying so easy was it for him. There was certainly also some inconsiderateness in the fact that he didn't help me at all, for I made my way to the top only with extreme effort, on all fours, frequently sliding back again, as if the wall had become steeper under me. At the same time it was also tormenting that it was covered with human muck, so that flakes of it stuck to me above all on my chest. I looked at them with my face bowed and ran my hand over them. When I at last reached the top, my father, who by then came from the inside of a building, immediately flung himself at me and kissed and hugged me. He had on an old-fashioned, short frock coat, padded inside like a sofa, with which I was well acquainted from memory. "That Dr. von Leyden![544] Isn't he an excellent person" he kept exclaiming. He hadn't visited him as a doctor at all, however, but only as a man worth knowing. I was a little afraid that I would have to go in to see him too, but it wasn't required. Behind me to the left I saw, sitting in a room positively surrounded by nothing but glass walls, a man who turned his back to me. It turned out that this man was the professor's secretary, that my father had actually spoken only with him and not with the professor himself, but that he had somehow recognized through the secretary the merits of the professor in the flesh, so that in every respect he was just as entitled to a judgment on the professor as if he had spoken with him in person.

Lessing Theater: Die Ratten[545]
Letter to Pick, because I haven't written to him. Card to Max, out of joy over Arnold Beer.[546]

---

9 v *(1912)* Yesterday evening with Pick in the coffeehouse.

How I hold on to my novel against all restlessness,[547] just like a monument figure that looks into the distance and holds on to the base.

Disconsolate evening today in the family. My sister weeps because of her new pregnancy, my brother-in-law needs money for the factory,[548] my father is upset because of my sister, because of the shop and because of his heart, my unhappy second sister, my mother unhappy about everything and I with my scribbling.

---

22 May *(1912)* Wonderful evening yesterday with Max. If I love myself, I love him even more strongly. Lucerna. Madame, la mort by Rachilde. Dream of a Spring Morning.[549] The merry fat woman in the box. The wild one with the rough nose, the ash-dusted face, the shoulders that pushed themselves out of her incidentally not low-cut dress, the back that was jerked this way and that, the simple white-dotted blue blouse, the fencing glove, which could always be seen, since she mostly let her right hand rest in its entirety or on its fingertips on the right thigh of her merry mother sitting next to her. The braids twisted over her ears, not the cleanest light blue ribbon on the back of her head, the hair at the front in a thin but dense bunch goes around her forehead and far beyond it in front. Her warm, wrinkled, light coat hanging carelessly in all its suppleness as she negotiated at the box office.

---

23 *(May 1912)* Yesterday: Behind us a man was so bored that he fell off his chair. Comparison by Rachilde: Those who take pleasure in the sun and demand pleasure from others are like drunkards who come at night from a wedding and force people they meet to drink to the health of the unknown bride.[550]

Letter to Weltsch, proposed the "Du" to him[551]
Yesterday good letter to Uncle Alfred about the factory.[552]
Day before yesterday letter to Löwy

This evening out of boredom washed my hands three times in succession in the bathroom.

Fear of being alone on Pentecost Sunday and Monday on the incredible grounds that my parents are traveling to Franzensbad.

The child with the two little braids, bare head, loose little white-dotted red dress, bare legs and feet, who, with a little basket in one hand, with a little box in the other, hesitantly crossed the road at the National Theater.

The actors performing with their backs to the audience at the beginning of Madame la mort according to the principle: The back of an amateur is, all else being equal, as beautiful as the back of a good actor. The conscientiousness of people!

In the past several days excellent lecture by Davis Trietsch on colonization in Palestine.[553]

25 *(May 1912)* Weak tempo, little blood.

27 *(May 1912)* Yesterday Pentecost Sunday, cold weather, unpleasant excursion with Max and Weltsch.
Coffeehouse in the evening, Werfel gives me "Besuch aus dem Elysium"[554]

Part of Niklasstrasse and the whole bridge turn around to look, touched, at a dog that, barking loudly, accompanies an automobile of the rescue service. Until the dog suddenly stops, turns back and reveals itself to be an ordinary unknown dog that meant nothing in particular by the pursuit of the car.

1 June 1912 Wrote nothing.

2 June *(1912)* Wrote almost nothing.
Yesterday lecture Dr. Soukup[555] in the Municipal House[556] on America [The Czechs in Nebraska, all officials in America are elected, everyone must belong to one of the three parties (republican, democratic, socialist), Roosevelt's election meeting, with his glass he threatened a farmer who made an objection, street orators who carry with them a small box as a podium] then spring festival,[557] met Paul Kisch who talks about his dissertation "Hebbel & the Czechs."[558] His terrible appearance. Growths on the back of his neck. The impression when he speaks of his darlings.

---

6 June *(1912)*. Thursday Corpus Christi
how one of the two horses in a race lowers its head for itself and out of the race and shakes its whole mane against itself, then raises its head and only now apparently recovered resumes the race, which it actually never broke off.

Now I read in Flaubert's letters:
My novel is the rock to which I cling and I know nothing of what is going on in the world—Similar to the way I put it in my own entry on 9 v[559]

Weightlessly, bonelessly, bodilessly walked for two hours through the streets and considered what I had come through in the afternoon while writing.

7 June *(1912)*. Awful. Wrote nothing today. No time tomorrow.

Monday 6 *(8)* July 1912 Began a little. Am a little sleepy. Also forsaken among these complete strangers.[560]

9 August *(July 1912)* Have written nothing for so long. Begin tomorrow. Otherwise I'll end up in a prolonged inexorable dissatisfaction; I'm actually already in it. The nervous states are beginning. But if I can do something, then I can do it without superstitious precautions.

The invention of the devil. If we are possessed by the devil, then it cannot be one, for otherwise we would live, at least on the earth, calmly, as with God, in unity, without contradiction, without reflection, always certain of who is behind us. His face wouldn't frighten us, for as devilish beings, while somewhat sensitive to this sight, we would be clever enough to prefer to sacrifice a hand, with which we would keep his face covered. If just a single devil had us with a calm undisturbed view over our whole being and with immediate discretion, then he would also have sufficient strength to hold and even to swing us for the length of a human life so high over God's spirit in us that we wouldn't get to see a glimmer of it thus wouldn't be troubled from there either. Only a multitude of devils can account for our earthly unhappiness. Why don't they exterminate each other until just one is left or why don't they subordinate themselves to one great devil; both would be in keeping with the devilish principle of deceiving us as completely as possible. What's the use, then, as long as unity is lacking, of the great pains all the devils take on our behalf? It stands to reason that the falling out of a human hair must matter more to the devils than to God, for the hair is really lost for the devil, not for God. Only, as long as the many devils are in us this still doesn't help us arrive at any well-being.

7 *(August 1912)* Long torment. Finally wrote to Max that I can't clean up the remaining little pieces, don't want to force myself and therefore will not publish the book.[561]

---

8 *(August 1912)* Finished "Confidence Trickster" roughly to satisfaction.[562] With the last strength of a normal state of mind. 12 o'clock, how will I be able to sleep?

---

9 *(August 1912)* The agitated night.—Yesterday the maid who said to the little boy on the stairs: "Hold on to my skirts."—My reading aloud, which flowed from inspirations, of "Der arme Spielmann."[563]—The recognition of what is manly about Grillparzer in this story. How he can risk everything and risks nothing, because from the outset only what is true is in him, which even in the face of a conflicting momentary impression will justify itself at the decisive time as true. The calm command over himself. The slow pace that neglects nothing. The immediate readiness, when it's necessary, no sooner, for he has long seen everything coming.

10 *(August 1912)* Wrote nothing. Was in the factory and breathed in gas for 2 hours in the engine room. The energy of the foreman and the stoker before the engine, which for an undiscoverable reason won't ignite. Wretched factory.

---

11 *(August 1912)* Nothing, nothing. Of how much time I am robbed by the publication of the little book and how much harmful ridiculous self-confidence arises while reading old things with an eye to publication.[564] Only that keeps me from writing. And yet I have in reality achieved nothing, the disturbance is the best proof of that. In any case I will now, after publication of the book, have to refrain far more than ever from reading magazines and reviews, if I don't want to content myself with sticking only my fingertips in the truth. How hard to move I've also become! Previously, if I said just one word opposed to the present direction, I immediately flew to the other side, now I merely look at myself and remain as I am.

14 *(August 1912)*

Letter to Rohwolt[565]

Dear Herr Rohwolt!

I am submitting here the little prose pieces you wished to see; they probably amount to a little book. As I was assembling them for this purpose, I sometimes had a choice between the appeasement of my sense of responsibility and the yearning to have a book of my own among your beautiful books. Certainly my decisions have not always been entirely pure. But now I would naturally be happy if the things pleased you even only to the extent that you printed them. In the end, even with the greatest practice and greatest understanding, the bad in the things cannot be seen at first glance. The most widespread individuality of writers consists, after all, in the fact that each conceals his bad qualities in an entirely particular way.

Yours faithfully

15 *(August 1912)* Useless day. Slept away, lounged away. Marian celebration on the Altstädter Ring.[566] The man with a voice as if out of a hole in the ground. Thought a lot about—what embarrassment before writing down names—Felice Bauer.[567] Yesterday "Polnische Wirtschaft"[568]—Ottla has just been reciting poems by Goethe for me. She selects with a true feeling. Trost in Tränen. An Lotte. An Werther. An den Mond.—Read old diaries again, instead of keeping these things away from me. I'm living as unreasonably as possible. But the publication of the 31 pages is to blame for everything.[569] Even more to blame, to be sure, is my weakness, which allows something of the sort to have an influence on me. Instead of shaking myself, I'm sitting here and thinking about how I could express all this as offensively as possible. But my terrible calm disturbs my inventiveness. I'm curious about how I will find my way out of this state. I don't let myself be pushed, nor am I aware of the right path, so how will things turn out? Have I, a large mass in my narrow paths, become stuck once and for all?—Then I could at least still turn my head.—But I do that.

16 *(August 1912)* Nothing either in the office or at home.[570] Wrote a few pages in the Weimar diary.[571]

In the evening my poor mother's whimpering because of my not eating.

20 August *(1912)*.

The little boys, both in blue blouses, one in a light-colored one, the other smaller one in a darker one, crossing the university building site[572] partly overgrown with grass outside my window, with arms full are each carrying a bundle of dry hay. They lug it up a slope. Pleasantness of the whole thing for the eyes.

This morning the empty cart and the thin large horse in front of it. Both, as they made the final effort to get up a slope, unusually elongated. Positioned at an angle for the viewer. The horse its forelegs a little raised, its neck stretched sideways and upward. Over it the whip of the coachman.

If Rohwolt sent it back and I could lock everything up again and undo it, so that I would be merely as unhappy as before.

Frl. Felice Bauer.[573] When I arrived at Brod's[574] on 13 VIII, she was sitting at the table and yet looked to me like a maid. I also wasn't at all curious about who she was, but rather immediately reconciled myself to her. Bony empty face, which wore its emptiness openly. Bare neck. Thrown-on blouse. Looked very domestically dressed, although, as it turned out later, she was not at all. [I estrange from her a little by getting so physically close to her. Indeed, what a state I'm in now, estranged from everything good in its entirety and moreover don't believe it yet. If the literary news at Max's doesn't distract me too much today, I will still try to write the story about Blenkelt.[575] It need not be long, but it must strike home to me] Almost broken nose. Blond, somewhat stiff charmless hair, strong chin. As I sat down I looked at her more closely for the first time, by the time I was sitting I had an unshakable judgment. How—

21 VIII *(1912)* Read Lenz incessantly and—this is how I'm doing—he brought me to my senses.[576]

The image of dissatisfaction represented by a street, since everyone is lifting his feet from the place on which he stands to get away.

---

30 August *(1912)* Did nothing the whole time. Visit of my uncle from Spain.[577] Last Saturday Werfel recited the "Lebenslieder" and the "Opfer" at Arco.[578] A monster! But I looked him in the eyes and held his gaze all evening.

I will be hard to rouse and yet am restless. When I was lying in bed this afternoon and someone quickly turned a key in the lock, for a moment I had locks on my whole body as at a costume ball and at brief intervals now here now there a lock was opened or closed.

Questionnaire by the magazine "Miroir" on love in the present and on the changes of love since the time of our grandparents. An actress answered: Never have people loved as well as today.[579]

How scattered and elevated I was after listening to Werfel! How I cast myself afterward downright wildly and flawlessly into the gathering at the Löwys'.[580]

This month, which due to the absence of my boss could have been used especially well, I have without much justification (sending the book off to Rohwolt, abscesses, my uncle's visit) idled away and slept away. Even this afternoon I stretched out on the bed with dreamy excuses for 3 hours.

4 Sept. *(1912)* My uncle from Spain. The cut of his coat. The effect of his nearness. The detailing of his nature.—His floating through the hall

to the water closet. On the way gives no reply to what is said to him.— Softens from day to day, if one judges not a gradual change but rather striking moments.—

5 Sept *(1912)* I ask him: How is one supposed to connect the idea that you're dissatisfied, as you recently said, and that you get on well in everything, as one sees again and again (and as is apparent with the coarseness that is always peculiar to such getting-on-well, I thought) He answered, as it dissolves in my memory: "In particulars I'm dissatisfied, it doesn't extend to the whole. I often have dinner in a small French pension, which is very elegant and expensive. For example, a room for a married couple costs, with board, 50 fr. a day. So I sit there, for example, between a legation secretary of the French embassy and a Spanish artillery general. Opposite me sit a high official of the navy ministry and some count. I already know them all well, sit down in my seat, greeting them on all sides, speak because I'm in a peculiar mood, not another word, except to say goodbye. Then I'm alone in the street and really can't see what purpose this evening is supposed to have served. I go home and regret not having married. Naturally, this fades again, whether because I think it through to the end or because my thoughts stray. But on some occasion it comes again."

---

8 Sept. *(1912)* Sunday morning

Yesterday letter to Dr. Schiller[581]

Afternoon

How my mother with the loudest voice among a crowd of women in the next room plays with small children and drives me out of the apartment: Don't cry! Don't cry! etc. That belongs to him! That belongs to him! etc. Two big people! etc. He doesn't want to!. . . . Well! Well!.. How did you like Vienna Dolphi?[582] Was it nice there? . . . I ask you just look at his hands.

---

11 Sept. *(1912)* Three days ago with Utitz in the evening.[583]

A dream: I was on a tongue of land built of square-hewn stones far out into the sea. Someone or several people were with me, but the consciousness of myself was so strong that I knew scarcely more about them than the fact that I was speaking to them. I can remember only the raised knees of someone sitting next to me. At first I didn't actually know where I was, only when I happened to stand up at one point did I see in front of me to the left and behind me to the right the wide clearly circumscribed sea with many firmly anchored warships arranged in rows. To the right one saw Newyork, we were in the harbor of Newyork. The sky was gray but evenly bright. Exposed to the air from all sides I turned freely back and forth in my spot to be able to see everything. Toward Newyork the gaze went a little downward, toward the sea it went upward. Now I also noticed that the water beside us was rising in high waves and an immense foreign traffic was taking place on it. I remember only that instead of our rafts long logs were tied together into a huge round bundle, which traveled with its cut surface repeatedly emerging either more or less depending on the height of the waves and at the same time also rolled lengthwise in the water. I sat down, drew up my feet, twitched with pleasure, positively burrowed into the ground with contentment and said: This is indeed even more interesting than the traffic on a Paris boulevard.

---

12 Sept. *(1912)* In the evening Dr. Löw at our apartment. Another traveler to Palestine. Is taking the bar examination a year before the end of his clerkship and traveling with 1200 K (in 14 days) to Palestine. Would look for a position at the Palestine Office. All these travelers to Palestine (Bergmann, Dr. Kellner)[584] have lowered eyes, feel blinded by their listeners, run their outstretched fingers over the table, their voices crack, they smile weakly and maintain this smile with some irony.—Dr. Kellner said that his students are chauvinists, constantly have the Maccabees[585] in their mouths and want to take after them.

I realize that I've written to Dr. Schiller so readily and well only because Frl. Bauer stayed in Breslau, albeit 14 days ago now, and a scent of her is still in the air, since I previously thought a lot about having flowers sent to her through Dr. Schiller.

---

15 *(September 1912)* Engagement of my sister Valli[586]

From the depths
of fatigue
we rise
with new powers

Dark lords
who wait
until the children
exhaust themselves

Love between brother and sister—the repetition of the love between mother and father

---

The presentiment of the sole biographer

The hollow burned into our surroundings by the work of genius is a good place to put in one's little light. Hence the incitement that emanates from genius, the general incitement that fires one not only to imitation.

---

18 *(September 1912)* Hubalek's[587] stories yesterday in the office. The stonebreaker who begged a frog from him on the country road, held it by the feet, and with three bites gobbled down first the little head, then the body and finally the feet.—The best method of killing cats, which have a very tenacious life: one squeezes the neck between a closed door and pulls on the tail.—His aversion to vermin. In the military one night something was itching him under his nose, he reached for it in his sleep and crushed something. But the something was a bug and he carried the stench of it around with him for days.—Four people were eating a finely prepared roast cat, but only three of them knew what they were eating. After the meal the three began to meow, but the fourth refused to believe

it, only when they showed him the bloody skin did he believe it, couldn't run out quickly enough to vomit everything up and was seriously ill for two weeks.—This stonebreaker ate nothing but bread and whatever else of fruit or living things came his way and drank nothing, but brandy. Slept in the brick shed of a brickyard. Once Hubalek met him at twilight in the fields. "Stop" said the man or—Hubalek stopped for the fun of it. "Give me your cigarette" the man went on. Hub. gave it to him. "Give me another!" So you want another? Hub. asked him, held his knotted cane ready in his left hand just in case and with his right gave him a blow in the face so that he dropped the cigarette. The man immediately ran away, cowardly and weak as such schnapps drinkers are.

Yesterday at Bergmann's with Dr. Löw. Song about Reb Dovidl, Reb Dovidl, der Wassilkower fährt heint nach Tale. In a city between Wassilko and Tale sung indifferently, in Wassilko tearfully, in Tale joyfully.

---

19 *(September 1912)* Controller Pokorny[588] tells about the trip he took as a 13-year-old boy with 70 Kreuzer in his pocket in the company of a schoolmate. How they arrived in the evening at a tavern where a huge drinking bout was going on, in honor of the mayor who had returned from the military. More than 50 empty beer bottles stood on the floor. Everything was full of pipe smoke. The stench of beer cheese. The two small boys against the wall. The drunken mayor, who in memory of the military wants to establish order everywhere, approaches them and threatens to have them sent home by force as runaways, for which he takes them despite all explanations. The boys tremble, show their Gymnasium identification cards, decline the word mensa, a half-drunken teacher watches without helping. Without getting a clear decision on their fate, they are compelled to join in the drinking, are very pleased to get for nothing so much good beer, which they never could have allowed themselves with their scant means. They drink their fill and then late at night after the last guests have marched off, lie down to sleep on thinly heaped straw in this room that hasn't been aired and sleep like lords. Except that at 4 o'clock a huge maid comes with a broom, declares she has no time and would have swept them out into the morning mist if they hadn't run away of their own accord. When the room had been

cleaned up a little, two large coffee pots filled to the brim were placed on the table for them. But as they stirred their coffee with the spoon, something big, dark, round kept coming to the surface from time to time. They thought it would be cleared up with time, and drank with relish until, in the face of the half empty pot and the dark thing, they became afraid after all and asked the maid for advice. Then it turned out that the blackness was old congealed goose blood, which had remained in the pots from the previous day's banquet and over which the coffee had simply been poured in a morning daze. Immediately the boys ran out and vomited everything to the last little drop. Later they were called before the priest, who after a brief examination in religion determined that they were good boys, had the cook serve them soup and then sent them off with his sacred blessing. As pupils of a Gymnasium run by priests they had this soup and this blessing given to them in almost all the parishes through which they passed.

20 *(September 1912)* Letters to Löwy and Frl. Taussig yesterday, to Frl. Bauer and Max today.

It was on a Sunday morning at the height of spring.[589] Georg Bendemann, a young businessman, was sitting in his private room on the second floor of one of the low lightly built houses that extended along the river in a long row differing almost only in height and coloring. He had just finished a letter to a friend of his youth who was now abroad, then sealed it in playful slowness and with his elbow resting on the desk looked out the window at the river, the bridge and the hills on the opposite bank with their pale green. He thought about how this friend, dissatisfied with his progress at home, had positively fled to Russia several years ago. Now he was running a business in St. Petersburg that had begun very promisingly, but for a long time now seemed to be stagnating, as the friend complained on his increasingly rare visits. Thus he toiled away uselessly in a foreign land, the foreign-looking full beard hardly covered the face so familiar from childhood, the yellow complexion of which seemed to indicate a developing illness. By his own account he had no real connection with the colony of his compatriots there, but also barely any social intercourse with native families and was thus preparing himself for a permanent bachelorhood.

What should one write to such a man, who had obviously lost his way, whom one could pity but not help. Should one perhaps advise him to come home again, transplant his existence here, to resume all his old friendly relations, which certainly nothing hindered him from doing and otherwise rely on the help of friends. But that was tantamount to telling him the more gently the more hurtfully that his efforts up to now had failed, that he should finally abandon them, that he had to return and be gaped at by all as a man who had returned forever, that only his friends understood anything and that he was an old child, who simply had to be guided by his successful companions who had stayed home. And was it certain even then that all the torment one would have to inflict on him would have a purpose. Perhaps it wouldn't even be possible to bring him home at all, indeed he himself said that he no longer understood the way things worked at home, and so he would then remain nonetheless in his foreign land, embittered by the advice and estranged a bit further still from his friends. But if he really did follow the advice and was then oppressed here, not intentionally, of course, but by the facts, got on well neither with his friends nor without them, suffered from humiliation, now really had no home and no friends, wouldn't it be much better for him if he stayed in the foreign land as he was. Under such circumstances, could one think that he would actually make headway here.

For these reasons, if one still wanted to maintain the correspondence at all, one couldn't send him any actual news such as one wouldn't hesitate to tell even the most distant acquaintances. The friend had not been home for over three years now and explained this very inadequately by the uncertainty of the political conditions in Russia, which apparently didn't permit even the briefest absence of a small businessman, while hundreds of thousands of Russians traveled around the world without difficulty. In the course of these three years, however, much had changed for Georg in particular. The death of Georg's mother, which had occurred about two years ago and since which Georg had lived in a shared household with his old father, had certainly come to his friend's knowledge, and he had expressed his sympathy in a letter with a dryness that could have stemmed only from the fact that the grief over such an event becomes completely unimaginable in a foreign land. But since that time Georg had tackled his business as well as everything else with greater determination. Perhaps while his mother was alive his father, by refusing to accept any view but his own in the business, had hindered him from taking any real initiative, perhaps since his mother's death his father although he still worked in the business, had grown more restrained, perhaps—it was even very probable—fortunate accidents played a far more important role—but in any case the business had developed quite unexpectedly in these two years, they had had to double the staff, the turnover had quintupled, further progress undoubtedly lay ahead.

The friend, however, had no inkling of this change. In the past, perhaps for the last time in that letter of sympathy, he had tried to persuade Georg to emigrate to Russia and had enlarged on the prospects that existed in St. Petersburg for Georg's line of business in particular. The figures were infinitesimal compared to the scale Georg's business had now assumed. But Georg hadn't felt inclined to write to his friend about his business successes and to do so belatedly now would have really looked odd.

So Georg confined himself to writing to his friend always only about insignificant events such as heap themselves up in one's memory when one is reflecting on a quiet Sunday. All he wanted was to leave undisturbed the image that his friend must have formed of his hometown in the long interval and to which he had also reconciled himself. So it happened to Georg that he announced to his friend the engagement of an inconsequential person to an equally inconsequential girl three times in letters written rather far apart, until quite contrary to Georg's intention his friend actually began to take an interest in this oddity.

But Georg much preferred to write to him about such things than to confess that he himself had become engaged a month ago to a Fräulein Frieda Brandenfeld a girl from a well-to-do family. Often he spoke with his bride about this friend and the special correspondence relationship he had with him. Then he definitely won't be coming to our wedding she said and yet I have the right to meet all your friends. "I don't want to bother him replied Georg, don't misunderstand me, he would probably come, at least I think so, but he would feel forced and aggrieved, would perhaps envy me and surely dissatisfied and unable to rid himself of the dissatisfaction would go back again alone. Alone—do you know what that is." "Yes but can't he find out about our marriage in another way." "I can't prevent that, certainly, but with his way of life it's unlikely." "But really if you have friends like that, Georg you shouldn't have married at all." "Well both of us are to blame for that, but I wouldn't want it any other way." And when, breathing rapidly under his kisses, she still asserted "Actually it does hurt me" he thought it really was harmless to write everything to his friend. This is the way I am and he has to take me as I am he said to himself. I can't cut a person out of myself who might be more suited to friendship with him than I am.

And in the long letter that he wrote on this Sunday morning he did indeed inform his friend of the engagement that had taken place with the following words: "The best news I have saved for the end. I've become engaged to a Fräulein Frieda Brandenhof a girl from a well-to-do family who settled here only long after your departure whom you could thus hardly know. There will be opportunity later to tell you more about my bride, today let it be enough for you that I'm very happy and that in our mutual relationship something has changed only to the extent that you will now have in me instead of an entirely ordinary friend a happy one. In addition you get in my bride, who sends her warm regards and will soon write to you herself, a genuine fem. friend which for a bachel. is not entirely without significance. I know all sorts of things are holding you back from visiting us, but wouldn't my wedding be just the right occasion to cast aside all obstacles? But be that as it may, act without any regard and only as you think best."

With this letter in his hand G. had been sitting for a long time at his desk his face turned toward the window. To an acquaintance passing by and greeting him from the street he had barely responded with an absent smile.

Finally he put the letter in his pocket and went out of his room across a small corridor into his father's room, which he had not entered for months now. Nor was there generally any need to do so, for he had constant dealings with his father in the business, they had lunch at the same time in an eating house, at dinner, it was true, each of them provided for himself as he pleased, but usually, unless Georg as happened most often was together with friends or now visiting his bride, they sat for a little while in the evening each with his newspaper in the shared living room.

Georg was astonished at how dark his father's room was even on this sunny morning. So the high wall that rose on the other side of the narrow courtyard cast such a shadow. His father was sitting by the window in a corner decorated with various mementos of his late mother, and was reading the newspaper, which he held to the side in front of his eyes in an attempt to make up for some weakness of vision. On the table were the remains of his breakfast, not much of which seemed to have been consumed. Ah Georg said his father, immediately going to meet him.

His heavy dressing gown opened a little as he walked, the ends fluttered around him, my father is still a giant Georg said to himself. It's unbearably dark in here he then said. Yes it is dark replied his father. You've closed the window too?

I prefer it like this.

It's very warm outside said Georg as if in an addendum to his previous remark and sat down.

His father cleared away the breakfast dishes and put them on a cabinet.

I actually only wanted to tell you Georg went on, following the old man's movements in great perplexity, that I've now sent word of my engagement to St. Petersburg after all. He pulled the letter out of his pocket a little and let it fall back in again.

Why to St. Petersburg? asked his father.

To my friend of course said Georg, seeking his father's eyes. He's really completely different in the business he thought. The way he sits here spread out and crosses his arms over his chest.

Yes.—To your friend. his father said with emphasis.

You know Father, that I at first wanted to keep my engagement from him. Out of consideration, for no other reason. You yourself know, he's a difficult person. I said to myself, he might hear about my engagement from somewhere else, even if that's hardly likely with his solitary way of life—that I can't prevent—but from me myself he is simply not going to hear about it.

And now you've changed your mind? asked his father, laying the large newspaper on the windowsill and on the newspaper his glasses, which he covered with his hand.

Yes now I've changed my mind. If he is my good friend I said to myself then my happy engagement will make him happy too. And so I have no longer hesitated to inform him of it. But before I mailed the letter, I wanted to tell you.

Georg said his father, stretching his toothless mouth wide listen. You've come to me about this matter to consult me. That does you credit no doubt. But it's nothing, it's worse than nothing, if you don't tell me the whole truth now. I don't want to stir things up that aren't pertinent. Since the death of our dear mother certain unpleasant things have occurred. Perhaps the time is coming for them too and perhaps it's coming sooner than we think. In the business much escapes me, perhaps it's not concealed from me—I don't at all want to make the assumption now that it's concealed from me—I'm no longer strong enough, my memory is deteriorating, I can no longer keep track of all the many things. That is first of all the course of nature and secondly the death of our sweet mother has cast me down far more than you.—But because we're keeping to this matter at the moment, to this letter, I beg you Georg don't deceive me. It's a trifle, it's not worth the breath, so don't deceive me. Do you really have this friend in St. Petersburg?

Georg stood up in embarrassment. Never mind my friends. A thousand friends can't replace my father for me. Do you know what I think? You're not looking after yourself enough. But age demands its due. You're indispensable to me in the business, you know that very well, but if the business should threaten your health, I would close it tomorrow forever. This won't do. We have to introduce a new way of life for you. And I mean thoroughly. You sit here in the dark and in the living room you'd have beautiful light. You nibble at your breakfast instead of strengthening yourself properly. You sit by a closed window and the air would do you such good. No my father. I will fetch the doctor and we will follow his orders. We will exchange rooms, you will move into the front room, I here. It will be no change for you, everything will be brought over with you. But there's time for all that, now lie down a little in bed, you really need rest. Come I'll help you get undressed, you'll see, I can do it. Or do you want to go straight to the front room, then you can lie down in my bed for the time being. That would actually be very sensible.

Georg stood just next to his father, who had let his head with its shaggy white hair sink to his chest.

"Georg" his father said softly without moving.

Georg immediately knelt down beside his father, he saw the pupils in his father's weary face, overlarge in the corners of his eyes, directed at him.

You have no friend in St. Petersburg. You've always been a joker and unfortunately haven't held yourself back even with me. How could you have a friend there of all places. I simply can't believe it.

"Just think Father" said Georg, lifting his father from the chair and as he stood there now quite weakly, taking off his dressing gown. Now it will soon be three years ago that my friend visited us. I still remember that you were not especially fond of him. At least twice I denied to you that he was there even though he was sitting in my room. I could actually understand your aversion to him quite well, my friend has his peculiarities. But then you had a really good talk with him after all. I was so proud at the time that you listened to him, nodded and asked questions. If you think, you're bound to remember. That was when he told incredible stories of the Russian Revolution. How, for example, on a business trip in Kiev during a riot he had seen an Armenian priest on a balcony who cut a broad blood cross into the palm of his hand, raised this hand and appealed to the crowd. You yourself have even retold this story now and then.

Meanwhile Georg had managed to sit his father down again and to carefully take off the knitted pants he wore over his white underpants, as well as his socks. At the sight of the not particularly clean underwear, he reproached himself for having neglected his father. It would certainly have been his duty to watch over the changing of his father's underwear. He had not yet spoken explicitly with his bride about how they wanted to arrange his father's future, for they had tacitly presumed that his father would remain alone in the old apartment. But now he abruptly resolved with all firmness to take his father with him into his future household. On closer inspection it almost seemed that the care that would be given to his father there might come too late.

In his arms he carried his father to the bed. He had a terrible feeling when he noticed during the few steps to the bed that his father was playing with his watch chain. He couldn't lay him in the bed right away, so firmly did he cling to this watch chain

But no sooner was he in the bed than everything seemed good. He covered himself up and then pulled the blanket especially high over his shoulder. He looked up at Georg in a not unfriendly way.

You're beginning to remember him aren't you asked Georg, nodding encouragingly to him.

"Am I well covered now" asked his father as if he couldn't see whether his feet were sufficiently covered.

So you already like being in bed said Georg, tucking the covers better around him

Am I well covered up his father asked again and seemed to be waiting especially intently for the answer

Just rest peacefully, you're well covered up.

No his father cried so that the answer collided with the question, threw the cover back with such strength that for a moment it completely unfolded in mid-air, and stood upright in the bed, he held only one hand lightly against the ceiling. "You wanted to cover me up, I know that my little scamp but I'm not covered up yet. And even if it's my last strength, enough for you, too much for you. Certainly I know your friend. He would have been a son after my own heart. And that's why you've been deceiving him all these years. Why else? Do you think I haven't wept for him? That's why you lock yourself in your office, no one is to disturb, the boss is busy just so that you can write your false little letters to Russia. But fortunately no one has to teach the father to see through the son. When you thought you'd brought him down brought him so far down that you could sit on him with your behind and he wouldn't budge, that's when my fine son decided to get married.

Georg looked up at the horrible vision of his father. The St. Petersburg friend, whom his father suddenly knew so well, moved him as never before. He saw him lost in vast Russia. He saw him at the door of the empty plundered shop. He barely remained standing among the wreckage of the shelves, the shredded wares, the falling gas fixtures. Why had he had to go so far away.

But look at me his father cried and Georg ran almost distractedly to the bed to take everything in but came to a stop halfway.

Because she lifted her skirts his father began to flute because she lifted her skirts like this, the disgusting goose, and to portray it he lifted his shirt so high that one could see the scar from his war years on his thigh because she lifted her skirts like this and like this and like this, you made advances to her and so that you can take your pleasure with her undisturbed, you have desecrated our mother's memory, betrayed your friend and stuck your father in bed so that he can't move. But can he move or not?

And he stood completely free and kicked his legs. He was radiant with insight.

Georg stood in a corner, as far as possible from his father. A long while ago he resolved firmly to observe everything with complete precision so that he couldn't somehow be caught indirectly, from behind, from above. Now he remembered the long-forgotten resolution again and forgot it, as one pulls a short thread through the eye of a needle.

But now your friend isn't betrayed after all his father cried and his wagging index finger reinforced it. I was his local representative here.

"Playactor!" Georg couldn't help crying, immediately realized the damage done and with staring eyes he bit his tongue only too late, so that he doubled over in pain.

Yes indeed I've been playacting. Playacting, good word. What other comfort remained for the old widowed father. Tell me—and for the moment of the answer still be my living son—what remained for me in my back room, plagued by a disloyal staff old to the marrow of my bones. And my son went through the world in jubilation, closed business deals that I had prepared, tumbled over himself with pleasure and walked away from his father with the reserved face of a man of honor. Do you think I didn't love you, I, from whom you came.

Now he will bend forward thought Georg. If he fell and shattered! These words hissed through his head.

His father bent forward, but didn't fall. Since Georg didn't approach, as he had expected, he straightened up again.

Stay where you are, I don't need you. You think you still have the strength to come here and are merely holding yourself back because you want to. Don't be mistaken. I'm still the much stronger one. Alone I might have had to retreat, but as it is your mother has given me her strength, with your friend I've formed a splendid alliance, your customers I have here in my pocket.

Even in his shirt he has pockets Georg said to himself, and believed that with this remark he could discredit him with the whole world. Only for a moment did he think so for he kept forgetting everything.

Just link arms with your bride and come toward me. I'll sweep her from your side, you don't know how.

Georg made grimaces, as if he didn't believe it. His father merely nodded affirming the truth of what he said, toward Georg's corner.

How you amused me today when you came and asked whether you should write to your friend about the engagement. He knows everything, stupid boy, he knows everything. I write to him, because you forgot to take my writing things away from me. That's why he hasn't come for years now, he knows everything a hundred times better than you yourself do. He crumples your letters unread in his left hand while in his right he holds up my letters to read.

In his enthusiasm he swung his arm over his head.

He knows everything a thousand times better cried his father.

Ten thousand times said Georg, to ridicule his father, but while still in his mouth the words took on a deadly serious tone.

"For years I've been waiting for you to come with this question. Do you think I care about anything else, do you think I read newspapers. Here!" And he threw him a newspaper sheet that had somehow been carried with him into the bed. An old newspaper with a name completely unknown to Georg.

How long you hesitated before you reached maturity. Your mother had to die, she couldn't live to see the joyful day, your friend is going to ruin in his Russia, 3 years ago he was already yellow enough to be thrown away, and I, well, you see how I'm doing. For that you have eyes.

So you've been lying in wait for me! cried Georg.

Pityingly his father said in passing: You probably wanted to say that earlier. It isn't even appropriate anymore

And louder: So now you know what else there was besides you, until now you knew only of yourself! You were truly an innocent child, but even more truly you were a devilish human being!

"And therefore know, I sentence you now to death by drowning!"

Georg felt himself cast out of the room, the crash with which his father collapsed behind him onto the bed he still carried away in his ears. On the staircase, hurrying down the steps as if down a flat slope, he took his cleaning woman by surprise on her way up to tidy the apartment after the night. "Jesus!" she cried, covering her face with her apron, but he was already gone. He leaped out the front door, was driven across the road to the water. Already he clung to the railing like a hungry man to food. He swung himself over, like the outstanding gymnast he had been in his youthful years to his parents' pride. Still he held on with weakening hands, spied through the bars of the railing an auto-omnibus, which would easily muffle the sound of his fall, cried softly, "dear parents I did always love you" and let himself fall.

At that moment a positively endless stream of traffic was going over the bridge.

---

23 *(September 1912)* This story "The Judgment" I wrote at one stretch on the night of the 22 to the 23 from 10 o'clock in the evening until 6 o'clock in the morning. My legs had grown so stiff from sitting that I could hardly pull them out from under the desk. The terrible strain and joy, how the story unfolded itself before me how I moved forward in an expanse of water. Several times last night I bore my weight on my back. How everything can be risked, how for all, for the strangest ideas a great

fire is prepared, in which they die away and rise again. How it turned blue outside the window. A carriage passed. Two men walked across the bridge.[590] At 2 o'clock I looked for the last time at the clock. As the maid walked through the hall for the first time, I wrote down the last sentence. Putting out the lamp and daylight. The slight heart pains. The tiredness passing away in the middle of the night. The trembling entrance into my sisters' room. Reading aloud. Beforehand stretching in front of the maid and saying: "I've been writing until now." The appearance of the untouched bed, as if it had just been carried in. The confirmed conviction that with my novel writing I am in disgraceful lowlands of writing. Only in this way can writing be done, only with such cohesion, with such complete opening of the body and the soul. Morning in bed. The always clear eyes. Many feelings carried along during the writing: for example, the joy that I will have something beautiful for Max's Arcadia,[591] thoughts of Freud naturally,[592] at one passage of Arnold Beer,[593] at another of Wassermann,[594] at one (shatter) of Werfel's Riesin,[595] naturally also of my "The Urban World"[596]

I, only I am the observer of the ground floor.

Gustav Blenkelt was a simple man with regular habits. He didn't like any extravagance and was certain in his judgment toward people who indulged in such extravagance. Although he was a bachelor, he felt himself entirely justified in having a decisive say in marital affairs of his acquaintances, and anyone who even cast doubt on such a justification would have fared badly with him. He was wont to express his opinion openly and never held back listeners whom his opinion didn't suit at the moment. As everywhere there were people who admired him, people who respected him, people who tolerated him and finally those who wanted nothing to do with him. Indeed every person even the most negligible if one only takes a proper look forms the center of a circle that is twisted together here and there, how could it have been different in the case of Gustav Blenkelt at bottom an especially sociable person?

In his 35th year the last year of his life he associated especially frequently with a young married couple named Strong. It's certain that for Herr Strong, who had just opened a furniture store with his wife's money, being acquainted with Blenkelt had various advantages, since the latter had the bulk of his acquaintances among young marriageable people, who sooner or later had to think about acquiring new furniture for themselves and who out of sheer habit generally didn't neglect Blenkelt's advice in this respect either. I keep them on tight reins Blenkelt was wont to say.[597]

---

24 *(September 1912)* My sister said: The apartment (in the story)[598] is very similar to ours. I said: how so? Then the father would have to be living in the water closet.

---

25 *(September 1912)* Restrained myself by force from writing. Rolled in bed. The congestion of blood in the head and the useless flowing by. What harmfulness!—Yesterday read at Baum's,[599] to the Baums,[600] my sisters,[601] Marta,[602] Frau Dr. Bloch with 2 sons[603] (one of them a one-year volunteer). Toward the end my hand moved around uncontrollably and genuinely before my face. I had tears in my eyes. The indubitableness of the story was confirmed.—This evening tore myself away from writing. Cinematograph at the National Theater.[604] Box. Frl. Oplatka,[605] whom a priest once pursued. She came home soaked in a cold sweat. Danzig. Körner's life. The horses. The white horse. The powder smoke. Lützow's Wild Hunt.

As the 17-year-old[606] Karl Rossmann, who had been sent by his poor parents to America because a maid had seduced him and had a child by him, entered the harbor of Newyork on the now slow-moving ship, he saw the long-observed statue of the goddess of liberty as if in a suddenly more intense sunlight. Her arm with the sword rose as if newly and around her figure blew the free winds.

"So high" he said to himself and, not thinking at all of leaving, was gradually pushed to the railing by the constantly swelling crowd of porters moving past him.

A young man with whom he had become casually acquainted on the voyage said as he passed: Well don't you feel like getting off yet? "Oh yes, I'm ready" said Karl, laughing at him, and in his exuberance and because he was a strong boy, lifted his suitcase onto his shoulder. But glancing over his acquaintance, who, swinging his cane a little, was now moving away with the others, he realized that he had forgotten his umbrella down in the ship. He quickly asked his acquaintance, who didn't seem very pleased, to be so kind as to wait for a moment with his suitcase, quickly surveyed his surroundings in order to find his bearings on his return and hurried away. Down below, to his dismay, he found a passage that would have considerably shortened his way barred for the first time, which probably had to do with all the passengers disembarking, and he had to find his way laboriously through countless little rooms, perpetually branching corridors, short flights of steps, which, however, kept following each other an empty room with an abandoned desk, until, since he had gone this way only once or twice and always in the company of others, he was indeed utterly lost. In his perplexity and having met no one and heard only the constant scraping of the thousand human feet over him and noticed from a distance like a breath the last workings of the now shut-off engine, he began without thinking to bang on a little door at which he happened to stop in his wandering. "It's open" called a voice from inside and with a genuine sigh of relief Karl opened the door. "Why are you banging so madly on the door?" asked a huge man, barely looking at Karl. Through some skylight hatch a dim light, long since expended up above on the ship, fell into the pitiful cabin, in which a bed, a wardrobe, a chair and the man stood closely side by side as if stored there. "I'm lost" said Karl "I never quite realized it during the voyage but it's a terribly big ship." "Yes you're right about that" said the man with some pride and didn't stop fiddling with the lock of a small suitcase, which he kept pressing shut with both hands in order to listen to the bolt snapping into place. "But do come in" the man went on "you're not just going to stand outside." Am I not disturbing you, asked Karl. "Oh how could you disturb me." "Are you a German?" Karl sought to reassure himself, for he had heard a lot about the dangers that threaten newcomers in America, especially from Irishmen. "I am, I am" said the man. Karl still hesitated. Then the man unexpectedly grabbed the door handle, and with the door, which he quickly closed, pushed Karl in with him. "I can't stand it when people look in at me from the corridor" said the man, who was again working on his suitcase. "Everyone runs by here and looks in, I'd like to see anyone bear it." "But the corridor is completely empty" said Karl, who stood there squeezed uncomfortably against the bedpost. "Yes, now" said the man. "But we're talking about now" thought Georg "it's hard to speak with this man." "Why don't you lie down on the bed, you'll have more room there," said the man. Karl crawled in as well as he could, laughing out loud at his first unsuccessful attempt to swing himself over. But no sooner was he in there than he cried "For God's sake, I've forgotten all about my suitcase." "Where is it, then?" "Up on the deck, an acquaintance is keeping an eye on it. What's his name again?" And from a secret pocket his mother had attached to the lining of his coat for the voyage he pulled a visiting card. Butterbaum, Franz Butterbaum. "Do you really need the suitcase?" "Of course." "Well then why did you give it to a stranger?" "I'd forgotten my umbrella down below and ran to get it, but didn't want to drag along the suitcase. And then I got lost." "You're alone? Unaccompanied." "Yes, alone." Perhaps I should stick with this man, it occurred to Karl, where am I going to find a better friend anytime soon. "And now you've lost the suitcase too. Not to mention the umbrella" and the man sat down on the chair as if Karl's affair had now begun to interest him somewhat. "But I believe the suitcase is not yet lost." "Blessed are those who believe" said the man, vigorously scratching his dark short thick hair. On the ship the morals change with the ports, in Hamburg your Butterbaum might have watched the suitcase, here there's most likely not a trace left of either of them. "But then I must go up and see immediately" said Karl, looking around for a way out. "Just stay" said the man and with one hand against his chest pushed him downright roughly back into the bed. But why Karl asked with annoyance. Because there's no sense in it said the man. In a little while I'll be leaving too, then we'll leave together. Either the suitcase has been stolen, then there's nothing to be done and you can mourn it to the end of your days or the man is still watching it, then he's an idiot and should go on watching or he's just an honest man and has left the suitcase where it was then we'll find it all the more easily once the ship is completely emptied out. And the same goes for your umbrella. Do you know your way around the ship? Karl asked mistrustfully and it seemed to him as if there were a hidden hitch in the otherwise convincing idea that his things would be easiest to find on the empty ship. I am a ship's stoker after all said the man. You're a ship's stoker Karl cried joyfully, as if this exceeded all expectations, and propped up on his elbow took a closer look at the man. "Just outside the small room where I slept with the Slovaks there was a hatch in the wall through which one could see into the engine room." "Yes, that's where I've been working" said the stoker. "I've always been so interested in technology" said Karl, pursuing a particular train of thought "and I would certainly have become an engineer later on if I hadn't had to leave for America." "Why did you have to leave, then?" "Oh, never mind that!" said Karl, casting the whole story away with his hand. At the same time he looked at the stoker with a smile, as if begging his indulgence even for what he hadn't confessed. There must have been a reason said the stoker and one wasn't quite sure whether he meant by this to demand or fend off the telling of this reason. "Now I could become a stoker too" said Karl "my parents don't care at all now what I become." "My job will be available" said the stoker, and in full consciousness of that fact he put his hands in his pants pockets and flung his legs, which were clad in wrinkled, leather-like, iron-gray pants, onto the bed to stretch them. Karl had to move closer to the wall. "You're leaving the ship?" "That's right, we're marching off today." "But why? Don't you like it?" Well, it's just the way things are, it's not always a matter of whether one likes it or not. Besides you're right I don't like it either. You probably aren't resolved to become a stoker, but that's just when it's easiest to become one. So I strongly advise you against it. If you wanted to study in Europe, then why don't you want to do the same here. After all, the American universities are incomparably better." "That's certainly possible, said Karl, but I have barely any money for studying. I did read about someone who worked in a shop during the day and studied at night until he became a doctor and I believe mayor. But that takes great perseverance, doesn't it? I'm afraid I lack that. Besides I was never an especially good student, leaving school really wasn't hard for me. And the schools here might be even stricter. I hardly know any English at all. On the whole people here are so prejudiced against foreigners, I believe." "Have you found that out already too? Well, then it's all right. Then you're my man. You see, we're on a German ship, it belongs to the Hamburg America line, why aren't we all Germans here? Why is the chief engineer a Romanian? His name is Schubal. It's incredible. And that dirty dog slave-drives us Germans on a German ship. Don't think—he ran out of breath, he made a fluttering movement with his hand—that I'm complaining for the sake of complaining. I know that you have no influence and are a poor boy yourself. But it's too awful." And he pounded on the table several times with his fist, not taking his eye off it as he pounded. I have served on so many ships—and he mentioned 20 names one after another as if it were one word, Karl grew quite confused—and have distinguished myself, have been praised, was a worker to the taste of my captains, I was even on the same merchant sailing vessel for several years he rose as if that had been the high point of his life—and here on this tub, where everything is done according to the rules, where no wit is required—here I'm good for nothing, here I'm always in Schubal's way, I'm a slacker deserve to be thrown out and am given my pay out of mercy. Do you understand that? I don't." "You mustn't put up with that" Karl said excitedly. He had almost lost the sense that he was on the unsteady ground of a ship on the coast of an unknown continent, so at home did he feel here on the stoker's bed. "Have you been to the captain yet? Have you appealed to him for your rights?" "Oh go away, just go. I don't want you here. You don't listen to what I say and then give me advice. How am I supposed to go to the captain." And wearily the stoker sat down again and buried his face in both hands. "There's no better advice I can give him" Karl said to himself. And on the whole it seemed to him that he should have fetched his suitcase rather than give advice here that was only considered stupid. When his father had handed the suitcase over to him forever, he had asked in jest: How long will you have it? and now that expensive suitcase was perhaps already lost in earnest. The only remaining consolation was that his father couldn't find out the least thing about his present situation, even if he were to make inquiries. All the shipping company could say was that he had reached Newyork. But Karl was sorry that he had hardly used the belongings in the suitcase yet, even though, for example, he would have needed to change his shirt a long time ago. So he had economized in the wrong place; now just at the beginning of his career when he would need to present himself cleanly dressed, he would have to appear in a dirty shirt. Those were beautiful prospects. Otherwise, the loss of the suitcase wouldn't have been so bad, for the suit he had on was even better than the one in the suitcase, which was actually only an emergency suit, which his mother had had to mend just before his departure. Now he also remembered that there was still a piece of Veronese salami in the suitcase, which his mother had packed for him as a special treat but of which he had been able to eat only the smallest portion, since he'd had no appetite at all during the voyage and the soup distributed in the steerage had been plenty for him. But now he would have liked to have the sausage at hand to offer as a gift to the stoker. For such people are easily won over when one slips them some trifle, Karl knew that from his father, who won over all the lower employees with whom he had business dealings by distributing cigars. All that Karl had left to give away now was his money, and if he had perhaps already lost his suitcase, he didn't want to touch that for the time being. Again his thoughts returned to the suitcase and now he really couldn't understand why he had kept such close watch over the suitcase during the voyage that the watch had almost cost him his sleep, if he had now let this same suitcase be taken away from him so easily. He remembered the five nights during which he had incessantly suspected a little Slovak, who slept two places to his left, of being after his suitcase. This Slovak had just been waiting for Karl finally overcome by weakness to doze off for a moment so that he could use a long rod, with which he was always playing or practicing during the day, to pull the suitcase over to him. By day this Slovak looked innocent enough, but no sooner had night come than he rose every so often from his bed and looked sadly over at Karl's suitcase. Karl could make this out quite clearly, for there was always someone here or there who with the restlessness of the emigrant had lit a small light, even though this was prohibited by the ship's regulations and was trying to decipher the incomprehensible brochures of the emigration agencies. If such a light was nearby, then Karl could doze a little, but if it was far away or if the room was dark, then he had to keep his eyes open. The strain of this had really exhausted him. And now it had perhaps been completely in vain. That Butterbaum, if he should ever meet him somewhere.

At that moment the silence outside, until then complete, was broken by the distant sound of short little taps like the patter of children's feet, they grew louder as they approached and now it was a steady march of men. They were evidently walking in a line, as was natural in the narrow corridor, one could hear clanking like that of weapons. Karl who had been on the verge of stretching out in the bed for a sleep freed of all worries about suitcases and Slovaks, gave a start and nudged the stoker in order to draw his attention at last, for the head of the procession seemed to have just reached the door. "That's the ship's band said the stoker. They were playing up above and are going to pack up. Now everything's finished and we can go. Come on." He seized Karl by the hand, took at the last moment a picture of the Mother of God from the wall over the bed, stuffed it into his breast pocket, grabbed his suitcase and hurriedly left the cabin with Karl.

Now I'm going to the office and will give the gentlemen a piece of my mind. There's no one left here, one needn't show any consideration the stoker repeated in various ways, and as he walked he kicked sideways, trying to crush underfoot a rat crossing his path, but merely driving it more quickly into the hole, which it had reached just in time. On the whole he was slow in his movements, for even though he had long legs, they were too heavy.

They passed through a section of the kitchen where some girls in dirty aprons—they splashed them intentionally—were washing dishes in large tubs. The stoker called a certain Line over to him put his arm around her hip and, while she kept pressing herself coquettishly against his arm, led her along for a short stretch. "It's time to get paid now, do you want to come along?" he asked. "Why should I bother just bring me the money." she replied, slipped out from under his arm and ran away. "Where did you pick up the beautiful boy" she called, but didn't wait for an answer. One could hear the laughter of all the girls, who had stopped their work.

But they walked on and came to a door, at the top of which was a small front gable borne by small gilded caryatids. For a ship's fixture it looked rather extravagant. Karl realized he had never entered this area, which had probably been reserved for the first- and second-class passengers during the voyage, whereas now before the great cleaning of the ship the dividing doors had been taken off their hinges. Indeed they had already encountered some men carrying brooms on their shoulders, who had greeted the stoker. Karl marveled at the great bustle, in his steerage he had certainly witnessed little of this. Wires of electric lines also ran along the corridors, and one constantly heard a small bell.

The stoker knocked respectfully on the door and, when someone shouted come in, gestured to Karl with his hand to enter without fear. He did enter, but remained standing at the door. Outside the room's three windows he saw the waves of the sea and as he contemplated their cheerful movement his heart pounded as if he had not been looking uninterruptedly at the sea for five long days. Great ships crossed each other's paths and yielded to the rising and falling waves only as far as their heaviness permitted. If one narrowed one's eyes, these ships seemed to be rocking from sheer heaviness. On their masts they bore narrow but long flags that, though tautened by the ships' motion, still wriggled back and forth. Gun salutes rang out, probably from warships, one such ship passed not too far away and its cannon barrels radiant with the reflection from their steel casing were as if caressed by the ship's sure, smooth and yet not horizontal motion. At least from the door one could observe the small ships and boats only in the distance, entering in droves the gaps between the large ships. But behind all this stood Newyort, looking at Karl with the hundred thousand windows of its skyscrapers. Yes in this room one knew where one was.

At a round table sat 3 gentlemen, one of them a ship's officer in a blue ship's uniform, the other two, officials of the harbor authority, in black American uniforms. Piled high on the table were various documents, which the officer first skimmed with pen in hand, then passed to the other two, who now read them, now made excerpts, now put them in their briefcases, unless one of them, almost uninterruptedly making little noises with his teeth, dictated something for his colleague to take down.

At a desk by the window, his back to the door sat a smaller gentleman who was busy with large folios that were lined up in front of him on a sturdy bookshelf at head level. Next to him stood an open cash box, which at least at first glance appeared empty.

The second window was empty and offered the best view. Near the third, however, stood two gentlemen conversing in low voices. One of them was leaning beside the window, also wearing the ship's uniform and playing with the handle of his sword. The man with whom he spoke was facing the window, and now and then one of his movements exposed part of the row of decorations on the other's chest. He was in civilian clothes and had a thin bamboo cane, which, since he had set both hands firmly on his hips, also stuck out like a sword.

Karl didn't have much time to look at everything, for soon a servant approached them and asked the stoker, giving him a look as if he didn't belong here, what it was he wanted. The stoker answered as softly as he had been asked that he wanted to speak with the chief purser. The servant for his part rejected this request with a hand movement, but nonetheless walked on tiptoe giving the round table a wide berth to the gentleman with the folios. This gentleman, one could see it clearly, positively stiffened at the servant's words, but finally turned around to face the man who wished to speak with him, then waved in a sternly dismissive manner at the stoker and for safety's sake at the servant too. Thereupon the servant returned to the stoker and said in a tone as if he were confiding something to him: "Get out of the room at once!"

After this response the stoker looked down at Karl, as if the latter were his heart to which he was silently pouring out his sorrow. Without further reflection Karl broke free, ran straight across the room, even lightly brushing against the officer's chair, the servant ran stooped with his arms prepared to clasp, as if he were chasing vermin, but Karl was the first to reach the chief purser's desk, to which he clung in case the servant should try to pull him away.

Naturally the whole room immediately came to life. The ship's officer at the table had jumped up, the gentlemen from the harbor authority watched calmly but intently, the two gentlemen by the window now stood abreast, the servant, believing he was out of place where his masters themselves showed an interest, stepped back. The stoker at the door waited tensely for the moment when his help would be needed. The chief purser finally made a great turn to the right in his armchair.

Karl rummaged in his secret pocket, which he had no qualms about revealing to these people's eyes, and pulled out his passport, which in lieu of further introduction he laid down open on the desk. The chief purser seemed to consider this passport irrelevant, for he flicked it aside with two fingers, whereupon Karl, as if this formality had been satisfactorily completed, put the passport back in his pocket. "I take the liberty of saying, he then began, that in my opinion injustice has been done to the Herr Stoker. There is here a certain Schubal who is giving him trouble. He himself has served to complete satisfaction on many ships, all of which he can name for you, is industrious, applies himself to his work and it's really incomprehensible why on this ship in particular, where the duties aren't as excessively onerous as, for example, on merchant sailing vessels, he should be inadequate. It can therefore only be slander that hinders him in his advancement and deprives him of the recognition he would otherwise most certainly not be denied. I've spoken only in general terms about this matter, his specific complaints he will present to you himself." Karl had addressed all the gentlemen with this matter because indeed all were listening, and it seemed far more likely that among all of them together a just man would be found than that this just man should be the chief purser in particular. Out of shrewdness Karl had also concealed the fact that he had known the stoker for only such a short time. Moreover, he would have spoken far better still if he hadn't been disconcerted by the red face of the gentleman with the bamboo cane, whom he saw for the very first time from where he was now standing.

"Every word of it is correct" said the stoker, before anyone had even asked him, indeed before they had so much as looked at him. This overhastiness on the stoker's part would have been a big mistake, if the gentleman with the decorations, who as it now dawned on Karl was definitely the captain, had not apparently already made up his mind to listen to the stoker. For he held out his hand and called to the stoker: Come here! in a voice firm enough to strike with a hammer. Now everything depended on the stoker's behavior, for as far as the justice of his cause was concerned, Karl had no doubt.

Fortunately it became clear at this juncture that the stoker had seen a great deal of the world. With exemplary calm he took out of his small suitcase at the first attempt a small bundle of papers as well as a notebook, then as if it were a matter of course walked with these to the captain while completely ignoring the chief purser and spread his evidence out on the windowsill. The chief purser had no choice but to make his way there. "The man is a notorious complainer" he said by way of explanation "he's in the purser's office more than in the engine room. He has driven Schubal that calm person to complete despair." "Now you listen!" he addressed the stoker "You're really pushing your importunity too far. How many times have you been thrown out of the disbursement rooms by now, just as you deserve with your wholly, completely and invariably unjustified demands! How many times have you come running here to the main purser's office from there! How many times have you been told kindly that Schubal is your immediate superior and it's with him alone that you as his subordinate must come to terms! And now you even come here when the Herr Captain is present, not only aren't ashamed to pester even him, but also have the effrontery to bring along as the trained spokesman of your tasteless accusations this little fellow, whom I'm seeing on the ship for the very first time."

Karl forcibly held himself back from jumping forward. But then the captain was already there, saying "Let's just listen to the man. Lately Schubal has been growing far too independent for my liking anyhow, though by this I don't mean to imply anything in your favor." The last remark was directed at the stoker, it was only natural that he couldn't take his side immediately, but everything seemed to be going in the right direction. The stoker began his explanations and at the very outset brought himself to refer to Schubal as Herr. How happy Karl was by the chief purser's abandoned desk, where he kept pushing down a letter scale in sheer pleasure. Herr Schubal is unjust. Herr Schubal favors the foreigners. Herr Schubal banished the stoker from the engine room and made him clean toilets, which certainly wasn't the stoker's job. Once doubt was even cast on Herr Schubal's capability, which was said to be more apparent than real. At this point Karl stared with all his might at the captain, trustingly as if he were his colleague, just so that he would not be influenced unfavorably by the stoker's somewhat awkward manner of expression. All the same, one learned nothing substantial from his many speeches and even though the captain kept looking straight ahead, his eyes revealing his determination to hear the stoker out this time, the other gentlemen were growing impatient and the stoker's voice soon no longer reigned absolutely in the room, which was cause for some fear. First the gentleman in civilian clothes set his bamboo cane in motion, tapping though only softly on the parquet floor. The other gentlemen naturally looked over now and then, the gentlemen from the harbor authority, apparently pressed for time, reached for their files again and began, even if still somewhat absentmindedly to look through them, the ship's officer moved closer to his table again and the chief purser, believing he had won the day, heaved a deep ironic sigh. The only one who seemed unaffected by the distraction generally setting in was the servant, who sympathized to some extent with the woes of the poor man placed among the great ones and nodded gravely to Karl as if trying to explain something.

Meanwhile the life of the harbor went on outside the windows, a flat cargo ship with a mountain of barrels, which must have been wonderfully stowed for them not to start rolling, passed by and plunged the room almost into darkness, small motor boats, which Karl could have examined closely now if he'd had time roared away in a straight line in accordance with the twitches of the hands of a man standing upright at the helm, peculiar floating objects emerged now and then of their own accord from the restless water, were immediately submerged again and sank before one's astonished eyes, boats of the ocean steamers were rowed forward by furiously working sailors and were full of passengers who sat in them quietly and expectantly just as they had been squeezed in, even though some of them couldn't refrain from turning their heads toward the changing scenery. A movement without end, a restlessness passed on from the restless element to the helpless people and their works.

But everything urged haste, clarity, completely precise description, but what was the stoker doing? He was certainly talking himself into a sweat, he had long been unable to hold the papers on the window with his trembling hands, from all points of the compass complaints about Schubal streamed toward him, every single one of which in his opinion would have sufficed to bury that Schubal completely, but what he could show the captain was only a sad jumble of all of them whirled together. For a long time now the gentleman with the bamboo cane had been whistling faintly up at the ceiling, the gentlemen from the harbor authority had been holding the officer at their table and showed no sign of ever letting go of him again, the chief purser was visibly held back only by the captain's calm from the intervention he was itching to make. The servant was standing at attention, waiting for his captain's command regarding the stoker at any moment.

At this point Karl could no longer remain idle. And so he walked slowly toward the group and while walking considered all the more quickly how he could tackle the matter as skillfully as possible. It was really high time, just a little while longer and both of them could quite easily be thrown out of the office. The captain certainly might be a good man and moreover might now of all times, as it seemed to Karl, have a special reason to show himself to be a just superior, but in the end he was not an instrument that one could play to its ruin—and that was exactly how the stoker was treating him, albeit out of his boundless inner indignation.

And so Karl said to the stoker "You must tell the story more simply, more clearly, the Herr Captain can't appreciate it the way you're telling it to him. Is he supposed to know all the engineers and errand boys by name, or even by their Christian names, so that you need only utter one of these names for him to know immediately whom you mean. Organize your complaints, say the most important first and the others in descending order then perhaps it will no longer be necessary at all even to mention most of them. You've always described it to me so clearly." If one can steal suitcases in America, one can also lie now and then, he thought by way of excuse.

But if only it had helped! Might it not already be too late? The stoker did break off immediately when he heard the familiar voice, but with his eyes, which were completely obscured by tears, of offended manly honor, of terrible memories, of extreme present distress, he could hardly even recognize Karl anymore. How should he now, Karl came to this realization silently before the now silent man, how should he now suddenly change his manner of speaking, when it seemed to him, after all, as if he had already brought up everything there was to say without the slightest acknowledgment and on the other hand as if he had said nothing at all yet and certainly couldn't now expect the gentlemen to listen to everything from the beginning. And at a moment like this Karl his sole supporter comes along, wanting to give him good advice, but instead shows him that all all is lost.

If only I had come sooner instead of looking out the window Karl said to himself, lowering his face before the stoker and slapping his hands against the seams of his pants as a sign of the end of all hope.

But the stoker misunderstood this, probably scenting in Karl some secret reproaches against him and with the good intention of talking him out of them he now crowned his deeds by beginning to quarrel with Karl. Now, when the gentlemen at the round table had long since grown indignant at the useless noise disturbing their important work, when the chief purser was gradually finding the captain's patience incomprehensible and was on the verge of an outburst, when the servant once again completely in the sphere of his masters was measuring the stoker with a wild look and when finally the gentleman with the bamboo cane, at whom even the captain occasionally cast a friendly glance having become entirely deadened to the stoker indeed disgusted by him, pulled out a small notebook and evidently preoccupied with completely different matters let his eyes wander back and forth between the notebook and Karl.

Yes I know, I know said Karl who was having difficulty fending off the torrent the stoker was now directing at him, but through all the quarreling could still spare a friendly smile for him. You're right, you're right, I've never once doubted it. He would have liked to hold his gesticulating hands for fear of being struck, though he would have liked even more to drive him into a corner and whisper a few soft soothing words to him, which no one else would have to hear. But the stoker was out of control. Karl now even began to draw a sort of consolation from the thought that if need be the stoker could vanquish all seven men present with the strength of his despair. To be sure, the desk as a glance in that direction revealed had an upper part with far too many push buttons of the electric line, and one hand, simply pressed down on them, could incite the whole ship with all its corridors filled with hostile people to rebellion.

Now the gentleman with the bamboo cane, who had been so uninterested, approached Karl and asked not too loudly, but clearly over all the stoker's shouting: What's your name anyway? At that moment, as if someone behind the door had been waiting for the gentleman to say these words there was a knock. The servant looked over at the captain, the latter nodded. And so the servant went to the door and opened it. Outside stood a man of medium proportions in an old frock coat, judging by his appearance not actually suited to work on the engines and yet he was—Schubal. If Karl hadn't recognized this in everyone's eyes, which expressed a certain satisfaction, of which not even the captain was free, he would inevitably have seen it, to his horror, in the stoker, who clenched his fists on his tensed arms as if this clenching were the most important thing about him, for which he was prepared to sacrifice all the life he had. All his strength was now concentrated there, even that which held him upright.

And so here was the enemy free and fresh in festive attire, under his arm an account book, probably the stoker's wage lists and work records and, boldly admitting that he wanted above all to determine the mood of every single one of them he looked into everyone's eyes in turn. All seven were already his friends anyhow, for even if the captain had previously had or perhaps only feigned certain objections to him, after the suffering the stoker had inflicted on him, he could probably no longer find even the slightest fault with Schubal. Against a man like the stoker one couldn't proceed severely enough and if

(Continuation of the text on page 86)

Seventh Notebook

11 II 13 On the occasion of the correction of "The Judgment"[607] I'm writing down all the relationships that have become clear to me in the story, as far as I can recall them. This is necessary because the story came out of me like a veritable birth covered with filth and slime and only I have the hand that can penetrate to the body and has the desire to do so:

The friend is the connection between father and son, he is their greatest commonality. Sitting alone by his window Georg rummages voluptuously in this commonality, believes he has his father in himself and regards everything as peaceful but for a fleeting sad reflectiveness. The development of the story now shows how from the commonality, the friend, the father rises forth and sets himself up in opposition to Georg, strengthened by other lesser commonalities namely by the love, devotion of the mother by the faithful memory of her and by the customers, whom the father, after all, originally acquired for the business. Georg has nothing, the bride, who in the story lives only through her relationship to the friend, that is, to the commonality, and who, since there hasn't been a wedding yet, cannot enter the circle of blood drawn around father and son, is easily driven away by the father. All the commonality is heaped up around the father, Georg feels it only as something foreign that has become independent, that has never been protected enough by him, that is exposed to Russian revolutions, and only because he himself has nothing left but the sight of the father does the judgment, which closes off the father to him completely, have such a strong effect on him.

Georg has the same number of letters as Franz. In Bendemann

"mann" is only a strengthening of "Bende" for the sake of all the still unknown possibilities of the story. But Bende has exactly the same number of letters as Kafka and the vowel e is repeated in the same places as the vowel a in Kafka.

Frieda has exactly the same number of letters as Felice and the same initial letter, Brandenfeld has the same initial letter as Bauer and through the word "Feld" a certain connection in the meaning too.[608] Perhaps even the thought of Berlin was not without influence and the memory of the Mark Brandenburg was perhaps involved.[609]

12 II *(1913)* During the description of the friend in a foreign land I often thought of Steuer.[610] Now when I met him by chance about three months after this story, he told me that he had become engaged about three months ago.

After I read the story yesterday at Weltsch's, Weltsch's father[611] went out and, when he returned after a little while, praised especially the visual description in the story. With an outstretched hand he said: I see this father in front of me and at the same time he was looking exclusively at the empty chair in which he had been sitting during the reading.

My sister said: "It's our apartment." I was astonished at how she misunderstood the setting and said: "Then the father would have to be living in the water closet."

---

28 II *(1913)* Ernst Liman[612] arrived in Constantinople on a business trip in the morning of a rainy autumn day and, as was his habit—he was now taking this trip for the tenth time—rode without paying attention to anything else through the otherwise empty streets to the hotel where he always stayed to his satisfaction. It was almost cool, the drizzle flew into the carriage and annoyed about the bad weather, which had been pursuing him all through this year's business trip, he pulled up the carriage window and leaned into a corner to sleep through the roughly 15 minute carriage ride that lay ahead of him. But since the ride was taking him through the business quarter at the moment he got no rest and the cries of the street peddlers, the rolling of the heavily laden carts, as well as other noise, senseless without closer examination, for example, the hand-clapping of a crowd, disturbed his usually sound sleep.

At the destination of his ride, an unpleasant surprise awaited him. During the last great fire in Stambul, about which Liman had certainly read on the trip, the Hotel Kingston, where he was in the habit of staying, had almost completely burned down, but the coachman, who had naturally known this, had nonetheless, with complete indifference toward his passenger, carried out the latter's instructions and without a word brought him to the site of the hotel fire. Now he climbed down calmly from the coach box and would even have unloaded Liman's suitcases if the latter hadn't seized him by the shoulder and shaken him, whereupon the coachman then let go of the suitcases, to be sure, but as slowly and sleepily as if not Liman had diverted him from it but his own changed decision.

The ground floor of the hotel was still partly preserved and had been made tolerably habitable by boarding it up with wooden slats on top and on all sides. A Turkish and a French inscription indicated that in a short time the hotel would be rebuilt more beautiful and modern than before. Yet the only sign of that was the work of three day laborers, who with shovels and hooks were heaping up rubble to the side and loading a small handcart with it.

As it turned out, part of the hotel staff, put out of work by the fire, was living in these ruins. A gentleman in a black frock coat and bright red tie also came running out immediately when Liman's carriage had stopped, told Liman, who listened morosely, the story of the fire, winding the ends of his long thin beard around his fingers and desisting from this only to show Liman where the fire had started, how it had spread and how finally everything had collapsed. Liman who all through this story hardly averted his eyes from the ground and had not let go of the handle of the carriage door, was just about to shout to the coachman the name of another hotel to which he should take him when the man in the frock coat implored him with upraised arms not to go to another hotel but to remain faithful to this hotel, where he had, after all, always been satisfied. Although this was certainly only an empty phrase and no one could remember Liman, just as Liman recognized hardly any of the male and female employees he saw in the doorway and in the windows, he nonetheless asked, as a person who cherished his habits, in what way, then, he was supposed to remain faithful to the burned down hotel at the moment. Now he learned—and couldn't help smiling involuntarily at the effrontery—that for former guests of this hotel, but only for them, beautiful rooms had been prepared in private apartments, Liman need only give the order and he would immediately be brought there, it was quite close he wouldn't lose any time and out of courtesy and since it was, after all, a substitute the price was quite especially low, even though the food made from Viennese recipes was possibly even better and the service even more conscientious than in the former Hotel Kingston, which in some respects had actually been inadequate.

"Thank you" said Liman, as he climbed into the carriage. "I'm staying in Constantinople only 5 days, for this time I will not install myself in a private apartment, no I'm going to a hotel. But next year, when I come back and your hotel has been rebuilt, I will certainly stay only with you. Pardon me!" And Liman tried to close the carriage door, the handle of which the representative of the hotel had now grasped. "Sir!" the latter said imploringly, looking up at Liman.

"Let go!" Liman cried, shook the door and gave the coachman the order: "To the Hotel Royal." But whether it was that the coachman didn't understand him, whether it was that he was waiting for the door to be closed, in any case he sat on his box like a statue. The representative of the hotel, however, by no means let go of the door, indeed he even waved eagerly to his colleagues to get moving and come to his aid. From some girl in particular he hoped for much and kept shouting "Fini! hey Fini! Where's Fini?" The people at the windows and in the doorway had turned toward the inside of the house, they were all shouting at the same time, one saw them running past the windows all of them were looking for Fini

Liman might well have been able to get the man who was preventing him from leaving and whom obviously only hunger gave the courage to behave like this off the door with a push,—the man realized this too and therefore didn't even dare to look at Liman—but Liman had already had too many bad experiences on his trips not to know how important it is, however much one might be in the right, to avoid causing any stir in a foreign land, he therefore calmly climbed out of the carriage again, for the time being disregarded the man, who was tenaciously holding the door, went to the coachman, repeated to him his instructions, explicitly adding the order to drive away from here quickly, then walked up to the man at the carriage door, grabbed his hand apparently with an ordinary grip, but secretly squeezed the wrist so hard that with the cry "Fini" which was at once a command and an outburst of his pain the man almost jumped up and removed his fingers from the handle.

"She's coming! She's coming!" came the shouts now from all the windows and a laughing girl with her hands still on her hair, which she had just finished fixing, ran with half bowed head out of the house toward the carriage. "Quick! Into the carriage! It's pouring" she cried, grasping Liman by the shoulders and holding her face very close to his. "I'm Fini" she then said softly and let her hands run caressingly along his shoulders.

"They really bear me no particular ill will" Liman said to himself and looked at the girl with a smile "too bad that I'm no longer a boy and don't let myself in for unsafe adventures." "There must be a mistake, Fräulein" he said, turning to his carriage "I neither had you called, nor do I intend to ride away with you." From the carriage he added: Don't trouble yourself further.

But Fini had already set a foot on the step and with her arms crossed over her chest she said: "Why won't you let me recommend an apartment to you?" Tired of the harassment he had already endured here, leaning out to her Liman said "Please don't detain me any longer with useless questions! I'm going to the hotel and that's all. Take your foot down from the step, or else you'll get into danger. Forward coachman!" "Stop" the girl cried, however, and now sought in earnest to swing herself into the carriage. Shaking his head, Liman stood up and blocked the whole door with his squat figure. The girl tried to push him away and even used her head and knees for this purpose, the carriage began to rock on its wretched springs, Liman could find no real handhold: Why won't you take me with you? Why won't you take me with you? the girl kept repeating. Certainly Liman would have managed to drive away the girl, strong though she was, without doing her particular violence if the man in the frock coat, who until now had behaved calmly as if he had been relieved by Fini, hadn't at this moment, when he saw Fini stagger, hurried over with a bound, held Fini from behind and, exerting all his strength, tried to lift the girl into the carriage against Liman's still gentle defense. Feeling this support, she actually penetrated the carriage, pulled the door shut at the same time as it was pushed shut from outside too, said as if to herself "Now then" and first hastily adjusted her blouse and then more thoroughly her hair. "This is unheard of" said Liman, who had fallen back onto his seat, to the girl sitting opposite him.

16 II 14

Useless day. The only joy I had was the hope, based on last night, for better sleep.

In the evening after closing time I was going home as usual when, as if I had been watched for, I was beckoned in a lively way from all three windows of the Genzmer apartment to come up.

22 II 14

Despite my head deprived of sleep (yesterday painter Dittrich,[613] a white-haired, black-eyed woman) and on the top left almost aching with restlessness, perhaps I am still capable of a calm construction of a larger whole, in which I could forget everything and be aware only of the good in me.

Director at his table. Servant brings a card.
D. Nitte again, he's a leech, the man is a leech.

---

23 II 14. I'm going.[614] Letter from Musil. Pleases me and makes me sad, for I have nothing.[615]

8 III 14 If F. has the same repugnance for me as I do, then a marriage is impossible. A prince can marry Little Briar Rose and even worse, but Little Briar Rose cannot be a prince.[616]

A young man rides on a beautiful horse out the gate of a villa.

When she died my grandmother happened to have only the nurse with her. The latter said that just before her death my grandmother had risen a little from the pillow, so that it appeared as if she were looking for someone, and that she had then lain back peacefully and died.[617]

Undoubtedly I am completely enclosed in an inhibition, with which I have, however, most certainly not grown together yet, the occasional loosening of which I notice and which can be burst. There are two means, marriage or Berlin, the second is surer, the first more immediately tempting.[618]

I dove under and soon found my way. A small school floated by in a rising chain and disappeared in the green. Bells borne back and forth by the drifting of the water—false

9 III 14

Rense walked a few steps through the dim corridor, opened the small concealed door of the dining room and said to the raucous gathering almost without looking: Please be a little quiet. I have a guest. I ask for some consideration. When he went back to his room and heard the unchanged noise, he hesitated for a moment, was about to go back again, but then changed his mind and returned to his room.

There a boy of about 18 years of age was standing by the window and looking down at the courtyard. It's quieter now he said as Rense entered, and lifted his long nose and his deep-set eyes to him. It's not quieter at all said Rense, taking a sip from the beer bottle standing on the table, one can never have peace and quiet here. You'll have to get used to that, boy[619]

I'm too tired, I must try to recover through sleep, or else I'm lost in every respect. What efforts to sustain oneself! No monument requires such an expenditure of strength to be erected.

The argument in general: I have lost myself to F.[620]

Rense, a student, was sitting in his small courtyard-facing room and studying. The maid came and announced that a young man wanted to speak with Rense. What's his name? asked Rense. The maid didn't know.

I won't forget F. here, therefore won't marry
Is that completely definite?
Yes, I can judge that, I'm almost 31 years old, have known F. for almost two years, so must have a general view by now. But aside from that my way of life here is such that I can't forget, even if F. had no such significance for me. The uniformity, regularity, comfort and dependence of my way of life hold me inescapably where I happen to be. Besides, I have a more than ordinary inclination toward a comfortable and dependent life, everything damaging is thus further strengthened by me. Finally, I am also aging, transformations become more and more difficult. But in all this I see a great unhappiness for me, which would be lasting and hopeless; I would drag myself along up the salary ladder and through the years and grow ever sadder and lonelier, as long as I could stand it at all
But didn't you want such a life for yourself?

The life of an official could be good for me, if I were married. It would give me good support in every respect in relation to society, to my wife, to writing, without demanding all too much sacrifice and without on the other hand degenerating into comfort and dependence, for as a married man I wouldn't have to be afraid of that. But as a bachelor I can't lead such a life to the end.
But couldn't you have married?

I couldn't marry at the time, everything in me revolted against it, much as I always loved F. It was mainly the consideration for my literary work that deterred me, for I believed this work to be endangered by marriage. I may have been right; but by bachelorhood within my present life it is annihilated. I have written nothing for a year, I can still write nothing, I have and keep in my head nothing but the one thought and it consumes me. At the time I couldn't weigh all this. Moreover, in my dependence, which is at least nourished by this way of life, I approach everything hesitantly and accomplish nothing at the first stroke. So it was here too.
Why do you give up all hope of getting F. after all?

I've already tried every self-humiliation. In the Tiergarten I once said: "Say "yes," even if you regard your feelings for me as insufficient for marriage, my love for you is great enough to compensate for the deficiency and in general strong enough to take everything on itself." F. seemed unsettled by my peculiarities, with which I'd frightened her in the course of a long correspondence. I said: "I love you enough to cast off anything that might bother you. I'll become a different person." Now, when everything must become clear, I can admit that even at the time of our warmest relationship I often had suspicions and fears, based on trifles, that F. doesn't love me very much, not with all the power of love of which she is capable. Now F., not without my help, to be sure, has realized it too. I'm almost afraid that after my last two visits F. even has a certain disgust for me, although we're outwardly friendly to each other, call each other Du, walk arm in arm. The last memory I have of her is the quite hostile grimace she made in the hall of her house when I didn't content myself with kissing her glove but tore it open and kissed her hand. Moreover, even though she had promised to be punctual in her further correspondence, now she hasn't answered two of my letters, has only promised letters by telegrams, but hasn't kept her promise, indeed she hasn't even so much as answered my mother. The hopelessness of this can therefore hardly be doubted.

One should actually never be permitted to say that. Didn't your previous behavior seem from F.'s point of view to be hopeless too.

That was something else. I always, even during the apparently final farewell in the summer, openly confessed my love for her; I was never so cruelly silent; I had reasons for my behavior that could be, if not approved, nonetheless discussed. F. has merely the reason of completely insufficient love. Still, it's correct that I could wait. To wait with a double hopelessness, however, is beyond my ability: first seeing F. slip ever farther away from me and in addition finding myself ever more unable to somehow escape. It would be the greatest risk I could take with myself, although or because it would most befit all the overpowering bad forces in me. "One can never know what will happen" is no argument in the face of the intolerability of a present state.

What do you want to do, then?

Leave Prague. Proceed against this most powerful human injury that has ever afflicted me with the most powerful means of reaction at my disposal.

Abandon your job?

Well, according to the above, the job is part of the intolerability. I'll be losing only something intolerable. The security, the calculation over a lifetime, the ample pay, the incomplete exertion of strength—those are all things, after all, with which I can do nothing as a bachelor, which turn into torments.

What do you want to do, then?

I could answer all such questions at once by saying: I have nothing to risk, every day and every slightest success is a gift, anything I do will be good. But I can also answer more precisely. As an Austrian lawyer, which in any serious sense I really am not at all, I have no prospects that are of use to me; the best I could attain for myself in this direction I possess, after all, in my position, and yet I can't use it. Moreover, in the event, in itself quite impossible, that I wanted to gain something for myself out of my legal education, only 2 cities would come into consideration: Prague which I must leave, and Vienna, which I hate and where I would surely be unhappy, for I would go there already having the deepest conviction of the necessity of it. Thus I must go outside of Austria and indeed, since I have no talent for languages and could do physical or commercial work only poorly, at least at first to Germany and there to Berlin, where there are the most possibilities to support oneself. There, in journalism, I can also best and most directly take advantage of my literary abilities and find a way of earning money that halfway suits me.[621] Whether I will perhaps be capable of inspired work beyond that too, on this subject I cannot express myself now with even the slightest confidence. But this I think I know for sure, that from this independent and free situation in which I will be in Berlin (however wretched it may otherwise be) I will draw the only feeling of happiness of which I am now still capable.

But you're spoiled

No, I need a room and vegetarian board, almost nothing else.

Aren't you going there because of F.

No, I choose Berlin only for the above reasons, though I love it too and perhaps I love it because of F. and because of the circle of associations around F.; that I can't control. It's also probable that I will meet F. in Berlin. If this togetherness will help me get F. out of my blood: so much the better, then it's a further advantage of Berlin.

Are you healthy?

No, heart, sleep, digestion

A small rented room. Dawn. Disorder. The student is lying in bed asleep, facing the wall. There's a knock. It remains silent. There's a louder knock. The student sits up in fright, looks at the door

Come in

Maid (frail girl): Good morning

St. What do you want? It's night.
M. Excuse me. A gentleman is asking for you
S. For me? (hesitates) Nonsense! Where is he?
M. He's waiting in the kitchen
S. What does he look like
M. (smiles) Well, he's still a boy, he's not very handsome, I think he's a Yid
S. And that's who wants to visit me at night? By the way, listen I don't need your judgment on my guests. And let him in. Now hurry!

The student stuffs the small pipe lying on the chair beside his bed and smokes.

Kleipe (stands at the door and looks at the student, who, his eyes turned toward the ceiling, puffs calmly away.)
(short, upright, a large, long, somewhat crooked, pointed nose, dark complexion, deep-set eyes, long arms)

St. How much longer? Come here to the bed and say what you want. Who are you? What do you want? Hurry! Hurry!
Kl. (walks very slowly to the bed and on the way tries to explain something with hand movements. He aids his speaking by stretching his neck and raising and lowering his eyebrows) As a matter of fact, I'm from Wulfenshausen too
S. Well; that's nice, that's very nice. Then why didn't you stay there?
Kl. Think about it! It's the hometown of both of us, nice, but still a wretched hole.

It was a Sunday afternoon, they were lying intertwined in bed. It was in winter, the room was unheated, they were lying under a heavy feather bed.

---

15 III 14 Behind Dostoyevsky's coffin the students wanted to carry his chains. He died in the workers' quarter on the 5th floor of an apartment building.[622]

Toward 5 o'clock one morning in winter, the half-dressed maid announced a guest to the student. "What's that? How's that?" the student, still drowsy, was asking, when a young man entered with a burning candle borrowed from the maid,

---

Nothing but an awaiting, eternal helplessness

---

17 III 14

Sat in the room with my parents, leafed through magazines for 2 hours, now and then just stared ahead, on the whole just waited until it's 10 o'clock and I can lie down in bed.

---

27 III 14 On the whole spent not much differently.

Hass hurried to get onto the ship, ran across the gangplank, climbed up onto a deck, sat down in a corner, pressed his hands against his face and from now on paid heed to no one. The ship's bell rang, people ran past, far away, as if it were at the other end of the ship someone sang at the top of his lungs

---

They were just about to pull back the gangplank when a small black carriage approached, the coachman cried from afar, the rearing horse had to be held with all his strength, a young man leaped out of the carriage, kissed an old white-bearded gentleman bending forward under the carriage roof and ran with a small suitcase onto the ship, which was immediately pushed off from the shore.

It was about three o'clock at night, but in summer, and already half light. In Herr von Grusenhof's stable his five horses Famos, Grasaffe, Tournemento, Rosina and Brabant arose. Because of the sultry night the stable door was ajar, the two grooms were sleeping in the straw on their backs flies hovered up and down over their open mouths, there was no hindrance. Grasaffe positioned himself so that he had the two men under him and, observing their faces, was ready to strike with his hoofs at the slightest sign of awakening. Meanwhile the other four left the stable one behind the other with two easy bounds, Grasaffe followed them.

---

30 III 14 Through the glass door Anna saw that it was dark in the tenant's room, she came in and turned on the electric light to prepare the bed for the night. But the student sat half lying on the sofa and smiled at her. She apologized and was about to leave. But the student asked her to stay and pay no attention to him. She did stay and did her work with several side glances in the student's direction.

5 IV 14

If it were possible to go to Berlin, to become independent, to live from day to day, even to go hungry, but to let all one's strength pour out instead of saving it here or rather turning away into nothingness! If F. wanted it, would stand by me!

7 IV 14

8 IV 14 Yesterday incapable of writing even a word. Today no better. Who will save me? And within me the throng, deep down, scarcely visible. I'm like a living latticework, a lattice that stands firm and wants to fall.

Today in the coffeehouse with Werfel.[623] How he looks from a distance, sitting at the coffeehouse table. Bowing his head, half lying even in the wooden chair, his face, beautiful in profile, pressed against him, almost panting in his fullness (not actually fatness), utterly independent of his surroundings, naughty and flawless. His hanging glasses, by their contrasting quality, make it easier to follow the delicate outlines of his face

6 V 14 My parents seem to have found a nice apartment for F. and me,[624] I spent a nice afternoon wandering around uselessly. Will they lay me in my grave too after a life made happy by their care.

A noble named Herr von Griesenau had a coachman Josef, whom no other employer could have tolerated. He lived in a ground-level room next to the porter's lodge, since due to his fatness and shortness of breath he was incapable of climbing stairs. His only occupation was driving the carriage, but even for that he was used only on special occasions, say, to honor a guest, but otherwise he lay for whole days whole weeks on a chaise longue near the window, and with his small eyes sunken deep in fat and blinking with striking rapidity he looked out the window at the trees, which

---

The coachman Josef lay on his chaise longue, sat up only to take from a little table a slice of buttered bread with herring, then leaned back again and stared around while chewing. Through his large round nostrils he drew in air with difficulty, sometimes, to get enough air, he had to stop chewing and open his mouth, his large belly trembled without interruption under the many folds of his thin dark-blue suit.

The window was open, one saw an acacia and an empty square. It was a low ground-floor window, from his chaise longue Josef saw everything and everyone could see him from outside. That was tormenting, but he had to live so low down, because for at least six months ever since he had put on a great deal of fat, he had no longer been able to climb stairs at all. When he had been given this room next to the porter's lodge, he had kissed and squeezed the hands of his employer, Herr von Griesenau, in tears, but now he knew the disadvantages of this room—the experience of perpetually being observed, the proximity of the unpleasant porter, the commotion of the driveway and the square, the great distance from the rest of the servants and the resulting estrangement and neglect—all these disadvantages he now knew thoroughly and he actually intended to petition the master about moving into his former room. What, then, were so many newly hired fellows standing around uselessly for especially ever since the master had become engaged, let them simply carry him, meritorious and unique man that he was, up and down the stairs.

An engagement was being celebrated. The banquet had ended, the guests stood up from the table, all the windows were opened, it was a beautiful warm evening in June. The bride was standing in a circle of friends and good acquaintances, the rest were together in small groups, now and then there was a great deal of laughter. The groom was alone, leaning against the entrance to the balcony and looking out.

After some time the mother of the bride noticed him, went to him and said: "You're standing here all alone? Not going to Olga? Did you have a quarrel?" "No" the groom replied "we didn't have a quarrel." "Well" said the woman "then go to your bride! Your behavior is beginning to attract attention"

The horribleness of the merely schematic

The landlady a frail black-clad widow wearing a straight-falling skirt stood in the middle room of her empty apartment. It was still completely quiet, the bell didn't stir. In the street it was quiet too, the woman had intentionally chosen so quiet a street, for she wanted good lodgers and those who demand peace and quiet are the best.

27 V 14 Mother and sister in Berlin.[625] I will be alone with my father in the evening. I think he's afraid to come up. Should I play cards with him? (I find my Ks ugly, they almost disgust me and yet I write them, they must be very characteristic of me)[626] How my father behaved when I touched F.

The white horse appeared for the first time on an autumn afternoon in a large but not very busy street in the city of A. It came out of the hall of a house, in the courtyard of which a freight business had vast storerooms, so that teams of horses often had to be led out of the hall, now and then a single horse too and hence the white horse didn't attract particular attention. But it wasn't one of the freight business's horses. A worker, tightening the cords on a bundle of goods outside the front door, noticed the horse looked up from his work and then into the courtyard to see whether the coachman wouldn't be following soon. No one came, but scarcely had the horse stepped on the sidewalk when it reared up powerfully, struck a few sparks from the pavement, for a moment was on the verge of falling, but immediately pulled itself together and then trotted neither quickly nor slowly up the street, which was almost completely empty at this twilight hour. The worker cursed the coachmen, who, in his opinion, had been negligent, shouted several names into the courtyard, people did come out but, immediately recognizing the horse as an unfamiliar one, merely stopped and stood side by side in the doorway in some astonishment. Only after a little while did a few think things over, they ran quite a stretch after the horse, but, having not so much as set eyes on it again, they soon returned.

In the meantime the horse had already reached the outermost suburban streets without being stopped. It blended in with the street life better than horses running alone usually do. Its slow pace couldn't frighten anyone, it never left the road or the prescribed side of the street, when it was necessary to stop for a carriage coming out of a cross street, it stopped, if the most careful coachman had led it by a halter, it could not have behaved more flawlessly. Still, it was naturally a striking sight, now and then someone stopped and watched it with a smile, from a passing beer wagon a coachman lashed down at the horse with his whip in jest, it was startled, to be sure, reared, but didn't quicken its pace.

But a policeman had observed this very incident, approached the horse, which at the last moment had tried to take a different direction, grabbed it by the rein (despite its not very strong build, it was harnessed as a packhorse) and said, actually in a very friendly way: Halt! Where are you running off to, then? For a while he held on to it here in the middle of the road, for he thought the owner would soon be coming after his runaway animal.

It has meaning, but is weak, the blood flows thin, too far from the heart. I still have pretty scenes in my head and yet I'm stopping. Yesterday the white horse appeared to me for the first time before I fell asleep, I have the impression that it first stepped out of my head, which was turned to the wall, jumped over me and down from the bed and then disappeared. The latter is unfortunately not refuted by the above beginning.

If I'm not very much mistaken, I'm actually getting closer. It's as if the spiritual battle were in a forest clearing somewhere. I penetrate the forest, find nothing and out of weakness soon hurry out again;

often when I leave the forest, I hear or think I hear the clashing of the weapons of that battle. Perhaps the eyes of the warriors are seeking me through the forest darkness, but I know only so little about them, and that is deceptive.

Heavy downpour. Confront the rain, let the iron rays penetrate you, slide in the water that wants to wash you away, but remain nonetheless, await upright in this way the suddenly and endlessly streaming-in sun.

The landlady flung her skirts and hurried through the rooms. A tall cold woman. Her protruding lower jaw scared off the lodgers. They ran down the stairs and when she watched them from the window, they covered their faces as they ran. Once a short lodger came, a strong thickset young man, who constantly kept his hands in the pockets of his coat. Perhaps it was his habit, but it was also possible that he wanted to conceal the trembling of his hands.

Young man said the woman, and her lower jaw moved forward you want to live here?

Yes said the young man, jerking his head upward.

You'll be happy here said the woman, leading him to a chair and sitting him down on it. In doing so she noticed that he had a stain on his pants, which prompted her to kneel down next to him and begin to scrape this stain with her nails.

"You're a sloven" she said

It's an old stain

Then you're simply an old sloven.

"Away with your hand" he said suddenly and really pushed it away. "What terrible hands you have" he said then grabbed her hand and turned it. "On top completely black, on the bottom whitish, but still black enough and—he put his hand up her wide sleeve—on your arm you're even a little hairy."

"You're tickling me" she said

"Because I like you. I don't understand how anyone can say you're ugly. People do say it. But now I see that it's not true at all."

And he stood up and walked up and down the room. She was still kneeling and examined her hand.

For some reason this drove him wild, he bounded to her and took her hand again.

"Such a woman" he then said, slapping her longish thin cheek. "It would be downright conducive to my contentment to live here. But it would have to be cheap. And you wouldn't be permitted to take in another tenant. And you would have to be faithful to me. I'm much younger than you, after all, I can certainly demand faithfulness. And you would have to cook well. I'm accustomed to good food and will never grow unaccustomed to it."

Dance on you pigs; what do I have to do with it?

But it's more real than anything I've written this past year. Perhaps it really is a matter of loosening the joint. I will be able to write again.

Every evening for a week my neighbor from the next room has been coming to wrestle with me. I didn't know him, even now have not yet spoken a word with him. We exchange only a few exclamations, which can't be called "speaking." With "all right" the fight is initiated, "wretch" one of us sometimes groans in the other's hold, "now" accompanies a surprising push, "stop!" means the end but we keep fighting a little while longer. Most of the time he even leaps from the doorway back into the room once more and gives me a push that makes me fall down. From his room he then shouts good night to me through the wall. If I wanted to abandon this acquaintance once and for all, I would have to move out of my room, for locking the door is no help. Once I had locked the door because I wanted to read, but my neighbor broke the door in two with an axe, and since once he has grasped something he can give it up only with difficulty, I was even endangered by the axe. I know how to adapt myself. Since he always comes at a particular hour, I undertake easy work that I can interrupt immediately if necessary. I must arrange things in this way, for no sooner has he appeared in the doorway than I must drop everything for he wants only to fight nothing else. If I feel strong, I provoke him a little by first trying to evade him. I crawl under the table to the other side I throw chairs at his feet, I wink at him from a distance, though it's naturally tasteless to make such jokes, which remain entirely one-sided, with a stranger. But most of the time our bodies immediately join together in battle. Apparently he's a student, studies all day and wants to quickly get some exercise in the evening before going to bed. Well, in me he has a good opponent, I am perhaps, leaving aside a change of fortune, the stronger and more skilled of the two of us. He, however, has more endurance.

---

28 / V 14 The day after tomorrow I'm leaving for Berlin.[627] Despite sleeplessness, headaches and worries perhaps in a better state than ever.

Once he brought a girl with him. While I'm saying hello and not paying attention to him, he jumps on me and yanks me into the air. "I protest" I cried, raising my hand. "Be quiet" he whispered in my ear. I realized that he would do whatever it took even use shameful holds to win in front of the girl and make himself shine. "He said 'Be quiet' to me" I therefore cried with my head turned toward the girl. "Oh scoundrel" the man groaned softly, he was using up all his strength on me. Still, he dragged me to the sofa, laid me down, knelt on my back, waited for his speech to return and said: "So there he lies." "Let him try it again" I wanted to say, but after the first word he was already pushing my face so hard into the upholstery that I was silenced. "Well" said the girl, who had sat down at my desk and was skimming an unfinished letter lying there. "Isn't it time we went? He has just begun a letter." "He won't continue it if we leave either. Come here. Grab here on the thigh, for example, he's trembling like a sick animal." "I say let him be and come." Very reluctantly the man crawled down off me. I could have beaten him up now, for I was rested now, whereas he had strained all his muscles to hold me down. He had been trembling and had thought I was trembling. He was still trembling even now. But I left him alone, because the girl was present. "You probably will have formed your own judgment on this fight by now" I said to the girl, walking past her with a bow and sitting down at the desk to continue the letter. "So who's trembling?" I asked, before beginning to write and, to prove that it was not I, held the penholder stiff in the air. Already writing, I shouted a brief adieu to them when they were in the doorway, but kicked out my foot a little to hint, at least to myself, at the goodbye the two of them probably deserved.

---

29 V 14 Tomorrow to Berlin. Is it a nervous or a real dependable cohesion that I feel? How would that be? Is it correct that once one receives the knowledge of writing, nothing can fall short, nothing sinks away, but at the same time only rarely does something rise to an excessive height. Would it be the dawning of marriage with F.? Strange state, though not entirely foreign to my memory.

Stood for a long time with Pick[628] outside the front door. Thought only of how I could get away soon, for my strawberry supper was prepared for me upstairs. Everything that I will now write about him is a meanness, for I'll let him see none of it or am content that he won't see it. But I even share guilt in his character, as long as I go around with him and so what I say about him applies to me too, even discounting the artificiality that lies in such a remark:

I make plans. I stare ahead, lest I move my eyes away from the imaginary peepholes of the imaginary kaleidoscope into which I'm looking. I jumble up good and selfish intentions, the good ones are washed out in the color that instead passes on to the merely selfish ones. I invite heaven and earth to participate in my plans, but I don't forget the little people who can be pulled out of any side street and who for the time being can be of more use to my plans. It's only the beginning, after all, perpetually only the beginning. I'm still standing here in my misery, but behind me the huge wagon of my plans is already driving up, the first little platform pushes itself under my feet, naked girls, as on the carnival wagons of better countries lead me backward up the steps, I float because the girls float and raise my hand, which commands silence. Rosebushes stand at my side, incense flames burn, laurel wreaths are lowered, people scatter flowers before and over me, two trumpeters as if built of square-hewn stones blow fanfares the little people run up in masses, arrayed behind leaders, the empty shiny clear-cut open squares grow dark, tumultuous and overcrowded, I feel the limit of human efforts and at this height, of my own accord and with skill that suddenly overcomes me I do the trick of a contortionist I admired many years ago by bending back slowly—at that moment the sky is trying to break open to clear the way for an apparition meant for me, but it hesitates—drawing my head and upper body through my legs and gradually rising again as an upright person. Was it the final heightening that is given to human beings. It seems so, for even now I see the little horned devils pushing their way out of all the gates of the land that lies deep and great below me, overrunning everything, under their steps everything breaks in the middle, their little tails wipe everything out, now 50 devil tails are scouring my face, the ground softens, one of my feet sinks, then the other, the cries of the girls follow me into my depths, into which I sink straight down, through a shaft that has exactly the diameter of my body but an endless depth. This endlessness tempts one to no special achievements, anything I would do would be petty, I fall senselessly and it is best.

Dostoyev.'s letter to his brother on life in prison.[629]

6 VI 14 Back from Berlin.[630] Was bound like a criminal. If one had sat me down in a corner with real chains and placed policemen in front of me and let me watch only in this way, it would not have been worse. And it was my engagement and everyone was making an effort to bring me to life and, since this didn't succeed, to tolerate me as I was. F., to be sure, least of all, with complete justification, for she was suffering the most. What was mere appearance to the others was a threat to her.

We couldn't bear it at home for an instant. We knew that they would search for us. But even though it was evening, we ran away. Our city was surrounded by hills. On these hills we climbed. We made all the trees tremble when we swung downward from one to the other.

The position at the shop in the evening shortly before closing time: Hands in pants pockets, slightly stooped, looking out from the vaulted depths through the wide-open front door at the square. Weary movements of the employees all around behind the desks. Weakly tying up a package, unconsciously dusting off some boxes, stacking up used packing paper.

An acquaintance comes and speaks with me. I positively lie down on him, so heavy am I. He makes the following assertion: Some say this, but I say just the opposite. He cites the reasons for his opinion. I waver. My hands lie in my pants pockets as if they had fallen in and yet as loosely as if I would have to turn out my pockets only slightly and they would quickly fall out again.

I had closed the shop, the employees, strangers, departed with their hats in their hands. It was an evening in June, already 8 o'clock but still light. I had no desire to take a walk, I never have any desire to take a walk, but I didn't want to go home either. When my last apprentice had turned the corner, I sat down on the ground outside the closed store.

An acquaintance with his young wife was passing by and saw me sitting on the ground. Look who's sitting here he said. They stopped and the man shook me a little, even though I was looking at him calmly from the very beginning. My God why on earth are you sitting here like this the young wife asked. "I'm going to shut down my shop I said. It isn't going particularly badly, I can even meet my obligations fully if only barely. But I can't bear the worries, I can't control the employees, I can't talk to the customers. From tomorrow on I'm not even going to open the shop anymore. It's all been well considered." I saw how the man tried to calm down his wife by taking her hand between both his hands.

"Well, all right" he said "you want to give up your shop. You're not the first to do it. We too—he looked across at his wife—will, once our wealth is enough for our needs—may it be soon—hesitate no less than you to give up our shop. The shop gives us no more pleasure than you, believe us. But why are you sitting on the ground?"

Where am I supposed to go? I said. I knew, of course, why they were asking me. It was sympathy, astonishment and also embarrassment that they felt, but I was by no means capable of helping them too.

"Don't you want to join us" an acquaintance recently asked me when he met me alone after midnight in a by then almost empty coffeehouse. No, I don't want to I said.

It was already after midnight. I was sitting in my room and writing a letter that was very important to me, since I hoped it would help me attain a good position abroad. I sought to remind the acquaintance to whom it was addressed, and with whom now after a 10-year separation I would by chance be brought back into contact by a mutual friend, of bygone days and at the same time make him understand how everything was driving me out of my country and how in the absence of other, good far-reaching connections I was placing my greatest hope in him.

The municipal official Bruder came home from his office only toward 9 o'clock in the evening. It was already completely dark. His wife was waiting for him outside the front door, holding their little girl pressed against her. "How do things stand?" she asked. "Very badly" said Bruder "Just come into the house, then I'll tell you everything." No sooner had they entered the house than Bruder locked the front door. Where is the maid he asked. "In the kitchen" said his wife. "Then it's all right, come!" In the large low-ceilinged living room the floor lamp was lit, everyone sat down and Bruder said: Well, the situation stands as follows. Our people are in full retreat. The battle at Rumdorf as I've learned from messages that have arrived in the municipal office and leave no room for doubt, has turned out wholly to our disadvantage. The majority of the troops have also already withdrawn from the city. This is still being kept secret to avoid heightening the terror in the city beyond measure. I consider that not entirely sensible, it would be better to tell the truth openly. But my duty demands that I remain silent. No one can prevent me from telling you the truth, to be sure. Besides, everyone suspects what's really going on, that's noticeable everywhere. All are locking their houses, hiding what can be hidden.

The municipal official Bruder came home from his office only at 10 o'clock in the evening, nonetheless he immediately knocked on the door that separated his room from the apartment of the furniture dealer Rumford, with whom he lodged. Even though he could hear only an indistinct word, he entered. Rumford was sitting at the table with a newspaper, his fat tormented him on this hot July evening, he had thrown coat and vest on the sofa; his shirt

---

Several city officials were standing at the stone balustrade of a town hall window and looking down at the square. The last part of the rearguard was waiting there for the command to withdraw. They were young tall red-cheeked fellows who held their jerking horses tightly reined. In front of them two officers rode slowly up and down. They were apparently waiting for a message. Often they sent away a rider, who disappeared in the greatest haste into a steeply rising side street of the Ringplatz. So far no one had returned.

The official Bruder, a still young but full-bearded man, had joined the group by the window. Since he had a higher rank and was held in particular regard for his talent, everyone bowed politely and let him go ahead to the balustrade. "So this is the end" he said, looking at the square "it's all too apparent." "Then you believe Herr Councilor said an arrogant young man, who despite Bruder's arrival hadn't stirred from his place and now stood so close to Bruder that they couldn't even look each other in the face then you believe that the battle is lost?" Most certainly. There's no doubt about it. Speaking in confidence we are badly led. We must atone for various old sins. This, to be sure, is no time to talk about it, now everyone has to fend for himself. We stand, after all, before the ultimate dissolution. By this evening the guests may be here. Perhaps they won't even wait until evening but will be here in ½ an hour.

---

12 VI 14

Kubin.[631] Yellowish face, sparse hair lying flat over his skull, gleam in his eyes incited from time to time. Fear of infection, he kissed her down below, even now he sees himself decaying, speaks of the "beloved woman" to whom he brings this misfortune. Blissfully seizes on the stupidest reassurance and after a little while wrests himself from it very cleverly.—Wolfskehl,[632] half blind, retinal detachment, must be careful of a fall or collision, or else the lens can fall out then it's all over. While reading must hold the book close to his eyes and try to catch the letters out of the corner of his eye. Was in India with Melchior Lechter,[633] fell ill with dysentery, eats everything, any piece of fruit he sees lying on the street in the dust.—Pachinger sawed a silver chastity belt off a corpse, shoved aside the workers who dug it up somewhere in Romania, reassured them with the remark that he saw here a worthless trifle he wanted to take with him as a souvenir, sawed the belt open and yanked it off the skeleton. If he finds in a village church a valuable Bible or a picture or a page that he wants to have, he tears what he wants out of books, from the walls, from the altar, leaves in return a 2-heller piece and is at ease.—Love for fat women. Every woman he has had is photographed. Pile of photographs that he shows every visitor. Sits in one corner of the sofa, the visitor, far away from him, in the other. Pachinger scarcely looks and yet always knows which photograph is next and gives his explanations accordingly: That was an old widow, those were the two Hungarian maids, etc.—On Kubin: "Yes, Master Kubin, you are indeed on the rise, in 10 to 20 years you can, if this lasts have a position like that of Bayros."[634]

Dostoyevsky's letter to a woman painter.[635]
Social life occurs in a circle. Only those suffering a particular affliction understand each other. By virtue of the nature of their affliction they form a circle and support each other. They glide along the inner edges of their circle, giving way to each other or gently pushing each other in the throng. Each encourages the other in the hope of a reaction on himself or, then it is done passionately, in the immediate enjoyment of this reaction. Each has only the experience that his affliction grants him, nonetheless one hears among such comrades the exchange of immensely varied experiences. "This is how you are" one says to the other "instead of complaining, thank God that this is how you are, for if this were not how you are then you would be in this or that misfortune, in this or that disgrace." Now how does this man know that? After all, he belongs, as this remark reveals, to the same circle as the person he is addressing, his need for consolation is of the same kind. But in the same circle one always knows the same things. There's not a hint of a thought that the consoler would have ahead of the consoled. Their conversations are therefore only unions of imagination, outpourings of wishes from one onto the other. At one point one of them looks down at the ground and the other up at a bird, in such differences their intercourse takes place. At one point they are united in faith and both look side by side in infinite directions of the heights. Recognition of their situation shows itself, however, only when they lower their heads together and the common hammer comes down on them.

14 *(June 1914)*

My calm gait, while there's a twitch around my head and while a branch scraping weakly across my head causes me the worst unease. I have the calm, I have the assurance of other people in me but somehow at the wrong end.

---

19 VI *(1914)* The excitements of the past several days. The calm that passes from Dr. W.[636] to me. The worries that he bears for me. How this morning, when I awoke at 4 after a sound sleep, they moved into me. Pištekovo divadlo.[637] Löwenstein![638] Now the crude exciting novel by Soyka. Fear. Conviction of the necessity of F.

24 VI 14 Elli[639] tells:
"Dearest sweetie! I long for your elastic body"

How we, O.[640] and I, give vent to our anger against human relationships.

The parents' grave in which the son ("Pollak, graduate of a commercial academy") is buried too.

25 VI 14

From early in the morning until now at twilight I had been walking up and down my room. The window was open, it was a warm day. The noise of the narrow street drifted in without interruption. By now I knew every trifle in the room from looking at it while walking around. I had scoured all the walls with my eyes. I had followed the pattern of the carpet and its marks of age into the last branches. I had measured the table in the middle with finger spans many times. I had already bared my teeth often at the portrait of my landlady's late husband. Toward evening I went to the window and sat down on the low balustrade. Then, for the first time, I happened to look calmly from one spot into the room and up at the ceiling. Finally, finally if I wasn't mistaken this room that I had so frequently shaken began to move. It began at the edges of the white ceiling lined with fragile plaster decorations. Little pieces of mortar broke off and fell here and there as if by chance, making a distinct crash on the floor. I held out my hand and some fell into my hand too, in my excitement I threw them over my head into the street without even turning around. The cracks above had no interconnection yet, but one could nonetheless somehow form it for oneself. But I desisted from such games when a bluish violet now began to mix with the white, it emanated from the ceiling's center, which remained white, indeed positively shone white, and in which, close to the top, the paltry electric light was stuck. In repeated bursts the color or was it a light pushed its way toward the now darkening edge. One no longer paid any attention at all to the falling mortar, which flew off as if under the pressure of a very precisely guided tool. Now yellow, golden-yellow colors surge into the violet from the sides. But the ceiling of the room didn't actually change color, the colors only made it somehow transparent, above it there seemed to be things hovering that wanted to break through, one could now almost see the activity there in outlines, an arm was stretched out, a silver sword hovered up and down. It was meant for me, there was no doubt about that, an apparition that would free me was preparing itself. I jumped onto the table to prepare everything, yanked out the electric light together with its brass rod and hurled it to the floor, then jumped down and pushed the table out of the middle of the room toward the wall. What wanted to come could easily settle on the carpet and announce to me what it had to announce. No sooner was I finished than the ceiling truly broke open. Still from a great height, which I had judged poorly an angel in bluish violet robes, wrapped with golden cords, descended slowly in the semidarkness on great white silkily shining wings, the sword in its upraised arm stretched out horizontally. "So it's an angel!" I thought "all day it's been flying toward me and in my unbelief I didn't know it. Now it will speak to me." I lowered my eyes. But when I raised them again, although the angel was still there, hanging quite low under the ceiling, which had closed again, it was not a living angel, but only a painted wooden figure from the prow of a ship, such as hang from the ceiling in sailors' taverns. Nothing more. The pommel of the sword was made to hold candles and catch the flowing tallow. I had yanked down the electric light, I didn't want to remain in the dark, a candle was still to be found, so I climbed onto a chair, stuck the candle into the sword pommel, lit it and then sat far into the night under the weak light of the angel.

30 VI 14

Hellerau Leipzig with Pick.[641] I behaved terribly. Couldn't ask a question, couldn't answer, couldn't move, could barely look anyone in the eyes. Man who advertises for the Navy League,[642] the fat sausage-eating couple, Thomas with whom we're staying,[643] Prescher who takes us there,[644] Frau Thomas, Hegner,[645] Fantl and wife,[646] Adler, wife and child Anneliese,[647] Frau Dr. Kraus, Frl. Pollak, Frau Fantl's sister, Katz,[648] Mendelssohn[649] (his brother's child,[650] alpine garden,[651] grubs, pine-needle bath) Waldschenke,[652] "Natura"[653] Wolff, Haas,[654] reading of Narcissus, in Adler's garden,[655] viewing of the Dalcroze house,[656] evening at the Waldschenke—Bugra[657]—horror upon horror. Failures: Not finding "Natura," searching all along Struvestrasse;[658] wrong tram to Hellerau,[659] no room at the Waldschenke; forgetting that I'm expecting a telephone call from Erna[660] there hence turning back; no longer met Fantl; Dalcroze in Geneva;[661] next morning arrived too late at the Waldschenke (F. telephoned to no avail); decision not to go to Berlin but to Leipzig; senseless trip; local train by mistake; Wolff is just going to Berlin; Lasker-Schüler takes up all Werfel's time;[662] senseless visit to the exhibition;[663] finally at the end in Arco[664] reminded Pick quite senselessly about an old debt.

---

1 VI *(July)* 14 Too tired.

5 VII 14 To have to bear and cause such woes!

29 VII 14 Wrote notes on the trip in another notebook.[665] Began failed works. But I won't yield despite sleeplessness, headaches, general inability. It is the last vital energy that has gathered itself in me for this. I've made the observation that I avoid people not in order to be able to live in peace, but in order to be able to die in peace. But now I will defend myself. For a month during my boss's absence I'll have time.

31 *(July 1914)* I have no time. It's general mobilization.[666] K. and P.[667] have been conscripted. Now I get the reward of being alone. It is, to be sure, hardly a reward, being alone brings only punishments. Still, I'm

affected little by all the misery and more determined than ever. In the afternoon I'll have to be in the factory, I won't be living at home, for E. is moving to our apartment with the 2 children.[668] But I will write despite all this, no matter what may happen, it's my struggle for self-preservation.

1 *(August 1914)* Accompanied K.[669] to the train. Relatives all around in the office. Desire to go to Valli.

2 *(August 1914)* Germany has declared war on Russia.—Swimming school in the afternoon[670]

3 VIII 14

Alone in my sister's apartment. It's lower down than my room, it's also an out-of-the-way street, hence loud talking of the neighbors outside down below. Whistling too. Otherwise complete solitude. No longed-for wife opens the door. In a month I was to have married. Terrible words: You have gotten what you wanted. One stands painfully pinned against the wall, fearfully lowers one's eyes to see the hand that pins and with a new pain that makes one forget the old, recognizes one's own crooked hand, which holds you with a strength it never had for good work. One raises one's head, again feels the first pain, again lowers one's eyes and this up and down never ceases.

---

4 VIII 14 When I rented the apartment for myself, I probably signed a document for the landlord in which I obligated myself to a two-year or even six-year lease. Now he is making the demand from this contract.[671] The stupidity or rather general and definitive defenselessness that my behavior shows. Sliding into the river. This sliding probably seems so desirable to me because it reminds me of "being pushed."

---

5 VIII *(1914)* almost straightened out with the last expenditure of my strength. Was there twice[672] with Malek[673] as witness, at Felix's about the drafting of a contract, at the lawyer's twice (6 K) and all of it unnecessary, I could and should have done it all myself.

---

6 VIII *(1914)* The artillery that marched across the Graben.[674] Flowers, shouts of Heil and Nazdar.[675] The tenaciously silent, astonished attentive black and black-eyed face.—I'm shattered instead of recovered. An empty vessel, still whole and already among fragments or already a fragment and still among the wholes. Full of falsehood, hatred and envy. Full of inability, stupidity, slow-wittedness. Full of laziness, weakness and defenselessness. 31 years old. I saw the 2 farmers M. in Ottla's picture. Young fresh people who know something and are strong enough to use it in the midst of people who necessarily offer some resistance.—One of them is leading the beautiful horses, the other is lying in the grass, the tip of his tongue playing between his lips in his otherwise unmoving and absolutely trustworthy face.

---

5 *(August 1914)* I discover in myself nothing but pettiness, indecision, envy and hatred toward those who are fighting, whom I passionately wish all evil.

---

6 *(August 1914)* From the perspective of literature my fate is very simple. The penchant for depicting my dreamlike inner life has pushed everything else aside and all this has atrophied in a terrible way and doesn't cease to atrophy. Nothing else can ever satisfy me. But now my strength for that depiction is quite incalculable, perhaps it has vanished forever, perhaps it will come over me again, the circumstances of my life are certainly not favorable to it. Thus I waver, fly incessantly to the peak of the mountain, but can keep myself up there for scarcely a moment. Others waver too, but in lower regions, with stronger powers; if they are in danger of falling, they are caught by the relative who walks beside them for that purpose. I, however, waver up there, it is, alas, not death, but the eternal torments of dying.

Patriotic parade. Speech by the mayor. Then disappearance, then emergence and the German exclamation: "Long live our beloved monarch, hurrah." I stand there with my evil eye. These parades are one of the most disgusting symptoms of the war. Emanating from Jewish merchants, who are now German, now Czech, do admit this to themselves, but are never permitted to shout it out as loudly as now. Naturally, they carry many others along with them. It was well organized. It's supposed to be repeated every evening, twice tomorrow Sunday.[676]

---

7 *(August 1914)* Even if one doesn't have the slightest apparent ability to individualize, one still treats everyone according to his nature. "L. from Binz," to draw attention to himself, extends his cane toward me and frightens me.[677]

The firm footsteps at the swimming school.

Yesterday and today wrote 4 pages, trivialities hard to surpass.

The tremendous Strindberg. That rage, those pages acquired in a fistfight.[678]

Choral singing from the tavern across the street.—I just went to the window. Sleep seems impossible. The full singing comes through the open tavern door. A girl's voice leads. They're innocent love songs. I long for a policeman. Now he's coming. He stops for a little while outside the door and listens. Then he shouts: "The proprietor!" The girl's voice: "Vojtíšku." A man in pants and shirt leaps from a corner. "Close the door! Who is supposed to listen to this noise?" "Oh sorry, oh sorry" says the proprietor and with gentle accommodating movements, as if he were negotiating with a lady he first closes the door behind him, then opens it to slip in and closes it again. The policeman (whose behavior particularly his anger is incomprehensible, for the singing can't disturb him, but can only sweeten his boring duty) marches off, the singers have lost interest in singing.

---

11 *(August 1914)* Fantasy that I've remained in Paris, walk through Paris arm in arm with my uncle pressed close to him[679]

12 *(August 1914)* Haven't slept at all. In the afternoon lay for 3 hours sleepless and dull on the sofa, likewise at night. But it must not hinder me.

15 *(August 1914)* I've been writing for a few days, may it last. Today I'm not quite as sheltered and burrowed away in the work as I was 2 years ago, nonetheless I do have a sense that my regular, empty, mad bachelor

life has a justification. I can again carry on a conversation with myself and don't stare so into complete emptiness. Only in this way is there an improvement for me.

During one period of my life—it's many years ago now—I had employment with a small railroad in the heart of Russia.[680] I have never been as forsaken as I was there. For various reasons not pertinent here, I was seeking such a place at the time, the more solitude engulfing me the more I liked it and so even now I don't want to complain about it. At first all I lacked was something to occupy me. The small railroad had perhaps originally been built with some economic intention or other, but the capital had been insufficient, construction came to a halt and instead of leading to Kalda the nearest sizable town a 5 days' journey from us by wagon the railroad stopped at a little settlement practically in a wasteland, from which another whole day's journey was necessary to reach Kalda. Now the railroad even if it had been extended to Kalda would have remained unprofitable for an indefinite period, because the whole plan for it was misconceived, the country needed roads but no railroads, in the condition in which the railroad now found itself, however, it couldn't survive at all, the two trains that ran daily carried loads that a light wagon could have transported, and the only passengers were a few field hands in the summer. But nonetheless they didn't want to shut down the railroad completely, for they were still hoping that by keeping it in operation they could attract capital for the further expansion. Even this hope was in my opinion not so much hope as despair and laziness. They let the railroad run as long as material and coal were still available, they paid the few workers their wages irregularly and cut down, as if they were gifts of charity and otherwise waited for the whole thing to collapse.

By this railroad, then, I was employed, living in a wooden shed that had been left there since the construction of the railroad and served at the same time as a station building. It had only one room, in which a plank bed had been set up for me and a desk for possible paperwork, over which the telegraph machine was installed. When I arrived in spring, one train passed the station very early—later this was changed—and it sometimes happened that some passenger came to the station while I was still asleep. Of course—the nights there were very cool into the middle of the summer—he did not then remain outside, but knocked, I unbolted the door and then we often spent whole hours chatting. I lay on my plank bed, my guest sat on the floor or followed my instructions to make tea, which we then both drank amiably. All these village people are distinguished by great agreeableness. Moreover, I realized that I wasn't quite suited to bear complete solitude, even if I had to tell myself that this solitude I had imposed on myself had already after a short time begun to dispel my past worries. I have found in general that it's a great trial of strength for a misfortune to lastingly dominate a person in solitude. Solitude is more powerful than anything and drives one back toward people. Naturally, one then tries to find other, seemingly less painful, in reality merely still unknown paths.

I became more attached to the people there than I had thought. It naturally wasn't a regular intercourse. Of the five villages that came into consideration for me, each was several hours from the station as well as from the other villages. I was not permitted to venture all too far from the station, if I didn't want to lose my job. And at least in the beginning I didn't want that at all. So I couldn't go to the villages themselves and remained dependent on the passengers or on the people who didn't shy from the long journey to pay me a visit. In the very first month such people arrived, but however friendly they were, it was easy to tell that they came only in the hope of perhaps doing some business with me; moreover, they didn't conceal their intention at all. They brought various wares and at first, as long as I had money, I usually purchased everything almost sight unseen, so welcome were the people to me, especially some of them. Later, to be sure, I limited these purchases, among other reasons because I thought I noticed that my manner of purchasing seemed to them contemptible. Besides, I also got food by train, though it was very bad and even far more expensive than what the peasants brought. Originally I had intended to plant a small vegetable garden, buy a cow and in this way make myself as independent as possible from everyone. I had even brought along garden tools and seed, there was an overabundance of soil, it stretched untilled in a single expanse around my hut without the slightest elevation as far as the eye could see. But I was too weak to conquer this soil. A recalcitrant soil, which was frozen solid into spring and resisted even my new sharp pickax. Whatever seed one sank into it was lost. I had attacks of despair during this work. Then I lay for days on my plank bed and didn't even come out when trains arrived. Then I only stuck my head out the small window directly over the plank bed and reported that I was sick. The train crew, which consisted of 3 men, then came into my hut to warm themselves, but they didn't find much warmth, for whenever possible I avoided using the old easily exploding iron stove. I preferred to lie wrapped in an old warm coat and covered up with various pelts I'd bought from the peasants over time. "You're often sick" they said to me "You're a sickly person. You'll never leave here." They didn't say this to make me sad, but rather they strove to tell the truth bluntly whenever possible. They usually did so with a peculiar goggling of their eyes.

Once a month, but always at different times an inspector came to examine my record book, to take the received money from me and—but not always—to pay me my wage. I was always notified of his arrival one day before by the people who had dropped him at the last station. They considered this notification the greatest favor they could do me, even though I naturally had everything in order every day. Nor was

(Continuation of the text on page 360)

Eighth Notebook

2 May 1913

It has become very necessary to keep a diary again.[681] My uncertain head, Felice, the decline in the office, the physical impossibility of writing and the inner need for it.

Valli walks out our door behind my brother-in-law,[682] who tomorrow is reporting for military training in Tschotkov. Strange the recognition that lies in this following-him of marriage as an institution to which one has thoroughly reconciled oneself.

The story of the gardener's daughter, who interrupted me the day before yesterday while I was working. I, who want to cure my neurasthenia through this work,[683] must hear that the young lady's brother, his name was Jan and he was the actual gardener and the prospective successor to old Dvorsky, indeed even now owner of the flower garden poisoned himself 2 months ago at the age of 28 due to melancholy. In the summer he felt relatively well despite his reclusive nature, since he at least had to have contact with the customers, in the winter, however, he was completely withdrawn. His beloved was an official—uřednice—an equally melancholy girl. They often went to the cemetery together.

The huge Menasse at the jargon performance.[684] Something magical that seized me at the sight of his movements in harmony with the music. I've forgotten it.

My stupid laughter when I told my mother today that I'm going to Berlin on Pentecost. "Why are you laughing?" said my mother (among several other remarks, including "Thus test, who would be bound forever" all of which I fended off, however, with remarks like "It's nothing, etc.") "In embarrassment" I said and was glad to have said something true in this matter for once.

Met Bailly yesterday.[685] Her calmness, contentment naturalness and clarity, even though in the past two years she has undergone the transition to old woman, that fullness that was burdensome even then will soon have reached the limit of sterile corpulence, her gait has taken on a sort of rolling and shuffling with her belly thrust forward or rather carried forward and on her chin—at a brief glance only on her chin—whiskers are curling out of the former down.

---

3 May *(1913)*

The terrible uncertainty of my inner existence.

Guardian[686]

How I unbutton my vest to show Hr. B. my rash. How I wave him into an adjoining room.

The leper and his wife. How her behind, she is lying in bed on her belly, keeps rising with all its ulcers, even though a guest is there. How her husband keeps shouting at her to remain lying covered up.

A stake—no one knows where it came from—has struck the husband from behind casting him down and impaling him. Lying on the ground he wails with upraised head and outspread arms. Later he is able to rise unsteadily for a moment. He knows how to talk about nothing but how he was struck and points in the approximate direction from which in his opinion the stake came. These never-changing stories are beginning to tire the wife, especially since the man is always pointing in a different direction.

---

4 *(May 1913)* Perpetually the image of a broad butcher's knife that in the greatest haste and with mechanical regularity pierces me from the side and cuts off very thin cross sections, which during the quick work fly away almost rolled up.

Early one morning, the streets were still empty far and wide, a man, he was barefoot and dressed in only a nightshirt and pants, opened the front door of a large apartment building on the main street. He held both door leaves firmly and took a deep breath. "You misery, you damned misery" he said, looking with apparent calm first down the street, then along some houses.

Despair, then, from here too. Nowhere taken in.

---

1. digestion 2. neurasthenia 3. rash 4. inner uncertainty

If only it would mingle
without tension in one's head

---

24 May 13 A walk with Pick.
Exuberance because I considered The Stoker so good.[687] In the evening I read it to my parents, there's no better critic than I while reading aloud in front of my extremely reluctantly listening father. Many shallow passages before apparently inaccessible depths.

5 VI 13

The inner advantages that mediocre literary works draw from the fact that their authors are still alive and pursuing them. The actual sense of growing obsolete.

Löwy story of crossing the border.[688]

21 VI *(1913)* The anxiety I endure in all directions. The examination at the doctor's, how he immediately presses forward against me, I positively hollow myself out and he makes his empty speeches in me disdained and unrefuted.

The tremendous world I have in my head. But how to free myself and free it without being torn to pieces. And a thousand times better to be torn to pieces than to retain or bury it in me. That's why I'm here, after all, that's completely clear to me.

One cold spring morning toward 5 o'clock a tall man in a coat reaching to his feet knocked with his fist on the door of a small hut, which stood in a bare hilly region. After each blow of his fist he listened, in the hut it remained silent.

1 VII 13

The desire for mindless solitude. To be confronted with only myself. Perhaps I'll have it in Riva.[689]

Three days ago with Weiss, author of Die Galeere.[690] Jewish doctor, Jew of the kind that is closest to the type of the Western European Jew and to whom one therefore immediately feels close. The tremendous advantage of Christians, who in general intercourse have and enjoy the same feelings of closeness all the time, for example, a Christian Czech among Christian Czechs.

The honeymoon couple that came out of the Hotel de Saxe.[691] In the afternoon. Dropping the card in the mailbox. Rumpled clothing, slack pace, gloomy warm afternoon. Scarcely characteristic faces at first glance.

The picture of the Romanov tercentenary celebration in Yaroslavl on the Volga. The Czar, the princesses standing morosely in the sun only one of them delicate, oldish, listless, leaning on her parasol, is looking ahead. The successor to the throne carried in the arms of the tremendous bareheaded Cossack.—In another picture men long since passed by are saluting in the distance.[692]

The millionaire in the picture in the cinema "Slaves of Gold."[693] Hold him fast! The calmness, the slow purposeful movement, when necessary rapid stride, jerk of the arm. Rich, spoiled, lulled to sleep, but how he jumps up like a servant and searches the room in which he has been locked in the forest tavern.

---

2 *(July 1913)* Sobbed over the report on the trial of a 23-yr.-old Marie Abraham, who because of destitution and hunger strangled her almost 9-month-old baby Barbara with a men's tie, which served her as a garter and which she untied. Quite schematic story.[694]

The fire with which I described a funny cinematographic picture to my sister in the bathroom. Why can I never do that in the face of strangers?

I would never have married a girl with whom I had lived in the same city for a year.

---

3 *(July 1913)* The expansion and elevation of existence through marriage. Sermon maxim. But I almost sense it.

When I say something it immediately and definitively loses its importance, when I write it down it always loses it too, but sometimes gains a new one.

A band of little golden beads around a tanned neck.

19 VII 13

Out of a house came four armed men. Each held a halberd erect in front of him. Now and then one of them turned his head back to see whether the man for whose sake they were standing here was coming. It was early in the morning, the street was completely empty.

What do you want then? Come!—We don't want to. Let us be!—

For this the inner effort. That's why the music from the coffeehouse rings so in one's ear. The stone's throw of which Elsa B.[695] spoke becomes visible.

A woman is sitting at a distaff. A man pushes the door open with a sword in its sheath (he is holding it loose in his hand).

M. He was here!

W. Who? What do you want?

M. The horse thief? He is hidden here. Don't deny it! (He brandishes the sword)

W. (raises the distaff in defense) No one was here. Let me be!

---

20 VII 13

Down on the river were several boats, fishermen had cast their rods, it was a gloomy day. Some fellows were leaning against the quay railing with their legs crossed.

By the time the people stood up and raised their champagne glasses to celebrate their departure, it was dawn. Their parents and several wedding guests escorted them to the carriage. It

---

21 VII *(1913)* Don't despair, not even over the fact that you don't despair. Just when everything seems to be over, new powers come forward after all, this simply means that you're alive. If they don't come, then everything here is over once and for all.

I can't sleep. Only dreams no sleep. Today in a dream I invented a new means of transportation for a steep park. One takes a branch, which needn't be very strong, braces it at an angle against the ground, keeps one end in one's hand sits down as lightly as possible on it, as if riding sidesaddle, the whole branch then naturally races down the slope, since one is sitting on the branch one is taken along and rocks comfortably at full speed on the elastic wood. It is then also possible to use the branch to ride upward. The main advantage aside from the simplicity of the whole device lies in the fact that the branch thin and mobile as it is, able to be lowered and raised as needed gets through everywhere where even a person by himself would have difficulty getting through

---

To be pulled in through the ground-floor window of a house by a rope around the neck and yanked up, bleeding and tattered, through all the ceilings, furniture, walls and attics without consideration as if by someone who is not paying attention, until up on the roof the empty noose appears, which has lost my remains only while breaking through the roof tiles.

---

21 VIII *(July)* 13 Special method of thinking. Emotionally permeated. Everything feels itself to be a thought even in the greatest indefiniteness. (Dostoyevsky)[696]

This block and tackle within. A little hook moves forward, in some secret recess, one scarcely knows it at first, and now the whole apparatus is in motion. Subject to an ungraspable power, as the watch seems subject to time, it creaks here and there and all the chains rattle one after the other down their prescribed stretch.

Compilation of all the arguments for and against my marriage: 1) Inability to endure life alone, not inability to live, on the contrary, it's even improbable that I know how to live with someone, but the onslaught of my own life, the demands I make on myself, the attack of time and age, the vague surge of the desire to write, the sleeplessness, the nearness of insanity—all this I'm unable to endure alone. Perhaps, I naturally add. The connection with F. will give my existence more power of resistance.

2. Everything immediately gives me pause. Every joke in the comic paper, the memory of Flaubert and Grillparzer, the sight of the nightshirts on my parents' beds, which have been prepared for the night, Max's marriage.[697] Yesterday my sister said: "All the married people (of our acquaintance) are happy, I don't understand it" this statement too gave me pause, I became afraid again.

3 I must be alone a great deal. What I have achieved is only a result of being alone.

4 I hate everything that doesn't relate to literature, it bores me to carry on conversations (even if they relate to literature) it bores me to pay visits, sorrows and joys of my relatives bore me to my soul. Conversations take from everything I think the importance, the seriousness, the truth.

5 The fear of the connection, of flowing across. Then I'll never be alone again.

6 In front of my sisters, especially in the past it was so, I have often been a completely different person than in front of other people. Fearless, exposed, powerful, surprising, moved as otherwise only while writing. If through my wife's mediation I could be like that in front of everyone! But then wouldn't it be at the expense of the writing? Anything but that, anything but that!

7. Alone I could perhaps one day really give up my job. Married it will never be possible.

In our class, the fifth grade of the Amaliengymnasium, there was a boy named Friedrich Guss, whom we all hated very much. When we came to class early and saw him sitting in his seat by the stove, we could hardly understand how he had been able to bring himself to come to school again. But I'm not telling it right. We didn't hate only him, we hated everyone. We were a terrible association. One day, when the regional school inspector was attending a lesson—it was a geography lesson and the professor his eyes turned to the blackboard or the window like all our professors, was describing the Morea Peninsula—

It was on the first day of school, evening was already approaching. The professors of the Obergymnasium were still sitting in the conference room, studying the lists of pupils, preparing new roll books, talking about their vacation trips.

Miserable person that I am!

Just whip the horse properly! Bore the spurs slowly into him, then pull them out with a jerk but now make them pierce the flesh with all one's strength.

What distress!

Were we crazy? We ran at night through the park and swung branches.

In my boat I entered a small natural bay.

During my Gymnasium days I was in the habit of visiting now and then a certain Josef Mack, a friend of my late father. When, after graduating from Gymnasium, I—

During his Gymnasium days Hugo Seiffert was in the habit of paying a visit now and then to a certain Josef Kiemann an old bachelor, who had been friendly with Hugo's late father. These visits suddenly ceased when Hugo unexpectedly received the offer of a job abroad starting immediately and left his hometown for several years. When he later returned, he did intend to visit the old man, but no opportunity arose, perhaps such a visit would not have suited his altered views anyhow, and although he often walked down the street where Kiemann lived indeed although he repeatedly saw him leaning in the window and was probably noticed too he neglected to visit.

Nothing, nothing, nothing. Weakness, self-annihilation, tip of a flame of hell penetrating the floor.

23 VIII *(July)* 13 With Felix in Rostock.[698] The bursting sexuality of the women. Their natural impurity. The game, senseless for me, with little Lenchen. The sight of the one fat woman, who, hunched in a wicker chair, one foot noticeably pushed back, was sewing something and conversing with an old woman, probably an old maid, whose teeth always appeared especially large on one side of her mouth. The full-bloodedness and cleverness of the pregnant woman. Her behind with straight divided planes, positively faceted. The life on the small terrace. How I quite coldly took the little girl on my lap, not at all unhappy about the coldness. The ascent in the "quiet valley"

How childishly a tinsmith, visible through the open door of the shop, sits at his work and keeps striking with the hammer

---

Roskoff, History of the Devil: Among the present-day Caribs "he who works at night" is considered the creator of the world.

13 Aug. *(1913)* Perhaps everything is now over and my letter of yesterday the last. It would absolutely be the right thing. What I will suffer,

what she will suffer—it can't be compared with the shared suffering that would arise. I will slowly collect myself, she will marry, it's the only way out among the living. We two can't smash a path into a rock for the two of us, it's enough that we've wept and tormented ourselves over it for a year. She will recognize it from my last letters. If not, then I will certainly marry her, for I'm too weak to resist her opinion on our shared happiness and incapable of not realizing, as far as it lies within my power, something she considers possible.

Yesterday evening on the Belvedere under the stars.

---

14 *(August 1913)* The opposite has occurred. Three letters arrived. The last one I couldn't resist. I love her, as far as I'm capable of it but this love lies buried to the point of suffocation under fear and self-reproaches.

Conclusions from the "Judgment" for my case. I owe the story indirectly to her. But Georg's downfall is precipitated by the bride.

Coitus as punishment of the happiness of being together. To live as ascetically as possible, more ascetically than a bachelor, that's the only way for me to endure marriage. But her?

And despite everything, if we, I and Felice, had completely equal rights, if we had the same prospects, and possibilities, I wouldn't marry. But this impasse into which I have slowly pushed her fate makes it into an unavoidable if by no means incalculable duty for me. Some secret law of human relationships is at work here.

The letter to her parents[699] caused me great difficulties especially because a draft written under especially unfavorable circumstances resisted revision for a long time. Yet today I have nearly succeeded, at least there's no untruth in it and it remains readable and comprehensible even for parents.

How coldly I played this evening—Oskar and his wife weren't home—with Leo, of whom I'm supposedly fond. I found him repugnantly strange and stupid.[700]

---

15 *(August 1913)* Agonies in bed toward morning. Saw the only solution in a leap out the window. My mother came to my bed and asked whether I'd sent off the letter[701] and whether it was my old text. I said it was the old text, only made even sharper. She said she didn't understand me. I replied that she certainly didn't understand me and not only in this matter. Later she asked me whether I was going to write to Uncle Alfred, he deserved to get a letter from me. I asked why he deserved it. He has telegraphed, he has written, he's so well-disposed toward you.[702] "Those are only appearances" I said "he's a complete stranger to me, he misunderstands me completely, he doesn't know what I want and need, I have nothing to do with him." "So no one understands you" my mother said "I'm probably a stranger to you too, and your father too. So we all want only what's bad for you." "Certainly you're all strangers to me, only the closeness of blood exists, but it doesn't express itself. You certainly don't want what's bad for me."

This and several other self-observations have led me to the conclusion that my ever-growing inner determination and conviction contain possibilities of persevering in a marriage despite everything, indeed even of leading it to a development advantageous to my destiny. This is, to be sure, a belief I take on to some extent already on the window ledge.

I will close myself off from everyone to the point of oblivion. Make enemies of everyone, speak with no one.—

The man with the dark, severely gazing eyes, who was carrying the heap of old coats on his shoulder.

Leopold S. tall strong man, awkward twitching movements, loosely hanging, wrinkled, black-and-white checkered clothes hurries through the door on the right into the large room, claps his hands and shouts Felice! Felice! Without waiting a moment for a reply to his shouting, he hurries to the middle door, which, again shouting Felice, he opens.

Felice S. enters through the door on the left, stops at the door, 40-year-old woman in a kitchen apron

Here I am Leo. How nervous you've become recently! What is it you want?

Leopold. turns around with a jerk, then stops and gnaws his lips

Well then! Come here! (he goes to the sofa)

F. (doesn't budge) Quick! What do you want? I have to go to the kitchen.

L. (from the sofa) Never mind the kitchen! Come here! I want to tell you something important. It's worth it. Come on!

F. (walks over slowly, pulls up the straps of her apron)

Now what is it that's so important? If you're making a fool of me, I'll be angry, seriously. (Stops in front of him)

L. Well sit down!

F. And what if I don't want to.

L. Then I can't tell you. I must have you close to me.

F. Well now I'm sitting.

---

21 VIII 13

Today I got Kierkegaard Buch des Richters.[703] As I suspected, despite essential differences his case is very similar to mine at least he is on the same side of the world. He confirms me like a friend. I'm drafting the following letter to her father, which if I have the strength, I will send off tomorrow.[704]

You hesitate to answer my request, that's completely understandable, any father would do so in the face of any suitor, it is thus by no means the reason for this letter, at most it increases my hope for calm evaluation of this letter. But I'm writing this letter out of fear that your hesitation or your consideration has more general grounds rather than resulting from that single passage of my first letter that by itself would make it necessary and that could have betrayed me. This is the passage that deals with the intolerability of my job.

You will perhaps pass over this word, but you shouldn't, rather you should ask quite precisely about it, then I would have to answer you precisely and briefly as follows. My job is intolerable to me because it is at odds with my only desire and my only calling that is literature. Since I am nothing but literature and can and want to be nothing else, my job can never seize me, but it can certainly shatter me completely. I'm not far from that. Nervous states of the worst sort dominate me without cease and this year of worries and torments about my and your daughter's future has fully proven my lack of resistance. You might ask why I don't give up this job and—I have no wealth—try to support myself by literary work. To this I can give only the pitiful answer that I don't have the strength for it and, as far as I have a general view of my situation, will more likely go to ruin in this job, indeed go to ruin quickly.

And now compare me with your daughter, this healthy, merry, natural strong girl. As often as I repeated it to her in about 500 letters and as often as she reassured me with a "no" that was, to be sure, not convincingly supported—it nonetheless remains true, she will surely be unhappy with me, as far as I can foresee. Not only due to my external circumstances but even far more due to my true nature I am a withdrawn, taciturn unsociable dissatisfied person, but without being able to call this a misfortune for me, for it is only the reflection of my goal. Conclusions can at least be drawn from my way of life at home. Well I live in my family, among the best and most loving people, stranger than a stranger. With my mother in recent years I haven't spoken an average of twenty words a day, with my father hardly ever exchanged more than words of greeting. With my married sisters and my brothers-in-law I don't speak at all, though I'm not angry with them. The reason for it is simply that I don't have even the slightest thing to speak with them about. Everything that isn't literature bores me and I hate it, for it disturbs me or hinders me, even if only supposedly. Therefore I lack any propensity for family life except that of the observer at best. I have no sense of kinship, in visitors I positively see malice directed against me.

A marriage couldn't change me, just as my job can't change me.

---

30 VIII 13 Where will I find salvation? How many untruths of which I was no longer even aware will be brought to the surface too. If the real relationship would be just as permeated by them as the real farewell then

I have definitely done the right thing. In me myself without human connection there are no visible lies. The bounded circle is pure.[705]

14 x 13.

The small street began with the wall of a churchyard on one side and a low house with a balcony on the other. In the house lived the retired official Friedrich Munch and his sister Elisabeth.

A troop of horses broke out of the enclosure.

Two friends took a morning ride.

"Devil, save me from benightedness!" cried an old merchant who had wearily lain down on the sofa in the evening and now at night rose with difficulty only by gathering all his strength. There was a dull knock at the door. "Come in, come in, all that is outside!" he cried

---

15 x 13 I have perhaps caught myself again, have perhaps secretly taken a shortcut again and stop myself, already despairing in loneliness, again. But the headaches, the sleeplessness! Well it's worth the struggle or rather, I have no choice.[706]

The stay in Riva[707] had a great importance for me. I understood a Christian girl[708] for the first time and lived almost entirely in her sphere. I'm incapable of writing down anything about it that would be decisive for the memory. Only to preserve itself does my weakness prefer to make my dull head clear and empty, insofar as the confusion can be pushed to the edges. But I almost prefer this state to the merely dull and vague surge the liberation of which, besides being uncertain, would require a hammer to smash me beforehand.

Failed attempt to write to E. Weiss.[709] And yesterday in bed the letter was boiling in my head.

Sitting in the corner of a tram, my coat wrapped around me.

Prof. Grünwald[710] on the trip from Riva. His German-Bohemian nose reminiscent of death, swollen, reddened, blistering cheeks of a face tending toward bloodless thinness, the blond full beard surrounding it. Possessed by the craving to eat and drink. The swallowing of the hot soup, the biting into and simultaneous licking of the unpeeled salami stump, the serious sipping of the already warm beer, the breaking out of sweat around his nose. A repulsiveness that the greediest staring and sniffing cannot savor to the full.

The house was already closed. There was light in two windows of the third floor and then in a window of the fifth floor too. A carriage stopped in front of the house. A young man came to the illuminated window on the fifth floor, opened it and looked down at the street. In the moonlight

---

It was already late in the evening. The student had lost all desire to keep working. Nor was it even necessary, he had really made great progress in the past few weeks, he could certainly rest a little and reduce the night work. He closed his books and notebooks, arranged everything on his small desk and was about to undress to go to bed. But by chance he looked toward the window and at the sight of the clear full moon it occurred to him to take a short walk first in the beautiful autumn night and possibly refresh himself somewhere with a black coffee. He put out the lamp, took his hat and opened the door to the kitchen. In gen. it didn't matter to him at all that he always had to go through the kitchen, this inconvenience also made his room significantly cheaper, but now and then when it was especially noisy in the kitchen or when as today for example he wanted to go out late in the evening, it was indeed bothersome.

Inconsolable. Today in half-sleep in the afternoon: In the end the pain will surely burst my head. And indeed at the temples. What I saw while imagining this was actually a gunshot wound, only around the hole the edges were turned up with sharp ends, as with a furiously torn-open tin can.

Don't forget Krapotkin![711]

---

20 X 13 The inconceivable sadness in the morning. In the evening read Jakobsohn "Der Fall Jakobsohn."[712] That strength to live, to decide, to set one's foot with pleasure in the right place. He sits in himself as a masterful rower would sit in his boat and in any boat. I wanted to write to him. Went for a walk instead, blurred all the absorbed feeling in a conversation with Haas,[713] whom I met, women excited me, now I've read "The Transformation"[714] at home and find it bad. Perhaps I'm really lost, the sadness from this morning will come back, I won't be able to resist it for long, it deprives me of all hope. I don't even feel like keeping a diary, perhaps because too much is already missing in it, perhaps because I would constantly have to describe only half and by all appearances <u>necessarily</u> half measures, perhaps because even writing contributes to my sadness. I would like to write fairy tales (why do I hate the word so?), which could please W.[715] and which she holds one day under the table during a meal, reads in the pauses and turns terribly red when she realizes that for a little while now the sanatorium doctor has been standing behind her and observing her. Her excitement sometimes, actually always, during the telling of stories (I notice that I fear the positively physical strain in remembering, the pain under which the floor of the mental vacuum slowly opens or even just buckles a little) Everything resists being written down. If I knew that her commandment to say nothing about her were at work in this (I've kept it strictly, almost effortlessly) then I would be satisfied, but it's nothing but inability. Besides, what do I think of the fact that for quite a stretch this evening I was reflecting on what the acquaintance with W. had cost me in pleasures with the Russian woman, who perhaps, it's by no means out of the question, would have let me at night into her room, which

was diagonally across from mine. While my evening intercourse with W. consisted in my knocking on the ceiling of my room, which was under hers, in a knock language we never definitively discussed, receiving her answer, leaning out the window, greeting her, once letting her bless me, once snatching at a lowered ribbon, sitting on the window balustrade for hours, hearing every one of her footsteps up above, mistakenly regarding every chance knock as a sign of understanding, hearing her coughing, her singing before falling asleep.

---

21 *(October 1913)* Lost day. Visit to the Ringhoffer factory[716] Ehrenfels's seminar,[717] at Weltsch's, dinner, walk, now 10 o'clock here. I keep thinking of the darkling beetle, but won't write.

In the small harbor of a fishing village a bark was being equipped for a voyage. A young man in baggy breeches was supervising the work. Two old sailors were carrying bags and boxes to a landing stage, where a tall man with his legs braced apart received everything and delivered it to various hands stretching toward him from the dark interior of the bark. On large square-hewn stones enclosing a corner of the quay sat five men half lying and blowing the smoke of their pipes in all directions. From time to time the man in baggy breeches came up to them, made a speech and patted them on the knees. Usually a wine jug was taken out from behind a stone where it was kept in the shade and a glass of opaque red wine was passed from man to man.

22 *(October 1913)* too late. The sweetness of grief and of love. Smiled at by her in the boat. That was the most beautiful of all. Always only the longing to die and the still-holding-out, this alone is love.

Yesterday's observation. The situation most suitable to me: To listen to a conversation between two people who are discussing a matter that closely concerns them while I have only a very remote interest in it, which is moreover completely selfless.

26 *(October 1913)* The family was sitting at dinner. Through the curtainless windows they looked out into the tropic night.

It was a quiet warm evening. In the moonlight the village street was completely

---

The family was sitting at dinner. Through the curtainless window holes they looked out into the tropic night.

"Who am I, then?" I scolded myself. I rose from the sofa, where I had been lying with my knees drawn up, and sat upright. The door which led directly from the stairwell into my room, opened and a young man with a bowed head and a scrutinizing gaze entered. As far as it was possible in the narrow room, he kept away from the sofa and stopped in the corner beside the window in the dark. I wanted to see what sort of apparition this was, walked over and grasped the man by the arm. It was a living person. He looked—a little shorter than I—up at me with a smile, the unconcern with which he nodded and said "Go ahead and examine me" should have been enough to convince me. Nonetheless I grabbed him in front by the vest and in back by the coat and shook him. His beautiful strong golden watch chain caught my eye, I seized it and pulled it down so that the buttonhole to which it was fastened tore. He put up with this, only looked down at the damage and tried in vain to hold the vest button in the torn buttonhole. What are you doing? he finally said, showing me the vest. "Be quiet!" I said threateningly.

I began to run around the room, from a walk I broke into a trot, from a trot into a gallop, whenever I passed the man I raised my fist to him. He wasn't watching me at all but was still working on his vest. I felt very free, even my breathing was occurring in an extraordinary way, my chest felt hindered only by my clothes from heaving gigantically.

For many months now Wilhelm Menz, a young bookkeeper, had been intending to speak to a girl whom he was in the habit of encountering regularly in the morning on the way to the office on a very long street now at this point now at that one. He had already reconciled himself to the fact that it would go no farther than this intention—he was very irresolute in the face of women and the morning was also an unfavorable time to speak to a girl who was in a hurry—when it happened that one evening—it was around Christmastime—he saw the girl walking just in front of him. "Fräulein" he said. She turned around, recognized the man whom she was in the habit of always encountering in the morning, without stopping let her eyes rest on him a little and, since Menz said nothing further, turned away again. They were on a brightly illuminated street in the middle of a large crowd of people and Menz was able, without attracting attention, to come up quite close to her. At this decisive moment Menz couldn't think of anything appropriate to say, but he didn't want to remain a stranger to the girl either, for he was determined to continue something begun so seriously, and so he dared to tug at the bottom of the girl's jacket. The girl put up with this as if nothing had happened.

---

6 XI 13 Whence the sudden confidence? May it remain! If I could go in and out through all doors as a halfway upright person. Only I don't know whether I want that.

Margarethe Bloch,[718] Ehrenstein[719]

We didn't want to tell our parents anything about it, but every evening after 9 o'clock we met I and two cousins by the cemetery fence at a point where a slight elevation of the ground made a good view possible.

The iron fence of the cemetery leaves a large grass-covered area open on the left.

Friedrich: I've had enough.

Wilhelm:

17 November 13

Dream: On a rising road about in the middle of the slope and mainly in the roadway there was beginning on the left when seen from below muck or hardened clay, which toward the right had been crumbling away into an ever lower heap, while on the left it stood as tall as fence posts. I walked on the right where the road was almost clear and saw a man on a tricycle coming toward me from below and apparently riding straight toward the obstacle. This man seemed to have no eyes at least his eyes looked like blurred holes. The tricycle was rickety, thus moved unsteadily and shakily, but still soundlessly, with an almost exaggerated silence and lightness. I grabbed the man at the last moment, held him as if he were the handlebar of his vehicle and steered the latter into the gap through which I had come. Then he fell toward me, I was now gigantic and yet held him only in a strained manner, moreover the vehicle as if it were now out of control began to move backward, even if slowly and pulled me along. We passed a cart on which several people stood crowded together, all dressed darkly, among them was a boy scout wearing a light gray hat with an upturned brim. From this boy, whom I had already spotted from some distance, I expected help, but he turned away and squeezed himself into the crowd. Then, behind this cart—the tricycle kept rolling and I bending down low with my legs spread had to follow—someone came toward me who brought me help, but whom I can't remember. I know only this, that it was a trustworthy person who is now hiding as if behind a black taut fabric and whose hiddenness I should respect.

---

18 *(November 1913)* I will write again, but how many doubts I've had in the meantime about my writing. At bottom I am an incapable ignorant person who if he hadn't been compelled, without any merit of his own, scarcely aware of the compulsion, to go to school, would have just barely been fit to sit in a dog house, to leap out when he is given food and to leap back when he has devoured it.

In a strongly sunlit yard two dogs were running toward each other from opposite directions.

18 *(November 1913)* Wrung from myself the beginning of a letter to Frl. Bloch.

19 *(November 1913)*
I'm moved by reading the diary. Is the reason for it that now in the present I no longer have the slightest certainty. Everything appears to me as a construction. Every remark by someone else, every chance sight turns everything in me over onto another side, even forgotten, utterly insignificant things. I'm more uncertain than I've ever been, I feel only the power of life. And I am senselessly empty. I'm really like a lost sheep in the night and in the mountains or like a sheep that is running after this sheep. To be so lost and not to have the strength to bemoan it.

I intentionally walk through the streets where there are whores. Passing them entices me, that remote but nonetheless existing possibility of going with one. Is that vulgarity? But I know no better and carrying this out seems to me basically innocent and causes me almost no remorse. I want only the fat older ones, with outmoded clothes made, however, to some extent luxurious by various adornments. One woman probably knows me by now. I met her this afternoon, she was not yet in professional clothing, her hair still lay flat against her head, she had no hat, a work blouse of the sort worn by cooks and was carrying some bundle perhaps to the laundress. No one would have found anything enticing about her, only I. We looked at each other fleetingly. Now in the evening, it has meanwhile grown cold, I saw her in a close-fitting, yellowish brown coat on the other side of the narrow street branching off from Zeltnergasse,[720] where she has her promenade. I looked back at her twice, she even caught the glance, but then I actually ran away from her.

The uncertainty surely stems from the thoughts of F.

---

20 *(November 1913)* Was at the movies. Wept. "Lolotte." The good priest. The little bicycle. The reconciliation of the parents. Boundless entertainment. Beforehand sad film "Das Unglück im Dock" afterward funny one "Endlich allein."[721] Am completely empty and insensible, the passing tram has more living feeling.

21 *(November 1913)*

Dream: The French ministry, four men, is sitting around a table. A deliberation is taking place. I remember the man sitting on the long right side with his face flattened in profile, a yellowish complexion, his quite straight nose protruding far protruding so far (due to the flatness) and an oily black, heavy mustache arching over his mouth.

Pitiful observation, which certainly proceeds again from a construction, the lowest end of which is hovering somewhere in emptiness: When I took the inkwell off the desk to carry it into the living room, I felt some sort of firmness in me, just as, for example, the edge of a large building appears in the mist and immediately disappears. I didn't feel lost, something was waiting in me, independent of people even of Felice. What if I now ran away from it, just as, for example, one at some point runs into the fields.

This predicting, this following of examples, this definite fear is ridiculous. These are constructions that even in the imagination where they alone reign, come only almost to the living surface, but always must be abruptly submerged. Who has the magic hand that he would stick into the machinery and it wouldn't be torn to pieces and scattered by a thousand knives.

I'm on the hunt for constructions. I come into a room and find them whitely growing muddled in a corner.

---

24 November 13 The evening before last at Max's. He's becoming more and more a stranger, he has often been one to me, now I'm becoming one to him too. Yesterday evening simply lay down in bed. Dream toward morning: I'm sitting in the garden of a sanatorium at a long table, even at the head, so that in the dream I actually see my back. It's a gloomy day, I must have gone on an outing, and I arrived a short while ago in an automobile that drove up in a curve to the sloping driveway. The food is just about to be served when I see one of the cleaning women, a young

delicate girl wearing a dress in the colors of autumn leaves, approaching with a very light or unsteady gait through the columned hall that served as the porch of the sanatorium and descending into the garden. I don't yet know what she wants but still point questioningly at myself to find out whether she means me. In fact she brings me a letter. I think this can't be the letter I'm expecting, it's a very thin letter and an unknown thin uncertain handwriting. But I open it and a great number of thin papers covered with writing come out, they are indeed all in the unknown handwriting. I begin to read, leaf through the papers and realize that it must be a very important letter after all and is apparently from F.'s youngest sister.[722] I begin to read eagerly, then my neighbor on the right, I don't know whether man or woman, probably a child, looks over my arm at the letter. I shout: "No!" The nervous people sitting around the table begin to tremble. I've probably caused a disaster. I try to apologize with a few quick words so that I can read again right away. Just as I'm bending over my letter again, I awake unavoidably, as if woken by my own scream. With clear consciousness I force myself back into sleep, the situation actually reappears, I quickly read another two or three hazy lines of the letter, of which I've retained nothing and lose the dream in further sleep.

The old merchant, a huge man, climbed the stairs up to his apartment with buckling knees, not holding but rather pressing the railing with his hand. Outside the door of his room a barred glass door he was about to pull his keys out of his pants pocket as always when he noticed in a dark corner a young man, who now gave a bow. "Who are you? What do you want?" asked the merchant still groaning from the exertion of climbing. "Are you the merchant Messner?" asked the young man. Yes said the merchant. "Then I have a message for you. Who I am is actually of no consequence here for I myself am not at all involved in the matter, am only the messenger. Nonetheless I'll introduce myself, my name is Kette and I'm a student." "Ah said Messner, thinking for a little while. Well and the message?" he then said. "It would be better for us to discuss that in your room" said the student "it's a matter that cannot be settled on the stairs." "I'm aware of no such message I'm supposed to receive" said Messner, looking sideways at the floor. "That may be" said the student. "Besides" said Messner "it's past 11 o'clock at night now, no one will listen to us here." "No replied the student I can't possibly say it here." "And I" said Messner "don't receive guests at night" and he stuck the key in the lock so forcefully that the other keys in the bunch kept jingling for a while. "But I've been waiting here since 8 o'clock, three hours" said the student. "That proves only that the message is important to you. I, however, don't want any messages. Every message I'm spared is a gain. I'm not curious, just go, go." He grabbed the student by his thin overcoat and pushed him away a bit. Then he opened slightly the door of the room, from which an immense heat penetrated the cold hall. "By the way, is it a business message" he then asked, already standing in the open doorway. "I can't say that here either" said the student. "Then I wish you a good night" said Messner, went into his room, locked the door with the key, turned on the light of the electric bedside lamp, filled a little glass at a small wall cabinet containing several liqueur bottles, drained it with a smack of his lips and began to undress. Leaning against the high pillows he was just about to begin reading a newspaper when it seemed to him as if someone were knocking softly at the door. He laid the newspaper back on the blanket, crossed his arms and listened. Indeed there was another knock and it was quite soft and practically at the bottom of the door. "Really, an intrusive monkey" thought Messner. When the knocking stopped, he picked up the newspaper again. But now there was a harder knocking and a downright banging against the door. The knocks came the way children at play spread their blows over the whole door, now dull against the wood down below now ringing against the glass up above. I'll have to get up Messner thought, shaking his head. I can't call the caretaker, for the telephone is over in the anteroom and I'd have to wake the landlady to get there. There's no choice but to throw the boy down the stairs myself. He pulled a felt cap over his head, drew back the blanket, pushed his way to the edge of the bed with his hands braced on it slowly set his feet on the floor and put on padded high slippers. "Well then" he thought, chewing his upper lip as he eyed the door "now it's quiet again." But I must get my peace once and for all he then said to himself, pulled a cane with a horn knob out of a rack, grasped it in the middle and went to the door. "Is anyone still out there?" he asked at the closed door. "Yes" came the answer "please just open the door." "I'm opening it" said Messner, opened it and stepped outside with the cane. "Don't hit me!" said

27 XI *(1913)*

the student warningly and took a step back. "Then go!" said Messner, pointing his index finger in the direction of the stairs. But I'm not permitted to said the student and ran so surprisingly toward Messner

---

27 XI *(1913)* I must stop, without having been downright shaken off. Nor do I feel any danger that I could lose myself, nonetheless I feel helpless and relegated to the outside. The firmness, however, that the slightest writing gives me is beyond doubt and wonderful. The gaze with which I surveyed everything yesterday on the walk!

The child of the female caretaker, who opened the front door. Wrapped in a woman's old scarf, pale, rigid fleshy little face. Is carried like this by the caretaker to the front door at night.

The caretaker's poodle, which sits down below on a step and listens to my stamping beginning on the fifth floor, looks at me when I arrive at his spot and watches me when I walk on. Pleasant feeling of intimacy, since he isn't frightened by me and includes me in the familiar house and its noise.[723]

Picture: Baptism of the ship's boys while crossing the equator. The sailors lounging around. The ship, climbed in all directions and at all heights, offers them places to sit everywhere. The tall sailors who cling to the ship's ladders and with one foot in front of the other press their powerful round shoulder against the body of the ship and look down at the spectacle.[724]

"Someone is ringing the bell!" said Elsa, raising her finger.

A small room. Elsa and Gertrud are sitting by the window with needlework. Twilight beginning.

E. Someone is ringing the bell.

Both listen.

G. The bell really rang? I didn't hear anything. I hear less and less.

E. It was only very quiet. (Goes into the anteroom to open the door)

In the anteroom some words are exchanged. Then E's voice.

Please come in here. Be careful not to stumble. Please walk ahead, it's only my sister in the room.

The Gelsenbauer sisters, Elsa and Gertrud, had three rooms to rent, one was rented to a piano teacher, the second to a cattle dealer

---

Recently the cattle dealer Morsin told us the following story. He was still agitated when he told it, although it had taken place several months ago now.

I very often have business in the city, it must be an average of 10 days a month. Since I usually have to spend the night there too and have always tried to avoid staying in a hotel if at all possible, I rented a private room that simply,

---

3 XII 13 Letter to Weiss[725]

4 XII 13

Seen from outside it is horrible to die or even to kill oneself grown up but young. To depart in complete confusion that would make sense within a further development, hopelessly or with the sole hope that this appearance in life will be regarded within the great reckoning as not having happened. I would now be in such a situation. Dying would mean nothing but sacrificing a nothingness to nothingness, but this would be emotionally impossible, for how could one even only as a nothingness consciously sacrifice oneself to nothingness, and not just to an empty nothingness but rather to a roaring nothingness, the nullity of which consists only in its ungraspability.

A circle of men, who are masters and servants. Well-wrought faces shining in vivid colors. The master sits down and the servant brings him food on a tray. Between the two there is no greater difference, no difference to be judged otherwise than, for example, between a man who due to the combination of countless circumstances is an Englishman and lives in London and another who is a Laplander and at the same time is sailing the sea in his boat alone in a storm. Certainly, the servant can—this too only under certain circumstances—become master, but this question, however it might be answered, does not intrude here, for it is a matter of the present evaluation of present conditions.

The unity of humanity, doubted now and then even if only emotionally by everyone even the most accessible and adaptable people, on the other hand also reveals itself to everyone, or seems to reveal itself in the complete, perpetually detectable commonality of general and individual human development. Even in the most hidden emotions of the individual.

The fear of folly. Seeing folly in every feeling that strives straight ahead and makes one forget everything else. What then is non-folly? Non-folly is standing like a beggar before the threshold, beside the entrance, decaying and falling over. But P. and O.[726] are actually disgusting fools. There must be follies that are greater than their bearers. This stretching of the little fools in their great folly is perhaps what is disgusting. But didn't Christ appear to the Pharisees in the same state?

Wonderful, completely contradictory idea that someone who has died, for example, at 3 o'clock at night enters a higher life immediately thereafter around dawn. What irreconcilability there is between the visibly human and everything else! How one mystery always gives rise to a greater one! At the first moment the human calculator is out of breath. Actually one should be afraid to step out of the house

---

5 XII 13 How I rage against my mother! I need only begin speaking with her and I'm annoyed, almost scream.

O.[727] is actually suffering and I don't believe that she is suffering can be suffering, don't believe it even though I know better, don't believe it so that I won't have to stand by her, which I couldn't do, for I'm annoyed at her too.

Externally, at least sometimes, I see only a few countable little details of F. That makes her picture so clear, pure, elemental, defined and airy at once.

8 XII 13 Constructions in Weiss's novel. The strength to abolish them, the duty to do so. I almost deny experiences. I want peace, step by step or running, but not calculated leaps of grasshoppers

9 XII 13 Weiss "Galeere" Weakening of the effect when the story begins to draw to a close. The world is overcome and we have watched with open eyes. Thus we can calmly turn around and go on living.[728]

Hatred toward active self-observation. Interpretations of one's soul: Yesterday I was like that and for that reason, today I'm like this and for this reason. It's not true, not for that reason and not for this reason and therefore also not like that and like this. To bear oneself calmly, without being overhasty, to live as one must, not to run around oneself like a dog.

I had fallen asleep in the thicket. A noise woke me. I found in my hands a book I had been reading earlier. I threw it away and jumped up. It was shortly after noon, in front of the hill on which I stood spread a great lowland plain with villages and ponds and uniform tall reedlike shrubs between them. I put my hands on my hips, searched everything with my eyes and at the same time listened to the noise

---

10 XII *(1913)* Discoveries have imposed themselves on people.

The laughing, boyish, sly, unrestrained, face of the chief inspector,[729] which I had never before seen on him and noticed only today at a moment when I was reading him something the director[730] wrote and happened to look up from it. At the same time he also put his right hand in his pants pocket with a jerk of his shoulders as if he were another person.

It is never possible to notice and judge all the circumstances that influence the mood of a moment and are even at work in it and are finally at work in the judgment, therefore it is false to say, yesterday I felt secure, today I am in despair. Such differentiations prove only that one wants to influence oneself and as separate from oneself as possible, hidden behind prejudices and fantasies to temporarily perform an artificial life, just as at some point someone in the corner of a tavern, sufficiently hidden by a little schnapps glass, alone exclusively with himself amuses himself with nothing but false unprovable imaginings and dreams.

Toward midnight a young man in a tight pale-gray checkered lightly snow-dusted overcoat climbed down the stairs to the small music hall. He paid at the cash desk, behind which a dozing young lady started and looked straight at him with large black eyes, and then he stopped for a little while to survey the hall lying 3 steps below him.

Almost every evening I walk to the state railroad station,[731] today, because it was raining, I walked up and down the hall there for ½ an hour. The boy who kept eating the sweets from the machines. The reaching of his hand into his pocket, out of which he pulls a lot of change, the careless inserting into the slot, the reading of the labels while eating, the falling of some pieces, which he picks up from the dirty floor and sticks straight into his mouth.—The calmly chewing man speaking intimately with a woman, a relative by the window.

---

11 XII 13 Read the beginning of Michael Kohlhaas at the Toynbee Hall.[732] Utter failure. Badly selected, badly presented, ultimately swam

around senselessly in the text. Exemplary audience. Very little boys in the first row. One of them tries to contend with his innocent boredom by carefully throwing his cap on the floor and then carefully picking it up and doing so repeatedly. Since he's too small to carry this out from his seat, he always has to slide off the chair a little. Read wildly and badly and carelessly and unintelligibly. And in the afternoon I was already trembling with eagerness to read, could hardly keep my mouth closed.

There's really no push necessary, only a withdrawal of the last strength devoted to me and I fall into a despair that tears me to pieces. When I imagined today that I would definitely be calm during the presentation, I asked myself what sort of calm it would be, on what it would be based, and I could say only that it would merely be a calm for its own sake, an incomprehensible mercy, nothing else.

12 *(December 1913)* And in the morning I got up relatively quite fresh.

Yesterday on the way home the little boy wrapped in gray running alongside a group of boys, slapping himself on the thigh, grabbing another boy with his other hand and shouting rather absentmindedly, which I must not forget: Dnes to bylo docela hezky.[733]

The freshness with which I walked on the street today around 6 o'clock after the day's somewhat altered schedule. Ridiculous observation, when will I eradicate this.

I looked closely at myself in the mirror a short while ago, and my face—albeit only in the evening lighting and with the light source behind me so that actually only the down at the edges of my ears was illuminated—even under closer examination appeared to me better than I know it to be. A clear well-formed, almost beautifully bounded face. The black of the hair, of the eyebrows and of the eye sockets issues like life from the rest of the waiting mass. The gaze isn't at all ravaged, there's no trace of that, but it's not childlike either, rather unbelievably energetic, but perhaps it was only observant, since at that moment I was observing myself and wanted to frighten myself.

---

12 XII 13 Didn't fall asleep for a long time yesterday. F. Finally had the plan and with that I fell asleep uncertainly, to ask Weiss to go to her office with a letter, and to write in this letter nothing more than that I must have a message from her or about her and have therefore sent Weiss there so that he would write to me about her. Meanwhile Weiss is sitting next to her desk, waits until she has finished reading the letter, bows, since he has no other instructions and is hardly likely to get an answer, and leaves.[734]

Discussion evening at the association of officials.[735] I led it. Funny sources of self-respect. My introductory sentence: "I must introduce today's discussion evening with the regret that it is taking place." For I had not been informed in time and was therefore not prepared.

14 XII *(1913)* Beermann lecture. Nothing, but presented with an occasionally contagious self-satisfaction. Girlish face with goiter. Before speaking almost every sentence the same muscle contractions in the face, as when sneezing. A verse from the Christmas market in his article in today's Tagblatt.

Sir, buy it for your little dears
So that they laugh and don't shed tears.

Quoted Shaw: "I am a sedentary timid civilian."[736]

Wrote letter to F. in the office.

The fright on the way to the office in the morning when I met the girl from the seminar who resembles F., at that moment didn't know who it was and only noticed that she did resemble F. and yet wasn't F., but had some further relationship to F. beyond that, namely that at the sight of her in the seminar I had thought of F. a great deal.[737]

Just now read in Dostoyevsky the passage that is so reminiscent of my "Unhappiness."[738]

When I slid my left hand into my pants along the side while reading and grabbed my lukewarm thigh.

---

15 *(December 1913)* Letters to Dr. Weiss and Uncle Alfred.
No telegram came.[739]

Read "Wir Jungen von 1870/71."[740] Again read of the victories and enthusiastic scenes with suppressed sobbing. To be a father and speak calmly with one's son. But then one must not have a little toy hammer in place of a heart.

"Have you written to your uncle yet?" my mother asked me, as I had long been maliciously expecting. She had been observing me anxiously for a long time, for various reasons hadn't dared firstly to ask me and secondly to ask me in front of my father and finally asked nonetheless in her worry when she saw that I was about to go out. When I passed behind her chair, she looked up from the playing cards, turned her face to me with a bygone gentle movement somehow revived for that moment and asked, glancing up only fleetingly, smiling shyly and humiliated in the mere asking of the question, before even receiving any answer.

16 XII 13
"The thunderous cry of delight from the seraphim"[741]

I sat at Weltsch's in the rocking chair, we spoke about the disorder of our lives, he at least with a certain confidence ("One must want the impossible") I without even that, looking at my fingers, feeling like the representative of my inner emptiness, which is exclusive and not even overly large.

Letter to Bl.

---

17 *(December 1913)* Letter to W. with the instructions.[742] "To be overflowing and yet only a pot on a cold stove"

Bergmann lecture "Moses and the Present."[743] Pure impression. How the man has lifted himself up, he has really wedged himself somewhere in the heights. And as a boy he could be blown away, in everything, but perhaps not in everything after all and it was only my lack of understanding that believed this.[744]—In any case I have nothing to do with it. Between freedom and slavery the real terrible paths cross without guidance for the coming stretch and with an immediate extinguishing of the distance already covered. There are countless such paths or only one it can't be determined for there's no overall view. That is where I am. I can't leave. I have nothing to complain about. I don't suffer excessively, for I don't suffer cohesively, it doesn't pile up, at least I don't feel it for the time being, and the magnitude of my suffering lies far below the suffering that might be my due.

The silhouette of a man who, with arms half raised in different positions in the air, confronts complete fog in order to enter it.

The beautiful strong separations in Judaism. One gets space. One sees oneself better, one judges oneself better.

18 *(December 1913)* I'm going to bed, I'm tired. Perhaps it has already been decided there.[745] Many dreams about it.

False letter from Bl.[746]

---

19 *(December 1913)* Letter from F.[747] Beautiful morning, warmth in my blood.

---

20 *(December 1913)* no letter

The effect of a peaceful face, a calm speech, especially from a stranger one hasn't seen through yet. The voice of God from a human mouth

---

An old man walked through the streets in the mist one winter evening. It was icy cold. The streets were empty. No one passed near him, only now and then he saw in the distance half in the mist a tall policeman or a woman in furs or shawls. Nothing concerned him, he thought only of visiting a friend at whose home he had not been for a long time and who had just now sent a maid for him.

It was already long after midnight when there was a soft knock on the door of the merchant Messner's room. He did not have to be roused, he always fell asleep only toward morning, but until then he was in the habit of lying awake in bed on his belly, his face pressed into the pillow, his arms outstretched and his hands interlaced over his head. He had immediately heard the knock "Who is it?" he asked. An unintelligible murmur, softer than the knock answered. It's open he said and turned on the electric light. A short frail woman in a large gray shawl entered.

---

2 1 14 Spent a lot of time well with Dr. Weiss[748]

4 1 14

We had dug a hollow in the sand in which we felt quite comfortable. At night we curled up inside the hollow, our father covered it up with tree trunks and underbrush thrown over them and we were as protected as possible from storms and animals. "Father" we often cried fearfully when it was already completely dark under the wood and our father still had not appeared. But then we saw his feet through a crack, he slid in with us, patted each of us a little, for it soothed us when we felt his hand and then we all fell asleep practically in unison. Besides our parents we were 5 boys and 3 girls, it was too cramped for us in the hollow, but we would have been afraid if we hadn't been so close to and on top of each other at night.

---

5 I 14 afternoon. Goethe's father died in a state of dementia, at the time of his final illness G. was working on Iphigenie[749]
"Get that woman home, she's drunk" some court official said to Goethe about Christiane

August, who drinks like his mother and runs around with women in a base way.

The unloved Ottilie, whom his father dictated to him as his wife out of social considerations.

Wolf the diplomat and writer

Walter the musician, cannot take the examinations. Withdraws for months to the Gartenhaus; when the czarina wants to see him: "Tell the czarina that I'm not a wild animal"[750]

"My health is more lead than iron."

Wolf's petty fruitless literary work.

Aged gathering in the attic rooms. The 80-year-old Ottilie, the 50-year-old Wolf and their old acquaintances.

Only in light of such extremes does one realize how everyone is irretrievably abandoned to himself and only the contemplation of others and of the law reigning in them and everywhere can provide comfort. How Wolf can be outwardly guided, moved here or there, cheered up, encouraged, induced to perform systematic work and how he is inwardly held back and immovable.

Why don't the Chukchi emigrate from their terrible country, they would live better anywhere else, in comparison to their present life and to their present desires. But they can't; everything that is possible does happen; only what happens is possible.[751]

In the little town of F. a wine merchant from the larger neighboring town had established a wine tavern. He had rented a small vaulted room in a building on the Ringplatz, painted Oriental ornaments on the walls and put in old by then almost unusable plush furniture

---

6 I 14. Dilthey: "Das Erlebnis und die Dichtung." Love for humanity, highest respect for all the forms developed by it, a calm standing back at the most suitable observation point. Luther's youthful writings
"the mighty shades that, from an invisible world, attracted by murder and blood enter the visible one" Pascal

---

Letter for Anzenbacher to his mother-in-law. L. kissed the teacher.[752]

8 I 14 Reading by Fantl "Goldhaupt," "he throws the enemy like a barrel."[753]

Uncertainty, dryness, peace, in these everything will pass.

What do I have in common with Jews? I have scarcely anything in common with myself and should stand completely silent in a corner, content that I can breathe.

Description of inexplicable feelings. Anzenbacher: Ever since it happened, the sight of women has been painful to me, but it's not sexual excitement, nor pure sadness, it's just painful to me. That's also how it was before I was sure of Liesl.

---

12 I 14
Yesterday: Ottilie's love affairs, the young Englishmen,—Tolstoy's engagement, clear impression of a delicate, tempestuous, self-restraining

young person full of presentiments. Beautifully dressed, dark and dark blue.

The girl in the coffeehouse. The narrow skirt, the white, loose, fur-trimmed silk blouse, the bare neck, the close-fitting gray hat with stiff, slanted and high [754] made of the same material. Her full, laughing, endlessly breathing, face, friendly eyes, though a little affected. My face growing hot in thoughts of F.

Way home, clear night, distinct consciousness of the merely dull in me, which is so far from great clarity fully spreading unhindered.

Nikolai, Litteraturbriefe.[755]

There are possibilities for me, certainly, but under what stone do they lie?

Yanked forward, on the horse—

Senselessness of youth. Fear of youth, fear of senselessness, of the senseless ascent of inhuman life.

Tellheim: He has that free agility of the inner life such as only the creations of true poets possess, which under changing life circumstances surprises us again and again by revealing completely new sides of itself.[756]

---

19 I 14 Fear at the office alternating with self-assurance. Otherwise more confident. Great aversion to "Transformation." Unreadable ending. Imperfect almost to its depths. It would have turned out much better if I hadn't been interrupted at the time by the business trip.[757]

---

23 *(January 1914)* Chief controller Bartl[758] tells of friend of his, a retired colonel, who sleeps by a wide-open window: "During the night it's very pleasant; on the other hand it becomes unpleasant in the morning when I have to shovel the snow off the ottoman by the window and then begin to shave.

Memoirs of Countess Thürheim:[759]
Her mother: "Racine was especially suited to her gentle nature. I often heard her praying to God to grant him eternal peace."

There's no doubt that he (Suwórow) at the great dinners given in his honor in Vienna by the Russian ambassador Count Rasumovsky, ate like a glutton from the food on the table without waiting for anyone. When he was full, he stood up and left the guests to themselves.

Judging by an engraving a delicate, resolute pedantic, old man.

"It wasn't meant for you" my mother's poor consolation. What's bad is that at the moment I almost don't need a better one. This is a sore point and remains a sore point with me, but otherwise the regular, scarcely varied, half-active life of the past several days (report on the "operations" at the office,[760] A.'s worries about his bride, Ottla's Zionism,[761] the girls' enjoyment of the Salten-Schildkraut presentation,[762] reading of the Thürheim memoirs, letters to Weiss and Löwy, correction of the "Transformation"[763]) fairly pulls me together and gives me some firmness and hope.

24 *(January 1914)* Napoleonic era: How there was a throng of celebrations, everyone was in a hurry "to savor the pleasures of the brief periods of peace." "On the other hand, the women exerted their influence on them in great haste, they really had no time to lose. Love at that time expressed itself in heightened enthusiasm and greater abandon" . . . "These days there's no longer any excuse for an hour of weakness."[764]

Incapable of writing a few lines to Frl. Bl., two letters had already gone unanswered, today came the third. I grasp nothing correctly and at the same time am quite solid, but hollow. Recently, when I got out of the elevator once again at the regular hour, it occurred to me that my life with its days growing uniform in more and more minute detail resembles the punishment in which the pupil has to write down the same sentence, senseless at least in its repetition, ten times, a hundred times or even more depending on his offense, except that in my case it's a punishment under the condition "as many times as you can stand it."

Anzenbacher cannot calm down. Despite the trust he has in me and although he wants advice from me, I always learn the worst details only in passing during the conversation, whereupon I always have to suppress my sudden astonishment as much as possible, not without the feeling that he must experience my indifference toward the terrible news either as coldness or as great reassurance. That's how it's intended too. I learned the story of the kiss in the following stages, some of them separated by weeks: A teacher kissed her—she was in his room—he kissed her several times—she was in his room regularly, because she was doing needlework for A.'s mother and the teacher's lamp was good—she let herself be kissed with no will of her own—he has declared his love to her before—despite everything she still goes for walks with him—wanted to give him a Christmas present, once she wrote something unpleasant has happened to me but nothing has remained.

A. questioned her in the following way: How was it? I want to know down to the last detail? Did he only kiss you? How often? Where? Didn't he lie on you? Did he touch you? Did he want to take off your clothes? Answers: I was sitting on the sofa with the needlework, he on the other side of the table. Then he came over, sat down next to me and kissed me, I moved away from him toward the sofa pillow and my head was pushed onto the pillow. Besides the kissing nothing happened.

During the questioning she said at one point: "What are you thinking? I am a girl."

Now it occurs to me that my letter to Dr. Weiss[765] was written in such a way that it could be shown to F. in its entirety. What if he had done so today and for that reason put off his reply.

---

26 I 14

Can't read the Thürheim, which has been my sole pleasure for the past few days. Just mailed the letter to Frl. Bl. at the railroad station. How it holds me and presses against my forehead. My parents' card playing on the same table.

The parents and their grown children, a son and a daughter were sitting at the table on Sunday at noon. The mother had just stood up and was dipping the ladle into the round-bellied soup pot to serve the soup when the whole table suddenly rose, the tablecloth fluttered, the hands lying on it slid off, the soup flowed with rolling bacon dumplings into the father's lap

---

How I almost berated my mother just now because she lent Elli "Die böse Unschuld,"[766] which I'd wanted to offer her myself only yesterday. "Leave me my books! I have nothing else." Speeches of this sort in true anger.

The death of Thürheim's father: "The doctors who entered soon thereafter found the pulse very weak and gave the sick man only a few hours to live. My God it was my father of whom they spoke—only a few hours' time and then dead."

---

28 I 14 Lecture on the miracles of Lourdes.[767] Freethinking doctor, energetic, baring of strong teeth, great pleasure in rolling the words "It is time that German thoroughness and honesty took a stand against Latin charlatanism." Newspaper criers of the Messager de Lourdes "Superbe guerison de ce soir" Guerison affirmée! Debate: "I'm a simple postal official nothing more"

Hotel de l'univers—Infinite sorrow while leaving in thoughts of F. Gradual calming by reflections.

Sent letter to Bl. and Weiss's Galeere[768]

Some time ago Anzenbach.'s sister was told by a fortune-teller that her oldest brother was engaged and that his bride was betraying him. At the time he had angrily fended off such stories. I: Why only at the time. After all, it's as false today as it was then. She hasn't betrayed you. He: She hasn't, has she?

2 II 14 Anzenbacher. Whorish letter to his bride from her friend. "If we were to take everything as seriously as when the confessional sermons held us under their influence." "Why did you hold yourself back so much in Prague, better to have one's fling on a small scale than a large." I interpret the letter, according to my conviction, in favor of his bride, with good points occurring to me. Yesterday A. was in Schluckenau.[769] Sits all day with her in the room and, holding the packet of all the letters (his only baggage) in his hand, doesn't stop questioning her. Learns nothing new, an hour before his departure he asks: "was the light out during the kissing?" and learns the news, which makes him inconsolable, that during the (second) kissing W. put out the light. W. was drawing on one side of the table, L. was sitting on the other side (in W.'s room, at 11 o'clock in the evening) and reading "Asmus Semper"[770] aloud. Then W. stands up, goes to the cabinet to get something (L. thinks a compass, A. thinks a condom) then suddenly puts out the light, assails her with kisses, she sinks against the sofa, he holds her by the arms, by the shoulders and from time to time says "Kiss me!"

L. on another occasion: "W. is very clumsy." Another time: "I didn't kiss him," another time: "I believed I was lying in your arms."

A: I must have clarity (he's thinking of having her examined by a doctor) what if I learn on my wedding night that she's been lying. Perhaps she's so calm only because he used a cond.

Lourdes: Attack on the belief in miracles also attack on the church. With the same justification he could proceed against the churches, the processions, the confessions, the unhygienic goings-on everywhere, since it can't be proven whether prayers help. Karlsbad is a greater swindle than Lourdes and Lourdes has the advantage that people go there because of their innermost belief. What about the stubborn opinions regarding operations, serum treatments, vaccinations, medicines?

Nonetheless: The huge hospitals for the seriously ill pilgrims; the dirty piscinae; the brancards waiting for the special trains; the medical commission; the great electrically illuminated crosses on the mountains; the Pope receives 3 mill. a year. The priest with the monstrance passes by, a woman cries out from her stretcher: "I am cured." Still has bone tuberculosis without any change.

The door opened a crack. A revolver appeared and an outstretched arm.[771]

Thürheim II[772] 35, 28, 37 (Nothing sweeter than love, nothing more amusing than coquetry)
45, 48 (Jews)[773]

20 *(10)* II 14 11 o'clock after a walk. Fresher than usual. Why?

1.) I told Max I was calm.
2.) Felix is getting married (was angry with him)[774]
3. I will remain alone, unless F.[775] wants me after all.
4. Invitation from Frau Thein[776] and consideration of how I will introduce myself to her.

By chance I was walking the opposite way of my usual route namely Kettensteg[777] Hradschin Karlsbrücke. Usually I practically fall down on this route, today coming from the opposite side I've lifted myself up a little.

---

21 *(11)* 11 14 "Goethe" Dilthey, read through hastily,[778] wild impression, carries one along, why couldn't one set oneself aflame and be destroyed in the fire. Or follow, even if one hears no commandment? Sit in the middle of one's empty room on a chair and look at the floor. Shout "forward" in a narrow pass and hear individual people shouting from all the side paths between the cliffs and see them emerging.

13 11 14

Yesterday at Frau Thein's.[779] Calm and energetic, an energy that flawlessly prevails, pierces, works its way in with glances hands and feet. Openness, open gaze. I keep remembering her ugly huge solemn Renaissance ostrich feather hats from the past, as long as I didn't know her personally she was repugnant to me. How her muff, when she hurries toward the point of a story, is pressed against her body and yet twitches. Her children Nora and Mirjam.

Very reminiscent of W.[780] in her look, in the way she loses herself in the story, in her complete involvement, in her small lively body, even in her hard dull voice, in her talk of beautiful dresses and hats, while nothing of the sort is to be seen on her.

View from the window over the river.[781] At many points in the conversation, although she allows no weariness to arise, my complete failure, senseless look, incomprehension of what she's saying, unreeling of the most simple-minded remarks while I am forced to see her listening attentively, senseless touching of the small child

Dreams: In Berlin, through the streets, to her house, the calm happy consciousness that, though I'm not yet at her house, I have the easy possibility of getting there, will definitely get there. I see the streets, on a white house a sign something like "The Magnificent Halls of the North" (read yesterday in the newspaper) in the dream "Berlin W" added. Ask an affable red-nosed old policeman who on this occasion is wearing a sort of servant's uniform. Receive overly detailed information, even a railing of a small park in the distance is pointed out to me, which I should hold on to for safety's sake when I pass by. Then advice regarding the tram, the subway, etc. I can no longer follow and ask in fright, knowing well that I'm underestimating the distance: "That must be ½ an hour away?" But he, the old man, answers: "I'll be there in 6 minutes." The joy! Some man, a shadow, a companion is always with me, I don't know who it is. Have positively no time to turn around, to turn sideways.—Stay in Berlin in some pension where apparently all the guests are young Polish Jews; very small rooms. I spill a bottle of water. Someone is writing incessantly on a small typewriter, scarcely turns his head when one asks for something. Can't get hold of a map of Berlin. In someone's hand I keep seeing a book that resembles a map. It keeps turning out that it contains something completely different, a list of Berlin schools, tax statistics or something of the sort. I don't want to believe it, but with a smile one proves it to me beyond any doubt.

---

14 II 14

If I should kill myself, there's most certainly no one to blame, even if, for example, the apparent immediate cause should be F.'s behavior. Once, in half-sleep, I even imagined the scene that would ensue if, foreseeing the end, I entered her apartment with the farewell letter in my pocket, were rejected as a suitor, laid the letter on the table, went to the balcony, broke free from the grasp of all who hurried over, and, while one hand after the other had to let go, jumped over the balcony balustrade. The letter, however, would say that, although I was jumping because of F., even if my proposal had been accepted nothing essential would have changed for me. I belong down below, I can find no other resolution, F. happens to be the one by whom my fate is proven, I am not capable of living without her and must jump, but—and F. suspects this—I would not be capable of living with her either. Why not use tonight for this purpose, even now the speakers from today's parents' evening,[782] who spoke of life and of the creation of its conditions, appear to me,—but I cling to fantasies, I live completely entangled in life, I won't do it, I am completely cold, am sad that a shirt is pinching my neck, am damned, gasp for breath in the mist.

---

15 II 14

How long this Saturday and Sunday seem to me in retrospect. Yesterday afternoon I had my hair cut, then wrote the letter to Bl., then visited Max for a moment in the new apartment,[783] then parents' evening[784] next to L. W.,[785] then Baum (met Krätzig[786] in the tram "emergency puncture"[787]), then on the way back Max's complaints about my silence, then the desire for suicide, then my sister returned from the parents' evening, incapable of reporting the slightest detail. In bed until 10, sleepless, sorrow and sorrow. No letter not here, not in the office,[788] mailed letter to Bl. on the Franz Josef Railroad,[789] Gerke in the afternoon,[790] a walk along the Moldau, reading aloud in his apartment, strange mother eating bread and butter and playing solitaire, walked around alone for 2 hours, resolved to go to Berlin on Friday, met Khol,[791] at home with brothers-in-law and sisters, then discussion of the engagement at Weltsch's[792] (Joine Kisch[793] putting out the candles) then at home attempts to elicit sympathy and help from my mother by remaining silent, now my sister, tells about the club evening, the clock strikes ¼ to 12.

I said at Weltsch's, to console his upset mother: "I'm losing Felix through this marriage too. A married friend is not one."[794] F.[795] said nothing, naturally couldn't say anything either, but he didn't even want to.

This notebook begins with Felice, who on 2 V 13 made my head uncertain,[796] with this beginning I can also close the notebook, if instead of uncertain I use a worse word.

Ninth Notebook

I step out of the house to take a short walk. It's nice weather but the street is strikingly empty, only a municipal worker is standing in the distance with a water hose in his hand and spraying a huge arc of water along the street. "Unheard of" I say, examining the span of the arc. "A little municipal worker" I say, looking again at the man in the distance. On the corner of the next cross street two men are fighting, collide, fly far apart, eye each other furtively and are now back together. "Stop fighting, gentlemen" I say.

The student Kosel was sitting at his desk and studying. He was so absorbed in his work that he didn't even notice it growing dark, which despite the bright May day had already begun toward four o'clock in the afternoon in this badly situated courtyard-facing room. Lips pursed, eyes unknowingly lowered far down toward the book, he read. Sometimes he paused, wrote short excerpts of what he had read in a small notebook and then with his eyes closed murmured to himself from memory what he had written. Opposite his window, not five meters away was a kitchen in which a girl was ironing linens and sometimes looked across at Kosel.

Suddenly Kosel put down the pencil and listened upward to the ceiling. In the room above someone was walking around, apparently barefoot, making circuit after circuit. With each step there was a loud slap, as when one steps into water. Kosel shook his head. Unless he defended himself in some way these walks up above, which he had been forced to endure ever since a new tenant had moved in, for about a week now, meant the end not only of his studies today, but also of his studies altogether. No head strained by intellectual work could bear it.

There are certain connections that I feel clearly but that I am incapable of discerning. It would be enough to dive down a little bit deeper, but that is just where the upthrust is so strong that I might believe myself to be on the bottom of the water if I didn't feel the pull of the currents below me. In any case I turn to face upward, from where the brilliance of the light, refracted a thousand times, strikes me. I rise and drift around up above, even though I hate everything up there and it

---

"Herr Director, a new actor has arrived" one clearly heard the servant announce, for the door to the anteroom was wide open. "I just want to become an actor" Karl said to himself and in this way corrected the servant's announcement. "Where is he?" the director said, craning his neck.

---

21 VI 14 Temptation in the Village

The old bachelor with the altered beard style

The woman dressed in white in the middle of the courtyard of the Kinsky Summer Palace.[797] Distinct shading of the high arch of her bosom despite the distance. Stiff sitting posture.

One summer I arrived toward evening in a village where I had never been before. It struck me how broad and clear the paths were. Everywhere one saw tall old trees in front of the farms. It was after a rain, the air blew fresh, I found everything so pleasant. I tried to show this to the people standing outside the gates by the way I greeted them, they answered in a friendly if restrained manner. I thought that it would be good to spend the night here if I could find an inn.

I was just walking past the tall greenery-covered wall of a farm when a small door opened in this wall, three faces looked out, disappeared and the door closed again. "Odd" I said, speaking sideways, as if I had a companion. And indeed, as if to embarrass me, there was a tall man standing next to me, without hat and coat, in a knitted black vest, smoking a pipe. I quickly composed myself and said, as if I had known of his presence beforehand: "That door! Did you see that small door open too." "Yes" said the man "but what's odd about that, it was the children of the tenant. They heard your footsteps and looked to see who was walking here so late in the evening." "That's certainly a simple explanation" I said with a smile "it's easy for everything to seem odd to a stranger. Thank you." And I walked on. But the man followed me. I wasn't actually surprised at this, the man could be going the same way, but that was no reason why we should walk one behind the other and not side by side. I turned around and said: "Is this the right way to the inn?" The man stopped and said: We don't have an inn or rather we have one, but it's uninhabitable. It belongs to the community and since no one applied for it, it was given away years ago to an old cripple whom the community had previously had to provide for. He now manages the inn with his wife and does so in such a way that one can hardly pass by the door, so great is the stench coming out. The taproom is slippery with filth. A wretched establishment, a disgrace to the village, a disgrace to the community. I had the urge to contradict the man, his appearance provoked me to do so, that basically thin face with yellowish, leathery poorly padded cheeks and black wrinkles wandering through the whole face in accordance with his jaw movements. "Ah" I said, expressing no further astonishment at these circumstances and then went on: "Well, I will stay there anyhow since I am simply determined to spend the night here." "By all means then" the man said hastily "but you must go this way to the inn" and he pointed in the direction from which I had come. "Go to the next corner and then turn right. You will then immediately see an inn sign. That's where it is." I thanked him for the information and now walked past him again while he observed me especially closely. Against the possibility that he had given me false directions I was, to be sure, defenseless, but I was definitely not going to let him confound me by forcing me to march past him now or by having desisted with such striking rapidity from warning against the inn. Someone else would show me the inn too and if it was filthy, I could sleep in filth once too, as long as my defiance was satisfied. Moreover, I didn't have much choice, it was already dark, the country roads were sodden from the rain and the journey to the next village was long.

The man was now behind me and I was intending to pay no more heed to him at all when I heard a woman's voice speaking to the man. I turned around. Out of the darkness under a group of plane trees stepped a tall upright woman. Her skirt shone yellowish brown, a black coarse-meshed shawl covered her head and shoulders. "Come home now, won't you" she said to the man. "Why aren't you coming?" "I'm coming" he said. "Just wait a little while longer. I just want to watch what this man here is going to do. He's a stranger. He's roaming around here quite unnecessarily. Just look." He was talking about me as if I were deaf or didn't understand his language. Now, to be sure, it didn't matter much to me what he said, but it would naturally have been unpleasant to me if he had spread any false rumors about me in the village. So I said to the woman: "I'm looking for the inn, nothing more. Your husband has no right to talk about me in that way and perhaps instill in you a false opinion of me." But the woman hardly looked at me, rather went to her husband—I had correctly discerned that he was her husband, there was such a direct natural relationship between them—and put her hand on his shoulder: "If you want something, then speak with my husband not with me." "I don't want anything at all" I said, annoyed at this treatment "I don't concern myself with you, don't concern yourself with me either. That's my only request." The woman jerked her head, that much I could see in the dark, but not the expression of her eyes. Apparently she wanted to make some reply, but her husband said: "Be quiet!" and she remained silent.

This encounter now seemed to me definitively concluded, I turned around and was about to walk on when someone called "Sir." This was probably directed at me. For a moment I had no idea where the voice was coming from, but then I saw a young man sitting above me on the farm wall, his legs dangling down and knees striking together, who casually said to me: "I just heard that you want to spend the night in the village. Apart from here on the farm you won't find suitable accommodations anywhere." "On the farm?" I asked and involuntarily, I was angry about it afterward, I looked questioningly at the married couple, who still stood there leaning against each other and observing me. "That's right" he said, in his answer as in his whole demeanor there was arrogance. "There are beds for rent here" I asked again, to make sure and to drive the man back into the role of landlord. "Yes" he said, having already averted his eyes from me a little "beds are provided here for the night, not to anyone but only to him to whom they are offered." "I accept" I said "but will of course pay for the bed, as at the inn." "Please" said the man, who had been looking past me for a long time "we won't take advantage of you." He sat up above like the master, I stood down below like a little servant, I had a strong urge to make him somewhat livelier up there by throwing a stone. Instead I said: "Then please open the door for me." "It's not locked" he said.

"It's not locked" I repeated grumbling almost without knowing it, opened the door and stepped in. Immediately after entering I happened to look up at the wall, the man was no longer up there, he had apparently jumped off the wall despite its height and was perhaps conferring with the married couple. Let them confer, what could happen to me a young person whose cash barely exceeded 3 guldens and the rest of whose property consisted of not much more than a clean shirt in his knapsack and a revolver in his pants pocket. Besides, the people did not look at all as if they would rob anyone. But what else could they want from me? It was the usual unkempt garden of large farms, the solid stone wall had led one to expect more. In the tall grass, at regular intervals, stood cherry trees that had shed their blossoms. In the distance one saw the farmhouse, an extensive one-story building. It was already growing quite dark; I was a late guest; if the man on the wall had in some way lied to me, I could end up in an unpleasant situation. On the way to the house I met no one, but just a few paces from the house I saw through the open door two tall old people, husband and wife, in the first room, side by side, facing the door, eating some sort of porridge out of a bowl. In the darkness I couldn't distinguish anything more precise, only the man's coat shone in places like gold, it was probably the buttons or the watch chain. I greeted them and then said, without crossing the threshold for the time being: "I was looking for overnight accommodations in the village when a young man sitting on the wall of your garden told me that one could pay to spend the night here on the farm." The two old people had stuck their spoons into the porridge, leaned back on their bench and looked at me silently. Their demeanor was not very hospitable. I therefore added: "I hope that the information I was given was correct and that I haven't disturbed you unnecessarily." I said this very loudly, for perhaps the two of them were hard of hearing. Come closer said the man after a little while. Only because he was so old did I obey him, otherwise I naturally would have insisted that he give a definite answer to my definite question. In any case I said, as I entered: "If taking me in should cause you even the slightest difficulties, then say so openly, I by no means insist on it. I'll go to the inn, it doesn't matter to me at all." "He talks too much" the woman said softly. It could only have been meant as an insult, so one responded to my courtesies with insults, but she was an old woman, I couldn't defend myself. And this very defenselessness was perhaps the reason that the woman's not-to-be-repelled remark had a much greater effect within me than it deserved. I felt some sort of justification for some sort of reproach, not because I had spoken too much, for I had actually said only what was strictly necessary, but for other reasons reaching very close to my existence.

I said nothing further, insisted on no reply, saw a bench in a nearby dark corner, went to it and sat down. The old people began to eat again, a girl came out of an adjoining room and placed a burning candle on the table. Now one could see even less than before, everything had contracted in the dark, only the little flame flickered over the slightly bowed heads of the old people. Several children ran in from the garden, one of them fell sprawling on the floor and wept, the others stopped running and now stood scattered around the room, the old man said: "Go to bed, children." Immediately they gathered, the weeping one was only sobbing now, a boy near me tugged at my coat as if to tell me to come along, I actually did want to go to bed too, so I stood up and as a grown man in the midst of the children, who loudly said good night in unison, I silently left the room. The friendly little boy held my hand, so that I found my way easily in the dark. But we also came to a ladder very soon, climbed up and were in the attic. Through a small open skylight one saw at the moment the narrow moon, it was a pleasure to step under the skylight, my head almost projected into it, and to breathe the balmy and yet cool air. Straw was heaped on the ground against a wall, there was enough room for me to sleep there too. The children—there were 2 boys and 3 girls—laughed while they undressed, I had thrown myself on the straw in my clothes, I was among strangers, after all, and had no claim to be admitted here. For a little while, propped up on my elbows, I watched the children playing half-naked in a corner. But then I felt so tired that I laid my head on my knapsack, stretched out my arms, took a few more glances at the roof beams and fell asleep. In the first moments of sleep I thought I still heard one boy shouting: Watch out he's coming! whereupon the sound of the hasty scurrying of the children running to their beds penetrated my already-waning consciousness. I had certainly slept only a very short time, for when I woke up the moonlight fell through the skylight almost unchanged on the same spot on the floor. I didn't know why I had woken up, for I had slept dreamlessly and deeply. Then I noticed beside me at about the height of my ear a very small bushy dog, one of those repugnant lapdogs with a relatively large head surrounded by curly hair, their eyes and snout loosely set into their head like pieces of jewelry made of some lifeless hornlike substance. How had a big-city dog like this ended up in the village? What drove it around the house at night? Why was it standing by my ear? I hissed at it to make it go away, perhaps it was a plaything of the children and had only strayed to me. It was frightened by my hissing, but didn't run away, instead only turned around, now stood there with crooked little legs and showed its—especially in comparison to its large head—stunted small body. Since it remained calm, I wanted to sleep again, but I couldn't I kept seeing in the air directly before my closed eyes the dog rocking and its eyes bulging. This was unbearable, I couldn't keep the animal beside me, I stood up and picked it up in my arms to carry it out. But the animal, so dull until now, began to defend itself and tried to grasp me with its claws. So I had to restrain its paws too, which was very easy, to be sure, I could hold all 4 of them together in one hand. "So my little dog" I said, speaking down to the agitated little head with its shaking curls and went into the dark with it to search for the door. Only now did it strike me how quiet the little dog was, it didn't bark or squeal, only the blood pounded wildly through all its veins I felt that. After a few steps—the attention the dog demanded had made me careless—to my great annoyance I bumped into one of the sleeping children. It was also now very dark in the attic room, only a little light still came through the small skylight. The child sighed, I stood still for a moment, didn't even move my toes away lest any change wake the child even more. It was too late, suddenly I saw all around me the children rising in their white shirts as if by arrangement, as if by command, it wasn't my fault, I had woken only one child and this waking had not been a waking at all but only a slight disturbance, which a child's sleep should have easily withstood. Well, now they were awake. "What do you children want I asked go back to sleep" You're carrying something said one boy and all five of them searched around on me. Yes I said, I had nothing to hide, if the children wanted to carry the animal out it was all the better. "I'm carrying this dog out. It wouldn't let me sleep. Do you know to whom it belongs?" "To Frau Cruster" at least this was what I thought I heard in their confused indistinct sleepy exclamations intended not for me but only for each other. "Who is Frau Cruster" I asked, but I got no further answer from the excited children. One of them took the dog, which had now become completely still, from my arms, and hurried away with it, the rest followed. I didn't want to remain alone here, my sleepiness had now passed away too, for a moment I did hesitate, it seemed to me as if I were meddling too much in the affairs of this house where no one had shown great trust in me, but in the end I ran after the children nonetheless. I heard the patter of their feet just ahead of me, but in the complete darkness and not knowing the way I stumbled often and once even banged my head painfully against the wall. We also came into the room where I had first met the old people, it was empty, through the still-open door one saw the garden in the moonlight. "Go outside" I said to myself "the night is warm and bright, one can march onward or even spend the night in the open air. After all, it's so senseless to run after the children here." But I kept running nonetheless, I did still have my hat, stick and knapsack up in the attic. But how the children ran! With fluttering shirts they had flown through the moonlit room, as I had seen clearly, in two bounds. It occurred to me that I was giving thanks in a manner befitting the lack of hospitality in this house by having rousted the children, holding a race around the house, myself making noise through the house instead of sleeping (the steps of the children's bare feet could hardly be heard beside my heavy boots) and not even knowing what would ensue from all this. Suddenly there was a bright light. In a room opening before us with several wide-open windows, a delicate woman was sitting at a desk and writing by the light of a tall beautiful floor lamp. "Children!" she cried in astonishment, she didn't see me yet, I remained outside the door in the shadow. The children put the dog on the desk, they must have loved the woman very much, they kept trying to look her in the eyes, one girl seized her hand and stroked it, she tolerated it and scarcely noticed it. The dog stood before her on the sheet of paper on which she had just been writing, and stuck out its trembling little tongue, clearly visible just in front of the lampshade, toward her. The children now asked permission to stay here and tried to wheedle consent out of the woman. The woman was indecisive, rose, stretched out her arms, pointed to the one bed and the hard floor. The children refused to accept this, and tentatively lay down on the floor where they were standing; for a little while everything was quiet. Her hands folded in her lap the woman looked down at the children with a smile. Now and then a child raised its head but seeing the others lying down too, it lay back again

---

One evening I came home from the office somewhat later than usual—an acquaintance had kept me down below for a long time outside the front door—and still absorbed in thoughts about the conversation, which had revolved mainly around professional questions, opened the door of my room, hung my overcoat on the hook and was about to go to the washstand when I heard strange short breaths. I looked up and at the height of the stove that stood deep in a corner I noticed in the semidarkness something alive. Yellowishly gleaming eyes looked at me, on both sides below the unrecognizable face the large round breasts of a woman rested on the ledge of the stove, the whole creature seemed to consist of only heaped-up soft white flesh, a thick long yellowish tail hung down from the stove, its end was constantly sweeping back and forth between the cracks of the tiles.

The first thing I did was to walk with long strides and deeply bowed head—folly! folly! I repeated softly like a prayer—to the door that led to my landlady's apartment. Only later did I realize that I had entered without knocking. Fräulein Hefter

---

It was at midnight. Five men were holding me, behind them a sixth raised his hand to grab me. "Let go" I cried, spinning to make all of them fall away. I felt certain laws reigning, had known during my last effort that it would be successful, saw all the men flying back now with upraised arms, realized that at the next moment they would all have to throw themselves at me together turned around to face the front door—I was standing just outside it—opened the lock, which sprang open positively of its own volition and in unusual haste, and escaped up the dark stairs. On the top floor my old mother stood in the doorway of the apartment with a candle in her hand. "Watch out, watch out" I shouted up from the floor below "they're following me." "Who? Who?" my mother asked. "Who could be following you, my boy?" "Six men" I said breathlessly. "Do you know them" my mother asked. "No, strangers" I said. "What do they look like?" "I hardly saw them. One has a black full beard, one a large ring on his finger, one has a red belt, one has his pants torn at the knees, one has only one eye open and the last bares his teeth." "Now don't think about it anymore" said my mother "go to your room, lie down to sleep, I've made the bed." My mother! this old woman! already unassailable by the living, with a sly expression around her mouth, which was unconsciously repeating 80-year-old follies. "Sleep now?" I cried "

---

23 VII 14.[798] The tribunal in the hotel.[799] The ride in the carriage. F.'s face. She runs her hands through her hair, wipes her nose with her hand, yawns. Suddenly gathers herself together and says well-thought-through, long-saved-up, hostile things. The way back with Frl. Bl. The room in the hotel, the heat reflected from the opposite wall. Also from the arching side walls that enclose the room's deep-set window comes heat. In addition, afternoon sun. The agile porter, almost Eastern Jewish. Noise in the courtyard, as in a machine factory. Bad smells. The bug. Difficult decision to crush it. Chambermaid is astonished: there are no bugs anywhere, only once did a guest find one in the corridor. At her parents'. Her mother's occasional tears. I recite the lesson. Her father grasps it correctly from all sides. Came specifically for my sake from Malmö, night journey, sits in his shirtsleeves. They admit that I'm right, nothing or not much can be said against me. Devilish in all innocence. Frl. Bloch's apparent guilt. In the evening alone on a chair under the lindens. Bellyache. Sad inspector. Stands in front of the people, fiddles with the slips of paper and one can get rid of him only by paying. Despite all apparent ponderousness performs his duty quite properly, one cannot fly back and forth while doing continuous work of this sort, he also has to try to remember the people. At the sight of such people always these reflections: How did he end up with this job, how is he paid, where will he be tomorrow, what awaits him in his old age, where does he live, in what corner does he stretch his arms before sleep, could I do it too, how would I feel. All this with a bellyache. Terrible night suffered through with difficulty. And yet almost no memory of it. In the Restaurant Bel-

vedere, on Strahlauer Brücke[800] with Erna. She's still hoping for a good outcome or acting as if she is. Drank wine. Tears in her eyes. Ships leave for Grünau, for Schwertau. A lot of people. Music. Erna consoles me, although I'm not sad, that is, I'm sad merely about myself and inconsolable in this. Gives me "Gothic Rooms."[801] Tells a lot of stories (I know nothing). Especially how she prevails against an old poisonous white-haired female colleague in the shop. She would like more than anything else to leave Berlin, to have her own business. She loves quiet. When she was in Sebnitz,[802] she often slept through Sunday. Can be funny too.—On the opposite riverbank Marinehaus. Her brother had already rented an apartment there.

Why did her parents and aunt[803] wave goodbye to me like that? Why did F. sit in the hotel and not stir, even though everything was already clear? Why did she telegraph me: "Expecting you, but have to go away on business on Tuesday." Were deeds expected of me? Nothing would have been more natural. From nothing (interrupted by Dr. Weiss, who walks to the window)[804]

27 VII *(1914)* Didn't visit her parents again the next day. Only sent a cyclist with a farewell letter. Letter dishonest and coquettish "Don't remember me unkindly." Speech from the gallows.[805] Was twice in the swimming school on the Strahlauer Ufer. A lot of Jews. Bluish faces, strong bodies, wild running. Evening in the garden of the "Askanischer Hof." Ate rice à la Trautmannsdorf and a peach. A wine drinker observes my attempt to cut up the small unripe peach with the knife. It's unsuccessful. Under the old man's glances I ashamedly abandon the peach altogether and leaf 10 times through the "Fliegende Blätter."[806] I wait to see whether he won't at last turn away. Finally I gather all my strength and in defiance of him bite into the completely juiceless expensive peach. In the arbor next to me a tall gentleman concerned with nothing but the roast he picks out carefully and the wine in the ice bucket. Finally he lights himself a large cigar, I observe him over my "Fliegende Blätter." Departure from the Lehrter railroad station.[807] The Swede in shirtsleeves. The strong girl with many silver bracelets. Changing trains in Büchen[808] at night. Lübeck. Terrible Hotel Schützenhaus. Overcrowded walls, dirty bedclothes under the sheet, forsaken building, an apprentice is the only waiter. Afraid of the room, I go into the

garden and sit there with a bottle of Harzer Sauerbrunn.[809] Drinking beer opposite me a hunchback and a thin bloodless young person who is smoking. Slept after all, but soon woken by the sun shining through the large window straight into my face. Window looks out on the railroad tracks, incessant noise of the trains. Salvation and happiness after moving to the Hotel Kaiserhof on the Trave. Journey to Travemünde. Bathing place—mixed bathing place. View of the beach. Afternoon in the sand. Due to my bare feet attracted attention as indecent. Next to me the apparent American. Instead of eating lunch, walked past all the pensions and restaurants. Sat on the tree-lined path in front of the Kurhaus and listened to the table music. In Lübeck a walk on the Wall. Sad forsaken man on a bench. Life on Sportplatz. Quiet square, people outside all the doors on steps and stones. Morning from the window, unloading of wood from a sailboat. Dr. W.[810] at the railroad station. Resemblance to Löwy now unceasing. Indecisiveness about Gleschendorf.[811] Meal at the Hansa dairy. "Errötende Jungfrau." Shopping for dinner. Telephone conversation with Gleschendorf. Journey to Marienlyst. Train ferry. Mysterious disappearance of a young man with raincoat and hat and mysterious reappearance of both. Trip in the carriage from Vaggerløse to Marienlyst.[812]

28 *(July 1914)* Despairing first impression of the desolation, the miserable building, the bad food without fruit and vegetables, the quarrels between W. and H.[813] Decision to leave the next day, giving of notice. Stay nonetheless. Reading of Der Überfall, my inability to listen, to share in the enjoyment, to judge. W.'s improvised speeches. Unattainable to me. The man writing in the middle of the garden, fat face, black-eyed, greased long smoothed-back hair. Fixed glances, winks, right and left. The children, uninvolved, sit like flies around his table.—

—My inability to think, to observe, to discern, to remember, to speak, to participate keeps growing, I am turning into stone, I am forced to realize this. My inability is growing even in the office. If I don't save myself in a work, I am lost. Do I know this as clearly as it is so? I hide away from people not because I want to live in peace but because I want to perish in peace. I think of the stretch we, Erna and I, walked from the tram to the Lehrter railroad station.[814] Neither of us spoke, all I was thinking was that each step was a gain for me. And E. is kind to me; incomprehensibly even believes in me, even though she saw me before the tribunal; now and then I even feel the effect of this belief in me, without, to be sure, quite believing this feeling. I felt life in me in the presence of people for the first time in many months opposite the Swiss woman in the compartment, during the return journey from Berlin. She reminded me of G. W.[815] Once she even shouted: Children!—She had headaches, so much did her blood plague her. Ugly, neglected small body, bad cheap dress from a Paris department store. Freckles on her face. But small feet, a body that despite ponderousness was completely under control due to its smallness, round firm cheeks, lively never-extinguished eyes.

The Jewish married couple who were staying next to me. Young people, both of them shy and modest, her big hooknose and slender body, he was slightly cross-eyed, pale, thickset and broad, at night he coughed a little. They often walked one behind the other. View of the disordered bed in their room.—Danish married couple. He often very proper in a suit jacket, she tanned, a weak but coarsely fashioned face. Are silent a lot, sometimes sit side by side, their faces placed side by side at an angle as on cameos.—The impertinent beautiful boy. Always smoking a cigarette. Looks at H. impertinently, challengingly, admiringly, mockingly and contemptuously, all in one glance. Sometimes he pays no attention to her at all. Silently demands a cigarette from her. Shortly thereafter offers her one from a distance. Has torn pants. If one wants to give him a beating, then one must do it this summer, by next summer he will be the one giving a beating. Grasps all the chambermaids caressingly by the arm, but not meekly, not in embarrassment, instead like some lieutenant who in light of his temporary childish form can in some respects take more liberties than later. How while eating he threatens to chop off the head of a doll with his knife.—Lancers. Four couples. By lamplight and to gramophone music in the great hall. After each figure a dancer hurries to the gramophone and puts on a new record. Especially on the part of the gentlemen a properly, lightly and seriously performed dance. The merry red-cheeked, urbane one, whose bulging stiff shirt made his broad high chest even higher—the carefree, pale one standing above everyone, joking with everyone; beginning of a paunch; light-colored baggy clothing; many languages; read the "Zukunft"[816]—the colossal father of the goitrous, hissing family, which one recognized by their heavy breathing and childish bellies; with his wife (with whom he danced quite gallantly) he sat pointedly at the children's table, where he did indeed occupy the most seats with his family.—The proper, neat, trustworthy one, whose face looked almost morose in its sheer seriousness, humility and manliness. Played piano.—The huge German with dueling scars on his square face, whose thick lips came together so peacefully when he was speaking. His wife, hard and friendly Nordic face, emphatic beautiful gait, emphatic freedom of her swaying hips.—Woman from Lübeck with gleaming eyes. Three children, including Georg, who, senseless as a butterfly, alights among complete strangers. Then in childish talkativeness he asks something senseless. We're sitting, for example, and correcting "Der Kampf."[817] Suddenly he appears and asks naturally, trustingly and loudly where the other children have run off to.—The stiff old gentleman who shows what the noble Nordic longheads look like in old age. Spoiled and unrecognizable, if beautiful young longheads were not running around here too.

29 VII *(1914)* The two friends, one of them blond, resembling Richard Strauss, smiling, reserved, adroit, the other dark, properly dressed, gentle and firm, all too supple, lisps, both epicurean, constantly drink wine, coffee, beer, schnapps, smoke uninterruptedly, one of them pours for the other, their room across from mine full of French books, write a great deal in the musty writing room when the weather is nice.

Josef K., the son of a rich merchant, one evening after a great quarrel he had had with his father—his father had reproached him for his dissolute life and demanded its immediate cessation—went without any particular intention only in complete uncertainty and exhaustion to the merchants' house, which stood all alone near the harbor. The doorkeeper bowed deeply. Josef looked fleetingly at him without a greeting. "These silent subordinates do everything one assumes of them" he thought. "If I think that he is observing me with inappropriate glances then he is really doing so." And he turned around once more again without a greeting to face the doorkeeper; the latter turned toward the street and looked up at the overcast sky.[818]

I was completely at a loss. Just a little while ago I had known what was to be done. With his hand held out my boss had pushed me to the door of the shop. Behind the two desks stood my colleagues, supposed friends, their gray faces lowered into the darkness to conceal their expressions. "Out" cried my boss, "thief! Out! I say: Out!" "It's not true" I cried for the hundredth time "I haven't stolen anything! It's a mistake or slander! Don't touch me! I'll sue you! There are still courts! I'm not leaving! For five years I've served you like a son and now I'm being treated as a thief. I haven't stolen anything, I haven't stolen anything, won't you listen for heaven's sake, I haven't stolen anything." "Not another word" said my boss. "You're leaving!" We were already at the glass door, an apprentice, who had run out before, hurriedly opened it, the noise penetrating from what was, to be sure, an out-of-the-way street made me more amenable to the facts, I stopped in the doorway, my hands on my hips, and said only, in all breathlessness as calmly as possible: "I want my hat." "You shall have it" my boss said, took a few steps back, received the hat from the clerk Grasmann, who had swung himself over the desk, tried to throw it to me, but missed his aim, also threw with too much strength so that the hat flew past me into the road. "The hat belongs to you now" I said and went out onto the street. And now I was at a loss. I had stolen, had pulled a five-gulden bill out of the till to be able to go to the theater with Sophie in the evening. She didn't even want to go to the theater, wages would be paid in three days, then I would have had my own money, moreover I had carried out the theft foolishly, in broad daylight, next to the glass window of the office, behind which the boss was sitting and watching me. "Thief!" he shouted and sprang out of the office. "I haven't stolen anything" was the first thing I said, but the five-gulden bill was in my hand and the till was open.

---

30 *(July 1914)* Tired of serving in other people's shops, I had opened a small stationery shop of my own. Since my means were only scant and I had to pay for almost everything in cash

---

I sought advice. I wasn't stubborn. It wasn't stubbornness when, my face convulsively contorted and my cheeks shining with heat, I laughed silently at someone who gave me some advice without knowing it. It was tension, receptiveness, pathological lack of stubbornness.

The director of the "Progress" insurance company was always extremely dissatisfied with his officials. Now every director is dissatisfied with his officials, the difference between officials and directors is too great to be balanced out by mere commands on the part of the director and by mere obedience on the part of the officials. Only mutual hatred achieves the balance and rounds off the whole enterprise.

Banz, the director of the Progress insurance company, looked doubtfully at the man standing in front of his desk and applying for a job as an assistant with the company. Now and then he also skimmed the man's papers lying in front of him on the desk. "You're certainly tall" he said "that much one can see, but what else are you? With us the assistants have to be capable of more than licking stamps and that's just what you don't have to be capable of, because such things are done automatically here. With us the assistants are half-officials, they have responsible work to do, do you feel equal to that. You have a peculiar head shape. How your forehead recedes. Strange! What was your last job? What? You haven't worked in a year? Why not? Because of pneumonia? Really? Well, that isn't much of a recommendation, is it? We can use only healthy people, of course. Before you are taken on, you must be examined by the doctor. You're better now? Really? Certainly, that is possible. If only you would speak louder! You're making me very nervous with your whispering. I also see here that you're married have four children. And you haven't worked in a year! Well, man! Your wife is a laundress? Ah! All right. Since you're already here, have yourself examined by the doctor at once, the assistant will lead you there. But you mustn't conclude from this that you're hired, even if the doctor's opinion is favorable. By no means. In any case you'll get a written notification from us. To be honest, I want to tell you at once: You don't appeal to me at all. We need completely different assistants. But have yourself examined in any case. Go ahead now, go. Begging won't help here. I'm not entitled to hand out favors. You're willing to do any work. Certainly. Everyone is. That's no special distinction. It shows only what a low estimation you have of yourself. And now

I will say for the last time: Go and don't keep me any longer. It's really enough." Banz had to strike the desk with his hand before the man let the assistant pull him out of the director's office.

I mounted my horse and sat down firmly in the saddle. The maid ran out the front door toward me and announced that my wife still wanted to speak to me about an urgent matter, I should wait just one moment, she was not yet fully dressed. I nodded and sat still on my horse, which now and then raised its forelegs slightly and reared a little. We lived at the end of the town, before me in the sun the country road stretched up a hill, which a small carriage had just climbed slowly from the other side to drive down rapidly now toward the town. The coachman brandished the whip, a woman in a quite provincial yellow dress sat in the dark, dust-covered interior of the carriage.

I was not at all surprised that the carriage stopped in front of my house.

Bundles of Paper

21 Aug. 14 Began with such hopes and was thrown back by all three stories,[819] today most of all. Perhaps it's correct that work could be done on the Russian story only always after the Trial. In this ridiculous hope, which is evidently based only on a mechanical fantasy, I begin the Trial again.—It wasn't completely in vain.

29 Aug *(1914)* End of a chapter failed, another beautifully begun chapter I will hardly or rather most definitely not be able to continue as beautifully, while at the time, in the night, I would certainly have succeeded in this. But I must not forsake myself, I am completely alone.

30 *(August 1914)* cold and empty. I feel all too keenly the limits of my ability, which, when I am not completely seized, are undoubtedly only narrowly drawn. And I believe that even when I am seized I am drawn only into these narrow limits, which, to be sure, I then do not feel, since I am being drawn. Nonetheless, in these limits there is space to live and for this I will probably take advantage of them to the point of contemptibility.

¼ to 2 at night. Across the street a baby is crying.[820] Suddenly a man speaks in the same room, as close as if he were outside my window. "I'd rather fly out the window than listen to this any longer." He then grumbles something about nervousness, his wife tries silently only with hissing sounds to put the baby back to sleep

I IX *(1914)* In complete helplessness wrote barely 2 pages. I have retreated considerably today, even though I had slept well. But I know that I must not yield, if I want to rise above the lowest woes of my writing, which is already held down by the rest of my way of life, into the greater freedom that might be waiting for me. The old dullness has not yet completely left me I realize and the coldness of my heart might never leave me. The fact that I recoil from no humiliation can just as well mean hopelessness as give hope.

13 IX *(1914)* Again barely 2 pages. At first I thought the sadness about the Austrian defeats[821] and the fear of the future (a fear that seems to me basically ridiculous and at the same time disgraceful) would hinder me altogether from writing. It wasn't that, only a dullness, which perpetually returns and must be perpetually overcome. For the sadness itself there's time enough when not writing. The trains of thought connected with the war are similar to the old worries about F. in the tormenting way they devour me in the most varied directions. I'm incapable of bearing worries and am perhaps meant to be destroyed by worries. When I am sufficiently weakened—and it needn't take very long—the slightest worry might suffice to drive me apart. In this prospect I can, to be sure, also find the possibility of staving off the misfortune as long as possible. Admittedly, with the exertion of all the strength of a then still relatively unweakened nature I did little against the worries about F, but only at the beginning of that time did I have the great help of writing, which I will never again allow to be wrested from me.

7 Oct. 14 I have taken a week of vacation to drive the novel forward.[822] Up to today—it is Wednesday night, Monday my vacation comes to an end—this has failed. I have written little and feebly. To be sure, even last week I was in decline; but I couldn't foresee that it would get so bad. Are these 3 days enough to permit conclusions that I am not worthy of living without the office?

15 *(October 1914)* 14 days, good work at times, complete grasp of my situation.—Today Thursday (Monday my vacation is over I have taken a further week of vacation) letter from Frl. Bl. I don't know what to do with it, I know that it is decided that I will remain alone (if I remain at all, which is by no means decided) I also don't know whether I love F. (I think of my aversion at the sight of her when she was dancing with a stern lowered gaze or when she ran her hand over her nose and through her hair at the Askan. Hof[823] shortly before leaving and the countless moments of fullest foreignness) but despite everything the endless temptation reappears, I played with the letter all evening, the work has come to a halt, even though I feel capable of it (albeit with agonizing headaches that I have had all week). I'm setting down from memory the letter I wrote to Frl. Bl.:

"It is a strange coincidence Frl. Grete that I got your letter today of all days. I don't want to mention with what it coincided, that concerns only me and the thoughts on which I was dwelling when I lay down in bed last night around 3 o'clock. (Suicide, letter to Max with many instructions)

Your letter surprises me very much. It doesn't surprise me that you're writing to me. Why shouldn't you write to me? You do write that I hate you, but it's not true. If everyone should hate you, I don't hate you and not only because I have no right to. You did sit in judgment over me at the Askanischer Hof, it was abhorrent for you, for me, for everyone—but it only appeared so, in reality I was sitting in your place and am there to this day.

You are completely mistaken about F. I'm not saying that to elicit details. I can think of no detail—and my imagination has by now chased itself around in these circles a great deal, so that I trust it—I say, I can think of no detail that could convince me that you are not mistaken. What you are implying is completely impossible, it makes me unhappy to think that F. for some inexplicable reason should perhaps be deceiving herself. But that too is impossible.

I have always regarded your sympathy as true and without consideration for yourself. Nor was it easy for you to write the last letter. I thank you warmly for it."

What does this achieve? The letter appears unyielding, but only because I was ashamed, because I considered it irresponsible, because I was afraid to be yielding, not because I didn't want to. I even wanted nothing more. It would be best for all of us if she didn't reply, but she will reply and I will wait for her reply.

.... st day of vacation.[824] ½ past two at night, almost nothing, read ....ter and found it bad. Failed ....in two respects. Ahead of me lies the office and ....of the failing factory. But I am ....completely without composure. And my strongest support is ....ly the thought of F., even though in yesterday's ....r I fended off any attempt at a connection. I have now lived in peace for two months without any actual contact with F. (except through the correspondence with Erna), dreamed of F. as of a dead woman who could never live again and now that I have been offered a chance to reach her, she is again the center of it all. She is probably disturbing my work too. Yet how she seemed to me, when I thought of her at times in recent days, the most distant stranger I had ever met, although I did tell myself that this quite special strangeness stemmed from the fact that F. came closer to me than any other person or was at least brought this close to me by the others.

Leafed through the diary a little. Had a sort of inkling of the organization of such a life.

21 *(October 1914)* Did almost no work for 4 days, always only an hour and only a few lines, but slept better, thereby almost lost my headaches. No reply from Bl., tomorrow is the last chance

25 *(October 1914)* Almost complete standstill of my work. What is written seems to be nothing independent, but rather the reflection of good previous work. Reply from Bl. arrived, I'm completely undecided about my reply. Thoughts so mean that I can't even write them down. Yesterday's sadness. When Ottla followed me to the stairs, told me about a picture postcard,[825] ....

and wanted some answer from me ....
say nothing. In my sadness completely incap ....
give a sign only with my shoulders ....
Pick's story[826] despite some merits ....
poem by Fuchs today in the newspaper[827]

1 XI 14 Yesterday after a long time made a little bit of good progress, today almost nothing again, the 14 days since my vacation are almost completely lost.—Today partly nice Sunday. Read Dostoyevsky's defense statement[828] in the Chotek Gardens.[829] The guard at the castle[830] and at the corps headquarters.[831] The fountain in the Thun Palace.[832]—Much self-satisfaction all through the day. And now complete failure in my work. And it's not even failure, I see the task and the way to it, I would only have to push through some thin obstacles and can't do it.—Playing with the thoughts of F.

3 XI 14 In the afternoon a letter to Erna, looked through a story Der blinde Gast by Pick and made corrections,[833] read a little Strindberg,[834] then didn't sleep, at home at ½ past 8, back at 10 o'clock, out of fear of headaches, which are already beginning, and because I had also slept only very little at night, didn't do any more work, partly also because I was afraid of spoiling a tolerable passage written yesterday. The fourth day since August when I have written nothing at all. The letters are to blame, I will try to write none at all or only very short letters. How bashful I now am too and how it flings me around! Yesterday evening the overjoyed state after I had read several lines of Jammes, with whom I otherwise have nothing to do, but whose French, it's about a visit with a poet friend[835] had so strong an effect on me.

(Continuation of the text from page 290)

the slightest effort necessary for it.[836] But the inspector too always entered the station with an expression as if this time he would definitely uncover my mismanagement. He always pushed the door of the hut open with his knee while looking at me. No sooner had he opened my book than he found a mistake. It took me a long time to prove to him by recalculating before his eyes that it was not I but he who had made a mistake. He was always dissatisfied with my receipts, then he slapped the book and looked at me sharply again. "We will have to shut down the railroad" he said every time. "It will come to that" I usually replied.

After the audit was completed, our relationship changed. I had always prepared schnapps and whenever possible some delicacy. We drank to each other, he sang with a tolerable voice, but always only two songs, one was sad and began: Where are you going little child in the forest?, the second was merry and began like this: "Boon companions, I'm one of you!" Subject to the mood I was able to put him in, I was paid my wage in installments. But only at the beginning of such amusements did I observe him with any intention, later we were completely united, shamelessly reviled the management, I received secret promises whispered in my ear about the career he would attain for me and finally we fell down together on the plank bed in an embrace that we often didn't release for ten hours. The next morning he departed as my superior again. I stood before the train and saluted he usually turned around to face me once more while boarding and said: "Well, little friend, we'll meet again in a month. You know what is at stake for you." I can still see his puffy face turned with difficulty toward me, everything in this face pressed forward, the cheeks, the nose, the lips.

This was the one great diversion of the month, when I let myself go; if some schnapps had been left by mistake, then I drank it up immediately after the inspector's departure, usually I could hear the train's departure signal even as it gurgled into me. The thirst after such a night was terrible; it was as if there were another person inside me, sticking his head and neck out of my mouth and screaming for something to drink. The inspector was provided for, he always carried a large supply of drinks on his train, but I was reliant on whatever was left over.

But then I drank nothing all month nor did I smoke, I did my work and wanted nothing more. It was as I mentioned not much work but I did it thoroughly. One of my duties, for example, was to clean and inspect the tracks daily for a kilometer to the right and to the left of the station. But I didn't keep to this requirement and often went much farther, so far that I could just barely see the station. In clear weather this was still possible at a distance of about 5 km, for the country was completely flat. When I was so far that the hut in the distance was almost only flickering before my eyes, I sometimes saw, my eyes deceiving me, many black dots moving toward the hut. They were whole crowds, whole troops. Sometimes, however, someone really came, then I ran, swinging my pickax, the whole long stretch back.

Toward evening I was finished with my work and withdrew for the night into my hut. Usually no visitors came at this time, for the journey back to the villages was not entirely safe at night. Various riffraff roved the area, but they weren't natives, they moved on to other places too, though they also came back. I got to see most of them, the secluded station attracted them, they were not actually dangerous, but one had to deal sternly with them.

They were the only ones who disturbed me during the long twilight hours. Otherwise I lay on the plank bed, didn't think about the past, didn't think about the railroad, the next train didn't come through until between 10 and 11 o'clock in the evening, in short I thought about nothing at all. Now and then I read an old newspaper that someone had thrown to me from the train, it contained scandalous stories from Kalda, which would have interested me but which I couldn't understand from the single issue alone. Moreover, in every issue there was an installment of a novel called "The Revenge of the Commander." I once dreamed of this commander, who always wore a dagger at his side, on a particular occasion he even held it between his teeth. Apart from that I could not read much, since it grew dark early and kerosene or a tallow candle was prohibitively expensive. For the month the railroad provided me with only ½ a liter of kerosene, which I had used up long before the month elapsed merely to keep the signal light for the train burning for ½ an hour in the evening. But this light was not even necessary and later at least on moonlit nights I no longer lit it at all. I foresaw quite correctly that after the summer elapsed I would be in desperate need of the kerosene. I therefore dug a hole in a corner of the hut, put an old small beer barrel in it and every month poured in the kerosene I had saved. The whole thing was covered up with straw and no one noticed anything. The more it stank of kerosene in the hut, the more satisfied I was; the stench became so great because it was a barrel made of old cracked wood that soaked up the kerosene. As a precaution I later buried the barrel outside the hut, for the inspector once flaunted a box of wax matches before me and, when I asked for them, threw them one after another burning into the air. Both of us and especially the kerosene were in real danger, I saved everything by choking him until he dropped all the matches.

In my free hours I often thought about how I could prepare for the winter. If I was freezing even now in the warm season—and it was, they said, warmer than it had been in many years—I would do very badly in winter. My hoarding of kerosene was only a whim, I should have had the good sense to stock up on all sorts of things for the winter; there was no doubt that the company would not take particular interest in my welfare, but I was too careless or rather I wasn't careless but I mattered too little to myself to have wanted to make much effort in this respect. Now in the warm season I was doing tolerably well, I left things as they were and undertook nothing further.

One of the temptations that had brought me to this station had been the prospect of hunting. I had been told that it was a region extraordinarily rich in game and I had already secured a rifle for myself that I wanted to have sent to me when I had saved some money. Now it turned out that there was no trace of huntable game here, only wolves and bears were said to be found here, in the first months I saw none, and apart from that there were peculiar large rats here, which I was immediately able to observe running across the steppe in droves as if blown by the wind. But the game I had been looking forward to was not there. People had not misinformed me, the region rich in game existed, only it was a three days' journey away,—I hadn't considered that the locations in these lands, which were uninhabited for hundreds of km, must necessarily be uncertain. In any case, for the time being I didn't need the rifle and could use the money for other things; for the winter, to be sure, I had to buy a rifle and I put aside money for it regularly. For the rats, which sometimes attacked my food my long knife sufficed. In the early days when I was still taking everything in with curiosity, I once speared one of these rats and held it in front of me at eye level against the wall. You see small animals clearly only when you have them in front of you at eye level; when you bend down toward them on the ground and look at them there, you get a false incomplete picture of them. The most striking thing about these rats was the claws, large, a little cupped and yet pointed at the end; they were very well suited to digging. Hanging in front of me against the wall in its final throes, the rat then spread its claws out straight seemingly against its living nature, they resembled a little hand reaching out toward you. In general these animals didn't bother me much, only at night they sometimes woke me when they hurried past the hut, clattering on the hard ground as they ran. If I then sat up and perhaps lit a little wax candle, I could see somewhere in a gap under the wooden posts a rat's feverishly working claws stuck in from outside. It was completely useless work, for to dig a sufficiently large hole for itself, it would have had to work for days and yet it fled as soon as the day brightened even a little, nonetheless it worked like a worker who knows his goal. And it did good work, they were admittedly imperceptible particles that flew up from its digging, but its claw was probably never applied without result. I often watched for a long time at night until the regularity and calm of this sight lulled me to sleep. Then I no longer had the strength to put out the little wax candle and it shone a little while longer for the rat at its work. Once on a warm night, when I again heard those claws working, I went out carefully, without lighting a candle to see the animal itself. It had lowered its head far down with its pointed snout, almost pushed it between its forelegs to get as close as possible to the wood and push its claws as deep as possible under the wood. One might have thought someone was holding on to the claws inside the hut and trying to pull the whole animal in, so tensed was everything. And yet everything was also ended with a kick, by which I struck the animal dead. Fully awake, I couldn't allow my hut, which was my only possession, to be attacked.

To secure the hut against these rats, I plugged all the gaps with straw and tow and every morning inspected the floor all around. I also intended to cover the floor of the hut, which until now was only hard-packed earth, with boards, which could also be useful for the winter. A peasant from the next village, named Jekoz, had promised me long ago to bring nice dry boards for this purpose, in the meantime I had also often received him hospitably for this promise, he also never stayed away for long, but came every 14 days, also sometimes had to send shipments by train, but he didn't bring the boards. He had various excuses for this, mostly that he himself was too old to haul such a load and that his son, who would bring the boards, was presently busy working in the fields. Now Jekoz was by his own account and it also seemed to be correct far over 70 years old, but a tall, still very strong man. Besides, he also changed his excuses and another time spoke of the difficulties of acquiring such long boards as I needed. I didn't press, I didn't absolutely need the boards, Jekoz himself had given me the idea of covering the floor in the first place, such a covering was perhaps not even very advantageous, in short, I could listen calmly to the old man's lies. My perpetual greeting was: "The boards, Jekoz!" Immediately the apologies began in a half-stammer, I was called inspector or captain or even just telegraphist, he promised me not only to bring the boards shortly but also, with the help of his son and several neighbors, to tear down my whole hut and build a solid house in its place. I listened until it made me tired and I pushed him out. But still standing in the doorway, seeking forgiveness, he raised his supposedly so weak arms, with which in reality he could have crushed a grown man. I knew why he didn't bring the boards, he thought that by the time the winter was approaching, I would need the boards more desperately and would pay better, besides, as long as the boards had not been delivered, he himself would be of greater value to me. Now he was of course not stupid and knew that I was aware of his ulterior motives, but in the fact that I didn't make use of this awareness he saw his advantage and he maintained it.

But all the preparations I was making to secure the hut against the animals and keep myself safe for the winter had to be abandoned when—the first three months of my service were approaching their end—I fell seriously ill. Until then I had for years been spared any illness, even the slightest indisposition, this time I fell ill. It began with a heavy cough. About two hours inland from the station was a small brook from which I usually fetched my water supply in a barrel on a wheelbarrow. I also bathed there often and this cough was the consequence of it. The coughing fits were so severe that I had to double up while coughing, I believed myself unable to withstand the coughing unless I doubled up and in that way gathered all my strength. I thought the train crew would be horrified by the coughing, but they were acquainted with it, they called it the wolf's cough. From then on I began to hear the howling in the cough. I sat on the small bench in front of the hut and greeted the train with a howl, with a howl I accompanied its departure. In the nights I knelt on the plank bed instead of lying and pressed my face into the pelts to spare myself at least the listening to the howling. I waited expectantly until the bursting of some major blood vessel would put an end to everything. But nothing of the sort happened and the cough had even gone away in a few days. But a fever remained and didn't subside.

This fever made me very tired, I lost all power of resistance, it could happen that sweat broke out on my forehead quite unexpectedly, then my whole body trembled and I had to lie down wherever I was and wait until my senses regathered.

Tenth Notebook

4 *(November 1914)* Pepa back.[837] Shouting, agitated, beside himself. Story of the mole that tunneled under him in the trench and that he regarded as a sign from God to move away from there. No sooner was he gone than a shot struck a soldier who had crawled after him and was now over the mole.—His captain. He could be seen clearly being taken captive. But the next day he was found naked in the woods impaled by bayonets. He probably had money on him, they had wanted to search and rob him, but he "the way officers are" had not voluntarily let himself be touched.—P.[838] almost wept with anger and agitation when, on the way from the railroad station, he met his boss (whom he had previously revered immoderately and ridiculously) going to the theater elegantly dressed, perfumed, with opera glasses hanging around his neck. A month later he did it himself with a ticket this boss had given him. He went to "Der ungetreue Eckehart" a comedy.[839]—Slept once in the castle of Prince Sapieha,[840] once just in front of Austr. firing batteries, where he was lying in reserve, once in a farmhouse room, where two women slept in each of the two beds against the walls to the right and left, a girl behind the stove, and eight soldiers on the floor.—Punishment for soldiers. Stand bound to a tree until they turn blue. Because, for example, he had left my sister's card somewhere against the rule, where it actually was lost too.—

---

12 *(November 1914)* Parents who expect gratitude from their children (there are even those who demand it) are like usurers, they are happy to risk the capital as long as they get the interest.

24 XI *(1914)* Yesterday on Tuchmachergasse, where the old linens and clothing are being distributed to the Galician refugees.[841] Max, Frau Brod,[842] Herr Chaim Nagel.[843] The intelligence, the patience, the friendliness, the diligence, the talkativeness, the wit, the trustworthiness of Herr Nagel. People who fill their circle so completely that one believes they must succeed in everything in the whole circle of the world, but it is also inherent to their perfection that they don't reach beyond their circle.—The clever lively, proud and modest Frau Kannegiesser from Tarnow,[844] who wanted only two blankets but nice ones, and yet despite Max's patronage got only old and dirty ones, while the new good blankets were in a separate room where all the good items of any kind were kept for the better people. Another reason they didn't want to give her the good ones was that she needed them only for 2 days before her linens came from Vienna and they couldn't take back used items due to the danger of cholera.—Frau Lustig with many children of all sizes and a small impertinent, self-confident agile sister. She spends so much time picking out a little children's dress that Frau Br.[845] shouts at her: "Now take this one already or you won't get any." But now Fr. Lustig responds with even much louder shouting and concludes with a large furious hand movement: "The mitzveh[846] is worth more than all these schmattes[847] (rags)"

---

25 XI 14 Empty despair, impossible to plant oneself, I can stop only at the satisfaction with the suffering.

I have almost no direct interest in the factory, but all the more indirect interest.[848] I don't want my father's money, which he put at K.'s disposal on my advice and at my request, to be lost that is my first concern, I don't want my uncle's money[849] to be lost, which he lent not so much to K.[850] as to us, that is my second concern and I also don't want E. and the ch.'s[851] money to be lost, that is my third concern. I'm not speaking at all of my money and my liability. Now I by no means consider the whole thing any more endangered than everything is endangered under the present circumstances. Of course, I also have complete confidence in the two of you; the fact that in the course of the last 3 months you yourself have withdrawn about 1500 K at least according to the cash book does not shake it in the slightest, you have according to the cash book deposited 400 K, will certainly pay back the rest too and are probably acting in accordance with Karl's wishes. To be sure, I knew nothing about this, but rather found out about it only from the book—by the way, no date has been entered in it recently—and thus for this reason and because at this time, after all, the management of the factory is especially sensitive, I was surprised at this nothing more, I was merely surprised and took notice of it. That was the end of the matter.

I want to say at the outset that I don't fully believe Elli's account, you caused her great agitation, moreover now during the war she is in constant agitation and in this state she then loses her perspective. But even if I regard much of what she told me as mere fantasy, there seems still enough left to assume that you treated her, incidentally here in front of the girls, outrageously. You forgot that she is a woman and that she is your brother's wife.

"She was lying in wait here and then sent you." That is an untruth and an insulting untruth. I believe you had and have the fullest freedom imaginable. Your work is certainly outstanding, I have no doubt at all about that. The concerns I have about the factory are of an entirely different sort than yours, they are completely passive, but no less serious as a result. You bear the responsibility for the work (and basically bear nothing more than that) but I bear the responsibility for the money. My responsibility is to my father and my uncle. Do not underestimate this, if it were my money, believe me, it would be child's play for me to attend to things. Unfortunately, however, I have merely the concerns, but for reasons that, to be sure, reside mainly in me cannot otherwise intervene myself. All I do is come once a month and sit here for one or two hours. In itself this is senseless, does no one any harm or good and is only a futile attempt to satisfy my sense of responsibility and my concerns. The fact that you find fault with this too is as ridiculous as it is presumptuous. I didn't come here to look at the cash book, that is untrue, even though I would have had the right and duty to do so; rather I came here for the same self-serving purpose as always, that is, to reassure myself; the fact that you were out would have been more a reason for me not to come, since I indeed always want to hear from you. Nonetheless I came, because it was a convenient time for me and because I also wanted to see whether something important didn't happen in your absence. The fact that I was looking through the cash book at that moment was a matter of chance and distractedness, I could just have well have been looking through the rubber newspaper,[852] for example. Then, to be sure, I found several items in the cash book that understandably interested me.

You supposedly also made a disparaging remark about the fact that my father accepts compensation for letting E. & the ch. live with us.[853] What concern is that of yours? How can you pass judgment on that.

30 XI 14 I can no longer go on writing.[854] I am at the final boundary, before which I shall perhaps again sit for years, only to perhaps again begin a new story that will again remain unfinished. This fate pursues me. I am also cold and senseless again, only an old person's love for complete peace has remained. And like some animal completely severed from human beings I swing my neck once again and for the intervening time would like to try to get F. again. I will really try it too, unless the nausea in the face of myself hinders me from it.

2 *(December 1914)* Afternoon at Werfel's[855] with Max and Pick. Read "In the Penal Colony" aloud,[856] not completely dissatisfied, but for the blatant ineffaceable flaws. Werfel poems and 2 acts from "Esther Kaiserin von Persien."[857] The acts sweep one away. But I am easily confused. The criticisms and comparisons brought up by Max, who is not quite satisfied with the play, bother me and I now retain the play in its entirety not nearly in the same way as I did while listening to it, when it assailed me. Memory of the jargon actors. W.'s beautiful sisters.[858] The older one leans against the chair, often looks sideways in the mirror, points, though already sufficiently devoured by my eyes, lightly with a finger to a brooch pinned in the middle of her blouse. It is a low-cut dark blue blouse, its neckline is filled with tulle. Repeated story of a scene in the theater: Officers who during Kabale und Liebe[859] often loudly made the remark among themselves: "Speckbacher is cutting a figure" by which they meant an officer leaning against the wall of a box.

Result of the day even before Werfel: Go on working under any circumstances, sad that it isn't possible today, for I'm tired and have a headache, had a hint of it in the morning in the office too. Go on working under any circumstances, it must be possible despite sleeplessness and the office.

Dream last night. With Kaiser Wilhelm. In the Beautiful View Castle. A room similar to the one in the "Tabakskollegium." Meeting with Matilde Serao. Unfortunately forgot everything.[860]

From Esther: God's masterpieces fart at each other in the bathhouse.[861]

5 XII 14

A letter from Erna about the situation of her family.[862] My relationship to the family takes on a consistent meaning for me only when I regard myself as the ruin of the family. It's the only organic explanation there is that smoothly overcomes everything astonishing. It's also the only active connection with the family that remains at the moment from my side, for otherwise I am emotionally completely cut off from them, though no more drastically than perhaps from the whole world. (A picture of my existence in this regard is provided by a useless pole covered with snow and frost, lightly driven into the ground at an angle, on a deeply churned-up field at the edge of a great plain on a dark winter night.) Only the ruin has any effect. I have made F. unhappy, weakened the power of resistance of all of them, who now need it so much, contributed to her father's death,[863] divided F. and E.[864] and finally made E. unhappy too, an unhappiness that in all probability will progress farther. I am harnessed in front of it and destined to pull it forward. My last letter to her, which I wrung from myself, she considers calm; it "breathes so much calmness" as she puts it.[865] Here, to be sure, it's not out of the question that she puts it this way out of delicacy, out of consideration, out of concern for me. I am indeed sufficiently punished within all this, even my position with respect to the family is punishment enough, I have also suffered so much that I will never recover from it (my sleep, my memory, my ability to think, my power of resistance against the tiniest worries have been incurably weakened, strangely these are roughly the same consequences that long prison sentences have) but at the moment I suffer little from my relationship to the family, in any case less than F. or E. There is something tormenting, to be sure, in the fact that I am now supposed to take a Christmas trip with E., while F. perhaps remains in Berlin.[866]

---

8 XII 14 Yesterday unquestionably capable of good work for the first time in a long while. And yet wrote only the first page of the mother chapter,[867] since I had barely slept at all for two nights, since a headache had already made its presence known in the morning and since I was all too afraid of the next day. Again realized that everything written down in fragments and not in the course of the greater part of the night (or even in its entirety) is inferior and that I am condemned to this inferiority by the circumstances of my life.

---

9 XII 14 Together with Emil Kafka from Chicago.[868] He is almost touching. Description of his quiet life. From 8 to ½ past 5 in the merchandise building. Inspection of the shipments in the hosiery department. 15 dollars a week. 14 days of vacation, 1 week of it with pay, after 5 years pay for all 14 days. For a while, when there was not much to do in the hosiery department, he helped out in the bicycle department. 300 bicycles a day are sold. A wholesale business with 10000 employees. Customers are solicited only by sending out catalogues. Americans like to change jobs, in the summer they don't throng to work much at all, but he doesn't like to change, he doesn't see the advantage of it, one loses time and money in the process. So far he has had 2 jobs each for 5 years and when he returns—he has unlimited vacation—will go back to the same job, they can always use him, though also always do without him. In the evening he is usually at home, a game of skat with acquaintances; for a diversion at some point an hour in the cinema, in summer a walk, on Sunday a boat ride on the lake. He is wary of marriage, even though he is already 34 years old, for the American women marry often only in order to get divorced, which is very simple for them, but very expensive for the husband.

---

13 XII 14 Instead of working—I have written only one page (exegesis of the legend)[869]—read parts of finished chapters and found some of them good.[870] Always in the awareness that every feeling of satisfaction and happiness, such as I have especially with respect to the legend, must be paid for and indeed in order to preclude any recovery must be paid for afterward.

Recently at Felix's. Impression of a great unhappiness. How he feverishly buries himself in the pillows, his lips dryly rubbing against each other. What I would find hard to bear about his wife he seems to bear relatively easily, but finds other things hard. On the way home I told Max that on my deathbed provided that the pains are not too great, I will be very content. I forgot to add and later omitted intentionally that the best of what I have written stems from this ability to die contentedly. All those good and strongly convincing passages always deal with the fact that someone is dying, that this is very difficult for him, that in it he experiences an injustice and at least a hardship and that for the reader at least in my opinion this is moving. For me, however, believing as I do in my ability to be content on my deathbed, such depictions are secretly a game, indeed I am happy to die in the dying man, therefore calculatingly take advantage of the attention the reader concentrates on death, am far more clearheaded than he, who I assume will lament on his deathbed, and my lament is therefore as perfect as possible, does not, for example, suddenly break off like a real lament, but rather trails away beautifully and purely. It's like my perpetual lamenting to my mother over woes not nearly as great as the lament led one to believe. For my mother, to be sure, I didn't need as much artistic effort as for the reader.

---

14 *(December 1914)* The work pitifully creeping forward, perhaps at its most important point where a good night would be so necessary.

At Baum's in the afternoon. He is giving a piano lesson[871] to a pale little girl with glasses. The boy is sitting quietly[872] in the semidarkness of the kitchen and playing carelessly with some unrecognizable object.

Impression of great ease. Especially compared to the bustling of the tall chambermaid, who is washing dishes in a bucket.

---

15 *(December 1914)* Did no work at all. Just spent two hours looking through classifications of businesses for the office.[873] Afternoon at Baum's. He was a little wounding and harsh. Dreary conversation due to my weakness, thoughtlessness, ponderousness and almost stupidity; was inferior to him in every respect, haven't spoken to him all alone in a long time, was happy to be alone again. The happiness of lying on the sofa without a headache in the quiet room, my steady breathing worthy of a human being.

The defeats in Serbia, the senseless leadership.[874]

19 *(December 1914)* Yesterday wrote the "Village Schoolteacher"[875] almost unconsciously, but was afraid to write past ¼ to 2, the fear was well founded, I barely slept at all, went through only about 3 short dreams and was then in the office in a corresponding state. Yesterday my father's reproaches about the factory: "You danced me into this."[876] Then went home and wrote calmly for 3 hours, in the awareness that my guilt is beyond doubt, even if not as great as my father portrays it. Today Saturday didn't go to dinner, partly out of fear of my father, partly in order to take full advantage of the night for my work, but I wrote only one page and not a very good one.[877]

Beginning of every novella ridiculous at first. It seems hopeless that this new still unfinished everywhere sensitive organism will be able to sustain itself in the finished organization of the world, which like every finished organization strives to close itself off. To be sure, one forgets here that the novella if it is justified, bears its finished organization in itself, even if it has not yet completely unfolded itself; therefore the despair in this regard in the face of the beginning of a novella is unjustified; parents would have just as much cause to despair in the face of their infant, for they had not wanted to bring this wretched and especially ridiculous being into the world. To be sure, one never knows whether the despair one feels is the justified or the unjustified one. But this consideration can provide a certain support, the lack of this experience has already done me harm.

---

20 *(December 1914)* Max's objection to Dostoyevsky, that he has too many mentally ill characters. Completely incorrect. They're not mentally ill. The designation of the illness is nothing but a means of characterization and indeed a very delicate and very fruitful one. For example, one need only keep saying of someone with the greatest stubbornness that he is simpleminded and idiotic and he will if he has the Dostoyevskian kernel in him be positively incited to his highest achievements. In this regard his characterizations have roughly the same meaning as insults among friends. If they say to each other You are a dolt then they don't mean that the other person is a real dolt and they have degraded themselves by this friendship, rather, if it's not merely a joke, but even if it is, it usually consists of an endless mixture of intentions. Thus the Karamazov father, for example, is by no means a fool, but rather a very clever, albeit wicked man who is almost Ivan's equal and in any case much cleverer than, for example, his cousin or nephew, the landowner, who feels so above him and is unchallenged by the narrator.[878]

---

23 XII *(1914)* Read a few pages of Herzen's "Fogs of London."[879] Had no idea what it's about and yet the whole unknown person steps out, resolute, self-tormenting, controlling himself and fading away again

---

26 *(December 1914)* In Kuttenberg[880] with Max and his wife. How I reckoned on the four free days, how many hours I thought about the correct use of them and now perhaps miscalculated after all. Wrote almost nothing this evening and perhaps no longer capable of continuing the Village Schoolteacher, on which I've been working for a week now and which I certainly would have finished in 3 free nights immaculately and without external flaws, now even though it is still almost at the beginning it already has two irremediable flaws in it and is moreover stunted.— New daily schedule from now on! Take even better advantage of the

time! Am I lamenting here to find an answer here? It will not come from this notebook, it will come when I am in bed, and will lay me on my back so that I lie beautiful and light and bluish-white, no other salvation will come.

Hotel in Kuttenberg. Morawetz, drunken porter, small covered courtyard with a skylight. The soldier leaning darkly circumscribed against the railing on the second floor of the courtyard building. The room I'm offered, the window faces a dark windowless corridor. Red sofa, candlelight. Jakobskirche, the pious soldiers, the girl's voice in the choir

---

27 *(December 1914)*

A merchant was hounded by misfortune. He bore it for a long time, but finally he didn't think he could bear it any longer and went to a man versed in the law. He wanted to ask his advice and find out what to do to fend off the misfortune or to make himself capable of bearing the misfortune. This man versed in the law always had the scripture open before him and studied it, he had the habit of receiving everyone who came for advice with the words: "I have just been reading about your case" while pointing with his finger at a passage on the page before him. The merchant, who had also heard of this habit, disliked it, the man versed in the law did, it was true, thereby immediately ascribe to himself the possibility of helping the petitioner and relieve him of the fear of being afflicted by a suffering that worked in the dark, could be communicated to no one and could arouse no one's sympathy, but the implausibility of the assertion was simply too great and it had even kept the merchant from going earlier to this man versed in the law. Even now he stepped hesitantly through his door.

31 XII 14 Have been working since August, in general not little and not badly, but neither in the former nor in the latter regard to the limit of my ability, as it should have been, especially since my ability in all likelihood (sleeplessness, headaches, weak heart) won't last much longer. Unfinished things I've worked on: The Trial, Memories of the Kalda Railroad, The Village Schoolteacher, The Assistant Prosecutor[881] and

smaller beginnings. Finished only: In the Penal Colony and a chapter of The Missing Person, both during the 14 day vacation. I don't know why I'm writing this summary, it doesn't suit me at all.

---

4 1 15 Didn't yield to my great desire to begin a new story. It's all useless. When I can't chase the stories through the nights, they escape and get lost, as "The Assistant Prosecutor" has now done. And tomorrow I'm going to the factory, might have to go there every afternoon after Paul reports for duty.[882] With that everything stops. The thoughts of the factory are my perpetual day of atonement.[883]

---

6 1 15 Have abandoned Village Schoolteacher and Assistant Prosecutor for the time being. But also almost incapable of continuing the Trial. Thoughts of the girl from Lemberg.[884] Promises of some sort of happiness, similar to the hopes of an eternal life. Seen from a certain distance they hold their ground and one doesn't venture closer.

17 1 15 Yesterday dictated letters at the factory for the first time. Worthless work (1 hour) but not without satisfaction. Terrible afternoon beforehand. Constant headaches, so that I had to hold my hand against my head uninterruptedly to soothe myself (condition at Cafe Arco) and heart pains at home on the sofa.

Read Ottla's letter to Erna: As if my ape had written it. I have really suppressed her and indeed heedlessly out of negligence and out of ineptitude. F. is right about that. Fortunately O. is so strong that alone in a strange city she would immediately recover from me. How many of her abilities for intercourse with people are unexploited because of me. She writes that she felt unhappy in Berlin. Untrue!

Realized that I have by no means taken sufficient advantage of the time since August. The constant attempts to make it possible to continue my work deep into the night by sleeping a lot in the afternoon were senseless, for I could see even after the first 14 days that my nerves would not permit me to go to bed after 1 o'clock, for then I no longer fall asleep at all, the next day is unbearable and I destroy myself. I thus lay down too long in the afternoon, but rarely worked past 1 o'clock at night, but always began toward 11 o'clock at the earliest. That was wrong. I must begin at 8 or 9 o'clock, the night is certainly the best time (vacation!) but it is inaccessible to me.

On Saturday I will see F.[885] If she loves me, I don't deserve it. Today I think I realize how narrow my limits are, in everything and hence in writing too. If one recognizes one's limits very keenly, one must be blown to pieces. It is probably Ottla's letter that made me aware of this. I've been very self-satisfied recently and had many objections for my defense and self-assertion against F. A shame that I had no time to write them down, today I wouldn't be able to.

Strindberg "Black Flags." On influence from a distance: You have surely felt how others have disapproved of your behavior, without their having expressed this disapproval. You have experienced a quiet contentment in solitude without having realized why; someone in the distance thought well of you, spoke well of you[886]

18 *(January 1915)* Worked, read, dictated, listened, wrote uselessly in the same way at the factory until ½ past 6. Same senseless satisfaction afterward. Headache, slept badly. Incapable of sustained concentrated work. Also have been in the open air too little. Nonetheless began a new story, I was afraid of spoiling the old ones. Now 4 or 5 stories stand upright before me like the horses before the circus director Schumann at the beginning of the show.[887]

19 *(January 1915)* As long as I have to go to the factory I will be able to write nothing. I believe it is a special inability to work that I feel now, similar to the one when I was employed at the Generali.[888] The immediate proximity of professional life deprives me even though I'm inwardly

as uninvolved as possible, of any overall view as if I were in a narrow pass where I am moreover bowing my head. In the newspaper today, for example, there's a statement by the competent Swedish authority according to which despite the threats of the Triple Entente neutrality shall unconditionally be maintained. At the end it says: In Stockholm the members of the Triple Entente will come up against a stone wall. Today I take this almost completely as it is meant. 3 days ago I would have felt to my depths that here a Stockholm ghost is speaking, that "threats of the Triple Entente" "neutrality" "competent Swedish authority" are only forms made of air balled up into a definite shape, which one can enjoy only with one's eye, but never touch with one's finger.[889]

I had arranged an excursion for Sunday with two friends, but quite unexpectedly slept past the hour of the meeting. My friends, knowing my usual punctuality, were surprised, went to the house where I lived, stood there for a while too, then went upstairs and knocked on my door. I was very startled, jumped out of the bed and attended to nothing but getting ready as quickly as possible. When I stepped out the door fully dressed, my friends backed away from me in apparent fright. "What do you have behind your head" they cried. Ever since I had woken up I had felt something hindering me from leaning my head back and now I groped with my hand for this hindrance. My friends, having pulled themselves together a little, cried "Be careful, don't hurt yourself" just as I grasped the hilt of a sword behind my head. My friends came closer, examined me, led me into the room to the wardrobe mirror and stripped me to the waist. A large old knight's sword with a cross-shaped hilt was stuck in my back to its handle, but in such a way that the blade had slid with incomprehensible precision between skin and flesh and caused no injury. But even at the point of penetration on my neck there was no wound, my friends assured me that the slit necessary for the blade had opened there completely bloodless and dry. And when my friends now climbed onto chairs and slowly pulled the sword out millimeter by millimeter, no blood followed and the opening on my neck closed, leaving only a scarcely perceptible slit. "Here's your sword" my friends said, laughing, and handed it to me. I weighed it in both hands, it was a precious weapon, crusaders might well have used it. Who tolerated old knights roaming around in dreams, irresponsibly brandishing their swords, piercing innocent sleepers with them and inflicting no severe wounds only because their weapons first of all probably glance off living bodies and because faithful friends are also standing on the other side of the door and knocking, ready to help.

20 *(January 1915)* End of writing. When will it take me in again? In what a bad state I'm meeting F.! The ponderousness of thinking arising immediately with the abandonment of writing, inability to prepare myself for the meeting, whereas last week I could hardly shake off important ideas for it. May I enjoy the only conceivable gain from this: better sleep.

Black Flags. How badly I even read. And how I maliciously and weakly observe myself. Apparently I cannot force my way into the world, but can calmly lie, receive, spread out within myself what I have received and then calmly step forward.

---

24 *(January 1915)* With F. in Bodenbach.[890] I believe it is impossible that we will ever unite, but dare say so neither to her nor at the decisive moment to myself. So I have held out hope to her again, senselessly, for every day makes me older and more ossified. The old headaches come back when I try to grasp that she is at the same time suffering and at the same time calm and cheerful. We must not torment each other again by writing a lot, it would be best to pass over this meeting as an isolated occurrence; or do I perhaps believe that I will free myself here, live off writing, go abroad or elsewhere and live there secretly with F. We have, after all, found each other otherwise completely unchanged. Each of us says to himself inwardly that the other is unshakable and merciless. I cede nothing of my demand for a fantasy life intended only for my work, she numb to all silent pleas wants the average, the cozy apartment, interest in the factory, ample food, sleep from 11 o'clock in the evening on, heated room, sets my watch, which for 3 months has been ahead by 1½ hours, to the actual minute. She is proven right and would continue to be proven right, she is right when she chides me for saying to the waiter: Bringen Sie die Zeitung, <u>bis</u> sie ausgelesen ist[891] and I can correct noth-

ing when she speaks of the "personal touch" (it cannot be pronounced in any way but creakily) of the desired apartment furnishing. She calls my two older sisters "shallow," doesn't ask at all after the youngest, she has almost no questions about my work and no visible receptiveness to it. That is one side.

I, however, am inept and dreary as always and should actually have no time to think about anything but the question of how it happens that someone even wants to reach for me with his little finger. In quick succession I have blown this cold breath on 3 different sorts of people. The Hellerau people,[892] the Riedl family in Bodenbach and F. F. said: "How good we are being here together." I was silent as if during this exclamation I'd lost my hearing. For two hours we were alone in the room. Around me nothing but boredom and hopelessness. We have not yet had a single good moment with each other during which I would have breathed freely. With F. I never had, except in letters, the sweetness of the relationship to a beloved woman as in Zuckmantel and Riva,[893] only boundless admiration, subservience, sympathy, despair and self-contempt. I also read to her, the sentences became disgustingly jumbled, no connection with the listener lying with her eyes closed on the sofa and silently taking it in. A lukewarm request to be permitted to take a manuscript with her and copy it. During the doorkeeper story[894] greater attention and good observation. The meaning of the story dawned on me for the first time, she too grasped it correctly, then, to be sure, we plunged into it with coarse remarks, I started it.

The difficulties I have with speaking, certainly incredible to other people, stem from the fact that my thinking or rather the contents of my consciousness are completely foggy, that as far as it is a question of myself alone, I rest in them undisturbed and sometimes self-satisfied, but that a human conversation requires sharpening, consolidation and continuous coherence, things that do not exist in me. No one will want to lie with me in clouds of fog and even if he wanted to, I cannot drive the fog out of my forehead, between two people it dissipates and is nothing.

F. takes the long detour to Bodenbach, goes to the trouble of obtaining her passport, must endure me after a sleepless night, even listen to another reading and all of it senseless. Does she feel this to be such an ordeal as I do? Certainly not, even assuming the same sensitivity. After all, she has no sense of guilt.

My statement was right and was acknowledged as right: Each of us loves the other just as this other is. But as he is, he doesn't think he can live with him.

This group: Dr. Weiss seeks to convince me that F. is detestable, F. seeks to convince me that W. is detestable. I believe both of them and love both of them or strive to.

---

29 *(January 1915)* tried to write again, almost to no avail. Past two days went to bed early, at 10 o'clock, for the first time in a long while, free feeling during the day, half-satisfaction, heightened usefulness in the office, possibility of speaking with people.—Now severe knee pains.

---

30 *(January 1915)* The old inability. Stopped writing for barely 10 days and already cast out. Again the great exertions lie ahead. It is necessary positively to dive under and sink more quickly than what is sinking away in front of you.

---

7 *(February 1915)* Complete standstill. Endless torments.

At a certain level of self-awareness and under other accompanying circumstances favorable to observation it will necessarily happen regularly that one finds oneself abhorrent. Every standard of the good—however varied the opinions on it may be—will appear too great. One will realize that one is nothing but a rat hole of wretched ulterior motives. Not the slightest action will be free of these ulterior motives. These ulterior motives will be so filthy that in a state of self-observation one will at first not even want to think them through, but rather content oneself with the sight of them from a distance. These ulterior motives will not consist merely of selfishness, compared to them selfishness will appear to be an ideal of the good and the beautiful. The filth one will find will be there for its own sake, one will recognize that one came into the world dripping with this burden and due to it will depart unrecognizably or all-too-recognizably. This filth will be the bottommost depth one will find, the bottommost depth will contain not lava but filth. It will be the bottommost and the uppermost and even the doubts of self-observation will soon be as weak and self-satisfied as the rolling of a pig in the muck.

9 II 15 Wrote a little yesterday and today. Dog story.[895]

Just read the beginning. It is ugly and causes a headache. It is despite all truth wicked, pedantic, mechanical, an only barely breathing fish on a sandbank. I'm writing Bouvard and Pecuchet very prematurely.[896] If the two elements—most pronounced in the "Stoker" and "Penal Colony"– do not unite, I'm finished. But is there any chance of this unification?

Finally took a room. In the same house on Bilekgasse.[897]

10 II *(1915)* First evening. The neighbor talks for hours with the landlady.[898] Both speak softly, the landlady almost inaudibly, all the worse. Having resumed for 2 days, stopped writing, who knows for how long. Sheer despair. Is it like this in every apartment? Does such ridiculous and absolutely deadly distress await me with every landlady, in every city? My classroom teacher's two rooms in the monastery.[899] But it is senseless to despair, better to seek means, however much—no it is not contrary to my character, there is still some tough Judaism in me, only it usually helps on the opposite side.

---

14 *(February 1915)* Russia's endless power of attraction. Dost.'s troika[900] captures it less well than the image of a great immense river of yellowish water rising everywhere in waves but not all-too-high waves. Desolate disheveled heath on the banks, bowed grasses. That captures nothing, rather extinguishes everything.

Saint Simonism[901]

15 II 15 Everything is at a standstill. Bad irregular schedule. The apartment is spoiling everything for me. Today again listened to the French lesson of the landlady's daughter.[902]

16 II 15 Am not finding my way. As if everything I possessed had run away from me and as if it would scarcely be enough for me if it came back.

22 II 15 Inability in every respect and complete.

25 II *(1915)* After days of uninterrupted headaches finally a little freer and more confident. If I were a stranger observing me and the course of my life, I would have to say that it all must end in uselessness, expended in incessant doubt, creative only in self-torment. But as a participant I hope.

1 III 15 With great effort after weeks of preparation and fear gave notice, not entirely with reason, for it's quiet enough, I simply have not yet done good work and therefore have sufficiently tried out neither quiet nor unquiet. Rather I have given notice out of my own unquiet. I want to torment myself, want to keep changing my condition, believe I have a presentiment that my salvation lies in the change and further believe that through the sort of little changes others make in half-sleep, but I only by stirring up all my intellectual powers, I can prepare myself for

the great change I probably need. I am certainly exchanging an apartment that is worse in many respects. All the same, today is the first (or second day) when, if I hadn't had a very severe headache, I could have done quite good work. Quickly wrote a page.[903]

11 III 15 How time passes, once again ten days and I attain nothing. I don't penetrate. A page is successful now and then, but I cannot hold my ground, the next day I am powerless.

Eastern and Western Jews, an evening.[904] The contempt of the Eastern Jews for the Jews here. The justification of this contempt. How the Eastern Jews know the reason for this contempt, but the Western Jews don't. For example, the horrible conception, beyond all ridiculousness, with which my mother seeks to grasp them. Even Max, the inadequacy weakness of his speech, unbuttoning his coat, buttoning his coat. And yet here there are good and the best intentions. In contrast a certain Wiesenfeld, buttoned into a wretched little coat, a collar that cannot get any dirtier worn as a formal collar, blares yes and no, yes and no. A devilish unpleasant smile around his mouth, wrinkles in his young face, movements of his arms, wild and embarrassed.[905] The best, however, the short fellow, who consists entirely of schooling, with a sharp voice incapable of rising, one hand in his pants pocket, with the other boring toward the listeners incessantly asks questions and immediately proves what is to be proven. Voice of a canary. With the filigree of his speech fills torturously burned-in labyrinthine grooves. Tossing of his head. I as if made of wood, a clothes rack pushed into the middle of the hall. And yet hope.

---

13 *(March 1915)* An evening: At 6 o'clock lay down on the sofa. Slept until about 8 o'clock. Was unable to get up, waited for the clock to strike and in my drowsiness didn't hear anything. Got up at 9 o'clock. Didn't go home for dinner, nor to Max's, where there was a gathering this evening. Reasons: the many unlocking fees,[906] lack of appetite, fear of returning late in the evening, but above all the thought that I wrote nothing yesterday, am getting farther and farther from it and am

in danger of losing everything I have laboriously gained in the past ½ a year. Provided evidence of this by writing 1 ½ wretched pages of a new and already definitively discarded story and then in a despair for which the condition of my listless stomach certainly shared the blame read Herzen, so that he might somehow carry me onward. Happiness of his first year of marriage, horror of seeing myself placed in such happiness, the great life in his circles, Belinsky, Bakunin on his bed for days in a fur coat.[907]

Sometimes the feeling of almost rending unhappiness and at the same time the conviction of its necessity and of a goal attained by every attraction of unhappiness, (now influenced by the memory of Herzen, but happens to me at other times too)

14 *(March 1915)* A morning: in bed until ½ past 11. Jumble of thoughts that forms slowly and solidifies in an implausible way. Read in the afternoon (Gogol, essay on lyric poetry)[908] in the evening a walk partly with the tenable but not trustworthy thoughts from the morning. Sat in the Chotek Gardens. Most beautiful place in Prague. Birds sang, the castle with the gallery,[909] the old trees bedecked with last year's foliage, the semidarkness. Later Ottla came with D.[910]

---

17 *(March 1915)* Pursued by noise. A beautiful much more congenial room than the one on Bilekgasse. I'm so dependent on the view, it's beautiful here, the Tein Church. But great noise of the carriages down below, to which, however, I'm already growing accustomed. Impossible, however, to grow accustomed to the noise in the afternoon. From time to time a crash in the kitchen or in the corridor. On the floor above me yesterday endless rolling of a ball as if someone were bowling incomprehensible purpose, then piano downstairs too. Yesterday evening relative quiet, did somewhat promising work (Assistant Prosecutor) began with enthusiasm today, suddenly next door or below me conversation of a gathering, as loud and fluctuating as if it were hovering around me. Fought a bit with the noise, then lay on the sofa with positively tattered nerves, quiet after 10 o'clock, but can no longer work.

23 III 15 Incapable of writing a line. The contentment with which I sat yesterday in the Chotek Gardens and today on Karlsplatz with Strindberg "By the Open Sea."[911] The contentment today in my room. Hollow as a shell on the beach, ready to be crushed by a footstep

25 *(March 1915)* Yesterday Max's lecture "Religion and Nation." Talmud quotations. Eastern Jews. The girl from Lemberg.[912] The Western Jew who has become assimilated to the Chassidim, the cotton plug in his ear. Steidler, a socialist, long shiny sharply cut hair. The way the Eastern Jewesses are one-sidedly delighted. The group of Eastern Jews by the stove. Götzl, in a caftan, the natural Jewish life. My confusion.[913]

9 IV 15 Torments of the apartment. Boundless. Did good work on a few evenings. If I could have worked at night! Today hindered by noise from sleeping, from working, from everything.[914]

14 IV 15 The Homer lesson of the Galician girls.[915] The one in the green blouse, sharp stern face; when she raises her hand, she holds her arm at a right angle; hasty movements while dressing; when she raises her hand and is not called on, she feels ashamed and turns her face to the side. The strong young girl dressed in green at the sewing machine.

27 IV 15[916] In Nagy Mihàly[917] with my sister. Incapable of living or speaking with people. Complete immersion in myself, thinking of myself. Dulled, unthinking, anxious. I have nothing to share, ever, with anyone. Trip to Vienna. The all-knowing, all-judging Viennese, an experienced traveler, tall, blond-bearded, legs crossed, reads "Az Est,"[918] obliging and yet, as E.[919] and I (in this regard on the lookout in the same way) notice, also restrained. I say: "What an experienced traveler you are!" [He knows all the train connections I need (as it later turns out, to be sure, the details are not quite correct) knows all electr. tram lines in Vienna, gives me advice on telephoning in Budapest to Banovce,[920] knows the parcel delivery services, knows that one pays less in the taximeter automobile when one takes one's luggage along into the car] to which he

does not reply, but sits motionless with bowed head. The girl from Žižkow,[921] tenderhearted, talkative, but rarely able to make herself heard, anemic, her body worthless, undeveloped and no longer capable of development. The old woman from Dresden with the Bismarck face, reveals herself later as a Viennese. The fat Viennese woman, wife of an editor of Die Zeit,[922] a lot of newspaper knowledge, clear speech, to my great repugnance usually holds my own opinion. I mostly silent, have nothing to say, in this circle the war elicits from me not the slightest opinion worth sharing. Vienna—Budapest. The two Poles, the lieutenant and the lady, soon get off, whisper at the window, she pale, not quite young, almost hollow-cheeked, often with her hands on her skirt-squeezed hips, smokes a great deal. The two Hungarian Jews, the one by the window resembling Bergmann,[923] supports with his shoulder the head of the sleeping other. All morning from about 5 o'clock onward business conversations, bills and letters go from hand to hand, samples of the most diverse wares are pulled out of a handbag. Opposite me a Hungarian lieutenant, in sleep an empty, ugly face, open mouth, funny nose, in the morning when he gives information about Budapest, heated, with gleaming eyes, lively voice infused with the whole personality. In the next compartment the Jews from Bistritz[924] who are returning home. A man is escorting several women. They find out that Körös Mezö[925] has just been closed to civilian traffic. They will have to ride for 20 hours or even more in a carriage. They tell a story of a man who stayed in Radautz[926] until the Russians were so close that his only remaining chance of escape was to sit on the last Austrian cannon passing through. Budapest. The most varied information about the connection with Nagy Mihály, the unfavorable accounts, which I don't believe, then turn out to be correct. The hussar in the railroad station in the laced fur jacket, dances and sets his feet like a horse on display. Bids farewell to a lady departing. Entertains her lightly and uninterruptedly, if not with words then with dance movements and manipulations of his saber hilt. Escorts her once or twice, out of precautionary fear that the train might be leaving already, up the steps to the carriage, his hand almost in her armpit. He is of medium height, strong large healthy teeth, the cut and waist accentuation of the fur jacket give his appearance something feminine. He smiles a great deal in all directions, a positively unconscious senseless smile, mere evidence of the natural complete and everlasting harmony of his being, which is almost required by the honor of the officer.—The old married couple saying goodbye in tears. Senselessly repeated countless kisses, just as one in despair keeps picking up a cigarette without knowing it. Familial behavior without regard for their surroundings. This is how it is in all bedrooms. Her facial features cannot even be perceived, an old unremarkable woman, if one takes a closer look at her face, if one tries to take a closer look at it, it positively dissolves and only a faint memory of some little likewise unremarkable ugliness such as the red nose or several pockmarks remains. He has a gray mustache, big nose and real pockmarks. Cape and cane. Controls himself well, even though he is very moved. In melancholy jest grasps the old woman by the chin. What magic lies in grasping an old woman under her chin. Finally, weeping, they look each other in the face. This is not how they mean it, but one could interpret it like this: Even this wretched little happiness that is the connection between us two old people is being disrupted by the war.—The huge German officer marches bedecked with various little pieces of equipment first through the railroad station then through the train. His sturdiness and height make him stiff; the fact that he is moving is almost astonishing; in the face of the firmness of the waist, the broadness of the back, the slender build of the whole figure one opens one's eyes wide to be able to take it all in at once.—In the compartment two Hungarian Jewesses, mother and daughter. Resemble each other and yet the mother in decent shape, the daughter a wretched but self-confident leftover. Mother—large well-wrought face, woolly beard on her chin. The daughter shorter, pointy face, blemished skin, blue dress, over the pitiful bosom a white blouse front.—Red Cross nurse. Very confident and resolute. Travels as if she were a whole family sufficient to itself. Like the father she smokes cigarettes and walks up and down the aisle, like a boy she jumps onto the bench to get something from her knapsack, like a mother she carefully slices the meat, the bread, the orange, like a coquettish girl which she really is, she shows on the opposite bench her beautiful little feet, her yellow boots and yellow stockings on her firm legs. She would have nothing against being spoken to, even begins herself to ask about the mountains one sees in the distance, gives me her guidebook so that I can search for the mountains on the map. Listlessly I lie in my corner, an aversion to asking her questions as she expects rises in me, even though I find her appealing. Strong brown face of indefinite age, coarse skin, arched lower lip, traveling clothes the nurse's uniform underneath, soft cap pressed at will over the tightly twisted hair. Since she isn't asked a question, she begins to tell stories bit by bit to no one in particular. My sister, who, as I later learn, didn't like her at all, supports her a little. She is going to Satoralja Ujhel[927] where she will find out her next destination, she likes best to be where there is the most to do, for there time passes most quickly (my sister concludes from this that she is unhappy, which I, however, think is incorrect). One experiences all sorts of things, a man, for example, was snoring intolerably in his sleep, he was woken up, asked to have consideration for the other patients, he promised, but no sooner did he fall back than there was the terrible snoring again. It was very funny. The other patients threw their slippers at him, he was lying in the corner of the room and was therefore an unmissable target. One must be very strict with the sick, otherwise one doesn't achieve anything, yes, yes, no, no, only don't let them bargain with you. Here I make a remark that is stupid but very characteristic of me, groveling, sly, beside the point, impersonal, indifferent, untrue, fetched from afar, from some ultimate pathological disposition moreover influenced by the Strindberg performance from the evening before,[928] to the effect that it must do women good to be permitted to treat men like that. She doesn't hear the remark or passes over it. My sister naturally understands it entirely in the sense in which it is meant, and by laughing adopts it as her own. Further stories of a tetanus patient who refused to die.—The Hungarian stationmaster who later gets on with his little boy. The nurse gives the boy an orange. The boy takes it. Then she gives him a piece of marzipan, touches his lips with it, but he hesitates. I say: He can't believe it. The nurse repeats it word for word. Very pleasant—Outside the windows Theiss and Bodrog with their huge springtime outflows. Lake landscapes. Wild ducks. Mountains with Tokay vines. Near Budapest suddenly amid plowed fields a semicircular fortified position. Wire barriers, carefully propped-up shelters with benches, model-like. Expression mysterious to me: "adapted to the terrain." Knowledge of the terrain requires the instinct of a quadruped.—Filthy hotel in Ujhel. Everything worn out in the room. The cigar ash of the previous sleepers still on the bedside table. The beds covered with only apparently clean sheets. Attempt in the squad headquarters, then in the rear headquarters to get permission to use a military train. Both in cozy rooms, especially the latter. Contrast between military and officialdom. Correct evaluation of paperwork: a table with inkwell and pen. The balcony door and the window open. Comfortable sofa. In a curtained area on the courtyard balcony clatter of dishes. The snack is being served. Someone—it is as later becomes clear the lieutenant colonel—lifts the curtain to see who is waiting here. With the words: "After all, one must earn one's salary" he interrupts the snack and comes to me. In the end I achieve nothing, even though I must go back home again to fetch my second proof of identity too. Military authorization to use the mail train the next day is simply written on my identification card, a completely superfluous authorization.—Area around the railroad station village-like, the square neglected (Kossut memorial,[929] coffeehouses with gypsy music, pastry shop, an elegant shoe store, crying of "Az Est," a one-armed soldier strolling around proudly with exaggerated movements, a crude color print depicting a German victory is when I pass by in the course of 24 hours, besieged and closely examined, met Popper)[930] cleaner suburbs. Evening in the coffeehouse, nothing but civilians, residents of Ujhel, simple and yet strange, partly suspicious people, suspicious not because there's a war but because they are incomprehensible. An army chaplain is reading newspapers alone.—In the morning the young beautiful German soldier at the inn. Has a great deal served him, smokes a thick cigar, then writes. Sharp stern but youthful eyes, clear regular clean-shaven face. Then puts on his knapsack. Saw him again later, saluting someone, but don't remember where.

---

3 V *(1915)* Complete indifference and dullness. A dried-out well, water at an unattainable depth and uncertain there. Nothing, nothing. Don't understand the life in "The Quarantine Master's Second Story" by Strindberg;[931] what he calls beautiful disgusts me when set in relation to myself. A letter to F., false, not sendable. What holds me for a past or future. The present is ghostly, I am not sitting at the table but fluttering around it. Nothing, nothing. Desolation, boredom, no not boredom just desolation, senselessness, weakness. Yesterday in Dobřichowitz.[932]

---

4 V *(1915)* Better state because I have read Strindberg (The Quarantine Master's Second Story). I'm not reading him to read him but to lie on his chest. He holds me like a child on his left arm. I sit there like a person on a statue. Am ten times in danger of sliding off, but on the eleventh attempt I sit firmly, have security and a great overall view.

Consideration of the relationship of others to me. As insignificant as I may be, there's no one here who has understanding for me on the whole. To have someone who has that understanding, such as a wife, this would mean having support on all sides, having God. Ottla understands some things, even many things, Max, F.[933] some things, some people like E.[934] understand only details, but these with abhorrent intensity, F.[935] understands perhaps nothing at all though here, where there's an undeniable inner connection, this provides a great special position. Sometimes I believed that she understood me without knowing it, for example, when, at the time when I was longing for her unbearably, she was waiting for me in the subway station, I in my craving just to reach her as quickly as possible, presuming her to be up above, was about to run past her and she grasped me quietly by the hand.

---

5 V *(1915)* Nothing, dull slightly aching head. In the afternoon Chotek Gardens, read Strindberg, who nourishes me.

The long-legged black-eyed yellow-skinned childlike girl, merry impertinent and lively. Sees a little friend carrying her hat in her hand. "Do you have two heads?" Her friend immediately understands the joke, in itself quite weak but enlivened by the voice and the infusion of the whole little personality. With a laugh she tells it to another friend, whom she meets a few steps farther: "She asked me whether I have two heads!"

In the morning met Frl. R.[936] Actually an abyss of ugliness, a man cannot change so. Clumsy body, relaxed as if still from sleep; the old jacket that I know; what she's wearing under the jacket is as unrecognizable as it is suspicious, perhaps only a shirt; it is apparently also unsettling for her to be encountered in this state, but she does something wrong, instead of hiding the place of embarrassment she reaches as if guiltily into the neckline of the jacket, pulls the jacket into place. Heavy down on her upper lip, but only in one spot, exceptionally ugly impression. Despite everything I find her very appealing even in unquestionable ugliness, moreover the beauty of her smile is unchanged, the beauty of her eyes has suffered from the diminishing of the whole. Besides, we are separated by continents, I certainly don't understand her, but have an inkling of her, she, however, contents herself with the first most superficial impression she received of me. In all innocence she asks for a bread card.

In the evening read a chapter of Die neuen Christen[937]

The old father and the oldish daughter. He reasonable with a pointed beard, slightly stooped, a cane behind his back. She broad-nosed, with a strong jaw, round but battered face, turns with difficulty at her broad hips. "They say I look bad. But I don't look bad."

---

14 v *(1915)* Fallen out of all regularity of writing. In the open air a great deal. A walk with Frl. Stein[938] to Troja,[939] with Frl. Reiss,[940] her sister, Felix, wife and Ottla to Dobřichowitz, Častalice. As if on the rack. Today religious service on Teingasse,[941] then Tuchmachergasse, then soup kitchen.[942] Today read old chapters from the Stoker. Strength seemingly inaccessible to me today (already inaccessible). Fears of being unfit due to a heart defect.[943]

27 *(May 1915)* Much unhappiness since the last entry. Am going to ruin. To go so senselessly and unnecessarily to ruin.

The facts initially established with regard to the sudden death of the attorney Monderry were as follows: One morning toward ½ past 4 it was a beautiful June morning and already very bright Frau Monderry ran out of her apartment on the fourth floor bent over the staircase railing and cried with outspread arms apparently intending to call the whole house to her aid "My husband has been murdered! Mercy! Mercy! My good husband has been murdered!" The first person to see and hear Frau Monderry was a baker's boy who just at that time was climbing the last steps to the fourth floor with a large basket of rolls in both hands. It was also he who during the first interrogation claimed to have remembered F. M.'s cry verbatim. Later, however, when he was confronted with F. M., he took this statement back and explained that he could have been mistaken, since he had at the first moment been all too shocked by the appearance of the woman. This was, to be sure, quite probable, for even after weeks had passed, whenever he described the incident he was so agitated that he accompanied his story with exaggerated movements of his hands and feet in an effort to produce an impression in the listener that even approximated the one he retained in himself. According to his story, F.M. had flown with a cry out the door, which he had not even noticed opening and which he therefore believed had already been open beforehand, had torn apart her hands clenched together over her head and had hurried to the railing. She was dressed in nothing but her nightshirt and a small gray sheet, which, however, did not even fully cover her upper body. Her hair was let down and hung partly over her face, which also contributed to making her cry unclear. No sooner did she see the baker's boy than she ran to the stairs, pulled him up to her with trembling hands, stepped behind him and pushed him along in front of her as a sort of protection while clasping his shoulders. In all this haste it didn't occur to the boy that he could put the basket of rolls down somewhere and he didn't let go of it the whole time. Thus they went—the woman in her mounting fear pressed the boy tighter and tighter against her—with fast but very short steps toward the apartment door, crossed the threshold and moved forward in the dark narrow anteroom. The woman's face was always leaning forward to the right or left of the boy, she seemed to be lying in wait for something, which should show itself in a moment, sometimes she yanked the boy back as if it were impossible to proceed, but then she pushed him forward again after all with her whole body. With one hand the woman opened the first room door they came upon, with the other she held on to the boy's neck from behind. She surveyed the floor the walls and the ceiling of the room, found nothing, left the door open and now went more resolutely, still with the boy, to the next door. This one was already wide open. Upon entering one saw not much more than two beds side by side. The room was dark, for the heavy completely closed window curtains let in a shimmer of daylight only in narrow gaps. On the little night table beside the bed closest to the door burned a small candle stub. About this bed there was also nothing unusual to be seen, but in the other something must have happened.

Now it was the boy who didn't want to go on, but the woman pushed him forward with fists and knees. During an interrogation he was asked why he had hesitated, whether perhaps out of fear of what he might have expected to see in the bed. To this he replied that he wasn't afraid of anything and hadn't been afraid at that time either, but at that time he had had a feeling as if something were hiding somewhere in the room and could suddenly jump out. At first he had wanted to wait for this "something" which he couldn't describe in any more detail, before he moved forward. But since it seemed so important to the woman to reach the second bed, he finally yielded.

Eleventh Notebook

13 Sept. 15 Eve of my father's birthday, new diary. It's not as necessary as usual, I don't have to make myself restless, I'm restless enough, but for what purpose, when will it come, how can a heart, a not entirely healthy heart bear so much dissatisfaction and so much uninterruptedly tugging desire.

The distraction, the weakness of memory, the stupidity!

14 *(September 1915)* with Max and Langer[944] on Saturday at the wonder rabbi's.[945] Žižkov, Harantova ulice. Many children on the sidewalk and the steps. An inn. Upstairs completely dark, a few steps blindly with hands held out. A room with wan dim light, whitish gray walls, several small women and girls, white headscarves, pale faces, are standing around, small movements; impression of bloodlessness. Next room. All black, full of men and young people. Loud praying. We squeeze ourselves into a corner. Scarcely have we looked around a little when the prayer is over, the room empties. A corner room with two window walls, each with 2 windows. We are pushed to a table, to the right of the rabbi. We resist, "You're Jews too, aren't you?" The strongest paternal nature makes the rabbi. All rabbis look wild, said Langer. This one in a silk caftan, underpants visible underneath. Hairs on the bridge of his nose. Fur-edged cap, which he keeps shifting back and forth. Filthy and pure, peculiarity of intensely thinking people. Scratches himself under his beard, blows his nose through his hand onto the floor, reaches into the

food with his fingers—but when he leaves his hand lying on the table for a little while, one sees the whiteness of the skin, a whiteness such as one thinks one has seen only in childhood imaginings. At that time, to be sure, one's parents too were pure.

---

16 *(September 1915)* Humiliation with Eisner.[946] Wrote the first line of a letter to him, because a worthy letter had quickly formed in my head. Nonetheless desisted after the first line. I used to be different. How easily, moreover, I bore the humiliation, how easily I forgot it, how little impression even his indifference made on me. I could have floated untouched through a thousand corridors, a thousand offices, past a thousand formerly friendly now cold people, without lowering my eyes. Untouchable but also unawakable. And in one office Max could have sat, in another Felix, etc.

New headache of a still unknown sort. Brief painful stabbing on the right over my eye. In the morning for the first time since then more frequently.

Sight of the Polish Jews going to Kol Nidre.[947] The small boy who, prayer shawls under both arms, runs along beside his father. Suicidal not to go to temple.

Opened the Bible. Of the unjust judges.[948] Thus find my opinion or at least the opinion that I have found in myself until now. Apart from that it has no meaning, I am never visibly guided in such things, the pages of the Bible do not flutter before me.

The most fruitful place to stab seems to be between neck and chin. Lift the chin and thrust the knife into the tautened muscles. But the place is probably fruitful only in one's imagination. There one expects to see a magnificent gush of blood and to tear apart a network of sinews and little bones, such as one finds in the roasted legs of turkeys.

Read Förster Fleck in Russia. Napoleon's return to the battlefield of Borodino. The monastery there. It is blown up.[949]

28 IX 15 Complete idleness. Memoirs of General Marcellin de Marbot[950] and Holzhausen "Leiden der Deutschen 1812"[951]

Senselessness of complaining. In response to it stabbing pains in the head.

A small boy was lying in the bathtub. It was the first bath at which in accordance with his old wish, neither his mother nor the maid was present. To fulfill the command of his mother, who shouted to him now and then from the next room he had hastily run the sponge over himself; then he had stretched out and was enjoying the immobility in the hot water. The gas flame hummed steadily and in the stove the dying fire crackled. In the next room it had been quiet for a long time now, perhaps his mother had gone away

---

Why is complaining senseless? Complaining means asking questions and waiting until an answer comes. But questions that do not answer themselves at their inception are never answered. There are no distances between questioner and answerer. There are no distances to overcome. Asking and waiting therefore senseless.

---

29 IX *(1915)* Various hazy decisions. That much I can manage. Chance glimpse of a not entirely unrelated picture on Ferdinandstrasse. A bad sketch of a fresco. Under it a Czech saying, something like: Blinded one you abandon the cup for the girl, soon you will come back the wiser

---

Bad miserable sleep, in the morning racking headaches but freer day.

Many dreams. Appearance of a mixture of Dir. Marschner and clerk Pimisker.[952] Red firm cheeks, blackly waxed beard, exactly the same thick wild hair.

I used to think: Nothing will kill you, this hard clear downright empty head, never will you, unconsciously or in pain, contract your eyes, wrinkle your forehead, twitch your hands, will always be able only to portray it.

How could Fortinbras say that H. would have proved most royally.[953]

In the afternoon couldn't keep myself from reading what I had written yesterday "the filth of the previous day," without harm, by the way.

---

30 *(September 1915)* Made sure that Felix didn't disturb Max. Then at Felix's.[954]

Rossmann and K.,[955] the innocent one and the guilty one, in the end both killed in punishment without distinction, the innocent one with a lighter hand, more pushed aside than struck down.

---

1 Oct. 1915
Volume III Memoirs of General Marcellin de Marbot
Polotsk—Beresina—Leipzig—Waterloo
Mistakes Napoleon made:

1 Decision to wage this war. What did he want to achieve? Strict enforcement of the continental blockade in Russia. That was impossible. Alexander I could not yield without endangering himself. After all, his father Paul I had been murdered because of the alliance with France and because of the war with England, which had damaged Russia's trade immeasurably. Nonetheless, Napoleon still

hoped Alex. would yield. Only to compel him to do so did he plan to assemble his army on the Niemen

2. He could have known what awaited him. Lieutenant Colonel de Ponthon, who had been in the Russian service for several years, implored him on his knees to refrain. The obstacles cited by him were: Apathy and lack of participation of the Lithuanian provinces, which had been subjugated by Russia for many years, the fanaticism of the Muscovites, scarcity of provisions and forage, the desolate land, the roads that the slightest rain made impassable for artillery, severity of the winter, impossibility of advancing during snowfall, which began even in early October.—Napoleon let Maret, Duke of Bassano and Davout influence him in the opposite direction.
3. He should have weakened Austria and Prussia as much as possible by demanding great contingents of auxiliary troops, but demanded only 30,000 men from each
   He didn't take the Prussian Crown Prince into his headquarters even though he had been asked to do so.
4. He should have taken them to the front, instead he placed them on the wings, the Austrians under Schwarzenberg in Volhynia, the Prussians under Macdonald on the Niemen, thereby sparing them and making it possible for them to block his retreat or at least endanger it, which actually happened, since in November the Austrians let Tchichagov's army, which had been freed after the peace with Turkey mediated by England pass undisturbed through Volhynia on its way north, which was to blame for the disaster on the Beresina.

5 He mixed all the corps heavily with the unreliable auxiliary troops (Badenese Mecklenburgers Hessians, Bavarians Württembergers Saxons Westphalians Spaniards Portuguese Illyrians, Swiss Croats, Poles, Italians) and thereby damaged their cohesion. Choice wine spoiled by adding murky water.

6 He set his hopes on Turkey, Sweden and Poland. The first made peace, because England paid, Bernadotte deserted N. formed an alliance with Russia through England's mediation, Sweden did lose Finland but was promised Norway, to be torn from Denmark, which was devoted to Napoleon, the Poles: Lithuania was too bound to Russia by 40 years of annexation to it. The Austr. and Prussian Poles did march with him, but without enthusiasm, they feared the devas-

tation of their country; only the now Saxon grand duchy of Warsaw could be counted on to some extent.

7. From Vilna he wanted to organize conquered Lithuania and make use of it. He might have received universal support 300,000 men, if he had proclaimed the Kingdom of Poland (with Galicia and Posen)—a national assembly in Warsaw did issue such proclamations itself—but that would have meant war with Prussia and Austria (and also made the peace treaty with Russia difficult). Besides, even then the Poles probably would have been unreliable. Vilna and its circle mustered only 20 men for Napol.'s bodyguard. N. chose the middle way, promised the kingdom in the event of their assistance and thereby achieved nothing. Besides, N. could not even have equipped a Polish army, he had not arranged for supplies of weapons and clothing to follow to the Niemen.
8. He gave Jerome Bonaparte who was completely inexperienced in military matters the command over an army of 60,000 men. Immediately upon entry into Russia Napoleon had broken the Russian army line. Emperor Alexander and Field Marshal Barkley marched north to the Dvina Bagration's corps was still near Mir on the lower Niemen. Davout had already occupied Minsk and cast Bagration, who wanted to pass through there on his way north, in the direction of Bobruisk toward Jerome. If Jerome had worked consistently with Davout—but he didn't find that compatible with his royal dignity—Bagration would have been annihilated or forced to capitulate. Bagration escaped, Jerome was sent to Westphalia, Junot took his place, but he too soon made a serious mistake.
9. He named the Duke of Bassano civil governor and General Hogendorp military governor of the province of Lithuania. Neither understood how to create a rear support for the army. The duke was a diplomat, understood nothing of administration, Hogendorp was unacquainted with French customs and military regulations. He spoke French very badly, thus found sympathy neither among the French nor among the local nobility.

10 a reproach leveled by other writers, not Marbot

He remained in Vilna for 19 days, in Vitebsk for 17 until 13 VIII, thus lost 36 days. But it can be explained, he was still hoping for an agreement with the Russians, wanted to maintain a center for directing the corps in pursuit of Bagration and to conserve the energy of the troops. The difficulties of provisioning began too, every evening after completing their day's march the troops were compelled to fetch their necessities often from very far away. Only Davout had a food train and herds for his corps.

11. Unnecessarily great losses at the siege of Smolensk 12,000 men. N. had not expected such a vigorous defense. If they had avoided Smolensk and thus put pressure on Barclay de Tolly's line of retreat, they could have taken it without a battle.

12. He has been reproached for his inaction during the Battle of Borodino (7 Sept.). He spent all day pacing in a ravine, only twice did he climb a hill. In Marbot's opinion this was not a mistake, but N. was ill that day, he had a severe migraine. On the evening of the 6th he had received news from Portugal. Marshal Marmont, one of the generals about whom Napoleon had been mistaken, had been heavily defeated at Salamanca by Wellington.

13 In principle the retreat from Moscow was decided quickly. Many things compelled it: the fires, the battles in Kaluga the cold, the desertions, the threat to the line of retreat, the situation in Spain, a conspiracy uncovered in Paris—nonetheless N. remained in Moscow from 15 Sept. to 19 October he was still hoping for an agreement with Alexander. Kutusov had not even replied to his last conciliatory proposal.

14 He tried to withdraw by way of Kaluga even though it was a roundabout route. He hoped to get provisions there, the road of retreat by way of Mozhaysk was despoiled over long stretches in both directions. But after several days he realized that he couldn't continue on this route without doing battle with Kutusov. Thus he returned to the old road of retreat.

15 The large bridge across the Beresina was covered by a fortress and protected by a Polish regiment. In his confidence that he would be able to use this bridge, N., to lighten and quicken the march, had all the pontoons burned. But in the meantime Tchichagov had taken the fortress and burned the bridge. Despite extreme cold the river was not yet frozen. The lack of pontoons was one of the main causes of the disaster.

16 The crossing of the 2 bridges built at Studianka was badly organized. In the afternoon of 26 Nov. the bridges were built (if they had had pontoons, they would have been able to begin the crossing

at daybreak) until the morning of the 28 they were unmolested by the Russians. Nonetheless only part of the train had crossed by then and the thousands of stragglers had been left for two days on the left bank. The French lost 25,000 men

17. The line of retreat was not protected. From the Niemen to Moscow with the exception of Vilna and Smolensk not a garrison, not a depot, not a hospital. In the whole country between roamed the Cossacks. Nothing could reach the army or leave it without the danger of being captured. This was also the reason that not one of the roughly 100,000 Russian prisoners of war was brought across the border.

18 Lack of interpreters. Partouneaux's division got lost on the way from Borisov to Studianka and ran into Wittgenstein's army and thus into their destruction. They had simply been unable to communicate with the Polish peasants, who were supposed to guide them.

Paul Holzhausen Die Deutschen in Russland 1812

Wretched condition of the horses, great exertions as fodder wet green straw, unripe grain, rotten thatch. Diarrhea emaciation, constipation. Enemas using smoking tobacco. An artillery officer says that his people had to insert the whole length of their arms into the horses' anuses to relieve them of the masses of feces that had accumulated in their bowels. Bloating of their bodies by the green fodder. Sometimes one could remedy it by arduous running. But many died, one saw hundreds with burst bellies on the bridges of Pilony. "They lie in ditches and holes with fixed dimming eyes and try strengthlessly to climb up. But the attempt is fruitless and only rarely do they get a foot onto the road, which then makes their condition even more pitiable. Unfeelingly, train and artillery soldiers drive over it with the ordnance, so that one hears the leg being crushed, the animal's dully screaming sound of pain and sees it driven by fear and horror, lifting its head and neck convulsively, falling back with all its load and immediately being buried by thick mud."

Despair even upon setting out. Heat, hunger, thirst, illness. A noncommissioned officer who cannot go on is admonished to pull himself together and lead his people by example. Soon he disappears into the bushes and kills himself with his own gun. (July Sunday) The next day a first lieutenant from Würtemberg is lambasted by the regimental commander, he snatches a bayonet from the nearest soldier and runs it through his own breast.

Objection to the 11th mistake. Due to the wretched condition of the cavalry and the lack of scouts, the fords to be found above the city were discovered too late.

---

6 Oct. 15 Various forms of nervousness. I think noise can no longer disturb me. To be sure, I'm not working now. To be sure, the deeper one digs one's pit, the quieter it becomes; the less anxious one becomes, the quieter it becomes.

Langer's stories:

A Zadik[956] is to be obeyed more than God. Balshem[957] once told one of his favorite disciples to get baptized. He got baptized, gained esteem, became a bishop. Then Balshem summoned him and gave him permission to return to Judaism. He obeyed again and did great penance for his sin. B. explained his command by saying that due to the disciple's outstanding qualities he had been hounded by the evil one and that the purpose of the baptism had been to divert the evil one. B. cast the disciple himself into the midst of evil, the disciple wasn't to blame for taking the step but was following a command and for the evil one there seemed to be no more work to do here.

Every 100 years a supreme Zadik appears, a Zadik Hador.[958] He need not even be known or be a wonder rabbi and yet he is the supreme one. B. was not Zadik Hador in his time, rather it was an unknown merchant in Drohobisz.[959] The latter heard that B. wrote amulets as other Zadiks did too, and had the suspicion that he was an adherent of Sabbatai Zevi[960] and wrote the latter's name on the amulets. Therefore, from a distance he took from him, whom he did not know personally, the power to give those amulets. B. soon recognized the powerlessness of his amulets—though he had never written anything on the amulets but his own name—and after some time also found out that the man from Drohobysc was the cause of it. When the man from Dr. one day came to Balshem's town—it was on a Monday—B. made him sleep away a day without realizing it; hence the man from Dr. always remained behind by a day in his time reckoning. On Friday evening—he thought it was Thursday—he wanted to go home to spend the holidays at home. Then he sees the people going into the temple and realizes his mistake. He decides to stay here and has himself taken to B. The latter has instructed his wife already in the afternoon to prepare a meal for 30 people. When the man from Dr. comes, he sits down to eat immediately after the prayers and in a short time eats up the food meant for 30 people. But he is not full, rather demands more to eat. B. says: "I was expecting an angel of the first degree, but I was not prepared for an angel of the second degree." He now had everything edible in the house brought in, but even that wasn't enough.

B. was not Zadik Hador, but he was even higher. Witness to this is the Zadik Hador himself. For he came one evening to the town where Balshem's future wife lived as a girl. He was a guest in the house of the girl's parents. Before he went to sleep in the attic, he asked for a candle, but there was none in the house. So he went up without a candle, but when the girl later looked up from the courtyard, it was bright up above as if in festive illumination. From this she recognized that it was a special guest and she asked him to take her as his wife. She was permitted to ask in this way because her higher destiny was proven by the fact that she had recognized the guest. But the Zadik Hador said: "You are meant for someone even higher." This proves that B. was higher than a Zadik Hador.

---

7 *(October 1915)* yesterday with Frl. Reiss for a long time in the vestibule of the hotel. Slept badly, headaches.

Frightened Gerti[961] by limping, the frightfulness of the clubfoot.

Yesterday on Niklasstrasse a fallen horse with a bloody knee. I look away and uncontrollably make grimaces in broad daylight.

Unsolvable question: Am I broken? Am I in decline? Almost all signs speak in favor of this (coldness, dullness, the state of my nerves, absent-mindedness, ineptitude in the office, headaches, sleeplessness) almost nothing but hope speaks against it.

---

3 Nov. *(1915)* Have seen a great deal recently, fewer headaches. Walks with Frl. Reiss. With her at "Er und seine Schwester," performed by Girardi.[962] (Do you have talent, then?—Permit me to intervene and answer for you: Oh yes, oh yes) In the municipal reading room.[963] Looked at the flag at her parents'.[964] The 2 wonderful sisters Esther and Tilka[965] like contrasts of glowing and dimming. Especially Tilka beautiful: olive-brown, arched lowered eyelids, the depths of Asia. Both with shawls drawn around their shoulders. They are of medium height, rather short and appear erect and tall as goddesses, one on the round pillow of the sofa, Tilka in a corner on some unrecognizable seat, perhaps on boxes. In half-sleep for a long time saw Esther, who, with the passion that according to my impression she seems to have for everything spiritual, had bitten firmly into the knot of a rope and was being swung powerfully back and forth in empty space like a bell clapper (memory of a movie poster)[966]—The two Lieblichs. The little devilish teacher whom I also saw in half-sleep, how she flew furiously up and down in a dance, in a Cossack-like but floating dance over a slightly sloping bumpy brick pavement lying there dark brown in the twilight.

---

4 *(November 1915)* Memory of the corner in Brescia where I distributed soldi to children on similar pavement, but in broad daylight.[967] Memory of a church in Verona where, completely forsaken, only under the light compulsion of the duty of a pleasure traveler and under the heavy compulsion of a person lapsing into uselessness I entered reluctantly, saw a larger than life-sized dwarf stooping under the holy water basin, walked around a little, sat down and just as reluctantly went out as if outside there were another such church attached door to door.[968]

Recently the departure of the Jews at the state railroad station.[969] The 2 men carrying a bag. The father loading his possessions onto his many children down to the littlest one in order to reach the platform more quickly. The strong healthy already shapeless young woman sitting on her suitcase with an infant, surrounded by acquaintances in lively conversation.

---

5 *(November 1915)* State of excitement in the afternoon. Began with the consideration whether and how much war loan I should buy.[970] Went to the shop twice to give the necessary instructions and returned twice without having entered. Feverishly calculated the interest. Then asked my mother to buy a 1000 K bond, but increased the amount to 2000 K. In the process it turned out that I had not even known about an investment amounting to roughly 3000 K that belonged to me and that it barely affected me at all when I found out about it. There was nothing in my head but the doubts about the war loan, which now didn't cease for about ½ an hour on a walk through the busiest streets. I felt directly involved in the war, weighed, albeit in accordance with my knowledge, quite generally the financial prospects, raised and reduced the interest that would one day be at my disposal, etc. Gradually, however, this excitement transformed, my thoughts were steered toward writing, I felt capable of it, wanted nothing but the chance to write, considered which nights in the near future I could set aside for it, ran with heart pains across the stone bridge,[971] felt the unhappiness, experienced so often before, of the consuming fire that was not permitted to break out, invented to express and calm myself the saying "Little friend, pour out," sang it incessantly to a special melody and accompanied the song by repeatedly pressing and releasing a handkerchief in my pocket like a bagpipe.

---

6 *(November 1915)* Sight of the antlike movement of the crowd in front of the trench and in it.[972]

At the home of Oskar Pollak's[973] mother. Good impression of his sister. Incidentally, is there anyone to whom I don't bow? In the case of

Grünberg,[974] for example, who in my opinion is a very significant person and is almost universally underestimated for reasons impenetrable to me: If I were faced with the choice, say, that one of the two of us would have to perish immediately (with regard to him it is very probable, for he is said to have a far-advanced tuberculosis) but that it would depend on my decision who it should be, I would find the question ridiculous to the outermost edge of its theoretical formulation, since obviously the incomparably more valuable Grünberg would have to be preserved. Grünberg too would agree with me. In the final uncontrollable moments, to be sure, I would as anyone else would have done much earlier invent evidence in my favor, evidence that due to its crudeness, bareness, falseness would at any other time have made me vomit. These final moments, to be sure, are happening now too, when no one is imposing a choice on me, they are those when I seek to examine myself while keeping away all distracting external influences.

"Silently the "black ones" sit around the fire. The glow of the flames flickers on their somber enthusiast faces."[975]

---

19 XI 15

Days spent uselessly, powers expended in waiting and despite all idleness the fluttering and piercing pains in my head.

Letter from Werfel. Reply.

At Frau Mirsky-Tauber's.[976] Defenselessness against everything. Malicious discussion at Max's. Disgust over it the next morning.

With Frl. Fanni Reiss and Esther.

In the Alt-Neu Synagogue[977] at the Mishna lecture.[978] With Dr. Jeiteles[979] at home. Great interest in individual disputed questions.

Self-pity in the face of the cold, in the face of everything. Now ½ past 9 in the evening someone in the next apartment is pounding a nail into the common wall.

---

21 XI 15 Complete uselessness. Sunday. At night special sleeplessness. Until ¼ past 11 in bed in the sunshine. Walk. Lunch. Read the newspaper, leafed through old catalogues. Walk Hybernergasse, Stadtpark, Wenzelsplatz, Ferdinandstrasse, then toward Podol.[980] Laboriously extended to 2 hours. Now and then felt severe headaches, once positively burning ones. Had dinner. Now at home. Who can survey this from above from beginning to end with open eyes?

---

25 XII *(1915)* Opening the diary for the special purpose of enabling me to sleep. But now see what happens to be the last entry and could imagine 1000 entries with the same content from the past 3–4 years. I am wearing myself out senselessly, would be overjoyed to be permitted to write, don't write. Can no longer get rid of the headaches. I have really squandered myself.—Yesterday spoke openly with my boss, since by deciding to speak and vowing not to shy away I enabled myself to sleep, albeit restlessly, for 2 hours the night before last. Presented 4 possibilities to my boss: 1.) continue to leave everything as it has been this last worst week of torture and end with nervous fever, insanity or otherwise 2.) out of some sense of duty I don't want to take a vacation, but it would be no help anyhow 3.) I can't give notice now because of my parents and the factory 4.) only military service remains. Answer: a week of vacation and hematogenic treatment, which my boss wants to undergo together with me. He himself is probably seriously ill. If I left too, the department would be deserted.

Relief to have spoken openly. For the first time almost officially shook the air in the institute with the word "notice."

Nonetheless hardly slept today.

Always this main anxiety: If I had left in 1912 in full possession of all my powers with a clear head, not gnawed away by the exertions of suppressing living powers![981]

With Langer: He won't be able to read Max's book[982] until 13 days from now. He could have read it on Christmas, since according to an old custom one is not permitted to read Torah on Christmas (one rabbi always cut up the toilet paper for the whole year on that evening) but this time Christmas fell on Saturday. In 13 days, however, it's Russian Christmas, then he'll read it. According to medieval tradition one is not supposed to occupy oneself with fine literature or other worldly knowledge until after one's 70th year, according to a milder view until after one's 40th year. Medicine was the only science with which one was permitted to occupy oneself. Today not even with that, since it is now too closely linked with the other sciences.—On the toilet one is not permitted to think about the Torah, hence one is permitted to read worldly books there. One very pious man from Prague, a certain Kornfeld, knew many worldly things, he studied everything on the toilet.

---

19 April 1916

He wanted to open the door to the corridor but it resisted. He looked up, down, the hindrance could not be found. Nor was the door locked, the key was in the lock on the inside, if someone had tried to lock it from outside, the key would have been pushed out. And who on earth should have locked it? He pushed against the door with his knee, the frosted glass rang, but the door remained stuck. Just look.—He went back into the room, stepped onto the balcony and looked down at the street. But he had not yet grasped with a single thought the usual afternoon life down below when he returned to the door and again attempted to open it. But now it was no attempt, the door opened immediately, it required scarcely any pressure, the breeze wafting here from the balcony made it positively fly open, effortlessly as a child who is allowed in jest to touch the handle while in reality someone bigger pushes it down, he gained entry to the corridor.

I will have 3 weeks to myself. Is that called being treated cruelly?[983]

Recently dreamed: We were living on the Graben near Cafe Kontinental. From Herrengasse a regiment turned into the street, heading toward the state railroad station. My father: "One must see something like this as long as one is capable of it" and swings himself (in Felix's[984] brown dressing gown, the whole figure was a mixture of the two of them) up to the window and with outstretched arms sprawls outside on the very wide, sharply sloping window balustrade. I seize him and hold him by the two little chains through which the dressing gown cord is drawn. Out of malice he stretches himself even farther out, I exert my strength to the limit to hold him. I think about how good it would be if I could fasten my feet with ropes to something firm to keep from being pulled along by my father. To achieve this, to be sure, I would have to let go of my father for at least a little while and that's impossible. Sleep—and especially my sleep can't bear all this tension and I wake up.

---

20 *(April 1916)* In the corridor the landlady came toward him with a letter. He examined the old lady's face, not the letter, while he opened it. Then he read: "Dear Sir. For several days you have been living across from me. A strong resemblance to an old good friend makes you remarkable to me. Give me the pleasure and visit me this afternoon. With regards Louise Halka." "All right" he said as much to the landlady still standing in front of him as to the letter. It was a welcome opportunity to make a perhaps useful acquaintance in this city where he was still a complete stranger. "You know Frau Halka" asked the landlady, as he reached for his hat. "No" he said questioningly. "The girl who brought the letter is her maid" the landlady said as if in apology. "That may be" he said, indignant at her interest and hurried to get out of the apartment. "She is a widow" the landlady breathed after him from the threshold.

A dream: Two groups of men were fighting with each other. The group to which I belonged had caught one of our opponents a huge naked man. Five of us were holding him one by the head, two each by the arms and legs. Unfortunately we had no knife with which to stab him to death, we hurriedly asked each other whether there was a knife, no one had one. But since for some reason there was no time to lose and there was an oven nearby, the unusually large cast-iron oven door of which was red-hot, we dragged the man to it, moved one of the man's feet closer to the oven door until it began to smoke, then pulled it back again and let it stop steaming, only to quickly move it closer once again. This we did regularly until I woke up not only in a cold sweat but really with chattering teeth.

Hans and Amalia, the butcher's two children, were playing with balls by the wall of the warehouse, a large old fortress-like stone building, which with its 2 rows of heavily barred windows extended far along the riverbank. Hans aimed carefully, examined ball path and pit before he took a shot, Amalia was squatting by the pit and knocking impatiently on the ground with her little fists. But suddenly both of them stopped playing with the balls, stood up slowly and looked at the nearest warehouse window. They heard a sound as if someone were trying to wipe clean one of the many little murky dark panes into which the window was divided, but it failed and now the pane was shattered a thin face smiling seemingly for no reason appeared indistinctly in the small square, it must have been a man and he said "Come children come. Have you ever seen a warehouse?" The children shook their heads, Amalia looked up heatedly at the man, Hans glanced back to see whether there were people nearby, but he saw only one man with bent back pushing a heavily laden cart along the quay railing, indifferent to everything. "Then you will really be amazed" said the man, very eagerly as if eagerness were necessary for him to overcome the unfavorable circumstances that separated him with wall bars and window from the children. "But come now. It is high time." "How are we supposed to get in" said Amalia. "I will show you the door" said the man. "Just follow me, I'm going to the right now and will knock on every window." Amalia nodded and ran to the next window, there really was a knock there and so too at the subsequent ones. But while Amalia obeyed the stranger and ran after him unthinkingly as one runs after, say, a wooden hoop, Hans followed only slowly. He felt uneasy, the warehouse, which it had never before occurred to him to visit, was certainly very much worth seeing, but whether it was really permitted to go there was not yet at all proven by the invitation of some chance stranger. Rather it was improbable, for if it had been permitted, then his father certainly would have taken him there by now, since he not only lived quite close by, but even knew all the people within a wide radius, was greeted and treated with great respect by them. And now it occurred to Hans that this must therefore be true of the stranger too, he ran after Amalia to determine this and reached her as she and with her the man stopped at a small sheet-iron door level with the ground. It was like a large oven door. At the last window the man again smashed a small pane and said: "Here is the door. Wait a moment, I'll open the inner doors." "Do you know our father?" Hans asked immediately, but the face had already disappeared and Hans had to wait with his question. Now they heard the inner doors actually being opened. The squeal of the key was at first scarcely audible, then louder and louder in closer doors. The thick masonry broken through here seemed to have been replaced here with many closely spaced doors. Finally the last one too opened inward, the children lay down on the ground to be able to see in and now there was the man's face too in the semidarkness. "The doors are open, so come. Quickly now quickly now." With one arm he was pressing the many door slabs against the wall. As if waiting outside the door had brought Amalia to her senses a little, she now slipped behind Hans and didn't want to be the first, but she pushed him forward, for with him she very much wanted to go into the warehouse. Hans was quite close to the doorway, he felt the cool breath coming out of it, he didn't want to go in, not to the stranger, not behind the many doors, which could be locked, not into the cool old huge building. Only because he was already lying here in front of the opening did he ask: "Do you know our father?" "No" replied the man "but come already, I must not leave the doors open so long." "He doesn't know our father" Hans said to Amalia and stood up; he felt relieved, now he would certainly not go in. "But I do know him" said the man, pushing his head farther forward in the opening "of course I know him, the butcher, the great butcher by the bridge, I myself sometimes get meat there, do you think I would let you into the warehouse if I didn't know your family?" "Why did you say at first that you don't know him" asked Hans, who with his hands in his pockets had already turned completely away from the warehouse. "Because here in this position I don't wish to carry on any long conversations. First come in, then we can talk about everything. Besides, you little boy don't have to come in at all, on the contrary I'd prefer if you stayed outside with your bad manners. Your sister however she is more reasonable, she will come and be welcome." And he held out his hand to Amalie. "Hans" said Amalia, moving her hand closer to the stranger's hand, but not yet grasping it. "Why don't you want to go in?" Hans, who after the man's last reply could cite no clear reason for his reluctance, only said softly to Amalia: "He hisses so." And indeed the stranger hissed not only while speaking but also when he was silent. "Why do you hiss" asked Amalia, who wanted to mediate between Hans and the stranger. "You Amalie I will answer" said the stranger. "My breathing is heavy it comes from being here in the damp warehouse without interruption, I wouldn't advise the two of you to stay here long either, but for a little while it's simply extraordinarily interesting."

"I'll go" Amalia said and laughed, she was now completely won over, "but" she then added more slowly Hans must come along too. Of course said the stranger, hopped out with his upper body, grasped the completely surprised Hans by the hands causing the latter to immediately fall down and pulled him with all his strength into the hole. "This is the way in my dear Hans" he said and dragged the struggling and loudly screaming boy with him without consideration for the fact that one of Hans's coat sleeves was being torn to shreds on the sharp edges of the doors. "Mali" Hans cried suddenly,—he was already in the hole to his feet, so quickly did it go despite all resistance—"Mali, get Father, get Father, I can't turn back, he's pulling me so hard." But Mali, completely confused by the stranger's rough intervention, moreover feeling a little guilty, for she had, after all, to some extent prompted him to commit this misdeed, but in the end also still quite curious as she had been from the very beginning, did not run away but held on to Hans's feet and let

---

11 V *(1916)* And so handed the letter over to the director.[985] Three days ago. Asked either if the war is over in autumn for a long leave later on and indeed without pay or if the war continues for cancellation of the exemption. That was a complete lie. Half a lie would have been if I had asked for an immediate long leave and in the event of refusal for dismissal. Truth would have been if I had given notice. I didn't dare to do either hence complete lie.

Useless discussion today. Director thinks I'm trying to extort the usual 3 weeks of vacation to which I, being exempted, am not entitled, therefore offers them to me without further ado, was supposedly resolved to do so even before the letter. He doesn't so much as speak of the military, as if it weren't in the letter. When I speak of it, he doesn't hear it. He apparently finds long leave without pay funny, mentions it carefully in that tone. Urges me to take the 3 weeks' vacation immediately. Makes incidental remarks as a lay neurologist, like everyone. After all, I have no responsibility to bear as he does, his position, that could certainly make one ill. How much he worked in the past too, when he was preparing for the bar examination and at the same time employed at the institute. For 9 months 11 hours of work a day. And then the main difference. Have I in any way and ever had to fear for my position, but he has had this fear. He has had enemies in the institute who tried all sorts of things, even to cut through the "sturdy branch of his life" in this way, to throw him on the scrap heap.

Strangely, he doesn't speak of my writing.

I weak, even though I see that my life is almost at stake. But insist that I want to join the military and that 3 weeks are not enough for me. Thereupon he postpones the continuation of the discussion. If only he weren't so friendly and sympathetic!

I will stick to the following: I want to join the military, to yield to this wish that has been restrained for 2 years; due to various considerations that don't pertain to me personally, if I were granted a long leave, I would prefer this. But due to official as well as military considerations it is probably impossible. By long leave I understand—the official is ashamed to say it, the sick man is not—six months or a whole year. I want no pay, because it is not a matter of an organic unquestionably diagnosable illness.

All this is a continuation of the lie, but in its effect, if I remain consistent, it comes close to the truth.

---

2 June 1916

What aberrations with girls despite all headaches, sleeplessness, gray hair, despair. I count: since the summer there have been at least 6. I can't resist, it positively tears my tongue out of my mouth when I don't yield to admire an admirable one and love her until the admiration (which indeed comes flying) is exhausted. Toward all six I have almost only inner guilt, but one of them had someone reproach me.

From "The Origin of the Belief in God" by N Söderblom Archbishop of Upsala quite scientific without personal or religious involvement.[986]

Primordial divinity of the Masai: how he lowers the first cattle from heaven on a leather strap into the first kraal.

Primordial divinity of some Australian tribes: he came as a powerful medicine man from the west, made people animals trees rivers mountains, introduced the holy ceremonies and determined from which clan a member of a particular other clan should take his wife. When he was finished he left. The medicine men can climb a tree or rope up to him and receive power

in the case of others: here and there during their creative wanderings they also performed the holy dances and rites for the first time

---

in the case of others: people themselves created the totem animals in primordial times by performing the ceremonies. The holy rites thus themselves brought forth the object at which they are directed

---

The Bimbinga near the coast know 2 men who created wellsprings forests and ceremonies on their wanderings in primordial times.

---

19 June 1916

To forget everything. To open windows. To empty the room. The wind blows through it. One sees only the emptiness, one searches in all corners and does not find oneself.

With Ottla. Fetched her from the English teacher. Home by way of the quay, stone bridge, short stretch of the Kleinseite, new bridge.[987] Exciting statues of saints on the Karlsbrücke. The strange evening light of summertime when the bridge is empty at night.

Joy over Max's liberation. I believed in the possibility, but now I see the reality too. Now again not for myself.[988]

And they heard the voice of the Lord God walking in the garden in the cool of the day.[989]

Calm of Adam and Eve

Unto Adam also and to his wife did the Lord God make coats of skin, and clothed them.[990]

God's raging against the human family[991]
the two trees[992]
the unexplained prohibition[993]
the punishment of all (snake woman man)[994]
the favoring of Cain
whom he still provokes by speaking to him[995]
my spirit shall not always strive with man[996]

Then began men to call upon the name of the Lord[997]

And Enoch walked with God: and he was not; for God took him.[998]

---

3 July *(1916)* First day in Marienbad with Felice. Door to door, keys on both sides[999]

Three houses abutted each other and formed a small courtyard. In this courtyard there were also two workshops housed in sheds and in a corner stood a high pile of small boxes. On an extremely stormy night—the wind drove the torrents of rain over the lowest of the houses sharply into the courtyard—a student still sitting over his books in an attic room heard a loud moan from the courtyard. He started and listened, but it remained quiet, continuously quiet. Must have been mistaken the student told himself and began to read again. "Not mistaken" these were the words into which, after a little while, the letters in the book positively assembled themselves. Mistaken he repeated and helped the lines, which were growing restless, by running his index finger along them.

---

4 July *(1916)* Confined in the square of a picket fence that left no more room than a step lengthwise and widthwise, I awoke. There are similar enclosures in which sheep are penned at night, but they aren't so cramped. The sun shone on me in a straight beam, to protect my head I pressed it to my chest and squatted there with hunched back.

What are you? I am miserable. I have two little boards screwed against my temples.

5 July *(1916)* Hardship of living together. Imposed by strangeness sympathy, lust, cowardice, vanity and only deep down perhaps a thin little stream worthy of being called love, inaccessible to searching, flashing once in the moment of a moment.

Poor Felice

6 July *(1916)* Unhappy night. Impossibility of living with F. Intolerability of living together with anyone. Not regret about this, regret about the impossibility of not being alone. But further: Senselessness of the regret, submission and finally understanding. Stand up from the ground. Cling to the book. But back again: Sleeplessness, headaches, jump down from the high window, but onto the rain-soaked ground, where the impact won't be deadly. Endless rolling with eyes closed, presented to any open gaze.

Only the Old Testament sees—say nothing yet about it.

Dream of Dr. Hanzal,[1000] was sitting behind his desk, somehow leaning back and bending forward at the same time, limpid eyes, explains slowly and precisely in his way a clear train of thought, even in the dream hear almost nothing of his words, follow only the methodicalness by which they are borne. Was then together with his wife too, she was carrying a lot of luggage, was astonishingly playing with my fingers, a piece was torn out of the thick felt of her sleeves, this sleeve, the smallest part of which was filled up by her arms, was filled with strawberries.

[To be laughed at troubled Karl indescribably little. What sort of fellows were they and what did they know. Smooth American faces with only two or three wrinkles, but those engraved deep and bulging, in the forehead or on one side of the nose and the mouth. Americans by birth, whose nature could be ascertained by no more than positively hammering on their stony foreheads. What did they know,][1001]

A man lay seriously ill in bed. The doctor sat at the little table that was pushed to the bed and observed the sick man, who looked back at him. "No help" said the sick man, not as if he were asking but as if he were answering. The doctor opened slightly a large medical work lying on the edge of the little table, cast a fleeting glance inside from a distance and said, snapping the book shut: "Help is coming from Bregenz." And when the sick man contracted his eyes in a strained way, the doctor added: Bregenz in Vorarlberg. "That is far" said the sick man

---

The eternal tension, walk to Auschowitz.[1002] Teacher Zeidler, the ladies with the cherries, looking for mushrooms, eating on the balcony, telling about her brother,[1003] lecture on Pestalozzi, reading "The Bachelor" aloud,[1004] she doing needlework, when "newspaper" is mentioned in the story,[1005] she exclaims: We wanted to buy a newspaper, about my notebook[1006] she says: it's beautiful, how do you come to have it and when I ask what she means by that: Well you haven't exactly spoiled me with good taste. In the end she wrests the notebook from me to briefly brush a page and snap the notebook shut. Is in a hurry to go have tea announced it even while I was reading.

Take me into your arms, that is the depth, take me into the depth, if you refuse now, then later

---

Take me, take me, web of folly and pain

The Negroes came out of the bushes. Around the wooden stake encircled by a silver chain they flung themselves in a dance. The priest sat apart a small rod raised over the gong. The sky was overcast but rainless and still.

I was never before intimate with a woman except in Zuckmantel. Then again with the Swiss girl in Riva. The first was a woman, I ignorant, the second a child, I utterly confused. With F. I was intimate only in letters, humanly only in the past 2 days. It's certainly not so clear, doubts remain. But beautiful the gaze of her soothed eyes, the opening of womanly depths[1007]

---

13 *(July 1916)* And so open yourself gate person come
forth
Breathe the air and the stillness

It was a cafe in a spa. The afternoon had been rainy, no guest had appeared. Only toward evening did the sky clear, the rain gradually stopped and the waitresses began to dry off the tables. The proprietor stood under the archway and looked out for guests. And indeed one was now coming up the forest path. He was wearing a long-fringed plaid over his shoulder, held his head bowed to his chest and with each step extended his hand to set his cane far from himself on the ground

---

14 *(July 1916)* Isaac denies his wife before Abimelech, as Abraham earlier had done his.

Confusion with the wells in Gerar. Repetition of a verse.

Jacob's sins. Esau's predestination.[1008]

Gloomily a clock strikes
Listen to it when you enter the house

15 *(July 1916)* He sought help in the forests, he almost leaped through the foothills, he hurried to the sources of the brooks that encountered him, he struck the air with his hands, he panted through nose and mouth

---

19 July 15 *(1916)*

Dream and weep poor race
you don't find the way, have lost it
Woe! is your greeting in the evening, Woe! in the morning
I want nothing only to wrest myself
from hands of the depths that reach out
to take me, powerless one, down.
Heavily I fall into the ready hands.

In the distance of the mountains
resounded slow speech. We hearkened.

Oh they bore, demons of hell,
veiled grimaces, the body pressed close to themselves.

Long procession, long procession bears the unfinished one

Strange court custom. The man condemned to death is stabbed there in his room by the executioner without the presence of other people. He is sitting at his table finishing the letter in which he writes:

---

20 July *(1916)*

A little bird emerged from a neighboring chimney, clung to the edge of the chimney, looked around the area, ascended and flew. No ordinary bird, no ordinary bird that flies up out of the chimney. From a window on the second floor a girl looked up at the sky, saw the bird rising high, cried: "There it flies, quickly, there it flies" and two children were now pressing to her sides to see the bird too.

Have mercy on me, I am sinful in every corner of my being. But had not entirely contemptible gifts, small good abilities, squandered them, unadvised being that I was, am now close to the end, just at a time when outwardly everything could take a turn for the better for me. Do not relegate me to the lost ones. I know it is a ridiculous self-love that speaks in this, ridiculous in the distance and indeed even nearby, but being alive, I also have the self-love of the living thing and if the living thing is not ridiculous, then neither are its necessary expressions. Poor dialectic. [If I am condemned, then I am not only condemned to the end but also condemned to resist until the end.]

On the Sunday morning shortly before my departure you seemed to want to stand by me, I hoped, to this day an empty hope. [And whatever I lament is without conviction, even without real suffering, swings like the anchor of a lost ship far over the depths that could provide a firm hold.] Give me only rest in the nights—childish lament.

---

21 July *(1916)*

They called. It was beautiful. We got up, the most varied people, gathered outside the house. The street was quiet, as it always is early in the morning. A baker's boy put down his basket and watched us. All of us came running down the stairs, one close behind the other, the occupants of all 6 floors were jumbled together, I myself helped the merchant from the second floor put on his overcoat, which he had until then been dragging along behind him. This merchant led us, that was proper, he had been sifted through the world more than any of us. First he arranged us into a cluster, admonished the most restless to be calm, he took the bank official's hat, which the latter kept waving, and threw it to the other side of the street, every child was taken by the hand by an adult.

22 *(July 1916)*

Strange court custom. The condemned man is stabbed to death in his cell by the executioner without other people being permitted to be present. He is sitting at the table finishing his letter or his last meal. There's a knock, it's the executioner. "Are you ready?" he asks. His questions and orders are prescribed to him in their content and sequence, he cannot deviate from them. The condemned man who at first jumped up from his seat, sits again stares ahead or has buried his face in his hands. Since the executioner receives no reply, he opens his instrument case on the plank bed chooses the daggers and tries even now to perfect their diverse cutting edges in places. It is already very dark, he sets up a small lantern and lights it. The condemned man furtively turns his head toward the executioner, but when he notices his work, he shudders, turns around again and wants to see nothing more. "I am ready" the executioner says after a little while. "Ready" the condemned man cries with a screaming question, jumps up and now does look fully at the executioner. "You won't kill me, won't lay me down on the plank bed and stab me to death, you are a human being after all can execute someone on the platform with assistants and before court officials, but not here in the cell one human being killing another." And since the executioner bent over the case says nothing, the condemned man adds more calmly: It is impossible. And since even now the executioner remains silent, the c. goes on: "It is precisely because it is impossible that this strange court custom was introduced. The form was to be preserved but the death penalty no longer carried out. You will take me to another prison, there I will probably remain for a long time, but I won't be executed." The execut. loosened a new dagger in its cotton sheath and said: "You must be thinking of the fairy tales in which a servant was ordered to expose a child, but didn't do this, instead apprenticing the child to a shoemaker. That is a fairy tale, but this here is no fairy tale." The not quite complete accord

21 Aug *(1916)* for the collection "all the beautiful words about rising above nature prove ineffectual in the face of the primordial forces of life" (Essays against Monogamy)

---

27 Aug 16

Final view after two ghastly days and nights: Thank your official's vice of weakness, thriftiness, indecisiveness, art of calculation, precaution, etc., that you haven't sent off the card to F. It's possible that you wouldn't have retracted it, I concede, it's possible. What would have been achieved? An act, a revival? no. You have already carried out this act several times, nothing improved. Don't try to explain it; certainly you can explain all the past, since you won't even take the risk of a future without having explained it beforehand. Which is simply impossible. What amounts to a sense of responsibility and as such would be very honorable is at bottom official's spirit, puerility, will broken by your father. The better, work on it, it lies directly before your hand. This means, then, do not spare yourself (moreover at the expense of F.'s human life that you do love), for sparing is impossible, the apparent sparing has almost brought you to ruin today. It's not only the sparing with regard to F., marriage, children, responsibility, etc., it's also the sparing with regard to the office in which you sit, with regard to the bad apartment out of which you don't stir. Everything. Stop doing it then. One cannot spare oneself, cannot calculate in advance. You know nothing about yourself when it comes to what would be better for you. Last night, for ex., at the expense of your brain and heart a battle was waged within you between two motives of completely equal value and strength, worries on both sides, that is, impossibility of calculation. What's left? To no longer degrade yourself into such a battlefield, where the battle is fought practically without consideration for you and you feel nothing but the blows of the terrible warriors. Rouse yourself, then, improve yourself, escape officialdom, just begin to see who you are instead of calculating what you shall become. The next task is imperative: become a soldier. Also abandon your senseless error of making comparisons, such as with Flaubert, Kierkegaard, Grillparzer.[1009] That is entirely puerile. As a link in the chain of calculations the examples can certainly be of use or rather with all the calculations they are unusable, but compared individually they are unusable even from the outset. Flaubert and Kierkegaard knew very well how things stood with them, had an unbent will, that wasn't calculation but act. In your case, however, a perpetual succession of calculations a monstrous undulation of 4 years. With Grillparzer the comparison is perhaps correct, but Grillparzer seems to you unworthy of imitation, an unhappy example, whom future generations should thank because he suffered for them.

---

8 October 16 Förster:[1010]

to make the treatment of the human relationships contained in school life into a subject of instruction

---

Education as a conspiracy of adults. We draw the freely frolicking under pretenses in which we too believe but not in the professed sense, into our cramped house. (Who wouldn't like to be a nobleman? Closing the door)[1011]

The ridiculousness in the explanation and combatting of Max and Moritz.

The value of giving free rein to the vices, which is irreplaceable, consists in the fact that they arise and become visible in their whole strength and size, even if in the excitement of participation one sees only a faint glimmer of them. One does not learn the life of a sailor by practicing in a puddle but by training all too much in a puddle one might well become incapable of being a sailor.

Page 98 "the younger then suspect"
99 "today for the first time when you came . . ."

16 Oct. *(1916)* Among the 4 conditions that the Hussites proposed to the Catholics as a basis for unification there was one that all mortal sins, among which they counted "gluttony, drunkenness unchastity lying perjury usury, accepting a confession- and mass-penny" should be punished

with death. One party even wanted to have the right granted to every single individual to carry out the death penalty as soon as he saw anyone besmirched with one of the above-mentioned sins.[1012]

Is it possible that I at first discern the future in its cold outlines with understanding and desire and only when pulled and pushed by them gradually enter the reality of this same future?

We are permitted to swing the will, the whip, over us with our own hand.

---

18 *(October 1916)* From a letter:[1013]

It is not so simple for me to simply accept what you say about my mother, my parents, flowers, the New Year and the company at the table. You say that for you too it "won't be among the most pleasant experiences to sit at the table in your home with your whole family." By saying this you are of course only expressing your opinion quite rightly without regard for whether it makes me happy or not. Well it doesn't make me happy. But it would certainly make me much less happy still if you had written the opposite. Please, tell me as clearly as possible, wherein will this unpleasantness consist for you and wherein do you see its causes? After all, in relation to myself, we have often spoken about the matter before, but here it is hard to grasp even a little what is correct. In general terms—and thus with a harshness not quite corresponding to the truth—I can describe my position roughly like this: Having mostly been dependent I have an infinite longing for independence autonomy, freedom in all directions, better to put on blinders and go my way to the limit than for my native pack to whirl around me and distract my gaze. That's why every word I say to my parents or they to me so easily becomes a wooden beam that comes flying in front of my feet. All connection that I do not myself create or struggle to attain, even if it be against parts of my nature, is worthless, hinders me from moving, I hate it or am close to hating it. The way is long, one's strength is scant, there's more than enough reason for such hatred. But I come from my parents, am bound to them and my sisters by blood, do not feel this in ordinary life and due to the necessary obsession with my special intentions, but at bottom respect it more than I know. At times I pursue this too with my hatred, the sight of the marriage bed at home, the used bedclothes, the carefully laid-out shirts can nauseate me, can turn me inside out, it is as if I were not definitively born, came again and again into the world from this musty life in this musty room, were compelled again and again to seek confirmation for myself there were indissolubly bound if not completely and utterly, nonetheless in part to these disgusting things, at least this still clings to my feet that want to run, they are still stuck in the original formless mush. But at other times I know again that they are my parents, after all, necessary constantly strength-giving components of my own being, belonging to me not only as hindrance but also as being. Then I want them as one wants the best; if in all malice, rudeness, selfishness, lovelessness I have nonetheless always trembled before them and actually do so even to this day, for that is something one cannot stop and if they Father from one side Mother from the other necessarily almost broke my will in their turn, then I also want to see them worthy of this. (Ottla sometimes seems to me what I would want a mother to be like from a distance: pure truthful honest consistent, humility and pride, receptiveness and restraint, devotion and independence, timidity and courage in unerring balance. I mention Ottla because my mother is in her too, after all, though utterly unrecognizable) I want, then, to see them worthy of this. Hence their uncleanliness is for me 100 times as great as it may be in reality, which doesn't concern me; their simplemindedness a hundred times, their ridiculousness a hundred times, their crudeness a hundred times. Their good qualities, on the other hand, a hundred thousand times lesser than in reality. I have been deceived by them and yet cannot revolt against the law of nature without going mad, thus again hatred and nothing but hatred. You belong to me, I have made you mine, I cannot believe that in any fairy tale there has been a greater and more desperate battle for any woman than for you within me, from the beginning and ever anew and perhaps forever. So you belong to me, therefore my relationship to your relatives is similar to my relationship to my own, though naturally incomparably more tepid in the good and the bad. They constitute a connection that hinders me (hinders, even if I should never speak a word with them) and they are not worthy in the above-mentioned sense. I am speaking to you as frankly as to myself, you won't take it amiss or look for arrogance in it, this isn't there at least not where you might look for it.

When you are now here and are sitting at my parents' table, my openness to attack by what is hostile to me in my parents has naturally grown much greater. My connection with the family as a whole seems to them to have grown much greater (but it has not and must not) I seem to them inserted into these ranks, one post of which is the bedroom next door (but I am not inserted) they believe that in you they have gained support against my resistance (they have not gained it) and their ugliness and contemptibility increases, since in my eyes it should be superior to something greater. If this is so, then why am I not happy about your remark? Because I am positively standing before my family incessantly swinging knives in a circle to constantly and simultaneously wound and defend my family, let me represent you completely in this without your representing me in this sense to your family. Is this sacrifice not too heavy for you dearest? It is immense, and will be lightened for you only by the fact that if you don't make it, I, by virtue of my nature, must wrest it from you. But if you make it, then you have done a lot for me. I intentionally won't write to you for 1 or 2 days so that, undisturbed by me, you can think about and reply to it. As a reply—so great is my confidence in you—even a single word will suffice.

---

30 x 16

Two gentlemen were speaking in the saddle room about a horse whose hindquarters a stable boy was massaging. "I have not" said the older white-haired one, squinting one eye somewhat and gnawing lightly on his lower lip "I have not seen Atro in a week, one's memory for horses remains uncertain even with the greatest practice. In Atro I now miss much that in my imagination he definitely possessed. I am speaking now of a general impression, the details may indeed be correct, even if I now notice here and there a slackness of the muscles. Look here and here." He moved his bowed head searchingly and groped with his hands in the air.

---

6 April 17

Today, in the small harbor where besides fishing boats only the 2 passenger steamers that provide sea transport usually stop, there was an unknown bark. A heavy old vessel, relatively low and very round-bellied, soiled, as if utterly inundated with dirty water, which still seemed to be dripping down the yellowish outer wall, the masts incomprehensibly tall, the main mast bent in its upper third, wrinkled, coarse, yellow-brown sailcloths pulled every which way between the wood, patchwork, equal to no gust of wind.

I marveled at it for a long time, waited for someone to show himself on the deck, no one came. A worker sat down beside me on the quay wall. "Whose ship is that?" I asked, "this is the first time I've seen it." "It comes every 2 or 3 years" said the man "and belongs to the hunter Gracchus"[1014]

---

29 July 17

Court jester. Study on the court jester.

The great days of jesterdom are probably over and are not coming back. Everything is aiming elsewhere, it cannot be denied. All the same, I have still savored jesterdom to the full, even if it should now be lost from the possession of humanity.

I always sat deep inside the workshop, completely in the dark, there one sometimes had to guess what one was holding in one's hand, but nonetheless for every bad stitch one received a blow from the master.

Our king did not live extravagantly; anyone who didn't know him from pictures would not have recognized him as a king. His suit was poorly sewn, not in our workshop, by the way, a thin material, his coat always unbuttoned, flying and rumpled, his hat battered, coarse heavy boots, careless broad movements of his arms, a strong face with a big straight manly nose, a short mustache, dark somewhat too-sharp eyes, a sturdy well-proportioned neck. Once, as he was passing, he stopped in the doorway of our workshop and asked his right hand up on the door beam: Is Franz here? He knew all the people by name. I pushed my way out of my dark corner through the journeymen. "Come along" he said after a brief glance. "He is moving into the castle" he said to the master.

30 *(July 1917)* Frl. Kanitz.[1015] Temptations with which her nature doesn't go along. The opening and closing, the stretching, pursing, blossoming of her lips, as if her fingers were invisibly shaping them. The always surprising movement executed suddenly, probably nervously but

with discipline, for example, arranging of her skirt on her knees, changing of her seat. The conversation with few words, few thoughts, without any support from the others, produced mainly by turns of her head, gesticulations of her hands, varied pauses, liveliness of her gaze, if necessary by clenching of her small fists.

Ride said the commandant.

He wrested himself from their circles. Mist blew around him. A round forest clearing. The phoenix bird in the bushes. A hand making the cross again and again on an invisible face. Cool perpetual rain, a changeable song as if from a breathing chest.

An unusable person. A friend? If I seek to recall to my memory what he possesses, then what remains, albeit only in the most favorable judgment, is his voice, somewhat deeper than mine. If I cry, "Saved," I mean, if I were Robinson and cried "Saved," he would repeat it with his deeper voice. If I were Korah and cried "Lost,"[1016] he would immediately be repeating it with his deeper voice. One gradually grows tired of always having this bass player in one's company. At the same time, he himself is not at all cheerful about it, he repeats only because he has no choice and can do nothing else. Occasionally during my vacation, when I have some time to turn my attention to these personal matters, I consult with him, perhaps in the arbor, about how I might free myself from him.

---

31 July 17 When Kaspar Hauser had woken up to the extent that he recognized people and things around him

---

To sit in a railroad train, forget it, live as if at home, suddenly remember, feel the power of the train sweeping one along, become a traveler, pull one's cap out of one's suitcase, encounter one's fellow travelers more freely, warmly, urgently, be borne toward one's destination through no merit of one's own, feel this in a childlike way, become a darling of the women, stand under the constant attraction of the window, always leave at least one outstretched hand on the windowsill. More sharply tailored situation: Forget that one forgot, all at once become a child traveling alone on an express train, around whom the carriage, moving so fast that it is trembling, astonishingly builds itself in the minutest detail as if out of the hand of a conjuror.

---

1 Aug *(1917)* Old Prague stories of Dr. Oppenheimer[1017] at the swimming school.[1018] The furious speeches against the rich that Friedrich Adler[1019] delivered in his student days and at which everyone laughed so much. Later he married rich and fell silent.—As a small boy, having come from Amschelberg to Prague to attend the Gymnasium, Dr. O. lived with a Jewish private scholar whose wife was a saleswoman in a junk shop. The food was fetched from a delicatessen. Every day O. was woken at ½ past 5 to pray.—He provided for the education of all his younger siblings, it took a great deal of effort, but gave him self-confidence and satisfaction. At the time a Dr. Adler, who later became a finance councilor[1020] and has long been retired (a great egoist), once advised him to go away, to hide, to simply run away from his family, for otherwise they would bring him to ruin

---

I tighten the reins.

---

2 Aug. *(1917)*
Usually he whom one is seeking lives next door. This cannot be explained easily, one must accept it at first as an empirical fact. It is so deep-rooted that one cannot prevent it, even if one is determined to. That's because one doesn't know of this neighbor one is seeking. Indeed one knows neither that one is seeking him nor that he lives next door, but then he most certainly lives next door. One may of course know the general empirical fact as such, this knowledge does not cause so much as the slightest disturbance, even if one intentionally always keeps it in mind. I'll tell the story of one such case:

Pascal arranges things quite tidily before God's appearance,[1021] but there must be a deeper more anxious skepticism than that of the enthroned man cutting himself up, admittedly with wonderful knives, but nonetheless with the calm of the butcher. Whence the calm? The sureness in wielding the knife? Is God a theatrical triumphal chariot that, granted all toil and despair of the workers, is pulled with ropes from a distance onto the stage?

---

3 Aug. *(1917)*

Once again I cried out into the world at the top of my lungs. Then they thrust the gag into my mouth bound my hands and feet and tied a cloth over my eyes. I was rolled back and forth several times, I was set upright and laid down again this too several times, they pulled jerkily at my legs so that I reared with pain, they left me lying quietly for a little while, but then they stabbed me deeply with something sharp, surprisingly here and there, wherever their whim prompted.

For years I have been sitting at the great crossroads, but tomorrow, because the new emperor is arriving, I shall leave my spot. As much on principle as out of aversion I interfere in nothing that goes on around me. I have even long since stopped begging; those who have been passing by for a long time give to me out of habit, out of loyalty, out of acquaintance, but the new ones follow their example. I have a little basket sitting beside me and everyone throws into it as much as he thinks best. For that very reason however because I pay heed to no one and in the noise and senselessness of the street preserve a calm gaze and a calm soul, I understand everything that concerns me, my position, my justified claims, better than anyone. About these questions there can be no dispute, here only my opinion can be valid. Therefore, when a policeman, who naturally knows me very well, but whom I have just as naturally never noticed before, stopped in front of me this morning and said: Tomorrow is the arrival of the emperor; don't you dare come here tomorrow, I replied with the question: How old are you?

---

4) *(August 1917)*

Literature spoken as a reproach is so stark an abbreviation of speech that—perhaps there was intent in this from the very beginning—it has gradually entailed an abbreviation of thought too, which deprives one of the correct perspective and makes the reproach fall far short and far wide of the mark. . . . .

The signal trumpets of nothingness. The A.

A. I want to ask you for advice.

B. Why me of all people?

A. I have trust in you.

B. Why?

A. I have often seen you at social gatherings. And at our gatherings it is in the end always a matter of advice. We agree on that, don't we? Whatever sort of gathering it may be, whether we are playacting together or drinking tea or summoning spirits or trying to help the poor it is always a matter of advice, isn't it? So many unadvised people! And even more than it seems, for those who give advice at such meetings give it only with their voices, with their hearts they want it themselves. They always have their double among the advice-seeking and especially have their eye on him. But he more than anyone leaves unsatisfied, disgusted and drags the advice-giver along behind him to other meetings and to the same game.

B. That's how it is?

A. Certainly, you recognize it too, don't you? Nor is there any merit in this, the whole world recognizes it and its plea is all the more urgent.

---

5 *(August 1917)* Afternoon in Radešowitz with Oskar.[1022] Sad, weak, often at pains to at least keep hold of the central question.

A. Good day.

B. You've been here before? Haven't you?

A. You recognize me? Amazing.

B. In my head I have already spoken with you several times. What was it you wanted the last time we met.

A. To ask you for advice
B. Right. And was I able to give you some.
A. No. Unfortunately, we could not agree even on how to ask the question.
B. So that's how it was.
A. Yes. It was very unsatisfying, but indeed only for the moment. One simply cannot deal with the matter all at once. Couldn't we repeat it once again?
B. Of course. Ask away!
A. Then I will ask
B. Go ahead
A. My wife—
B. Your wife?
A. Yes, yes
B. I don't understand this. You have a wife?
A.

---

6 August *(1917)*

A. I am not satisfied with you.
B. I won't ask why. I know.
A. And?
B. I am so powerless. I can change nothing. Shrugging my shoulders and screwing up my mouth, that's all I can do.
A. I will take you to my master. Do you want to come?
B. I feel ashamed. How will he receive me? To go straight to the master! It's brazen.
A. Leave the responsibility to me. I'll take you. Come!

They go down a corridor. A. knocks on a door. A voice calls "Come in." B. wants to run away, but A. grabs him and so they enter.

C. Who is the master?
A. I thought—

---

at his feet, fall down at his feet.

A. No way out, then?
B. I have found none.
A. And you know the area better than any of us.
B. Yes.

---

7 Aug. *(1917)*

A. You keep roaming around the door here. What is it you want?
B. Nothing, please.
A. Really?! Nothing? I know you, by the way.
B. You might be mistaken.
A. No, no. You are B. and went to school here 20 years ago. Yes or no?
B. Well, then, yes. I didn't dare to introduce myself.
A. You do seem to have become fearful, with the years. In those days you were not.
B. Yes, in those days. I regret everything as if I had done it this hour.
A. So are penalties paid in life?
B. Oh!
A. Didn't I say so?
B. You said so. But that's not how it is. Penalties are not paid directly. What does my employer care if I chattered in school. That was no hindrance to my career, no.

"How?" said the traveler[1023]

The traveler felt too tired to give another order or do anything more at all here. He just pulled a handkerchief out of his pocket, made a movement as if he were dipping it into the distant bucket, pressed it against his forehead and lay down beside the pit. He was found thus by two men the commandant had sent out to fetch him. As if refreshed he jumped up when they spoke to him. His hand on his heart, he said: "I'll be a dirty dog if I permit this." But then he took it literally and began to run around on all fours. Only sometimes he jumped up, positively broke free, clung to the neck of one of the men exclaimed in tears: "Why is all this happening to me" and hurried back to his post.

8 *(August 1917)* And even if everything was unchanged, the spike was still there, crookedly jutting out of his shattered forehead.

As if all this made the traveler aware that what was to follow was solely his and the dead man's affair, he sent away the soldier and the condemned man with a movement of his hand, they hesitated, he threw a stone at them, they kept deliberating, then he ran to them and struck them with his fists.

"How?" the traveler suddenly said. Had something been forgotten? A decisive word? A grasp? The extending of a hand? Who can penetrate the confusion? Damned evil tropical air, what are you doing to me? I don't know what's happening. My power of judgment has stayed home in the North.

"How?" the traveler suddenly said. Had something been forgotten? A word? A grasp? The extending of a hand? Quite possibly. Most probably. A gross miscalculation, a fundamental misconception, a screeching ink-spraying stroke goes through the whole thing. But who will set it right? Where is the man to set it right. Where is the good old miller, a countryman from the North, who will stuff the two grinning fellows over there between the millstones?

"Prepare the way for the snake!" came a shout. "Prepare the way for the great madam." "We are ready" came a shout in reply "we are ready." And we preparers of the way, we widely lauded stonebreakers, marched out of the thicket. "Get to work" cried our ever cheerful commandant "get to work you snake food." Thereupon we raised our hammers and for miles the most diligent smashing began. No pause was permitted, only changing of hands. The arrival of our snake was announced for that very evening, by then everything had to be smashed to dust, our snake tolerates not even the smallest pebble. Where else is so sensitive a snake to be found. She is indeed a unique snake, she is incomparably spoiled by our work, therefore by now incomparable in her nature too. We don't understand, we regret the fact that she still calls herself a snake. She should always call herself a madam at least, even though as a madam too she is of course incomparable. But that is not our concern, our job is to make dust.

Hold the lamp up high, you in front! You others quiet behind me! Everyone in a line. And calm. That was nothing. Don't worry. I bear the responsibility. I will lead you out.

---

9 Aug. *(1917)*

The traveler made a vague movement of his hand, abandoned his efforts, pushed the two away from the corpse again and pointed out to them the colony where they were to go immediately.[1024] With gurgling laughter they showed that they gradually understood the order, the condemned man pressed his repeatedly greased face against the traveler's hand, the soldier slapped the traveler on the shoulder with his right hand—in his left he was brandishing the rifle—all three now belonged together.

The t. had to forcibly fend off the feeling coming over him that in this case a perfect order had been established. He grew tired and abandoned the plan of burying the corpse now. The heat that was still rising—only to keep from staggering did the t. avoid raising his head toward the sun—the sudden final silence of the officer, the sight of the two over there, who were staring at him strangely and with whom he had lost all connection by the death of the off., finally this smooth mechanical refutation the off.'s opinion had found here—all this—the t. could no longer stand upright and sat down on the cane chair. If his ship had slid to him here through this trackless sand to take him aboard,—this would have been the most beautiful thing of all. He would have climbed aboard, only from the steps would he have reproached the officer for the cruel execution of the condemned man. I will tell them at home he would have said, raising his voice so that the captain and the sailors bending over the railing above with curiosity heard it too. "Executed?" the officer would then have asked with reason. "But here he is" he would have said, pointing to the man carrying the traveler's suitcase. And indeed it was the condemned man, as the t. persuaded himself by sharp observation and close examination of his facial features. "My compliments" the t. had to say and said it gladly. "A conjuror's trick?" he then asked. "No" said the o. "an error on your part I was executed as you ordered." The captain and sailors were now listening even more attentively. And all saw how the o. now ran his hand over his forehead and exposed a spike crookedly jutting out of his shattered forehead.

It was already the period of the last major battles that the American government had to wage with the Indians. The fort deepest in Indian territory—it was also the strongest—was commanded by General Samson, who had distinguished himself here many times by now and had the unswerving confidence of the people and the soldiers. Against an individual Indian the cry "General Samson!" was worth almost as much as a rifle.

One morning a raiding party captured a young man in the woods and in accordance with the standing order of the general, who personally dealt with even the most trivial things, brought him to headquarters. Since the general was at the moment having a consultation with several farmers from the frontier territory, the stranger was first taken to the adjutant Lieutenant Colonel Otway.

"General Samson!" I cried and staggered a step back. It was he who came out of the tall thicket here. "Quiet" he said, pointing behind him. A retinue of about 10 men stumbled after him.

---

10 *(August 1917)*

I was standing with my father in the entrance hall of a house; outside it was raining very hard. A man was about to turn hurriedly out of the street into the hall when he noticed my father. That made him stop. "Georg" he said slowly, as if he gradually had to retrieve old memories, and, holding out his hand, approached my father from the side.

"No, let me be, no let me be!" thus I cried incessantly along the streets and again and again she took hold of me, again and again the siren sank her claw hands from the side or over my shoulders into my breast

---

It is always the same, always the same

Twelfth Notebook

15 Sept. 17 You have as far as this chance exists at all, the chance to make a beginning. Do not waste it. You won't be able to avoid the filth that wells up out of you, if you want to penetrate. But don't wallow in it. If the lung wound[1025] is only a symbol, as you claim, symbol of the wound the inflammation of which is called Felice and the depth of which justification,[1026] if this is so, then the medical advice too (light air sun rest) is symbol. Take hold of this symbol.

O beautiful hour, masterful composure, overgrown garden. You turn out of the house and on the garden path the goddess of happiness drifts toward you.

Majestic apparition, prince of the realm

Bulldogs, five,
Phillipp, Franz, Adolf Isidor and Max

Not so

The village square abandoned to the night. The wisdom of the little ones. Predominance of the animals. The women—cows moving across the square with extreme naturalness. My sofa over the land.

18 IX *(1917)* Tear everything up.

---

19 *(September 1917)* Instead of a telegram: "Very welcome station Michelob[1027] health excellent Franz Ottla" which Mařenka[1028] twice took to Flöhau[1029] supposedly without being able to send it because the post office had closed shortly before her arrival, I wrote a farewell letter[1030] and all at once suppressed torments that arose powerfully yet again. Farewell letter ambiguous, to be sure, like my opinion

---

It is the age of the wound more than its depth and overgrowth that makes it painful. To be torn open again and again in the same wound channel, to see the wound that has been operated on countless times taken under treatment again, this is what is awful.

The fragile moody negligible being—a telegram flings it down, a letter helps it up, revives it, the silence after the letter dulls it

---

The cat's playing with the goats. The goats resemble:[1031] Polish Jews, Uncle Siegfried,[1032] Ernst Weiss,[1033] Irma[1034]

Different but similarly stern unapproachability of the overseer Hermann[1035] (who left today without dinner or goodbye; the question is whether he is coming tomorrow) of the young lady, of Mařenka.[1036] Fundamentally constricted in their presence, as in front of the animals in the stable when one instructs them to do something and they astonishingly obey. The case is more difficult here only because they so often seem approachable and completely understandable for a moment.

Always incomprehensible to me that it is possible for almost anyone who can write, suffering pain, to objectify the pain, so that I, for example, suffering unhappiness, my head perhaps still burning with unhappiness, can sit down and communicate to someone in writing: I am unhappy. Indeed, I can even go beyond that and in various flourishes depending on my talent, which seems to have nothing to do with the unhappiness, improvise on it simply or antithetically or with whole orchestras of associations. And it is not at all a lie and does not still the pain, is simply a merciful surplus of powers at a moment when the pain has actually visibly used up all my powers to the bottom of my being, which it scrapes. What sort of surplus is it, then?

Yesterday's letter to Max. Mendacious, vain, theatrical.

One week in Zürau.

In peace you make no progress, in war you bleed to death.

Dream about Werfel: He was telling how, in Lower Austria where he is currently staying,[1037] by accident he slightly jostled a man on the street, whereupon the latter reviled him terribly. I've forgotten the individual words, I remember only that "barbarian" was among them (from the World War) and that it ended with "you proletarian Turch." An interesting formation: Turch dialect for Turk, "Turk" an insult apparently still from the tradition of the old Turkish wars and sieges of Vienna and added to it the new insult "proletarian." Characterizes well the simple-mindedness and backwardness of the reviler, since these days neither "proletarian" nor "Turk" is an actual insult.

21 *(September 1917)* Felice was here, travels 30 hours to see me, I should have prevented it. As I imagine it, she bears, primarily because of me, an extremity of unhappiness. I myself don't know how to compose myself, am completely emotionless, equally helpless, think of the disturbance of some of my comforts and as my only concession playact somewhat. In

details she is wrong, wrong in the defense of her supposed or even real right, but on the whole she is an innocent woman condemned to severe torture; I have done the wrong for which she is being tortured and moreover wield the torture instrument.—With her departure (the carriage with her and Ottla drives around the pond, I go straight to head them off and come close to her once again) and a headache (earthly remnant of the playactor) the day ends.

Dream about my father.—There is a small audience (Frau Fanta[1038] for the sake of characterization among them) before which my father is imparting a social reform idea to the public for the first time. It's important to him that this select audience, select especially in his opinion, undertake the propaganda for the idea. Outwardly he expresses this far more humbly by asking the gathering only to inform him afterward, once they have become acquainted with everything, of the addresses of people who might be interested in it and therefore might be invited to a large public assembly that is to take place soon. My father has never before had anything to do with all these people, hence he takes them excessively seriously, has even put on a black dress suit and presents the idea in extreme detail, with all the signs of dilettantism. The gathering recognizes, even though they were not at all prepared for a lecture, immediately that nothing but an old stale, long since thoroughly discussed idea is being brought up here with all the pride of originality. They let my father feel this. He, however, was expecting the objection, but with great conviction of the nullity of the objection, though he himself seems quite often to have been tempted by it, he presents his case with a faint bitter smile even more emphatically. When he has finished, one hears in the general morose murmur that he has convinced them neither of the originality nor of the usefulness of his idea. Not many will be interested in it. Still, here and there someone is to be found who, out of good-naturedness and perhaps because he knows me, gives him some addresses. My father, completely undeterred by the general mood has cleared away the lecture notes and picked up little piles of white slips of paper he has prepared to write down the few addresses. I hear only the name of a Hofrat Střižanowski or something like that—Later I see my father sitting on the floor and leaning against the sofa in the same way as when he plays with Felix.[1039] Taken aback, I ask him what he is doing. He is thinking about his idea.

22 *(September 1917)* Nothing.

25 *(September 1917)*

Way to the woods. You have destroyed everything without having actually possessed it. How do you intend to reassemble it? What powers remain to the wandering spirit for this greatest of tasks?

"Das neue Geschlecht" by Tagger,[1040] wretched, loudmouthed, agile, experienced, well written in places, with faint shivers of dilettantism. What right does he have to show off? Is at bottom as wretched as I and everyone.

Not entirely reprehensible to have children as a tubercular man. Flaubert's father tubercular. Choice: Either the child's lung fizzles out (very nice expression for the music the doctor puts his ear to the patient's chest to hear) or the child becomes Flaubert. Trembling of the father while this is being discussed in the emptiness.[1041]

I can still have temporary satisfaction from works like "Country Doctor," provided that I can still achieve something of the sort (very improbable) but happiness only if I can raise the world into the pure, true, immutable.[1042]

The whips with which we lash each other have grown quite knotty in these 5 years.[1043]

---

28 *(September 1917)* Outline of the conversations with F.

I: So I have brought things this far

F. I have brought things this far

I. I have brought you this far

F. That's true

So I would entrust myself to death. Remnant of a faith. Return to the father. Great Day of Atonement.

From a letter to F., perhaps the last (1 Oct)

When I probe myself for my ultimate goal, it turns out that I am not actually striving to be a good human being and to measure up to a supreme tribunal, but rather, quite the opposite, to survey the whole human and animal community, to recognize their fundamental predilections, desires, moral ideals, to trace them back to simple rules and to adapt myself to them as quickly as possible in order to please absolutely all and indeed (here comes the leap) please them so much that in the end, without losing the universal love, as the only sinner who is not roasted, I might carry out the vulgarities residing in me openly, before the eyes of all. To sum up, then, only the human tribunal matters to me and moreover I want to deceive it, albeit without deception.[1044]

---

8 *(October 1917)* In the meantime: Felice's letters of complaint, G. B.[1045] threatens to write a letter, desolate state (courbature),[1046] feeding the goats, field tunneled by mice, digging potatoes ("How the wind blows into our arses") plucking rose hips, farmer Feigl[1047] (7 girls, one of them short, a sweet look, white rabbit on her shoulder) in the room a picture "Kaiser F. J. in the Capuchin crypt," farmer Kunz[1048] (powerful, haughtily telling the world history of his farm, but friendly and good) General impression of the farmers: Noblemen who have escaped into agriculture, where they have arranged their work so wisely and humbly that it fits seamlessly into the whole and they are protected from any rocking and seasickness until their blissful death. Real earth dwellers.—The boys who hasten across the vast fields on the hill in the evening in pursuit of the fleeing scattered cattle herd and at the same time must keep yanking around a young tethered bull that refuses to follow.—Dickens Copperfield ("The Stoker" sheer imitation of Dickens, the planned novel even more so.[1049] Suitcase story, the delightful and charming young man, the lowly jobs, the beloved on the country estate the dirty houses, among other things, but above all the method. My intention as I now see was to write a Dickens novel, only enriched by the sharper lights I would have taken from the time and the duller ones I would have found in myself. Dickens's richness and unreserved powerful onrush, but as a result of

this passages of horrible strengthlessness, where he wearily stirs only what he has already achieved into a jumble. Barbaric the impression of the senseless whole, a barbarism that I, to be sure, thanks to my weakness and the wiser for my epigonism have avoided. Heartlessness behind the style overflowing with feeling. Those blocks of coarse characterization, which are artificially driven in for every person and without which Dickens would not be capable of even only once hastily climbing up his story. Walser's connection with him in the blurring use of abstract metaphors)

9 *(October 1917)* At the farmer Lüftner's.[1050] The great hall. The whole thing theatrical: he nervous with hee-hee and ha-ha and pounding-on-the-table and arm raising and shoulder shrugging and beer glass raising like a Wallensteiner. Beside him his wife, an old woman,[1051] whom he married 10 years ago when he was her hired hand. Is a passionate hunter, neglects the farm. Huge two horses in the stable, Homeric figures, in a fleeting sunshine that came through the stable window.

---

14 Oct. *(1917)*

An 18-year-old boy comes to say goodbye to us, he is reporting for duty tomorrow: "Because I am reporting for duty tomorrow, I've come to take my leave of you."

15 *(October 1917)* On the country road toward Oberklee,[1052] in the evening; went because the overseer and 2 Hungarian soldiers were sitting in the kitchen

---

the view from Ottla's window in the twilight, over there a house and behind it already open field

---

Kunz and wife, on their fields, on the slope opposite my window.

---

21 *(October 1917)* Beautiful day, sunny warm windless.

Most dogs bark senselessly even when someone is approaching in the distance, but some, perhaps not the best watchdogs, but reasonable creatures, calmly walk up to the stranger, sniff at him and bark only when there's a suspicious smell.

---

6 Nov. *(1917)* Sheer incapacity

10 Nov *(1917)* I have not yet set down the decisive in writing, I am still flowing in two branches. The work waiting is immense.

Dream about the battle on the Tagliamento:[1053] A plain, river actually not there, many thronging, excited spectators, ready, depending on the situation, to run forward or back. Before us a plateau, the edge of which, alternately bare and covered with tall bushes, one sees very clearly. Up on the plateau and beyond it Austrians are fighting. One is in suspense; how will it turn out? Now and then one sees, apparently in order to recover, isolated thickets on a dark slope, from behind which one or two Italians are shooting. But this is meaningless, though we do begin to run a little. Then the plateau again: Austrians run along the bare edge, stop with a jerk behind the bushes, run again. It is apparently going badly, it is also becoming incomprehensible how it could ever go well, how can one, being only human oneself, after all, ever overpower human beings who have the will to defend themselves. Great despair, general flight will be necessary. Then a Prussian major appears, who has actually been observing the battle with us the whole time, but when he now steps calmly into the suddenly empty space, he is a new appearance. He sticks two fingers of each hand into his mouth and whistles, just as one whistles for a dog, but lovingly. The signal is for his division, which has been waiting not far away and now marches forward. It is Prussian Guard, young quiet people, not many, perhaps only a company, all of them seem to be officers, at least they have long sabers, the uniforms are dark. When they now march past us with short steps, slowly, compactly, look at us now and then, the naturalness of this death walk is at once moving, uplifting and victory-assuring. Released by the intervention of these men I awake.

---

27 June 1919 new diary,[1054] actually only because I've been reading the old one. Several reasons and intentions, now, ¼ to 12, no longer ascertainable.

---

30 June *(1919)* Was in Riegerpark.[1055] Walked up and down with J.[1056] past the jasmine bushes. False and true, false in sighing, true in attachment, in trust, in security. Restless heart.

---

6 June *(July 1919)* Perpetually the same thought, the longing, the fear. But still calmer than usual, as if a great development were unfolding, the distant trembling of which I sense. Said too much.

---

5 Dec. 19. Again yanked through this terrible long narrow crack, which can actually be conquered only in a dream. Of one's own volition when one is awake it would certainly never happen.

---

8 XII *(1919)* Monday holiday[1057] in the Baumgarten, in the restaurant, in the gallery.[1058] Sorrow and joy, guilt and innocence like two indissolubly intertwined hands, one would have to cut through them through flesh blood and bone.

---

9 XII *(1919)* A lot of Eleseus.[1059] But wherever I turn, I am met by the black wave.

---

11 XII *(1919)* Thursday. Cold. Silent with J.[1060] in Riegerpark. Seduction on the Graben. All this is too difficult. I am not sufficiently prepared. In a spiritual sense it is just as the teacher Beck,[1061] without realizing the prophetic joke, to be sure, said 26 years ago: "Let him stay in the fifth grade, he is too weak, rushing him so much will take its toll later on." Indeed I have grown like seedlings driven up all too quickly and forgotten, a certain artistic daintiness in the elusive movement when a draft

blows; if you will, even something touching in this movement, that is all. As with Eleseus and his spring business trips to the cities. Although one need not at all underestimate him: Eleseus could even have become the hero of the book, it would even have been probable in Hamsun's youth.

---

6 I 20 All that he does seems to him extraordinarily new. If it did not have this freshness of life, it would, according to its own value, this he knows, inevitably be something out of the old infernal swamp. But this freshness deceives him makes him forget it or take it lightly or indeed see through it, but painlessly. It is, after all, undoubtedly today, this very day, on which progress sets off to progress farther

---

9 I 20 Superstition and principle and making life possible: Through the heaven of vices, the hell of virtues is gained. Superstition is simple

10 I *(1920)*
The sad consequences of the afternoon (Baumgarten)

A segment-like piece is cut out of the back of his head. With the sun the whole world looks in. It makes him nervous, it distracts him from his work, he is also annoyed that he of all people should be excluded from the spectacle

---

It is no refutation of the presentiment of a final liberation if the next day the imprisonment remains unchanged or even grows more severe or even if it is explicitly declared that it shall never cease. Rather, all this can be a necessary prerequisite of the final liberation.

He is on no occasion sufficiently prepared, but cannot even reproach himself for it, for where in this life, which so tormentingly demands readiness at every moment, would there be time to prepare oneself and even if there were time, could one prepare oneself before one knows the task, that is, can one tackle a natural, a not merely artificially assembled task at all? That's why he is also long since under the wheels, strangely but also comfortingly he was least prepared for that.

He found the Archimedean point, but used it against himself, apparently he was permitted to find it only under this condition

---

13 *(January 1920)*

All that he does seems to him, it is true, extraordinarily new, but also in accordance with this impossible fullness of the new extraordinarily dilettantish, hardly even bearable, incapable of becoming historic, bursting the chain of generations, breaking off the music of the world, which until now could always at least be sensed, for the first time down to the utmost depths. Sometimes in his arrogance he is more afraid for the world than for himself.

He would have reconciled himself to a prison. To end as a prisoner—that would be a life's goal. But it was a barred cage. Indifferently, imperiously, as if at home, the noise of the world streamed out and in through the bars, the prisoner was actually free, he could take part in everything, nothing escaped him outside, he could even have left the cage, the bars were meters apart, after all, he was not even imprisoned.

He has the feeling that by being alive he blocks his own way. From this obstruction he then in turn derives the proof that he is alive.

---

14 *(January 1920)* Himself he knows, the others he believes, this contradiction saws up everything for him.

He is neither bold, nor careless. But nor is he fearful. A free life would not frighten him. Now such a life has not been granted him, but even this doesn't worry him; just as he doesn't worry about himself at all.

But there is a someone completely unknown to him who continuously worries a great deal about him only about him. These worries of the someone regarding him, especially the continuousness of these worries sometimes in a quiet hour cause him agonizing headaches.

He lives in dispersion. His elements, a freely living horde, roam around the world. And only because his room too is part of the world does he sometimes see them in the distance. How is he supposed to bear the responsibility for them? Is it still called responsibility?

Everything; even the most ordinary things, such as being served in a restaurant he must attain by force with the help of the police. This deprives life of all comfort.

17 I *(1920)* His own forehead bone bars his way (against his own forehead he beats his forehead bloody)

He feels imprisoned on this earth, he feels cramped, the sorrow, the weakness, the illnesses, the delusions of prisoners break out in him, no consolation can console him, because it is indeed only consolation, delicate head-aching consolation in the face of the crude fact of imprisonment. But if one asks him what he actually wants, he cannot answer for—this is one of his strongest pieces of evidence—he has no conception of freedom.

Some deny the misery by pointing to the sun, he denies the sun by pointing to the misery.

He has two opponents, the first presses him from behind from his origin, the second obstructs his way forward. He struggles with both. Actually the first supports him in the struggle with the second, for he wants to push him forward and likewise the second supports him in the struggle with the first, for he drives him backward. But this is so only theoretically, for not only the 2 opponents are there, after all, but also he himself and who actually knows his intentions?

He has many judges, they are like a host of birds sitting in a tree. Their voices are jumbled, the questions of rank and jurisdiction cannot be disentangled, there is also a constant changing of places. But one still makes out individuals

---

In three ways:

The self-tormenting ponderous often long-halting but at bottom still incessant undulation of all life, others' and his own, torments him, because it brings with it an incessant compulsion to think. Sometimes it seems to him that this torment precedes the events. When he hears that a child is to be born to his friend, he recognizes that he has already suffered for this as a thinker beforehand.

He sees in two ways: The first is calm contemplation, consideration, investigation, outpouring, filled with life and impossible without a certain contentment. Their number and possibility are endless, even a woodlouse needs a relatively large crack to find shelter, but for these tasks no space at all is necessary, even where there's not the slightest crack they can still live interpenetrating by the thousands upon thousands. That is the first. The second, however, is the moment when one is summoned to give an account, utters not a sound, is cast back into the contemplations, etc., but now faced with the hopelessness cannot possibly go on splashing in them, makes oneself heavy and with a curse sinks.

---

2 II 20

He remembers a picture representing a summer Sunday on the Thames. A long stretch of the river was filled in its whole breadth with boats waiting for a lock to open. In all the boats were merry young people in light pale clothing, they were almost reclining, freely abandoned to the warm air and the coolness of the water. Because they had all this in common, their sociability was not confined to the individual boats, joking and laughter were communicated from boat to boat.[1062]

He now imagined that on a meadow on the bank—the banks were barely suggested in the picture, everything was dominated by the gathering of boats—he himself was standing. He was contemplating the celebration, which was not actually a celebration but which could be called one. He naturally very much wanted to participate in it, he was positively reaching for it, but he had to tell himself frankly that he was excluded from it, it was impossible for him to fit in there, it would have demanded such great preparation that in the process not only this Sunday but many years and even he himself would have passed away, and even if time here would have stood still, no other result would have been attainable, his whole lineage, education, physical training would have had to be conducted otherwise.

So this was how far he was from those excursionists, but then again he was at the same time very close and that was harder to comprehend. After all, they were human beings like him, nothing human could be completely foreign to them, if one were to thoroughly investigate them one would surely find that the feeling that dominated him and excluded him from the boat trip lived in them too, except that, to be sure, it was far from dominating them, rather only haunted some dark corners.

---

15 II 20

It is a matter of the following: I was sitting once many years ago, certainly sad enough, on the slope of the Laurenziberg.[1063] [I examined the wishes I had for life. It turned out that the most important or the most appealing wish was to gain a view of life (and—this was, to be sure, necessarily connected—to be able to convince others of it in writing) in which life, while retaining its natural heavy falling and rising, would at the same time be recognized with no less clarity as a nothing, as a dream, as a hovering. A beautiful wish, perhaps, if I had wished it correctly. Say, as the wish to hammer together a table with painstakingly proper craftsmanship and at the same time do nothing and indeed not in such a way that one could say: "to him the hammering is a nothing" but rather "to him the hammering is a real hammering and at the same time also a nothing," whereby the hammering truly would have become even bolder, even more resolute, even more real and if you will even madder. But he could not wish in that way at all, for his wish was no wish, it was only a defense, a domestication of the nothing, a touch of liveliness that he wanted to give to the nothing, into which at that time he had, it is true, scarcely taken the first conscious steps, but which he already felt to be his element.] It was a sort of farewell that he bid the illusory world of youth at that time; it had, by the way, never directly deceived him but only let him be deceived by the speeches of all the authorities surrounding him. Thus had the necessity of the "wish" arisen

---

He proves only himself, his only proof is himself, all opponents defeat him immediately, but not by refuting him, he is irrefutable rather by proving themselves.

Human unifications are based on one's seeming by one's own strong existence to have refuted other individuals irrefutable in themselves, this is sweet and comforting for those individuals, but it lacks truth and therefore never lasts.

He used to be part of a monumental group. Around some elevated center stood symbols of the military, the arts, the sciences, the trades in a well-thought-out arrangement.[1064] He was one of these many. Now the group has long since been dissolved or at least he has left it and makes his way alone through life. He no longer has even his old profession, indeed he has even forgotten what he represented then. It is probably this very forgetting that gives rise to a certain sadness, uncertainty, restlessness, a certain longing for bygone days that clouds the present. And yet this longing is an important element of vital energy or perhaps the energy itself.

He does not live for the sake of his personal life, he does not think for the sake of his personal thought. He feels as if he were living and thinking under the compulsion of a family, which, it is true, itself has an overabundance of vital and mental energy, but for which, according to some law unknown to him, he signifies a formal necessity. Because of this unknown family and these unknown laws he cannot be released.

The original sin, the ancient wrong that man has committed, consists in the accusation, which man makes and from which he does not desist, that a wrong has been done to him, that the original sin was committed against him.

18 II 20 In front of Casinelli's display[1065] 2 children were loitering, a roughly 6-year-old boy, a 7-year-old girl, richly dressed, speaking about God and sins. I stopped behind them. The girl perhaps Catholic regarded only lying to God as an actual sin. With childish stubbornness the boy, perhaps a Protestant, asked what lying to people or stealing was. "Also a very great sin" said the girl "but not the greatest, only the sins against God are the greatest, for the sins against people we have confession. When I confess the angel immediately stands behind me again; for when I commit a sin, the devil comes behind me, only one doesn't see him." And tired of the half-seriousness, she turned around for the fun of it on her heel and said: "You see no one is behind me." The boy likewise turned around and saw me there. "You see" he said without consideration for the fact that I would certainly hear it, but also without thinking about it "behind me stands the devil." "I see him too" said the girl "but I don't mean him"

He wants no consolation, but not because he doesn't want it—who wouldn't want it—rather because seeking consolation means: dedicating one's life to this work, always living at the edge of one's existence, almost outside it, scarcely knowing anymore for whom one is seeking consolation and therefore not even being capable of finding effective consolation (effective, not true, which doesn't exist)

He defends himself against fixation by his fellow human being. (The human being even if he were infallible sees in the other only that part for which the strength and nature of his gaze suffice. He has, like everyone, but in extreme exaggeration the craving to limit himself to the same extent as the gaze of his fellow human being has the strength to see him.) If Robinson had never left the highest or more correctly the most visible point of the island, out of defiance or humility or fear or ignorance or yearning, he would have soon perished, but since without regard for the ships and their weak telescopes he began to explore his whole island and take pleasure in it, he kept himself alive and in the end—in what was, to be sure, rationally not a necessary consequence—was found after all.

---

19 II *(1920)*

"You make a virtue of your necessity."

"Firstly everyone does that and secondly I of all people do not. I let my necessity remain necessity, I do not drain the swamps, but rather live in their feverish haze."

"That's exactly what you make your virtue of"

"Like everyone, as I said. Besides, I do it only for your sake; so that you remain friendly to me, I suffer harm to my soul."

My prison cell—my fortress.

Everything is permitted him except to forget himself, whereby, to be sure, everything is again prohibited but the one thing that is necessary at the moment for the whole.

The narrowness of consciousness is a social requirement

All virtues are individual, all vices social; what is regarded as a social virtue, such as love, unselfishness, justness, self-sacrifice, are only "astonishingly" weakened social vices.

The difference between the "yes and no" that he says to his contemporaries and that which he should actually say, might correspond to that of death and life; is also graspable to him only in just as faint presentiments.

The reason that the judgment of posterity on the individual is more correct than that of his contemporaries lies in the dead man. One unfolds in one's nature only after death, only when one is alone. Being dead is for the individual like Saturday evening for the chimney sweep, they wash the soot from the body. It becomes visible whether his contemporaries have done him more harm or he his contemporaries, in the latter case he was a great man.

The power to say no, this most natural expression of the perpetually changing, renewing, dying reviving human fighting organism, is something we always have, but not the courage, although living is saying no, thus saying no saying yes.

With his dying thoughts he does not die. The dying is only a phenomenon within the inner world (which endures, even if it too were only a thought) a natural phenomenon like any other neither joyful nor sad.

"He is hindered from rising by a certain heaviness, a feeling of being secure for any eventuality, the vague sense of a bed that is prepared for him and belongs only to him, but he is hindered from lying still by a restlessness that drives him from the bed, he is hindered by his conscience, his endlessly beating heart, the fear of death and the longing to refute it, all this will not let him lie and he rises again. This up and down and some random, fleeting, remote observations made on these paths are his life."

"Your description is bleak, but only for the analysis, the fundamental error of which it shows. It is indeed the case that the human being rises, falls back, rises again, etc., but it is also at the same time and with still far greater truth not the case at all, for he is one, thus in his flying there is resting too, in his resting flying and both united again in each individual, and the unification in each, and the unification of the unification in each, etc., to the point, well, to the point of real life, although this description too is just as false as and perhaps even more deceptive than yours. From this region there is simply no path to life, whereas there must have been a path from life to here. So astray are we."

The current against which one is swimming is so furious that in a certain absentmindedness one sometimes despairs over the desolate calm in the midst of which one is splashing, so infinitely far has one been driven back in a moment of failure.

---

29 *(February 1920)* He is thirsty and is separated from the spring only by a thicket. But he is divided, one part looks over the whole, sees that he is standing here and the spring is nearby, but a second part notices nothing, has at most an inkling that the first part sees everything. But since he notices nothing, he cannot drink.

15 X 21[1066] About a week ago gave M.[1067] all the diaries. A little freer? No. Am I still capable of keeping a sort of diary? It will certainly be different, or rather it will hide itself away, it will not be at all, about Hardt, for example, with whom I have indeed been relatively quite occupied,[1068] I would be capable of noting something down only with the greatest effort. It's as if I had long since written everything about him or what's the same thing, as if I were no longer alive. I could probably write about M., but not of my own volition, it would also be directed too much against myself, I no longer need to make myself elaborately conscious of such things, as in the past, I am no longer as forgetful as I used to be in this respect, I am a memory come alive, hence the sleeplessness too.

In Hebel's letter the passage on polytheism.[1069]

16 X 21 Sunday The unhappiness of a perpetual beginning, the lack of illusion about the fact that everything is only a beginning and not even a beginning, the folly of others who don't know it and, for example, play football, in order to at last "make progress," bury their own folly in themselves as in a coffin, the folly of others who believe they see a real coffin here, thus a coffin that one can transport, open, destroy, exchange.

Among the young women up in the park. No envy. Enough imagination to share their happiness, enough judgment to know that I am too weak for this happiness, enough folly to believe that I penetrate my own and their circumstances. Not enough folly, there's a tiny crevice there, the wind whistles through it and prevents the full resonance.

If I have the great wish to be a track and field athlete, it is probably the same as if I wished to go to heaven and to be permitted to be as despairing there as here.

However wretched my resources may be, even if, "all else being equal," (especially in light of my weakness of will) they be the most wretched on earth, I must still seek to attain the best with them, even in my sense, and it is empty sophistry to say one could attain only one thing with them and this one thing would therefore also be the best and it would be despair

---

17 XI *(October 1921)* It's possible that there's an intention behind the fact that I have learned nothing useful and—this is connected—also let myself decline physically. I wanted to remain undistracted, undistracted by the joy a useful and healthy man finds in life. As if illness and despair would not distract at least as much!
I could round off this thought in various ways and thereby bring it to a conclusion in my favor, but I don't dare and believe—at least today and so in the majority of days—in no solution favorable to me.

I don't envy the particular married couple, I envy only all married couples, even if I envy only one married couple, I actually envy marital happiness as a whole in its infinite variety, in the happiness of a single marriage even in the most favorable case I would probably despair.

I don't believe that there are people whose inner condition is similar to mine, nonetheless I can imagine such people, but that around their head as around mine the secret raven constantly flies, that I cannot even imagine.

The systematic destruction of myself in the course of the years is astonishing, it was like a slowly developing dam breach, a purposeful action. The spirit that has accomplished it must now be celebrating triumphs; why doesn't it let me take part in this? But perhaps it is not yet finished with its work and can therefore think of nothing else.

---

18 (October 1921) Eternal childhood. Again a call of life.

It is very easily conceivable that the glory of life lies ready around everyone and always in its complete fullness, but veiled, deep down, invisible, very distant. But it lies there, not hostile, not reluctant, not deaf. If one calls it with the right word, by the right name, then it comes. That is the essence of magic, which does not create but calls.

---

19 *(October 1921)* The essence of the desert road. A person who takes this road as the popular leader of his organism, with a remnant (more is not conceivable) of consciousness of what is happening. He has scented Canaan all his life; that he should see the land only before his death is unbelievable. This final prospect can only have the purpose of representing how incomplete a moment human life is, incomplete because this sort of life could last forever and yet the result would again be nothing but a moment. It is not because his life was too short that Moses does not reach Canaan, but because it was a human life. This end of the 5 books of Moses has a similarity with the concluding scene of the Education sentimentale.[1070]

He who does not deal with life while alive needs one hand to fend off a little the despair over his fate—this is done very incompletely—but with his other hand he can record what he sees among the ruins, for he sees different things and more than the others, he is, after all, dead during his lifetime and the actual survivor. Provided that he does not need both hands and more than he has for the struggle with the despair.

---

20 *(October 1921)* Afternoon Langer,[1071] then Max, reads Franzi aloud[1072]

A dream, short, in a fitful short sleep, held on desperately, in boundless happiness. A many-branched dream, containing 1000 connections becoming clear all at once, what remains is scarcely the memory of the basic feeling: My brother has committed a crime, a murder, I think, I and others are involved in the crime, the punishment, the resolution, the salvation is approaching from a distance, it grows powerfully, many signs indicate its inexorable approach, my sister, I think, keeps announcing these signs, which I keep greeting with ecstatic exclamations, the ecstasy increases with the approach. I thought I could never forget my individual exclamations, short sentences, because of their perspicuity and now cannot clearly remember a single one. They could only be exclamations because speaking caused me great difficulty, I had to puff out my cheeks and at the same time twist my mouth as if I had a toothache before I could utter a word. The happiness consisted in the fact that the punishment came and I welcomed it so freely, with such conviction and joy, a sight that must have moved the gods, I felt this emotion of the gods too almost to the point of tears.

---

21 *(October 1921)* Afternoon on the sofa

It had been impossible for him to enter the house, for he had heard a voice saying to him: "Wait until I lead you." And so he was still lying in the dust outside the house, even though by now everything was probably hopeless (as Sarah would say)[1073]

All is fantasy, the family, the office, the friends, the street, all fantasy, more distant or closer, the woman the closest, but truth is only that you are pressing your head against the wall of a windowless and doorless cell.

---

22 *(October 1921)* A connoisseur, an expert, someone who knows his share, a knowledge, to be sure, that cannot be imparted but fortunately also seems to be necessary to no one.

---

23 *(October 1921)* Palestine film in the afternoon.[1074]

---

after dinner
25 *(October 1921)* Ehrenstein yesterday[1075]

My parents were playing cards; I was sitting alone, a complete stranger; my father said I should play with them or at least watch; I made some excuse. What was the meaning of this refusal, repeated many times since childhood? The invitation made common, to some extent public life accessible to me, I would have achieved the performance demanded of me as participation not well but tolerably, the playing would probably not even have bored me all too much—nonetheless I refused. Judging by this, I'm wrong when I complain that the stream of life never seized me, that I never got away from Prague, was never thrust into sports or a trade and the like—I probably would have always refused the offer, just as I did the invitation to the game. Only the senseless was allowed in, the law studies, the office, then later on senseless supplements, such as a little gardening, carpentry and the like,[1076] these supplements are to be understood in the same way as the conduct of a man who throws the needy beggar out the door and then by himself plays the benefactor by passing alms from his right hand to his left.

And so I always refused, probably out of general weakness and especially out of weakness of will, I comprehended this only relatively quite late. In the past I regarded this refusal mostly as a good sign (seduced by the general great hopes I set on myself), today only a vestige of this congenial view remains.

---

29 *(October 1921)* One of the next evenings I then really participated by keeping score for my mother. But this did not result in more close-

ness, and even if there was a trace of it, it was inundated with fatigue, boredom, grief over the lost time. So it would always have been. I have crossed this borderland between loneliness and community only extremely rarely, I have even settled there more than in loneliness itself. What a lively beautiful land Robinson's island was in comparison to it.

---

30 *(October 1921)* Afternoon, theater, Pallenberg[1077]

My inner possibilities for (I don't want to say acting or writing the miser but rather for) the miser himself.[1078] Only a quick resolute hand movement would be necessary, the whole orchestra looks with fascination at the place over the conductor's stand where the baton is to rise.

The feeling of complete helplessness.

What connects you to these firmly bounded, speaking, eye-flashing bodies more closely than to anything, say, the penholder in your hand? That you are of their kind, perhaps? But you are not of their kind, indeed that's why you raised this question.

The firm boundedness of human bodies is ghastly

The strangeness, the unfathomability of this not-perishing, of this silent guidance. It drives one to the absurdity: "I for my part would have long since been lost." I for my part.

1.) Werfel's "Bocksgesang"[1079]

The discretion over a world in flouting its laws. The imposition of the law. Happiness of this law-abidance.

It is not possible, however, to impose on the world only the law that everything else remains unchanged but the new lawmaker shall be free. That would be no law, but arbitrariness, revolt, self-condemnation.

2.) vague hope, vague confidence

An endless gloomy Sunday afternoon, consuming whole years, an afternoon consisting of years. Alternately despairing in the empty streets and at ease on the sofa. Astonishment sometimes at the colorless, senseless clouds almost incessantly drifting by. "You are being preserved for a great Monday!" "Well said, but Sunday will never end"

3.) The call

---

7 *(November 1921)* Inescapable duty of self-observation: If I am observed by someone else, naturally I must observe myself too, if I am observed by no one else, I must observe myself all the more closely.

Everyone who falls out with me or grows indifferent to me or feels burdened by me is to be envied for the ease with which he can get rid of me (provided probably that my life is not at stake; once, with F., when my life seemed to be at stake, it was not easy to get rid of me, certainly I was young and had my strength, my wishes too had their strength)

---

1 XII *(1921)* After four visits M.[1080] left, is leaving tomorrow. 4 calmer days within tormented ones. A long way from not being sad about her departure, not actually being sad to being infinitely sad about her departure. Admittedly: Sadness is not the worst thing

---

2 *(December 1921)* Writing letters in my parents' room. The forms of decline are inconceivable.—Recently the idea that I was defeated by

my f.[1081] as a small child and now out of ambition have been unable to leave the battlefield through all the years, even though I am defeated again and again.—Always M.,[1082] or not M. but a principle, a light in the darkness.

6 *(December 1921)* From a letter: "I warm myself by it in this sad winter."[1083] Metaphors are one among many things that make me despair of writing. Writing's lack of independence, its dependence on the maid tending the fire, on the cat warming itself by the stove, even on the poor old man warming himself. All these are independent, autonomous activities, only writing is helpless, doesn't dwell in itself, is amusement and despair.

Two children, alone in the apartment, climbed into a large suitcase, the lid fell shut, they couldn't open it and suffocated.

---

20 XII *(1921)* Suffered much in my thoughts

I was startled out of a deep sleep. In the middle of the room a stranger was sitting at a little table by candlelight. He was sitting in the semi-darkness broad and heavy, the unbuttoned winter coat made him even broader.

Better to think through:
Raabe while dying, when his wife stroked his forehead: That's wonderful[1084]

The grandfather laughing at his grandchild with a toothless mouth.

There is undeniably a certain happiness in being able to calmly write down: "Suffocation is inconceivably horrible." Indeed inconceivable, thus nothing would be written down after all.

---

23 XII *(1921)* Sat again over "Náš Skautík"[1085]

Ivan Ilyich[1086]

---

16 I *(1922)* This past week there seemed to be a breakdown, as complete as perhaps only on that night 2 years ago, I have not experienced another precedent. Everything seemed over and even today seems not to have changed very much at all. One can understand it in two ways and it is also probably to be understood in both at the same time. First: Breakdown, impossibility of sleeping, impossibility of waking, impossibility of enduring life, or more precisely the succession of life. The clocks are not synchronized, the inner one races in a devilish or demonic or in any case inhuman way, the outer one haltingly takes its usual course. What else can happen but that the two different worlds separate and they are separating or at least tugging at each other in a terrible way. There may be various reasons for the furiousness of the inner movement, the most visible one is the self-observation that lets no idea come to rest, chases each one upward only in turn to be chased further itself as an idea by new self-observation. Second: This chasing is heading in a direction out of humanity. The loneliness that has always for the most part been imposed on me, in part been sought by me—yet what was this but compulsion too—is now becoming completely unambiguous and is going to the extreme. Where is it leading? It can, this seems most compulsory of all, lead to insanity, about that nothing more can be said, the chase goes through me and tears me up. Or I can—I can?—be it even only to the tiniest extent maintain myself, thus let myself be borne by the chase. Then where will I end up? "Chase" is only an image, after all, I can also say "onslaught against the last earthly boundary" and indeed an onslaught from below, from humanity and can, since this too is only an image, replace it with the image of the onslaught from above, down toward me.

This whole literature is an onslaught against the boundary and, if Zionism had not intervened, it could easily have developed into a new secret doctrine, a Kabbalah. There are rudiments of this. To be sure, a practically incomprehensible genius is required here, which strikes its roots anew into the old centuries or creates anew the old centuries and does not expend itself with all this but only now begins to expend itself.

---

17 I *(1922)* Hardly different.

---

18 I *(1922)* That somewhat calmer, instead comes s.[1087] Salvation or exacerbation as you will.

A moment of thought: Content yourself, learn (learn 40-year-old) to rest in the moment (really, once you could do it). Yes in the moment, the terrible moment. It is not terrible, only the fear of the future makes it terrible. And admittedly looking back too. What have you done with the gift of sex? It has failed, one will ultimately say, that will be all. But it could easily have succeeded. Admittedly a trifle and not even discernible, so small is it, decided this. What do you find in it? At the greatest battles of world history it has been so. The trifles decide on the trifles

---

M.[1088] is right: fear is unhappiness, but therefore it's not courage that is happiness but fearlessness, not courage, which perhaps wants more than strength (in my class there were probably only 2 Jews who had courage and both shot themselves dead while still in Gymnasium or shortly thereafter),[1089] not courage, then, but fearlessness, resting, openly gazing, all-enduring. Don't force yourself to do anything, but don't be unhappy that you don't force yourself or that, if you were to do it, you would have to force yourself. And when you don't force yourself, don't keep lustfully running around the possibilities of compulsion. Admittedly it is never so clear or actually it is always so clear, for example: s. presses me,[1090] torments me day and night, I would have to overcome fear and shame and probably even sorrow to satisfy it, but on the other hand it is certain that if an opportunity presented itself quickly and attainably and willingly, I would immediately take advantage of it without fear and sorrow and shame; according to the above, what remains then is simply the law not to overcome the fear etc., (but not to play with the thought of overcoming either) but certainly to take advantage of the opportunity (but not to complain when it doesn't come) Admittedly there is something between the "act" and the "opportunity" namely the eliciting, enticing of the "opportunity," a practice that I have unfortunately followed not only here but everywhere. The "law" has scarcely anything to say against it, even though this "enticing" especially when it is done with unsuitable means bears a suspicious resemblance to "playing with the thought of overcoming" and there's not a trace of resting, openly gazing fearlessness in it. Indeed, despite "literal" compliance with the "law," it is something abhorrent and to be avoided at all costs. Admittedly it requires compulsion to avoid it and I do not come to an end with this.

---

19 *(January 1922)* What do yesterday's conclusions mean today? They mean the same thing as yesterday, are true, except that the blood seeps away in the channels between the great stones of the law.

The infinite deep warm saving happiness of sitting beside the basket of one's child opposite its mother.
There is also something in this of the feeling: things no longer hinge on you, unless you want them to. In contrast the feeling of the childless man: things constantly hinge on you whether you want them to or not, every moment until the end, every nerve-racking moment, things constantly hinge on you and to no purpose. Sisyphus was a bachelor.

Nothing bad; once you have crossed the threshold, everything is good. Another world and you need not speak.

The two questions:[1091]

From several trifles, which I am ashamed to mention, I had the impression that the recent visits were indeed kind and proud as always, and yet also somewhat tired, somewhat forced, like visits to a sick person. Is this impression correct?

Have you found something decisive against me in the diaries?

20 *(January 1922)* A little calmer. How necessary it was. No sooner is it a little calmer than it is almost too calm. As if I got the true feeling of myself only when I am unbearably unhappy. That's probably correct too.

Seized by the collar, dragged through the streets, pushed into the door. Schematically it is like that, in reality there are counterforces, only a trifle—the life- and torment-sustaining trifle—less unbridled than those. I the victim of both.

This "too calm." As if—somehow physically, physically as a result of the years of torments (confidence! confidence!)—the possibility of the peacefully creative life were closed off to me, thus the creative life in general, for the condition of torment is for me absolutely nothing but torment closed off in itself, closed off against everything, nothing beyond that.

The torso: seen from the side from the upper edge of the stocking upward knee, thigh and hip, belonging to a dark woman.

The longing for the country? It is not certain. The country strikes up the longing, the infinite longing.

M.[1092] is right about me: "everything glorious just not for me and rightly so." Rightly I say and show that I have at least that confidence: Or do I not have even that? For I am not actually thinking of "right," life in its sheer power of persuasion has no space in it for right and wrong. Just as you cannot meditate on right and wrong in the despairing hour of death, you cannot do so in despairing life. It is enough that the arrows fit perfectly in the wounds that they have made.

On the other hand, there is no trace in me of a general condemnation of the generation.

21 *(January 1922)* It is not yet too calm. In the theater in the face of Florestan's prison the abyss suddenly opens. Everything, singers, music, audience, neighbors, everything more distant than the abyss.[1093]

No one's task was so difficult, as far as I know. One might say: it is no task, not even an impossible one, it is not even impossibility itself, it is nothing, it is not even as much of a child as the hope of a barren woman. But it is nonetheless the air in which I breathe, as long as I shall breathe.

I fell asleep after midnight, awoke at 5, an extraordinary achievement, extraordinary happiness, moreover I was still sleepy. But the happiness was my unhappiness, for now came the thought, not to be fended off: you do not deserve so much happiness, all the gods of revenge came crashing down on me, I saw their raging chief wildly spread his fingers and threaten me or horribly strike cymbals. The agitation of the 2 hours until 7 o'clock not only consumed the sleep gains but also made me shaky and restless all day.

Without ancestors, without marriage, without descendants, with fierce desire for ancestors, marriage and descendants. All hold out their hand to me: ancestors, marriage and descendants, but too distant for me.

For everything there is an artificial, pitiful substitute: for ancestors, marriage and descendants. One strains to create it and, if one has not already been destroyed by the strain, is destroyed by the hopelessness of the substitute

---

22 *(January 1922)* Nocturnal resolution

The remark regarding the "bachelors of memory" was clairvoyant, albeit clairvoyance under very favorable conditions.[1094] But the similarity to U. R.[1095] is astonishing even beyond that: both quiet (I less so) both dependent on our parents (I more so) fallen out with our fathers, loved by our mothers (he still condemned to live together horribly with his father, admittedly the father too condemned) both shy overmodest (he more so) both regarded as noble good people of which in my case nothing and to my knowledge in his case too not much was to be found (shyness, modesty, anxiousness are considered noble and good, because they offer little resistance to one's own expansive impulses) both hypochondriacal at first, then really ill, both, being do-nothings, fairly unspoiled by the world (he, because he was less of a do-nothing, in much worse condition, as far as one can compare as yet) both officials (he a better one) both living with the utmost uniformity without development young to the end, more correct than young is the expression well preserved, both close to insanity, he, remote from Jews, with tremendous courage, with tremendous leaping power (by which one can gauge the magnitude of the danger of insanity) rescued in the church, remaining loosely restrained to the end, as far as one could tell, he himself had probably not restrained himself for years. A difference in his favor or disfavor was that he had less artistic talent than I, thus could have chosen a better path in his youth, was not so torn apart, not even by ambition. Whether he struggled (with himself) over women, I don't know, a story I read by him suggested as much, when I was a child there was also talk about something of the sort. I know far too little about him, I don't dare ask about it. Besides, up to this point I've been writing about him frivolously as if about someone living. It's also untrue that he wasn't good, I noticed not a trace of miserliness, envy, hatred, greed in him; he was probably inadequate to the task of providing help himself. He was infinitely more innocent than I, here there's no comparison. He was in particulars a caricature of me, but in essence I am his caricature.

23 *(January 1922)* Restlessness came back. From where? From certain thoughts, which are quickly forgotten but leave the restlessness unforgettably behind. More easily than the thoughts I could name the place where they occurred to me, one of them, for example, on the small grassy path that runs past the Altneu Synagogue. Restlessness also from a certain feeling of comfort that now and then approaches timidly and distantly enough. Restlessness also from the fact that the nocturnal resolution remains only resolution. Restlessness from the fact that my life

until now has been a marching in place, a development at most in the sense a tooth becoming hollow and decaying undergoes one. The way I led my life never proved its worth in the slightest. It was as if I like every other person had been given the center of a circle, as if I then like every other person had to follow the decisive radius and then draw the beautiful circle. Instead I have perpetually started the radius, but again and again had to break it off immediately (examples: piano, violin, languages, German studies, anti-Zionism, Zionism, Hebrew, gardening, carpentry, literature, marriage attempts, an apartment of my own) The center of the imaginary circle bristles with beginnings of radii, there is no more space for a new attempt, no space means age, weakness of nerves, and no further attempt means the end. If I have ever brought the radius a little bit farther than usual, perhaps in the case of my law studies or engagements, everything was simply worse by this little bit, instead of better.

Told M. about the night,[1096] inadequately. Accept symptoms, don't complain about symptoms, descend into the suffering.

Heart palpitation

The other view: saved for later. The third view: already forgotten.

---

24 *(January 1922)* The happiness of the young and old husbands in the office. Inaccessible to me and if it were accessible to me unbearable to me and yet the only thing with which I have the inclination to satisfy myself.

Proposal for E. P.[1097]

The hesitation before birth. If there is a transmigration of souls, then I am not yet on the lowest rung. My life is the hesitation before birth.

Steadfastness. I don't want to develop in a particular way, I want to go to a different place, it is in truth that "desire to go to another star," it would be enough for me to stand just next to myself, it would be enough for me to be able to perceive the place where I am standing as a different one

---

The development was simple. When I was still satisfied, I wanted to be dissatisfied and with all the means of the time and tradition that were accessible to me thrust myself into dissatisfaction, now I wanted to be able to turn back. I was thus always dissatisfied, even with my satisfaction. Strange that playacting, if it is systematic enough, can turn into reality. My spiritual decline began with childish albeit childishly conscious play. For example, I made my face muscles jerk artificially, I walked across the Graben[1098] with my arms crossed behind my head. Childishly repugnant but successful play. (It was similar with the development of my writing, except that this development unfortunately later came to a halt.) If it is possible to bring about unhappiness in this way by force, it should be possible to bring about anything by force. However much the development seems to refute me and however much it is altogether contrary to my nature to think like this, I can in no way admit that the first beginnings of my unhappiness were inwardly necessary, they may have had necessity, but not inner necessity, they came flying like flies and would have been as easy as they are to drive away.

The unhappiness on the other shore would be just as great, probably greater (due to my weakness), I have the experience of it, after all, the lever is still trembling to some extent from the time when I last shifted it, but then why do I increase the unhappiness of being on this shore by longing for the other.

---

25 *(January 1922)* Sad with reason. Dependent on this reason. Always in danger. No way out. How easy it was the first time, how difficult this time. How helplessly the tyrant is looking at me: "That's where you're leading me?" Thus despite everything still no peace, in the afternoon the hope of the morning is buried. To reconcile oneself to such a life in love is impossible, there has certainly never been anyone who could have

done so. When other people came to this boundary—and merely having come here is pitiful—they veered off, I cannot. It also seems to me as if I had not come here at all, rather while still a small child had been pushed to this point and held fast there with chains, only the consciousness of the unhappiness gradually dawned, the unhappiness itself was finished, it required only a penetrating, not a prophetic gaze to see it.

In the morning I thought: "Perhaps you can live in this way after all, now just guard this life from women." Guard it from women, but they are already in the in-this-way.

To say that you abandoned me would be very unjust, but that I was abandoned, and at times horribly, is true.

Even in the sense of the "resolution" I have the right to be in boundless despair over my situation.

---

27 *(January 1922)* Spindelmühle.[1099] Necessity of independence from the unhappiness mixed with clumsiness of the double sleigh, the broken suitcase, the wobbly table, the bad light, the impossibility of having peace in the hotel in the afternoon and the like. It is not to be attained by neglecting it, for it cannot be neglected, it is to be attained only by summoning new powers. Here, to be sure, there are surprises, the most disconsolate person must admit it, experience shows that something can come out of nothing, the coachman with the horses can crawl out of the dilapidated pigpen.[1100]

The powers crumbling away during the sleigh ride. One cannot arrange a life as a gymnast a handstand

---

Strange, mysterious, perhaps dangerous, perhaps saving consolation of writing: the leap out of the killers' ranks deed—observation, deed—

observation, in that a higher kind of observation is created, a higher, not a sharper kind, and the higher it is and the more unreachable from the "ranks," the more independent it becomes, the more obedient to its own laws of motion, the more incalculable, joyful, rising its path.

Although I wrote my name clearly for the hotel, although they too have now written my name correctly twice, downstairs on the board it says Josef K.[1101] Shall I enlighten them or shall I let them enlighten me?

28 *(January 1922)* A little faint tired from sledding,[1102] there are still weapons, so rarely wielded, I have such difficulty reaching them, because I don't know the pleasure in their use, didn't learn it as a child. It is not only "my f.'s[1103] fault" that I didn't learn it, but it is also because I wanted so to destroy the "calm," to upset the balance and therefore could not let someone be newly born over there when I was taking pains to bury him over here. Admittedly, I return to "fault" here too, for why did I want out of the world? Because "he" didn't let me live in the world, in his world. I cannot judge so clearly now, to be sure, for now I am already a citizen in this other world, which is to the ordinary world as the desert to cultivated land (I have been wandering for 40 years from Canaan), look back as a foreigner, am admittedly the smallest and most anxious in that other world too—I have brought this with me as my patrimony—and am capable of living only by virtue of the special organization there according to which even the lowliest there can undergo lightning-like elevations though also sea-pressure-like thousand-year shatterings. Must I be grateful despite everything? Would I have necessarily found the way here? Couldn't the "banishment" there in conjunction with the rejection here have crushed me at the border? Didn't my f.'s power make the expulsion so strong that nothing could resist it (it, not me)? Admittedly, it is like the wandering in the desert in reverse with the constant approaches to the desert and the childlike hopes: (especially with regard to women) "perhaps I will stay in Canaan after all" and in the meantime I have long since been in the desert and they are only visions of despair especially at those times when I am the most wretched of all even there and Canaan must present itself as the only land of hope, for there is not a third land for human beings.

---

29 *(January 1922)* Attacks on the road in the snow in the evening. Always the mixture of ideas something like this: In this world the situation would be horrible, here alone in Sp.,[1104] moreover on a forsaken road, on which one is constantly slipping in the snow in the dark, moreover a senseless road without an earthly goal (to the bridge? Why there? Besides, I have not even reached it), moreover I too forsaken in the town,[1105] (I cannot count the doctor as a humanly personal helper, I haven't earned him, have at bottom only the fee relationship with him),[1106] incapable of becoming acquainted with anyone, incapable of bearing an acquaintance, at bottom full of endless astonishment in the face of a cheerful gathering (here in the hotel, to be sure, there is not much cheerfulness, I won't go so far as to say that I am the cause of it, perhaps as the "man with the all-too-great shadow" but in this world my shadow is indeed all too great, and with new astonishment I see that some people have the resilience to want to live nonetheless "despite everything" even in this shadow, especially in it; but here there is still more to add) or even in the face of parents with their children moreover so forsaken not only here but in general, even in Prague my "home" and indeed forsaken not by people, that would not be the worst, I could run after them as long as I am alive, but by myself in relation to people, by my strength in relation to people, I have lovers but I cannot love, I am too far away, am expelled, have since I am human after all and the roots want nourishment, my representatives "down" (or up) there too, pitiful unsatisfactory playactors, who can satisfy me (admittedly, they don't satisfy me at all and that's why I'm so forsaken) only because my main nourishment comes from other roots in other air, those roots pitiful too, but nonetheless more capable of living.

This brings me to the mixture of ideas. If things were only as they can seem on the road in the snow, then it would be horrible, then I would be lost, this understood not as a threat but as an immediate execution. But I am elsewhere, only the attraction of the human world is tremendous, in a moment it can make one forget everything. But the attraction of my world too is great, those who love me love me because I'm "forsaken," and indeed perhaps not as a Weissian vacuum,[1107] but because they feel that I have the freedom of movement I am completely lacking here on another level in happy times.

If M.,[1108] for example, suddenly came here, it would be horrible. Externally, it is true, my position would immediately be comparatively splendid. I would be honored as a human being among human beings, I would get more than only formal words, I would sit (admittedly less upright than now, when I am sitting alone, and even now I'm sitting slumped) at the table of the theater company, externally I would be socially almost on a par with Dr. H.[1109]—but I would be plunged into a world in which I cannot live. It only remains to solve the riddle of why I was happy in Marienbad for 14 days[1110] and why I might consequently be the same, albeit after painfully breaking through the boundary, here with M. But probably with much more difficulty than in Marienbad, the ideology is firmer, the experiences greater. What used to be a dividing band is now a wall or a mountain range or more correctly: a grave.

30 *(January 1922)* Waiting for pneumonia. Fear not so much of the illness as for my mother and of her, of my father, the director and everyone else. Here it seems to be clear that the 2 worlds exist and that I am as ignorant, as unconnected, as anxious in the face of the illness as, say, in the face of the h.[1111] Otherwise, however, the division seems to me to be all too definite, dangerous in its definiteness, sad and too imperious. Am I living in the other world, then? Dare I say that?

When someone says: "What does life matter to me? It is only for my family's sake that I don't want to die." But the family is, after all, the representative of life, thus it is indeed for the sake of life that he wants to stay alive. Now this seems as far as my mother is concerned, to apply to me too, but only recently. But is it not gratitude and emotion that bring me to this, gratitude and emotion because I see how she strives with strength that is infinite for her age to compensate for my lack of connection to life. But gratitude is life too.

31 *(January 1922)* That would mean that I am alive for the sake of my mother. That can't be correct, for even if I were infinitely more than I am, I would be only an emissary of life and bound to it, if by nothing else, by this mission.

The negative alone, however strong it may be, cannot suffice, as I believe in my unhappiest times. For if I have climbed only the smallest step, am in any be it even the most questionable safety, I stretch out and wait—not until the negative climbs after me—but until it yanks me down the small step. Therefore it is a defensive instinct that doesn't tolerate the production of the slightest lasting contentment for me and, for example, smashes the marriage bed before it is even set up

---

1 II *(1922)* Nothing, only tired. Happiness of the coachman, for example, who experiences every evening as I do mine today and even much more wonderfully. Evening, say, on the stove. The person purer than in the morning, the time before wearily falling asleep is the actual time of purity from ghosts, all of them are expelled, only as the night progresses do they approach again, in the morning they are all there even if still unrecognizable, and now in the case of the healthy person their daily expulsion begins again.

Seen with a primitive eye the actual, indisputable truth, disturbed by nothing outside (martyrdom, sacrifice for a person), is only physical pain. Strange that the god of pain was not the chief god of the first religions (rather perhaps only of the later ones) For every sick man his household god, for the man with lung disease the god of suffocation. How can one bear his approach if one has no share in him even before the terrible union.

---

2 *(February 1922)* Struggle on the path to the Tannenstein in the morning, struggle while watching the ski-jumping competition.[1112] The little cheerful B. in all his innocence somehow shadowed by my ghosts, at least in my eyes, especially the one leg placed forward in the gray rolled-up stocking, the aimlessly wandering gaze, the aimless words. Here it occurs to me—but this is already artificial—that toward evening he would like to accompany me home.

The "struggle" would probably be horrible while learning a trade.

The probable maximum strength of the negative achieved by the "struggle" makes the decision between insanity or security imminent.

Happiness of being together with people.

3 *(February 1922)* Sleepless, almost completely; plagued by dreams, as if they were being scratched into me, into a reluctant material.[1113]

A weakness, a deficiency is clear, but hard to describe, it's a mixture of anxiousness, restraint, talkativeness, tepidness, with this I am trying to outline something definite, a group of weaknesses that in a particular aspect represent a single precisely characterized weakness (which is not mixed with the great vices like mendacity, vanity, etc.). This weakness holds me back from insanity as much as from any ascent. Because it holds me back from insanity, I cultivate it; out of fear of insanity I sacrifice ascent, a bargain that on this level, which knows no bargains, I will certainly lose. Unless sleeplessness intervenes and with its nightly-daily work breaks down all hindrances and clears the way. But then again only insanity will receive me, since one attains ascent only if one wants it, and I didn't want it.

---

4 *(February 1922)* In the desperate cold, the changed face, the incomprehensible others,

---

What M.[1114] said, without being able to fully understand the truth of it (there is also a justified sad arrogance) about the happiness of chatting with people. How chatting can delight people other than me! Too late probably and by a peculiar detour a return to people.

---

5 *(February 1922)* Run away from them. Some nimble leap. At home by the lamp in the quiet room. Careless to say it. It calls them out of the forests, as if one had lit the lamp to help them get on one's trail.

6 *(February 1922)* Consolation in hearing that someone has served in Paris, Brussels, London, Liverpool on a Brazilian steamer that followed the Amazon river to the border of Peru, has borne with relative ease the terrible sufferings of the winter campaign in the 7 Gemeinden[1115] during the war, because he was accustomed to hardships from childhood. The consolation lies not only in the demonstrative presentation of such possibilities, but also in the feeling of pleasure that with these achievements of the first level much must at the same time necessarily have been won, much wrested from clenched fists on the second level. So it is possible.

7 *(February 1922)* protected and depleted by K. and H.[1116]

8 *(February 1922)* extremely misused by the two of them and yet—I certainly could not live like this and it is no life, it is a tug-of-war in which the other is constantly working and winning and yet never gets me across, but it is a peaceful numbness similar to that time with W.[1117]

9 *(February 1922)* lost two days but used the same 2 days to get settled

10 *(February 1922)* sleepless, without the slightest connection with people except for that made by them themselves, which convinces me for the moment like everything they do

---

New attack by s.[1118] It is clearer than anything else that, attacked from the right and left by overpowering enemies, I can evade them neither to the right nor to the left, the path to edible nourishment, breathable air, free life, even if it be beyond life, leads only forward hungry animal. You lead the masses, great tall commander, lead the desperate through the mountain passes detectable to no one else under the snow. And who gives you the strength? He who gives you the clarity of vision.

The commander stood at the window of the dilapidated hut and looked with wide-open, unclosable eyes into the ranks of the troops marching past outside in the snow and dim moonlight. Now and then it seemed to him as if a soldier out of ranks were stopping at the window, pressing his face against the panes, looking briefly at him and then moving on. Although it was always a different soldier, it always seemed to be the same one, a face with strong bones, thick cheeks, round eyes, rough yellowish skin and always while he was walking away, he adjusted his straps, shrugged his shoulders and swung his legs to get back into step with the mass marching unchanged in the background. The commander did not intend to tolerate this game any longer, lay in wait for the next soldier, flung open the window in front of him and seized the man by the breast. "In with you" he said, making him climb in through the window. There he drove him from behind into a corner, stood in front of him and asked: "Who are you?" "Nothing" the soldier said anxiously. "That was to be expected" the commander said. "Why were you looking in?" To see whether you are still here.

In his hand he held a letter

---

11 *(February 1922)* Three spurs of my life

---

12 *(February 1922)* The form of rejection with which I was always met was not the one that says: I don't love you, but the one that says: "You cannot love me, however much you want to, you are unhappily in love with the love for me, the love for me doesn't love you." Hence it is incorrect to say that I have experienced the words "I love you," I have experienced only the expectant silence that should have been broken by my "I love you," that is all I have experienced, nothing else.

The fear while sledding, the anxiousness of walking on slippery snow, a short story I read today,[1119] brings to the surface again the long unheeded, always readily available thought of whether the cause of my decline was not merely insane self-interest, fear for myself and indeed not fear for a higher self but fear for my ordinary well-being, such, it is true, that I have sent the avenger from myself (a special case of the-right-hand-doesn't-know-what-the-left-hand-is-doing). In my office the accounting is still being done[1120] as if my life were beginning only tomorrow, meanwhile I have reached the end.

13 *(February 1922)* The possibility of serving with all one's heart

14 *(February 1922)* The power of contentment over me, my powerlessness without contentment. I know no one for whom both are so great. Hence everything I build is airy, impermanent, the chambermaid who forgets to bring me the warm water in the morning overturns my world. At the same time contentment has always pursued me and has deprived me not only of the strength to bear other things but also of the strength to create contentment myself, it creates itself around me of its own accord or I attain it by begging, weeping, forgoing more important things.

15 *(February 1922)* A little singing below me, a little slamming of doors in the corridor and all is lost.

16 *(February 1922)* The story of the crevasse in the glacier[1121]

17 *(February 1922)* (came back from Spindelmühle. Germanist woman)

18 *(February 1922)* Theater director who must create everything himself from the ground up, even the actors he must first beget. A visitor is not admitted, the director is busy with important theater work. What is it? He is changing the diapers of a future actor.

19 *(February 1922)* Hopes?

Path to L. Press back!

20 *(February 1922)* Imperceptible life. Perceptible failure.

21 *(February 1922)* A walk through the streets in the evening. The back and forth of the women

22 *(February 1922)* In the streets. A thought

23 *(February 1922)*

24 *(February 1922)* Helplessness. The dog on the chain, the look back at the dark house

25 *(February 1922)* A letter

26 *(February 1922)* I admit—to whom do I admit it? to the letter?—that there are possibilities in me, close possibilities of which I am not yet aware; but just find the way to them and when I have found it, venture! This means a great deal: there are possibilities, it even means that a scoundrel can turn into an honorable man, a man happy in his honorableness.

Your half-sleep fantasies recently.

---

27 *(February 1922)* A bad afternoon sleep, everything is changed, the distress is again pushed against the body

28 *(February 1922)* View of the tower and the blue sky. Calming.

1 III *(1922)* Richard III.[1122] Powerlessness

5 III *(1922)* Three days in bed. Small gathering in front of the bed. Turnabout. Flight. Complete defeat. Always this world history confined in rooms.

6 III *(1922)* New seriousness and fatigue

7 *(March 1922)* Yesterday the worst evening, as if everything were at an end

9 *(March 1922)* But that was only fatigue, but today a new attack that brings sweat to my brow. What would it be like if one choked to death on oneself? If pressing self-observation made the opening through which one pours out into the world too small or completely closed it? At times I am not far from it. A river flowing back. This has been happening in large part for a long time.

Use the attacker's horse for one's own ride. Sole possibility. But what powers and skills does this demand? And how late it is already!

Jungle life. Jealousy of nature, which is happy, inexhaustible and yet visibly working out of necessity (no differently than I), but always fulfilling all the demands of its opponent. And so easily, so musically.

In the past when I had a pain and it went away, I was happy, now I am only relieved, but have the bitter feeling: "again only healthy, nothing more"

Somewhere help is waiting and the drivers are guiding me there.

9 III *(1922)* The wretchedness. The insults. The inner enemy (Hardt)[1123]

13 *(March 1922)* The pure feeling and the clarity about the reasons for it. The sight of the children, especially one girl (upright gait, short black hair) and another (blond, indefinite features, indefinite smile), the enlivening music, the marching step. The feeling of someone who is in distress and help is coming, but who is happy not because he is being rescued—he is not being rescued at all—but rather because new young people are coming, confident, prepared to take up the battle, admittedly ignorant of what lies ahead but in an ignorance that doesn't make the spectator hopeless, rather moves him to admiration, to joy, to tears. Also hatred of him against whom the battle is being waged, is mixed in (but little Jewish feeling, I believe)[1124]

---

15 *(March 1922)* Objections taken from the work: Popularization and indeed with pleasure—and magic. How he gets past the dangers. (Blüher)[1125]

To escape into a conquered land and soon find it unbearable, for one can escape to nowhere

---

16 *(March 1922)* The attacks, the fear. Rats that tear at me and that I multiply with my gaze

17 *(March 1922)* 37° 4[1126]

18 *(March 1922)* The chance encounter (with H. and Th.) the wincing, the wandering constrained gaze, the fatigue afterward, almost a need to lean against something, moans

---

To not yet be born and already be forced to roam the streets and speak with people

19 *(March 1922)* Hysteria (Bl.)[1127] compelling and for unknown reasons pleasing.

20 *(March 1922)* Yesterday a failed, today a lost (?) evening. Difficult day. Reveries concerning Bl. Also, more anxiously, Mi.[1128]

The dinner conversation about murderers and execution. All fear unknown in the calmly breathing breast. The difference unknown between committed and planned murder

22 *(March 1922)* Dream of the boil on my cheek in the afternoon. The perpetually trembling boundary between ordinary life and the terror that is seemingly more real.

24 *(March 1922)* How it lies in wait! On the way to the doctor, for example, so often there.

29 *(March 1922)* In the stream

4 April *(1922)* How long the road is from the inner distress to, say, a scene like the one in the courtyard and how short the road back. And since one is now in one's home one can no longer leave[1129]

6 *(April 1922)* Sensed for two days now, yesterday an outbreak, further pursuit, the enemy's great strength. One of the causes: conversation with my mother, jokes about the future.—Planned letter to Milena.

The 3 Erinyes. Flight into the grove. Milena

7 *(April 1922)* The 2 pictures and the 2 terracottas in the exhibition

Fairy Tale Princess (Kubin) naked on the divan, looks through the open window, landscape penetrating powerfully, in its manner open air as in the picture by Schwind

Naked Girl (Bruder) German-Bohemian, faithfully captured by a lover in her grace that is inaccessible to anyone else, noble, convincing, seductive.

Pietsch { Sitting Peasant Girl, one foot under her, resting with pleasure, bent at the ankle,
Standing Girl, right arm clasps her body across her belly, left hand supports her head under her chin, a flat-nosed, simplemindedly profound, unique face.[1130]

Letter by Storm[1131]

---

10 IV *(1922)* The 5 guiding principles to hell: (genetic succession)

1.) "The worst is behind the window." Everything else is angelic, conceded either explicitly or (the more frequent case) silently when not paying attention
2.) "You must possess every girl!" not in a Don Juan fashion but according to the devilish phrase "sexual etiquette"
3.) "This girl you are not permitted to possess!" and therefore also cannot. Heavenly mirage in hell.
4.) "Everything is only bare necessity"; since you have it, content yourself
5.) "Bare necessity is everything." How could you have everything? Hence you do not have even the bare necessity.

As a boy I was (and would have remained so for a very long time if I had not been forcibly pushed into sexual things) as innocent and uninterested with regard to sexual matters as I am today with regard to, say, the theory of relativity. Only trifles (but those too only after precise instruction) struck me, such as the fact that the very women who on the street seemed to me the most beautiful and the most beautifully dressed were supposed to be bad.[1132]

Eternal youth is impossible; even if there were no other hindrance, self-observation would make it impossible

---

11 *(April 1922)* "The only woman suitable for him is the dirty, oldish complete stranger with wrinkled thighs, who extracts his semen in an instant, puts the money in her pocket and hurries into the next room, where another guest is already waiting for her."

At Fr.'s[1133] with Max, at once the letter

13 *(April 1922)* Max's suffering.[1134] In the morning in his office[1135]

In the afternoon in front of the Thein Church (Easter Saturday)[1136]

Fear of disturbances (Tr. M. Pe. Va. K.)[1137] Sleeplessness due to this fear

---

Nightmare recently because of M.'s[1138] letter in my portfolio

---

1) Young little girl 18 years old, nose, head shape, blond, seen fleetingly in profile, came out of the church.

---

16 *(April 1922)* Max's suffering. A walk with him. On Tuesday he is leaving[1139]

II 5-year-old girl, Baumgarten,[1140] little path to the main alley, hair, nose, bright face. Asks: "Jak se jmenuje ten který to dělá slinama?" "Ty myslíš vlaštovku"[1141]

23 *(April 1922)* III brownish yellow velvet jacket in the distance toward the fruit market

---

helpless days, yesterday night

---

so much strength and abundance, useless, everyone sees it, nothing can conceal it

27 *(April 1922)* IV Makkabi girl[1142] talking on the telephone in the Selbstwehr office[1143] yesterday: "Přišla jsem ti pomoct."[1144] Pure warm voice and speech

---

Shortly thereafter opened the door for M.[1145]

8 v *(1922)* Work with the plow. It bores its way in deep and yet moves along easily. Or it only scratches the ground. Or it moves along emptily with raised useless plowshare; with it or without it, it makes no difference

---

The work closes as an unhealed wound can close

Is it called carrying on a conversation when the other person is silent and in order to maintain the appearance of conversation one seeks to take his place, thus imitates him, thus parodies him, thus parodies oneself.

M. was here,[1146] is not coming again, probably wise and true and yet there is perhaps a possibility, the closed door of which we both are guarding, so that it doesn't open or rather so that we don't open it, for it won't open by itself.

Maggid[1147]

---

12 V *(1922)* The uninterrupted manifoldness and in the midst of it once the moving sight of a momentarily waning power of variation

---

from Pilgrim Kamanita, from the Vedas: "Just as, O dear one, a man whom they have led here blindfolded from the land of the Gandharans and then let loose in a desolate place, is cast eastward or northward or southward, because he had been led here blindfolded and had been let loose blindfolded; but after someone removed his blindfold and said to him: 'Out there live the Gandharans go out there' asking his way from village to village, instructed and wise, reaches his home among the Gandharans: so too is a man who has found a teacher here below aware: 'I will belong to this worldly bustle only until I am released, and then I will go home.' "[1148]

---

in the same place: "Such a man, as long as he is in the body, is seen by men and gods; but after his body is decomposed in death, he is no longer seen by men and gods. And even nature, the all-seeing, no longer sees him: he has blinded the eye of nature, he has vanished from the sight of the evil."

13 V *(1922)* Nothing

17 *(May 1922)* Sad

19 *(May 1922)* Reading by Eva Vischer[1149]

With a second person he feels more forsaken than when alone. When he is with a second person, the latter reaches for him and he is helplessly at his mercy. When he is alone, it is true, all humanity reaches for him, but the countless outstretched arms become entangled with each other and no one reaches him.

20 *(May 1922)* The Freemasons on the Altstädter Ring. The possible truth of every speech and doctrine.

The little, dirty, barefoot running girl in the little chemise dress with her hair blowing.

23 *(May 1922)* Incorrect to say about someone: he had an easy time of it, he suffered little more correct: he was such that nothing could happen to him most correct: he suffered everything, but everything together in a single moment; how could anything still have happened to him when in reality or at his command the variations of suffering were completely exhausted (2 old Englishwomen in Taine)[1150]

25 *(May 1922)* The day before yesterday "H. A."[1151] Beautiful walk today. Everywhere people sitting, wearily standing, dreamily leaning.—Much disturbed

26 *(May 1922)* The severe "attacks" on the evening walk [resulting from 4 tiny unpleasant things during the day (dog at the summer house,[1152] Mareš's book,[1153] registration as a soldier, borrowing of money by P.[1154])] in short spells a shattered state helplessness, hopelessness, immeasurable abyss, nothing but abyss, only on turning into the front door the possibility of a helpful thought, a possibility that is usually readily available to me but had not occurred to me this time for the whole way, apparently because in my complete despair I had not even sought it

30 *(May 1922)* The "attack" at night

---

5 VI *(1922)* Bad days (s.)[1155] Four or 5 days now. Talent for "patchwork"

Myslbeck's funeral[1156]

12 VI *(1922)* Eleven days now. Yesterday Frána.[1157] Today letter to M.[1158]

---

16 VI *(1922)* Outbreaks of tastelessness, confusion.—G. to H.[1159]

In reviewing this book,[1160] one is, quite apart from the insurmountable difficulties always caused by Blüher's intellectual and visionary power in a difficult position also because one comes remarkably easily, with almost every remark, under the suspicion of wanting to ironically dismiss the ideas of this book. One comes under this suspicion even when, as in my case, nothing is farther from one's mind in the face of this book than irony. This difficulty in reviewing is countered by a difficulty that Blüher in turn cannot surmount. He calls himself an anti-Semite without hatred, sine ira et studio, and he really is, but he arouses very easily, almost with every remark, the suspicion that he is an enemy of the Jews, be it in happy hatred, be it in unhappy love. These difficulties stand opposed to each other like facts of nature and it is necessary to call attention to them so that in thinking through this book one does not crash into these errors and thereby make oneself from the outset incapable of penetrating further.

According to Blüher, one cannot refute Judaism statistically, inductively empirically, this method of the old anti-Semitism cannot prevail against Judaism, one can refute all other peoples in this way, not the Jews the chosen people, to all the individual reproaches of the anti-Semites the Jew will be able to respond individually with justification. Blüher provides a very cursory overview, to be sure, of such individual reproaches and the responses to them.

This insight as far as it pertains to the Jews, not as far as it pertains to the other peoples, is deep and true. Blüher draws two conclusions from it a whole one and a half one.

The whole one:

23 VI *(1922)* Planá[1161]

27 VII *(1922)* The attacks. Yesterday an evening walk with the dog.[1162] Tvrz Sedlec.[1163] The alley of cherry trees on the way out of the woods,

which produces almost the privacy of a room. Return of man and woman from the field. The girl in the stable door of the dilapidated farm seems to be in battle with her ample breasts, innocently attentive animal gaze.[1164] The man with glasses who is wheeling the cart with the heavy load of fodder, elderly, a little deformed, nonetheless very upright due to the strain, high boots, the woman with the sickle, next to him and behind him.

26 *(August 1922)* No entries for two months. With interruptions a good period, thanks to O.[1165] For a few days breakdown again. On its first day made a sort of discovery in the woods

14 XI 22 In the evening always 37°6, 37°7.[1166] Sit at the desk, accomplish nothing, hardly set foot on the street. Nonetheless Tartuffery to complain about the illness.

18 XII *(1922)* The whole time in bed. Yesterday Either/Or[1167]

12 VI 23 The horrible recent periods, impossible to enumerate, almost uninterrupted. Bergmann,[1168] Dobřichowitz,[1169] M.,[1170] P., walks, nights, days, incapable of anything except pain.

And yet. No "and yet," however anxiously and tensely you look at me, Krizanowskaja on the picture postcard in front of me[1171]

More and more anxious while writing. It is understandable. Every word, twisted in the hand of the spirits—this flourish of the hand is their characteristic movement—becomes a spear, turned against the speaker. A remark like this most especially. And so on to infinity. The consolation would be only: it happens whether you want it or not. And what you want helps only imperceptibly little. More than consolation is: You too have weapons.

TRAVEL DIARIES

January-February 1911 Trips

Friedland Trip	January	1911
Reichenberg[1172]	February	

I would have to write through the night, so much is coming over me, but all of it is impure. What a power this has gained over me, whereas in the past as far as I remember I was capable of evading it with a turn, a slight turn that in itself still made me happy.

Reichenberg Jew in the compartment makes his presence felt at first with brief exclamations about express trains that are such only judging by the fare. Meanwhile a thin passenger, what is known as a windbag, is devouring ham, bread and two sausages, the skin of which he scrapes transparent with a knife, until he finally throws all the scraps and paper under the bench behind the heating pipe. While eating he sat facing me as he finished reading two evening papers in this unnecessary heat and haste that I find so appealing but cannot successfully imitate. Protruding ears. An only relatively broad nose. Wipes hair and face with his greasy hands without making himself dirty, which I am not permitted to do either. His apparently sizable member makes a large bulge in his pants.

Across from me a thin-voiced, hard-of-hearing gentleman with a pointed beard and a mustache laughs derisively at the Reichenberg Jew, silently at first without exposing himself, while after communicating by glances I join in always with some reluctance but out of a certain respect. Later it turns out that this man, who reads the Montagsblatt,[1173] eats something, buys wine at one station and drinks in sips the way I do, is worth nothing at all.

The thin passenger then introduces a high-chested short passenger who sits down next to me and is too heavy and self-confident to make his presence felt with anything but loud (moreover not derisive) smiling and now and then a word. Joke with Protiwin.[1174] Moreover, he gets off later

---

Then another young red-cheeked fellow who spends a great deal of time reading Das interessante Blatt,[1175] which he recklessly tears open with the edge of his hand, only finally to fold it up with that carefulness of unoccupied people that I always admire, as if it were a silk cloth, frequently pressing together, pressing in the edges from inside, smoothing down, brushing off the surfaces from outside and thick as it is to stuff it in his breast pocket. So he will read it more at home. I have no idea where he got off.

The hotel in Friedland. The large foyer. I remember a Christ on the cross, which perhaps wasn't there at all. No water closet, the snowstorm came up from below. For a while I was the only guest. Most of the weddings in the vicinity are celebrated in the hotel. I remember quite vaguely a glance into a hall the morning after a wedding celebration. Throughout the foyer and the corridor it was very cold. My room was over the building's driveway; I noticed the cold immediately, all the more when I realized the reason. Outside my room was a sort of sideroom of the foyer; there on a table were two forgotten bouquets in vases from a wedding. Locking of the windows not with handles but with hooks on the top and bottom. Now I remember that I once heard music, for a little while. But there was no piano in the dining room, perhaps in that wedding room. Whenever I closed the window, I saw a delicatessen on the other side of the market. The room was heated with large pieces of wood. Chambermaid with a large mouth, once despite the cold with her neck and the upper part of her bosom bare; now aloof now surprisingly affectionate, I always immediately respectful and embarrassed, as I usually am in the presence of all friendly people. When I had a stronger electric light put in for my work in the afternoon and evening, she was very happy when she saw it while tending the fire "yes, one couldn't work by the old light," she said. "Not by this light either" I said after several lively exclamations of the sort that unfortunately always come into my mouth in my embarrassment. And I didn't know what else to do but to recite my opinion, which I had already learned by heart, that electric light was both too harsh and too weak. Thereupon she went on tending the fire silently. Only when I said "besides I have only made the old lamp stronger" did she laugh a little and we were in accord.

On the other hand, I can do things like this: I had always treated her like a young lady and she had adapted herself to it; once I came home at an unusual time and see her washing the floor in the cold foyer. At that moment it caused me not the slightest difficulty to protect her from any shame by greeting her and making a request regarding the heating.

Next to me on the return journey from Raspenau[1176] to Friedland that stiff corpse-like person whose mustache went down over his mouth, which hung open, and who, when I asked him about a station, amiably turned to me and gave me the liveliest information.

The castle in Friedland. The many ways to see it: from the plain, from a bridge, from the park, between leafless trees, from the woods through tall firs. The castle surprisingly built one part above another, still far from orderly when one steps into the courtyard since the dark ivy, the grayish black wall, the white snow, the ice covering the slate-colored slopes increase the manifoldness. The castle is simply not built on a broad summit but around the fairly pointed summit. Constantly slipping, I walked up a road, while the castellan, whom I met farther up, easily made his way up by two flights of stairs. Ivy everywhere. Great view from a sharply jutting point. A staircase along the wall ends uselessly halfway up. The chains of the drawbridge hang down neglected from their hooks.

Beautiful park. Because it lies with various groupings of trees on the slope in the form of a terrace but also partly down below around a pond one cannot even imagine its summer appearance. In the icy cold pond water sit two swans (I learned their names only later in Prague), one of them sticks its neck and head in the water. I follow two girls who keep looking back uneasily and curious about me the uneasy and curious but moreover indecisive man, let them lead me along the mountain across a bridge a meadow, under a railroad embankment into a surprising rotunda formed by the forest slope and railroad embankment farther up high into a forest apparently not ending so soon. At first the girls walk slowly, when I begin to marvel at the size of the forest they walk more quickly, then we are already on a plateau with a strong wind a few paces from the town.

Kaiserpanorama.[1177] Only amusement in Friedland. Am not really at ease in it because I had not been prepared for such a beautiful setup as I found there, had entered with snow-covered boots and now sitting in front of the lenses touched the carpet with only my toes. I had forgotten the setup of the panoramas and was afraid for a moment that I would have to go from one chair to the next. An old man reading a volume of Illustrierte Welt[1178] at an illuminated little table runs the whole thing. After a while plays an Ariston[1179] for me. Later 2 old ladies come too, sit down to my right, then another to my left. Brescia, Cremona, Verona. People in there like wax dolls fastened to the ground to the pavement by their soles. Funerary monuments: a lady with the train of her dress dragging across a low flight of steps opens a door slightly while still looking back.[1180] A family, in front a young man is reading one hand on his temple, a boy to the right is tensing an unstrung bow. Monument to the hero Tito Speri:[1181] the clothes flutter neglected and enthusiastic around his body. Blouse, broad-brimmed hat. The pictures more alive than in the cinematograph, because they allow the gaze the repose of reality. The cinematograph gives what is viewed the restlessness of its movement, the repose of the gaze seems more important. Smooth floor of the cathedrals in front of our tongue. Why is there no union of cinema and stereoscope in this way? Posters of Pilsen Wihrer familiar from Brescia.[1182] The distance between merely hearing a story and seeing a panorama is greater than the distance between the latter and seeing reality. Scrap iron market in Cremona. At the end wanted to tell the old gentleman how much I liked it, didn't dare. Got the next program. Open from 10 o'clock to 10 o'clock.

In the display of the bookshop I had noticed the Literarischer Ratgeber of the Dürerbund. Decided to buy it, then changed my mind, reconsidered again, while I often stopped in front of the display at all hours of the day. The bookshop seemed to me so forsaken, the books so forsaken. I felt the connection of the world with Friedland only here and it was so thin. But just as all forsakenness in turn generates warmth for me, I quickly felt the happiness of this bookshop too and eventually I went in, just to see the inside. Because one doesn't need scholarly works there, the shelves looked even more full of fine literature than in the urban bookshops. An old lady was sitting under a green-shaded electric lamp. Four or five just-unpacked copies of Kunstwart[1183] reminded me that it was the beginning of the month. Declining my help the woman pulled the book, which she had hardly known existed, out of the display, handed it to me, marveled that I had noticed it behind the icy pane (indeed I had seen it before) and began to search for the price in the account books, for she didn't know it and her husband was out. I'll come later in the evening, I said (it was 5 o'clock in the afternoon) but didn't keep my word.

Reichenberg:[1184]

One is completely in the dark as to the actual intention of people who walk quickly in the evening in a small town. If they live out of town, then they surely have to use the tram because the distances are too great. But if they live in the town itself, then there are indeed no distances and no reason to walk fast. And yet people take long strides across this square, which would not be too large for a village and is made even smaller by the unexpected size of its town hall (which can amply cover it with its shadow), while from the small square one cannot quite believe the size of the town hall and would like to explain one's first impression of its size by the smallness of the square.

One policeman doesn't know the address of the workers' insurance office, another that of the institute branch, a third doesn't even know where Johannesgasse is. They explain this by saying that they have been serving only for a short time. For an address I have to go to the station, where enough policemen are resting in various ways, all in uniforms whose beauty, newness and colorfulness is surprising, since everywhere on the street one usually sees only the dark winter coats.

In the narrow streets only one track could be laid. The tram to the railroad station therefore runs through different streets than the one from the railroad station. From the railroad station through Wiener Strasse, where I stayed in the Hotel Eiche, to the railroad station through Schückerstrasse.

In the theater three times always a full house: Des Meeres & der Liebe Wellen:[1185] I sat on the balcony, an all-too-good actor makes too much noise with Naukleros, I had tears in my eyes several times such as at the end of the first act when Hero's and Leander's eyes cannot break away from each other. Hero steps out the temple door, through which one sees something that can be nothing but an icebox. In the second act a forest of the sort in old deluxe editions, it's deeply moving, lianas wind from tree to tree. Everything mossy and dark green. The background wall of the tower chamber returns the next evening in Miss Dudelsack.[1186] From the third act on decline of the play as if an enemy were after it

August-September 1911 Trip

Departure 26 VIII 11 Noon
the bad idea: Simultaneous description of the trip and our inner responses to each other concerning the trip. Its impossibility proven by a passing carriage with peasant women. The heroic peasant woman (Delphic Sibyl). In a laughing one's lap sleeps one who, waking up, waves. The description of Max's greeting would bring false enmity into the description.

A girl, who later turns out to be Alice Rehberger, gets on in Pilsen.[1187] The coffee ordered during the journey is indicated to the restaurateur by little green slips of paper that are stuck to the windows. But with a slip of paper one doesn't have to take it and gets it even without one. At first I can't see her because she's sitting next to me. First shared situation: Her packed-up hat flies down onto Max. Thus do hats come in with difficulty through the carriage doors and go back out with ease through the large windows.—Max probably destroys the possibility of a later description in that, as a married man, he must say something to deprive the occurrence of dangerousness, in doing so leaves out what is important, emphasizes what is didactic and makes it a little ugly.—"impeccable, to fire out 0 point 5 acceleration, prompt," the nestling in the office, views on the military, jokes in the office (mixing up the hats in the office, nailing down the croissants), our joke with the card, which she will write in Munich, which we will send to her office from Zürüch and which will say: "The prediction has unfortunately come true . . wrong train . .

now in Zürich . . 2 days of the trip lost." Her joy. But she expects us as men of honor to add nothing. Automobile in Munich. Rain, quick drive (20 min.) basement apartment perspective, driver calls out the names of the invisible sights, the tires whir on the wet asphalt like the apparatus in the cinematograph, what is clearest: the uncurtained windows of the "Vier Jahreszeiten,"[1188] the reflection of the lamps in the asphalt as in a river

---

Washing hands and face in a "cubicle" in the railroad station in Munich.

Left suitcases in the carriage. Got Angela settled in a carriage where a lady who was more to be feared than we offers her her protection, which is enthusiastically accepted. Suspicious.

Max's sleep in the compartment. The 2 Frenchmen, the dark one keeps laughing, once at the fact that Max hardly leaves him room to sit (so much does he stretch out) then at the fact that he takes advantage of a moment and doesn't leave Max room to lie. Max in the canopy of his Inverness cape.[1189] The cigarettes of the other burlier Frenchman. Eating at night. Incursion of three Swiss. One of them smokes. One, who later stays behind even after the other 2 get off, is at first insubstantial grows clearer only toward morning. Lake Constance. Seen carelessly as from the quay.—Switzerland during the first morning hours left to itself. I wake Max at the sight of a bridge like this

I wake Max and thereby get my first strong impression of Switzerland even though I have been looking at it for a long time already from inner in outer half-light.— The impression of upright, independent houses in Gallen without street formation.—Winterthur.—Man in the illuminated villa in Würtemberg, leaning over the railing on the veranda at 2 o'clock at night. Door to the study open.—The cattle already awake in sleeping Switzerland.—Telegraph poles cross-section of clothes hooks.—Meadows paling as the sun rises—Memory of the prison-like station building in Cham with its sign inscribed in biblical seriousness. Window decoration seems despite its poverty to violate rules. In two of the large building's windows far apart from each other stand small trees swaying in the wind a larger one there a smaller one here.

Ragged fellow in the railroad station in Wintertur with a cane, singing and one hand in his pants pocket.

Inquiry in the window: How will Zürich the first big Swiss city be formed out of the individual houses?

Business activities in villas.

A lot of singing in Lindau in the railroad station at night.

Patriotic statistics:[1190] the area of a Switzerland stretched out flat.

---

foreign chocolate companies

(lost things)

Zürich
Emergence of the railroad station from several intermingled railroad stations of recent memory—(Max takes possession of it for a + x)[1191]

Historical impression of a foreign military. Absence of this impression in the case of one's own—argument of anti-militarism.

Armed men in Züruch in the railroad station. Our fear of the guns going off when they run.

Map of Zurück is purchased.

Back and forth on a bridge because of indecisiveness about the sequence of cold, warm bathing and eating breakfast.

Direction of the Limmat,[1192] Urania observatory.

Main traffic artery, empty tram, pyramids of cuffs in the foreground of a display of an Italian men's wear shop

---

only artists' posters (spa hotels, festival performance "Marigagno" by Wiegand, music by Jermoli.)[1193]

Extension of a department store. Best advertisement. Years of attention of the whole population. (Dufayel)[1194]

Postmen as first cowl-wearers of the approaching south and west appear to be in nightshirts. Carrying small boxes in front of them, letters arranged like the fortunes at the Christmas market,[1195] heaped up high on top.

Lake view. Strong Sunday feeling in imagining being a resident here. Air reservoir of the lake, not to be built on. Rider. Startled horse. Educational inscription perhaps relief of Rebecca at the well, the calm of the inscription and of the relief above the positively strongly blown glass form of the flowing water.

Old town: Narrow steep street, which a man in a blue blouse descends with difficulty. By way of stairs.

Memory of the water closet threatened by traffic outside Saint Roche[1196] in Paris.

Breakfast in a nonalcoholic restaurant. Butter like egg yolk. Zürcher Zeitung[1197]

Grossmünster: old or new? Men belong at the sides. The sexton directs us to better seats. We follow him since it is on our way out. Since, when we are already at the exit, he seems to believe we can't find these seats he sets off straight across the church toward us. We push each other out. A lot of laughter.

Max: Confusion of languages as solution to national difficulties. The chauvinist loses his bearings.

Bathhouse in Zürich: Only men's bathhouse. Everyone packed together. Swiss dialect. Lead-filled German. Partly no cubicles, republican freedom of getting undressed in front of one's clothes hook, likewise freedom of the swimming master to empty the full sun bath with a fire hose. This emptying, moreover, will have been no more groundless than the language is incomprehensible. Diver: with feet spread apart on the railing he first jumps onto the diving board and thereby increases his momentum.—Bathhouse facilities can be appreciated only after fairly long use. No swimming lessons. Some naturopath with long hair behaves forlornly. Low shores of the lake.

Open-air concert of the officers' tourist association. Among the listeners a writer with a companion is writing in a notebook filled with little lines and after the conclusion of one number on the program is pulled away by his companion. No Jews. Max: The Jews have missed out on this great business. Beginning: Bersaglieri March. End: Pro patria March. There are no open-air concerts for their own sake in Prague (Luxembourg Park[1198]) republican according to Max, military in Paris.

Keller room locked. Tourist office. Bright house behind a dark street. Houses with terraces on the r. bank of the Limmat. Blue-and-white-flamed window shutters. Slowly walking soldiers are policemen. Concert hall. Polytechnikum not sought and not found. Stadthaus. Lunch on the second floor. Meilen wine (Sterilized wine of fresh grapes). A waitress from Lucern tells us what trains go there. Pea soup with sago, beans w. roasted potatoes. Lem. cream.—Respectable, craftsmanlike houses. Departure around 3 o'clock to Luzern around the lake. The empty, dark hilly, wooded shore of Lake Zug in many tongues of land. American appearance. Aversion on the journey to comparisons with lands not yet seen. Great panoramas in the Luzern railroad station. Skating rink to the right of the railroad station. We step into the midst of the porters and shout Rebstock.[1199] Is the hotel among the hotels as the porter is among the porters? Bridge (according to Max) divides lake from river as in Zürich. Where is the German population that justifies the German signs? Kursaal. The visible Swiss in Zürich did not seem to be hotelier talents, here, where they are, they're disappearing, perhaps even the hoteliers are French. The empty balloon hangar opposite. Hard to imagine an airship gliding in. Roller rink. Resemblance to Berlin. Fruit. In the evening the darkness of the beach promenade remains defined under the treetops. Gentlemen with daughters or whores. Rocking of the boats visible down to their lowest sharp edge. Ridiculous reception lady in the hotel, laughing girl leads us farther and farther up to the room, serious, red-cheeked chambermaid. Small stairwell. Locked walled-in wardrobe in the room. Glad to be out of the room. Would have liked to have fruit for dinner. Gotthard-Hotel, girls in Swiss costume. Apricots compote Meilen wine. Two older women and a gentleman speak about aging. Discovery of the gambling hall in Luzern. 1 fr. admission, 2 long tables. Sights really worth seeing are unpleasant to describe, because it must be done positively before waiting people. At each table a crier in the middle with a guard on either side.

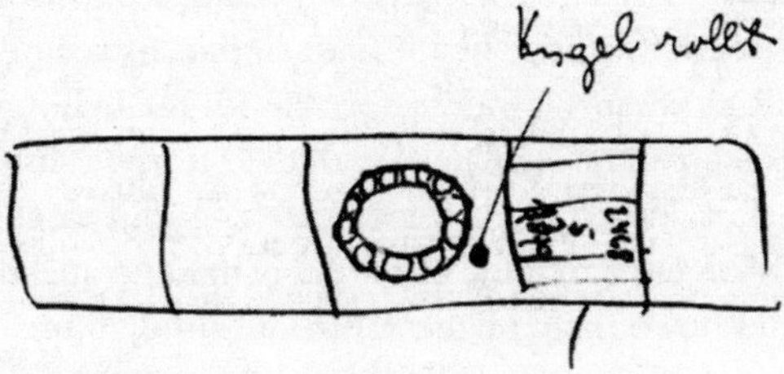

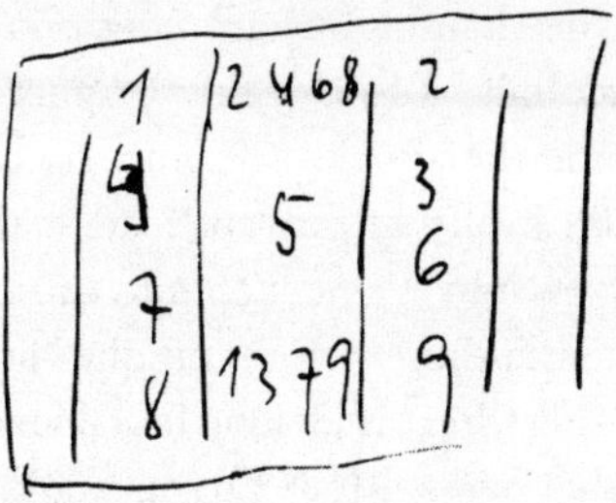

Maximum wager 5 f. "The Swiss are asked to let the foreigners go first, since the game is intended for the entertainment of the guests." One table with a ball, one with little horses. Croupiers in frock coats. Messieurs faites votre jeu—marquez le jeu—les jeux sont faits—sonts marqués—rien ne va plus. Croupiers with nickel-plated rakes on wooden rods. What they can do with them: Pull the money onto the right fields, separate it, pull money to themselves, catch money thrown by them onto the winning fields. Influence of the different croupiers on chances of winning or rather one likes the croupier with whom one wins. Excitement before the mutual decision to gamble, one feels alone in the hall. The money (10 fr) disappears on a gently sloping plane. The loss of 10 fr. is experienced as too weak a temptation to continue gambling, but still as a temptation. Anger at everything. Prolonging of the day by this gambling.

Monday 28 August *(1911)*. Man in high boots is having breakfast against the wall. 2nd-class steamer. Luzern in the morning. Worse appearance of the hotels. Married couple is reading letters from home with newspaper clippings about cholera in Italy.[1200] The beautiful residences only visible from a boat on the lake, one is riding at their level. Changing shape of the mountains. Vitznau Rigi Railroad. Lake seen through leaves, southern impression. Surprise by the sudden flat surface of Lake Zug. Bouquet with Rigi, what is it waiting for? Woods like at home. Railroad built in 75, look it up in the old Über Land und Meer.[1201] Historical Engl. ground, here they still wear checkered clothing and sideburns. Telescope. Jungfrau far away, rotunda of the Mönch, wavering hot air moves the picture. Laid-down palm of the Titlis. Cut-through bread loaf of a snowfield. False estimate of the heights from above as from below. Unresolved dispute about the slanting or level position of the Arth-Goldau railroad station. Table d'hôte. Black woman serious, sharp beginning of her mouth, seen already down below next to the carriage, is sitting in the hall. English girl at the departure, each tooth the same all around. Small Frenchwoman gets into the next compartment, with outstretched arm declares our full compartment not "complet" and pushes her father in and her innocent- and whorish-looking older small sister, who tickles me on the hip with her elbows. More English spoken with the teeth by the old lady on Max's right, for which one searches for the name of a county. Journey Vitznau-Fluelen. Gersau, Beckenried, Brunnen (nothing but hotels) Schillerstein, Tellplatte, the Rütli skipped,[1202] 2 loggias on Axenstrasse (Max imagined several here, because in photographs one always sees these 2) Uri basin, Fluelen. Hotel Sternen.

Tuesday 29 August *(1911)*

This beautiful room with a balcony. The friendliness. Too hemmed in by mountains. A man and 2 girls, in raincoats, one behind the other, walk through the hall in the evening with alpenstocks, when all of them are already on the stairs they are stopped by a question from the chambermaid. They thank her, they already know about it. In reply to a further question about their mountain excursion: Well, it wasn't so easy either, I can tell you that. In the hall they seemed to me like something out of Miss Dudelsack,[1203] on the stairs to Max like something out of Ibsen, then to me too. Forgotten binoculars. At the railroad station one learns that even an old lady is going to Genoa. Boys with the Swiss flag. Bathing in Lake Lucerne. Married couple. Life ring. People strolling on Axenstrasse. Nicest bathing place because one could fend for oneself. Fisherwomen in pale yellow dresses. Boarding the Gotthard railroad. Reuss. Milk-mixed water of our rivers. The Hungarian flower.[1204] Her thick lips. Exotic line from her back to her behind. The beautiful man there among the Hungarians. In Italy spits grape skins on the ground, but toward the south they disappear. Jesuit general at the railroad station in Göschenen. Sudden Italy, tables strewn outside the osterias, a young man in all colors who cannot contain himself, hand movements of the women saying goodbye (imitation of a sort of pinching), black combed-up one to the side of a railroad station, light pink houses, blurred signs. Later the Italian quality disappears and the Swiss core comes forward. Women in the crossing-keeper's huts, reminiscent of battle. Ticino falls, jerky falls everywhere. German Lugano. Noisy palestra. Post office newly built. Hotel Belvedere.[1205] Concert in the Kurhaus. No fruit.

30 August. From 4 to 11 at night with Max at a table, first in the garden, then in the reading room, then in my room. Morning was bathhouse, post office.

31 August. Clock-hand-like looming up of the snowy mountains on the Rigi—

Friday 1 IX 11. Departure 10:15 from Place Guglielmo Tell.—Formulaic analogy of the backseat in a carriage and on a ship. Frame for cloth covering on the boats as on milk wagons—Every ship's landing an attack.

Trip without luggage, hand free to hold my head—Gandria one house stuck behind the other, loggias with colored cloths, no bird's-eye view, streets and no streets—S. Margeritha with fountain[1206] on the landing place. Villa with 12 cypresses at Oria.[1207]

Balcony entrance in a shirt—One cannot and dares not imagine a house in Oria that has a terrace in front with Greek columns—burnt-out houses proper only in a fire—Mamette: mediev. magician's hat on a bell tower[1208]—Donkey in the trellis-covered walk earlier along one side of a harbor—on Lake Lucerne one thought too much about oneself—Osteno—The priest in the company of ladies

Special incomprehensibility of the exclamations. In sentences one's incomprehension can crawl around. Child in the window behind the

pissoir tunnel. Tickling sight of the lizard movement on a wall—Psyche's falling hair[1209]—Soldiers riding by on bicycles and porters of the hotels dressed up as sailors—Bathing place between Cadenabbia. People passing in a carriage show each other the Ital. boys.[1210] After the landing recoiling from the departure

---

Carlotta[1211]—Ilex holm oak stripped-off skin of small animals—Passiflora physical balancing feat—bamboo—palm trunks wrapped in old men's scalps—Bux (myrtle) aloe (double saw) cedar (a larch enswirled by its branches) hanging limp bells that have stopped ringing (fuchsias) Jubaea (rhinoceros trunk) plane tree—cacti magnolias (untearable leaves) Australian ferns (palms)—myrtle (delicate Bux)—Delicate laurel Dome-shaped rhododendr. Eucalyptus—exposed muscle trunk—lemons papyrus three-edged stalk rush-shaped on top wisteria entwining itself—gigantic plane tree—banana

---

Children on the landing stage in Menaggio, father, the woman's body proud of her children

---

Statesman with half-open mouth (Villa Carlota)

Frenchwoman with the voice of my aunt and a straw parasol with a frayed thick border is writing in a small notebook about montagne, etc.—black man in a boat standing in the frame of the hoops, bent over the oars. Customs official quickly looks over and rummages through a little basket as if it were all a gift for him.—Italian man on the Porlezza Menaggio train. Every Italian word addressed to one penetrates the great space of one's own ignorance and hence occupies one whether understood or not for a long time. One's own uncertain Ital. cannot hold out against the Italian man's certainty and whether understood or not is easily ignored.—Joke of the train going backward before Menaggio nice conversation topic[1212]—Boathouses made of stone with terraces and decorations on the other side of the street in front of the villas—Extensive business in antiques.—Boatman: peu de commerce—Customs cutter (story of Captain Nemo and Journey through the Solar World).—[1213]

2 September *(1911)*. Saturday

Trembling of my face on the small steamer—gathered-up curtains (brown with white border design) in front of the stores (Cadenabbia)—Bees in the honey—solitary morose woman with short upper body language teacher—proper gentleman with pants pulled up. His forearms hover over the table, as if his hands were clasping not the knife and fork handles but the ends of armrests.—Listens to the proprietor—leg to leg—Children watching the weak rockets: encore un—hissing—reaching up of arms—Bad ride on the small steamer. Participation in the motion too great—not high enough to feel the fresh air and freely survey the area—closer to the position of the stokers—Bathing place between Cassagnola[1214] and Gandria on seats we built—Passing group, man cow and woman. She is talking. Black turban, loose dress.—Heartbeat of the lizards—Energy expended by a gentleman: late serving in the reading room, at the same time beer, wine, Fernet branca, postcards, light sighing—Though I hadn't spoken to him earlier, the proprietor's small boy, at his mother's urging, offers me his mouth for a good night kiss. I enjoyed it—Gandria instead of streets cellar stairs and cellar corridors—a boy is being thrashed, dull sound of beds being beaten—house overgrown with ivy, at the edge sprinkled with ivy—in Gandria seamstress at the window without blinds, curtains or panes—We support each other on the way from the bathing place to Gandria, so tired are we—solemn procession of boats behind a small black steamer—young gentlemen looking at pictures kneeling squatting on the landing stage in Gandria, one of them completely white, well known to us as a ladies' man and a jester.—In Porlezza in the evening on the quay.—At the Wilhelm Tell monument an already forgotten Frenchman with a full beard reminds us of his peculiarity—This monument with a drainpipe of a kitchen sink, brass out of stone

3 September *(1911)* Sunday

A German with a gold tooth, to which a describer can hold fast even amid the otherwise vague impression, gets an entrance ticket to the swimming facilities at ¼ to 12, even though they close at 12, which the swimming master inside immediately points out to him in incomprehensible, hence somewhat stern Italian. Confused by this Italian even within his native language the German asks in astonishment why in that case he was sold a train ticket at the cash desk and complains that he was sold a train ticket and asserts that he should not have been sold a train ticket anymore. From the Italian answer one makes out that he does still have almost 15 minutes to swim and get dressed. Shed tears.—Sat on the barrel in the lake.—Hotel Belvedere "With all respect to the proprietor, the food is miserable"

4 September *(1911)* Cholera information:[1215] Tourist office, Corriere della Serra, Norddeutscher Lloyd,[1216] Berliner Tageblatt, chambermaid brings information from a Berlin doctor, depending on the group and one's own physical condition the average character of these reports changes, at the departure from Lugano to Porte Ceresio[1217] 1:05 it is rather favorable.—Fleeting enthusiasm for Paris, in the wind that billows the Excelsior[1218] of 3 Sept 11 held in front of us, with which we run to a bench.—On the bridge over Lake Lugano there are still several billboard spaces for rent.—

---

on Friday the 3 fellows drive us away from the bow of the ship because perhaps the helmsman must have an unobstructed view of the light in front, but then push a bench over and sit down themselves—I would have liked to sing.

Friday *(1 September 1911)*
Under the eyes of the Italian man who advises us to travel to Turin (exposition)[1219] and to whom we nod, mutual resolution confirmed by a handshake not to go to Turin at any price—praise of reduced tickets. Cyclist circling on the lakeside terrace of a house in P. Ceresio—Whip that instead of a strap has only a little tail of horsehair—Cycling cyclist holds a horse trotting alongside him by a rope

Milan: Forgot guidebook in a shop. Went back & stole it—in the courtyard of the Mercanti[1220] ate apple strudel—Health cake—Theatro

Fossati[1221]—All hats and fans in motion—Laughter of a child up above—Program sealed by an advertising leaflet—an elderly lady in the male orchestra—Poltrone[1222]—Ingresso[1223]—Orchestra level with the auditorium—Lancia advertisement included in the ceiling decoration of a salon—all windows of the back wall open—tall strong actor with delicately dabbed nostrils, the black of which strikingly endures even when the edges of the bent-back face blur in the light—Girl with long thin neck runs with short steps and stiff elbows out of the room and gives a sense of the high heels that suit the high neck. Overestimation of laughter, for it is a greater distance from uncomprehending seriousness to laughter than from initiated seriousness—Significance of each piece of furniture—5 doors in both plays for any eventuality—A girl's nose and mouth shone down on by her painted eyes.—Gentleman in the box opens his mouth while laughing all the way to a gold tooth in the back, which then holds the mouth open like that for a little while. Impossible to attain in any other way a unity between stage and auditorium such as that which is formed for and against the spectator who doesn't understand the language

---

—Young Italian woman[1224] with otherwise Jewish face that shifts into non-Jewishness in profile.—How she stood up extended her hands to the railing and only her narrow body could be seen without the broadening of her arms and shoulders, how she stretched her arms out to the window posts, how she held on to one post with both hands in the train wind as if to a tree.—She was reading a detective paperback for which her little brother had long been asking her in vain.—Her father next to her with a sharply crooked nose whereas hers in the same place was curved gently therefore more Jewishly—she looked at me often, out of curiosity whether I might not finally cease my bothersome staring—her dress made of raw silk—fat tall fragrant lady next to me who spreads her perfume in the air with her fan—her abundant flesh cannot bear it in her flat foot and rises immediately behind the toes—I feel myself shriveling up next to her—in the luggage room[1225] the metal shade of the gas flame has the shape of a girl's flat hat—entertaining variety of gates in the houses—under the arch of the entrance to the Skala we were searching for it and, confronted with its simple scraped-off facade, were not astonished at this error even when we stepped out onto the square[1226]—growing approval of the increasing traffic toward the center of the city until on the cathedral square one sees nothing but the tram slowly going around the monument to Vittorio Emanuel, turns away and searches for a hotel—Joy at the connection between the 2 rooms, which is made by a double door. Each of us can open one of the doors. Max considers this suited even to married couples.—First write down a thought, then read it aloud, don't write while reading aloud, for then only the inwardly initiated impetus succeeds, while what is still to be written breaks away.—Conversation about apparent death and piercing the heart[1227] at a small coffeehouse table on the cathedral square. Mahler[1228] asked for his heart to be pierced too. During this conversation the intended time of the stay in Milan dwindles a great deal despite a slight resistance on my part.—The cathedral is importunate with its many spires.—Development of the decision to go to Paris: the moment in Lugano over the Excelsior,[1229] trip to Milan due to the not entirely voluntary purchase of the tickets to Milan by way of Porte Ceresio, from Milan to Paris out of fear of cholera and out of the desire to be compensated for this fear. Moreover, calculation of the financial and time advantages of this trip

I Rimini—easternmost point[1230]—Genoa Nervi (Prague)

II Upper Ital. lakes, Milan (Prague) Genoa (vacillation between Locarno & Lugano)

III Leave out Maggiore, Lugano Milan, trip through cities as far as Bologna

IV in (Lugano) Lugano—Paris

V Lugano—Milan (several days)—Maggiore

VI in Milan: directly to Paris (poss. Fontainebleau)

VII got off in Stresa giving the trip a good retrospective and prospective view for the first time, it has grown and is therefore clasped around the waist—I have never seen people as small as in the galleria[1231]—Max claims the galleria is only as high as houses one sees in the open air too, I deny it with a forgotten objection, as I will in general always stand up for this galleria.—It has almost no superfluous ornamentation, doesn't arrest one's gaze, due to this and also due to its height seems short, but tolerates that too—it forms a cross, through which the air freely blows—from the roof of the cathedral the people opposite the galleria seem to have grown larger—with the galleria I can console myself completely about the fact that I haven't seen the ancient Roman remains—

Transparent inscription in the depths of the hall over the brothel: Al vero Eden. Heavy traffic with the street mostly by individuals. Back and forth in the narrow streets of the surrounding area. They are clean, despite their narrowness have several sidewalks, once we see from one narrow street in another that turns into it at a right angle a woman leaning against the window grate on the top floor of a house—I was at the time easily determined to do anything and as always in such a mood felt my body grow heavier.—The girls spoke their French like virgins.—Milanese beer smells like beer, tastes like wine.—Max regrets what he has written only during the writing, never later on

---

Out of fear Max is taking a cat for a walk in the reading room.

The girl whose belly while she was sitting was without doubt unshapely over and between her outspread legs under her translucent dress, whereas when she stood up it dissipated like theater scenery behind veils and formed an ultimately tolerable girl's belly. The French girl whose sweetness showed itself to the concluding glance above all in her round and yet detailed, chatty and affectionate knees.—An imperious monumental figure, pushing the money just earned into her stocking.—The old man laying one hand over the other on his knee.—The girl by the door, whose scowling face is Spanish, whose putting her hands on her hips is Spanish and who stretches in a bodice-like dress of prophylactic silk. Hair runs thickly from her navel to her private parts.—At home the German girls in the brothels estrange their guests for a little while from their nation, here the French ones do it. Perhaps insufficient knowledge of these native circumstances.—Punished passion for iced drinks: 1 grenadine, 2 aranciatas in the theater, 1 in the bar on Corso Emanuele, 1 sorbet in the coffeehouse in the galleria, 1 French Thierry mineral water, which suddenly revealed the effects of all that had preceded it, going to bed sad while looking from there at a strongly Italian sweeping prospect produced by a somewhat protruding window of a side facade, waking up disconsolate with the dry pressure against all throat walls.—Not at all official elegance of the policemen, when they make their rounds with their removed knitted gloves in one hand, their cane in the other.—Whores striding on the cathedral square and in the galleria.—Apology to Max about the brothel in the morning

5 Sept. *(1911)*
Banca Commerciale on the Skala square—Letter from home.—Considerable stool.—Card to my boss: "With this and with a second card I seek to serve you with It. stamps and permit myself under this pretext to send you warm regards"[1232]—Marveling entrance into the cathedral between portieres, brown as in Cadenabbia.—Desire to provide an architectural picture of the cathedral, because the cathedral in its entirety is a pure representation of architecture, for the most part has no benches, few statues on the pillars, few and always dark pictures on the distant walls and the individual visitors are arrayed on the floor tiles as a measure of its size or move as a measure of its extent.—Sublime, but much too quickly reminded of the galleria.—Irresponsible to travel, even to live without taking notes. The deadly feeling of the monotonous passing of the days is impossible.—Climb to the roof of the cathedral. A young Italian man walking ahead makes the climb easier for us by humming a tune, trying to take off his coat, looking through slits through which only sunny haze can be seen and constantly tapping on the numerals that indicate the number of steps.—View from the front roof gallery. The mechanism of the trams down below is somewhat damaged, so weakly do they roll, carried along only by the bend of the tracks. A conductor hurries slanted and pressed down from our vantage point, to his tram and jumps on.—A gargoyle in the shape of a man, whose spinal column and brain have been taken out to make a path for the rainwater.—Each of the great stained glass windows is dominated by the color of a garment that keeps recurring in the individual pictures.—Max: Railroad station in the display of a toyshop, rails that close themselves into a circle and lead nowhere, is and will remain the strongest impression of Milan. The fact that in the display the railroad station is put together with the cathedral could be explained by the striving to show the variety of the stock.—From the rear facade of the cathedral one looks a large roof clock straight in the face.—Max: spared the journey to the castle[1233] by the sight of it.—Teatro Fossati[1234]—Ride to Stresa. The movements in relief of the sleeping people in the packed compartment.—Pair of lovers Afternoon in Stresa, Wed. 6 Sept. Getting angry, in the evening inventions[1235] & hotels. Thurs. 7 Sept. Bathing, letters, departure.—Sleep in public—Friday 8 Sept. Trip Italian couple, supposed Frau Salus[1236]—priest—American—the 2 short Frenchwomen with a great deal of flesh around their behinds, Montreux

One's legs diverge on the large Paris streets—footbath from the edge of the bedpost—little night lamps of the summer cafés—cores of ordinary & of cushioned chairs on the Champs Elisées—the arrangement of the Place de la Concorde which casts the attractions into the distance where the gaze finds them easily but only if it is looking for them

---

école Florentine (XV century) apple scene—[1237]

Tintor—Suzanne

Simone Martini 1285 (Ecole de Sienne) Jesus Christ marchant au Calvaire

---

Mantegna La sagesse victorieuse des Vices 1431–1506 école Venetienne

---

Titian Le concile de Trente 1477–1576

Rafael: Apollo and Marsyas

Velasquez 1599–1660 Port. de Philippe IV roi d'Espagne

Jakob Jordaens 1593–1678 Le concert apres le repas

Rubens Kermesse

Confiserie de l'enfant gaté
rue de petits champs

Laundresses in morning negligée—

---

rue de pet. champs, so narrow that it remains entirely in the shade, even when one row of houses is completely bathed in sunshine, this difference in the lighting of houses pushed so close together

---

Le sou du soldat
societé anonyme Avenue de l'Opera
Capital 1 mill

Robert—Samuel—[1238]

Ambassadeur[1239]—drum roll with a brass band announcing itself in the double-s before which in the eur the drumsticks still in motion rise and are silent.

Gare de Lion—Compteur francaises.[1240]—As a substitute for suspenders excavators wear sashes in many colors around their waists—I didn't quite know whether I was sleepy and was preoccupied with this in the carriage and all morning—be careful not to mistake the nursemaids for French governesses of German children—misunderstanding about the length of a little morning toilet rooted in Max's innermost nature[1241]—because the French

---

Uncertainty about the character of a person standing on the stage in front of the curtain who directs the conductor[1242]

Rehearsal (often interrupted) before the audience. For which performance are they rehearsing

---

Ground covered with small pebbles

Prise de Salins 17 v 1668 par Mr Lafaye[1243]
2 friends one dressed in red on a white horse, one dark on a dark horse recover from the siege of a city in the background by taking a ride as a storm approaches[1244]

---

voyage de Louis XVI à Cherbourg 23 Juin 1786[1245]
while Louis with his hand extended toward Cherbourg is making a lively remark to 2 courtiers standing behind him, particularly to one who is laying his hand on his breast, the boat he's on is being carried ashore on the tied-together oars by the boatmen in 3 rows on each side. Women lightly dressed are bounding toward them from the shore, a man is looking through a telescope. The carriage is waiting. From other boats they will have to disembark on gangplanks, one is presently being pulled out.

Bivouak de Napoleon sur le champ de bataille de Wagram nuit du 5 au 6 juillet 1809.[1246] N. is sitting alone with one leg resting on a low table. Behind him a smoking campfire. The shadows of his r. leg and of the table and chair legs lie in front radiating around him. Peaceful moon. The generals in a distant semicircle are looking into the fire and at him.

the characteristic condition of flatness: shirts, linens in general, napkins in the restaurant, sugar, large wheels of the mostly 2-wheeled carriages, horses harnessed one behind the other, flat steamers on the Seine, the balconies divide the houses crosswise and broaden these flat cross-sections of the houses, the flattened broad chimneys, the folded newspapers

the lines of Paris:
the tall thin chimneys growing out of the flat chimneys (with the many little flower-pot-like ones), the extremely silent old gas candelabra, the horizontal lines of the blinds, which in the suburbs are joined by the

streaks of dirt on the outside wall of the house, the thin molding on the roofs, which we saw on rue Rivoli, the lines of the glass roof of the Grand Palais des Art, the windows of the business premises divided by lines, the lattices of the balconies, the Eifel Tower formed out of lines, the greater linear effect of the side and center strips of the balcony doors opposite our windows, the little chairs in the open air and the little coffeehouse tables, the legs of which are lines, the gold-pointed gates of the public gardens

Reflection on department stores

how easily grenadine with seltzer goes through one's nose when one laughs (bar outside the Opera comique[1247])

Things worthy of imitation: Café Biard,[1248] traveling merchants, Duval,[1249] the trains in the station hall are in the open air
Lash of the whip on the boulev.
Max has a cold
keeping a game chip so that one can't get it

Airplane

Platform ticket, that coarse intervention in family life is unknown

rue de Cléry rises into the sky and falls into it.

Colonel Arthur Boucher
La france viktorieuse dans la guerre du demain. L'auteur ancien chef des operations militaires à l'Etat major de l'armee demontre que si la France etait ataquée elle saurait se defendre avec la certitude absolue de la victoire[1250]

Alone in the reading room[1251] with a hard-of-hearing lady to whom I introduced myself in vain when she was looking elsewhere and who considers the rain I indicated outside a lingering sultriness. She is telling fortunes with cards according to a book lying beside her into which she is looking intently, her head resting on her hand closed into a fist, in which there must be 100 still-unused little miniature cards printed on both sides. Next to me his back turned to me an old gentleman dressed in black is reading the Münchner neueste Nachrichten.—A heavy thick rain.—Traveled with a Jewish goldsmith. He is from Krakow, a little over 20 years old, was in America for 2 ½ years, has now been living in Paris for 2 months and has had only 14 days of work. Badly paid (only 10 fr daily) bad business environment. When someone newly arrives in a city, he doesn't know what his work is worth. Beautiful life in Amsterdam. Nothing but Krakovians. One knows every day what's new in Krakow, for someone is always going there or coming from there. Along whole streets only Polish is spoken. Great earnings in New York, for there all the girls earn a lot and can deck themselves out. Paris cannot compare with that, the first step onto the boulevards makes it apparent. Left New-York because his people are here, after all, and because they wrote to him, we're living in Krakow and earning money too, how much longer are you actually going to stay in America? Quite right. Enthusiasm for the life of the Swiss. Those must indeed be tremendously strong people, living in the country as they do and raising cattle. And the rivers! Certainly the main thing is to get into running water after waking up.—He has long, curly hair only occasionally worked through by his fingers, a strong gleam in his eyes, a slowly crooked nose, hollows at the bottom of his cheeks, an American cut suit, a frayed shirt, overhanging socks. His suitcase is small, but while getting off he carries it like a burden. His German unsettled by English stresses and phrases, the jargon can take a rest so strong is the English. Liveliness after traveling through the night. "You're an Austrian? Yes you have one of those rain capes too. All Austrians have them." I prove by showing my sleeves that it's not a cape but a coat. He continues to insist that all Austrians have capes. They put it on like this.—He turns to a third person and shows him how they do it. He pretends to fasten something to the back of his shirt collar, jerks his body to see whether it holds, then pulls this something first over his right arm, then over his left and finally wraps himself up in it completely until, as one can tell, he is feeling pleasantly warm. Movements of his legs show, although he is sitting, how easily and downright unconcernedly an Austrian can walk in one of those capes. There's almost no mockery at all in this, rather it is presented as if by someone who has traveled and hence seen some things. A somewhat childlike quality is mixed in.

My walk in the dark little garden in front of the sanatorium.

Morning gymnastics with singing of a Wunderhorn song[1252] that someone first plays on the cornet.

The secretary who takes journeys on foot every winter to Budapest, Southern France, Italy. Barefoot, then nourishes himself only on raw food (wholewheat bread, figs, dates) lives with 2 others for 14 days in the region around Nice mostly naked in an abandoned house.

Fat little girl, who often picks her nose, is clever but not especially pretty, has a nose without a future, is named Waltraute and who a young lady says has something radiant about her.

The columns in the dining hall, of which I was frightened from the picture in the prospectus (tall, shiny, marble through and through), because of which I cursed myself during the passage on the small steamer and which were in the end very plain, built of bricks, bear a bad marble design and are strikingly low.

Merry conversation of a man in the pear tree opposite my window with a girl not visible to me on the ground floor.

Pleasant feeling when the doctor listened to my heart again and again, kept wanting my body in a different position and could not sort things out. He felt the area around my heart for an especially long time, it lasted so long that it seemed almost unthinking.

Quarrel of the women at night in the compartment, the lamp of which they covered. How the Frenchwoman lying down screamed out of the darkness and the elderly woman pressed by her feet against the wall who spoke French badly didn't know what to do. In the Frenchwoman's opinion she should have left that seat, hauled all her luggage to the other side, the backseat and let her stretch out there. The Greek doctor from my compartment emphatically disagreed with her in bad clear French apparently based on the German language. I fetched the conductor who separated them.

Once again together with that lady, who moreover is a writing fiend too. She carries with her a writing case full of stationery, cards, pens and pencils, which on the whole is very encouraging.

Now it's like being in a family here. Outside it's raining, the mother is telling fortunes with cards and the son is writing. There's no one else in the room. Since she's hard of hearing, I could even call her Mother.

Despite my extreme aversion to the word "type" I do think it's true that naturopathy and all that goes with it is giving rise to a new type, represented, for example, by Hr. Fellenberg,[1253] whom I admittedly know only superficially. People with thin skin, rather small heads, exaggeratedly clean-looking, with one or two little details not befitting them (in Hr. F.'s case missing teeth, the beginning of a paunch), greater meagerness than seems appropriate to the structure of their bodies, that is, suppressed fat, treatment of their health as if it were an illness or at least a merit (by which I mean no reproach) with all the other consequences of so forced a feeling of health.

At the Opera comique on the gallery. In the first row a gentleman in a frock coat and top hat, in one of the last a man in a shirt (which he has even folded in at the front to uncover his chest), ready to climb into bed.[1254]

The trumpeter whom I would have regarded as a merry, happy person [for he is agile, has sharp ideas, his face is surrounded by a low growth of blond beard and ends in a pointed beard, he has reddened cheeks, blue eyes, is dressed practically], today in a conversation about his digestive complaints gave me a look that came strikingly with equal intensity from both eyes, that positively tensed his eyes, met me and went at an angle into the earth.

National disputes in Switzerland. Biel a completely German city a few years ago is in danger of being Frenchified by the immigration of many French watchmakers. Ticino the only Italian canton wants to secede from Switzerland. There's an irridentist[1255] movement. For the Ital. have no representation in the 7-member Federal Council, with their small number (perhaps 180,000) they would be entitled to it only in a 9-mem.

one. But they don't want to change the number. The Gotthard railroad was a German private enterprise, had German officials, they founded a German school in Bellinzona, now that it is state-run, the Italians want Italian officials and abolition of the German school. And indeed only the cantonal government has authority over the school system. Total population ⅔ German, ⅓ French & Italian.

The sick Greek doctor, who drove me out of the compartment in the middle of the night with his coughing, can as he claims digest only mutton. Since he must spend the night in Vienna, he asked me to write down the German term for him.

Despite the fact that it was raining, that I was later completely alone, that my unhappiness is always present to me, that in the dining hall they were playing parlor games in which I didn't participate due to inability, indeed despite the fact that I finally wrote only bad things I still felt neither the ugliness nor the dishonor nor the sadness nor the pain of this moreover organic aloneness, as if I consisted only of bones. At the same time it made me happy that on top of the block of my clogged intestines I thought I felt a bit of an appetite. The lady who fetched milk for herself in a tin cup, came back and asked me, before she worked her way back into her cards: What are you writing anyway? Observations? Diary? and since she knew that she wouldn't understand my answer, she immediately asked further "Are you a student?" I answered without thinking of her hardness of hearing: "No, but I was one" while she had already returned to her fortune-telling cards, I remained alone with this sentence and compelled by its weight looked at her for a while longer.

We are two men at a table with 6 or 7 Swiss women. How the most distant bowls, when my plate is only half empty or I look around the hall out of boredom, rise, quickly approach in the hands of the women (I address them as Frau and Fräulein in confusion) and when I say thank you and don't want any more slowly go back the way they came.

Le siège de Paris
par Francisque Sarcey[1256]
19 July 1870 Declaration of war. The changing celebrities of several days.—changing character of the book itself while it describes the changing character of Paris.—Praise and censure of the same things. The calm of Paris after defeats is at one point French levity at another Fr. resilience—4 Sept after Sedan the Republic—Workers and national guards on ladders knock the N off the pub. buildings with hammers—Even 8 days after proclamation of the Republic the enthusiasm was so great that they couldn't get anyone for the fortification work—The Germans are advancing. Parisian jokes: Mac-Mahon was captured at Sedan, Bazaine had surrendered Metz, finally the 2 armies have accomplished their unification—the order to destroy the suburbs—for 3 months no news—Never had Paris had such an appetite as at the beginning of the siege—Gambetta organized the uprising of the provinces. Once a letter from him was successfully received. But instead of providing the exact dates everyone was burning to know he wrote only que la resistance de Paris faisant l'admiration de l'univers.—Thiers tours the courts—Insane club meetings. A women's meeting au gymnase Triat. "How are the women to protect their honor from the enemy?" With the doigt de Dieu or better le doigt prussique. Il consiste en une sorte de dé en caoutchouc que les femmes se mettent au doigt. Au bout de ce dé est un petit tube contenant de l'acide prussique. When a German soldier comes, the hand is extended to him, he is pricked and sprayed—The institute sends out a scholar by balloon to study the solar eclipse in Algiers—They ate chestnuts from the previous year, the animals of the jardin des plantes—There were a few restaurants where one could get everything to the last day—That sergent Hoff who had become so famous for his murders of Prussians to avenge his father, then disappeared and was considered a spy—State of the army: particular advanced posts fraternize with the Germans over drinks—Louis Blanc compares the Germans with Mohicans who have studied at a technical university—on 5 I the bombardment begins. Makes little difference. It was ordered when one hears shells hissing to fling oneself down. Street boys even adults positioned themselves near puddles and cry from time to time "Gare l'obus"—For a while General Chanzy was the hope in Paris, he lost like everyone else, even at the time no one knew any reason for his celebrity, nonetheless the enthusiasm in Paris was so strong that Sarcey even when

he is writing his book feels a vague groundless admiration for Chanzy in himself—A day in Paris at that time: On the boulevards it was sunny and beautiful, people calmly strolling, things change toward Hotel de Ville, where there is a revolt of the Communards with many dead, troops are coming. On the left bank the Pruss. shells are hissing. Quay and bridges are quiet. Back to the Théâtre-Français. The audience is coming out of a performance of the Mariage de Figaro. The evening papers are just appearing, this audience gathers in groups around the kiosks, on the Champs Elysées children are playing, people on Sunday walks watch with curiosity a cavalry squadron riding by with trumpets. From a German's letter to his mother: Tu n'imagines pas, comme ce Paris est immense mais les Parisiens sont de drôles de gens; ils trompettent toute la journée.—For 14 days there was no warm water in Paris—End of January end of the 4 ½ mo. siege

20 *(September 1911)* comradely intercourse of old women in the compartment. Stories about old women run over by automobiles; their methods while traveling: never eat sauce, take out the meat, keep your eyes closed during the journey, but at the same time speak, with fruit eat bread, no hard veal, ask gentlemen to escort you across the streets, cherries are the heaviest fruit, the salvation of the old woman.[1257]

Siamese compartment[1258] in the Milan railroad station

Young Italian married couple on the train to Stresa mingles with another on the train to Paris. One husband only let himself be kissed and while looking out the window offered only his shoulder for her cheek. When he took off his coat in the heat and closed his eyes she seemed to look at him more closely. She wasn't pretty, she had only thin curly hair around her face. The other woman, however, with the veil, one of the blue dots of which often covered her eye, whose nose seemed cut off too soon, whose wrinkles around her mouth were youthful wrinkles, for the purposes of her youthful liveliness. Her eyes moved, when she lowered her face, back and forth, as I have seen at home only among people who wear eyeglasses.

[Efforts of all Frenchmen with whom one comes into contact to correct bad French at least for the moment.]

Young, badly shaven priest with the traveling picture postcard salesman, who is showing cards packed by the dozens, on which the priest is commenting. I look at him, also influenced a little by the heat so intently that I ultimately step on his cowl with the whole heel of my boot. Niente he says and goes on speaking always with a strong addition to his breathing indicated by an Italian Ah!

Sitting inside our carriage with the uncertain decisions regarding the hotel[1259] we seem to be driving the carriage uncertainly too, once turning it into a side street, then bringing it back onto the main route and this in the morning traffic of rue de Rivoli near the Halles

---

Stepping out onto my balcony for the first time and looking around as if I

Description of the gradual improvements of the Cafe Biard breakfasts[1260]

Euripides—King of Greece

Bettina and a colonel in the theater: May Bettina rest her head on your arm? If Bettina has no lice.[1261]

Stepping out onto my balcony for the first time and looking around as if I had just woken up in this room, while I'm actually so tired from the night journey that I don't know whether I'll be capable of running out into these streets for the whole day, especially the way I now see them from above, still without me.

Beginning of the Paris misunderstandings. Max comes up to my hotel room and is annoyed that I'm not ready yet and am washing my face, even though I had said before that we should just wash up a little and leave at once. Since with washing up a little I excluded only washing the whole body but meant washing the face in particular and am not yet finished doing precisely that, I don't understand his reproaches and keep washing my face even if not as thoroughly as before, while Max sits down on my bed to wait with the whole filth of the night journey in his clothes. When he is leveling reproaches, he has the habit and performs it now too of contracting his mouth but also his whole face in a saccharine way as if thereby seeking on the one hand to promote understanding of his reproaches and wanting on the other hand to show that this saccharine face he has at the moment is the only thing keeping him from slapping me. In the fact that I am forcing him into this hypocrisy against his nature lies another reproach, which he seems to level at me when he falls silent and in order to recover from the saccharine expression his face stretches apart in the opposite direction, that is, away from his mouth, which naturally has a much stronger effect than the original face. I, however, know how to be so withdrawn into myself with fatigue—so it was in Paris too—that the influence of such faces doesn't reach me at all, which is why I can be powerful enough in my misery to be able to apologize to him straight out of the most complete indifference and without any sense of guilt. In Paris at that time this appeased him at least apparently to the extent that he stepped out onto the balcony with me and commented on the view, above all how Parisian it was. I actually saw only how fresh he was, how he assuredly fit into some Paris that I didn't even perceive, how coming from his dark back room he now stepped out onto a Paris balcony in the sun for the first time in a year and was worthily aware of this, while I unfortunately was distinctly more tired than when I stepped out onto the balcony for the first time a little while before Max's arrival. And my fatigue in Paris cannot be remedied by sleeping but only by leaving. Sometimes I even regard this as a peculiarity of Paris.

I actually wrote this without antipathy, but he was at my heels with every word

---

At first I'm against Cafe Biard, because I believe that one can get only black coffee there. It turns out that milk is available too, even if only with bad spongy pastries. Almost the only improvement that has occurred to me for Paris is to provide better pastries in these cafes. Later I come up with the idea of wandering in the side streets and looking for fruit before breakfast while Max is already sitting. On the way to the cafe I always eat a bit up so that Max isn't too astonished. When we make a successful attempt in a good cafe near the station of the Vers. steam tram[1262] to finish eating apple strudel and almond pastries from a bakery under the eyes of a waiter leaning over us in the doorway, we introduce this in Cafe Biard too and find that apart from the enjoyment of the fine pastries one arrives at the more distinct enjoyment of the actual advantage of this cafe, namely being completely disregarded in a rather empty establishment, with good service, near all the people behind the counter and outside the always open shop door. Only one must reconcile oneself to the floor being swept, which because of the guests coming in directly from the street and shuffling back and forth at the counter is done often and during which the habit of disregarding the guests is not abandoned.

At the sight of the small bars on the route of the Versailles steam tram it seems easy for a young married couple to open such a bar and thus lead an outstanding interesting life free of risk and strenuous only at certain times of day. Even on the boulevards cheap bars of this sort are inserted in the side darkness between two side streets at the point of a wedge-shaped block of houses.

The guests in lime-spattered shirts around the small tables of the suburban taverns.

The cries of a woman with a small handcart of books in the evening on the Boulevard Poissoniere: Leaf through them, leaf through them gentlemen, take your pick, everything here is for sale. In the midst of her cries without urging him to buy it without even looking at him obtrusively she immediately names the price of the book that one of the surrounding people picks up. She seems to demand only that the books are leafed through more quickly, are exchanged more quickly, which one can understand when one watches how now and then someone, myself, for example, slowly picks up a book, slowly leafs through it a little, slowly puts it down and finally slowly walks away. The serious naming of the prices of books the indecency of which is so ridiculous that one at first cannot imagine making a purchase under the eyes of the whole crowd.

How much more decisiveness the purchase of a book demands outside the shop than inside, because this selection is actually only a free consideration in the chance presence of the books on display

---

Sitting on the two little chairs facing each other on the Champs Elysees. Children staying up much too late are still playing in the semidarkness in which they can no longer see well the lines they have drawn in the sand.

The closed bathhouse with a painted exterior that in my memory appears Turkish. It is illuminated iron gray in the middle of the afternoon, because sunlight only comes through the gaps in the cloths stretched above in individual rays in a corner and down below the river water helps darken the whole thing. Large room. In a corner a bar. The swimming masters run along either side of the pool snatching the customers from each other. They approach the visitor in front of his cubicle threateningly from the side and, speaking incomprehensibly but insistently, demand an unlocking fee. A demand in an incomprehensible language seems to me to be made discreetly. Grand bains du pont Royal. In the corners people stand on the steps washing themselves thoroughly with soap. The soapy water around them doesn't move. Through the gaps facing the river one sees something moving past, it's steamers. The paltriness of this swimming amusement becomes apparent when two men are entertaining themselves with an old rowboat that is no sooner pushed off from one wall than it crashes into the opposite one. Cellar smell. Beautiful green garden benches. A lot of German. In a swimming school a knotted rope hangs down over the water for any desired gymnastics.[1263] We ask about Musee Balzac,[1264] a pretty boy with his hair puffed up from the wetness explains to us that we mean the Musee Grevin (a wax museum).[1265] Ready to be of service, he has his cubicle opened, brings a small guidebook (perhaps a New Year's gift from some establishment) and doesn't find the Musee Balzac there either. We have already been inwardly thanking him continuously, since we foresaw it; and also urged him not to look for it. After all, it's not even in the Bottin.[1266]

Why was a policeman gendarme or soldier sitting in the box office of the Theatre Francais[1267] in the morning?

A fat placeuse in the Opera Com. rather condescendingly takes our tip.[1268] I thought it was due to the fact that we had come up somewhat too gradually one behind the other with our theater tickets in our hands and I resolved to refuse the placeuse a tip to her face the next evening at the Comedie, while now feeling ashamed before her and myself I gave her a large tip. Even as everyone else was coming in without a tip. At the Comedie I even uttered my remark calling the tip something in my opinion "not inevitable," but had to pay again when the placeuse, this time a thin one, complained that she wasn't compensated by the management and leaned her face toward her shoulder

---

Boot polishing scene in the beginning. How the children accompanying the guard walk down the stairs in step. Impression of the casually played overture so that those coming late have an easy entrance, usually only operettas are treated like this. Real simplicity of the staging. Sleepy extras, as at all performances I saw in Paris whereas at home they often have a poorly restrained liveliness. The donkey for the first act of Carmen surrounded outside the theater entrance in the narrow street by theatergoers and some street spectators, waits in the semidarkness until the small entrance doorway is clear. On the outside steps I buy almost consciously one of those false programs that are sold outside all theaters. A ballerina dances for Carmen in the smugglers' tavern. How her silent body works while Carmen is singing.[1269] Later Carmen's dance composed of individual elements, which is actually much more beautiful due to her merits in the performance up to now. It looks as if she had taken a few hasty lessons with the leading ballerina before the performance. The footlights make her soles white when she leans against the table, listens to someone and lets her feet play against each other under her green skirt.

A person who has no diary is in a false position in the face of a diary. When, for example, he reads in Goethe's diary that on 11 January 1797 the latter was busy at home all day with various arrangements, it seems to this person that he himself has never done so little.[1270]

For the last act we are already too tired (I was even for the next to last) leave and sit down in a bar across from the Opera comique where Max in his tiredness sprays soda water all over me and I in my tiredness can't contain myself and laugh so hard that the grenadine comes out of my nose. In the meantime the last act has probably begun, we walk home

---

On this square, after the heat in the theater, where I had fanned the hot air on my chest through my open shirt, I became especially conscious of the night air, of sitting outdoors, of stretching out my legs onto a city square, even though the illuminated large theater facade with the side lights of the theater cafes sufficed to light up the small square, especially its ground to under the little tables like a room.

Gentleman in the foyer, who is entertaining two ladies, in a dress suit, which hangs somewhat loosely and which if it weren't new weren't worn here and fit better could be historical. Monocle dropped and picked up again. When the conversation falters, taps his cane on the floor uncertainly. Stands with his arm jerking constantly, as if he intended at any moment to clear the way for his ladies through the middle of the crowd with outstretched arm. Faded worn skin of his face.

The German language's quality of becoming beautiful in the mouths of foreigners who have no command of it and usually want none. As far as we have observed Frenchmen, we could never see that they took pleasure in our errors in French or so much as found those errors worth hearing and even we whose French can bring forth only little feeling for the French language,

to be continued!

The—from my point of view—happy cooks and waiters who after the general meal eat salad beans and potatoes, make mixtures of them in large bowls, take only a little of each dish, even though a lot is served them and from a distance look like cooks and waiters at home.—Waiter whose mouth and little beard are elegantly contracted and who serves me one day, in my opinion, only because I'm tired, awkward, unthinking and disagreeable and therefore could not get food for myself, whereas he brings it to me almost without being aware of it.

At Düval[1271] on the Boulevard Sebastopol at twilight. Three guests scattered in the establishment. The waitresses speaking softly with each other. The counter still empty. I order a yogurt then another. The waitress brings it silently, the semidarkness of the establishment also contributes to the silence, she is also silent as she takes away the cutlery that had been set at my place in preparation for dinner and could hinder my drinking. I found it very pleasant to be able to sense tolerance and understanding of my woes in a woman who was so silent.

Ridiculous restaurant on Rue Richelieu. Densely packed. Ugly sight of the smoke in front of plate-glass panes. Clothes hooks full of hats at regular intervals like trees. Custom of the railings between small tables. Immediately after the awkward foreigner's illusion that where there's a railing-like frame there must also be a glass pane is cleared up by looking boldly into the pane in which one believes one sees the reflection of distant guests and realizing from their looking back that one is dealing with real faces—one feels how such railings between small tables placed side by side are especially conducive to closeness.

In the Louvre from one bench to the next. Pain when one is skipped.

Crowd in the Salon Carré,[1272] excited mood, standing in groups as if the Mona Lisa had just been stolen.[1273]

Convenience of the crossbars in front of the pictures, on which one can lean, especially in the hall of the primitives.[1274]

This compulsion to look with Max at his favorite pictures, since I'm too tired to look around by myself. Looking up admiringly

---

The strength of a tall young Englishwoman who walks with her companion from one end of the longest hall[1275] to the other.

Sight of Max reading Phaedra[1276] under a street lamp outside Aristide[1277] and ruining his eyes with the small print. Why does he never follow my lead. Unfortunately I still benefit from it, since on the way to the theater he tells me everything he read in his Phaedra on the street while I was having dinner. Short walk, Max's straining to tell me everything, everything, a straining on my part too.

Military spectacle in the foyer. Soldiers regulate in accordance with military principles the forward movement of the crowd pushed back several meters from the box office.

Supposed claqueur in our row. Her applause seems to follow the cane taps of the chief claqueur busy above us in the last balcony. She claps with her absent face bent so far forward that, when the applause is over, she looks with astonished concern at the palms of her openwork gloves. But immediately begins again if necessary. But ultimately claps independently too and is not a claqueur at all.

The feeling of equality with the play that theatergoers must have to arrive toward the end of the first act and make whole rows of people stand up. A set that remains in place through 5 acts contributes a great deal to the seriousness and, even if it is only made of paper, is more solid than a changing one made of wood and stone.

A group of pillars held up against the sea and the blue air, overgrown with climbing plants on top. Direct influence of the Banquet by Veronese, also of Claude Lorrain.[1278]

Hypolit's mouth calmly curved in the same way whether closed, opening or open.[1279]

Oenone, easily falling into enduring positions, at one point upright, her legs tightly bound by her robe, her arm raised, with a steady fist, she recites a verse.[1280] Much slow covering of faces with hands. Gray color of the advisers of the main characters.

Dissatisfaction with the actress playing Phaedra in the memory of the satisfaction I've had with Rachel as a memb. of the Comedie Francais whenever I have read about her.[1281]

At a sight as surprising as the first scene, where Hypolite is holding the motionless bow as tall as a man beside him, intending to confide in his tutor, and with his calm proud gaze directed at the audience recites his verses like a celebratory poem, I had, as often in the past, the impression, though it was very weak, that this is happening for the first time and the rest of my admiration mingled with the admiration for its succeeding at the very first attempt.

Memory of the performance of "Des M. & d. L. Wellen" in Reichenberg.[1282] The actors there were more delicate, weaker,

to be continued

Rationally arranged brothels. The clean blinds of the large windows of the whole house lowered. In the porter's lodge instead of a man a respectably dressed woman, who could be at home anywhere. Even in Prague I have always taken passing notice of the Amazon-like character of the brothels. Here it is even more distinct. The female porter who sounds her electr. bell, who keeps us in her lodge because she is informed that guests are presently coming down the stairs, the two respectable women upstairs (why two?) who receive us, the turning on of the electr. light in the next room where the unoccupied girls were sitting in the dark or half-dark, the ¾ circle (we complete the circle) in which they stand around us in upright positions intentionally favorable to them, the long stride with which the selected one steps forward, the grasp of the madam with which she encourages me . . . I feel pulled to the exit. Impossible to imagine how I got onto the street, so quick was it. It's hard to take a closer look at the girls there, because they are too many, blink their eyes, above all stand too close. One would have to open one's eyes wide and that takes practice. In my memory I have actually only the one who was standing directly in front of me. She was gap-toothed, stretched herself upward, held her dress together with her fist clenched over her private parts and opened and closed immediately and quickly her large eyes and large mouth. Her blond hair seemed tousled. She was thin. Fear lest I forget not to take my hat off. One must tear one's hand away from the brim. Lonely, long senseless walk home.

Gathering of the visitors before the opening of the Louvre. The girls sit between the tall columns, read the Bädeker,[1283] write postcards.

Venus de Milo, the sight of which changes quickly and surprisingly no matter how slowly you circle it. Unfortunately made a forced remark (about waist and drapery) but also some true ones, for the memory of which I would need a sculptural reproduction, especially about how the bent left knee influences the sight from all sides, but sometimes only very weakly. The forced remark: One expects that above the point where the drapery ends the body will immediately narrow, but it first grows even broader. The falling garment held by the knee.

The Borghese Gladiator, the front view of which is not the main view, for it makes the viewer back away and is more scattered. Seen from behind, however, where the foot first begins on the ground, the surprised gaze is lured along the tensed leg and flies safely over the inexorable back to the arm and sword raised forward.[1284]

The metro seemed very empty to me at that time, especially when I compare it with the ride I took sick and alone to the race.[1285] Even leaving aside the number of passengers, the appearance of the metro is subject to the influence of Sunday. The dark steel color of the walls was predominant. The work of the conductors pushing the carriage doors open and shut and swinging themselves in and out between them presented itself as Sunday afternoon work. The long passageways to the correspondance were walked down slowly. The unnatural indifference of the passengers with which they submit to the ride in the metro became more distinct. Facing the glass doors, getting off individually at unknown stations far from the Opera is experienced as capricious. Despite the electr. lighting the changing daylight is definitely noticeable in the stations, one notices it especially when one has just climbed down, especially that afternoon light just before it grows dark. The arrival in the empty terminus of porte Dauphine, a lot of tubes becoming visible, view into the loop where the trains are permitted to make their only turn after so long a ride in a straight line. Rides through tunnels on the railroad are much worse, no trace of the oppression that the passenger feels under the pressure, even if held back, of the mountain masses. One is also not far from people but rather an urban facility, like the water in the pipes, for example. The recoiling when getting off, followed by the now stronger forward movement. This getting off onto the same level. Mostly abandoned little offices with telephones and signal bells direct the traffic. Max likes to look in. The noise of the metro was horrible when I rode it for the first time in my life from Montmartre to the great boulevards. Otherwise it's not bad, even strengthens the pleasant calm feeling of speed. The Dubonnet advertisement is very well suited to being read, awaited and observed by sad and unoccupied passengers. Elimination of speech from the transportation system, since neither when paying nor when getting on & off does one have to speak. Because it is easily understood, the metro is the best opportunity for an expectant and frail foreigner to acquire the belief that at the first attempt he has correctly and quickly penetrated the essence of Paris.

One recognizes the foreigners by the fact that up on the last landing of the metro stairs they no longer know their way around, unlike the Parisians they don't disappear without transition from the metro into the street life. When we come out reality also corresponds to the map only slowly, since this place where after coming up we are now deposited is somewhere we never would have reached on foot or by carriage without the guidance of the map. The memory of walks in parks is always wonderful.[1286] Pleasure in the fact that it is still so light, watching out that it doesn't get dark quickly, this and fatigue govern one's way of walking and looking around. The tight driving of the automobiles on the large smooth street. The red-clad orchestra that in the noise of the automobiles is working inaudibly at its instruments in a small garden restaurant only for the enjoyment of its immediate surroundings. Never-seen Parisians lead each other by the hand. Burnt earth-colored grass. Men in shirtsleeves with their families in the semidarkness of the trees in flowerbeds even after being warned to keep off. Here the absence of Jews was the most conspicuous. The look back at the little steam train, which seems to have unreeled from a merry-go-round and rolled away. The path to the lake. My strongest memory of the first sight of this lake[1287] is the bent back of the man who leaning toward us in the boat under the taut cloth covering, handed us the tickets. Probably due to my worry about the ticket and my inability to compel the man to explain whether the boat goes around the lake or crosses to the island and whether it makes stops. Therefore I fell so under his spell that I sometimes see him alone, just as bent over the lake but without the boat. Many people in summer clothes on the landing place. Boats with clumsy rowers. Low shore of the lake without a railing. Slow ride, reminds me of walks I took alone every Sunday several years ago. Pulling my feet out of the water on the floor of the boat. Astonishment of passengers listening to our Czech[1288] at having sat down with such foreigners in a boat. Many people on the slopes of the western shore, canes planted, newspapers spread, man with his daughters flat in the grass, little laughter, low eastern shore, path boundary long since abolished at home made of small, conjoined curved pieces of wood, suited to keeping lapdogs off the grass, a wild dog runs across the meadows, seriously working rowers with a girl in their heavy boat. I leave Max especially lonely with a grenadine in the darkness at the edge of a half-empty café garden, near which a street passes, which is itself crossed downright casually by another unknown one. Automobiles and carriages drive from this dark intersection into even more desolate areas. A large iron gate belongs perhaps to the consumption tax office, but is open and lets anyone through. Nearby one sees the harsh light of Luna Park[1289] that increases the disorder of this semidarkness. So much light and so empty. On the way to Luna Park and back to Max I stumble perhaps 5 times.

Monday 11 Sept. *(1911)* On asphalt pavement automobiles are easier to steer but also harder to stop.[1290] Especially when a private individual is at the wheel, taking advantage of the size of the streets, the beautiful day, his light automobile, his driving skills for a short business trip and at the same time is supposed to weave his way in the car at intersections like the pedestrians on the sidewalk. That's why such an automobile, just before the entrance to a small street while still on the large square drives into a tricycle, but stops elegantly, doesn't do much damage to it, practically just steps on its foot, but while a pedestrian whose foot is stepped on like that hurries onward all the more quickly, the tricycle doesn't move and has a bent front wheel. The baker's assistant who until now has been driving along on this vehicle belonging to the——— company in a completely carefree manner with that ponderous rocking peculiar to three-wheelers, dismounts, walks up to the motorist, who likewise dismounts, and levels reproaches at him that are dulled by the respect for an automobile owner and spurred on by the fear of his boss. First it's a matter of explaining how the accident happened. The automobile owner represents the approaching automobile with his raised palms, now he sees the trycycle getting in his way, his right hand breaks free and waves back and forth to warn the tricycle, his face is worried, for what automobile can brake at this distance. Will the tricycle realize it and let the automobile go first? No, it's too late, his left hand stops warning, both hands unite for the collision, his knees bend to observe the last moment. It has happened and the bent tricycle standing there motionless can now help with the further description. Against this the baker's assistant cannot easily prevail. Firstly the motorist is an educated lively man, secondly he has been sitting in the automobile until now, has rested, can soon sit down in it again and rest more and thirdly he really had a better view of the event from the height of the automobile. In the meantime several people have gathered and as the motorist's performance deserves are not actually standing in a circle around him but rather before him. The traffic meanwhile must manage without the space taken up by this group, which, moreover, shifts back and forth in accordance with whatever occurs to the motorist. Thus, for example, they all move to the tricycle at one point to take a closer look at the damage about which so much has been said. The motor. doesn't consider it bad, (some side with him in moderately loud discussions) although he doesn't content himself with merely looking but also walks around it, looks in from above and through from below. Someone who wants to shout advocates, since the mot. doesn't need shouting, for the tricycle; but he is answered very well and very loudly by a newly appearing stranger, who if one is unswayed, was accompanying the mot. Several times some spectators can't help laughing together, but always calm themselves down with new sober ideas. Now there's actually no great diff. of opinion bet. mot. & bak., the mot. finds himself surrounded by a small friendly crowd of people he has convinced, the baker's boy gradually stops monotonously stretching out his arms and leveling reproaches, the mot. doesn't deny, after all, that he has caused some slight damage, by no means puts all the blame on the bak. either, both of them are to blame, thus neither, these things just happen, etc. In short the affair would end in embarrassment, the votes of the spectators, who are already conferring about the price of the repair, would have to be demanded, if they did not remember that they could fetch a policeman. The baker's boy who has fallen into a more and more subordinate position to the mo., is simply sent by him for a pol. and entrusts his tricycle to the protection of the mot. Not with ill intent, for it isn't necessary for him to form a party in his favor, he doesn't cease his descriptions even in his opponent's absence. Because one tells stories better while smoking, he rolls himself a cigarette. In his pocket he has a supply of tobacco. Uninformed new arrivals and even if they are only shop assistants are led systematically first to the automobile, then to the tricycle and only then provided the details. If he hears an objection from someone standing farther back in the crowd, he answers him on tiptoe in order to be able to look him in the face. It turns out that it's too cumbersome to lead the people back and forth between aut. & t., therefore the automobile is driven into the street closer to the sidewalk. An intact tricycle stops and the driver takes a look at the situation. As if to teach a lesson about the difficulties of automobile driving a large motor omnibus has stopped in the middle of the square. The engine is being worked on in front. The first to bend down around the vehicle are its disembarked passengers, rightly feeling their closer connection. In the meantime the mot. has established a little order and pushed the tr. closer to the sidewalk too. The situation is losing its pub. interest. New arrivals now have to guess what has actually happened. With several old spect. who have value as witnesses the mot. has positively withdrawn and is speaking softly with them. But where has the poor boy been wandering around in the meantime? Finally they see him in the distance, beginning to cross the square with the pol. They weren't impatient but their revived interest is immediately apparent. Many new spectators appear, who will have the extreme pleasure of the statement-taking at low cost. The mot. parts from his group and approaches the pol., who takes in the affair immediately with the same calm that the involved parties have attained only after waiting for half an hour. The st.-taking begins without a long investig. With the ponderousness of a construction worker the p. pulls an old dirty but blank sheet of paper out of his notebook, takes down the names of the inv. parties, writes down the baking company and to get it right walks around the tricycle while writing. The unconscious unreasonable hope of everyone present for an immediate objective conclusion of the whole affair by the pol. passes into the joy in the details of the st.-tak. This st. falters at times. The pol. has somewhat muddled his notes and in the effort to restore them hears and sees nothing else for brief stretches. Namely, he began writing on the sheet in a place where for some reason he should not have begun. But now it has indeed happened and his astonishment at this is often renewed. He must keep turning the sheet around in order to believe the bad beginning of his notes. But since he quickly abandoned this bad beginning and began writing elsewhere too, when a column is finished, he cannot possibly know without a great deal of unfolding and searching where the correct place is for him to continue. The calm the affair thereby gains cannot even be compared with the earlier one attained by the inv. part. alone.

June-July 1912 Trip

Weimar-Jungborn Trip
from 28 June 1912–29 July

Friday 28 v *(June 1912)* Departure state railroad station. Feeling well. Sokols delay the train's departure.[1291] Lay undressed stretched out to my full length on the bench. Bank of the Elbe. Beautiful situation of the villages and villas, similar to lake shores. Dresden. Great quantities of fresh goods everywhere. Clean proper service. Calmly spoken words. Massive appearance of the buildings due to the concrete engineering, yet in America, for example, it doesn't have the same effect. The otherwise calm Elbe water marbled with eddies.—Leipzig. Conversation with our porter. Max asks him even though he looks like our grandfather about girls. Opels Hotel.[1292] The half-built new railroad station. Beautiful ruin of the old one.[1293] Shared room. From 4 o'clock on buried alive, because Max has to close the windows due to the noise. Great noise. Judging by ear, one carriage is pulling the next behind it. Because of the asphalt the horses sound like running riding horses. The ringing of the tram receding, its interruptions suggesting streets and squares. Evening in Leipzig. Max's topographic instinct, my lostness. On the other hand, I discover, later confirmed by the guidebook, a beautiful oriel on the Fürstenhaus.[1294] Night work on a construction site, probably on the site of Auerbachs Keller.[1295] Irremediable dissatisfaction with Leipzig. Indecisiveness in the narrow brothel streets. My shoelace tying is discussed from the street to the window. Enticing Café Oriental. "Taubenschlag" beer tavern. The lumbering long-bearded beer father. His wife pours.

Two tall strong daughters serve. Compartments in the tables. Lichtenhainer in wooden mugs. Foul smell when one opens the lid. A frail regular guest, reddish gaunt cheeks, wrinkled nose is sitting with a large group, then stays behind alone, the girl sits down with her beer glass at his table. The picture of the regular guest who died 12 years ago, who had been coming here for 14 years. He is raising his glass, behind him a skeleton. Many heavily bandaged students in Leipzig. Many monocles. Brief visit to a b.[1296] A girl with breast jewelry is having a rib for dinner. Our unclear information about the reason for our immediate departure. Friday *(Saturday)* 29 *(June 1912)* Breakfast. Misjudgment of an encounter between the hotelier and his daughter. The gentleman who on Saturday won't sign the receipt of a remittance. A walk. Max to Rohwolt.[1297] Book trade museum.[1298] Can't contain myself in the presence of all the books. The antiquated streets of this publishing quarter, despite straight streets and newer albeit unadorned houses. Public reading room.[1299] Lunch at "Manna."[1300] Bad. Met Brandeis there.[1301] Rendezvous with Max in front of the Goethe monument[1302] at 2. Goodbye to Brandeis. Wilhelms Weinstube,[1303] dim establishment in a courtyard. Rohwolt. Young red-cheeked, sweat standing still between nose and cheeks, moving only from the hips on. Count Bassewitz, author of "Judas"[1304] tall, nervous, a dry face, play in his waist, well-treated strong body. Hasenclever,[1305] Jewish, loud, a lot of shadow and brightness in his small face, bluish colors too. All 3 swing canes and arms. Peculiar daily lunch in the wine tavern. Large broad wine cups with slices of lemon. In the Cafe Francais[1306] later, Pinthus,[1307] correspondent for the B. T.,[1308] fat, a rather flat face, corrects the typescript of a review of "Johanna v. Neapel"[1309] (premiere the previous evening). Hasencl.'s proposal to have our afternoon coffee in a b.[1310] Not admitted, because the ladies sleep until 4 o'clock. The madams coming together out of the darkness. Café Francais. R. quite seriously wants a book from me.[1311] Personal obligations of the publishers and their influence on the daily average of German literature. At the publishing house.—Departure for Weimar 5 o'clock. The old maid in the compartment. Dark skin. Beautifully rounded chin and cheeks. How the seams of the stockings twisted around her legs, her face was covered with her newspaper and we looked at her legs. Weimar. She gets off there too after she had put on a large old hat. I saw her once later when I was observing the Goethe House from the marketplace. Long way to Hotel Chemnitius.[1312] Almost lost heart. Search for bathhouses.

Three-part suites assigned to us. Max is to sleep in a hole with a skylight. Open-air bathhouse on Kirschberg.[1313] Schwanensee.[1314] A walk at night to the Goethe House. Immediate recognition. Yellowish-brown color of the whole thing. Tangible participation of our whole previous life in the present impression. The darkness of the windows of the uninhabited rooms. The light-colored Juno bust. Touching the wall. White shades lowered a little in all the rooms. 14 street-facing windows. The chain on the door. No picture captures the whole thing. The uneven square, the fountain, the broken alignment of the house following the rising square. The dark somewhat oblong windows set into the brownish yellow. Even in itself the most striking middle-class residential house in Weimar.

Sunday 30 *(June 1912)* Morning. Schiller House.[1315] Deformed woman who comes forward and with a few words, mainly by her tone apologizes for the presence of these souvenirs. On the stairs Clio as a diarist. Picture of the 100th birthday celebration 10 Nov. 1859, the decorated, widened house. Italian views, Bellagio, gifts from Goethe. No-longer-human locks of hair, yellow and dry as beards of grain. Maria Pavlovna,[1316] delicate neck, face no wider, large eyes. The most varied Schiller heads. Good arrangement of a writer's dwelling. Waiting room, reception room, study, sleeping alcoves. Frau Junot,[1317] his daughter resembles him. "Baumzucht im Grossen nach Erfahrungen in Kleinen," his father's book.[1318]

Goethe House. Reception rooms. Glimpse of the study and bedroom. Sad sight reminiscent of dead grandfathers. That garden growing continuously since Goethe's death. The beech tree darkening his study. She had already run past us with her little sister when we were sitting at the foot of the stairs.[1319] In my memory the plaster cast of a greyhound at the foot of the stairs is associated with this running. Then we saw her again in the Juno room, then while looking out from the garden room. Many other times I thought I heard her footsteps and her voice. Two carnations handed through the balcony railing. Went into the garden too late. Max sees her up on a balcony. She comes down, only later, with a young man. As we pass I thank her for having called our attention to the garden. But we don't leave yet. Her mother comes, some intercourse develops in the garden. She is standing by a rosebush. Pushed by Max I go to her, learn of the excursion to Tiefurt. I'll go too.[1320] She's going with her parents. She mentions an inn from which one can observe the door of the Goethe House. Gasthaus zum Schwan.[1321] We sit between ivy trellises. She comes out the front door. I run over, introduce myself to everyone, get permission to go with them and run back again. Later the family comes without her father. I want to join them, no, they're going to have coffee first, I am to follow with her father. She tells me to go into the house at 4. I fetch her father after saying goodbye to Max. Conversation with the coachman outside the gate. Walk with her father. Conversation about Silesia, Grand Duke, Goethe, National Museum,[1322] photography and drawing and the nervous age. Stop outside the house where they are having coffee. He runs up to call everyone to the oriel window because he wants to take a photograph. Out of nervousness played ball with a little girl. Walk with the men, in front of us the two women, in front of them the 3 girls. A small dog runs back and forth among us. Castle in Tiefurt.[1323] Tour with the 3 girls. She has a lot of these things in the Goethe House too and better. Explanations in front of the Werther pictures. Room of Fräulein von Göchhausen.[1324] The walled-up door. The replica of a poodle. Then setting off with her parents. Taking photographs twice in the park. Once on a bridge, which won't turn out well. Finally on the way back definite connection without a real relationship. Rain. The stories of Breslau carnival jokes at the archive. Goodbye outside the house. My standing around on Seifengasse.[1325] Max has slept in the meantime. Incomprehensibly meeting 3 times in the evening. She with her girlfriend. The first time we accompany them. In the evening after 6 I can always come into the garden. Now she has to go home. Then meeting again on the circle, which has been prepared for a duel. They are speaking with a young man in a manner more hostile than friendly. But why didn't they stay home, since we had escorted them to Goetheplatz.[1326] Hadn't they had to get home as quickly as possible? But why were they running now, apparently without having been home at all, pursued by the young man or in order to meet him out of Schillerstrasse, down the small staircase, onto the out-of-the-way circle?[1327] Why, after having spoken a few words with the young man at a distance of 10 paces and apparently declined his company, were they turning around again there and running back alone? Had we disturbed them when we had passed by with only a simple greeting? Later we walked back slowly; when we arrived on Goetheplatz, they ran, apparently very frightened, once again out of another street almost into our hands. We turned around out of consideration. But they had thus taken a detour once again.

Monday 1 July *(1912)*. Garden house on the Stern. Made a drawing in the grass in front of it.[1328] Learned the verse on the resting spot by

heart.[1329] Suitcase bed. Sleep. Parrot in the courtyard calling Grete. Went in vain to Erfurter Allee,[1330] where she is learning to sew. Bathing. Tuesday 2 *(July 1912)* Goethe House. Attic rooms. Looked at the photographs with the caretaker. Children standing around. Photography conversations. Constant watching out for a chance to speak with her. She goes to sewing with a friend. We stay behind.—Liszt House in the afternoon.[1331] Virtuosic. Old Pauline.[1332] Liszt worked from 5–8 o'clock, then church, then second sleep, visitors from 11 on. Max at the bathhouse, I fetch the photographs, meet her beforehand, come with her up to the door. Her father shows me the pictures, I bring photograph stands, but finally I have to go. She smiles at me senselessly uselessly behind her father's back. Sad. Idea of having the photographs enlarged. To the druggist's. Back again to the Goethe House for the negatives. She sees me from the window and opens the door.—Frequently meeting Grete. While eating strawberries; outside Werthers Garten, where there's a concert. The agility of her body in her loose dress. The tall officers coming out of the "Russischer Hof."[1333] All sorts of uniforms. The slender, strong ones in the dark clothes.—The fight in the out-of-the-way street. "You must be the greatest dirty scoundrel!" The people at the windows. The departing family, a drunkard, an old woman with a back basket and 2 boys as appendages.—The fact that I have to leave soon constricts my throat. Discovery of "Tivoli." The old snake lady, her husband, who serves as magician. The female Deutschmeisters.[1334]
Wednesday 3 July *(1912)*. Goethe House. Photographs are to be taken in the garden. She is nowhere to be seen, I am then permitted to fetch her. She is always quite trembling with movement, but moves only when one speaks to her. Photographs are taken. The two of us on the bench.[1335] Max shows the man how to do it. She grants me a rendezvous for the next day.—Öttingen[1336] looks through the window and forbids Max and me, presently standing alone at the camera, to take photographs. But we aren't taking photographs!—At that time her mother was still friendly. Leaving aside the schools and the nonpaying visitors 30,000 people come a year.—Bathhouse. Serious, calm wrestling matches of the children.—Grand ducal library[1337] in the afternoon. Trippel bust.[1338] The guide's praise. The always recognizable Grand Duke.[1339] Massive chin and thick lips. Hand in his buttoned coat. Goethe bust by David,[1340] with hair bristled back and large tense face. The transformation, undertaken by Goethe, of a palace into a library.[1341] Busts of Passow[1342] (pretty

curly-haired boy), Zach. Werner,[1343] narrow, searching, penetrating face. Gluck. "Cast from life." The holes in the mouth from the tubes through which he breathed.[1344] Goethe's study. Through a door one steps directly into the garden of Frau v. Stein. The staircase fashioned by a convict out of a gigantic oak without a single nail.[1345]—A walk in the park with the carpenter's son Fritz Wenski.[1346] His serious speeches. At the same time he strikes the bushes with a branch. He will be a carpenter too and wander. Now people no longer wander as in his father's time, the railroad spoils them. To become a guide one would have to know languages, thus either learn them in school or buy books of that sort. What he knows about the park he either learned in school or heard from the guides. Striking guide-remarks that are incongruous with the rest, for example, about the Roman House[1347] nothing but: The door was meant for the purveyors. Bark Hut.[1348] Shakespeare monument.[1349]—Children around me on Karlsplatz. Conversations about the navy. The seriousness of the children. Discussion of shipwrecks. Superiority of the children. Promise of a ball. Giving out of cookies. Garden concert Carmen.[1350] Completely thrilled by it.

Thursday 4 July *(1912)* Goethe House. Confirmation of the promised rendezvous with a loud yes. She was looking out the door. False explanation of this, for even while we were present she looked out. I asked once again: "Even if it's raining?" "Yes." Max leaves for Jena to visit Diederichs.[1351] I to the ducal vault.[1352] With the officers. Over Goethe's coffin golden laurel wreath donated by the German women of Prague in 1882. Found everyone again at the cemetery. Tomb of the Goethe family. Walter von Goethe b. Weimar 9 Apr. 1818, † Leipzig 15 Apr. 1885 "with him expired the house of Goethe, whose name outlasts all ages," epitaph of Fr. Karoline Falk: "Though God took 7 of her own children, she became a mother to the children of strangers. God will wipe away all tears from her eyes." Charlotte von Stein: 1742–1827.—Bathhouse—Didn't sleep in the afternoon in order to keep an eye on the uncertain weather. She didn't come to the rendezvous.—Meet Max dressed in bed. Both unhappy. If one could pour the sorrow out the window.—In the evening Hiller with his mother.[1353]—I run away from the table, because I thought I saw her. Was mistaken. Then everyone to the Goethe House. Greeted her.

Friday 5 July *(1912)* A walk to the Goethe House in vain.—Goethe-Schiller Archive.[1354] Letters from Lenz.[1355]—Letter from the citizens of

Frankfurt to Goethe 28 August 1830: "Some citizens of the old city on the Mayn, long accustomed here to greeting the 28th of August with cups in their fists, would praise the favor of heaven if they could welcome personally to the precincts of the Free City the rare Frankfurt man whom this day brought.

But because from year to year they go on hoping and waiting and wishing, for the time being they extend the gleaming goblet across woods and meadows, borders and tolls to the lucky city on the Ilm and ask their revered compatriot to grant them the privilege of clinking glasses with him in their thoughts and singing:

Willst Du Absolution
Deinen Treuen geben
Wollen wir nach Deinem Wink
Unablässig streben
Uns vom Halben zu entwöhnen
und im Ganzen Guten Schönen
resolut zu leben."[1356]

1757 "Sublime Grandma! . . ."[1357]

Jerusalem to Kestner: "Might I most humbly request Your Excellency's pistols for a planned journey?"[1358]
Mignon's Song with nothing struck through.—
Fetched the photographs. Brought them there. Stood around uselessly, delivered only 3 of the 6 photographs. And precisely the worse ones in the hope that to vindicate himself, the caretaker will take photographs anew. Not a trace.—Bathhouse—Directly from there to Erfurter Strasse. Max for lunch. She comes with 2 girlfriends. I take her aside. Yes she had to leave 10 min. earlier yesterday, has learned only now from her girlfriends of my waiting yesterday. She also had trouble because of her dancing lessons. She definitely doesn't love me, but she has some respect. I give her the box of chocolates entwined with the little heart and the chain and accompany her a stretch. A few words back and forth about a rendezvous. Tomorrow at 11 in front of the Goethe House. It can only be an excuse, she certainly has to cook, and then in front of the Goethe House, but I still accept it. Sad acceptance. Go to the hotel, sit for a

little while with Max, who is lying in bed. Excursion to Belvedere in the afternoon.[1359] Hiller and his mother. Beautiful ride in the carriage down a single alley. Surprising arrangement of the castle, which consists of a main part and 4 small houses arranged at its sides, all low and delicately colored. A low fountain in the middle. View forward toward Weimar. The Grand Duke has not been here for several years. He's a hunter and there's no hunting here. The calm accommodating servant with a clean-shaven angular face, sad as perhaps all people are who move among masters. Sorrow of the pets. Maria Pavlovna, daughter-in-law of the Grand Duke Karl August, daughter of Maria Feodorovna and of Emperor Paul, who was strangled. Many Russian things. Cloisoné copper vessels with hammered-on wires between which the enamel is poured. The bedrooms with the dome of the sky. Photographs in the still habitable rooms the only modernization. How they will also integrate themselves unobserved! Goethe's room, a corner room downstairs. Several ceiling paintings by Oeser, touched up beyond recognition. Many Chinese things. The "dark room of the lady's maids." The nature theater with the two rows of seats. The carriage consisting of back-to-back benches, dos à dos, in which the ladies sat while their escorting cavaliers rode alongside them. The heavy carriage in which Maria Pavlovna and her husband rode with three horses from St. Petersburg to Weimar in 26 days on their wedding journey. Nature theater and park laid out by Goethe.—To Paul Ernst's in the evening.[1360] In the street asked 2 girls about the apartment of the writer P. E. At first they look at us thoughtfully, then one nudges the other, as if she wanted to remind her of a name that isn't coming to her mind at the moment. Do you mean Wildenbruch?[1361] the other then asks us.—Paul Ernst. Mustache going over his mouth and pointed beard. Clings to the chair or his knees, though even when he is agitated (due to his critics) he doesn't go off.—Lives on the Horn.[1362] A villa apparently completely filled with his family. A bowl of strong-smelling fish, which was supposed to be carried up the stairs, is at the sight of us brought back to the kitchen again.—Entrance of Father Expeditus-Schmitt, with whom I collided once on the hotel stairs. Works in the archive on an Otto Ludwig edition.[1363] Wants to introduce narghiles into the archive. Reviles a newspaper "pious poisonous toad" because it attacked his edition of "Heiligenlegenden."

Saturday 6 July *(1912)* —To Schlaf's.[1364] Old sister who resembles him receives us. He's not home. We'll come back in the evening.—One-hour walk with Grete. She apparently comes with the consent of her mother, with whom she still speaks from the street through the window. Pink dress, my little heart. Restlessness because of the big ball in the evening. Had no relationship to her. Broken-off, constantly resumed conversation. Walking now especially fast, then especially slow again. Straining not to let it become clear at any price how we are connected by not one little thread. What drives us through the park together? Only my defiance?—At Schlaf's toward evening. Visit at Grete's beforehand. She stands outside the slightly open kitchen door in the ball dress praised long before, which is not even as beautiful as her usual one. Eyes very red with tears, apparently because of her main dancing partner, who has already caused her a great deal of trouble in general. I say goodbye forever. She doesn't know and if she did know, it wouldn't matter to her at all. A woman bringing roses even disturbs the little goodbye.—In the streets dancing lesson gentlemen and ladies from all sides.—Schlaf. Lives not exactly in a garret, as Ernst, who has fallen out with him, wanted to persuade us.[1365] Lively man, his strong upper body embraced by a tightly buttoned coat. Only his eyes twitch in a nervous and sick way. Speaks mainly about astronomy and his geocentric system.[1366] Everything else literature, criticism, painting still clings to him only because he doesn't cast it off. On Christmas, moreover, everything will be decided. He has not the slightest doubt in his victory. Max says his position with respect to the astronomers is "similar to Goethe's position with respect to the opticians." "Similar" he replies, his hands constantly busy on the table, "but much more advantageous, since I have indisputable facts in my favor." His small telescope for 400 M. For his discovery he doesn't need it at all, or mathematics either. He lives in complete happiness. His field of work is endless, since his discovery once recognized will have tremendous consequences in all fields (religion, ethics, aesthetics, etc.) and he is of course first called to elaborate them.—When we arrived, he was just gluing reviews that had appeared on the occasion of his 50th birthday into a large book. "On such occasions they go easy on you."—A walk with Paul Ernst in the Webbich[1367] beforehand. His contempt for our time, for Hauptmann, Wassermann, Thomas Mann. Without consideration for our possible opinion, in a little subordinate clause that one comprehends only long after it is spoken, Hauptmann is called a scribbler. Otherwise vague utterances about Jews, Zionism, races, etc., in all this only remarkable that this is a man who has vigorously used all his time well.—Dry, automatic "Yes, yes" at brief intervals when the other is speaking. Once this went so far that I no longer believed it.—

7 July *(1912)*

27 No. of the porter in Halle.—Now ½ past 6 near the Gleim memorial fell down on the long-sought bench.[1368] If I were a child, I would have to be carried from here, so much do my legs hurt.—After taking leave of you didn't feel alone for a long time.[1369] And then was so dulled again that it was still not aloneness.—Halle, little Leipzig. These pairs of church towers here and in Halle that are connected up in the sky by a small wooden bridge.—The mere feeling that you will read these things not immediately but only later makes me so uncertain.—The cycling club that gathers on the marketplace in Halle for an excursion. The difficulty of viewing a city or even only a street by oneself.—Good vegetarian lunch. In contrast to the other innkeepers, it's precisely the veg. innkeepers with whom vegetarianism doesn't agree. Anxious people who approach one from the side.

Ride from Halle with 4 Prague Jews: two pleasant merry elderly strong men, one resembling Dr. Klemens, one my father only much shorter, then a weak young husband afflicted by the heat and his abhorrent well-built young wife, whose face somehow comes from the Berg butcher family. She's reading a 3 M Ullstein novel by Ida-Boy-Ed, with the excellent title, probably invented by Ullstein, "A Moment in Paradise."[1370] Her husband asks her how she likes it. But she has just begun. "As yet there's nothing to say." A good German with dry skin and a whitish blond beard beautifully spread over cheeks and chin takes a strangely friendly interest in everything going on among the 4 of them.—

Railroad hotel, room down on the street with a little garden in front of it. Any passerby who wants can see me taking care of all my business naked in the room. Off into the city. An utterly old city. Half-timbered construction seems to be the building technique calculated to last the longest. The timbers warp everywhere, the filling sinks in or bulges out, the whole thing remains and at most collapses a little with time and thereby becomes even firmer. I have never before seen people leaning so beautifully in windows. The center strips of the windows are mostly affixed too. One leans one's shoulder against them, children spin around them. In a low hall strong girls, spread out in their Sunday dresses, are sitting on the first steps.

Drachenweg. Katzenplan.[1371]

In the park with little girls on a bench, which we defend as a girls' bench against boys. Polish Jews. The children shout Itzig at them and don't want to sit down on the bench immediately after them. Jewish inn Nathan Eisellsberg with Hebrew sign. It is a neglected castle-like building with a large staircase, which stands out from narrow streets. I walk behind a Jew who comes out of the inn and speak to him. After 9. I want to know something about the community.[1372] Learn nothing. Am too suspicious to him. He keeps looking at my feet. But I'm a Jew too. Then I can lodge at Eiselsberg's.—No I already have a place to stay.—All right.—Suddenly he comes close to me. Was I not in Schöppenstedt 1 week ago. Outside his front door we part; he is happy to be rid of me; without my asking, he tells me how to get to the synagogue.—People in dressing gowns on the doorstep. Old meaningless inscriptions. Thought through the possibilities of being abundantly unhappy on these streets, squares, garden benches, stream banks. Whoever can weep should come here on Sunday. In the evening after 5 hours of walking around in my hotel on the terrace in front of a little garden. At the next table the hotelkeepers with a young, lively woman who looks like a widow. Cheeks unnecessarily gaunt. Hair parted and puffed up.

8 July *(1912)* My house is called "Ruth."[1373] Furnished practically. 4 skylights, 4 windows, 1 door. Fairly quiet. Only in the distance they are playing football, the birds are singing loudly, several naked people are lying still outside my door. Everyone except me without swimming trunks. Beautiful freedom. In the park, reading room, etc. one gets to see pretty, fat little feet.

9 July *(1912)* Slept well in the hut, which is open on 3 sides. I can lean against my door like a house owner. Woke up at the most varied times in the night and kept hearing rats or birds cooing or fluttering around the hut in the grass. The gentleman spotted like a leopard. Yesterday evening lecture on clothing. Chinese women's feet were stunted so that they would get a large behind.

9 July *(1912)* The doctor, former officer, affected laughter that looks insane, tearful, unrestrained. Walks in a sprightly manner, disciple of Mazdaznan.[1374] A face made for seriousness. Clean-shaven, lips for pressing together. He steps out of his consulting room, one walks in past him, "Please come in" he laughs after one. Forbids me to eat fruit with the qualification that I don't have to obey him. I am an educated man, should listen to his lectures, which have also been printed, should study

the matter, form my own opinion and then act accordingly. (From his lecture yesterday: "When one's toes are even completely stunted, but one pulls on such a toe and at the same time breathes deeply, one can straighten it with time." After a certain exercise the genitals will grow. From the rules of conduct: "Air baths at night are highly recommended (I simply slide out of my bed when it suits me and step into the meadow outside my hut) only one should not expose oneself too much to the moonlight, that is harmful") Our present clothes cannot be washed at all!! This morning: Washing, Müller exercises, group gymnastics (I'm known as the man with the swimming trunks), singing several chorales, playing ball in a large circle. 2 beautiful Swedish boys with long legs, which are so formed and taut that one could really only run one's tongue along them. Concert by a military band from Goslar. In the afternoon turned hay. In the evening so upset my stomach that in my chagrin I don't want to take a single step. An old Swede is playing tag with several little girls and is so involved in the game that at one point while running he calls out: Wait, I will block these Dardanelles for you. Means the passage between 2 thickets. When an old not pretty nursemaid passes by: that's certainly something one could knock on (her back in the black dress with white dots). The perpetual groundless need to confide in someone. Looking at every person to see whether it is possible with him and whether he has an opportunity for himself.

10 *(July 1912)* Sprained my ankle, pain, loaded green fodder. In the afternoon a walk to Ilsenburg[1375] with a very young Gymnasium professor Lutz from Nauheim; might be in Wickersdorf next year. Coeducation, naturopathy, Kohen,[1376] Freud. Story of the excursion of girls and boys he led. Storm, all of them soaked, have to completely undress in a room at the next inn.—At night fever from the swollen foot. The noise made by the rabbits running by. When I get up at night, 3 of those rabbits are sitting on the meadow outside my door. I dream that I hear Goethe declaiming, with an infinite freedom and arbitrariness.

11 *(July 1912)* Conversation with a Dr. Friedrich Schiller,[1377] municipal official of Breslau, who spent a long time in Paris to study the urban institutions. Stayed in a hotel with a view into the courtyard of the Palais Royal. Previously in a hotel at the Observatoire. One night a pair of lovers was in the next room. The girl was screaming with delight in a shameless way. Only after he offered through the wall to fetch a doctor was she quiet and he could sleep.—My two friends disturb me, their

path runs past my hut and they always stop for a little while at my door for a brief conversation or invitation to a walk. But I'm also grateful to them for this.—In the "Evangelische Missionszeitung" July 1912 on missions in Java: "As much as objections can rightly be made to the amateur medical activity of the missionaries, which they practice to the greatest extent, it is nonetheless the main aid of their missionary activity and indispensable."

Now and then I get slight superficial nausea when, albeit usually at some distance, I see these completely naked people moving slowly past among the trees. Their running doesn't make it better.—Now a naked complete stranger has stopped at my door and has asked me slowly and amiably whether I am living here in my house, of which there is, after all, no doubt.—They approach so inaudibly too. Suddenly someone is standing there, one doesn't know where he came from.—Old gentlemen who jump naked over haystacks don't appeal to me either.—In the evening a walk to Stapelburg. With the two whom I introduced and recommended to each other. Ruin. Return 10 o'clock. Among the haystacks on the meadow outside my hut several creeping naked people who fade away in the distance. At night when I walk across the meadow to the water closet, three of them are sleeping in the grass.

12 *(July 1912)* Dr. Schiller's stories. Traveling for a year. Then long debate in the grass about Christianity. The old blue-eyed Adolf Just,[1378] who cures everything with clay and warns me about the doctor who forbade me fruit. The defense of God and the Bible by a member of the "Christian Community"; as proof, which is needed at the moment, reads a psalm aloud. My Dr. Schiller makes a fool of himself with his atheism. The foreign words illusion, autosuggestion are no help to him. A stranger asks why the Americans are doing so well even though they curse with every other word.—For most of them it's not possible to determine their real opinion, despite their lively participation. The one who spoke so impetuously of Flower Day[1379] and how the Methodists of all people restrained themselves. The one from the "Christ. Com." who eats cherries and dry bread out of a small bag for lunch with his beautiful little boy and otherwise lies in the grass all day, has three Bibles open in front of him and takes notes. He has been on the right path for only 3 years. Dr. Sch.'s[1380] oil sketches from Holland. Pont neuf.—Loaded hay.—At the Eckar seats.—Two sisters. Little girls. One with a narrow face, careless posture, one lip moving over the other, a nose com-

ing delicately to a point, clear eyes not completely open. Her face shines with such cleverness that I have been looking at her excitedly for several minutes now. Something comes over me when I look at her. Her more feminine little sister intercepts my glances.—A newly arrived stiff young lady with a bluish glow.—The blond with short tousled hair. Supple and thin as a leather strap. Skirt, blouse and shirt, nothing else. The stride!—With Dr. Sch. (43 years old) in the evening on the meadow. Strolling, stretching, rubbing, slapping and scratching. Completely naked. Shameless.—The scent when I stepped out of the writing room in the evening.

13 *(July 1912)* Picked cherries. Lutz reads Kinkel "Die Seele"[1381] to me.—After eating I always read a chapter from the Bible, which is in every room here. Evening, the children at play. Little Susanne von Puttkammer. 9 years old, in pink panties.

14 *(July 1912)* Picked cherries on a ladder with a little basket. Was high up in the tree. In the morning religious service at the Ecker seats. The Ambrosian song of praise. In the afternoon sent the two friends to Ilsenburg.—I'm lying in the grass when the man from the "Christ. Community" (tall, beautiful body, tanned, pointed beard, happy appearance) goes from his studying spot to the dressing hut, I follow him unsuspectingly with my eyes, but instead of returning to his spot he comes toward me, I close my eyes, but he is already introducing himself: Hitzer, land surveyor, and gives me 4 pamphlets as Sunday reading. While leaving he still speaks of "pearls" and "casting," by which he is implying that I am not to show the pamphlets to Dr. Schiller. They are "the prodigal son," "Bought or No longer mine (for unbelieving believers)" with short stories, "Why can't the educated man believe the Bible?" and "Hurrah for freedom! but: What is true freedom?" I read a little and then go back to him and, unsettled by the respect I have for him, try to make clear to him why at present there is no prospect of grace for me. In response he speaks to me for 1 ½ hours (toward the end an old white-haired, thin, red-nosed gentleman in a sheet joins us with several unclear remarks) with a beautiful command of every word, which only truthfulness makes possible. The unhappy Goethe, who made so many existences unhappy. Many stories. How he, Hitzer, forbade his father to speak when he blasphemed God in his house. "May you Father be horrified at this and too frightened to go on speaking, it's all right with me." How his father heard God's voice on his deathbed.—He can tell by looking at me that I am close to grace.—How I myself cut short all his evidence and refer him to the inner voice. Good effect.—

15 *(July 1912)* Read Kühnemann "Schiller."[1382]—The man who always carries a card to his wife in his pocket, in case of an accident.—Book of Ruth—I'm reading "Schiller." Not far away a naked old man is lying in the grass, an umbrella open over his head, his behind turned toward me and blasts several times loudly in the direction of my hut.—The brown and the blue dress of the stiff young lady who was at first dressed in white and how the skin of her face changes so clearly, downright methodically, under the influence of these colors.

15 *(July 1912)* Plato "The Republic"—Served as a model for Dr. Schiller. Without swimming trunks. Exhibitionistic experience.—The page in Flaubert about prostitution.[1383]—The great participation of the naked body in the overall impression of the individual.—A dream: The gathering of air bathers is destroyed by a fight. After the bathers, divided into two groups, have joked with each other, someone steps forward out of one of the groups and shouts to the others: "Lustron and Kastron!" The others: "What? Lustron and Kastron?" The first: "That's right." Beginning of the fight.

16 *(July 1912)* Kühnemann.—Herr Guido von Gillhausen, ret. capt., writes poetry and composes music "To my sword" and the like. Beautiful man. Out of respect for his nobility don't dare to look up at him, break out in a sweat (we're naked) and talk too softly. His signet ring.—The bowing of the Swedish boys. The older, red-haired one's habit of breathing heavily while speaking.—Talk in the park while dressed with a man who is dressed. He blasts so frequently and loudly that I can't understand a word he says.—Missed mass excursion to Harzburg.—Evening. Marksmen's festival in Stapelburg. With Dr. Schiller and a Berlin master hairdresser. The large plain gently rising toward the Stapelburg castle hill, led by old lindens, falsely cut through by a railroad embankment. The marksmen's hut from which they shoot. Old peasants make the entry in the marksmen's book. The 3 fifers with women's headscarves hanging down from their backs. Old inexplicable custom. Some in old simple blue inherited smocks, which are made of the finest linen and cost 15 M. Almost everyone has his rifle. A muzzle-loader. One has the impression that all of them are somehow bent from the work in the fields, especially when they form two lines. Several old leaders in top hats with sabers buckled on. Horse-tails and several other old symbols are carried over, excitement, then the band playing, greater excitement, then silence and drumming and fifing, even greater excitement, finally in the midst of the last drumming and fifing three flags

are brought out, last excitement, command and forward march. The old man in a black suit, black cap, somewhat pinched face and not-too-long, thick, silky unsurpassably white beard surrounding his face. The previous king of the marksmen, also with a top hat, with a porter-like sash around his body, which has little metal plates sewn all over it, on each of which the king of the marksmen of a year is engraved with the corresponding sign of his trade. (The master baker has a loaf of bread there, etc.) The forward march with music in the dust and the changing lighting of the heavily clouded sky. Doll-like appearance of one of the marching soldiers (a marksman who is currently serving) and his hopping step. People's armies and peasant wars. We follow them through the streets. Now they're closer, now farther away, since they stop at the homes of individual master marksmen, play and are given some refreshments. Toward the end of the procession the dust steadily disperses. The final pair is the clearest. At times we completely lose sight of them. The tall peasant with somewhat sunken chest, fixed face, top boots, clothes seemingly made of leather, how elaborately he detached himself from the post of the gate. The 3 women who stood in front of him, one in front of the other. The middle one dark and beautiful. The two women at the gate of the opposite farm. The 2 huge trees in both farms, which united over the wide road. The large targets on the houses of former kings of the marksmen. The dance floor, divided in two, in the middle the band partitioned off in a two-row section. Empty for the time being, little girls slide across the smooth boards. (Resting talking chess players disturb me in my writing) I offer them my soda, they drink, the oldest first. Lack of a true common language. I ask whether they have eaten dinner yet, complete incomprehension, Dr. Sch. asks whether they have already had their "Abendbrot," beginning of an inkling, (he doesn't speak clearly, breathes too much) only when the hairdresser asks whether they have "gefuttert"[1384] can they answer. A second soda that I order for them they no longer want, but they do want to ride the merry-go-round, I with the 6 girls (from 6–13 years old) around me fly to the merry-go-round. On the way the one who suggested riding the merry-go-round boasts that the merry-go-round belongs to her parents. We sit down and spin around in a coach. The girlfriends around me, one on my knees. Girls crowding around who want to enjoy my money too are pushed away by mine against my will. The owner's daughter checks the bill so that I don't pay for the strangers. I am prepared, if they want, to ride again, but the owner's daughter herself says that it's enough, however she wants to go to the candy tent. I in my stupidity and curiosity lead them to the wheel of fortune. As far as it's possible, they are very frugal with my money. Then to the candy. A tent with a large stock, which is as clean and neat as on the main street of a city. At the same time they are cheap goods, as at our markets too. Then we go back to the dance floor. I felt the experience of the girls more strongly than my giving. Now they are drinking the soda again too and thanking me nicely, the oldest for all of them and each for herself. At the beginning of the dance we have to leave, it's already ¼ to 10. The incessantly talking hairdresser. 30 years old, angular beard and elongated mustache. Chases after girls, but loves his wife, who is running the business at home and can't travel because she is fat and can't bear riding. Even when they go to Rixdorf one day, she has to get off the tram twice to walk a little and recover. She doesn't need vacation, she's satisfied just to be able to sleep later a few times. He is faithful to her, has all he needs with her. Temptations to which a hairdresser is exposed. The young wife of a restaurateur. The Swedish woman who has to pay more for everything. He buys hair from a Bohemian Jew, named Puderbeutel. When a social democratic delegation came to him and demanded that the Vorwärts[1385] be put out too, he said "If you demand that, then I haven't called you." But in the end gave in. As a "young man" (assistant) he was in Görlitz. He is an organized bowler. Was at the big bowlers' day in Braunschweig a week ago. There are about 20,000 organized German bowlers. For 3 days they bowled at 4 alleys of honor from early in the morning to late at night. But one cannot say that anyone is the best German bowler.—When I entered my hut in the evening, I couldn't find the matches, borrowed them from the neighboring hut and held a light under the table to see whether they hadn't perhaps fallen. They weren't there, but the water glass was there. Gradually it became apparent that my sandals were behind the wall mirror, the matches on a windowsill, the hand mirror was hanging from a protruding corner. The chamber pot was on the wardrobe, the Education sentimental[1386] was in the pillow, a clothes hook under the sheet, my traveling inkwell and a wet washcloth in the bed and so on. All in punishment, because I hadn't gone to Harzburg.

19 *(July 1912)* Rainy day. One lies in bed and the loud knocking of the rain on the roof of the hut seems to be against one's own chest. On the edge of the protruding roof the drops appear mechanically like lights

being lit along the line of a street. Then they fall. Like a wild animal an old man suddenly races across the meadow and takes a rain bath. The patter of the drops at night. One sits as if in a violin case. Running in the morning, the soft earth under one's feet.

20 *(July 1912)* In the morning with Dr. Schiller in the woods. The red soil and the light spreading out from it. The soaring of the tree trunks. The hovering broad flat-leaved branches of the beeches.—Arrival of a masquerade from Stapelburg in the afternoon. The giant with the dancing man dressed as a bear. The swinging of his thighs and back. The marching through the garden behind the music. The running of the spectators across the grass, through the thickets. Little Hans Eppe when he sees them. Walter Eppe on the mailbox. The men dressed as women completely veiled with curtains. The indecent sight when they dance with the kitchenmaids and these abandon themselves to the seemingly unknown dressed-up man.

In the morning read the first chapter of the Education to Dr. Sch. In the afternoon a walk with him. Stories of his girlfriend. He is a friend of Morgenstern, Baluschek, Brandenburg, Poppenberg.[1387] His horrible complaining in the evening in the hut in his clothes on the bed. First conversation with Frl. Pollinger, but she already knows everything worth knowing about me. She knows Prague from "Zwölf aus d. Steiermark."[1388] Light blond, 22 years old, appearance of a 17-year-old, always worrying about her hard-of-hearing mother; engaged and coquettish.—Departure at noon of that leather-strap-like Swedish widow Frau von Wasman. Over her usual clothing only a little gray jacket, a little gray hat with a small veil. In this frame her brown face becomes very delicate, the impression of regular features is decided only by distance and covering. Her luggage is a small knapsack, not much more than a nightshirt is in it. Thus she travels incessantly, came from Egypt, is going to Munich.—This afternoon when I was in bed, the people here made me hot, so much do some of them interest me.—A song by H. v. Gillhausen is called: "You know, little mama, you're so sweet."—Dance in Stapelburg in the evening. The festival lasts 4 days, hardly any work is done. We see the new king of the marksmen and read on his back the names of the kings of the marksmen from the beginning of the 19th century on. Both dance floors full. All around the hall couple stands behind couple. Each has a brief dance only every fifteen minutes. Most of them are silent, not out of embarrassment or for any other particular reason, but simply silent. A drunkard is standing at the edge, knows all the girls, assails them or at least reaches his arm out to hug them. Their dancing partners don't budge. There's enough noise from the music and the shouting of the people sitting below at the tables and those standing at the bar. We walk around uselessly for a long time (I and Dr. Sch.) I'm the one who speaks to a girl. I already noticed her outside when she and 2 girlfriends were eating little Halberstadt sausages with mustard. She has a white blouse with an inlay adorned with flowers that goes over her arms and shoulders. Her face is bowed in a sweet and melancholy way, thereby slightly compressing her upper body and puffing out her blouse. Her small upturned nose increases the sorrow in this bowed posture. Indiscriminate reddish brown across her whole face. I speak to her just as she is climbing down the 2 steps from the dance floor. How we stand chest to chest and she turns around. We dance. Her name is Auguste, she's from Wolfenbüttel and has been employed on the farm of a certain Klaude in Appenroda for 1½ years. My peculiarity of not understanding proper names even after several repetitions and then not retaining them either. She's an orphan and will enter a convent on 1 October. She hasn't told her friends yet. She already wanted to go in April, but her masters wouldn't let her. She's entering the convent because of the bad experiences she's had. She cannot tell about them. We walk up and down in the moonlight in front of the dance hall, my recent little girlfriends pursue me and my "bride." Despite her sorrow she likes to dance very much, as is especially apparent when I lend her to Dr. Sch. later. She is a field hand. At 10 o'clock she had to go home.

22 *(July 1912)* Frl. Gerloff, teacher, owlish young fresh face, full of lively tense features. Her body is laxer.—Hr. Eppe private school headmaster from Braunschweig. A person who defeats me. Dominant, when necessary fiery, well-thought-out, musical speaking that even makes a show of wavering. Delicate face, delicate sideburns and pointed beard nonetheless covering his whole face. Mincing gait. I sat diagonally across from him when he sat down simultaneously with me at the common table for the first time. A silently chewing group. He cast words here and there. If it nonetheless remained silent, then it simply remained silent. No sooner did a distant person say a word, however, than he held him, but without overstraining, rather he spoke to himself as if he had been addressed and was being listened to and at the same time looked at the tomato he was peeling. Everyone paid attention, except for those who felt humili-

ated and defiant as I did. He laughed at no one, rather let everyone's opinion rock on his words. If no one stirred, then he sang softly while cracking nuts or performing the many procedures that are necessary when eating raw fruit and vegetables. (The table is covered with bowls and one mixes as one pleases) In the end he involved everyone in his affairs by pretending he had to note down all the dishes and send the list to his wife. After he had delighted us for several days with his wife, he began to tell new stories about her. She was emotionally disturbed, had to go to a sanatorium in Goslar, would be admitted only if she pledged herself for 8 weeks, brought along an attendant, etc., the whole thing, as he calculated and as he again calculates for us at the table would cost over 1800 M. But no inkling of an intention to arouse sympathy. But still, so expensive a matter demands to be thought over, everyone thinks it over. A few days later we hear that his wife will come, perhaps this sanatorium will suffice for her. During the meal he gets the message that his wife has just arrived with their 2 boys and is waiting for him. He is happy, but calmly eats to the end, even though there is no end to this meal, since all the dishes are on the table at the same time. His wife is young, fat, with a waist suggested only in her clothing, clever blue eyes, upswept blond hair, understands cooking, market conditions, etc., very well. At breakfast—his family was not yet at the table—while cracking nuts he tells Frl. Gerloff and me: His wife is emotionally disturbed, has failing kidneys, her digestion is bad, she suffers from agoraphobia, falls asleep only toward 5 o'clock at night, if she is then woken up at 8 in the morning, "she is naturally terribly annoyed" and grows "furious." Her heart is in the greatest disorder, she has severe asthma. Her father died in the madhouse,

September 1913 Trip

on 10 Sept. 1913

Between the pillars of the portico of the parliament.[1389] Waiting for my director.[1390] Heavy rain. In front of me Athena Parthenos with a golden helmet.

6/IX *(1913)* Trip to Vienna. Stupid literary chatter with Pick.[1391] Considerable aversion. In this way (like P.) one clings to the ball of literature and cannot break away, because one has bored one's fingernails into it, but otherwise one is a free man and wriggles one's legs pitifully. His nose-blowing tricks. He tyrannizes me by claiming I tyrannize him.—The observer in the corner.—Heiligenstadt station,[1392] empty with empty trains. In the distance a man is scrutinizing the posted timetable. (Now I'm sitting on the step of the herm of a Teophil Hansen[1393]) Bent, in a coat, his face fades held up against the yellow poster. Riding past a small inn with a terrace. Raised arm of a guest. Vienna. Stupid uncertainties, all of which I ultimately respect. Hotel Matschakerhof.[1394] 2 rooms with one entrance. Choose the front one. Unbearable hubbub. Have to go into the street again with P. Supposedly run too much, run even more. Windy air. Recognize everything I've forgotten. Bad sleep. Full of worries. A repugnant dream (Malek).[1395] (The question of the diary is at the same time the question of the whole, contains all the impossibilities of the whole. I thought about this on the train during the conversation with P. It is impossible to say everything and it is impossible not to say everything. Impossible to preserve one's freedom, impossible not to preserve it. Impossible to lead the only possible life, namely, to live together, each free, each for himself, to be married neither outwardly nor actually, merely to be together and thereby to have taken the last possible step beyond male friendship, just short of the boundary set for me, where my foot is already raised. But that too is simply impossible. One morning last week it occurred to me as a way out, I wanted to write it in the afternoon. In the afternoon I got a biography of Grillparzer.[1396] He did it, that very thing. (At the moment a gentleman is contemplating the Theophil Hansen, I'm sitting like his Clio) But how unbearable, sinful, repugnant this life was and yet just the sort I might achieve with greater woes than he, for I am much weaker in some ways. (Come back to this again later—dream) In the evening met Lise Weltsch.[1397]

7/IX *(1913)* Aversion to P. A very good person on the whole. Has always had a small unpleasant gap in his nature and out of this very gap he creeps, now that one is watching continuously, in his entirety.

At the parliament in the morning. Beforehand fetched tickets to the Zionist Congress from Lise W. at the Residenzkafe. Went to Ehrenstein's.[1398] Ottakring. I can't do much with his poems. (I'm very uneasy and hence also a little false and that because I'm not writing this for myself alone) At the Thalisia[1399] with the two of them. With them and Lise W. in the Prater. Sympathy and boredom. She is coming to Berlin to the Zionist office. Complains about the sentimentality of her family, but only squirms like a pinned-down snake. She cannot be helped. Compassion for such girls (on some detour by way of myself) is perhaps my strongest social feeling. Taking photographs,[1400] shooting, "A Day in the Jungle" merry-go-round (how she sits helplessly up there, the billowing dress, well made, wretchedly worn). With her father[1401] in the Prater cafe. Gondola pond. Incessant headaches. The W.'s go to Monna Vanna.[1402] Lie for 10 hours in bed, sleep for 5. Give up the theater ticket.

8 *(September 1913)* Zionist Congress. The type with small round heads, firm cheeks. The workers' delegate from Palestine, perpetual shouting. Herzl's daughter. The former Gymnasium director from Jaffa. Upright on a step, blurred beard, agitated coat. Fruitless German speeches, much Hebrew, main work in the small meetings. Lise W. just lets herself be dragged along by the whole thing without taking part, throws little balls of paper into the hall, disconsolate. Frau Thein.[1403]

Notes

Translated from the German critical edition of Kafka's diaries edited by Hans-Gerd Koch, these notes have been abridged and adapted for this English edition. For full citations of all German sources, see Franz Kafka, *Tagebücher: Kommentarband,* edited by Hans-Gerd Koch, Michael Müller, and Malcolm Pasley. *Franz Kafka: Schriften, Tagebücher, Briefe: Kritische Ausgabe* (Frankfurt am Main: Fischer, 1990). All quotations from German sources have been translated by Ross Benjamin.

Key to Abbreviations

B: Franz Kafka, *Beschreibung eines Kampfes. Novellen, Skizzen, Aphorismen aus dem Nachlaß.* Edited by M. Brod. Frankfurt, 1954.

BKB: *Max Brod, Franz Kafka: Eine Freundschaft.* Vol. 2: *Briefwechsel.* Edited by M. Pasley. Frankfurt, 1989.

BKR: *Max Brod, Franz Kafka: Eine Freundschaft.* Vol. 1: *Reiseaufzeichnungen.* Edited by M. Pasley in collaboration with H. Rodlauer. Frankfurt, 1989.

Br: Franz Kafka, *Briefe 1902–1924.* Edited by M. Brod. Frankfurt, 1958.

F: Franz Kafka, *Briefe an Felice und andere Korrespondenz aus der Verlobungszeit.* Edited by E. Heller and J. Born. Frankfurt, 1967.

FK: Max Brod, *Über Franz Kafka. Eine Biographie.* Frankfurt, 1974.

H: Franz Kafka, *Hochzeitsvorbereitungen auf dem Lande und andere Prosa aus dem Nachlaß.* Edited by M. Brod. Frankfurt, 1953.

KKA: *Kritische Ausgabe der Schriften, Tagebücher, Briefe.* Frankfurt, 1982ff. Appended by: *S, V, P, NII, NI, D, A* for the volumes: *Das Schloß,* edited by Malcolm Pasley, 1982; *Der Verschollene,* edited by Jost Schillemeit, 1983; *Der Prozeß,* edited by Malcolm Pasley, 1990; *Nachgelassene Schriften und Fragmente II,* edited by Jost Schillemeit, 1992; *Nachgelassene Schriften und Fragmente I,* edited by Malcolm Pasley, 1993; *Drucke zu Lebzeiten,* edited by Wolf Kittler, Hans-Gerd Koch, and Gerhard Neumann,1996; further appended by *App.* for the respective apparatus volume. Appended by *B1, B2,* and *B3* for the volumes: *Briefe 1900–1912,* edited by Hans-Gerd Koch, 1999; *Briefe 1913–1914,* edited by Hans-Gerd Koch, 2001; *Briefe 1914–1917,* edited by Hans-Gerd Koch, 2005; *A* for the volume: *Amtliche Schriften,* edited by Klaus Hermsdorf and Benno Wagner, 2004; *KKAA* further appended by *Mat.* for the materials on CD-ROM.

KP: Hartmut Binder, *Kafka in Paris. Historische Spaziergänge mit alten Photographien.* Munich, 1999.

KWBr: Kurt Wolff, *Briefwechsel eines Verlegers 1911–1963*. Edited by B. Zeller and E. Otten. Frankfurt, 1966.
M: Franz Kafka, *Briefe an Milena*. Edited by J. Born and M. Müller. Frankfurt, 1983.
O: Franz Kafka, *Briefe an Ottla und die Familie*. Edited by H. Binder and K. Wagenbach. Frankfurt, 1974.
T: Franz Kafka, *Tagebücher 1910–1923*. Edited by M. Brod. Frankfurt, 1951.
WB: Klaus Wagenbach, *Franz Kafka: Bilder aus seinem Leben*, 2nd ed. Berlin, 1989.

1. After a guest performance in 1908, the Imperial Russian Ballet of St. Petersburg appeared in Prague for the second time on the occasion of the Maifestspiele (May Festival) on May 24 and 25, 1909. Yevgenya (Eugenie) Eduardova (1882–1960) belonged to the ensemble. Regarding the performance on May 24 at the Neues Deutsches Theater (New German Theater) on the Stadtpark, Wenzel Ritter von Bělský, the critic for the *Prager Tagblatt*, wrote: "The evening reached its climax . . . in the lively gypsy dance, in which Frl. Eduardova claimed victory with what was in my view an unprecedented wild gracefulness." The details of Kafka's diary entry suggest that he attended this performance. When the "Czar's Ballet" gave a guest performance in Prague again in 1913, Kafka wrote (on January 17–18) to Felice Bauer: . . . *tomorrow the Russian Ballet will appear. I saw it once 2 years ago and dreamed of it for months, especially of one very wild dancer Eduardova* (KKAB2 no. 398). Since Kafka often displays considerable uncertainty about the dates of past events, and since between 1909 and 1913 no further guest performance of the ballet company in Prague is documented, it can be assumed that he is referring here to the guest performance of May 24–25. Although it's impossible to determine definitively the date of the diary entry *I . . . dreamed of it for months* means that May 24, 1909, should be regarded as the earliest possible time it was written.
2. See note 176.
3. Refers—as the entry on p. 66 in the Second Notebook makes clear—to Gerhart Hauptmann's *Die Jungfern vom Bischofsberg*. In the first act of this comedy, the bride Adelheid says: "I must go to the seamstresses anyhow. I have three of them in the house."
4. See note 178.
5. From November 16 to 30, 1909, the Japanese acrobats the Mitsutas appeared in the Prague Theater Variété on Palackystraße. An announcement in the *Bohemia* on November 17, 1909, mentioned: "On their ladder, which is a good eight meters tall and which one of them balances on his extended legs through the whole production, they develop a catlike agility." The fact that Kafka captured this feat in a drawing too (see the facsimile on p. 6) suggests that he saw one of the performances at the Theater Variété.
6. Since the autumn of 1909, readers of Prague daily newspapers had been informed about the approach of Halley's comet. On January 2, 1910, the *Prager Tagblatt* noted: "For the time being the comet cannot yet be seen with small binoculars."
7. In Prague, it was announced that Halley's comet would pass in front of the sun on May 19, 1910, between about four and five o'clock in the morning. In their May 19 editions, the Prague daily newspapers reported that on the night of May 18–19, hundreds of spectators gathered at the city's elevated points. Apparently Kafka was off by a day in his subsequent dating of the entry, because Max Brod recorded in his diary on May 18, 1910, that Kafka and Brod's sister Sophie picked up the writer Franz Blei (1871–1942), who was living in Munich at the time, from the railroad station. On the *Comet Night*, that is, on the evening of May 18, Kafka and Brod went with Blei, his wife Maria (1867–1943), and his son Peter Maria (born 1905) to the

Laurenziberg. Kafka had become acquainted with Blei through his friend Brod. In March 1908 eight pieces by Kafka had appeared under the collective title *Betrachtung* (*Contemplation*) in *Hyperion*, the magazine published by Blei, followed in May 1909 by the stories "Gespräch mit dem Beter" ("Conversation with the Praying Man") and "Gespräch mit dem Betrunkenen" ("Conversation with the Drunken Man"). In February 1909 Kafka had reviewed Blei's book *Die Puderquaste* (*The Powder Puff*) under the title "Ein Damenbrevier" ("A Ladies' Breviary") in the magazine *Der neue Weg*.

8. On May 28, 1910, Max Brod noted in his diary that he was with Kafka at the bathhouse in the afternoon, where they sunbathed and rowed for an hour (unpublished, privately owned).
9. This fragment and the five variations that follow, in which Kafka incorporates details of his biography, are apparently related to the title "The Little Ruin Dweller," which Kafka set down in the Second Notebook (p. 56).
10. (taken up again on pp. 8, 9, 12) In a letter written ten years later, on June 21, 1920, to Milena Pollak, née Jesenská, this youthful memory of Kafka's can be found: *For example in the first grade. Our cook, a small dry thin woman with a pointed nose, hollow-cheeked, yellowish, but strong, energetic and superior took me to school every morning. . . . And now the same thing was repeated every morning for about a year* (M 71).
11. From 1907 to 1913, the Kafka family lived at Niklasstraße 36 on the top floor of the house "Zum Schiff," which was newly built, was equipped with an elevator, and had a view of the river and the Civilschwimmschule (Civilian Swimming School). In late October 1907, when only the approach road but not the bridge (the Svatopluk Čechbrücke) itself had been finished, Kafka called Niklasstraße the *approach road for suicides*.
12. Kafka had probably read Robert Walser's piece "Theater Fire," published on July 9, 1908, in the magazine *Die Schaubühne*, which begins with the words "That was a peculiar time" and exhibits a close kinship with Kafka's fragment: "Mothers trampled their own sweet flowers; men tore whole tufts of hair off children, and there was a beautiful little girl who was kicked in the eyes. A struggle arose such as later cultures perhaps never again witnessed in the midst of everyday life. Women were crushed to death against columns and railings, and meanwhile people too began to burn, to burn as paper burns."
13. A bon mot by the writer George Sand, passed down in one of Heinrich Heine's contributions to the *Allgemeine Zeitung* in the following form: "You see, the French are all born actors, and each plays his role in the world more or less brilliantly; but those among my compatriots who have the least talent for the noble art of acting devote themselves to the theater and become actors."
14. Notes written in pencil, partly in shorthand, probably during the Paris trip with Max and Otto Brod from October 8 to 17, 1910. Further notes on Paris can be found on the front flyleaf and the last page of the First Notebook as well as the back flyleaf of the Second Notebook. These notes are apparently based on observations Kafka made on October 15, 1910, during a performance of the drama *Manette Salomon* by Edmond de Goncourt in the Paris Théâtre de l'Odéon; see also p. 537. In a March 26, 1911, article for the *Frankfurter Zeitung*, Max Brod wrote about the "claque in French theaters" as he perceived it on the trip with Kafka: "It's not at all calculated to deceive. It works openly, in response to a signal that everyone hears. The cane knocks, applause."
15. Draft of a letter to Chief Inspector Eugen Pfohl (1867–1919), Kafka's immediate superior. Kafka had met Pfohl in the spring of 1908 as a lecturer at the Prager Handelsakademie (Prague Academy of Commerce), when he attended a course there on workers' insurance. When he entered the Workers' Accident Insurance Institute for the Kingdom of Bohemia in Prague (Arbeiter-Unfall-Versichungs-

Anstalt für das Königreich Böhmen in Prag, or AUVA) in late July 1908, Kafka was assigned to the *versicherungstechnische Abteilung* or the "actuarial department" (known as the *Kontrollabteilung* or "supervisory department" from 1910 on, after consolidation with several other departments), of which Pfohl was the head. Numerous statements in the letters to Felice Bauer make clear Kafka's high regard for his *admirable boss* (KKAB1 no. 361). Throughout the diary entries that follow, *boss* means Eugen Pfohl.

16. Here and in the diary entries that follow, *office* means the Workers' Accident Insurance Institute.
17. This fragment might be related to the following passages in the Second Notebook: pp. 56–60, 61–63, 64–65, 71–72. Two entries in the First Notebook, on pp. 17 and 18 (both of them beginning *I sensed at the sight of him . . .*), appear to be further approaches to this text.
18. The notes that follow, together with another diary entry dated March 26 (p. 99), deal with a visit by Rudolf Steiner (1861–1925) to Prague. At the invitation of the Prague chapter of the Theosophical Society, Steiner gave a total of eleven lectures from March 19 to 28, 1911: on the nineteenth a public lecture on the subject "How Does One Refute Theosophy," on the twenty-fifth another titled "How Does One Defend Theosophy," on the other days the eight lectures making up the cycle "Occult Physiology," and on the twenty-eighth an additional lecture for members "Aphorisms on the Relationship between Philosophy and Theosophy." Steiner stayed in Prague until March 30.

    Ten days before the beginning of Steiner's lectures, on March 9, after a visit to the Fanta house, Max Brod noted in his diary (unpublished, privately owned): "Frau F. lends me writings by Dr. Steiner, theosophist, which I'm reading quite eagerly." And a day later: "In the evening Café City with the Brentanists—theosophy—'Higher Worlds' by Dr. Rudolf Steiner, very inspiring." Brod's first entry refers to a circle interested in general philosophical subjects that met regularly in the house of the pharmacist Max Fanta on the Altstädter Ring; his second entry refers to a circle consisting of adherents to the philosopher Franz Brentano. Berta Fanta (1865–1918), the pharmacist's wife, who occupied a leading role in Prague's intellectual and cultural life, belonged to both circles; besides Brod, other friends and acquaintances of Kafka's who belonged to both circles included Hugo Bergmann, Felix Weltsch, and Emil Utitz, while Kafka himself, according to Brod, participated in the meetings only sporadically. Brod's diary notes indicate that Berta Fanta steered the interest of her friends and acquaintances toward Steiner and the lecture series in March 1911.

    Max Brod attended the public lectures on March 19 and 25. The latter began at four o'clock in the afternoon; for the evening of the twenty-fifth, Brod noted: "In the evening theosophical social gathering. Audience with Steiner." On the twenty-sixth, he went to the sixth lecture of the cycle, "The Blood as Expression and Instrument of the Human Self," and on March 28 to the lecture for members. On March 30 Brod noted: "Aftern. private audience with Dr. Steiner." Several weeks later he reported his impressions in an article titled "Higher Worlds" in the magazine *Pan*.

    Kafka too seems to have attended the two public lectures (on March 19 and 25), judging by his entry in the Second Notebook about Steiner's rhetorical techniques with respect to the defense of theosophy and the refutation of counterarguments. See pp. 80–81. Among other things, his remark on the *few drawings, which recall those from the lectures on occult physiology* (p. 16) suggests that he might have attended other lectures too.

    The first part of the entry dated March 28 probably records either observations and parts of the conversation from the social evening on March 25 or from the periphery of the additional lecture for members on the afternoon of March 28. Most of the details mentioned in this passage are verifiable events in Steiner's life.

19. Richard Pollak-Karlin (1867–1943), a painter from Prague; Hilda Kotányi-Pollak (1874–1943), a painter and craftswoman. Both had taken part in the painting of the dome of the first Goetheanum in Dornach; they painted the Lemuria and Atlantis motifs (see p. 15).
20. Xaverine Bittner was the widow of a *kaiserlich-königlicher Hofrat* (imperial-royal court councilor) and mother of the composer Julius Bittner, who mainly worked as a judge in Vienna.
21. On August 15, 1910, the premiere of Steiner's mystery drama *Die Pforte der Einweihung* (*The Portal of Initiation*) took place at the Munich Schauspielhaus.
22. Kafka evidently means Eugène Lévy, an adherent of Rudolf Steiner's teachings who tried to popularize them in France. At least Lévy's address, which corresponds to Kafka's information, suggests this: He lived in Paris, 10 Square Moncey. Lévy was the author of the book *Quelques réflexions sur "l'initation" de Rudolf Steiner* (Paris, 1910). Rudolf Steiner's book *Wie erlangt man Erkenntnisse der höheren Welten?* (*How Does One Attain Knowledge of Higher Worlds?*) had been published in 1909 in Berlin.
23. As an eighteen-year-old, Steiner encountered the herbalist Felix Kogutzki (1833–1909): "And so gradually I came to feel as if I were together with a soul from the very distant past who, untouched by the civilization, science and outlook of the present, brought close to me an instinctive knowledge of former times."
24. Dr. Felix Peipers (1873–1944), in his private clinic in Munich, used not only the first anthroposophic remedies but also a special color therapy in accordance with Steiner's instructions.
25. The audience Kafka describes probably took place on March 29, the first of the two days that Steiner remained in Prague after the end of his lectures and that were apparently reserved for personal conversations. It's not out of the question that Kafka added the date to the first line of his entry, which is indented very far, after the event and was mistaken with respect to the day or applied the date only to the first part.
26. This refers to the Hotel Victoria at Jungmannsgasse 18, at the corner of Palackygasse, where Rudolf Steiner resided during his stay in Prague.
27. The *Kaiserrock,* as Kafka wrote in the original German, was a sort of frock coat that civilians had to wear on official occasions at the Austrian imperial court.
28. Occult physiology was the overarching subject of Steiner's Prague lecture cycle.
29. The *Annalen der Naturphilosophie,* edited by Wilhelm Ostwald, had appeared since 1901 as a quarterly published by Verlag Veit & Comp. in Leipzig.
30. Kafka is referring to Rudolf Steiner's description in his third lecture on "Occult Physiology" of a "mystical immersion in the self, as well as the reverse, the lifting of oneself out of one's own consciousness."
31. Attempt at a review of Max Brod's novel *Jüdinnen* (*Jewish Women*), which was published in May 1911 by Axel Juncker Verlag in Berlin. There are further attempts in the Second Notebook (pp. 81–82).
32. See note 17. There's a second attempt, textually identical in its final stage, on p. 18.
33. Term for the guarded bathhouses on the river, where swimming lessons were also given.
34. Königsaal, Černoschitz: excursion villages and summer resorts on the Moldau, about ten miles south of Prague.
35. Kafka is referring to the August-September 1911 trip, taken together with Max Brod. See pp. 503ff.
36. See note 17.
37. Erroneously dated by Kafka. He meant August 25, since he departed on August 26. See p. 503.
38. Kafka is referring to the vacation trip with Max Brod. See pp. 503ff.
39. Hermann Kafka (1852–1931) and his wife Julie (1855–1934) both worked in the "shop," the fancy goods store on Zeltnergasse. See also note 115.

40. Ottilie, known as Ottla (1892–1943), was Kafka's youngest sister.
41. This probably refers to the owner of Niklasstraße 36, the jeweler Alfréd Nikodém, who lived in the same house.
42. On September 18, 1911—following their trip together, Kafka was still staying in the sanatorium Erlenbach near Zurich (September 13–19)—Max Brod met the painter, graphic artist, and writer Alfred Kubin (1877–1959) in Prague. When Kafka returned to Prague—probably on September 26, the day of this entry—Brod brought him together with Kubin. The entries about Kubin on pp. 22 and 24 were written later from the memory of this encounter.
43. The German publisher of the Norwegian author Knut Hamsun, whom Kafka regarded highly, was Albert Langen (1869–1909).
44. In his memoirs, Arthur Holitscher reported as an eyewitness on this episode, which occurred during Hamsun's stay in Munich in 1896: "In the editorial office I saw him [Hamsun] suddenly, as if startled out of his thoughts, which had taken him far away, reach into his breast pocket, pull out a long pair of scissors and begin to cut off the fringes at the bottom of his defective pants legs."
45. By *Belvedere,* Kafka means the Belvedere hill on the left bank of the Moldau with its extensive gardens, which was regularly the destination of his walks (see pp. 145 and 301) and not the summer palace of the same name in the Chotek Gardens (see p. 386).
46. See the corresponding passage in August-September 1911 Trip, p. 535.
47. See Goethe's diary entry of August 26, 1797: "a group of Austrian officers, partly from the army, partly from the boardinghouse, the usual guests, were conversing cheerfully and quite courteously in their various circumstances of age and rank."
48. Goethe's diary entry of August 27, 1797: "Wiesenbach . . . The men wear blue coats and white vests adorned with woven flowers."
49. See Goethe's diary entry of September 18, 1797. See also p. 24.
50. The Lucerna is a multipurpose building with a passage that connects Stephansgasse (Czech: Štěpánská) and Wassergasse (Czech: Vodičkova). In the basement of the Lucerna was the Orangensaal, also known as the "Kleine Lucerna-Saal," and in this hall the Cabaret Lucerna was established in September 1910. Kafka is describing the opening program of the 1911–12 season.
51. A Viennese singer and dancer.
52. Emil Artur Longen (also: Longhen), actually Emil Artur Pittermann (1885–1936), actor, playwright, director and painter, was friendly with Max Brod, Jaroslav Hašek, and Egon Erwin Kisch, among others.
53. Rudolf Vašata (1888–1953).
54. Fritz Grünbaum (1880–1941), a cabaret performer and writer.
55. Actually Auguste "Gusti" von Erler (?–1931), a Viennese dancer.
56. Helene Haas (born 1890), a cousin of Willy Haas. See p. 217 and note 543.
57. With *bathhouse,* Kafka is referring to one of Prague's swimming facilities on the Moldau.
58. Stands for "brothel."
59. Kurt Tucholsky (1890–1935), at the time of the diary entry, was a law student in Berlin. His friend, the artist Kurt Szafranski (1890–1964), visited Prague in September 1911.
60. Szafranski was a student of Lucian Bernhard (1883–1972), who made the cover and book jacket drawings for most of Max Brod's books published by Axel Juncker Verlag.
61. In all the entries that follow, *Max* means Kafka's closest friend Max Brod (1884–1968), here mentioned in the diaries for the first time.
62. Located between Maislgasse and Niklasstraße, the "Alt-Neu-Synagoge" (Old New Synagogue), also known as the "Alt-Neuschule," is Prague's oldest synagogue.
63. Kafka made an error in the subsequent addition of the day of the week. Kol Nidre

is the name of the introductory prayer on the eve of the Day of Atonement (Yom Kippur); in 1911 it fell on Sunday, October 1. Kafka's uncertainty about the date is also made clear in the manuscript by the multiple corrections of the date.

64. Located on Josefsgasse adjacent to the old Jewish cemetery.
65. *B.* for brothel. The Salon Šuha (U Šuhů) on Benediktgasse was among the more well-known Prague establishments. It is mentioned in Jaroslav Hašek's 1921–23 novel *The Good Soldier Švejk.*
66. See also p. 21. Kafka is alluding to Goethe's September 25, 1797, letter to Schiller from Stäfa.
67. See Goethe's diary entry of September 30, 1797.
68. Karoline Kohn (1856–1929) was the widow of Heinrich Kafka, an uncle who died in 1886. Kafka mentioned a visit to their shop, which she kept running with her second husband Sigmund Kohn, in a December 9–10, 1912, letter to Felice Bauer (KKAB1 no. 345). She had three sons from her first marriage, Viktor, Emil, and Rudolf, and two sons from her second marriage, Fritz and Robert.
69. Dr. Robert Anton Marschner (1865–1934) was the director of the AUVA. His daughter was named Berta (1900–72).
70. Regarding the regular evening card game in the Kafka household, see note 227.
71. Bialli, at first written down in the manuscript, then crossed out except for the initial. This refers to Louise Bailly (1860–1942), a former governess of the Kafka family from Coeuve, Switzerland.
72. Renamed Náměstí Republiky (Republic Square) after the proclamation of the Czechoslovak Republic. Na Poříčí, the street that Kafka's office, the AUVA, was on, starts out heading east from Josefsplatz.
73. In the Austro-Hungarian Empire, as in Austria today, *Bezirkshauptmannschaft* was the term for the administrative office of a district.
74. Kafka's range of duties at the time included "preparing licenses and other documents (correspondence; commenting on and composing objections, appeals and complaints; composing reports of all sorts)" (KKAB1 no. 164).
75. Julie Kaiser (1887–1941), a typist in the AUVA, is also mentioned in letters of Kafka's later years (KKAB3 nos. 923 and 1062) and visited him in Zürau (KKAB3 no. 1083). A photograph of Julie Kaiser together with Kafka and others in Zürau is reproduced in WB 198.
76. This refers not to Kafka's office but rather to an office in which other typists also sat. Thus Kafka wrote in a letter to Felice Bauer of his *dictation room* (KKAB3 no. 892).
77. The street is Niklasstraße and the bridge is the Čechbrücke.
78. Probably Valerie (1890–1942), known as Valli, or Ottla Kafka, who were both still living with their parents at the time.
79. From September 24, 1911, to January 21, 1912, a Yiddish theater troupe from Lemberg gave guest performances in Prague, first at the Hotel Central at Hibernergasse 10 (September 24–28), then in Herrmann's Café Savoy on Ziegenplatz, where Kafka attended numerous performances. He developed a friendly relationship with members of the ensemble, from whom he received his first insights into the history of Yiddish literature and theater, which developed into a continuing interest, as reflected in the entry on p. 34 beginning *Desire to see a large Yiddish theater* . . . and in his reading of Pinès (pp. 188–191). Kafka's diary entries contain numerous inaccuracies, especially in the spelling of Yiddish expressions and in the reproduction of names and biographical details of Yiddish authors. In places where incorrect or misleading material is demonstrable, it is corrected in these notes.

    The performances of the Yiddish troupe usually consisted of solo acts by the members of the ensemble in the first part of the evening and plays by Yiddish authors in the second. Kafka's writing of his first impressions extended over several days (October 5–8, 1911).
80. With respect to Kafka's description, see the facsimile of one of her picture postcards

(p. 110: *she didn't offer me her picture postcards*) in Franz Kafka, *Tagebücher: Kommentarband*, edited by Hans-Gerd Koch, Michael Müller, and Malcolm Pasley (Frankfurt, 1990), p. 32.

81. Hebrew: *meshumad*, literally "destroyed one"; a label for baptized Jews (apostates).
82. Kafka apparently repeated an error of attribution from the announcement in the October 5, 1911, issue of the *Prager Tagblatt*, which misidentified the author of *Der Meschumed* as Joseph Latteiner. The actual author, correctly named in later announcements, was Abraham Scharkansky.
83. A Czech folk dance.
84. Yiddish for "little child."
85. A representative of the censorship authorities had to monitor public events in order to ensure that they proceeded according to the rules.
86. Yiddish for "father dear."
87. In accordance with the convention of the time, Kafka called Yiddish "the jargon" or simply "jargon" (Jargon).
88. A *mezuzah* (plural: *mezuzot*), Hebrew for "doorpost," is a piece of parchment inscribed with verses from the Fifth Book of Moses (Deuteronomy 6:4–9 and 11:13–21), which is kept rolled up in a case with an opening through which the word *Shaddai* ("Almighty") is visible. In the homes of observant Jews, the case is affixed to the right doorpost and is touched when one enters or leaves.
89. From April 25 to mid-May 1910, a Jewish theater company led by Moritz Weinberg gave guest performances in Café Savoy. Besides Weinberg's wife Pepi, the singer Salcia Weinberg was a member of the ensemble. Max Brod attested to the fact that Kafka attended at least one of the performances at the time: "On May 1 of that year I find noted in my diary: 'Café Savoy. Lemberg company. Very important for J.P.' (a novel I was planning at the time). On May 4: 'In the evening with Kafka at the Savoy. Excellent'" (FK 98).
90. *The Bartered Bride* is a comic opera in three acts by the Czech composer Bedřich Smetana.
91. Probably Rosa Kaufmann (1878–1942), daughter of Adolf and Regine Kaufmann. Her brother Hugo was married to Olga Ehrmann, the daughter of Kafka's aunt Julie Ehrmann.
92. Kafka's article appeared under the title "Die Arbeiterunfallversicherung und die Unternehmer" ("Workers' Accident Insurance and Employers") in the *Tetschen-Bodenbacher Zeitung* of November 4, 1911.
93. Along with Ferdinandstraße, later renamed Nationalstraße (Czech: Národní; known at the time as the Czech "boulevard"), the Graben (Czech: Na Příkopě; known at the time as the German "boulevard") marks the boundary between Prague's Old Town and New Town, following the former course of the Old Town wall.
94. Announced in an advertisement in the *Prager Tagblatt* of October 8, 1911, for the same evening as "'Die Sejdernacht' by Gordon." It's actually a play by Joseph Latteiner.
95. Since mid-August, Max Brod had rented a room at Schalengasse 4 in the immediate vicinity of his parents' apartment (Schalengasse 1).
96. Reproduced in this edition as August-September 1911 Trip, pp. 503ff.
97. Refers to Angela Rehberger (born 1887), an acquaintance whom Kafka and Brod included in *Richard und Samuel* as "Dora Lippert." See also August-September 1911 Trip, pp. 503ff. In Brod's travel notes she is called "Angela" (BKR 74), while Kafka names her "Alice" (p. 503).
98. In Prague there are often passages through buildings connecting two streets.
99. The Schützeninsel is an island in the Moldau, accessible from the middle of the Kaiser-Franzens-Brücke (today: Most Legií, or Legion Bridge) by a staircase, with a restaurant of the same name and green spaces. According to an advertisement in

the *Prager Tagblatt* of October 12, 1911, the band of the 91st Infantry Regiment (the Prague "House Regiment") gave a concert that evening in the hall of the restaurant on the Schützeninsel.

100. In mid-December 1911, together with his brother-in-law Karl Hermann (1883–1939), the husband of Gabriele (known as Elli, 1889–1941), Kafka founded as a silent partner an asbestos factory, the Prager Asbestwerke Hermann & Co. This diary entry records a meeting with the attorney Dr. Robert Kafka—son of Heinrich Kafka, a cousin of Kafka's father—who was entrusted with giving legal advice and carrying out the authorization procedures. The lawyer's office was at Wenzelsplatz 35, his private apartment on Na Smetance 6, southeast of the Franz-Josephs-Bahnhof, in the Prague suburb Königliche Weinberge (Czech: Královské Vinohrady).
101. Here and in all the diary entries that follow, *factory* means the Prager Asbestwerke Hermann & Co., which was located in Žižkov, in the rear courtyard of Boriwogasse (Bořivojova) 27.
102. Alludes to the entry about Kubin on p. 22.
103. On October 12, 1911, Kafka wrote on a postcard to Max Brod: *Dear Max, we're in luck! Sulamit by Godfaden will be performed!* (KKAB1 no. 210). In the *Prager Tagblatt* of October 13, 1911, an advertisement announced the performance of Abraham Goldfaden's operetta *Sulamit* for that evening. See also p. 48.
104. Mania Tschisik, née Firstenfeld (1881–1976).
105. Emanuel Tschisik (born 1867).
106. Mano Pipes.
107. S. Klug. The initial of the first name is mentioned several times in advertisements; the complete first name could not be determined.
108. Flora Klug.
109. "Many people go to Jerusalem and find their peace" (or, to give the general sense, "and return as whole people"); *beshulim*, Yiddish (Hebrew: *beshalom*) for "in peace."
110. Probably Schamai (Sami) Urich.
111. Jizchak Löwy (1887–1942).
112. Yiddish for "truth" (Hebrew: emet).
113. Yiddish for "mercy" (Hebrew: *rachmānut*).
114. For October 14, 1911, at Café Savoy, the Zukunft support association organized a Simchat Torah celebration that included a performance of Joseph Latteiner's *Gabriel oder Chinke-Pinke.*
115. Hermann Kafka was the owner of a fancy goods shop (notions, gloves, slippers, umbrellas, walking sticks, and the like). At that time his shop was located on Zeltnergasse 12.
116. Anton Tullach (1883–1948).
117. Žižkov was a suburb on the east side of Prague with numerous factories where mostly Czech workers resided (incorporated into Prague as a district in 1922).
118. The printer Karel Tulach lived on the same street as the bookkeeper Anton Tullach.
119. A town on the Prague-Pilsen railroad line of the Böhmische Westbahn, fifteen kilometers south of Prague.
120. The issue of the biweekly *Pan* of October 15, 1911, included Max Brod's "Kommentar zu Robert Walser." This issue was among Kafka's possessions.
121. Kafka used the term *Pawlatsche,* which is derived from the Czech (*pavlač*) and entered Austrian parlance, designating a balcony or covered passageway that runs along the outside of a building connecting several apartments.
122. Probably paraphrased from volume two of *Napoleon-Anekdoten,* collected and edited by Gustav Kuntze: " 'When I was still a simple lieutenant in the artillery,' began the Emperor . . . At these words the royal guests were taken aback and all their faces expressed the greatest tension. 'When I had the honor of still being a simple lieutenant,' he repeated calmly."

123. This refers to the diary of the August-September 1911 Trip. See pp. 503ff.
124. See note 127.
125. In the second act of the opera *The Fair Maid of Perth* by Georges Bizet, this gypsy dance is performed.
126. The volume *Berühmte Aussprüche und Worte Napoleons von Corsika bis St. Helena,* a collection of Napoleon's sayings, was among the books in Kafka's possession at the time of his death. Kafka also mentioned it later in a letter to Felice Bauer (KKAB1 no. 376).
127. Jizchak Löwy's reading might have been part of the weekly evening presentations at the Jüdische Toynbeehalle (Jewish Toynbee Hall). For these evenings—which were only rarely reviewed in the daily press—there were frequent advertisements seeking participants. In December 1913, Kafka read there from Heinrich von Kleist's *Michael Kohlhaas.* See p. 320 and KKAB2 no. 428.
128. The Yiddish writer Sholem Aleichem (actually Sholem Rabinovich) was the author of "Tevye the Milkman" and many humorous stories and plays.
129. Isaac Loeb Peretz. See note 151.
130. "In the City of Slaughter," Chaim Nachman Bialik's poem about the Kishinev pogrom of 1903.
131. Morris Rosenfeld. See note 149.
132. Probably Valli and Ottla Kafka. See note 78.
133. See note 100.
134. Karl Hermann, Kafka's brother-in-law. See note 100.
135. On February 4–5, 1913, Kafka wrote to Felice Bauer: *Löwy and Winterberg is certainly a large company, the third largest timber merchant in Bohemia, as far as I know* (KKAB2 no. 423).
136. Chuchle, known as Kuchelbad in German, was the next station after Prague on the Prague-Pilsen railroad line.
137. The drama of that name by Ivo Vojnović was performed at the Czech National Theater (corner of Ferdinandstraße and Riegerquai).
138. Possibly a misspelling of *gospodars* (from *gospodar,* Slavic for "lord" or "master"), the title for princes of the old Danube principalities Moldavia and Wallachia.
139. Jizchak Löwy.
140. Apparently sisters of Kafka's brother-in-law Karl Hermann.
141. Kafka had seen Mania Tschisik on October 13, 1911, in the title role of Goldfaden's operetta. See his entry on pp. 40–41.
142. Hatikvah, Hebrew for "The Hope," written in 1878 by Naphtali Herz Imber, was initially the unofficial and later the official anthem of the Zionist movement; today it is Israel's national anthem.
143. An advertisement in the *Prager Tagblatt* of October 21, 1911, announced the performance of Abraham Scharkansky's *Kol-Nidre* that evening at Café Savoy.
144. The three previous evenings were on October 5, 8, and 13.
145. This might refer to Ottla Kafka.
146. In his biography of Kafka, Max Brod recalls: "A strange sort of shy love and veneration bound him to one of the actresses, who most likely noticed hardly any of it" (FK 98–99).
147. Annie Tschisik (1903–83).
148. Probably Ottla Kafka.
149. The Yiddish authors Edelstadt and Rosenfeld played a decisive role in the development of Yiddish literature. However, their similar life paths led to confusions in the debate between the actors. David Edelstadt, one of the first socialist Yiddish authors, left Russia in 1882 and went to America. He worked as a tailor and joined an anarchist group whose journalistic organ, the *Fraye Arbeyter Shtime,* he edited as of 1890. As a labor poet, he became—after his death of tuberculosis at the age of twenty-six in 1892—one of the heroes of the still-young Jewish labor movement.

His collected works appeared in London in 1910. Morris Rosenfeld, a Yiddish labor poet like Edelstadt, also emigrated from Russia, went first to London and in 1886 to New York. Like Edelstadt, he worked as a tailor and with the growth of the labor movement became known beyond that circle and was translated into various languages. As of 1905, he was editor of the Yiddish daily *New Yorker Morgenblatt.*

150. The poet, playwright, and composer Abraham Goldfaden founded the first Yiddish theater troupe in Romania in 1876; he is regarded as the founder of the Yiddish theater. See pp. 40–41 and note 103.

151. Isaac Loeb Peretz is regarded as one of the Yiddish folk authors. In 1910 the Prague publisher Richard Brandeis reissued a selection of Peretz's stories and sketches, *Ausgewählte Geschichten und Skizzen,* in a German translation by Mathias Acher (actually Nathan Birnbaum; see also notes 454 and 456), which had been published by Jüdischer Verlag in 1905.

152. Yiddish (Hebrew: *bachur*) for "young man," "Yeshiva student."

153. Jacob P. Adler, a member of Abraham Goldfaden's theater troupe (see note 150) in Russia, emigrated to New York via London. As of 1891, he worked with the playwright Jacob Gordin. With roles in Gordin's plays, he became popular as "der groyser Adler" (Yiddish for "the great eagle"), while at the same time this collaboration helped Gordin achieve his breakthrough as a Yiddish dramatist.

154. The title role in *Der vilder Mensh* by Jacob Gordin (and not the poet Judah Leib Gordon, as the mistake suggests) was among Jacob P. Adler's most brilliant roles.

155. Located at Wintergartenstraße 17–19 in Leipzig, the Kristall-Palast with the Alberthalle, a domed building with a circus and concert space, was among the largest and most renowned entertainment venues in Germany.

156. Eugen Lederer (1861–1937) was imperial councilor and director of the AUVA's accident department. From April 17 to September 17, 1909, Kafka had been temporarily transferred to the accident department.

157. Included by Kafka under the title "Unglücklichsein" ("Unhappiness") in his book *Betrachtung* (*Contemplation*), published by Ernst Rowohlt in 1912. The handwritten version in the diaries does not contain the entirety of the printed text; the passage that follows *ghosts?* (p. 55) was presumably written on a separate sheet of paper that has not survived.

158. Entry referring to the fragments on pp. 7–13 (see also note 9); probably intended as a title for a clean copy that was not made here.

159. The first of a series of fragments that—like those written later in the First Notebook (see note 17)—document Kafka's attempts to resume his work on the second version of his novella "Beschreibung eines Kampfes" ("Description of a Struggle"), to "jump into" his novella (see p. 63).

160. On three evenings in early November 1910, the Parisian elocutionist Marguerite A. Chenu gave guest lectures at the Palace-Hotel (Herrengasse, at the corner of Heinrichsgasse). The second of her "Conférences françaises" was dedicated to Alfred de Musset and took place on November 5.

161. "Un souper chez Mademoiselle Rachel" was Alfred de Musset's description of a supper at the home of the actress Elisa Rachel Félix (1821–58), who became famous with the title role of Racine's *Phaedra.* See also the mention in August-September 1911 Trip, p. 538.

162. The literary historian, essayist, and translator Paul Wiegler (1878–1949), feuilleton editor of the Prague daily *Bohemia* from 1908 to early 1913, spoke on November 6, 1910, in the Deutsches Studentenheim (German Student Residence) on Mariengasse 34 before the Verein Deutscher Arbeiter (Association of German Workers). The occasion for the lecture was a performance of *Maria Magdalena* given a week later at the Deutsches Landestheater (German National Theater, located at Obstmark 13). The *Bohemia* of November 8, 1910, reported: "The lecture, which took place in the

Adlersaal of the Deutsches Studentenheim, described the course of Hebbel's life and closed with an introduction to his drama." Paul Wiegler belonged to Brod and Kafka's circle of friends and acquaintances. At Brod's recommendation, he twice accepted contributions by Kafka to the feuilleton section of the *Bohemia*: On September 29, 1909, the article "Die Aeroplane in Brescia" ("The Airplanes in Brescia") dating from the preceding trip to Italy; and on March 27, 1910, under the title "Betrachtungen" ("Contemplations"), five pieces that were later included by Kafka in his book *Betrachtung* (*Contemplation*). See also note 157. In addition, he published two reviews by Kafka and the piece "Kinder auf der Landstraße" ("Children on the Country Road") from *Betrachtung*, on the occasion of the collection's publication.

163. See note 159.
164. The drawing described by Kafka appeared in 1910 in the *Mitteilungen der Gesellschaft für vervielfältigende Kunst*, a supplement to the magazine *Die graphischen Künste*. The ambiguous caption to the illustration reads "Julius Schnorr von Carolsfeld, Portrait Study after Friedrich Olivier." See the facsimile in Kafka, *Tagebücher: Kommentarband*, p. 43. It apparently led to Kafka's consideration of who was the model here and who the artist. The fact that the word "after" is not fully written out in *Karolsfeld aft drawing* is evidence of this.
165. See note 159.
166. Kafka is commenting on his numerous attempts in his diary to find an approach to his aborted writing of the second version of "Beschreibung eines Kampfes" ("Description of a Struggle") and to continue this writing. See pp. 56ff. and note 159.
167. A play by Goethe.
168. On November 27, 1910, the writer Bernhard Kellermann (1879–1951) read in the Spiegelsaal of the Deutsches Kasino (German Casino) in the Deutsches Haus (German House) at Graben 26. In contrast to Paul Wiegler's positive review in the *Bohemia* of November 28, 1910, Ludwig Steiner, the reviewer for the *Prager Tagblatt*, confirmed Kafka's remarks on the reading and the reaction of the listeners: "Unfortunately the writer had the strange ambition to try their patience rather sorely. His program included a lengthy prose work, which took considerably more than an hour to read aloud. . . . As a result, after an hour, the audience began to trickle out of the hall drop by drop, then streamed out in a broader current, and the end was greeted—if one may say so—with deferential applause by only a remnant of the listeners. The writer then read to the decimated audience the tender fairy tale of the princess who lost her eyelash."
169. The "prose work" mentioned in the review is the story "Die Heiligen" ("The Saints"), first published in *Die neue Rundschau* in June 1911.
170. "Die Geschichte von der verlorenen Wimper der Prinzessin. Ein Märchen" ("The Story of the Princess's Lost Eyelash: A Fairy Tale") was first published posthumously in 1979.
171. Possibly Rudolf Hermann, known as Rudl, brother of Kafka's brother-in-law Karl Hermann.
172. Probably the painter and lithographer Georg Kars (1882–1945), who was a friend of Max Brod. Kars (actually Karpeles) had gone to Prague in 1908 and repeatedly stayed in Prague for brief periods in order to participate in exhibitions of contemporary artists, among other things.
173. See note 159.
174. Quoted verbatim from Friedrich Hebbel's diaries. The four-volume 1903 edition was among the books in Kafka's possession at the time of his death; the relevant passage there is marked with pencil in the margin. Justinus Kerner's book appeared anonymously in 1811 under the title *Reiseschatten. Von dem Schattenspieler Luchs* (*Travel Shadows: By the Shadow Player Luchs*).
175. In this phase, Kafka revisits his First Notebook and expands here on the entries

contained there only in brief form. In the entry on the *seamstresses in the downpours*, Kafka himself makes the reference; the preservation of the sequence and the conceptual proximity to the brief notes in the First Notebook suggest that the other three entries too are further elaborations.

176. The writer W. Fred (actually Alfred Wechsler, 1879–1922) was surely known to Kafka due to his articles in the *Prager Tagblatt*, among other things; he was also among the authors of the volume *Französische Meister* (Berlin, ca. 1908), which Kafka owned. The novel *Die Straße der Verlassenheit. Zehn Jahre* had been published in 1905 in Berlin. The entry *Writers speak stench* (p. 5) probably refers to the reading of this novel.
177. A more detailed formulation of the thoughts connected with the entry *The seamstresses in the downpours*. See note 3.
178. In his paradoxes of motion, the Greek philosopher Zeno of Elea tried to prove that the assumption of the plurality of space and of motion leads to contradictions. The note on the paradox of the "flying arrow" is apparently connected with the image of the "moving train" used by Kafka, that is, probably with the entry *From the train compartment window* (p. 5) and the first entry in the diaries: *The spectators stiffen when the train passes* (p. 3).
179. This entry is probably connected with the notes from the Paris trip in October 1910, p. 13.
180. Elli, Kafka's oldest sister, and Karl Hermann had gotten married on November 27, 1910.
181. Possibly passages from attempts at the second version of "Beschreibung eines Kampfes" ("Description of a Struggle").
182. Kafka's entries are based on his reading of the German edition of Mikhail Kuzmin's *The Exploits of Alexander the Great:* Michail Kusmin, *Taten des großen Alexander* (Munich, 1910).
183. "She told the king that she had given birth to a strange child whose upper half was dead but whose lower half had all the signs of life, and a miracle voice had commanded her to bring the child to the palace. Alexander, filled with presentiments, looked with horror at the child's corpse with the moving little red legs" (ibid., pp. 147–48).
184. "With this head, which produced a horror that turned people to stone, the king defeated many peoples of the desert and the impure kings Gog and Magog, who fed on worms and flies, driving them into cracked cliffs and sealing them in until the end of the world with the seal of Solomon" (ibid., pp. 141–42).
185. "Past the sweet rivers and the stone streams, where instead of water stones rolled with a roar, past the sand brooks that flow for three days toward the south and for three days toward the north, they came to an island from where the sun rises" (ibid., pp. 138–39).
186. "After some time a hundred tall man-like women with burnt-off right breasts, short hair, wearing men's footgear and armed with spears, arrows and quivers came with the returned Ptolemy" (ibid., p. 136).
187. "After a solemn meal Kandake took her guests to show them the city, golden apples, melon-sized nuts, roosters on which warriors rode, panthers whose bones cut glass, crocodiles that burned down trees with their urine, one-eyed people, giants and the evil race of the viper" (ibid., p. 129).
188. Along with Max Brod and Felix Weltsch (see note 389), the blind writer Oskar Baum (1883–1941), whom he met in the autumn of 1904 (see FK 96), belonged to the circle of Kafka's closest friends, which Brod later called the "inner Prague Circle." Among the customary activities of the circle of friends were excursions together in the vicinity of Prague and regular evening meetings at which they read to each other from their literary works. At that time Baum lived with his family at Stockhausgasse 8.

189. A number of governesses were employed by the Kafka family. Due to the lack of further details, it's not possible to determine which of them this entry refers to. Hartmut Binder surmises that the passage refers to Louise Bailly.
190. Leo Tolstoy's novella *The Kreutzer Sonata,* in a later edition (Jena, 1914), was among the books in Kafka's possession at the time of his death.
191. See note 159.
192. Karl Schönherr's tragedy was performed on January 1, 1911, as a "popular performance at reduced prices" in the Deutsches Landestheater, and on January 5 as a regular performance in the Neues Deutsches Theater; there's no substantiation of a performance on January 4. According to a diary entry by Max Brod (unpublished, privately owned), the friends attended the performance together on January 5.
193. See note 159.
194. Sophie Brod (1892–1963) had become engaged on December 4, 1910, to her later husband Max Friedmann (1885–1963). See Kafka's December 17, 1910, letter to Max Brod: *I haven't congratulated your sister yet either* (KKAB1 no. 177).
195. January 7, 1911, was a Saturday; Kafka probably made a mistake in the date of the entry.
196. See note 159.
197. Leonie Frippon was a member of the ensemble of the Prague cabaret Stadt Wien on Hibernergasse.
198. In 1909 a reproduction of Schadow's profile drawing of Schiller (see the facsimile in Kafka, *Tagebücher: Kommentarband*, p. 52) appeared in the magazine *Die graphischen Künste* (see also note 164), accompanying the essay "Gottfried Schadows Familienalbum" by Hans Mackowsky. Mackowsky wrote: "Schiller in Berlin, a year before his death, enjoyed all the inconveniences of a sightseeing attraction." Regarding his reception, the essay notes, among other things, that "the Berliners at the *Braut von Messina* gave him cheers of 'vivat,'" that he was received by Queen Louise and "was introduced to the royalty in Potsdam." Regarding the drawing, Mackowsky remarks: "Schadow presented what he saw, the high noble forehead, around which the straggly reddish hair hung, the beak-shaped nose, which had been deformed by the wretched habit of pulling at it while working."
199. Martin Beradt's novel *Eheleute* had recently been published by S. Fischer Verlag.
200. *Abschied von der Jugend,* Max Brod's "Romantic Comedy in Three Acts," was published in February of the subsequent year by Axel Juncker Verlag. The first edition, with Brod's handwritten dedication, was among the books in Kafka's possession at the time of his death.
201. Jakob Löwy (1824–1910) and his second wife Julie, née Heller (1827–1908).
202. In February 1911 the ensemble of the Viennese Kleine Bühne with Mella Mars and Béla Laszky, and as of February 15 with Egon Friedell, gave guest performances at the Cabaret Lucerna with great success. Whether Kafka saw the Kleine Bühne's program before or after February 15 cannot be determined with certainty, since this entry—like the entry beginning *Marc Henry—Delvard* . . . on p. 76—might have been written from memory.
203. Probably an impression from the business trip to Friedland from January 30 to ca. February 6, 1911. See January-February 1911 Trips, pp. 497ff.
204. Max Brod asserted that this was a "memory of the Paris trip of the previous year (1910)" (T 697). But *promenoir* could also refer to the arcade in the Prague Cabaret Lucerna, which Kafka described visiting in the entry on Mella Mars.
205. Kafka is quoting from Heinrich von Kleist's March 18–19, 1799, letter to Christian Ernst Martini: "They made objections, asked me which breadwinning field I would take up; for it occurred to no one to doubt that this would be my intention. I faltered. They gave me the choice between jurisprudence and cameralism. I conveyed that I was not averse to those but without making a commitment. They asked

me whether I could count on connections at court? I said no at first in some embarrassment, but then declared all the more proudly that, even if I had connections, according to my current notions I should be ashamed of counting on them. They smiled, I felt that I had been overhasty. One must beware of speaking such truths."

206. Due to an illness, Kafka was forced to break off early the Paris trip he had begun on October 8, 1910, with Max Brod and the latter's brother Otto (1888–1944) and return to Prague alone.
207. Marya Delvard and Marc Henry gave guest performances on February 13 and 17, 1911, in the banquet hall of the Hotel Central.
208. Emanuel Wetzler was the owner of Prague's largest "Concert Management, Music Supplies and Piano Store."
209. Depicted by Bertold Löffler in a color lithograph for the program of the Viennese Cabaret Fledermaus, 1907.
210. A *chanson* by Aristide Bruant. Les Batignolles is the Paris district north of the Champs-Elysées.
211. A term for Parisian muggers, crooks, and pimps.
212. Aristide Bruant was a writer and singer of satirical, humorous songs, infused with argot expressions, that he performed in Parisian cabarets.
213. Kafka later connected the fragment "The Urban World" with his story "The Judgment." See his entry of September 23, 1912, after writing "The Judgment" (pp. 241–242).
214. For Kafka's entries on Rudolf Steiner, see pp. 14–17 and notes 18–30.
215. The reading by Karl Kraus (1874–1936) took place on March 15, 1911, at the Hotel Central and included, among other pieces, "Heine und die Folgen" ("Heine and the Consequences"), "Desperanto, Übersetzungen aus Maximilian Harden" ("Desperanto: Translations from Maximilian Harden"), and "Erdbeben" ("Earthquake"). The lecture by the Viennese architect Adolf Loos (1870–1933) was on the subject of "Ornament und Verbrechen" ("Ornament and Crime") and took place on March 17, 1911, in the lecture hall of the Deutsche Technische Hochschule (German Technical University) on Franzensquai.
216. See note 31.
217. Draft of a letter to Max Brod for his birthday on May 27, 1911.
218. On the August–September 1911 trip, conversations between Kafka and Brod gave rise to the idea to write a novel together on the basis of their travel notes. This diary entry is probably an attempt by Kafka to write a sort of prologue to the story during his stay in the Erlenbach Sanatorium near Zurich (September 14–19, 1911) following the trip. The novel, which at first was to be titled *Robert und Samuel* (see also pp. 107 and 521), then *Richard und Samuel,* didn't succeed beyond the first chapter, which appeared in May 1912 in *Herder-Blätter*. See also p. 217 and note 543.
219. Continuation of the first part, contained in the Sixth Notebook (pp. 244–256), of the text published by Kurt Wolff Verlag in May 1913 under the title "Der Heizer" ("The Stoker"). The writing of this first chapter of the novel *Der Verschollene* (*The Missing Person*) ends with *heaving around their boat* (p. 96). The passage that follows—*In his uncle's house . . . an exagger*—(pp. 97–98)—belongs to the later second chapter of the novel.
220. Jacob Gordin's adaptation of the Faust legend. On the confusion of the names of the authors "Gordon" and "Gordin," see also note 154.
221. Jacob Gordin's *Der vilder Mensh* was announced in the *Prager Tagblatt* of October 24, 1911, for that evening in Café Savoy with the subtitle "Lebensbild von Gordon" ("Picture of a Life by Gordon").
222. This refers to the authors Jacob Gordin, Joseph Latteiner, Abraham Michael Scharkansky, and Sigmund Feinmann.
223. Jacob Gordin's *Gott, Mensch und Teufel.*

224. *Der wilde Mensch.* For the casting of the play reproduced in the passage that follows, see also the facsimile of the playbill, which survived among Kafka's posthumous materials, in Kafka, *Tagebücher: Kommentarband,* p. 58.
225. Regarding Kafka's comments, see the facsimile of the playbill (ibid.).
226. This refers to the slash, conspicuously large in the manuscript, after *nothing for the spectator to see* (p. 100)

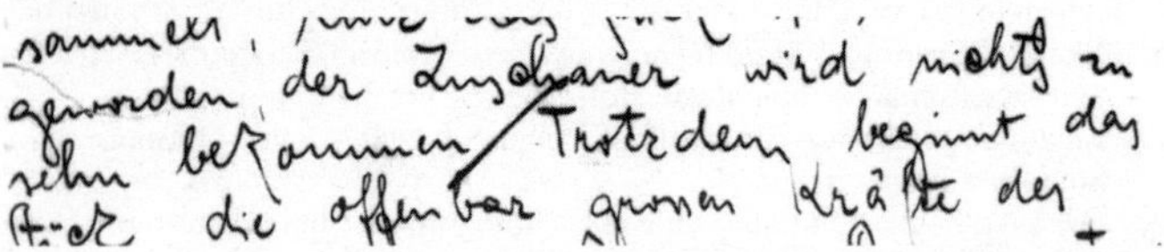

227. The card game every evening, Franzefuß, was among the customs of Kafka's parents. He himself participated in it only rarely—*perhaps the only thing I haven't been able to force myself to do even for my father's sake except on extremely rare occasions* (KKAB1 no. 313)—but often kept them company. See pp. 463–464. How noisy it was during the card playing Kafka also describes in a March 3, 1914, letter to Grete Bloch: *Now my parents are sitting at the table, I can no longer write so peacefully, my father is breathing heavily through his mouth, now he's still reading the evening paper, but then he begins to play the usual card game with my mother with exclamations, laughter and quarreling not to mention whistling* (KKAB2 no. 661).
228. Ottla Kafka.
229. Refers to Jizchak Löwy's diaries about Paris. See p. 99.
230. The quote comes from the autobiographical preface to George Bernard Shaw's second novel *The Irrational Knot.* Which German edition was the basis of Kafka's excerpt could not be determined. The original English reads: "I was an ablebodied and ableminded young man in the strength of my youth; and my family, then heavily embarrassed, needed my help urgently. That I should have chosen to be a burden to them instead was, according to all the conventions of peasant lad fiction, monstrous. Well, without a blush I embraced the monstrosity. I did not throw myself into the struggle for life: I threw my mother into it. I was not a staff to my father's old age: I hung on to his coat tails."
231. In addition to his memories of Paris, Kafka's subsequent entries repeatedly return to Jizchak Löwy's life story, his reports on life in Eastern European Jewish communities, and the Jewish legends he recounted. See pp. 102, 106, 114, 134, 135, 142, 163, 183–185.
232. Kafka made further remarks on the stage and the dressing rooms in Café Savoy in the First Notebook (see pp. 35 and 51).
233. Refers to the performance of *Der vilder Mensh* on October 24, 1911. See note 221.
234. What follows is Kafka's response to Max Brod's article "Axioms on Drama," which had appeared on September 21, 1911, in the magazine *Die Schaubühne.*
235. The theater term for painted lengths of fabric that form the upper edge of the scenery.
236. Apparently a memory of the August–September 1911 trip; on August 27, Kafka and Brod had stopped in Zurich (see Travel Diaries, pp. 505ff.), although there are no notes on a Salvation Army event in the travel writings.
237. Kafka had traveled with Max Brod and his brother Otto to Lake Garda in September 1909 and to Paris in October 1910.
238. Refers to Café Savoy. See note 79.
239. See note 221.
240. Actually by Jacob Gordin.
241. Café City was located on Niklasstraße 30, near the Kafkas' apartment.

242. See note 11. On his walks, Kafka favored the quay plateau that ran along the river at the foot of the quay; see *Elisabethbrücke,* p. 151 and note 363.
243. Notes on Jizchak Löwy's stories about the Tannaim (derived from the Aramaic word for "teacher"), the teachers of the law from the first to third centuries, whose teachings make up the Mishnah (Hebrew for "instruction," "repetition"). Among them were Akiva ben Joseph, a founder of Talmudic Judaism; Elisha ben Abuyah, known as "Acher" ("the other one"); Meir ("the illuminator"), a student of Akiva's and Acher's; and Eliezer ben Hyrcanos ("the great"), who was excommunicated for deviating from a majority decision of his colleagues. See also note 231.
244. Kafka's impressions of one of the weekly meetings of the "inner Prague Circle" follow. See note 128.
245. Brod's note in the edition of Kafka's diaries he published: "At the time I wrote the novella Weiberwirtschaft with the girl I later married [i.e., Elsa Taussig]" (T 700).
246. Regarding Oskar Baum's drama *Konkurrenz,* see note 261.
247. At that time their collaboration on the novel project *Robert and Samuel,* also abbreviated R. & S., came to a halt, but was shortly thereafter continued under the altered title *Richard and Samuel.* See p. 128.
248. Franz Blei, Max Brod, Oskar Baum, Franz Werfel, and numerous other friends and acquaintances of Kafka often contributed to the weekly *Die Aktion,* which had been appearing since February 1911.
249. Wilhelm Schäfer's 1909 novella *Die Mißgeschickten.*
250. This refers to the writings on Paris in August-September 1911 Trip.
251. Refers to the catalogue of the publishing house S. Fischer Verlag for 1911, the *Insel Almanach auf das Jahr 1912,* and the magazine *Die neue Rundschau* published by S. Fischer Verlag.
252. At that time Max Brod rented a room at Schalengasse 4. See note 95.
253. Kafka's second oldest sister.
254. Yiddish for "crazy hothead."
255. Heinrich Graetz's 1888 history of the Jews, *Volkstümliche Geschichte der Juden in drei Bänden.* The entry relates to the beginning of the first volume, *Von der Entstehung des jüdischen Volkes bis zur zweitmaligen Zerstörung Jerusalems unter Kaiser Vespasian* (*From the Emergence of the Jewish People to the Second Destruction of Jerusalem Under Emperor Vespasian*). The second and third volumes—in later editions—were among the books in Kafka's possession at the time of his death.
256. The Yiddish theater troupe at first planned an interruption of the guest performances in Café Savoy from October 31 to November 15, 1911. Herr and Frau Klug departed on October 31, but the rest of the ensemble still appeared on November 3, 4, and 5 with *Bar-Kochba* (see p. 115) before it set off on November 6 on a tour with Pilsen as the first stop. See pp. 118–120 and 121–122.
257. See the facsimile in Kafka, *Tagebücher: Kommentarband,* p. 32.
258. A saying attributed to Fromet, the wife of the philosopher Moses Mendelssohn.
259. The owner of Café Savoy was Josef Herrmann.
260. Karl Hermann, Kafka's brother-in-law.
261. Kafka's envy was probably connected with the success of Oskar Baum's drama *Konkurrenz.* See note 246.
262. A "wonder rabbi" (Wunderrabbi) was a rabbi believed to perform miracles.
263. The Jewish Pesach, or Passover, festival commemorates the exodus from Egypt.
264. Yiddish (Hebrew: *matzah*; plural: *matzot*) term for the unleavened bread baked on the occasion of the Passover festival.
265. During the guest performance break from October 31 to November 15, 1911, the ensemble performed Abraham Goldfaden's *Bar-Kochba* on November 3, 4, and 5, without Herr and Frau Klug, who had departed. See note 256.
266. At that time Oskar Baum lived with his family at Mariengasse 26.

267. Published in slightly altered form under the title "Großer Lärm" ("Great Noise") in October 1912 in the magazine *Herder-Blätter*, edited by Norbert Eisler, Willy Haas, and Otto Pick.
268. For Kafka's literary treatment of a traffic accident he and Brod witnessed in Paris, see August-September 1911 Trip, pp. 542–544.
269. Kafka's description was based on the performance he attended on November 4, 1911, in Café Savoy. See also p. 115.
270. Václav Pokorny, controller in the AUVA. *Kontrollor* was the official title of the engineers entrusted with supervisory and appraisal duties in the operations department (*Betriebsabteilung*).
271. Max Brod's article "Eine Jargonbühne in Prag" ("A Jargon Theater in Prague") had appeared a week earlier, on October 27, 1911, in the *Prager Tagblatt*.
272. Kafka's youthful friend and former schoolmate Hugo Bergmann (1883–1975) was a leading member of the Zionist organization Bar-Kochba: Verein jüdischer Hochschüler in Prag (Bar-Kochba: Association of Jewish University Students in Prague). *Bar Kochba* (Hebrew for "son of the star") was the name given to Simon bar Kosiba, the leader of the final revolt of the Jews in Palestine against the Romans. As of 1899, the Association of Jewish University Students was probably named after an 1897 epic about this revolt by Jaroslav Vrchlický; see note 372.
273. See note 256.
274. The tour was to lead to Nuremberg; see p. 121. After their return, on November 16, 1911, the theater troupe continued their guest performances in Prague's Café Savoy.
275. Kafka visited the lawyer Dr. Robert Kafka concerning the drafting of the partnership agreement for the asbestos factory; see note 100.
276. In October 1910 Kafka and Brod had seen a performance of the play *Manette Salomon* by Edmond de Goncourt at the Paris Théâtre de l'Odéon. The actress who played Manette Salomon was Mademoiselle Barjac.
277. The *Doktor* here and in the following entry refers to the lawyer Dr. Robert Kafka.
278. Frau Tschisik. See note 104.
279. A spa town in northwestern Bohemia, at the foot of the Erzgebirge (Ore Mountains).
280. Translation: if one earned a living. *Parnussa* is Yiddish (Hebrew: *parnāssā*) for "livelihood."
281. Dr. Josef Poláček (1874–1943), a stepson of Kafka's uncle Filip Kafka (1846–1914), was an active member of the Teplitz Jewish community.
282. Altstädter Ring is the German name of Prague's Old Town Square (Czech: Staroměstské náměstí). The Kafka family had lived in a house at Altstädter Ring 2 from June 1889 to September 1896. The other sites mentioned in the entry also have links to Kafka's biography. In Kinsky Palace, Kafka had gone to school (at the Altstädter Deutsches Gymnasium); the Kafka family had lived at Niklasstraße 36 since June 1907. The Old Town Hall with the astronomical clock as well as the Tein (Týn) Church and the Niklas (St. Nicholas) Church with the fountain are located on the Altstädter Ring (also known as the Großer Ring). Until 1918 the Marian Column stood in the middle of the square, and in 1915 the Jan Hus memorial was unveiled there. Niklasstraße meets the Altstädter Ring on the northern side, Eisengasse on the southern side. The old fountain in front of the town hall was apparently known to Kafka from historical depictions, since the Krocín Fountain, erected in 1591–93, was demolished in the 1860s.
283. "If the affect, turned into a proficiency, becomes enduring character, those consensual features of the machine also become more deeply entrenched, they remain behind, if I may borrow the word from the pathologists, deuteropathically and finally become organic." From Friedrich Schiller's treatise *Über den Zusammenhang der tierischen Natur des Menschen mit seiner geistigen* (*On the Connection between the Animal and Spiritual Nature of Man*).
284. Max Brod's book *Über die Schönheit häßlicher Bilder. Ein Vademecum für Romantiker* (*On the*

Beauty of Ugly Pictures: A Vade Mecum for Romantics) was published in May 1913 by Kurt Wolff Verlag. Brod had originally intended to include the unabridged version of Kafka's piece "Die Aeroplane in Brescia" in his book (only a shortened version had appeared in the daily *Bohemia;* see also note 162), but at the publisher's request, the already-typeset book had to be reduced in length, and as a result Kafka's contribution was cut.

285. Kafka was supposed to accompany Brod to a reading in Brünn (Czech: Brno). See p. 127 and note 292.
286. See note 135.
287. Thomas Alva Edison's interview with the New York correspondent of the *Neues Wiener Tagblatt* was reprinted on November 5, 1911, by the *Prager Tagblatt.*
288. Elli Hermann.
289. On November 11, 1911, in the Rudolfinum, the French poet Jean Richepin (1849–1926) lectured on the Napoleonic legend and recited poems by Barbier, Hugo, and Heine, to an enthusiastic reception, as reported in the *Bohemia* of November 12, 1911. Located on the Kronprinz Rudolf-Quai, the Künstlerhaus Rudolfinum housed, among other things, the music conservatory, concert halls, and an art gallery.
290. Alfons Maria Mucha (1860–1939) was a painter, graphic artist, and craftsman from Eibenschütz, in Moravia, who later lived in Paris.
291. "Les deux Grenadiers" ("Die Grenadiere") by Heinrich Heine, translated by Edouard Grenier. The fact that Gérard de Nerval translated all the other poems of the *Nocturnes* cycle and published them in *Poèmes et légendes* in 1855 apparently led to Kafka's error with respect to the translator.
292. Kafka was originally supposed to have accompanied Brod to Brünn for the evening reading. See pp. 123–124. On November 17, 1911, the *Prager Tagblatt* reported: "Last Sunday in Brünn Max Brod read his own works with great success." This notice is followed by a review of the reading by Karl Hans Strobl reprinted from the *Brünner Tagesbote* of November 12, 1911.
293. Included by Kafka under the title "Das Unglück des Junggesellen" ("The Unhappiness of the Bachelor") in his first book publication, *Betrachtung.* See also note 157.
294. See note 218 and note 247.
295. Note by Max Brod: "Refers to studying for the bar examination and oral examinations" (T 700–1).
296. According to the *Prager Tagblatt* of February 19, 1911, the French singer Yvonne de Tréville had given guest performances in Prague in November 1910 and in February 1911.
297. The Prague suburb in which Kafka and his brother-in-law's asbestos factory was located. See notes 101 and 117.
298. On October 30, 1911, the fourth performance of Arthur Schnitzler's tragicomedy *Das weite Land* (*The Distant Land*) was given in the Neues Deutsches Theater, with the author present; Schnitzler was staying in Prague for a reading that was to take place the following day. There was another performance on Saturday, November 18, 1911. The dream recorded by Kafka a day later might be based on his attendance at one of these performances, although the people mentioned in the entry have no connection with Schnitzler's play or the Prague performances.
299. Emil Utitz (1883–1956) was a former schoolmate of Kafka with whom Kafka remained in contact; see p. 228. Both of them were associated with the Brentanist and Fanta circle; see note 18. In 1910 Utitz had gone to the University of Rostock, where he worked at the time of this entry as a *Privatdozent* (lecturer) of philosophy.
300. The Prague Kisch family had five sons. Paul, Kafka's former schoolmate, was the oldest (1883–1944), followed by Egon Erwin (1885–1948), Wolfgang (1887–1914), Arnold (1889–1942), and Friedrich (1894–1968).
301. Paul Kisch. The name the German Kisch goes back to Kisch's time as a *Couleurstu-*

dent, as members of student associations who wore distinctive colors were known, and his German nationalist sentiments.

302. Although Gertrud Hackelberg was a member of the Deutsches Landestheater ensemble, she didn't appear in any of the performances of *Das weite Land.*
303. Probably the manuscript of the book reviews by Max Brod that appeared in the *Prager Tagblatt* on November 26, 1911, under the title "Neue Literatur" ("New Literature").
304. Refers to their collaboration on *Richard und Samuel.* See note 218.
305. A dream sequence probably based on the painting *L'Age d'or* by Jean A. D. Ingres. Kafka might have been familiar with a publication that had appeared in Paris that April: Henri Lapauze, *Ingres, sa vie, son œuvre illustré de 400 reproductions et de 11 héliogravures.*
306. Notes for a planned drama are followed by a draft of a first scene.
307. The English teacher Emil Weis was a friend and distant relative of Max Brod. In an obituary in the *Selbstwehr* of October 6, 1922, Brod wrote: "All Prague knew him as a figure who was part of the Prague cityscape: the short red-haired man."
308. Marie Werner, who was employed by the Kafka family for many years, was generally referred to as "*das Fräulein,*" the term Kafka uses here in the original German.
309. A further attempt at a scene of the planned drama (see p. 133). The replacement of the name *Emil* by *Karl,* not yet executed consistently, suggests that these attempts belong together.
310. On November 22, 1911, under the headline "Trauerfeier am Grabe Kleists" ("Memorial Service at Kleist's Grave"), the *Prager Tagblatt* reported: "In addition, wreaths were laid by the Kleist family, with the inscription 'To the greatest of their house.'"
311. Since there is no documented performance of this play (*Die Schechite*) by Jacob Gordin from the time the Yiddish theater troupe resumed their guest performances on November 16, 1911, this entry apparently relates to Löwy's reading in the coffeehouse mentioned in the next entry.
312. A side street of Ferdinandstraße, one of Prague's boulevards.
313. See note 241.
314. Eduard Mischka (Czech: Myška).
315. The introduction of "Compulsory Pension Insurance for Employees" meant a considerable financial burden for business owners like Hermann Kafka. In February 1912 the Prague notions and fancy goods trade association (Zentralverein der Kurz- und Galanteriewaren-Interessenten zu Prag) therefore appealed to the Ministry of the Interior and the Social Policy Committee with a telegram in which it "strongly protested against a further expansion of compulsory pension insurance" and implored them "not to endorse this intolerable new burden on the dealers," as reported in the *Prager Tagblatt* of February 15, 1912.
316. "Die Häßlichen" was written by the Prague author Norbert Eisler, who founded the magazine *Herder-Blätter* with Otto Pick and Willy Haas in the spring of 1912. "Die Häßlichen" appeared in the January 1912 issue of the magazine *Deutsche Arbeit* with the note "From the novel *Der Doktor mit dem Heiligenschein,* which will appear in the beginning of 1912."
317. Collaboration with Max Brod on the novel project *Richard und Samuel.* See note 218.
318. Anton Max Pachinger (1864–1938), Hofrat (court councilor) from Linz, wrote on November 25, 1911, to his friend Alfred Kubin: "On Sunday I'm heading to Prague, Monday Vienna . . . Unfortunately the message came from Prague that Dr. B[rod]. isn't free on Saturday evening (I had reserved that evening for Prague). He mentioned nothing at all about his friends." Pachinger had been inspired to establish contact with Max Brod and to visit Prague by Kubin's enthusiastic reports on his wanderings in Prague's nightlife with Brod, Kafka, and others; see p. 20 and

note 42. Kafka's note *recommended by Kubin* also indicates this connection. Max Brod mentioned Pachinger's visit in a review of *Glaube und Aberglaube im Steinreich* (*Belief and Superstition in the Mineral Kingdom*), published on January 28, 1912, in the *Prager Tagblatt* immediately following an article on Kubin.

319. Pachinger published several works on pilgrimage medals (*Wallfahrtsmedaillen*) and other religious medals and coins.

320. In the above-mentioned review of January 28, 1912 (note 318), Max Brod wrote: "At the 'Hygiene Exhibition' in Dresden, Pachinger's collection devoted to 'Historical Medicine' was a sight worth seeing."

321. The Hotel Graf was located on Komenskyplatz 4.

322. Kubin had recently made a bookplate for Pachinger. In the above-cited November 25, 1911, letter (note 318), Pachinger wrote to Kubin: "Many thanks for the letter and bookplate!"

323. Pachinger's book *Glaube und Aberglaube im Steinreich* (*Belief and Superstition in the Mineral Kingdom*), rendered by Kafka as *Zauberei und Aberglaube im Steinreich (Magic and Superstition in the Mineral Kingdom),* appeared in late 1911.

324. The title was actually *Die Mutterschaft in der Malerei und Graphik* (*Motherhood in Painting and Graphic Art*).

325. Little soul
you leap in dance
lay your head in warm air
lift your feet from glistening grass
which the wind gently stirs

Preserved on a calendar page with "September. / 17. Freitag" printed on it. Inferred year: 1909. See KKANI 181.

326. By reproducing Persian *ghazals,* Friedrich Rückert had introduced this poetic form into German literature.

327. The writer Max Halbe (1865–1944).

328. Franz Blei (see note 7) was regarded as a "master of literary erotomania." Franz Blei, *Erzählung eines Lebens* (Vienna, 2004), p. 515.

329. Maria Blei (see note 7) ran a dental practice in Munich; the daughter was Maria Sybille Blei (1897–1963?).

330. Carl Sternheim's comedy *Die Hose* had recently—on November 20, 1911—been performed for the first time under that title for an invited audience in Munich. The actual premiere had taken place under the altered title *Der Riese* on February 15, 1911, in Berlin.

331. *Am ha'aretz* (Hebrew): Talmudic term for uneducated people (also illiterates), in contrast to scholars.

332. Adherents to Chassidism, a religious mystical movement in Judaism, which arose in the eighteenth century in Ukraine, rapidly spread to Poland and Romania, and became a prevailing form of Jewish piety.

333. Hebrew for "tradition": a term for medieval Jewish mysticism. Chassidism is a popularization of the doctrines of the Kabbalah.

334. Probably title ideas for a literary treatment of Kafka's encounter with the Yiddish theater troupe.

335. Preserved on a notepad with tear-off pages is a series of entries consisting of keywords, sometimes crossed out to mark them as "used," which almost all served as a source for diary entries in the Fourth and Fifth Notebooks. For the corresponding diary entries, the notes that follow indicate the respective notepad entry that may be related to them. The first of these notepad entries were apparently written during the reading of Wilhelm Schäfer's book *Karl Stauffers Lebensgang. Eine Chronik der Leidenschaft* (Munich, 1911).

336. Eduard Mörike (1804–75) was a German poet and writer.
337. See note 218 and the passage in *Richard und Samuel* that begins with the words *Wir steigen in das Koupee ein* in KKAD 431–432.
338. See note 283.
339. Until 1918 the hunting castle on the hill over the Baumgarten (Czech: Stromovka), commonly known as the Statthalterschloß (the governor's castle), served the sitting governor of the Kingdom of Bohemia as a summer residence. From Paul Wiegler's 1934 novel *Das Haus an der Moldau* (*The House on the Moldau*): "Through the iron-barred gate, which was open for the wagons, Manja reached the castle of the governor, a Norman fort. From there the path led to the Baumgarten . . . they entered the Baumgarten. Behind them the Norman battlements of the governor's villa faded."
340. Prague's largest island in the Moldau was popular as an excursion destination because of its park facilities and outdoor restaurants.
341. This refers to the Yiddish theater troupe.
342. *Castle* here refers to the Prague Castle, the Hradschin (Czech: Hradčany).
343. See pp. 144–145 and note 337.
344. Probably the same as the above-mentioned Helli Haas. See p. 22 and note 56.
345. Maria Blei. See also p. 7 and note 7.
346. See p. 103 and note 221.
347. Café Central, located on the second floor of the building at Graben 15, reopened on November 18, 1911, according to an advertisement in the *Prager Tagblatt* of the same day.
348. See note 98.
349. Jizchak Löwy.
350. Probably the Franzens-Quai, the oldest Moldau promenade in Prague.
351. Refers—as does the entry on p. 148 beginning *Only later can it surprise us . . .*—to Otto Brahm's 1892 book *Karl Stauffer-Bern: sein Leben, seine Briefe, seine Gedichte.*
352. Quote from Karl Stauffer-Bern's January 15, 1886, letter.
353. Felix Hermann (1911–40), the first child of Kafka's sister Elli and Karl Hermann, had been born the previous day, December 9.
354. See note 351.
355. In an April 19, 1887, letter, Stauffer-Bern wrote about the death of his friend Lissel. Kafka's notepad contains the note *death of Lissner and contemplation.*
356. On December 12, 1911, the actress Else Lehmann (1866–1940) from the Berlin Lessing Theater played Mother Wolffen in Gerhart Hauptmann's *Der Biberpelz,* in the second and final performance of her guest appearance at Prague's Neues Deutsches Theater.
357. After a break in the guest performances, an advertisement in the *Prager Tagblatt* of December 9, 1911, announced the "Continuation of the Guest Performances of the German-Jewish [*Deutsch-jüdischen,* i.e., Yiddish] Company from Lemberg" for the same evening at Café Savoy "with the participation of the famous comedian and the singer Herr and Frau Liebgold from the Jewish theater in Lemberg."
358. On December 10 and 11, 1911, Herrmann's Café-Restaurant Savoy announced the premiere of Moses Richter's *Mojsche Chajet oder: Der Schneider als Gemeinderat* in the *Prager Tagblatt.* Kafka probably attended the December 11 performance.
359. On December 13, 1911, the "Brahms Evening" of the Deutscher Singverein (German Choral Society) and the Deutscher Männergesangverein (German Men's Choral Society) took place in the Rudolfinum, conducted by Gerhard von Keußler.
360. The asbestos factory, in which Hermann Kafka also had a financial stake, increasingly became a point of contention between father and son in the period that followed; see p. 169. Apparently in connection with this confrontation, Kafka noted on his notepad: *My hatred of my father.*
361. On December 16, 1911, Max Brod "read with great success in the Harmoniumsaal

in Berlin his own works and poems by the young Prague poet Franz Werfel," as reported in the *Prager Tagblatt* of December 19, 1911. See also p. 154 and note 378.

362. Elsa Taussig (1883–1942), Max Brod's later wife.
363. Seen from the quay plateau (see p. 106 and note 242) down by the river, the Elisabethbrücke (known by this name among Prague residents because Elisabethstraße led to it, but officially the Kaiser Franz Josefs-Brücke) offered the described nocturnal impressions due to its suspended structure. See also the picture in WB 69.
364. "Beethoven und das Liebespaar" ("Beethoven and the Lovers"), a story by Wilhelm Schäfer.
365. December 16, 1911, was a Saturday. Kafka probably added the date subsequently in the space that remained after the beginning of a paragraph.
366. Possibly "Das ist ein Anblick" ("What a sight it is"), Kafka's review of the recent book *Heinrich von Kleist: Anekdoten.* There's no evidence of a publication of this review in Kafka's lifetime.
367. In his 1912 collection of reportage, *Aus Prager Gassen und Nächten*, Egon Erwin Kisch describes the Prague Christmas Market as follows: "While other cities have long had their Luna Park, . . . at the Old Town Christmas Market there are still just merry-go-rounds with visible manual operation. And while elsewhere they threaten to probe the depths of fate in spiritistic séances, here—though with the same effect—the Prague maid has white mice or canaries draw 'fortunes' [*'Planeten'*] for her, slips of paper with printed prophecies and—though for this you pay a higher charge—with a picture of the future . . . and the artificial flowers being peddled are so honestly imitated that no one could take them for real ones." The Czech saying, which—with the addition of the word *planéty*—is also written on Kafka's notepad, means: "That is a rose made of leather."
368. Kafka's notepad contains the keywords: *covered with splinters of glass—sweat.*
369. On Kafka's notepad is the entry: *warm shadow in the throat.*
370. This entry might derive from a conversation with Jizchak Löwy, who had stayed in Paris and related his impressions to Kafka. Without the addition of *Jewish streets in Paris,* this entry is also written on Kafka's notepad.
371. Kafka's notepad contains the note: *disordered called-upon education.*
372. The drama *Hippodamie* by Jaroslav Vrchlický (actually Emil Frída, 1853–1912) premiered on December 17, 1911, at the Czech National Theater. See also the entry beginning *Hippodamie the day before yesterday* . . . .
373. Kafka made an error in dating the entry after the event. According to the announcement in the *Selbstwehr* of December 15, 1911, *Hippodamie* was performed at the Czech National Theater on December 17.
374. Jaroslav Kvapil (1868–1950) was the dramaturge and director of the Czech National Theater.
375. Max Reinhardt (1873–1943) regularly directed guest performances at Prague's German-language theaters by the ensembles of Berlin's Deutsches Theater and the Kammerspiele. Apparently Kvapil was influenced by Reinhardt beyond the particular case judged by Kafka. "Jaroslav Kvapil . . . directed in the manner of M. Reinhardt," wrote Antonín Měšťan in a history of nineteenth- and twentieth-century Czech literature.
376. At the time of the entry, Prince Franz Anton von Thun und Hohenstein (1847–1916) was governor of the Kingdom of Bohemia and official representative of the Austrian Kaiser.
377. The reviewer, Albert Ehrenstein, was a friend of Viennese satirist Karl Kraus and a contributor to Kraus's journal *Die Fackel* (*The Torch*). At that time, Brod's relations with Kraus and his circle had soured.
378. Regarding Max Brod's reading in Berlin's Harmoniumsaal on December 16, 1911 (see also p. 185), the *Prager Tagblatt* published three days later (December 19, 1911)

an excerpt from a positive review in the *Berliner Lokal-Anzeiger* and the one mentioned from the *Berliner Tageblatt* of December 17, 1911. In the latter, however, two passages that apparently displeased Brod were omitted, as well as the last section in which his musical performance following the reading is panned with, among other remarks, the sentence: "If he hadn't prudently covered himself with Werfel beforehand: the audience would have had a hard time sitting so patiently through this part of the program." In the excerpt from the *Prager Tagblatt* reproduced here, the passages deleted by Brod—Kafka alludes to the second one—are provided in brackets: "In the [poorly attended] Harmoniumsaal, Max Brod, the author of the peculiar novella 'Ein tschechisches Dienstmädchen,' first read several of his unpublished works. . . . Simple, plain people from the provinces are well drawn with a few substantial strokes, and one supposed the evening would also go on without any particular emotions. One hadn't reckoned with a selflessness on Brod's part worthy of the highest praise. He made a change to the program that was greeted with approval and suddenly began to read five quite incredibly strong poems by a [far more talented] twenty-two-year-old Prague poet whose discovery German literature might owe to him." The poems presented by Brod were from Werfel's recent poetry collection *Der Weltfreund* (*The Friend of the World*); see also note 388. In his memoirs, Brod was still offended decades later by the review attributed to Albert Ehrenstein.

379. Franz Werfel (1890–1945). Through his schoolmate and friend Willy Haas (see note 543), Werfel had become acquainted with Brod, who then brought him together with his friends Kafka and Weltsch.
380. Unidentified.
381. Kafka probably added the date subsequently in the space left after the beginning of a paragraph. According to an advertisement in the *Prager Tagblatt* of December 19, 1911, the performance of *David's Geige* took place the same evening in Café Savoy.
382. See p. 173.
383. Probably Lise Weltsch (1889–1974), a cousin of Kafka's friend Felix Weltsch. Her father, Dr. Theodor Weltsch, was a board member of the Centralverein zur Pflege jüdischer Angelegenheiten (Central Association for the Promotion of Jewish Affairs), and in 1911 her brother, Robert, was head of Bar-Kochba: Verein jüdischer Hochschüler in Prag (Bar-Kochba: Association of Jewish University Students in Prague). Lise Weltsch was on the board of the Klub jüdischer Frauen und Mädchen (Jewish Women and Girls' Club). The possibility that Kafka is referring to Felix Weltsch's sister Elizabeth (see p. 160) cannot be ruled out with certainty.
384. Frau Tschisik. See note 104.
385. Alfred Löwy (1852–1923), a brother of Julie Kafka, was director of a Spanish railroad company and lived in Madrid.
386. Rudolf Löwy (1861–1921) was a half-brother of Julie Kafka. He was a bookkeeper in a Prague brewery, converted to Catholicism out of conviction, and was regarded as the family eccentric. See also p. 472.
387. The next day, December 24, 1911, under the headline "Neue Farbelithographien von Willy Nowak" ("New Color Lithographs by Willy Nowak"), the *Prager Tagblatt* wrote: "Willi Nowak, our country's great artist, has just now created four new color lithographs, which attest once again to the greatness of this master. They are four pieces of rare perfection and harmony in the style of the old masters. The 'Walk' in particular will enchant all connoisseurs. The 'Girl with Apples' shows his delicate coloring, the portrait of Max Brod his fabulous nobility, the 'Bathing Girls' a gracefulness of forms reminiscent of the French greats. All four sheets can be seen in our picture exhibition and purchased in the Hübscher art gallery (Elisabethstraße)."
388. Franz Werfel's poetry collection *Der Weltfreund* (*The Friend of the World*) had appeared in the first half of December.

389. Here and in all the entries that follow, unless otherwise indicated: Felix Weltsch (1884–1964). Kafka probably became acquainted with Weltsch, whose connection with Max Brod went back to a childhood and school friendship, in 1903, either in the Brentanist circle, to which both belonged, or through Brod, who refers in his book *Der Prager Kreis* (*The Prague Circle*) to "the triumvirate Kafka, Weltsch, Brod."
390. The café and cinematograph theater of the same name in the building at Hibernergasse 20.
391. Max Brod.
392. Felix Weltsch.
393. Elizabeth Weltsch (1888–1944), known as Betty.
394. Felix Hermann.
395. Lev Austerlitz, rabbi of the Prague Jewish community.
396. Yiddish for "circumciser" (Hebrew: *mohel*). The Yiddish phonetic form in Prague was actually *moyel,* in West Bohemia *mou(h)el.*
397. This entry and the one that follows apparently record stories told by Jizchak Löwy (see note 231) inspired by Kafka's account of the ceremony on the occasion of his nephew's circumcision.
398. Hebrew for "Hear, Israel"; the central Jewish prayer named after the first words of Deuteronomy 6:4–9, usually expanded by Deuteronomy 11:13–21 and Numbers 15:37–41.
399. Adam Porias (1794–1862), whose name in Yiddish was "Amschel Brias."
400. Esther Löwy, née Porias (1830–59).
401. Sara Porias, née Levit (?–1860).
402. Nathan Porias (1824–?)
403. Schloss Stern (Czech: Letohrádek Hvězda, English: Star Villa), a castle located in a park outside Prague to the west, built in Renaissance style in the shape of a star.
404. Joseph Latteiner's *Blümale* was performed by the Lemberg theater company on December 25, 1911, in Café Savoy, with Frau Tschisik in the title role.
405. Elsa Taussig.
406. A continuation of the entries beginning *What I discern of contemporary Jewish literature* . . . (pp. 161–163) and *By the power of his works* . . . (p. 164). See also the entry beginning *Schema for the characterization of small literatures* . . . (p. 168).
407. On all Prague's bridges, with the exception of the Karlsbrücke (Charles Bridge), a bridge toll was charged. In *Aus Prager Gassen und Nächten,* Egon Erwin Kisch wrote: "the bridge toll is an inconvenience for the rich, a tangible expense for the poor. Whenever a bridge is built in Prague, modern transportation is swindled and logic vanquished by the placing of a tollbooth at either end of the bridge."
408. The page numbers subsequently noted by Kafka show that his diary entries on *Dichtung und Wahrheit* are based on the 1910 Tempel-Klassiker edition of Goethe's works. See pp. 169 and 195.
409. Hermann Kafka's sister Julie Ehrmann (1855–1921) from Strakonitz. Regarding Kafka's description of her appearance, see the photograph in WB 95.
410. Probably related to the entry on Kafka's notepad: *Not happy even in a child.*
411. Relates to the entries on pp. 161–163, 164, and 166.
412. The confrontation in the entry on p. 151 had apparently resulted in Kafka's commitment to attend to the family's asbestos factory in the afternoon (that is, after his work in the AUVA).
413. The inspection was apparently carried out in connection with the authorization procedure, which was initiated by the December 18, 1911, application for the "Errichtung einer offenen Handelsgesellschaft" ("The Establishment of an Open Trading Company") from the commercial court (*Handelsgericht*) in Prague.
414. Refers to Kafka's work and his superior in the AUVA, Chief Inspector Eugen Pfohl; see note 15. In a March 14–15, 1913, letter to Felice Bauer, Kafka wrote: *in his absolute*

firmness my boss in the office gives me strength, I can't follow him but can imitate him consciously up to a certain limit, unconsciously up to a further limit and continue at least to observe him and hold on to that (KKAB2 no. 466).

415. See also p. 167 and note 408.
416. See the entry on p. 175 beginning *New Year's Eve* . . .
417. *Die christliche Welt*, a Protestant magazine, was first published in 1887.
418. Hugo Bergmann (see note 272) confirms the debate on God and his possibility in his "Erinnerungen an Franz Kafka" ("Memories of Franz Kafka").
419. On Kafka's notepad is the entry: *I had bad clothes.*
420. A suburb located southeast of Prague, incorporated into the city as a district in 1922.
421. The January 1912 issue of *Die neue Rundschau* included Emil Strauß's "Der nackte Mann," chapters 1 and 2, and Gerhart Hauptmann's "Gabriel Schillings Flucht."
422. See the entry on p. 171 beginning *In the morning I felt so fresh* . . .
423. *Richard and Samuel.* See note 218.
424. Located across the street from the Neues Deutsches Theater, the Stadtpark-Restaurant (Mariengasse, at the corner of Bredauergasse), which had been reopened in late 1910, was run by Karl Čáda. Kafka's notepad also records the name of the tenant as a keyword.
425. Probably Egon Erwin Kisch. Paul Kisch, the older brother who was friendly with Kafka, spent Christmas and New Year's Eve in Vienna in 1911.
426. An expansion of the entry on Kafka's notepad: *ferns fire.*
427. The brand name for fruit juices from the Ceres factory in Ringelshain, Bohemia.
428. Refers to the plan to read to each other on New Year's Eve, which fell on a Sunday in 1911. See pp. 171–172, 175.
429. Apparently a reflection on the use of *often* in the entry on pp. 172ff. Kafka's notepad contains the entry: *the often in diaries.*
430. Though written in the middle of the line in the style of a heading, this entry is separated by a short horizontal line from the text that follows and therefore probably should not be understood as the title of that text.
431. Included by Kafka under the title "Der plötzliche Spaziergang" ("The Sudden Walk") in his book *Betrachtung* (*Contemplation;* see note 157), published in December 1912. Kafka's notepad contains the note: *the unhappiness from staying home.*
432. The *Prager Tagblatt* of January 5, 1912, announced the "great benefit performance by the popular soubrette Frau Flora Klug," together with the performance of *Der Vicekönig,* for that evening in Café Savoy.
433. Sigmund Feinmann's *Der Vitse-Kenig.*
434. Frau Tschisik.
435. Hersh David Nomberg (1876–1927), essayist and short story writer, co-founder of the Polish-Jewish Folkspartei (People's Party).
436. Herr and Frau Tschisik.
437. The play by Abraham Scharkansky. See also note 143.
438. See note 264.
439. Kafka had attended a performance of *Die Sejdernacht* by Joseph Latteiner on October 8, 1911. See p. 37 and note 94.
440. Hebrew for "Creator of Israel."
441. Traditional Jewish schools devoted chiefly to the study of the Talmud. *Yeshivas* is also a keyword on Kafka's notepad.
442. Hebrew for "head of the Yeshiva."
443. On Kafka's notepad are the two entries: *Ostro, 10 hours' journey* and *count's carriage.*
444. Yiddish (*kloyz*) for a house of study.
445. Kafka's nephew Felix Hermann.
446. In 1912 the writer Karl Hans Strobl (1877–1946) was living as a tax official in Brünn

(Czech: Brno). As a literary and theater critic, he wrote for the *Brünner Tagesbote,* among other publications. See note 292.

447. By the feuilleton "on the folk song," Kafka apparently meant Oskar Baum's feuilleton article "Ghettolieder" ("Ghetto Songs"), which appeared in the *Prager Tagblatt* on January 14, 1912. There's no record of a publication by Baum with the title "Des Schicksals Spiele und Ernst"; possibly this refers to the story "Ein Schicksal" that appeared in 1912 in Heidelberg.
448. Either an unrealized "plan" or one that ended up having another name. Neither this title nor a character with this name is to be found in Brod's published oeuvre.
449. Morris Rosenfeld, "Sturm" ("Storm"), the sixth strophe of which reads, in a 1903 German translation from the Yiddish by Berthold Feiwel:

    "Da wimmern die Kleinen und klagen die Weiber,
    Und alles bekennt voll Reu' seine Schuld.
    Es flattern die Seelen, es zittern die Leiber:
    'Erbarme dich unser in deiner Huld!'"

    ("The little ones whimper and the women lament,
    And full of remorse all confess their guilt.
    The souls flutter, the bodies tremble.
    'Take pity on us in your grace!'")

450. Ernst Ascher (1888–?).
451. Meyer Isses Pinès, *Histoire de la Littérature Judéo-Allemande* (Paris, 1911). See also Kafka's excerpts on pp. 188–191. The appearance of this publication might have been brought to Kafka's attention or the attention of one of his friends by a reference in the magazine *Selbstwehr* of November 3, 1911, titled "Eine Geschichte der Jargon-Literatur in französischer Sprache" ("A French-Language History of Jargon Literature").
452. Jakob Fromer, *Der Organismus des Judentums* (Charlottenburg, 1909).
453. On January 26, 1912, under the headline "Jüdisches Theater," the weekly *Selbstwehr* wrote: "A Jewish theater company, which has just completed a four-month guest appearance in Prague and is now performing in Pilsen, would be available to give guest performances in the Bohemian provinces as of the 27th of this month. Because the troupe has excellent talent and puts on extremely interesting plays, so that a guest performance conveys a truly valuable picture of Eastern Jewish life in a very entertaining form, the organization of one or two theater evenings (for which a special stage isn't necessary) would be wholeheartedly recommended to the Jewish associations in those cities where a substantial Jewish population resides. In order to avoid drawn-out negotiations, the editorial office of the *Selbstwehr* is prepared to serve as an intermediary."
454. The Lemberg Jewish theater company performed *Sulamit* by Abraham Goldfaden on January 12, 1912, in Café Savoy. Kafka had already seen the operetta on October 13, 1911; see pp. 40–41. On January 19, 1912, the Jewish folk play *Herzele Mejiches* by Moses Richter was performed there too, announced in an advertisement in that day's *Prager Tagblatt* "in honor of the guest Dr. Nathan Birnbaum (M. Acher)." The day before, January 18, 1912, Birnbaum, known under the pen name "Mathias Acher," gave the introductory lecture to Bar-Kochba's festive evening. On January 22, 1912, the play *Der Graf von Gleichen* by Wilhelm Schmidtbonn premiered at the Neues Deutsches Theater.
455. Probably Dr. Theodor Weltsch (1861–1922), uncle of Kafka's friend Felix and father of Robert and Lise Weltsch; lawyer and board member of the Centralverein zur Pflege jüdischer Angelegenheiten (Central Association for the Promotion of Jewish Affairs).

456. The Jewish folk song evening organized by the Bar-Kochba Association took place on January 18, 1912, in the sold-out large banquet hall of the Hotel Central at Hibernergasse 10. The program that followed Nathan Birnbaum's introduction, "Das Lied der Ostjuden" ("The Song of the Eastern Jews"), included the performance of Jewish folk songs by the Berlin singer and cantor Leo Gollanin as well as recitations of Eastern European Jewish poems in German translation by Margarethe Neff, an actress of the Deutsches Landestheater.

457. See also note 451. The bibliographic reference, which is roughly in the middle of the right side of a diary page, is followed by a series of excerpts from the French edition in Kafka's translation. The missing text after the bibliographic reference and after *Marek 1901)* resulted from the subsequent removal of the lower half of the first page. Kafka probably used these notes for his introduction to Jizchak Löwy's recitation evening; see p. 196.

458. Probably the titles mentioned in the entry on p. 192.

459. In the Prague premiere of the tragedy *Erdgeist* on February 1, 1912, at the Neues Deutsches Theater, the author Frank Wedekind gave a guest performance in the role of the editor-in-chief Schön and his wife Tilly as Lulu, as reported in that day's *Bohemia*.

460. The performance of Jacques Offenbach's operetta *Orpheus in der Unterwelt* with Max Pallenberg as Jupiter took place on January 31, 1912, at the Neues Deutsches Theater. Pallenberg had been celebrated enthusiastically during his Prague guest performance, so that, according to the *Prager Tagblatt* of January 29, 1912, this performance was scheduled as a sort of encore.

461. Apparently after a reply to the circular and the appeal in the *Selbstwehr*. See p. 187 and note 453.

462. *Goethes Gespräche*, ed. Woldemar Frhr. v. Biedermann (see pp. 255–259 and notes 525–526); *Goethes Studentenjahre (1765–1771). Novellistische Schilderungen aus dem Leben des Dichters* (Leipzig, 1910); *Stunden mit Goethe*, ed. W. Bode (Berlin, 1904ff). *A Stay of Goethe's in Frankfurt* (*Ein Aufenthalt Goethes in Frankfurt*) might refer to Ludwig Geiger, *Goethe in Frankfurt am Main 1797. Aktenstücke und Darstellung* (Frankfurt, 1899).

463. Salomon Schmerler, an active member of the Prague Jewish community, participated in the organization of Jizchak Löwy's recitation evening. It's possible that this entry records Kafka's impressions from the preliminary conversation that he mentions later; see p. 196 and note 476. Schmerler's name is also on a list on Kafka's notepad in which he apparently recorded the proceeds from collections for the recitation evening.

464. Apparently Kafka attended the performance of Frank Wedekind's *Erdgeist* (p. 191) with Elsa Taussig.

465. As in the case of "Weiberwirtschaft" (see note 245), this refers to a story Elsa Taussig wrote in collaboration with Max Brod, which the latter included under the title "Aus einer Nähschule" in his book *Weiberwirtschaft. Drei Erzählungen* (Berlin, 1913).

466. The *Selbstwehr* of February 2, 1912, reported: "On January 28 Dr. Felix A. Theilhaber, the author of the book *The Decline of the German Jews*, spoke in Prague's Jewish Town Hall; from the material he dealt with in his book he tried to extract the fundamental features that necessarily lead in such a convincing way to the insight: German Jewry has fallen into decline. In general the speaker limited himself to summarizing in broad outlines what he had said in the book."

467. Christian Freiherr von Ehrenfels (1859–1932) was a professor of philosophy at the German Karls-Universität (Charles University) and founder of gestalt theory. During his studies, Kafka had attended Ehrenfels's lectures and as late as 1913 participated in sessions of a seminar of his. See p. 308.

468. Dr. Siegmund Fleischmann (1878–1935) was a clerk in the AUVA. Kafka had met him in 1908 as an instructor in a preparatory course for those aspiring to work in the AUVA. In later years, Kafka expressed high regard for his colleague.

469. Included by Kafka under the title "Entschlüsse" ("Decisions") in his book *Betrachtung* (*Contemplation*), published in December 1912.
470. See also note 408.
471. Kafka was organizing a recitation evening with Jizchak Löwy. Initially Oskar Baum was supposed to say the introductory words, but after some hesitation he declined, and Kafka took on the task himself. His introduction has survived as "Einleitungsvortrag über Jargon" ("Introductory Lecture on Jargon") in a transcription by Elsa Taussig-Brod (KKANI 188–93).
472. A review in the *Selbstwehr* of February 23, 1912, reported that on February 18 "the announced recitation evening by the Warsaw actor Herr J. Loewy took place in the banquet hall of the Jewish Town Hall. After a fine and gracious lecture given by Herr Dr. Kafka, Herr Loewy opened his performances with his own recitations and offered a colorful abundance of serious and light-hearted pieces, dramatic scenes and song."
473. At Kafka's request the Zionist Bar-Kochba Association of Jewish University Students took on the patronage of the event and rented the banquet hall of the Jewish Town Hall on Maiselgasse from the religious community council.
474. See note 732.
475. While the *Prager Tagblatt* alerted its readers to the event only in brief form, the *Bohemia* provided more details, including information on individual items on the program.
476. The *Selbstwehr* wrote in the above-cited review: "Herr Schneller explained the texts in a speech tirelessly opening every section of the program." This is probably an incorrect rendering of the name *Schmerler*. On Salomon Schmerler, see also p. 192 and note 463.
477. See p. 195 and note 471.
478. The cousins Hugo and Leo Hermann were leading members of Bar-Kochba. In late 1910, Leo Hermann had taken over the editorial leadership of the Zionist weekly *Selbstwehr*, for which Hugo also wrote regularly.
479. Café Arco, at Hibernergasse 16, was the meeting place of young literati, where Franz Werfel was also a regular visitor.
480. Robert Weltsch (1891–1983), a cousin of Kafka's friend Felix Weltsch, was at that time head of the Bar-Kochba Association.
481. Possibly the lawyer Dr. Arthur Bloch, an active member of the Prague Jewish community.
482. Dr. Emanuel Hanzal (1880–?), a colleague in the AUVA, was promoted together with Kafka to the position of *Concipist* (a clerk responsible for drafting legal documents) in April 1910. See also Kafka's *Dream of Dr. Hanzal*, p. 419.
483. Dr. Siegmund Fleischmann was a colleague of Kafka's in the AUVA. See also note 468.
484. Elsa Taussig.
485. At the invitation of the "Verein zur Förderung und Verbreitung der Wissenschaft des Judentums, Afike Jehuda" ("Association for the Promotion and Dissemination of the Study of Judaism, Afike Jehuda"), the Munich rabbi Dr. Chanoch Heinrich Ehrentreu spoke on February 13, 1912, at the Hotel Bristol at Langegasse 11 (according to an announcement in the *Selbstwehr* of February 9, 1912).
486. Emil Weis. See note 307.
487. Probably Jizchak Löwy.
488. Dr. Karl Bendiener, his father, Dr. Ludwig Bendiener, and Siegfried Liebers were members of the Jewish religious community council.
489. At that time, the writer and translator Otto Pick (1887–1940) was employed in a bank.
490. Probably the evening presentation of the Jewish Toynbee Hall on February 15, 1912, in the Jewish Town Hall, the last event before Jizchak Löwy's recitation evening

(see also note 497). For further information on the Jewish Toynbee Hall, see also note 732.

491. Ida Freund, née Sohr (1868–1931), who was the sister of Berta Fanta (see note 18) and was married to a Prague lawyer, was co-founder of the Klub deutscher Künstlerinnen (Club of German Women Artists), whose exhibition "Der gedeckte Tisch" ("The Set Table") began on February 15 and ended on February 18 (according to the *Prager Tagblatt* of February 3, 1912).
492. Apparently in connection with the references to the recitation evening that appeared under the title "Ostjüdischer Abend" ("Eastern Jewish Evening") in the *Prager Tagblatt* of February 17 and 18, 1912.
493. The village of Košíře was incorporated into Prague as a district in 1922.
494. Jizchak Löwy.
495. On February 18, 1912, the *Prager Tagblatt* wrote: "A group of young Prague residents who have come together to promote humanitarian and intellectual efforts and have chosen Johann Gottfried Herder as their patron saint entered the public life of German Prague on Friday with an event that, if nothing else, may be called a social occurrence." The event of the Johann Gottfried Herder-Vereinigung zu Prag took place on February 16, 1912. It was opened by Oskar Bie with a lecture "on dance," which he illustrated with slides and piano performances. Next Hugo von Hofmannsthal read a selection of his poems, including the prologue to the celebration of Kainz. Grete Wiesenthal danced to Johann Strauss's "Frühlingsstimmen" and "Donauwalzer" and to Franz Liszt's "Hungarian Rhapsody No. 2." Willy Haas also recounts this event in his memoirs. The magazine *Herder-Blätter* was sponsored by the J. G. Herder-Vereinigung. See notes 267, 316, 543.
496. A Prague island in the Moldau with gardens and a restaurant, in the Großer Saal ("Great Hall") of which the event took place.
497. Probably refers to Kafka's attendance at the event on February 15, 1912 (see note 490), at which, following an engineer's remarks on "railroad accidents," the Prague chief cantor Siegmund Schwarz performed secular songs (according to that day's *Prager Tagblatt*).
498. At the invitation of Prague's Zionist student associations, Kurt Blumenfeld, the general secretary of the World Zionist Organization, spoke on February 22, 1912, in the Kleiner Saal of the Produktenbörse on Havlíčekplatz about "Jews in academic life" (according to that day's *Prager Tagblatt*).
499. In the account that follows, *the reciter Reichmann* (see p. 209) refers to Oskar Reichmann (1886–1934), an employee of the Union Bank in Prague.
500. One of the Andreas Felix Hess Company's two shops was at Zeltnergasse 38.
501. The actor Josef Kainz (1858–1910) had regularly given guest performances in Prague.
502. Apparently Richard Dehmel, "Nachtgebet der Braut" ("The Bride's Night Prayer").
503. Pseudonym of the lawyer and writer Fritz Oliven, who was successful with humorous writings in particular.
504. The career of the actor Alexander Moissi (1880–1935) had begun in Prague. In later years he often gave readings and guest performances there, for example, on February 28, 1912. See p. 205.
505. Kafka meant the American writer Orison Swett Marden. At the time of the diary entry, two of his numerous books were available in German translation: *Wille und Erfolg* (Stuttgart, 1909) and *Wege zum Erfolg* (Stuttgart, 1911), to which the reciter Reichmann is apparently referring.
506. The Verein zur Förderung des Wohles und der Bildung der Frauen (Association for the Promotion of the Welfare and Education of Women), also known as the Frauenfortschritt or Women's Progress, organized language, stenography and needlework courses as well as lecture cycles. See p. 216 and note 540.
507. Jenny Durège-Wodnanski, a lady of Prague society, was also active in other Prague

associations—for example, in the Klub deutscher Schriftstellerinnen (Club of German Women Writers).

508. "Das Kind als Schöpfer" ("The Child as Creator") appeared in the entertainment supplement of the *Prager Tagblatt* of February 25, 1912.
509. "Die Armen" ("The Poor") by Hedwig Feldstein.
510. Hugo Löw.
511. The office of the *Prager Tagblatt* was on Herrengasse, a cross street of Heinrichsgasse, on which the main post office was located.
512. Egon Erwin Kisch worked for the Prague daily *Bohemia* until 1913.
513. The *Deutsches Abendblatt,* founded in 1896, was published by Gottlieb Schmelkes.
514. On February 28, 1912, Alexander Moissi gave a reading in the Rudolfinum.
515. The concluding song of the fool, Feste, in *Twelfth Night.*
516. Café Radetzky on the Kleinseitner Ringplatz (Czech: Malostranské námêstí, the main square of Prague's Malá Strana district).
517. Regarding Kafka's attitude toward conventional medicine and naturopathy, Max Brod wrote: "Kafka was very sensitive toward all damage to his health . . . he was mistrustful toward medicines and doctors—he demanded that nature itself should restore the balance, he disdained all 'unnatural' remedies. This tendency grew stronger in 1911 when he met the manufacturer Schnitzer, an apostle of naturopathy, on a (probably official) trip to Warnsdorf" (FK 97). Brod went on to quote from his diary what Kafka told him about Schnitzer after this trip in April 1911: "As a remedy he recommends: sleeping by an open window, sunbathing, gardening, being active in a naturopathic association and subscribing to the magazine published by this association, that is, by the manufacturer himself. Speaks against doctors, medicines, vaccination" (FK 97). Kafka himself followed these principles. For example, a few months after this entry, in July 1912, he went to the naturopathic Jungborn sanatorium in the Harz Mountains; see June-July 1912 Trip, pp. 555ff. Despite this fierce criticism, however, Dr. Heinrich Kral, physician at Niklasstraße 11 (at that time, the Kafka family lived at Niklasstraße 36), remained the family doctor and was consulted by Kafka even in later years.
518. Title of an apparently unpublished one-act play by Oskar Baum.
519. Oskar Baum's son Leo (1909–46).
520. Café Continental, Prague's largest coffeehouse, was located on the second floor of the building at Graben 17. It had four separate game rooms and made 250 different newspapers available to the guests. The café was a meeting place for the German-speaking middle class.
521. On Sunday, March 3, 1912, the actor Leopold Kramer of the Deutsches Volkstheater in Vienna gave a guest performance as editor Konrad Bolz in the production of Gustav Freytag's comedy *Die Journalisten* at the Deutsches Landestheater.
522. On March 7, 1912, the writer and journalist Maximilian Harden (1861–1927) spoke at the invitation of the Concordia (Verein deutscher Schriftsteller und Künstler in Böhmen: Association of German Writers and Artists in Bohemia) in the Rudolfinum.
523. A mountain range located northwest of the Riesengebirge (Krkonoše Mountains). The towns at the foot of or in the Isergebirge (Reichenberg, Neustadt an der Tafelfichte, among others) were frequently the destination of Kafka's business trips, for example, in late February 1911. See January-February 1911 Trips, pp. 497ff.
524. Addendum to the entry on pp. 199ff.
525. The title (see also p. 192) is followed by excerpts from and summaries of *Goethes Gespräche.*
526. From a letter written by David Veit, quoted in *Goethes Gespräche* and reproduced by Kafka with his preceding comment (*always Jewish observation* . . .) and his abridgement (———*brief dialogue about the play*——).
527. On May 1, 1912, the *Prager Tagblatt* reported: "Today is the beginning of the great

March program, which was assembled with painstaking care. Curt Warnebold, the famous piano humorist and reciter, Rocking Girls, four enchanting young Englishwomen (song and dance quartet), Fatinizza, a charming Viennese singer, Thea Degen, irresistible not only in her chanson, but this time also in dances—these are the main numbers of the new rich program, which has generated quite extraordinary interest."

528. Apparently this Viennese singer reminded him of Julianne Szokoll (known as "Hansi"; 1886–?), who was from Vienna and with whom he had an unhappy love affair in 1908. On Kafka's relationship with her, Max Brod wrote: "I remember his passion for a wine tavern waitress named Hansi, of whom he once said that whole cavalry regiments had ridden over her body. Franz was very unhappy in this affair. This can be seen in a photograph taken of him together with Hansi" (FK 104). The photograph is reproduced in WB 55.
529. Thea Degen was a *chanson* singer about whom Franz Werfel was so enthusiastic that he dedicated a poem to her.
530. *Aus dem Leben eines Schlachtenmalers* (*From the Life of a Battle Painter*) is the autobiography of German painter Albrecht Adam (1786–1862).
531. The novel *Morgenrot* by Otto Stoessl had recently been published by Verlag Georg Müller.
532. On March 17, 1912, with the singer Valesca Nigrini and the violinist Dr. Erwin Stein, Max Brod gave a concert at the meeting place of the Klub deutscher Künstlerinnen (Club of German Women Artists) on Postgasse, where he presented himself as a composer with, among other pieces, songs to texts by Goethe, Shakespeare, Li Tai-peh, and Hugo Salus, as well as his own poems. The concert, in which Brod himself sat at the piano, received some quite critical reviews in the Prague daily press, with the exception of a more sympathetic review in the *Prager Tagblatt* of March 18, 1912.
533. Elsa Taussig.
534. The performance of "Mam'zelle Nitouche: Vaudeville in 3 Acts (4 Tableaux) by H. Meilhac and A. Millaud . . . Music by Hervé" (actually Florimond Ronger) at the Neues Deutsches Theater was announced in the *Prager Tagblatt* of March 18, 1912, for that evening.
535. Erroneously dated by Kafka, as he noted a few days later in the next entry: *the last few days I've written wrong dates*. The earliest possible date for the entry is March 19, 1912, since the performance of *Mam'zelle Nitouche* had been on March 18, 1912, and there was at least one afternoon between that event and this entry, as reflected in the remark: *Today spent the afternoon with painful fatigue on the sofa*.
536. On March 21, 1912, Oskar Baum read from his collection *Uferdasein* (*Shore Existence*), among other things, in the Lese- und Redehalle der deutschen Studenten (Reading and Lecture Hall of German Students) on Krakauergasse.
537. Margarethe Fischer (1892–1943) married the lawyer Dr. Leo Zuckermann on April 18, 1912, at the age of nineteen.
538. On March 23, 1912, the *Prager Tagblatt* announced for that evening the premiere of the drama *Die Sternenbraut* by Christian von Ehrenfels (see note 467) at the Neues Deutsches Theater.
539. Possibly Filip and Rosa Lebenhart, a married couple active in the life of Prague's Jewish community. The name *Lebenhart* is also on a list on Kafka's notepad, in which he apparently recorded the proceeds from collections for Jizchak Löwy's recitation evening.
540. On March 25, 1912, Berta Fanta (see note 18) spoke on her "Berlin Impressions" in the Soziale Hilfe (Social Assistance) division of Women's Progress: "After a brief characterization of the daily life and nightlife, the speaker described the University of Berlin, presenting concise portraits of several lecturers in the philosophy department (Simmel, Riehl, among others). The riveting lecture went on to discuss

exhibitions, religious sects, theatrical events. The individually tinged remarks, which a substantial audience followed with rapt attention, finally culminated in the confession that the speaker preferred the calmer stream of intellectual stimulation in Prague to the nervous hustle of Berlin." On the Women's Progress, see note 506.

541. In the production of *Hamlet* at the Neues Deutsches Theater on April 3, 1912, Albert Bassermann gave a guest performance in the title role. Kafka had seen Bassermann as Hamlet in Berlin in December 1910. The sister he is referring to is probably Ottla.

542. Erroneously dated by Kafka. In 1912 Holy Saturday was on April 6.

543. Willy Haas (1891–1973) was co-founder of the Johann Gottfried Herder-Vereinigung zur Förderung ideeller Interessen (Johann Gottfried Herder-Association for the Promotion of Ideal Interests; see note 495) and co-editor of the magazine *Herder-Blätter* in which the *travel account* he praised appeared in June 1912 under the title "Erstes Kapitel des Buches 'Richard und Samuel' von Max Brod und Franz Kafka: Die erste lange Eisenbahnfahrt (Prag-Zürich)" ("First Chapter of the Book 'Richard and Samuel' by Max Brod and Franz Kafka: The First Long Train Trip (Prague-Zurich)"). On *Richard and Samuel,* see also note 218.

544. During Kafka's stay in Berlin from December 3 to 9, 1910, the memorial services for the director of the Klinik für innere Medizin (Department of Internal Medicine) of the Charité hospital and renowned lung specialist Prof. Dr. Ernst von Leyden (1832–1910), co-founder of the *Zeitschrift für physikalische und diätetische Therapie,* were widely reported in the Berlin daily newspapers. The name of the doctor, whose memoirs had been published by the Deutsche Verlags-Anstalt, was evidently familiar to Kafka.

545. On May 2, 1912, Berlin's Lessing Theater opened the Prague Maifestspiele (May Festival) with a performance of Gerhart Hauptmann's *Die Ratten* at the Neues Deutsches Theater.

546. Otto Pick's book of poems *Freundliches Erleben* (*Kindly Experience*) and Max Brod's novel *Arnold Beer. Das Schicksal eines Juden* (*Arnold Beer: The Fate of a Jew*) had recently been published by Axel Juncker Verlag. For Kafka's May 7, 1912, letter card to Max Brod about *Arnold Beer,* see KKAB1 no. 227. A copy of *Arnold Beer* with a handwritten dedication from Brod was among the books in Kafka's possession at the time of his death.

547. Possibly an early draft of the novel *Der Verschollene* (*The Missing Person*) that has not survived.

548. Gerti (1912–72), the second child of Elli and Karl Hermann, was born six months later, on November 8, 1912. Regarding the financial problems of the asbestos factory, see also p. 221 and note 552.

549. On May 21, 1912, the Czech Divadlo Umění performed *Madama la Mort* by Rachilde (actually Marguerite Vallette) and *The Dream of a Spring Morning* by Gabriele d'Annunzio in the hall of the Lucerna.

550. Kafka misunderstood Rachilde's comparison. In the first act of *Madame la Mort,* it's not the sun lovers who are compared with pushy drunkards but the sun itself, which illuminates "annoying creatures" ("*créatures bien agaçantes*") and has a "triumphant attitude" ("*air vainqueur*") in the face of "dreadful situations" ("*situations épouvantables*").

551. In this letter to Felix Weltsch, which has not survived, Kafka evidently proposed that they use the familiar form of address ("*Du*") with each other.

552. In this letter, which has not survived, Kafka probably asked his uncle Alfred Löwy (see note 385), who lived in Madrid, for advice and financial support for the asbestos factory.

553. The *Selbstwehr* of May 17, 1912, reported: "Palestine as land of colonization. On May 16, in the Großer Saal of the Jüdisches Vereinsheim (Langegasse 41), the Zion-

ist District Committee for Bohemia organized a lecture by Davis Trietsch from Berlin, the well-known expert on Palestine and the Orient." The Zionist leader and writer Davis Trietsch (1870–1935) was among the founders of the Berlin publishing house Jüdischer Verlag and was a coeditor of the Palestine magazine *Volk und Land* as well as other Zionist periodicals.

554. Franz Werfel's drama *Der Besuch aus dem Elysium* had recently been published in *Herder-Blätter.*

555. In the autumn of 1911, the Czech social democratic politician Dr. František Soukup (1871–1939) had been in America on a lecture tour speaking before workers' associations. After his return he described his impressions in lectures and in the book *Amerika: Řada obrazů amerického Života* (*America: A Series of Pictures from American Life*).

556. The magnificent art nouveau building on Josefsplatz (next to the Powder Tower) was erected from 1906 to 1911 and was used by the Czech middle class.

557. The annual charity event of the German associations of Prague took place in the garden of the Deutsches Haus (the German House, meeting place of the social club known as the Deutsches Kasino, or German Casino) at Graben 26 and was one of the highlights in the social life of the German-speaking middle class. Kafka's friends and relatives had participated in this event at various times. In a letter to Felice Bauer, Kafka described the German Casino as a "general association that is nonetheless of the highest prestige among the local Germans" (KKAB2 no. 446).

558. Paul Kisch's dissertation (full title: *Hebbel und die Tschechen. Das Gedicht "An seine Majestät König Wilhelm I. von Preußen." Seine Entstehung und Geschichte*) was published in 1913.

559. Kafka is quoting from a 1909 edition of Flaubert's "letters on his works" that was among the books in his possession at the time of his death: *Briefe über seine Werke*, volume seven of the complete works in German translation edited by E. W. Fischer. In the remark that follows—*Similar . . . 9 V*—Kafka is referring to his May 9 entry on p. 220.

560. Following a trip with Max Brod to Leipzig and Weimar, Kafka stayed from July 7 to 27, 1912, in the naturopathic Jungborn sanatorium, near Stapelburg in the Harz Mountains. For further notes from this trip, see June-July 1912 Trip, pp. 555ff.

561. In Leipzig, Max Brod had arranged a meeting on June 29, 1912, between Kafka and the publisher Ernst Rowohlt (1887–1960), who offered to publish a book by Kafka (see also p. 546). After his return from the naturopathic Jungborn sanatorium, Kafka was occupied with assembling the pieces for the collection *Betrachtung* (*Contemplation*) and making clean copies. See the subsequent entries of August 8, 11, and 14. For the letter mentioned here, see KKAB1 no. 247.

562. "Unmasking of a Confidence Trickster" is among the pieces that Kafka included in his book *Betrachtung.*

563. On April 15, 1914, Kafka wrote to Grete Bloch (see note 718), to whom he had given an edition of Franz Grillparzer's story "Der arme Spielmann" ("The Poor Musician"): *Der arme Spielmann is beautiful isn't it? I remember having read it once to my youngest sister as I've never read anything. I was so filled with it that there was no room in me for any mistake of emphasis, of breathing, of sound, of sympathy, of understanding, it really burst forth from me with an inhuman naturalness, I was happy about every word I uttered. That won't be repeated, I would never dare to read it aloud again* (KKAB3 no. 702).

564. Refers to the preparation of the collection *Betrachtung.*

565. What follows is a draft of a letter originally intended to be sent to Rowohlt Verlag with the manuscripts for the collection *Betrachtung*. The letter written the same day on a typewriter corresponds—with the exception of the handwritten addition *Manuscript will follow separately by parcel post*—word for word to the draft. The misspelling of the name (*Rohwolt*) is in the original letter and in all subsequent diary entries. See, for example, p. 226.

566. August 15, the Assumption of Mary, was a public holiday in Bohemia. The celebra-

tion took place at the Marian Column erected in 1650 on the Altstädter Ring (see also note 282).

567. Kafka had met the Berliner Felice Bauer (1887–1960), his later fiancée, on August 13, 1912, at Max Brod's. See p. 226.
568. The operetta *Polnische Wirtschaft* by Jean Gilbert (actually Max Winterfeld) was performed in Prague under the title *Tolle Wirtschaft*. The *Prager Tagblatt* of August 14, 1912, announced the performance for that evening at the Neues Deutsches Theater.
569. This refers to the thirty-one manuscript pages for the collection *Betrachtung*, which Max Brod—whose main job at the time was as a postal official—sent to Ernst Rowohlt Verlag on Kafka's behalf on August 14.
570. Kafka was apparently waiting for an immediate acknowledgment from Rowohlt Verlag. See also the entry on p. 226 beginning *If Rohwolt sent it back* . . .
571. This refers to the section on Weimar in June-July 1912 Trip, pp. 546–554.
572. Outside Kafka's window in the house "Zum Schiff" (Niklasstraße 36) "an elongated open area with its long side running parallel to the bank of the Moldau had been created by the sanitation [of the former ghetto]. . . . On both sides of Niklasstraße this 'university building site' displayed wide rectangular hollows quite steep at their edges, which hadn't even been filled in after the demolition of the houses between the south side of the former Johannisplatz (Jánské naměstí) and the bank of the Moldau, so that they wouldn't have to be excavated again for the planned new buildings." Kurt Krolop, "Zu den Erinnerungen Anna Lichtensterns an Franz Kafka." *Germanisitica Pragensia* 5 (1968): 21–60.
573. What follows is Kafka's description of the first impression Felice Bauer made on him.
574. This refers to Brod's parents' apartment on Schalengasse 1. See note 95.
575. First reference to the planned writing of the narrative fragment that survives in this diary notebook only following "The Judgment" (p. 242).
576. Refers to the writings of Jakob Michael Reinhold Lenz.
577. Alfred Löwy. See note 385 and the subsequent entry of September 4.
578. "Ein Lebenslied" ("A Song of Life") and the dramatic poem "Das Opfer" ("The Sacrifice") appeared in May 1913 in Franz Werfel's collection of poems *Wir sind* (*We Are*). "Das Opfer" was also later included in Max Brod's *Arkadia. Ein Jahrbuch für Dichtkunst.*
579. Among the answers to the survey "Où en est l'Amour," *Le Miroir* (Sunday supplement to the *Petit Parisien*) of August 4, 1912, published a photograph of the actress Louise Silvain captioned with the quotation: "Jamais on n'aima tant ni si bien qu'à notre époque." See also the facsimile in Kafka, *Tagebücher: Kommentarband,* p. 126.
580. Perhaps a family reunion at the home of Julie Kafka's brother Richard Löwy (1857–1938), who lived in Prague, on the occasion of Alfred Löwy's visit from Madrid.
581. *Dr. Friedrich Schiller, municipal official of Breslau,* whom Kafka met at the naturopathic Jungborn sanatorium. See June-July 1912 Trip, p. 556.
582. Adolf Ernst Kaufmann (born 1910), a distant relative.
583. Emil Utitz. See note 299.
584. Dr. Hugo Löw later reported on his experiences in Palestine in letters to the *Selbstwehr,* among other places. Kafka's schoolmate Hugo Bergmann had been in Palestine in 1910. Viktor Kellner (1887–1970), a leading member of the Bar-Kochba Association, had emigrated to Palestine and taught there at the Hebrew Gymnasium in Jaffa. On a visit to Prague in September 1911, he had on various occasions, in public lectures and in private circles, reported on his life in Palestine.
585. Maccabees (also Hasmoneans), a dynasty named after Judah Maccabee, which liberated the Jewish people from Syrian rule and reestablished the Jewish state in 142 B.C.
586. Kafka's second-oldest sister became engaged to Josef Pollak (1882–1942), her later husband.

587. Heinrich (Jindřich) Hubalek (1866–1939), an official of the AUVA, was possibly Kafka's "typist."
588. Václav Pokorny. See note 270.
589. First published in June 1913 under the title "Das Urteil" ("The Judgment") in *Arkadia. Ein Jahrbuch für Dichtkunst,* edited by Max Brod.
590. This refers to the Čechbrücke. See also note 11.
591. See note 589.
592. Further mentions of the name and their respective contexts suggest that Kafka was familiar with Sigmund Freud's theories. See June-July 1912 Trip, p. 556, as well as Br 169 and BKB 248.
593. Max Brod's novel *Arnold Beer. Das Schicksal eines Juden* had been published in May.
594. Jakob Wassermann (1873–1934) had visited Prague to give evening readings at various times. He was known to Kafka at least from his articles in S. Fischer Verlag's *Die neue Rundschau.*
595. "Die Riesin. Ein Augenblick der Seele" ("The Giantess: A Moment of the Soul"), by Franz Werfel, appeared in October 1912 in the same issue of *Herder-Blätter* in which Kafka's "Großer Lärm" ("Great Noise") was first published. See p. 115 and note 267.
596. See p. 76 and note 213.
597. See also the mention of the story about Blenkelt on p. 226.
598. This refers to "The Judgment."
599. The circle of listeners mentioned suggests that Kafka read "The Judgment" to a gathering at Oskar Baum's house and not at a meeting of the circle of friends.
600. The Baum family.
601. Ottla and Valli, the two sisters not yet married at that time.
602. Probably Martha Löwy (1891–?), *a pleasant, pretty, elegant and above all very considerate and modest cousin* (KKAB2 no. 390), daughter of Kafka's uncle Richard, who lived in Prague. See also note 580.
603. Possibly the family of the above-mentioned Dr. Bloch. See p. 196 and note 481.
604. On September 25, 1912, the premiere of the "Volkstümliche Lichtspiele" ("Popular Moving Pictures") took place at the Deutsches Landestheater. According to the announcement in the *Bohemia* of the same day, the program of these "Wissenschaftl. kinematographische Vorstellungen" ("Scientific cinematographic showings") included: "1. Seltsame Insekten. 2. Die Insel Ceylon. 3. Danzig. 4. Zur Erinnerung an den Geburtstag Theodor Körners: Theodor Körner. Sein Leben und Dichten.—Aus der Jugendzeit.—Der Student.—Der Theaterdichter und seine Braut.—Der Freiheitskämpfer" ("1. Strange Insects. 2. The Island of Ceylon. 3. Danzig. 4. In Memory of the Birthday of Theodor Körner: Theodor Körner: His Life and Writing.—The Early Years.—The Student.—The Playwright and his Bride.—The Freedom Fighter").
605. Probably Grete Oplatka, who—like Kafka's sister Ottla—was active in the Klub jüdischer Frauen und Mädchen (Jewish Women and Girls' Club).
606. Beginning of the novel *Der Verschollene* (*The Missing Person*), which is continued in the Second Notebook. See p. 86 and note 219.
607. The correction for the first printing of "The Judgment" in Max Brod's yearbook *Arkadia,* which appeared in late May 1913.
608. In German *Bauer* means "farmer" and *Feld* means "field."
609. In a June 3, 1913, letter to Felice Bauer, Kafka took up again these considerations on the names in "The Judgment" (KKAB2 no. 541). As early as October 24, 1912, with regard to the story's publication in the *Arkadia* yearbook and his intention to dedicate it to Felice Bauer, he had written: *Besides, as far as I can see, the story in its essence has not the slightest connection with you, except that a girl appearing fleetingly in it is named Frieda Brandenfeld, that is, as I realized later, shares your initials* (KKAB1 no. 269).

610. Otto Steuer (1881–?), a former schoolmate of Kafka's.
611. Heinrich Weltsch (1856–1936), the father of Kafka's friend Felix Weltsch.
612. On March 1, 1913, Kafka wrote to Felice Bauer: *Yesterday I began a little story, it's still so little it's barely sticking its head out, nothing can be said, it's all the more sinful that today, against all good resolutions, I abandoned it and went to Max's. But if it's worth anything, it will perhaps be able to wait until tomorrow* (KKAB2 no. 452). On the night of March 2–3, Kafka wrote: *it's past 1 o'clock, in the meantime, dearest, I've been completely cast off by my story—today was the decision and it was made against me—and now, if you want me, I'm positively crawling back to you* (KKAB2 no. 453). With the "Ernst Liman fragment," the entries from 1913 in the Seventh Notebook break off; beginning from the other end of the notebook, Kafka used it again starting on February 16, 1914, for the entries that follow here. The entries from 1913 he continued in the Eighth Notebook starting on May 2. See pp. 291ff.
613. Possibly refers to a number on the program of the Kabarett Lucerna, often attended by Kafka, which announced on February 19, 1914, in the daily *Bohemia:* "Munich Painting at the Peak of Perfection."
614. In late 1913 Kafka sought Felice Bauer's hand in marriage, but she responded only hesitantly to his pressing questions. She didn't reply to a January 2, 1914, letter from Kafka until February 9 with *a short but nonetheless friendly card* (KKAB2 no. 651). Because he didn't receive any further word in the weeks that followed, Kafka decided, on the day of this diary entry, to go to Berlin and clear things up with Felice Bauer. On the weekend of February 27 to March 1, 1914, Kafka and Felice Bauer had several meetings during which she explained to him her objections to getting married. For Kafka, the situation remained unsettled for the time being—which finds expression in the subsequent entries dealing with Felice Bauer on pp. 262–269. On another visit to Berlin, from April 11 to 13, 1914, they finally became unofficially engaged, and Felice Bauer agreed to marry Kafka in September.
615. Robert Musil (1880–1942), editor of the magazine *Die neue Rundschau* since the beginning of 1914, had asked Max Brod for Kafka's address. The contribution he sought from Kafka for *Die neue Rundschau* did not come to pass.
616. "Little Briar Rose" is a closer translation of the German name for the fairy tale character more commonly known in English as "Sleeping Beauty."
617. The entry probably refers to Kafka's grandmother Julie Löwy (born 1827), who died on May 22, 1908, and not to his grandmother Franziska Kafka (born 1816), who apparently died before her husband Jakob (1814–89).
618. Kafka was considering either marrying Felice Bauer and living with her in Prague or, instead of this more conventional existence, moving to Berlin to live as a freelance writer.
619. Attempt at a story to which Kafka returns repeatedly in subsequent entries: see pp. 263, 266–268, 269.
620. Here and in all the diary entries that follow, unless otherwise indicated: Felice Bauer.
621. Regarding the decision to go to Berlin recorded here in the diary, Kafka wrote to Grete Bloch on April 14, 1914: *This decision was that, in the event that I had not married F., I would have given up my job here or, if possible, taken an extended leave without pay and gone to Berlin (not for F., but for Berlin and its many possibilities) and become a journalist or something similar* (KKAB3 no. 702).
622. Kafka's entry is based on his reading of the article "Dostojewski: Die Tragödie seines Lebens" by Stefan Zweig, which had appeared in the first February issue of the magazine *Der Merker*: "he died in a workers' quarter, in a fifth-floor corner apartment"; "The police chief wants to prohibit the public funeral, during which the students plan to carry the convict's chains behind his coffin."
623. See note 479.
624. In light of the decision that had now been made for the marriage to take place in

September (see note 614), Kafka and his family were looking for an apartment in Prague.

625. In late May, Julie and Ottla Kafka traveled to Berlin, where Kafka's official engagement to Felice Bauer was celebrated on June 1, 1914 (Pentecost Monday).

626. Refers to the "*K*" in Kafka's handwriting with its conspicuously sweeping curve:

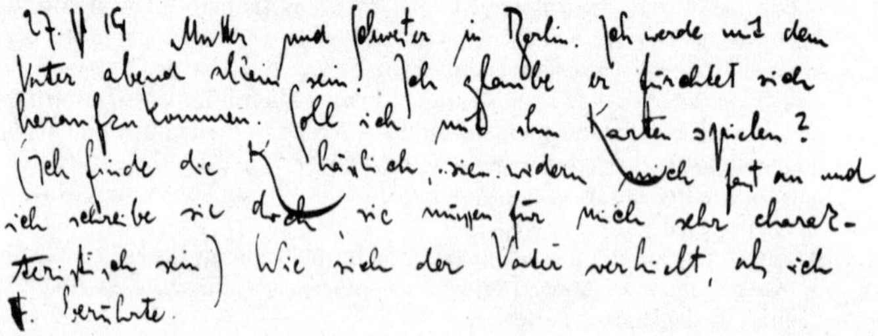
27. V 14 Mutter und Schwester in Berlin. Ich werde mit dem Vater abend allein sein. Ich glaube er fürchtet sich heraufzukommen. Soll ich mit ihm Karten spielen? (Ich finde die K häßlich, sie widern mich fast an und ich schreibe sie doch, sie müssen für mich sehr charakteristisch sein) Wie sich der Vater verhielt, als ich F. berührte.

627. Kafka traveled to Berlin on Pentecost Saturday, May 30, 1914.

628. Otto Pick. See note 489.

629. Probably Dostoyevsky's February 22, 1854, letter to his brother Mikhail. A 1914 German edition of Dostoyevsky's letters was among the books in Kafka's possession at the time of his death.

630. Kafka had returned to Prague on June 2, 1914.

631. This entry recalls Alfred Kubin's and Anton M. Pachinger's visits to Prague in the autumn of 1911 (see pp. 20, 22, 24, 139–142), of which Kafka was probably reminded by a card from Kubin, which—as can be inferred from Kafka's reply on July 22, 1914—he received around this time (see KKAB3 no. 777). Kafka's entry apparently describes further details from his past conversations with Kubin and Pachinger.

632. The writer Karl Wolfskehl (1869–1948), a friend of Alfred Kubin.

633. Wolfskehl and his friend Melchior Lechter (1865–1937), a painter and book designer, had set off on their India trip in late September 1910. Having fallen ill with dysentery, Wolfskehl returned alone in mid-December.

634. Franz von Bayros was an Austrian painter, book designer and bookplate artist, also known for his erotic drawings.

635. Fyodor Dostoyevsky's April 11, 1880, letter to Yekaterina Fyodorovna Yunge. See note 629.

636. Since the summer of 1913, Kafka and the doctor and writer Ernst Weiß (1882–1940) from Brünn (Czech: Brno) had developed a friendly relationship. At Kafka's request, Weiß, who lived in Berlin, had visited Felice Bauer several times since December 1913 and taken on a sort of intermediary role. On June 16 or 17, 1914, Weiß came to Prague for a few days, where he met Kafka before he returned to Berlin on June 19.

637. The popular Czech theater named after its founder Jan Pištěk was located in the Prague suburb Königliche Weinberge (Czech: Královské Vinohrady).

638. Kafka described his encounter with Eugen Löwenstein (1877–1961) in a letter to Grete Bloch dated June 20, 1914: *A few days ago I spoke with one of the heads of a large linen factory Joss and Löwenstein, his name is Eugen Löwenstein* (KKAB3 no. 759). Löwenstein made a name for himself as a writer and patron. Starting in 1914, he also wrote reviews for the *Prager Tagblatt,* including one of Kafka's story "Die Verwandlung" ("The Transformation," also known in English as "The Metamorphosis") on April 9, 1916.

639. Elli Hermann, Kafka's sister.

640. Ottla Kafka.

641. The main destination of the trip taken with Otto Pick (see note 489) on June 27–29,

1914, was the garden city of Hellerau founded in 1906 and located outside the gates of Dresden (incorporated into Dresden as a district in 1950). Hellerau was known as the seat of the Deutsche Werkstätten für Handwerkskunst (German Workshops for Craftsmanship) and the Bildungsanstalt Jaques-Dalcroze, an educational institute founded in 1911. Among the colony of artists residing permanently in Hellerau at that time were the publisher Jakob Hegner, the writer Paul Adler from Prague, and the artist blacksmith Georg Mendelssohn.

642. The German Navy League (Deutscher Flottenverein) had been founded in 1898 in Berlin to arouse public interest in the significance and the missions of the navy and of imperial naval policy. As of 1908, it had more than a million members.

643. Because there was no vacancy in the *Waldschenke* (that is, the Waldschänke), Kafka and his companion Otto Pick stayed with *Gymnasium* teacher Kurt Thomas and his wife at Breiter Weg 10 in Hellerau.

644. Hermann Prescher managed the Waldschänke inn in Hellerau.

645. Jakob Hegner (1882–1962) founded the publishing house Hellerauer Verlag and was editor of the biweekly *Neue Blätter*.

646. The Prague writer Leo Fantl (1885–1944) and his wife Grete, née Theiner, hosted a small literary salon in their Hellerau apartment (Am Schänkenberg 24), which earned her the jocular nickname “Rahel von Hellerau.”

647. Paul Adler (1878–1946), his life companion and later wife Anna Dusik (1874–?), and their daughter Elisabeth (born 1912; known as “Nise,” interpreted by Kafka as a shortened form of *Anneliese*).

648. Possibly the Prague writer Richard Katz (1888–1968).

649. The artist blacksmith Georg Mendelssohn (1886–1955). Kafka described him in a 1921 letter to Robert Klopstock as follows: *I’m casually acquainted with Georg von Mendelssohn, he certainly won’t remember me, but one cannot forget him, a huge tall Nordic-looking person with a small, horribly energetic bird-face, one is frightened by his disposition, his terse choppy speech, his attitude dismissive seemingly of anything that might arise, but one should not be frightened, he means no harm, at least not in his average behavior and is absolutely reliable. He is a central figure in German applied arts, has an artist’s smithy in Hellerau and belongs in every respect to the “connoisseurs” of the applied arts* (Br 355).

650. After the early death of his brother Erich (1887–1913), Georg von Mendelssohn took his son Harald, born in 1911, into his family for several years.

651. Georg von Mendelssohn lived with his family in a villa built by Richard Riemerschmid on Moritzburger Weg in Hellerau; the large property included a little rock garden with alpine plants.

652. The Waldschänke inn (Am grünen Zipfel) is the oldest building in Hellerau and existed before the founding of the garden city, into which it was incorporated as the only building. In the 1920s it was known for offering health food according to the reform efforts of the garden city movement and was a popular excursion destination not least of all due to the restaurant garden and the attached bowling alley.

653. This refers to the vegetarian restaurant Natura on Struvestraße 5, second floor, in Dresden, which was run by Hedwig Jentsch.

654. Kafka’s publisher Kurt Wolff (1887–1963) and Willy Haas (see note 543).

655. From 1912 to 1920, Paul Adler lived with his family in a house on Tännichtweg 6, “surrounded by pines, shrubbery and flower bushes in the garden.” Ludo Abicht, *Ein Dichter aus Prag* (Wiesbaden/Frankfurt, 1972), p. 19.

656. During his time in Hellerau (1910–14), the music educator Émile Jaques-Dalcroze lived in the villa Auf dem Sand 10, designed by Richard Riemerschmid.

657. Abbreviation for the Internationale Ausstellung für Buchgewerbe und Graphik (International Exhibition for the Book Industry and Graphic Arts), which took place in 1914 in Leipzig.

658. See note 653.

659. Hellerau was connected to Dresden by a tramline.
660. Erna Bauer (1886–1972) was the older sister, by one year, of Kafka's fiancée Felice.
661. Since 1911 the Swiss Émile Jaques-Dalcroze (1865–1950) had run his Hellerau school for rhythm, music, and physical education with great success. The educational institute was carried on under new leadership when he returned to Geneva in 1914 to found a new school. On March 7, 1911, at the invitation of the Klub deutscher Künstlerinnen (Club of German Women Artists), Dalcroze had presented his method of music education in the Rudolfinum in Prague, and on March 1, 1914, he also demonstrated the "Dalcroze method" in Prague, portrayed by a group of Hellerau students. It's possible that these presentations were the basis of Kafka's continuing interest in this method in later years. See KKAB2 no. 398 and Br 418.
662. Apparently Kafka visited the Kurt Wolff Verlag in Leipzig, but for the reasons given couldn't speak with either the publisher Kurt Wolff or the editor Franz Werfel, who was tied up in a conversation with Else Lasker-Schüler.
663. Refers to the "Bugra." See note 657.
664. Café Arco. See note 479.
665. This refers to the entries in the Ninth Notebook on the trip to Berlin, Travemünde, and Marielyst, July 11–26, 1914. See pp. 346–350 and notes 798–817.
666. Egon Erwin Kisch also recorded the outbreak of the First World War on July 31, 1914, in his diary: "In the afternoon posters were put up announcing that the Kaiser had ordered general mobilization."
667. Karl Hermann and Josef (Pepa) Pollak, the husbands of Kafka's two sisters.
668. The AUVA had declared Kafka "indispensable." Because he stayed in Prague as a "recruit for unarmed service," after the conscription of his brother-in-law Karl Hermann, he had to devote increased attention to the asbestos factory. Shortly thereafter Karl Hermann's brothers Rudolf and Paul took on management responsibilities. Elli Hermann, Kafka's sister, moved into their parents' apartment with her children Felix and Gerti, while Kafka at first moved into his sister Valli's apartment (Bilekgasse 10); Valli had gone to stay with her parents-in-law in Böhmisch-Brod after her husband's conscription. See the subsequent entry of August 3, 1914. From September to February 9, 1915, he then moved into Elli Hermann's apartment in the suburb Königliche Weinberge (Czech: Královské Vinohrady) at Nerudagasse 48.
669. Karl Hermann.
670. Among Prague's river bathing facilities, Kafka favored the Civilschwimmschule (Civilian Swimming School) located across from the family's former apartment (see note 11) as well as the swimming school on the Sophieninsel.
671. In light of the wedding with Felice Bauer planned for September 1914, Kafka entered into a rental agreement for an apartment at Langegasse 5. After the engagement was broken off, Kafka faced the problems described here with the termination of the agreement.
672. Meeting with the landlord of the apartment on Langegasse.
673. Probably an employee of Hermann Kafka.
674. The *Prager Tagblatt* of August 5, 1914, reported: "An artillery division that traversed the city today was applauded enthusiastically by the public. Women threw flowers to the soldiers and the artillerymen constantly had to wave their caps to thank the crowd for their enthusiastic cheers."
675. *Nazdar* is Czech for the German *Heil* ("hail").
676. Under the headline "Wiederholte patriotische Kundgebungen in Prag" ("Repeated Patriotic Rallies in Prague"), the *Bohemia* of August 9, 1914, reported: "The parade then proceeded to the Old Town Hall, where the demonstrators gathered in front of the loggia: Silence was ordered and Mayor Dr. Groš appeared at a second-floor window and gave a speech to the crowd in which he thanked them on behalf of the

city council for the patriotic rally. . . . Dr. Groš expressed reverence for the Kaiser and . . . concluded his speech with three shouts of 'Slava' to the Kaiser, which were followed by shouts of 'Slava,' 'Heil' and 'Hoch' from the crowd." Starting on Friday, August 7, 1914, the Prague public held daily patriotic rallies and parades. On August 9, the Prague daily press published the governor's request "not to repeat the street parades and to stem the entirely justified urge to express personal sentiments in street rallies."

677. Kafka was never in Binz; this might be a reflection on the photograph he received in the autumn of 1912 from Felice, which shows the Bauer family in Binz on the island of Rügen (see opposite F 177). The quotation marks suggest that *"L. from Binz"* is probably a quote from Felice Bauer's letter explaining the photograph.
678. Probably refers to Kafka's reading of August Strindberg's *The Gothic Rooms.* The 1912 German edition of the novel, among the books in Kafka's possession at the time of his death, was a belated birthday gift from Felice Bauer's sister (see p. 347); the dedication inscribed on the flyleaf reads "Zum 3. Juli 1914 Erna."
679. Kafka is reminiscing about his stays in Paris in October 1910 and September 1911 and his uncle Josef Löwy (1858–1932), who lived in Versailles at that time and whom Kafka might have met during his first stay in Paris.
680. First part of a fragment that Kafka later titled "Erinnerungen an die Kaldabahn" ("Memories of the Kalda Railroad"); see p. 376. The continuation survives on six of the remaining pages of a lost notebook; see Bundles of Paper, pp. 360–365.
681. In early 1913 Kafka had broken off his writing in the Seventh Notebook with the "Ernst Liman fragment." In a new notebook, the Eighth Notebook, he resumed his diary entries with this remark on May 2. See also note 612.
682. Kafka's sister Valli and her husband, Josef Pollak.
683. Since early April 1913, Kafka had been spending his free afternoons working at the Dvorský Nursery on Slupergasse 19. On April 7, 1913, he wrote to Felice Bauer: *Can you tell by my handwriting that I've done hard work today and the penholder is now too light a thing for me? Yes today I worked for the first time at the gardener's out in Nusle, a suburb, in the cool rain in only shirt and pants. . . . My main purpose was to liberate myself for a few hours from self-torment, in contrast to the ghostly work in the office, which positively flies away from me when I try to grasp it—there in the office is the true hell, I no longer fear any other—to do some dull, honest, useful, silent, solitary, healthy, strenuous work* (KKAB2 no. 495).
684. Since April 13, 1913, the Viennese Jüdische Bühne had given guest performances in Café-Restaurant Piccadilly on Ziegenplatz (formerly Café Savoy, see note 79). On May 2 the ensemble performed a play entitled *Die Goldene Hochzeit.*
685. Louise Bailly. See note 71.
686. The day after this entry, on May 4, 1913, Kafka wrote in a letter to Felice Bauer: *Yesterday Felix said to me in some connection that I would need a guardian. That's not a bad idea, I would need one in the ordinary and in the highest sense, if it's not too late* (KKAB2 no. 523).
687. That day Kafka received the first printed copies of his story "Der Heizer" ("The Stoker," published by Kurt Wolff Verlag as the third volume in the series "Der jüngste Tag"). The day after this entry, on May 25, 1913, he confirmed receipt in a letter to his publisher. On "The Stoker," see also note 219.
688. In early June 1913, Jizchak Löwy was staying in Prague again. As he had in February 1912, Kafka organized a recitation evening for the actor, who was currently having financial difficulties: *if Löwy weren't here and I didn't have to organize a performance for the poor fellow . . . didn't have to sell tickets, didn't have to make arrangements for the hall and finally if this irrepressible fire of Löwy's didn't affect me and send me into apparent haste and activity—I wouldn't know how these few days would have gone by* (letter to Felice Bauer, June 1, 1913, KKAB2 no. 540). Löwy's recitation evening, organized by the Bar-Kochba Association of Jewish University Students, took place on June 2, 1913, in the Hotel Bristol at Langegasse 11, which recommended itself as a venue for Jewish events and celebra-

tions, especially marriage ceremonies. It advertised itself as the "only strictly ritual [i.e., kosher] restaurant in Prague" (*Selbstwehr* of June 9, 1911).

689. Kafka planned a vacation in Riva on Lake Garda for September. On August 1, 1913, he wrote to Felice Bauer: *I feel miserable, I'll fall apart, if they don't put me back together there in the south* (KKAB2 no. 577).

690. Kafka's first meeting with Ernst Weiß. See note 636. The novel *Die Galeere* (*The Galley*) had been published in June by S. Fischer Verlag. See also p. 319.

691. Prague Hotel at Hibernergasse 2.

692. Kafka's entry is probably based on images he saw in a newsreel.

693. On July 1, 1913, the *Prager Tagblatt* provided a description of the movie *Sklaven des Goldes* (*Slaves of Gold*) at the Grand Theatre Bio "Elite" on Poříčerstraße (Na Poříčí): "There's also something of a detective novel in the second drama 'Slaves of Gold.' It too is about the robbery of a millionaire, but in the end the criminals are stricken with terror, because the chests of gold contain—living snakes. The Wild West milieu in which these events take place does the rest to grip the viewer."

694. The *report on the trial* appeared under the headline "Ihr Kind erwürgt. Das Motiv: Hunger" ("Strangled Her Baby. The Motive: Hunger") on July 2, 1913, in the column entitled "Gerichts-Zeitung" ("Court News") of the *Prager Tagblatt.* The "terrible tragedy of woe" suffered by Marie Abraham and her youngest child "Barbara, who was born on September 30, 1912 and murdered by her own mother on May 22, 1913," the background, and the murder are described in detail: "Almost mad, she took her baby, ran with her into a nearby forest. There she untied from her foot a thin men's tie, which had served her as a garter, and wound it twice around the little one's neck . . . all those elements that come into consideration for an acquittal, Abraham's terrible destitution through no fault of her own, her despair and her weakened ability to think as a result of hunger and privations" lead to an acquittal. The report ends: "The jurors have meanwhile organized a collection among themselves and their chairman presents to the loudly sobbing accused woman, who can't even believe that she is now free, the sum of sixty kronen: 'So that you can get over this initial time!'"

695. Elsa Brod, née Taussig. See note 697.

696. Kafka is probably alluding to Fyodor Dostoyevsky's novel *The Adolescent,* which, according to Brod, he held in particularly high regard and from which he read aloud "with enthusiasm" (FK 46). The third chapter includes the following passage: "Not all natures are the same; for many people a logical conclusion sometimes turns into the strongest feeling, which seizes the whole person and is very difficult to drive out or change. . . . The thought arises from the feeling and, when it becomes dominant in a person, formulates a new feeling in its turn!" It's also possible, however, that the entry is based on N. N. Strachoff's introduction to the volume *Literarische Schriften* of the 1913 German edition of the complete works of Dostoyevsky. He wrote of Dostoyevsky: "Many a simple thought, indeed occasionally even some entirely ordinary thought already known to everyone, could suddenly excite him tremendously, when it dawned on him all at once in its whole significance. The reason for this was undoubtedly that he, it's safe to say, *felt thoughts* in an extraordinarily vivid way" (Strachoff's emphasis). And shortly thereafter, referring to the tendency of the magazine *Vremya*: "The indefiniteness of the thought in itself didn't worry him, since he didn't have the slightest doubt in the development of that thought."

697. Max Brod and Elsa Taussig had gotten married on February 2, 1913.

698. Regarding Rostok (Czech: Roztoky), an excursion town twelve kilometers from Prague, Grieben's guidebook remarks: "Village in picturesque surroundings, with a number of villas; several restaurants. Pleasant walk in the Quiet Valley." 15th ed., rev. by O. Klauber (Berlin, 1911), p. 145.

699. . . . *the letter to your parents will leave at the same time as this letter,* Kafka wrote in his

August 14, 1913, letter to Felice Bauer (KKAB2 no. 590). The letter to Anna and Carl Bauer has not survived.

700. Refers to a visit to Oskar Baum's apartment, where the son Leo was apparently the only family member present.
701. Refers to the above-mentioned letter to Felice Bauer's parents.
702. In early August 1913, Kafka had sent his uncle Alfred Löwy in Madrid the yearbook *Arkadia* (in which the story "The Judgment" had appeared; see note 589) with an accompanying letter. On August 5, 1913, Kafka received a telegram from Alfred Löwy in reply. That day he wrote to Felice Bauer: *I poured out my complaints thoroughly in the letter and with an elegant transition also wrote (this uncle actually should have heard about our engagement before my parents) that I would soon become officially engaged. . . . Well, my uncle must have misunderstood my letter and must think we were already officially engaged, for the telegram lying in front of me says in these exact words: "warmest congratulations to the engaged couple with great joy from Uncle Alfred"* (KKAB2 no. 582).
703. Søren Kierkegaard, *Buch des Richters* (*Book of the Judge*), a selection from Kierkegaard's diaries, 1833–55, published in 1905 in a German translation by Hermann Gottsched.
704. Regarding the draft of a letter to Carl Bauer, Kafka wrote to Felice on August 22, 1913: *. . . and drafted a letter that would make it clear to him. It isn't finished nor will I send it off, it was only an outburst, which didn't even relieve me* (KKAB2 no. 596).
705. Apparently relates to the contents of Kafka's August 30, 1913, letter to Felice Bauer (KKAB2 no. 601).
706. The surviving letters show that the crisis in the relationship with Felice Bauer had escalated during the trip to Vienna and Riva (see the following note). His correspondence with her had been broken off since September 20, 1913.
707. On September 6, 1913, Kafka had set off on a trip that took him first to Vienna, accompanying the director of the AUVA, Dr. Robert Marschner, and his immediate superior, Chief Inspector Eugen Pfohl, to the "Second International Congress for Rescue Services and Accident Prevention." Following this business portion of the trip, Kafka traveled on September 14 via Trieste, Venice, Verona, and Desenzano to Riva on Lake Garda. From September 22 to (probably) October 12, he stayed there in the sanatorium of Dr. von Hartungen. On the stay in Vienna, see the entries in September 1913 Trip, pp. 565–566.
708. In Riva, Kafka *fell in love with a girl, a child, about 18 years old, who is Swiss* (KKAB2 no. 641), whose name he renders as *W.* or *G. W.* in the text that follows.
709. Kafka had met Ernst Weiß during his stay in Vienna. See note 636.
710. Josef Grünwald, professor of mathematics at the University of Prague.
711. Prince Peter Kropotkin's memoirs.
712. Siegfried Jacobsohn, *Der Fall Jacobsohn* (Charlottenburg, 1913).
713. Willy Haas. See note 543.
714. Kafka's story "Die Verwandlung," also known in English as "The Metamorphosis," was written in November–December 1912.
715. See note 708.
716. The Franz Ringhoffer Werke, a machine factory in the Prague suburb Schmichow (Czech: Smíchov; incorporated into Prague as a district in 1920), was at that time one of the largest concerns in Austria-Hungary. It manufactured not only railroad vehicles of all sorts but also installations for sugar factories, distilleries, breweries, etc. As part of his job at the AUVA, Kafka was responsible for the risk classification of this company, among others.
717. Meetings of a seminar given by the Prague philosophy professor Christian von Ehrenfels (see note 467), in which, according to Max Brod's memoir *Streitbares Leben* (*Contentious Life*), the book *Anschauung und Begriff* (*Intuition and Concept*), co-written by Brod and Felix Weltsch and published in 1913, was discussed.

718. Margarethe Bloch, known as Grete (1892–1944), was asked by her friend Felice Bauer to serve as an intermediary in her relationship with Kafka, which had entered a serious crisis. In late October 1913 she met Kafka in Prague. The diary entry probably relates to the receipt of a letter from Grete Bloch. See Kafka's November 10, 1913 letter: *you might be angry with me that I haven't yet answered your nice letter, the clear kindness of which is interrupted by an incomprehensibility only in the passage about the roses* (KKAB2 no. 627).
719. On November 7, 1913, the writer Albert Ehrenstein (1866–1950), whom Kafka had encountered in Berlin in March and in Vienna in September (see September 1913 Trip, p. 566), read in Prague at the invitation of the Klub deutscher Künstlerinnen (Club of German Women Artists) "for a circle of numerous literary friends," as reported in the *Prager Tagblatt* of November 8, 1913.
720. Probably refers to Tempelgäßchen.
721. On November 19, 1913, the Grand Théâtre Bio "Elite," located directly next to the AUVA, announced: "'Die kleine Lolotte.' aus 'Das Kind von Paris' spielt die Hauptr. in 'Es gibt keine Kinder mehr.' Tragikomödie in 3 Akten. 'Die Katastrophe im Dock.' Großes sensationelles Schauspiel in 4 Akten. Gespielt von d. ersten Kopenhagener Schauspielern. . . . 'Isidors Hochzeitsreise.' (oder 'Endlich allein!') Großes Lustspiel in 4 Akten mit Hanny Weiße in der Hauptrolle" ("'Little Lolotte.' from 'The Child of Paris' plays the lead in 'There Are No More Children.' Tragicomedy in 3 acts. 'The Catastrophe at the Dock.' Great sensational spectacle in 4 acts. Performed by the foremost Copenhagen actors. . . . 'Isidor's Honeymoon.' (or 'Alone at Last!') Great comedy in 4 acts with Hanny Weiße in the lead").
722. The youngest of Felice Bauer's sisters was Toni (1892–1919).
723. In November 1913, the Kafka family had moved from Niklasstraße 36 to the Oppelt House at Altstädter Ring 6 (today no. 5).
724. Probably a description of a film scene, for which Kafka uses the then-common term *Bild* (translated here as "picture").
725. This letter has not survived. It's possible that at that point Kafka had already asked Ernst Weiß to serve as an intermediary in his relationship to Felice Bauer. See also p. 322 and note 734.
726. The subsequent entries of December 5, 1913, suggest that Kafka's abbreviations stand for his sister Ottla and her later husband Josef (known as "Pepo" or "Pepa") David (1891–1962). Kafka's parents were strongly opposed to their daughter's relationship to a Catholic Czech. Ottla and Josef David got married on July 15, 1920.
727. Ottla Kafka.
728. Entries based on the reading of the novel *Die Galeere* by Ernst Weiß.
729. Eugen Pfohl.
730. Robert Marschner.
731. Located at the corner of Hibernergasse and Havlíčekgasse.
732. The Jüdische Toynbeehalle (Jewish Toynbee Hall, an organization named after Arnold Toynbee) was, as Max Brod wrote in his memoir *Streitbares Leben* (*Contentious Life*), "a charitable institution in which the audience consisted predominantly of very poor people. For it was stipulated that no entrance fee be charged and that every audience member even receive a free cup of tea and piece of cake." The Toynbee Hall organized weekly evening presentations, for which participants were often sought in classified ads.
733. Czech for "Today it was quite nice."
734. The carrying out of the plan described here is later confirmed by Kafka in a January 28, 1914, letter to Grete Bloch: *I have a very good friend in Berlin, Dr. E. Weiss. . . . Well, in early December I asked this Dr. Weiss to go to F.'s office with a letter from me* (KKAB2 no. 645).
735. An event of the Verein der deutschen Beamten der AUVA (Association of German

Officials of the AUVA, which names Kafka in its January 17, 1912, statement of accounts as one of the two auditors), a branch of the Prague Staatsbeamtenverein (Association of State Officials), which customarily held meetings in the beer hall at Stefansgasse 40.

736. On December 14, 1913, in the Kleiner Spiegelsaal of the Deutsches Haus at Graben 26, the journalist and writer Richard Arnold Bermann (1883–1939), who at that time lived in Berlin, spoke at the invitation of the Lese- und Redehalle der deutschen Studenten (Reading and Lecture Hall of German Students) under the title "Literary Snapshots" on his "impressions of modern literary and artistic life" (*Bohemia* of December 7, 1913). In the entertainment supplement of the December 14 *Prager Tagblatt,* the article "Damit sie lachen und nicht weinen" ("So that they laugh and don't cry") on the Christmas market in Berlin appeared under his pseudonym "Arnold Höllriegel." It contains the advertising slogan quoted by Kafka:

> "Kaufen Sie etwas für die Kleinen,
> Damit sie lachen und nicht weinen!"
>
> ("Buy something for the little ones,
> So that they laugh and don't cry!")

737. On October 19, 1913, Kafka mentioned in a letter to Felice Bauer the seminar participant who resembled her: *Yesterday I stared at a girl in the seminar for an hour because she resembled you a little* (KKAB2 no. 623). On the seminar of the philosophy professor Ehrenfels, see note 717.

738. Kafka relates the appearance of the "gentleman" in the chapter "The Devil. Ivan Fyodorovich's Nightmare" of Dostoyevsky's novel *The Brothers Karamazov* to the appearance of the child introduced as a small ghost in his piece "Unhappiness" (see pp. 53–55): "And so he was sitting in his room now, was almost aware himself that he was delirious with fever, and, as I have already said, was gazing intently at the opposite wall, as if he were staring at an object on the divan there. Someone was suddenly sitting there! God knows how and when he came in, for when Ivan Fyodorovich had entered the room on his return from visiting Smerdyakov no one had been there."

739. Kafka was awaiting a reply from Felice Bauer to his letters and telegrams.

740. Hermann Schaffstein, *Wir Jungen von 1870/71. Erinnerungen aus meinen Kinderjahren,* the 32nd of the Little Green Books, ed. N. Henningsen (Cologne, 1913).

741. Quoted from *The Brothers Karamazov.*

742. This letter has not survived—apparently the letter to Ernst Weiß requesting that he personally deliver the enclosed letter to Felice Bauer. See Kafka's thoughts on this in the entry on p. 322 about his *plan . . . to ask Weiss to go to her office with a letter.* . . .

743. On December 17, 1913, in the Hotel Bristol, Hugo Bergmann spoke at an event of the Afike Jehuda Association on "Moses and our Present," a further "explanation of the ethics of the Pentateuch discussed in the lecturer's recently published book 'Moses'" (announced in the *Prager Tagblatt* of December 12, 1913).

744. Kafka is referring to their time together in *Gymnasium,* during which he *debated . . . with Bergmann in a Talmudic way either found within or imitated from him about God and his possibility.* See p. 172 and note 418.

745. Refers to Kafka's "intermediary" Ernst Weiß's visit to Felice Bauer.

746. Grete Bloch.

747. Apparently the few lines that Felice Bauer gave Ernst Weiß in reply to Kafka's letter: *W. got a few lines for me in which F. promised me to write at length that same day. This announced letter didn't come,* Kafka wrote in a letter to Grete Bloch, January 28, 1914 (KKAB2 no. 645).

748. Ernst Weiß was staying in Prague for the turn of the year. See Kafka's Decem-

ber 29, 1913, letter to Felice Bauer: *In the evening I then wanted to visit Dr. Weiss, who is now in Prague* (KKAB2 no. 641).

749. Kafka's notes are based on his reading of J. Höffner, "Die Tragödie im Hause Goethe," *Velhagen und Klasings Monatshefte* 28 (January 1914): 97ff.

750. In his notes, Kafka mixes up Wolf and Walter. *"Wolf withdraws for months to the Gartenhaus . . . and the severe temper of the young soul is evident in his vexed words when the Russian Empress wishes to see him: Tell the czarina I'm not a wild animal! Still, Wolf at least manages to pass the Abiturium with 'excellent.' Walter, too sickly for regular work, studies music with Felix Mendelssohn, who 'cannot encourage' him"* (ibid. p. 101).

751. Kafka probably read Oskar Iden-Zeller's 1913 account "Als Knecht unter heidnischen Nomaden im Tschuktschen-Lande" in Hermann Schaffstein, *Auf einsamen Wegen in Nordost-Sibirien,* the 39th of the Little Green Books, ed. N. Henningsen (Cologne, 1913), pp. 49ff.

752. Albert Anzenbacher (1885–1916) was a colleague of Kafka's who believed that his fiancée had betrayed him with the teacher W. See p. 332. Kafka *learned the story of the kiss in . . . stages, some of them separated by weeks;* see p. 330. Further entries about Anzenbacher and his fiancée Elisabeth Rämisch (1894–1931), known as Liesl (L.), are on pp. 327 and 329. The two of them married at the outbreak of the war.

753. The Prague writer Leo Fantl, a friend of the translator Jakob Hegner (see note 645), probably read in an interested private circle from the German edition of Paul Claudel's tragedy *Tête d'Or,* which had not yet appeared at that time. The exact words of the passage quoted by Kafka from memory are: "So sind wir unter dies Heer gedrungen und haben es aufgehoben / Und haben es hingeworfen, wie eine Tonne, hin auf die andere Seite" ("Thus we made our way under this army and lifted it up / And threw it like a barrel, overturning it"), quoted from Paul Claudel, *Goldhaupt. Ein Trauerspiel in drei Teilen,* German translation by Jakob Hegner (Hellerau, 1915), p. 81.

754. In the manuscript Kafka left a space here, apparently intending to fill in later the name of the article of clothing that had not occurred to him while writing.

755. Refers to his reading of Wilhelm Dilthey's *Das Erlebnis und die Dichtung.*

756. Quoted from Dilthey's *Das Erlebnis und die Dichtung.*

757. On November 25 and 26, 1912, Kafka had to interrupt the work on his story "Die Verwandlung" ("The Transformation," also known in English as "The Metamorphosis"), written between November 17 and December 6, for a business trip to Kratzau. See also p. 329 and note 763.

758. Johann Bartl was chairman of the appeals department in the AUVA.

759. Kafka's notes are based on his reading of Countess Lulu Thürheim, *Mein Leben. Erinnerungen aus Österreichs großer Welt 1788–1819,* ed. René van Rhyn (Munich, 1913), vol. 1.

760. Probably for the "Bericht der Arbeiter-Unfall-Versicherungs-Anstalt für das Königreich Böhmen über ihre Tätigkeit während der Zeit vom 1. Jänner bis 31. Dezember 1913" ("Report of the Workers' Accident Insurance Institute for the Kingdom of Bohemia on its Activities during the Period from January 1 to December 31, 1913"), Prague 1914. See KKAA, pp. 272–75 and 857–59.

761. Kafka's youngest sister was active, among other places, in the Klub jüdischer Frauen und Mädchen (Jewish Women and Girls' Club) (see p. 336), the chairwoman of which was Lise Weltsch (see note 383) and the leading members of which included Klara Thein (see note 776) and Grete Oplatka (see note 605).

762. The festive evening of the Bar-Kochba Association on January 21, 1914, in the ceremonial hall of the Hotel Central was introduced with a lecture by Felix Salten (actually Siegmund Salzmann, 1869–1947) on "Jewish Modernity." Then the actor Rudolf Schildkraut (1862–1930) read, among other things, poems by Max Brod.

763. Reading (see p. 328) and correction of the typescript of "Die Verwandlung" ("The Transformation," also known in English as "The Metamorphosis") were probably

undertaken in anticipation of a possible publication in the monthly *Die weißen Blätter*, which then didn't come to pass until October 1915.

764. Further notes on his reading of Countess Thürheim, *Mein Leben*.
765. Apparently refers to the letter to Ernst Weiß mentioned in the entry on p. 329.
766. Oskar Baum's 1913 novel *Die böse Unschuld. Ein jüdischer Kleinstadtroman* (*Evil Innocence: A Jewish Small-Town Novel*).
767. On January 29, 1914, at the Deutsches Vereinshaus (Smečkagasse 22), the Munich doctor Eduard Aigner spoke on the "Miracle Cures of Lourdes." Regarding the event of the Freie Deutsche Schule (Free German School) Association, the *Bohemia* of January 31, 1914, reported: "His seriously, thoroughly and scientifically conducted investigations have led Dr. Aigner, conscious of his medical duty, to take up the battle against the belief in the miracle cures of Lourdes. . . . Dr. Aigner . . . concluded with a rapturously received appeal to the German people to tell the truth. . . . After several questions had been answered by Dr. Aigner, the postal official Heermut was the first to speak up in opposition, defending the miracle cures of Lourdes as a firm believer."
768. Kafka's January 28, 1914, letter to Grete Bloch (KKAB2 no. 645), which he sent to her together with the novel *Die Galeere* by Ernst Weiß.
769. Czech: Šluknov, a town in North Bohemia.
770. Otto Ernst, *Asmus Sempers Jugendland* (Leipzig, 1905).
771. Probably a description of a film scene.
772. Kafka's notes on the corresponding pages of Countess Lulu Thürheim, *Mein Leben. Erinnerungen aus Österreichs großer Welt 1788–1819*, ed. René van Rhyn (Munich, 1913), vol. 2. See note 759.
773. "Outside Rzeszow Nany and I were riding in front of the Goëß' wagon, but o horror, at the town stood two rows of Jews, who as if possessed received us with cries of 'vivat' and waving of their flags and finally presented us with their Torah to kiss. In my modesty I didn't know where to hide myself away, but Nany responded to these accolades with loud laughter. Since we couldn't communicate with the Jews, we were forced to wait for the wagon behind us. When it finally appeared, the Israelites' attention immediately turned to it; they abandoned us in the middle of the street and hurried away with their flags and Tablets of Moses in order to rectify their error" (ibid., p. 48).
774. See also Kafka's February 15, 1914, entry on p. 336.
775. Felice Bauer.
776. Klara Thein (1884–1974) was a Prague Zionist whom Kafka had encountered on September 8, 1913, at the Eleventh Zionist Congress in Vienna. See September 1913 Trip, p. 566.
777. A footbridge that was replaced in 1914 by the Erzherzog Franz Ferdinand-Brücke (Archduke Franz Ferdinand Bridge, as of 1920 the Mánes Bridge). See note 987. See also the photograph in WB 136–137.
778. Refers to his reading of the chapter on Goethe in Wilhelm Dilthey's *Das Erlebnis und die Dichtung*.
779. Klara Thein lived with her family at Königstraße 120 in the district of Karolinenthal (Czech: Karlín).
780. Possibly the young woman G. W., whom Kafka had met on vacation in Riva. See note 708.
781. The apartment of the Thein family was located on the third floor, with a view over the Moldau.
782. See note 784.
783. Since their wedding, Max Brod and his wife had been living at Eliška Krásnohorskýgasse 3 in Prague's center.
784. On February 14, 1914, in the Hotel Bristol, the Zionistische Kulturkommission für Böhmen (Zionist Cultural Commission for Bohemia) organized for interested par-

ents a "public discussion evening ('parents' evening')" on "The Education of Jewish Youth" (announced in the *Prager Tagblatt* of February 12, 1914).

785. Lise Weltsch.
786. Vice-Secretary Josef Krätzig (1874–?) was a colleague of Kafka's at the AUVA.
787. The German term Kafka uses in this diary entry, *Notstich*, can have broadly the same sense as "emergency puncture," but the translation might well vary depending on the context, which could not be determined. See the Translator's Preface (pp. xxii–xxiii) for further discussion of the translation of this term.
788. Kafka had received a card from Felice Bauer, immediately replied with a letter, and was now awaiting a reply.
789. The railroad line from Prague's Kaiser Franz Josefs-Bahnhof via Wesseli-Gmund to Vienna.
790. Hans (Jan) Gerke (1895–1968) moved in the Café Arco literary circle while still a *Gymnasium* student and at the time of the diary entry had made a name for himself with publications in the *Prager Tagblatt.*
791. František Khol (1877–1930) was, at the time of the diary entry, a librarian at the National Museum and later was a dramaturge at the Czech National Theater.
792. At that time, the Weltsch family lived at Gemsengasse 4. Felix Weltsch was getting engaged to Irma Herz (1892–1969), his later wife.
793. Klaus Wagenbach remembers an anecdote told by Max Brod, according to which Jonas Enoch Kisch, the grandfather of Paul and Egon Erwin (see note 300), blew out the already-lit candles at such an engagement negotiation when he found the dowry too small.
794. In his February 19, 1914, letter to Grete Bloch, Kafka wrote: *Since my last letter a peculiar fortune has befallen me, which I must not keep from you, whom I don't spare my suffering. The last of my close unmarried or unengaged friends has become engaged. . . . To be sure, I am thus to some extent losing a friend, for a married friend is not one* (KKAB2 no. 654). Felix Weltsch's mother was Louise Weltsch, née Pereles (1861–1942).
795. Felix Weltsch.
796. See the first entry on p. 291.
797. Kafka is evidently referring to the former Kinsky villa (housing the ethnographic museum) built in the Empire style in the Kinsky Garden at the border of Prague's Malá Strana district with the suburb of Schmichow (Czech: Smíchov).
798. On July 11, 1914, Kafka traveled to Berlin, where on July 12 his engagement to Felice Bauer was dissolved. Probably on the night of July 13–14 he left Berlin for Lübeck and on July 16 or 17 continued to the Danish Baltic Sea resort of Marielyst to vacation with Ernst Weiß and his girlfriend Rahel Sanzara (actually Johanna Bleschke; 1894–1936). On July 26 Kafka set out on his return journey via Berlin to Prague. Kafka began writing the diary entries about his trip on July 23 in Marielyst. He broke them off midsentence (p. 347) and resumed them only after his return to Prague, from July 27 to 29.
799. Kafka used the image of a "tribunal" for the dissolution of the engagement in the Hotel Askanischer Hof, during which, besides Felice Bauer and her sister Erna, Grete Bloch too was present. On October 15, 1914, he wrote to Grete Bloch: *You did sit in judgment over me at the Askanischer Hof—it was abhorrent for you, for me, for everyone—but it only appeared so, in reality I was sitting in your place and haven't left it to this day* (KKAB3 no. 781).
800. An der Stralauer Brücke was a street on the bank of the Spree River in the center of Berlin.
801. See note 678.
802. Town near Pirna, on the Bohemian border at that time.
803. Emilie, a sister of Carl Bauer.
804. Kafka resumed his entries about the trip only on July 27, 1914, after his return to Prague.

805. In his July 13, 1914, letter to Anna and Carl Bauer, Kafka wrote: *Farewell, especially after your conduct yesterday you have earned my unconditional admiration, don't remember me unkindly* (KKAB3 no. 771).
806. An illustrated humorous weekly founded in 1844, published by Braun & Schneider in Munich.
807. The Berlin terminus for the Berlin-Hamburg railroad line.
808. The junction of the Berlin-Hamburg and Lüneburg-Lübeck railroad lines.
809. Mineral water from a spring in Grauhof near Goslar.
810. Dr. Ernst Weiß.
811. Kafka had originally planned to spend his vacation in Gleschendorf and not in Marielyst: *I was then in Lübeck, went bathing in Travemünde, in Lübeck received a visit from Dr. Weiss, who was on his way to this Danish resort, and traveled here instead of to Gleschendorf,* Kafka wrote in a July 19 or 20, 1914, letter from Marielyst to Max Brod and Felix Weltsch (KKAB3 no. 774).
812. The crossing to the Danish island of Falster was made by a train ferry. From Væggerløse, passengers then took a carriage to Marielyst—not Marienlyst, the seaside resort near Helsingør, as Kafka's misspelling suggests.
813. Here and in the rest of the entry: Ernst Weiß and his girlfriend Rahel Sanzara, whom Weiß called "Hansi."
814. Refers to Kafka's meeting with Erna Bauer before his departure for Lübeck. A further meeting with her on the return to Prague is documented by a card to Ottla Kafka (KKAB3 no. 778).
815. The young woman Kafka met on his vacation in Riva. See note 708.
816. *Die Zukunft,* a weekly edited by Maximilian Harden.
817. Kafka is referring to *Der Kampf* (titled *Franziska* in later editions) by Ernst Weiß. The first edition (Berlin, 1916) was among the books in Kafka's possession at the time of his death.
818. Attempt at a story that converges with the novel *Der Proceß* (*The Trial*) in the identically named protagonist.
819. Refers to Kafka's simultaneous work on "Erinnerungen an die Kaldabahn" ("Memories of the Kalda Railroad," called "the Russian story" in this entry), on *Der Proceß* (*The Trial*), and possibly on *Der Verschollene* (*The Missing Person*).
820. Kafka was staying temporarily in his sister Elli's apartment at Nerudagasse 48 in the Prague suburb Königliche Weinberge (Czech: Královské Vinohrady). See note 668.
821. For the Danube monarchy, the beginning of the First World War was characterized by numerous defeats, the shocking scale of which became clear despite the strict censorship of the press.
822. Kafka is referring to *Der Proceß* (*The Trial*).
823. The Berlin hotel Askanischer Hof. See note 799.
824. The top right corner of the diary page was torn after the writing of the entry. As a result, text is missing from this passage on the recto side and from the passage on pp. 358–359 on the verso side.
825. See note 824.
826. Perhaps the story "Der blinde Gast" ("The Blind Guest") by Otto Pick mentioned shortly thereafter in the entry of November 3, 1914.
827. The poem "Die Feuertaufe" ("The Baptism of Fire") by Rudolf Fuchs appeared in the entertainment supplement of the *Prager Tagblatt* of October 25, 1914.
828. Nina Hoffmann, *Th. M. Dostojewsky. Eine biografische Studie* (Berlin, 1899), pp. 73ff. The volume was among the books in Kafka's possession at the time of his death.
829. Along with the Belvedere gardens, the Chotek Gardens, adjoining the Belvedere summer palace, were among Kafka's preferred destinations on his walks. See also note 45 and the entries on pp. 386 and 392.
830. Kafka is referring to the Prague Castle, the Hradschin (Czech: Hradčany), and the guard of honor stationed there. See p. 145.

831. The seat of the Imperial and Royal Eighth Corps headquarters as well as Prague's main police station was the former Ledebour Palace on the Kleinseitner Ring (Czech: Malostranské námêstí).
832. Both the Thun-Hohenstein Palace at Nerudagasse 20 and the nearby Thun Palace at Thunschengasse 14 have fountains.
833. See also the entry of October 25, 1914; no copy of the story could be found.
834. For Kafka's reading of Strindberg, see note 678 and pp. 347, 378, 387, 391.
835. Probably: "Le poète et l'ami causent," from "L'église habillée de feuilles" in Francis Jammes, *Clairières dans le Ciel, 1902–1906*. See also the July 25, 1914, letter from Jakob Hegner to Kafka, in which Francis Jammes is also mentioned; apparently Hegner was hoping that Kafka would translate a text by the French writer into German. See KKAB3 no. 43 of the letters to Kafka.
836. Continuation of the fragment "Erinnerungen an die Kaldabahn" ("Memories of the Kalda Railroad"). See note 680.
837. Kafka's brother-in-law Josef Pollak was staying in Prague from the beginning of November on convalescent leave. Regarding the length of the leave, Julie Kafka wrote in a November 27, 1914, letter to Felice Bauer: "Our son-in-law Peppo came home 3 weeks ago with a wounded hand. How long it will take to heal, we don't yet know" (F 623).
838. Pepa, i.e., Josef Pollak.
839. This remark, inserted subsequently into the manuscript by Kafka, refers to a performance of *Der ungetreue Eckehart* by Hans Sturm at the Neues Deutsches Theater on December 4 or 7, 1914.
840. The Polish princely family had several estates in Galicia, the main combat zone between Austrian and Russian troops.
841. The course of the war in Galicia led to a great influx of Eastern Jewish refugees into Prague. The Prague Jewish community established an aid committee for these refugees in which Max Brod's parents, among others, became involved. In the *Bohemia* of November 22, 1914, the Relief Committee for Jewish Refugees asked for donations in kind to be deposited at Tuchmachergasse 7.
842. Fanny Brod, Max Brod's mother.
843. Chaim Nagler, head of the Relief Committee for Jewish Refugees.
844. A county seat in Galicia.
845. Frau Brod.
846. Yiddish (Hebrew: *mitzvah*) for "good deed."
847. *Schmattes*: Yiddish (Slavic) for "rags."
848. Draft of a letter—which has not survived—to Paul Hermann, who had been looking after the asbestos factory since his brother, Kafka's brother-in-law Karl Hermann, had been conscripted. See note 668.
849. Alfred Löwy (see note 385) too had a financial stake in the asbestos factory. See also p. 220 and note 552.
850. Karl Hermann.
851. Elli and the children's; Kafka's sister and her children Felix and Gerti.
852. Either of two rubber industry publications: the *Gummi- und Asbest-Zeitung. Organ des Verbandes der österreichisch-ungarischen Kautshukwaren-Fabriken*, which appeared as a biweekly in Vienna, or the *Gummi-Zeitung. Fachblatt für die Gummi-, Guttapercha-, Asbest- und Celluloid-Industrie*, which appeared as a weekly in Berlin.
853. Since her husband's conscription, Elli Hermann and her two children had been living at her parents' apartment. See p. 285.
854. It cannot be determined with certainty which text Kafka is referring to, though the entries on pp. 372 and 373 suggest that the writing of the novel *Der Proceß* (*The Trial*) had stalled.
855. In November 1914, Franz Werfel had been given three months' leave from military service and was staying in Prague with his parents, who lived at Mariengasse 41.

856. Kafka had finished writing "In der Strafkolonie" ("In the Penal Colony") during his two-week vacation from October 5 to 18. See the entry of December 31, 1914, p. 377.
857. Franz Werfel's fragmentary dramatic poem "Esther, Kaiserin von Persien" ("Esther, Empress of Persia").
858. Hanna Werfel (1894–1964) and Marianne, known as Mizzi (1899–1965).
859. A play by Friedrich Schiller.
860. Kafka is apparently referring to the Berlin castle Bellevue, the contemporary depiction of King Friedrich Wilhelm I's Tabakskollegium, and the Italian writer and newspaper publisher Matilde Serao. It's possible that Kafka was familiar with Serao's novel *Dopo il perdono* (*After the Pardon*), published in German translation in 1908 as *Nach der Verzeihung,* in which the author describes in detail a ball held in honor of Kaiser Wilhelm II in a princely palazzo on the occasion of his state visit to Rome.
861. In Werfel's "Esther, Kaiserin von Persien," the Supreme Doorkeeper says: "But before a general's sash all humanity falls over, while in the bathhouses one of God's masterpieces farts at the other."
862. On December 2, 1914, Erna Bauer wrote an "immediate reply" to a letter from Kafka that has not survived. Her letter has survived, tucked inside a book that was in Kafka's possession.
863. Carl Bauer had died of a heart attack on November 5, 1914.
864. Kafka is apparently referring to a remark made by Erna Bauer in her letter: "Dear Franz, the relationship between Felice and me always remained the same good one, it never suffered from all the ugliness, only something new, disturbing had come between us, and it is still still there" (KKAB3 no. 47 of the letters to Kafka).
865. Referring to Kafka's letter, which has not survived, Erna Bauer wrote: "Your last letter breathes so much calmness that I dare to hope you now possess this often."
866. In her letter Erna Bauer inquires: "What do you want to do about Christmas? Make your decisions, then everything else will work out."
867. Kafka is referring to the unfinished chapter "Fahrt zur Mutter" ("Journey to His Mother") in *Der Proceß* (*The Trial*).
868. Emil Kafka (1881–1963), second oldest son of Heinrich and Karoline Kafka from Leitmeritz, had immigrated to America in July 1904. The description of his quiet life reproduced here deals mainly with his work for the mail-order company Sears, Roebuck & Co. The course of Emil Kafka's life and the lives of another two cousins of Franz Kafka who immigrated to America might have provided inspiration for the novel *Der Verschollene* (*The Missing Person*).
869. The exegesis that follows the legend of the doorkeeper ("Vor dem Gesetz"/"Before the Law") in the novel *Der Proceß* (*The Trial*).
870. Refers to Kafka's work on the novel *Der Proceß* (*The Trial*).
871. Oskar Baum earned his living as a piano teacher; his apartment was located at Mariengasse 26.
872. Oskar Baum's son Leo.
873. The classification of businesses subject to compulsory insurance by accident risk was part of Kafka's job at the AUVA.
874. The headline of the heavily censored evening edition of the *Prager Tagblatt* of December 15, 1914, read: "Withdrawal of our right wing in Serbia."
875. Kafka is referring to the text (included in KKANI 194–216) that Max Brod published under the title "Der Riesenmaulwurf" ("The Giant Mole").
876. In light of the economic difficulties, Hermann Kafka was worried about the family's investments in the Prager Asbestwerke.
877. Kafka was living temporarily in his sister Elli Hermann's apartment (see note 668) and came to his parents' apartment only for meals.
878. For Kafka's reading of *The Brothers Karamazov,* see note 738. The *cousin or nephew*

mentioned here by Kafka is not the Karamazov father's cousin or nephew but Pyotr Alexandrovich Miusov, the cousin of his deceased first wife.

879. Kafka is referring to the chapter "Fogs of London" in Alexander Herzen's autobiography.
880. Evidently Kafka was staying for several days with Max and Elsa Brod in this city (Czech: Kutná Hora), located ninety kilometers east of Prague; among its sights was the Gothic *Jakobskirche*, the Church of St. James.
881. A narrative fragment that survived among Kafka's posthumous materials. See KKANI 217–24.
882. Paul Hermann had been running the asbestos factory since the conscription of his brother Karl (see also note 848) and had now himself been called up to serve in the war.
883. A reference to the Jewish High Holy Day of Yom Kippur, Hebrew for "Day of Atonement."
884. Fanny Reiß, who was from Lemberg, was one of the pupils in the school for Galician refugee children where Max Brod taught classes. Kafka occasionally attended Brod's class as a listener (see p. 387), presumably met Fanny Reiß on one of these occasions, and befriended her and her sisters Esther and Tilka. See also pp. 393, 406, 407.
885. For Kafka's meeting with Felice Bauer, see pp. 380ff.
886. The passage quoted by Kafka is from the seventeenth chapter and begins as follows: "You have also felt influence from a distance, though you may have observed it poorly. You have surely felt . . ."
887. The circus director Schumann, famous for his horse training, had performed in Prague with his circus on various occasions.
888. From October 1907 to July 1908, Kafka had been employed in the Prague branch of the insurance company Assicurazioni Generali.
889. Kafka is referring to an article from the *Vossische Zeitung* with the headline "Sweden Is Not a Balkan State," reprinted in the supplement to the morning edition of the *Bohemia* of January 19, 1915.
890. Kafka and Felice Bauer met on the weekend of January 23–24, 1915, in Bodenbach, a border town in the district of Tetschen in North Bohemia, a station of the Prague-Dresden railroad connection.
891. In Kafka's request to a waiter—to bring him the newspaper as soon as another guest had finished reading it—he underscored his use of the conjunction *bis* to mean "when" or "as soon as." Felice criticized this common Austrian usage, arguing that as a conjunction *bis* could mean only "until." For the "*bis*"*-Streit,* Kafka's dispute with Felice over the proper usage of *bis*, see also his September 23, 1917, letter to Felix Weltsch with a *library request* to check a dictionary or another authoritative source to determine *whether F. is right* (KKAB3 no. 1065).
892. Probably the acquaintances whom Kafka had met during his visit to Hellerau in late June 1914. See p. 284.
893. In an entry from July 1916, Kafka takes up these reflections again (p. 421). Kafka had the relationship with a woman in Zuckmantel during his sanatorium stays in 1905 and 1906. For his relationship to the young Swiss woman G. W. during his sanatorium stay in Riva in September 1913, see note 708.
894. Kafka is referring to the doorkeeper legend from the novel *Der Proceß* (*The Trial*), which he published on September 7, 1915, under the title "Vor dem Gesetz" ("Before the Law") in the Rosh Hashana issue of the *Selbstwehr*.
895. Kafka is referring to the text that begins "Blumfeld an elderly bachelor," in which the protagonist in the beginning considers buying a dog (KKANI pp. 229–66).
896. In connection with the above-mentioned *dog story*, the protagonist of which is the elderly bachelor Blumfeld, Kafka is alluding to Gustave Flaubert's posthumously

published unfinished satirical novel, the title characters of which are the two elderly bachelors Bouvard and Pécuchet.

897. Kafka rented a room in the house at Bilekgasse 10 where his sister Valli Pollak and her family also had an apartment. See also p. 285 and note 668.

898. Kafka's landlady, the widow Justine Nalos, née Propper (1859–?).

899. Emil Gschwind, Kafka's classroom teacher during his *Gymnasium* days, lived as a member of the Piarists in their monastery at Herrengasse 1. His pupils had to submit the results of their "private reading" to him there on Sundays.

900. Kafka is alluding to an image coined by Gogol in *Dead Souls*: "Are you, Russia, not also racing along like a bold troika that cannot be overtaken?" Dostoyevsky takes up this image in his novel *The Brothers Karamazov*. See also note 738. In the chapter titled "Psychology at Full Steam. The Galloping Troika. The Finale of the Prosecutor's Speech," the prosecutor uses the image of the racing troika, and in the chapter titled "An Adulterer of Thought," the defense attorney uses it in his counterargument.

901. In the first part of Alexander Herzen's autobiography, which Kafka was reading at the time of this entry (see pp. 375 and 386), Herzen gives an account of his relationship to Saint Simonism.

902. Ida Nalos was the almost-thirteen-year-old daughter of Kafka's landlady.

903. In his March 3, 1915, letter to Felice Bauer, Kafka mentioned once again the circumstances and reasons that led him to give up his room: *It was perhaps not so much the unquiet in the apartment that drove me away from there, for I have recently achieved almost nothing at all in my work anyhow, thus have at bottom been able to test neither the quiet nor the unquiet of the apartment, rather it was my own unquiet, a feeling that I don't want to interpret further* (KKAB3 no. 793). Shortly after giving notice, he moved into a room on the sixth floor of the house *Zum goldenen Hecht* at Langegasse 18 (today no. 16), from which he had a nice view of Prague's old town. See p. 386.

904. On March 12, 1915, the weekly *Selbstwehr* on the second discussion evening of the cycle "Ost und West" ("East and West") organized by the Jüdischer Volksverein (Jewish People's Association), which took place on March 9, 1915, in the Hotel Bristol: "In a continuation of the discussion from the previous lecture evening, Herr Gabriel Leipen spoke about 'Eastern and Western Jewry.' With the intention not to give a comprehensive talk but above all to open the debate, the speaker emphasized that there was no contradiction of any kind between Zionism and the Jewish religion, which he supported with many passages from our writings. His remarks concluded by declaring the unified national foundation of Eastern and Western Jewry. Among others who participated in the debate were Univ.-Prof. Dr. Raudnitz, the Prague writer Dr. Max Brod, Herr Dr. Simon Adler, etc., as well as several Eastern Jews."

905. On April 9, 1915, the *Selbstwehr* reported that "Herr L. Wiesenfeld," whom Kafka characterizes here, spoke not long after this second discussion evening, on March 18, 1915, "in the Jewish language on 'Eastern Jewish Problems.'" Wiesenfeld and his brother Moses played a part in founding the *Prager jüdische Zeitung*, a half-Yiddish, half-German organ initiated by the refugee committee in March 1915.

906. *Sperrsechser*, the term Kafka uses in the original German, designates the fee collected by building caretakers for opening and locking the front door after nightfall.

907. Kafka's entry is based on his reading of chapters sixteen and seventeen of Alexander Herzen's autobiography.

908. Probably "On the Lyricism of Our Poets: A Letter to V. A. Zhukovsky" or "Subjects for the Lyric Poets of the Present Time: Two Letters to N. M. Yazykov," both included in the volume of Gogol's correspondence with his friends in the 1913 German edition of Gogol's complete works. The volume was among the books in Kafka's possession at the time of his death.

909. The Chotek Gardens with the Belvedere summer palace. The building's *gallery* is an exterior walkway freely accessible from the palace garden with an arrangement of columns that reproduces that of the famous Temple of Poseidon in Paestum. From here Kafka had a view of Prague and the nearby Hradschin, the Prague Castle. See also note 45.
910. Kafka's sister Ottla with her later husband Josef David.
911. The 1912 German edition of the novel was among the books in Kafka's possession at the time of his death and is inscribed with a handwritten dedication from Erna Bauer dated March 10, 1915.
912. Probably Fanny Reiß. See p. 377 and note 884.
913. Regarding the lecture cycle "Ost und West" ("East and West") of the Jüdischer Volksverein (Jewish People's Association) (see note 904), the *Selbstwehr* of April 9, 1915, wrote: "The fourth lecture in the cycle was delivered on Wednesday, March 24, 1915, by Dr. Max Brod. . . . During the discussion Dr. S. Adler spoke for the Orthodox and H. Getzler from the point of view of the Galician Orthodox. Herr Steigler took an anti-religious position." Evidently, Kafka rendered the name *Getzler* as *Götzl* and the name *Steigler* as *Steidler*.
914. Several days earlier, on April 4, 1915, Kafka had already described the *torments of the apartment* in detail to Felice Bauer: *In my room, to be sure, the noise is probably infernal.* (KKAB3 no. 797).
915. Max Brod offered a weekly ninety-minute course on "World Literature," in which the Galician female pupils were studying Homer's *Iliad*. See also note 884.
916. On April 22, 1915, Kafka accompanied his sister Elli on a trip to visit his brother-in-law Karl Hermann, who was stationed near the Hungarian Carpathian town of Nagy Mihály. While Elli Hermann remained there, Kafka returned alone to Prague on April 27. The April 27 diary entry records the legs of the outbound journey: Prague–Vienna: pp. 387–388; Vienna–Budapest: pp. 388–389; Budapest–Sátoralja-Ujhely: pp. 389–390; the stay in Ujhely, where Kafka and his sister spent the night: pp. 390–391.
917. Nagy Mihály, municipality in the county of Zemplin, on the railroad line Sátoralja-Ujhely–Przemysl.
918. *The Evening*, Budapest daily newspaper.
919. Elli.
920. Bánovce, town located about twenty-five kilometers north of Sátoralja-Ujhely.
921. Žižkov, a Prague suburb. See notes 101 and 117.
922. Viennese daily newspaper.
923. Hugo Bergmann.
924. Capital of the Hungarian county of Bistritz-Naszód (Transylvania), which borders the county of Mármaros (see below).
925. A village in the Hungarian county of Mármaros on the Galician border.
926. A city in Bukovina.
927. Sátoralja-Ujhely was capital of the county of Zemplin, a railroad junction.
928. On April 21, 1915, at the Deutsches Landestheater in Prague, the Neue Wiener Bühne gave a guest performance of August Strindberg's drama *The Father*.
929. Memorial to the leader of the Hungarian independence movement of 1848–49, Lajos Kossuth.
930. Probably Ernst Popper (1890–1950), a former schoolmate of Franz Werfel and Willy Haas who belonged to their circle of friends.
931. Included in the 1913 German edition titled *Entzweit. Einsam.* Among the books in Kafka's possession at the time of his death, the volume was probably a gift from Felice Bauer. See Kafka's May 2, 1915, postcard from Dobřichowitz (KKAB3 no. 807).
932. A popular excursion destination and summer resort about twenty kilometers south of Prague.
933. Felix Weltsch.

934. Elli Hermann or Erna Bauer.
935. Felice Bauer.
936. Probably Angela (Alice) Rehberger. See note 97.
937. Max Brod's annotation: "An unfinished novel of mine" (T 712). An excerpt appeared with the note "From an unpublished novel" in *Der neue Roman. Ein Almanach* (Leipzig, 1917), pp. 174–86.
938. Irma Stein (1890–?), a daughter of Kafka's landlord. See also note 903.
939. Suburb on the right bank of the Moldau across from the Baumgarten (Czech: Stromovka; see note 1058) with the Baroque summer palace of the same name.
940. Fanny Reiß. See note 884.
941. Possibly Kafka is referring to a Mass witnessed through a side entrance of the Tein Church on Teingasse.
942. "At Petersgasse 3, an old house that previously served as a hospital, a welfare committee has established a soup kitchen for the Galician Jews, who receive strictly ritual [i.e., kosher] food here for a very minimal price, often even for nothing. This soup kitchen is always overfilled at lunch and dinner. 1800 portions are served daily." Richard Katz, "Galizien in Prag," *Prager Tagblatt*, December 25, 1914. For the Relief Committee for Jewish Refugees, see also note 841.
943. A week before this entry, probably on May 3, 1915, Kafka had already written to Felice Bauer: *Why don't you know that it would be my good fortune . . . to become a soldier, provided, to be sure, my health can stand it, which I do hope it can. At the end of this month or the beginning of next I'll be examined. You should want me to be accepted as I wish* (KKAB3 no. 808).
944. Georg (Jiří Mordechai) Langer (1894–1943) had devoted himself to Eastern Jewish Chassidism and in the years 1913 and 1914 temporarily belonged to the court of the Rabbi of Belz, one of the wonder rabbis of the Orthodox sect, who had to leave Galicia with his adherents when the war broke out. Shortly after being called up for military service, Langer was discharged for "mental disturbance," because he refused to give up his Orthodox way of life (sidelocks and beard, clothing, etc.). For a brief time afterward, he lived in Prague again before returning to the Rabbi of Belz, who was now living in exile. At that time—most likely through his distant relative Max Brod—he became acquainted with Kafka.
945. Max Brod recalls: "At that time, together with my Kabbalist friend Georg Langer, I spent a lot of time at the home of a wonder rabbi [Brod's annotation: the Rabbi of Grodeck], a refugee from Galicia who lived in dark, unfriendly, crowded rooms in the Prague suburb of Žižkov. . . . It is notable that Franz, whom I took with me to one of the 'Third Meals' at the end of the Sabbath, with its whispering and Chassidic singing, actually remained quite aloof" (FK 137).
946. Probably Ernst Eisner (1882–1929), director of the Assicurazioni Generali. Even after resigning from the insurance company (on July 15, 1908), Kafka remained in contact with his former superior, who took a great interest in literature.
947. The prayer opening the service on the eve of the Day of Atonement (Yom Kippur). See note 883.
948. Regarding the Bible passage on which Kafka's entry is based, Martin Buber wrote: "The 82nd Psalm, of which he is clearly speaking here, has as its subject God's judgment over those 'sons of God' or angels to whom he had entrusted the rule over the human world and who had despicably abused their office and 'judged falsely.' The content of this late psalm is connected with that of the Oriental myth, incorporated by Gnosticism, of the astral spirits who fatefully determine the destiny of the world, but from whose power the human being is capable of liberating himself by consecrating himself to the hidden highest light and entering rebirth. I have reason to assume that Kafka was also acquainted with this myth: He had asked me about it when he visited me in Berlin in 1914." Martin Buber, *Schuld und Schuldgefühle* (Heidelberg, 1958), pp. 61–62.

949. *Förster Flecks Erzählung von seinen Schicksalen auf dem Zuge Napoleons nach Rußland und von seiner Gefangenschaft 1812–1814,* the 18th of the Little Green Books, ed. N. Henningsen (Cologne, 1912–13), pp. 30ff.
950. *Memoiren des Generals Marcellin Marbot* (Stuttgart, 1907). See also pp. 400ff.
951. Paul Holzhausen, *Die Deutschen in Rußland 1812. Leben und Leiden auf der Moskauer Heerfahrt* (Berlin, 1912). See also pp. 404–405.
952. Dr. Robert Marschner was director of the AUVA. Pimisker refers to the clerk Herrman Pimiskan (1869–1926).
953. The German edition of *Hamlet* published by the Leipzig Bibliographisches Institut was among the books in Kafka's possession at the time of his death. Act 5, Scene 2: "Let four captains / Bear Hamlet, like a soldier, to the stage; / For he was likely, had he been put on, / To have prov'd most royally."
954. At that time Felix Weltsch lived with his wife on Kirchengasse in the district of Holleschowitz-Bubna (Czech: Holešovice-Bubny).
955. Karl Roßmann, main character of Kafka's novel *Der Verschollene* (*The Missing Person*); Josef K., protagonist of the novel *Der Proceß* (*The Trial*).
956. Yiddish (Hebr.) for "the pious one, the righteous one, the miracle worker." Based on the Kabbalist formula "the righteous one or the pious one is the foundation of the world," in Chassidism the *tzadik* is the appointed religious and moral leader of the community.
957. Israel ben Eliezer, the Baal Shem Tov (abbreviated by Kafka as B. in the text that follows), founded Chassidism in the eighteenth century.
958. Hebrew for "the pious (righteous) one of his generation."
959. Drohóbycz was a district capital at the edge of the Carpathians.
960. Sabbatai Zevi, born in 1626 in Smyrna, claimed to be the expected Messiah. The Sabbatian movement named after him—regarded by Orthodox Jews as heretical—spread across Europe and continued to exert an influence into the eighteenth century.
961. Kafka's then-three-year-old niece (1912–72) was the daughter of Elli and Karl Hermann.
962. During his Prague guest performance, Alexander Girardi appeared in Bernhard Buchbinder's farce *Er und seine Schwester* on Sunday, October 31, 1915, in an afternoon performance at the Neues Deutsches Theater.
963. At that time, the *Städtische Volksbibliothek* (municipal public library) was housed in a building at Valentinergasse 4.
964. Possibly a Torah flag rescued from Galicia by the Reiß family.
965. Sisters of Fanny Reiß. See also note 884.
966. Kafka is remembering the poster for one of the *Fantomas* films that had been showing in the Prague cinemas since the summer of 1913 with great success. See the facsimile in Kafka, *Tagebücher: Kommentarband,* p. 190.
967. Brescia was one of the places Kafka visited during his September 1909 trip to Italy.
968. In September 1913, Kafka traveled from Vienna to Riva by way of Trieste, Venice, Verona, and Desenzano. On September 20, 1913, he wrote to Felice Bauer from Verona: *In the church of St. Anastasia in Verona, where I'm sitting wearily in a pew, opposite a life-size marble dwarf bearing a holy water basin with a happy expression on his face* (KKAB2 no. 612).
969. Due to the intermittently favorable course of the war for Austria-Hungary, some Galician districts had become free again, and the first refugees could return.
970. The last day to subscribe to the "third tax-free 5½% Austrian war loan" (*Prager Tagblatt,* November 3, 1915) was November 6, 1915. On November 5, the *Prager Tagblatt* wrote: "Only a day and a half now separates us from the end of subscriptions to the third war loan. Tomorrow at noon the subscription period will end. That's why everyone who has not yet subscribed should hurry to take advantage of the short

time left to take on a share of the war loan. The choice of a secure investment, which over 15 years will yield more than 6% interest, certainly cannot be difficult. Everyone should just consider what assets had to be chosen in the past to earn so high a return. So take proper advantage of the final hours remaining for the subscription."

971. The Karlsbrücke (Czech: Karlův most; English: Charles Bridge) links Prague's Kleinseite (Czech: Malá Strana; English: Little Side) and the Altstadt (Czech: Staré Město; English: Old Town).
972. Regarding the rush of visitors to the model of a trench on exhibition on the Kaiserinsel (Czech: Císařský ostrov), an island in the Moldau between Troja and the Baumgarten (Czech: Stromovka), the *Prager Tagblatt* of November 11, 1915, reported: "Last Sunday the crowds visiting the Prague trench were so massive that besides the permanent ticket counters, several temporary sites for the sale of entrance tickets had to be opened in order to be able to even halfway meet the needs of the public. More than 10,000 people passed through the turnstiles. On weekdays too, in good weather, there was a lively bustle at the Prague trench, and the perfect replica of a military installation left every visitor with valuable and instructive impressions."
973. Kafka's schoolmate and youthful friend had fallen on June 11, 1915.
974. Abraham Grünberg (1889–?), a Jewish writer from Galicia, was staying in Prague during the war years. Among the books in Kafka's possession at the time of his death was Grünberg's account of the "great pogrom of Siedlce in the year 1906," which appeared in October 1916 under the title *Ein jüdisch-polnisch-russisches Jubiläum*. The book contains a handwritten dedication to Kafka from November 29, 1916.
975. Quoted from Max Dreyer, *Der deutsche Morgen: das Leben eines Mannes* (Leipzig, 1915), p. 232.
976. Regine Mirsky-Tauber (1865–?), a writer and the wife of a Prague cantor, was one of the leading members of the Klub deutscher Künstlerinnen (Club of German Women Artists). The purpose of Kafka's visit was probably the preliminary discussion of a lecture that Kafka's director Robert Marschner intended to give at the Klub deutscher Künstlerinnen. It was an event dedicated to the subject of relief for disabled veterans, for which Kafka was officially responsible. Frau Mirsky-Tauber lived at Altschulgasse 2A.
977. See note 62.
978. The Mishna (Hebrew: "repetition," "instruction"), the originally orally transmitted Jewish religious law, forms the basis of the Talmud.
979. In Max Brod's edition of the *Diaries*, he noted: "A Talmudic scholar belonging to the pious Lieben family of Prague" (T 713).
980. A village located south of Prague on the Moldau.
981. On a postcard to Felice Bauer, which arrived in Berlin on December 24, 1915, Kafka wrote: *Certainly I want to arrange my life differently after the war. I want to move to Berlin, despite the official's characteristic fear of the future, for here things cannot go on. But what sort of person will be moving by then? From the perspective of my present condition, a person who at best will be able to work for himself for a week, only to find himself definitively at the end of his strength. What a night this has been! What a day! I should have left in 1912* (KKAB3 no. 829).
982. Probably Max Brod's novel *Tycho Brahes Weg zu Gott* (*Tycho Brahe's Path to God*), published in December by the Kurt Wolff Verlag.
983. A trip to Marienbad originally planned for Easter 1916—in conjunction with official duties on the Tuesday after Easter—had to be postponed on short notice by about a month. Kafka then intended to combine it with a three-week vacation. See his April 25, 1916, postcard to Felice Bauer: *Dear Felice I was not in Marienbad, the business trip had to be postponed, perhaps it will be in mid-May, then I will combine it with my vacation and stay in Marienbad for 3 weeks, live in peace the way I wish and as far as headaches and self-reproaches will permit* (KKAB3 no. 841).

984. Felix Hermann, Kafka's nephew.
985. Dr. Robert Marschner, director of the AUVA.
986. Kafka's notes are based on his reading of the 1916 German edition of Nathan Söderblom's *The Origin of the Belief in God* (*Das Werden des Gottesglaubens*).
987. The Erzherzog Franz Ferdinand-Brücke (Archduke Franz Ferdinand Bridge; as of 1920 the Mánes Bridge), completed in the spring of 1915, replaced the Kettensteg often used by Kafka. See p. 333.
988. Might refer to the new recruitment of the so-called Landsturm reserve force on July 21, 1916. Although Kafka was deemed fit, he was—contrary to his hope—not conscripted, but at the request of the AUVA, he continued to be exempted from military service for an unlimited period.
989. Genesis 3:8. Further quotes from Genesis follow. In subsequent days—including during the vacation in Marienbad—Kafka continued his reading of the Bible. See pp. 419 and 421–422. On July 8, 1916, he wrote to Max Brod: *I'm doing only a little reading in the Bible nothing else* (KKAB3 no. 886).
990. Genesis 3:21.
991. Genesis 8:21.
992. Genesis 2:9.
993. Genesis 2:16–17.
994. Genesis 3:14–19.
995. Not Cain but Abel is favored. See Genesis 4:3–16.
996. Genesis 6:3.
997. Genesis 4:26.
998. Genesis 5:24.
999. Kafka and Felice Bauer's vacation together had been planned since April; see p. 411 and note 983. They met in Marienbad on July 2, 1916; Felice Bauer stayed until July 13. The rapprochement between her and Kafka at this time led to the plan of marrying after the end of the war. On July 13 they traveled together to Franzensbad, where Kafka's mother and his sister Valli were staying. From there Felice Bauer returned to Berlin, while Kafka stayed in Marienbad until July 24, 1916.
1000. See note 482.
1001. This entry is connected with the novel *Der Verschollene* (*The Missing Person*).
1002. A village near Marienbad.
1003. Felice Bauer's brother Ferdinand (1884–1952) had immigrated to America in 1913.
1004. The *dog story* begun in February 1915, without a title in the manuscript. See p. 383 and note 895.
1005. *Thanks to the balls Blumfeld has come out of his room much earlier than usual, even the newspaper he has forgotten unread on the table* (KKANI 247, lines 9–12).
1006. The text of "The Bachelor" is to be found in one of the brown quarto notebooks used by Kafka at that time.
1007. Kafka makes similar remarks in a letter to Max Brod written between July 12 and 14: *At bottom I was never before intimate with a woman, except in two cases, the one in Zuckmantel (but there she was a woman and I a boy) and the one in Riva (but there she was half a child and I utterly confused and sick in all directions). Now, however, I saw intimacy in a woman's eyes and could not close myself off* (KKAB3 no. 872). See also p. 381 and note 893.
1008. Entries based on Kafka's reading of Genesis 20–29.
1009. On various occasions Kafka compared these authors' difficulties reconciling their relationships to women and their literary work with his own. See, among other places, KKAB3 no. 732.
1010. Kafka's notes are based on his reading of Friedrich Wilhelm Foerster's 1904 pedagogical manual *Jugendlehre*.
1011. In a December 10, 1917, letter to Max Brod, Kafka wrote: *An example from Förster occurs to me, though very vaguely, which shows how one can unfailingly instill in a child the convic-*

tion that not only every person has to close the door behind him upon entering a room but also this very child this door (KKAB3 no. 1096).

1012. Quoted from Johann Adam Möhler, *Symbolik oder Darstellung der dogmatischen Gegensätze der Katholiken und Protestanten nach ihren öffentlichen Bekenntnisschriften*. The title of the book is written among the notes on the endpaper of the Eleventh Notebook.

1013. Draft of a letter to Felice Bauer subsequently written on a typewriter without significant alterations and dated October 19, 1916 (KKAB3 no. 977).

1014. Connected with the "Hunter Gracchus" fragments that survived among Kafka's posthumous materials. See KKANI 305–13 and 378–84.

1015. Gertrud Kanitz (1895–1946), an actress from Vienna who was staying in Prague for family reasons. In a December 27, 1920, letter to Kafka, Max Brod described a theater performance in which Gertrud Kanitz played the lead role (BKB 286).

1016. Kafka is probably alluding to Numbers 16.

1017. Dr. Adolf Oppenheimer (1857–1929), vice-secretary of the Verein der Prager Geschäftsreisenden (Association of Prague Business Travelers).

1018. See note 670.

1019. Friedrich Adler (1857–1938) was a lawyer in Prague, known also as a poet and translator, and regarded as the doyen of the turn-of-the-century Prague German poets. Max Brod reported on a visit Kafka paid Friedrich Adler (see FK 295–296).

1020. Evidently the chief finance councilor Dr. Jakub Adler, by then retired.

1021. This entry reflects Kafka's reading of the *Pensées* by Blaise Pascal.

1022. Evidently an excursion with Oskar Baum to the town, located about ten kilometers east of Prague.

1023. The first of a series of attempts at revision of "In der Strafkolonie" ("In the Penal Colony").

1024. See note 1023.

1025. After hemorrhages on the nights of August 10–11 and August 13–14, 1917, Kafka visited various doctors. Probably on September 7, he wrote to Felice: *The outcome, without going into all the medical details, is that I have tuberculosis in both lung apices* (KKAB3 no. 1053). Since the doctors strongly recommended a stay in the country, on September 12—the AUVA refused to grant him an early retirement but approved three months' convalescent leave—Kafka traveled to his sister in Zürau in northwestern Bohemia. There, since mid-April, Ottla Kafka had taken over the management of a farm belonging to the family of her brother-in-law Karl Hermann.

1026. Kafka took the outbreak of tuberculosis as an opportunity to break off for good his five-year relationship with Felice Bauer, to whom he had become engaged for the second time in July 1916. Two days before the diary entry, he had already written to Max Brod: *To be sure, there's still the wound of which the lung wound is only a symbol. . . . Sometimes it seems to me as if brain and lung had come to an understanding without my knowledge. "It can't go on like this" the brain said and after 5 years the lung declared itself ready to help* (KKAB3 no. 1057).

1027. The nearest railroad station to Zürau.

1028. A hired hand on the Zürau farm.

1029. The postal station responsible for Zürau.

1030. This probably refers to a telegram to Felice Bauer, who had *announced in a few lines* (KKAB3 no. 1062) that she was coming to visit him in Zürau on September 20–21, 1917. The *farewell letter* written instead of the telegram has not survived.

1031. In early October 1917, Kafka wrote to Elsa Brod: *These goats, by the way—outwardly they're perfectly Jewish types, mostly doctors, though there are also approximations of lawyers, Polish Jews and sporadically even Jewish girls* (KKAB3 no. 1071).

1032. Siegfried Löwy (1867–1942), Julie Kafka's youngest brother, was a country doctor in Triesch.

1033. See note 636.

1034. Irma Kafka (1889–1919), a cousin, worked in her uncle Hermann Kafka's shop after her father died and was close friends with Ottla.

1035. Ernst Hermann, a relative of Kafka's brother-in-law Karl, worked on the farm as an overseer.

1036. The *young lady* (*Fräulein*) Maria, called *Mařenka* in the diminutive—her surname is unknown—worked on the farm managed by Ottla Kafka. In a December 1917 letter to Oskar Baum (KKAB3 no. 1108), Kafka hints at the fine distinction between calling someone in Maria's position *Magd*—in this context, a female farm hand—and *Fräulein*—"young lady" or "Miss"—as it was customary to call her in Zürau.

1037. At that time Franz Werfel was assigned to the Kriegspressequartier (war press office) in Vienna.

1038. Berta Fanta. See note 18.

1039. Felix Hermann.

1040. Theodor Tagger, *Das neue Geschlecht. Programmschrift gegen die Metapher* (The New Generation: Programmatic Essay Against Metaphor) (Berlin, 1917).

1041. In early October 1917, Kafka wrote to Elsa and Max Brod: *Incidentally, Flaubert's father, as I have just read, was tubercular too, thus for a number of years the question may have been asked in secret whether a child's lung would fizzle out (I propose this phrase for "rattle") or whether it would be Flaubert* (KKAB3 no. 1071).

1042. Refers to the publication of the volume *Ein Landarzt. Kleine Erzählungen* (*A Country Doctor: Short Stories*), planned as of the summer of 1917, published by Kurt Wolff Verlag in late 1919.

1043. This entry and the next should probably be seen in relation to the aftermath of Felice Bauer's visit to Zürau.

1044. Included, with only minor discrepancies, in Kafka's September 30, 1917, letter to Felice Bauer (KKAB3 no. 1068).

1045. Grete Bloch.

1046. In a letter to Max Brod probably written on September 30 or October 1, 1917, Kafka wrote: *In the meantime, however, I have completely changed, not in my relationship to Zürau, which is still good, but in my capacity for direct intercourse with people. It's not sadness, it's heaviness in the limbs, "courbature" I keep reading now in a French book. It's not headaches, on the contrary, my head is light, but somewhere in the vicinity of my throat a lid has snapped shut and under it there's steady pressure* (KKAB3 no. 1069).

1047. Josef Feigl (1844–1926).

1048. Konrad Kunz (1859–1936).

1049. Kafka's reflections relate to his unfinished novel *Der Verschollene* (*The Missing Person*).

1050. Franz Lüftner (1872–1924).

1051. Anna Lüftner (1845–1926).

1052. A village near Zürau.

1053. Kafka's dream was probably influenced by the daily newspaper reports detailing the victorious advance of the united Austro-Hungarian and German forces on the Tagliamento from late October to mid-November 1917.

1054. Immediately following the final entry of November 1917, Kafka continued his diary entries in the Twelfth Notebook on June 27, 1919.

1055. An extensive park in the Prague suburb Königliche Weinberge (Czech: Královské Vinohrady).

1056. Julie Wohryzek (1891–1944). Kafka had met his later second fiancée during a convalescent stay at the Pension Stüdl in Schelesen (Czech: Želízy) in the winter of 1918–19. She came from the suburb Königliche Weinberge, where her father was a temple caretaker of the Jewish community.

1057. The Feast of the Immaculate Conception was at that time a public holiday in Bohemia.

1058. The Baumgarten (Czech: Stromovka), originally royal hunting grounds, is Prague's largest public park and a popular excursion destination; with *restaurant,* Kafka is probably referring to the Haupt-Restauration in the western part of the park. The Moderne Galerie, with works of contemporary Czech and German artists of Bohemia, was housed at the edge of the exhibition grounds into which the eastern part of the park was converted on the occasion of the Jubilee National Exhibition of 1891.

1059. Eleseus is a character in Knut Hamsun's novel *Growth of the Soil,* the German edition of which (*Segen der Erde*) was among the books in Kafka's possession at the time of his death.

1060. Julie Wohryzek.

1061. Matthias Beck, Kafka's teacher in the third and fourth grade.

1062. Kafka is describing the 1895 oil painting *Boulter's Lock, Sunday Afternoon* by the British genre and landscape painter Edward John Gregory. See the facsimile in Kafka, *Tagebücher: Kommentarband,* p. 203.

1063. Hill on the left bank of the Moldau with a view of Prague and its environs.

1064. Apparently an allusion to the 1851 memorial dedicated to Kaiser Franz I: "The monument stood on the Franzenskai, later Masarykovo, surrounded by statues representing the estates paying homage to the Kaiser. The removal of the statue of Kaiser Franz took place in 1919, in the first months of the Czechoslovak Republic." David Flusser, "Franz Kafka und Kaiser Franz," *Mitteilungsblatt des Irgun Ole Merkaz Eropa* 32, no. 13 (February 27, 1964): 13.

1065. Hermann Cassinelli's bookshop and lending library was on Husgasse 4. Regarding Cassinelli, Max Brod remarks: "Here new literature was always displayed. Kafka told me once that he read the titles with special avidity" (B 352).

1066. Beginning from the other end of the Twelfth Notebook, on October 15, 1921, Kafka resumed his diary entries, which he had broken off on February 29, 1920. *About a week ago* he had removed from the notebook the pages on which he had already written and handed them over to Milena Pollak (see note 1067), together with his other diary notebooks.

1067. Here and in the rest of the entry, Kafka's abbreviation for Milena Pollak, née Jesenská (1896–1944). A Prague-born Czech journalist and translator, she lived with her then-husband Ernst Pollak (1886–1947) in Vienna. A request for his permission to translate his story "Die Heizer" ("The Stoker") into Czech and an encounter in Prague shortly thereafter in the autumn of 1919 marked the beginning of her acquaintance with Kafka. In April 1920, while staying in a sanatorium in Meran, Kafka struck up an intensive correspondence with her that in the summer of 1920—in conjunction with the dissolution of his engagement to Julie Wohryzek—led to a closer relationship lasting until about the turn of the year 1920–21. Afterward they exchanged letters and met in Prague only occasionally. When Milena Pollak visited Kafka in early October 1921, he handed over to her his diary writings.

1068. The reciter Ludwig Hardt (1886–1947) had been staying in Prague from October 1 to 14, 1921, for several recitation evenings. His program included pieces by Kafka—on October 1, 1921, he recited, among other things, "Elf Söhne" ("Eleven Sons")—with which he was evidently acquainted from earlier recitation evenings in Prague.

1069. Kafka is referring to a letter from Johann Peter Hebel to Friedrich Wilhelm Hitzig: "If the Theol. Society still existed, this time I would have written an essay for them on polytheism. I confess to you—for a confession among friends is as holy as one at the altar, that it makes more and more sense to me, and only the captivity, or tutelage, in which we're kept by the faith in which we've been baptized and raised and preached to, has prevented me until now from building little churches to the blessed gods." Friedrich Becker, *J. P. Hebel. Festgabe zu seinem hundersten Geburtstage* (Basel, 1860), p. 221.

1070. Max Brod reported that he and Kafka had already read Gustave Flaubert's *Education sentimentale* together in a French edition in the first years of their friendship (FK 54). Kafka probably read the volume *L'éducation sentimentale. Histoire d'un jeune homme* (Paris, 1910), which was among the books in his possession at the time of his death, during his stay in Jungborn. See June-July 1912 Trip, pp. 559, 561, and 562.
1071. Georg Langer. See note 944.
1072. Max Brod's novel *Franzi, oder Eine Liebe zweiten Ranges* (*Franzi, or A Second-Rate Love*). An advance publication appeared several weeks later, starting in December 1921, in installments in the magazine *Der Feuerreiter*, the book edition not until November of the following year.
1073. An allusion to Genesis and Sarah's hopelessness of bearing children.
1074. On October 21, 1921, the *Prager Tagblatt* reported: "The Central Office of the Jewish National Fund in Prague has managed to acquire an original film from Palestine, *Schiwath Zion* (*Return to Zion*), which presents in a characteristic manner life during the building of Jewish Palestine and the industriousness of the pioneers (Chaluzim)." Kafka attended the showing that began at two o'clock in the afternoon on Sunday, October 23, 1921, at the "Lido-Bio" on Havlíčekgasse.
1075. In late October 1921 the Viennese writer Albert Ehrenstein (see note 719) was staying in Prague, where he spoke on the twenty-second in the hall of the Volksbildungsverein Urania (Urania Association for Popular Education) at Smečkagasse 22. As he had last done a year earlier, he took advantage of his stay to meet with Kafka.
1076. Kafka had engaged in gardening several times: in 1913 in a nursery (see p. 291 and note 683), and in the summer of 1918, inspired by the garden work in Zürau, at the Pomologisches Institut (Institute for Pomology, which was also connected with an agricultural school) in Troja, a village north of Prague. See also p. 473.
1077. During his Prague guest performance, the Viennese actor Max Pallenberg appeared as Alexander Badekow in Paul Schirmer's comedy *Der Herr Minister* on October 30, 1921, in an afternoon performance at the Neues Deutsches Theater.
1078. Max Pallenberg had begun his Prague guest performances at the Neues Deutsches Theater with the role of Harpagon in *Der Geizige*, Carl Sternheim's adaptation of Molière's *The Miser*, on October 25, 1921.
1079. Franz Werfel's tragedy *Bocksgesang* (*Goat Song*) appeared in installments starting on October 30, 1921, in the *Prager Presse*. In a November 1921 letter, Kafka recommended this publication to Robert Klopstock (1899–1972), whom he had befriended when they were both staying at a sanatorium in Matliary in the High Tatras from December 1920 to August 1921.
1080. Milena Pollak.
1081. His father, Hermann Kafka.
1082. Milena Pollak.
1083. The concluding sentence of a letter to Robert Klopstock from early December 1921.
1084. The words of Wilhelm Raabe, reproduced here by Kafka, are found in Hans Martin Schultz's personal recollections, which appeared under the title "Der alte Herr" in the 1921 commemorative volume *Raabe-Gedenkbuch*.
1085. *Our Scout*, magazine of the Boy Scouts in the Czechoslovak Republic. Kafka's interest in the Scout movement is also evinced by a remark in a letter to Robert Klopstock from early October 1921: *it's as if, say, I would yield today to my dream and join a scout troop of 10-year-old boys* (Br 359).
1086. Kafka's reading of Leo Tolstoy's novella *The Death of Ivan Ilyich* is confirmed in a letter he wrote several weeks later, on February 17, 1922, to Johannes Urzidil: *Many thanks for the book. In its essence, but also in its structure, it reminded me very much of Ivan Ilyich!* (see Br 371).
1087. Kafka's abbreviation in the original German, *G.*, might stand for *Geschlecht*, or "sex." See note 1090.

1088. Probably Milena Pollak.
1089. The two classmates who committed suicide are Karl Kraus (1883–1902) and Camill Gibian (1883–1907).
1090. The possibility that Kafka's abbreviation in the original German, *G.*, stands for *Geschlecht,* or "sex," is suggested by the incomplete word *Ges* over which the initial *G* is written in the manuscript; see also the entry *instead comes s.* and note 1087. Four days after this entry, on January 23, 1922, Max Brod noted in his diary: "At Kafka's. I'm profoundly shaken by him. He told . . . of a brothel visit. Torment of the sex organs. Is it not necessary that I support the cause of M. in this way?" Brod had always tried to encourage Kafka's relationship to Milena Pollak ("M."). On July 5, 1920, he had recorded in his diary: "I understand very well that this great passion means for him salvation from sex" (unpublished, privately owned). It's possible that the entries on pp. 469 and 470 beginning *Nothing bad* . . . and *A little calmer* . . . relate to the brothel visit mentioned by Brod.
1091. The questions addressed to Milena Pollak might have been included in a letter that has not survived. For Milena Pollak's visits, see p. 465. For the handing over of the diaries, see p. 459 and note 1066.
1092. Max Brod, whose first name Kafka shortened to an initial in the manuscript by crossing out the other letters.
1093. On January 21, 1922, at the Czech National Theater, there was an afternoon performance of Ludwig van Beethoven's *Fidelio,* which Kafka evidently attended.
1094. Refers to the entry *to model oneself in appearance and behavior on the one or two bachelors of our youthful memories* (p. 127).
1095. Uncle Rudolf. For a description of Rudolf Löwy, see also p. 157 and note 386.
1096. Max Brod. See note 1090.
1097. Probably Ernst Pollak, Milena Pollak's husband.
1098. See note 93.
1099. On January 27, 1922, Kafka traveled with one of his doctors, Dr. Otto Hermann, to Spindelmühle (also: Spindlermühle) in the Riesengebirge (Giant Mountains). Dr. Hermann had proposed spending a vacation there together. The following diary entries until February 17 (p. 483) were written during the stay in Spindelmühle.
1100. An allusion to Kafka's story "Ein Landarzt" ("A Country Doctor"), published in May 1920 in his book of the same title (see note 1042): . . . *distracted, tormented, I kicked the cracked door of the pigpen, which had not been used for years. It opened and clapped back and forth on its hinges. Warmth and a smell as of horses came out. A dim stable lantern swayed inside on a rope. A man, huddled up in the low shed, showed his open blue-eyed face. "Shall I hitch up?" he asked, crawling out on all fours.*
1101. The name of the protagonist of Kafka's novel *Der Proceß* (*The Trial*).
1102. In late January 1922, Kafka wrote to Robert Klopstock: *But apart from that I can go sledding and mountain climbing, high enough and steep, without particular harm, the thermometer is disregarded* (Br 370).
1103. His father's (Hermann Kafka).
1104. Spindelmühle.
1105. There may be resonances in this passage with the opening of the novel *Das Schloß* (*The Castle*), begun in Spindelmühle.
1106. This refers to Kafka's doctor and traveling companion to Spindelmühle, Dr. Otto Hermann. See also note 1099.
1107. An allusion to the novel *Die Galeere* by Ernst Weiß (see p. 294 and note 690), in which the protagonist, Dr. Erik Gyldendal, is compared by his beloved, Dina Ossonskaja, with an X-ray tube: "If, for example, someone is alone, completely without relationships, without any common interests with others—a vacuum encased in glass, would not a person so utterly alone, without kindness and without hatred—necessarily have a strong influence on other people, so that his gaze would pass through them?" And in another passage: "you're like your X-ray tube. Empty, completely

empty, only the electric current passes through you. This is the effect you have on other people, you can make them happy or destroy them. But nothing touches you yourself. You know neither shared pain nor shared pleasure. What is there to love about you? What is good about you? What is beautiful about you? And yet I cannot break away, I love you."

1108. Here and in the rest of the entry: Milena Pollak.
1109. Dr. Otto Hermann.
1110. This refers to Kafka and Felice Bauer's vacation together in July 1916. See pp. 418ff. and note 999.
1111. Kafka's abbreviation in the original German, *O.*, stands for *Oberkellner* or "head-waiter." In the manuscript the word has been crossed out with thick lines, except for the initial.
1112. The Tannenstein was a viewpoint about forty-five minutes' walking distance from Spindelmühle; the numerous winter sports competitions made possible by the exceptionally good weather conditions in Spindelmühle were also reported in the Prague daily newspapers.
1113. On February 8, 1922, Kafka wrote to Max Brod: *Up to now I have had 5 good nights, but the 6th and 7th were bad, I have been unmasked* (BKB 369).
1114. Milena Pollak.
1115. Ital. *Sette Comuni*: The seven former German-language islands—fiercely fought over during the First World War—in the northern Italian province of Vicenza.
1116. Possibly two female hotel guests, as the following entry suggests.
1117. G. W., Kafka's sanatorium acquaintance in Riva. See note 708.
1118. For the possibility that Kafka's abbreviation in the original German, *G.*, stands for *Geschlecht*, or "sex," see p. 468 and note 1090.
1119. Possibly one of the prose pieces in Karl Brand, *Das Vermächtnis eines Jünglings*, ed. Johannes Urzidil, with a foreword by Franz Werfel (Vienna, Prague, Leipzig, 1920). Kafka had received the volume—which was among the books in his possession at the time of his death—in January 1922 from Urzidil with a dedication. Several days after this entry, in a February 17, 1922, letter from Spindelmühle, Kafka thanked him for it (Br 371).
1120. An allusion to the text that Max Brod titled "Poseidon," in which Poseidon *sat here in the depths of the ocean, endlessly doing the accounting* (KKANII 302).
1121. Kafka's entry is probably based on his reading of Einar Mikkelsen, "Ein arktischer Robinson," an account of an Arctic expedition that had to surmount multiple large glacial crevasses. The account was among the books in Kafka's possession at the time of his death.
1122. In a production by guest director Leopold Jessner, the Neues Deutsches Theater offered William Shakespeare's tragedy *King Richard III* on March 1, 1922.
1123. On March 11, 1922, Ludwig Hardt (see note 1068) recited again in Prague (in the Mozarteum at Jungmannstraße 30), presenting for the first time from Johann Peter Hebel's *Schatzkästlein des rheinischen Hausfreundes.*
1124. Kafka's entry relates to the children's Purim celebration of the Jüdischer Turn- und Sportverein Makkabi (Maccabi Jewish Gymnastics and Sports Association) held on March 12 in the Heinesaal. The *Selbstwehr* of March 17, 1922, highlighted "the clear and pure reading of the Purim story by the clever Marianne Pollak," Kafka's then-nine-year-old niece, as well as "dance and gymnastics performances during which the girls in particular shone due to good discipline and gracefulness."
1125. Refers to Hans Blüher, *Secessio Judaica. Philosophische Grundlegung der historischen Situation des Judentums und der antisemitischen Bewegung* (Secessio Judaica: Philosophical Foundation of the Historical Situation of Judaism and the Anti-Semitic Movement) (Berlin, 1922). See also p. 493 and note 1160.
1126. Kafka's illness required regular checking of his body temperature. See also p. 494.

1127. *Bl.* probably stands for Hans Blüher, whom Kafka mentioned reading on March 15; see note 1125. The possibility cannot be excluded, however, that Kafka was still in contact with Grete Bloch at this time.
1128. Perhaps Grete Bloch and Milena Pollak.
1129. This entry might relate to the eighth chapter of the novel *Das Schloß* (*The Castle*).
1130. On Sunday, April 8, 1922, an opening for an exhibition of the artist group Die Pilger (The Pilgrims) was held in the Künstlerhaus of the Rudolfinum for invited guests. As of the fifteenth, the exhibition was open to the public. While Jost Pietsch was among the members of Die Pilger, Alfred Kubin and Anton Bruder participated in the exhibition as guests. During the exhibition, Kubin's picture *Die Märchenprinzessin* (*The Fairy Tale Princess*) (see the facsimile in Kafka, *Tagebücher: Kommentarband*, p. 214) was acquired by the Moderne Galerie. See note 1058.
1131. At this time, Max Brod had a relationship with Emmy Salveter, who lived in Berlin. Since he found himself incapable of making a decision for or against a life with Emmy Salveter or with his wife Elsa (the two entries on p. 489 beginning *Max's suffering* . . . relate to this situation), in an August 16, 1921, letter Kafka advised his friend to attempt a three-person living arrangement. He suspected that Elsa Brod might agree to it because she had once taken pleasure in showing him a letter written by Theodor Storm (BKB 412). Gertrud Storm reproduces excerpts of this letter in her biography *Theodor Storm. Ein Bild seines Lebens*: "Yes, there was a time in his life when his love vacillated painfully between these two women, Constanze and Dorothea Jensen, and visited much bitter suffering on these three people. 'Two women share in my life as in my poetry,' thus begins the confession that Storm made to his friend Brinkmann in a letter of April 21, 1866."
1132. In an unpublished 1921 letter to his sister Ellie Hermann, Kafka gave an account of how he was enlightened in school: *Consider, for example, the 2 boys who instructed me, today they surely know no more than they did then, although, as it turned out, they were particularly uniform consistent characters. They instructed me simultaneously, one from the right, the other from the left, the one on the right merry, fatherly, urbane, with exactly the same laugh I later heard among men of all ages, even myself (there's surely also a free laugh, a different laugh that stands above things, but I have not yet heard it from a living man) the one on the left objective, theoretical, which was far more abhorrent. Both have long since married and have remained in Prague, for many years now the one on the right has been ravaged by syphilis to the point of unrecognizability, I don't know whether he's still alive, the one on the left is a professor of venereal diseases and founder and chairman of an association to combat venereal diseases. I don't want to weigh them against each other, besides, they were not even friends, at the time they had come together only by chance for the purpose of my instruction.* One of the boys was Kafka's schoolmate Hugo Hecht (1883–1970).
1133. Possibly the Czech writer Fráňa Šrámek (1877–1952), with whom Kafka and Brod were acquainted.
1134. See note 1131.
1135. Max Brod worked "as a cultural officer on the presidium of the ministerial council," according to his memoir *Streitbares Leben (Contentious Life)*.
1136. In 1922, Easter Saturday fell on April 15.
1137. Hartmut Binder deciphers the abbreviations as follows: "Dr. Treml, Milena, Josef David or Josef Pollak, Valli and Klopstock." Hartmut Binder, *Kafka in neuer Sicht. Mimik, Gestik und Personengefüge als Darstellungsformen des Autobiographischen* (Stuttgart, 1976), p. 348.
1138. Probably Milena Pollak.
1139. See note 1131.
1140. See note 1058.
1141. Czech: "What's the name of the one that makes it with saliva?" "You mean the swallow."
1142. Makkabi, or Maccabi, a Jewish gymnastics and sports association.

1143. The building housing the editorial office of the *Selbstwehr* (edited since 1919 by Kafka's friend Felix Weltsch) was on Zeltnergasse.
1144. Czech: "I came to help you."
1145. Milena Pollak.
1146. Milena Pollak.
1147. Martin Buber, *Der große Maggid und seine Nachfolge* (Frankfurt, 1921).
1148. Kafka is quoting from the German edition of Danish writer Karl Gjellerup's "legendary romance" *The Pilgrim Kamanita.*
1149. On May 19, 1922, Eva Vischer recited in the Kleiner Saal of the Volksbildungsverein Urania (Urania Association for Popular Education) at Smečkagasse 22, among other things, Gustave Flaubert's "The Legend of Saint Julian the Hospitaller," passages from Friedrich Hebbel's tragedy *Judith,* the Samson legend, animal fables by Vladimir Sollogub, and texts by Else Lasker-Schüler. She also recited the second chapter ("Der Hase, der einen Mord erlebt") of an unpublished book by her husband, the Prague writer Melchior Vischer (1895–1975), entitled *Der Hase.* Several weeks later Kafka received from Melchior Vischer the story "Der Hase" with a handwritten dedication dated July 13, 1922; the volume was among the books in Kafka's possession at the time of his death.
1150. Kafka is probably referring to French writer Hippolyte Taine's *Notes on England,* which appeared in German as *Aufzeichnungen über England.* In the chapter titled "Mores and Households," Taine described two old ladies, about whom he wrote in conclusion: "In all this, I believe, two things are visible: one is the native and acquired energy, the strength of character by which man masters himself, always keeps himself in check, is self-sufficient, risks and resists misfortune, sorrow and despondency; the other is the institution of a hierarchy which, even in private life, establishes inequality, subordination, authority and order."
1151. Kafka's abbreviation *H.-K.* in the original German stands for his short story "Ein Hungerkünstler" ("A Hunger Artist"), the title story of his final book, published posthumously by Die Schmiede in 1924.
1152. Kafka's sister Ottla was already on summer vacation in Planá with her family, where Kafka would follow about a month later; see note 1161. The note in the diary probably refers to the dog mentioned again later; see p. 493.
1153. During a chance encounter, the Czech writer Michal Mareš (1893–1971) asked Kafka, with whom he was acquainted, *whether he might send me his books; moved, I begged him to do so. The next day came his book of poems with a beautiful dedication: "dlouholetému príteli"* ("to a longtime friend") *but a few days later a second book with a postal invoice. I did what was easiest, neither thanked nor paid.* Kafka told Milena Pollak about this unpleasantness in a September 1922 letter (M 306).
1154. Abbreviation for "Pepa" (or "Pepo"), Kafka's brother-in-law Josef David.
1155. For the possibility that Kafka's abbreviation in the original German, *G.*, stands for *Geschlecht,* or "sex," see p. 468 and note 1090.
1156. The Czech sculptor and academy professor Josef V. Myslbek had died on June 2, 1922; he was buried on Pentecost Monday, June 5, after a funeral service in the assembly room of the Old Town Hall.
1157. Possibly Fráňa Šrámek. See note 1133.
1158. Possibly a letter to Milena Pollak that has not survived.
1159. This could stand for "Gerti to Hellerau." Kafka had urged his sister Elli Hermann and her husband to send their children Felix and Gerti to the international school just founded by Alexander S. Neill in Hellerau near Dresden.
1160. Attempt at a review of Hans Blüher's book *Secessio Judaica;* see also p. 486 and note 1125. On June 30, 1922, Kafka wrote to Robert Klopstock: *Secessio Judaica, won't you write about it? . . . I cannot do it; when I try, my hand immediately sinks, although naturally I, like everyone, would have much to say about it* (Br 380).

1161. In Planá an der Luschnitz (in southern Bohemia), Kafka's sister Ottla David had rented a summer apartment with her family. In late June 1922—after the AUVA, at his request, granted his transfer into temporary retirement effective July 1, 1922—Kafka followed. With brief interruptions, he remained in Planá until September 18.
1162. See also p. 492 and note 1152.
1163. The Sedlec fortress (Czech: *tvrz*) is located in the forest areas around Planá.
1164. In a letter to Max Brod, which can be dated around August 13, 1922, Kafka described the women in Planá: *They don't get fat until very late in life and only an occasional young girl is voluptuous (a stable maid, for example, on a half-dilapidated farm, which I often pass in the evening, sometimes she stands in the stable door and positively battles with her breasts)* (BKB 407).
1165. Ottla Kafka.
1166. In a November 29, 1922, letter addressed to Max Brod, Kafka mentioned a *lung fever* that had lasted a month (BKB 421). See also note 1126.
1167. There is evidence that Kafka first read *Either/Or* by Søren Kierkegaard during his stay in Zürau. On January 20, 1918, Kafka wrote to Max Brod: *And moreover . . . I have started reading* Either/Or (BKB 228).
1168. In May 1920 Kafka's friend Hugo Bergmann (see also note 272) had moved to Jerusalem with his family. In the early summer of 1923, he stayed in Prague for several weeks. At a number of events, he lectured on his experiences and advocated the further development of Palestine.
1169. For several days in the first half of May 1923, Kafka stayed in the Prague summer resort.
1170. Probably Milena Pollak. There might be a connection with the *last time we were together* mentioned by Kafka at the beginning of his letter from the second half of November 1923, after which Milena Pollak *suddenly (but not surprisingly) disappeared* (M 319) and which probably took place close in time to the diary entry.
1171. In June 1923 the Moscow Art Theater gave a guest performance in the Stadttheater Königliche Weinberge (the City Theater of Královské Vinohrady, the former suburb incorporated into Prague as a district since 1922). In a review of the performances in the *Prager Presse* of June 6, 1923, the actress Maria Alexeyevna Kryshanovskaya—to whose portrait card Kafka was evidently referring—was among those mentioned (as "Kryžanovska").
1172. Friedland, Reichenberg, Rumburg, and Gablonz were the four *Bezirkshauptmannschaften*, or district administrations, in the northern Bohemian industrial area for which Kafka was responsible as an AUVA official. It was part of his job to inspect the industrial enterprises of this region on business trips.
1173. A Prague weekly founded in 1878 as the *Montags-Revue*, which continued as of 1894 under the title *Montagsblatt aus Böhmen*.
1174. Town in southern Bohemia on the Prague-Gmünd-Vienna railroad line.
1175. An illustrated weekly that first appeared in 1882.
1176. A town about four kilometers southeast of Friedland.
1177. The Kaiserpanorama, first presented to the public in 1880 by its inventor and operator August Fuhrmann, consisted of a "wooden cylinder about 5 meters in diameter, around which 25 spectators could be seated. They looked through the peepholes at colored glass stereoscopic slides of exotic locales or current events, separately illuminated from behind for each seat. . . . They saw each image for only a few minutes, then the ring of a bell startled them out of their contemplation, and shortly thereafter the image slid jerkily, the whole machinery shaking, to the next station. One show was made up of two different series of 50 slides each." Stephan Oettermann, *Das Panorama. Die Geschichte eines Massenmediums* (Frankfurt, 1980), p. 184. At times Fuhrmann was showing his stereoscopic images in more than 250 establishments in Germany alone.

1178. A magazine that appeared in Vienna from 1908 to 1913.
1179. The name of mechanical musical instruments played with perforated circular cardboard disks by turning a crank.
1180. For a picture of the funerary monument Kafka describes, see WB 135.
1181. The Tito Speri monument by Domenico Ghidoni in Brescia.
1182. During Kafka's vacation trip with Max Brod in September 1909, they had been in Brescia (see p. 407), where Kafka evidently saw posters for this beer brand.
1183. At times Kafka was a regular reader of the magazine *Der Kunstwart. Halbmonatsschau über Dichtung, Theater, Musik, bildende und angewandte Künste,* edited by Ferdinand Avenarius.
1184. The center of the northern Bohemian industrial area and most significant of the four *Bezirkshauptmannschaften*, or district administrations. See also note 1172.
1185. For the performance of Franz Grillparzer's tragedy *Des Meeres und der Liebe Wellen* (*Waves of the Sea and of Love*), which Kafka attended on February 24, 1911, at the Stadttheater Reichenberg (City Theater of Reichenberg), see also p. 538.
1186. During Kafka's stay, the operetta by Fritz Grünbaum and Heinz Reichert was offered at the Stadttheater Reichenberg on February 25 and 26.
1187. See note 97.
1188. Refers to the Munich hotel Vier Jahreszeiten.
1189. *Havelock* in the German original; a sleeveless men's coat with a capelike cloak hanging down to the hips.
1190. In Max Brod's parallel travel diary, he wrote: "Kafka: Has no patriot yet come up with the idea of calculating the area of Switzerland by measuring the surfaces of the mountains as planes side by side. Would surely be larger than Germany" (BKR 76).
1191. Refers to the philosophical treatise *Anschauung und Begriff* (*Intuition and Concept*) by Max Brod and Felix Weltsch. In it, the symbol (A + x) is introduced for the "general memory picture": "The A of such a formation therefore contains that which was common to the experienced images, while that which varied blurs in the x."
1192. See Max Brod's travel diary: "Difficult orientation on the Limmat bridge, whether the Limmat flows from the lake—we think it leads into it" (BKR 76).
1193. *Marignano,* a five-act popular drama by Carl Friedrich Wiegand, with music by Hans Jelmoli, premiered in the summer of 1911 at an open-air theater in Morschach, a village in the canton of Schwyz.
1194. Kafka is referring to the Grands Magasins Dufayel, Parisian department stores on rue Clignancourt and Boulevard Barbès.
1195. See note 367.
1196. The Church of St. Roch on rue St. Honoré; a memory of Kafka's October 1910 Paris trip.
1197. A daily newspaper founded in 1780 as *Zürcher Zeitung* and continued in 1821 as *Neue Zürcher Zeitung und schweizerisches Handelsblatt.*
1198. A memory of Kafka's October 1910 Paris trip.
1199. See Max Brod's travel diary: "We chose the 'Hotel Rebstock' from the guidebook" (BKR 80).
1200. In Prague too there had been press reports since July on cases of cholera in Italy. On September 4, 1911, under the headline "Cholera in Italy," the *Prager Tagblatt* reported on new cases and deaths in Venice, among other places. These incidents would also find their way into the collaborative novel *Richard und Samuel* planned by Kafka and Brod: "In the preface we included in the publication in *Herder-Blätter,* the plan, which unfortunately remained a sketch, is developed. It should be added that the 'conflict' that would temporarily cloud the friendship between Richard and Samuel was the occurrence of cholera in Milan (whispered surreptitiously, denied in the press)." Max Brod, "Zusammenarbeit mit Franz Kafka," *Herder-Blätter,* facsimile ed. on the occasion of the 70th birthday of Willy Haas (Hamburg, 1962), p. IX.

1201. An illustrated entertainment weekly founded in 1859 in Stuttgart with the subtitle *Allgemeine illustrierte Zeitung*.
1202. Evidently the steamer did not dock at the Rütli pier on the trip from Schillerstein to Tellsplatte.
1203. See note 1186.
1204. See Max Brod's parallel travel diary: "A Hungarian woman whom Kafka finds so appealing that he calls her 'the Hungarian flower'" (BKR 84).
1205. In Lugano, Kafka and Max Brod stayed in the Hotel Belvedere au Lac, a low-priced hotel on Piazza Guglielmo Tell with a beer restaurant and a small lakeside terrace. Only five hundred meters away was the only open-air bath in Lugano.
1206. Santa Margherita "in Kafka's time consisted of only a few buildings. The only one that caught the eye was a small Romanesque church, next to which plague victims of the region were buried in the seventeenth century. . . . Seen from the water, there's a small square to the right of the church, which presents itself to today's visitor as a grassy patch. At its rear stands a completely preserved fountain, which naturally no longer has running water. Embedded in the mountain face, which here rises almost vertically, it serves at the same time as a retaining wall. Grass has grown in its façade, and the two stone frogs flanking it on small pedestals, marking the point where the arch and the basin of the fountain meet, are weathered. . . . Kafka must have been taken with this composition, which he could admire from the ship, for he not only mentions the fountain in his notes but also supplements them with a small sketch, unidentified until now, which captures its appearance in simplified form." Hartmut Binder, *Mit Kafka in den Süden* (Furth im Walde, 2007), pp. 285–286, photograph of the fountain on p. 289.
1207. According to Hartmut Binder, the villa seen by Brod and Kafka during their steamer trip was the "'Villa Urie già Brusati' (also 'Villa Nisciorée')." Into the 1970s the building was flanked on either side by six cypresses (ibid., p. 286).
1208. Refers to the bell tower of the Church of Albogasio Superiore at San Mamette. See the picture in Binder, *Kafka in neuer Sicht,* facing p. 64.
1209. Refers to the sculpture *Cupid and Psyche* by Antonio Canova in the Villa Carlotta; see note 1211.
1210. See Max Brod's travel diary: "Passing travelers point us out to each other as Italian fellows" (BKR 91).
1211. The Villa Carlotta, near Cadenabbia on Lake Como. The entries that follow relate to its park.
1212. "Because the mountains fall away very steeply toward Lake Como, the train tracks coming from Grandola could not run directly toward Menaggio, but first proceeded south toward Griante on a slight incline for about a kilometer, where they ended in a railroad yard about 140 meters long. There the locomotives were detached, rotated on a turntable and reattached to the other end of the train, which was now shunted onto another track and traveled in the opposite direction at an acute angle down the mountainside toward the shore of Lake Como. Thus someone unaware of the route might have the misconception that he was heading back the way he came." Binder, *Mit Kafka in den Süden,* pp. 290–291.
1213. The first reference is to the protagonist in Jules Verne's novel *Twenty Thousand Leagues Under the Sea* and the second is to his novel *Hector Servadec: Journeys and Adventures Through the Solar World.*
1214. Correct: Castagnola.
1215. See note 1200.
1216. A newspaper appearing in Bremen since 1899, subtitled *Lloyd-Zeitung für Reise und Außenhandel.*
1217. Correct: Porto Ceresio.
1218. Parisian daily newspaper.
1219. In 1911 an international exposition took place in Turin.

1220. Here Kafka means: on the Piazza dei' Mercanti.
1221. Popular plays were performed in the Teatro Fossati near the Piazzale Marengo.
1222. *Poltrona,* Italian for "orchestra seat."
1223. *Ingresso,* Italian for "entrance."
1224. These notes are based on the journey to Milan.
1225. Refers to the arrival in the Milan central train station.
1226. From Via Manzoni, one can reach the Piazza della Scala without seeing the opera house itself.
1227. During this conversation, Kafka and Brod also discussed the further plot outline of their novel project *Richard und Samuel* in light of the danger of the cholera outbreak; see note 1200. Regarding this threat, Brod made a request: "in stiflingly hot Milan (where I moved Franz almost to tears by begging him not to let me be buried without piercing my heart if I should die abroad)" (FK 111).
1228. Gustav Mahler had died on May 18, 1911.
1229. See p. 515 and note 1218.
1230. Evidently Rimini was planned to be the eastern endpoint of their itinerary.
1231. The Galleria Vittorio Emanuele, a covered, cross-shaped arcade, connects the Milan Cathedral Square with the Piazza della Scala.
1232. The card, evidently addressed to Eugen Pfohl (see note 15), has not survived.
1233. Kafka is referring to the Castello Sforzesco, which can be seen from the roof of the cathedral.
1234. See note 1221.
1235. During the trip, the friends not only pursued the project of the collaborative travel novel *Richard and Samuel* but also developed, among other things, the idea of a series of travel guides under the title *Billig,* or *On the Cheap.* See Max Brod/Franz Kafka, "Unser Millionenplan 'Billig'" (BKR 189–92). Looking back on their shared journey, Brod wrote later: "we came up with the strangest, loveliest jokes" (FK 90).
1236. This refers to Olga Salus, the wife of the Prague poet Hugo Salus.
1237. Kafka's notes were written during his visit to the galleries of the Louvre; he evidently copied the titles of the paintings from their captions. The first painting noted by Kafka, the apple scene, is an exception: he probably means the altarpiece *La Vierge et l'enfant entourés d'anges, de saint Frédiano et de saint Augustin* by Fra Filippo Lippi, depicting the baby Jesus holding a pomegranate in his hand. At that time, this altarpiece—like the painting by Simone Martini noted by Kafka—hung in the Salle des primitifs italiens, Tintoretto's *Suzanne au bain* in the Salon Carré, and the other paintings listed by Kafka in the Grande Galerie. The erroneous assigning of Mantegna to the Venetian School and the attribution of *Apollo and Marsyas* to Raphael instead of Perugino, which had by then been revised, Kafka evidently reproduced from the captions on the picture frames.

    The memorandum for a reform of travel guides drafted by Brod and Kafka in Lugano, "Unser Millionenplan 'Billig,'" includes the lines: "Art gallery, on the cheap day. Only a small number of important pictures. But these in depth (in the manner of Kunstwart) educational" (BKR 191). This entry suggests that Kafka's listing of selected paintings—in the Louvre and in the Palace of Versailles (see p. 522 and note 1244)—was connected with the *Billig* plan.
1238. See note 218.
1239. The restaurant and Café-Concert des Ambassadeurs on the Champs-Elysées.
1240. *Compteurs français* (also called *taximètres*): term for the carriages for hire equipped with taximeters.
1241. See p. 531.
1242. This note and the two that follow probably relate to a visit to the Café-Concert des Ambassadeurs. See note 1239.
1243. Prosper Lafaye was a genre and history painter.

1244. This and the following descriptions of paintings were written during Kafka's visit to the art galleries of the Palace of Versailles.
1245. A painting by Louis-Philippe Crépin, a marine painter.
1246. A painting by Adolphe Roehn, a genre and history painter. See the picture in WB 111.
1247. For the Opéra-Comique, see also p. 526 and note 1254.
1248. The name of a chain of small, uniformly furnished cafés; see also p. 532.
1249. The name of a chain of uniformly furnished *bouillons,* simple restaurants with meals à la carte. See also p. 536.
1250. In a September 17, 1911, letter to Brod from Erlenbach, Kafka wrote: *For your war feuilleton* [i.e., for Brod's essay that appeared as "Das kriegerische Paris" in the magazine *März* in November 1911], *in Paris I copied the title of a book together with the blurb: [a second copy of the French text follows] I copied this in front of a bookshop on the Boulevard St Denis as a German literary spy. May it be of use to you!* (KKAB1 no. 208).
1251. This refers to the reading room in the Erlenbach Sanatorium on Lake Zurich, where Kafka stayed on his own from September 14 to 20, 1911, after the end of the trip with Brod and the latter's return to Prague.
1252. Refers to the 1805–1808 anthology of German folk songs *Des Knaben Wunderhorn* (*The Boy's Magic Horn*), ed. Achim von Arnim and Clemens Brentano.
1253. Friedrich Fellenberg-Egli was the director of the Erlenbach Sanatorium, also known as Fellenbergs Naturheilanstalt. Abbreviated in the rest of the entry as Hr. F.
1254. Memory of a visit to a performance in the Paris Opéra-Comique on September 8. See also pp. 534–535.
1255. Correct: irredentist. The term designates a political independence movement striving for the annexation of cut-off regions—in this case, of the Italian-speaking Ticino (Tessin)—to the motherland.
1256. Kafka's excerpts are based on his reading of Francisque Sarcey, *Le siège de Paris. impressions et souvenirs* (Paris, 1871).
1257. An entry evidently written during the train trip to Prague.
1258. Train carriages of a new type, first introduced in 1909 on international routes from Milan, these so-called *gemelli siamesi* (Italian for "Siamese twins") consisted of two carriages attached so that it was possible to cross from one into the other.
1259. The beginning of the Paris recollections written in Prague. The hotel where Kafka and Brod ultimately stayed was the Hotel Sainte Marie, rue de Rivoli 83 (BKR 105). A photograph of the hotel is reproduced in KP 129.
1260. See p. 532.
1261. Entries evidently not connected with Kafka's travel writings.
1262. Versailles steam tram; a double-decker "compressed-air" tram that took an hour and a half for the journey to Versailles. See KP 223, p. 224, for a photograph of this tram.
1263. With regard to this, Max Brod records in his travel diary: "Kafka does gymnastics very well on the rope" (BKR 123).
1264. The Maison Balzac, where Balzac lived from 1840 to 1848, had been established shortly before as a museum, on rue Raynouard 47.
1265. Musée Grévin was the wax museum founded in 1882 on the Boulevard Montmartre.
1266. An address book available to the public in all hotels and cafés.
1267. At the Théâtre-Français (also known as the Comédie-Française), Brod and Kafka attended a performance of Racine's *Phèdre*. See also pp. 537–538.
1268. In the entry beginning *Boot polishing scene . . .*, Kafka records his impressions of the performance of Georges Bizet's opera *Carmen,* which he attended with Brod, on September 8 at the Opéra-Comique.
1269. The title role was sung by the French soprano Geneviève Vix (1879–1939).
1270. A parallel entry is found in the First Notebook. See p. 21.

1271. See note 1249.
1272. An exhibition room of the Louvre adjacent to the longest hall (see note 1275), the Grande Galerie.
1273. Leonardo's *Mona Lisa* had been stolen from the Louvre on August 21, 1911, and wasn't found until two years later in Florence.
1274. For the Salle des primitifs italiens, see also p. 520 and note 1237.
1275. The Grande Galerie. See note 1237.
1276. On September 9, 1911, Brod and Kafka attended a performance of Racine's *Phèdre* in the Théâtre-Français. These notes convey Kafka's impressions before and during the theater visit.
1277. Like Duval (see note 1249), a restaurant belonging to a chain of *bouillons*.
1278. Aftereffect of the visit to the Louvre: *Les noces de Cana* by Veronese was exhibited in the Salon Carré, several works by Claude Lorrain in the Galerie français du XVIIe siècle.
1279. The actor playing the male lead in Racine's play was René Alexandre (1885–1946).
1280. Oenone was played by the actress Jeanne Even.
1281. Kafka was familiar with Friedrich Hebbel's description of a visit to the Théâtre-Français and of Rachel (for Elisa Rachel Félix, see also p. 60 and note 161) in his Paris diary on December 13, 1843 (see also note 174). He was probably also familiar with Flaubert's essay "Mademoiselle Rachel," which had been published in 1910 by Conard. The leading role in this performance was played by Madeleine Roch.
1282. For *Des Meeres und der Liebe Wellen,* see p. 502 and note 1185.
1283. Short for the guidebook published by Karl Baedeker. Kafka and Brod too evidently oriented themselves mainly with the help of Baedeker's guidebook *Paris et ses environs,* probably the 17th ed. (Leipzig, 1911). Under the date September 11, 1911, Brod wrote in his travel diary: "A Bädecker is among the most easily lost objects. . . . It happened to me several times that I returned and in a very bustling place saw the book lying very still where I had left it" (BKR 137–38).
1284. Kafka's descriptions of the ancient sculptures go back to his visit to the Musée des marbres antiques in the Louvre on September 10, 1911.
1285. A reminiscence of the Paris trip in October 1910: On October 16, Kafka had attended a horse race in the Paris suburb of Longchamp.
1286. Kafka's notes go back to an excursion to the Bois de Boulogne on September 10, 1911.
1287. Refers to the Lac inférieur, the largest of the artificial lakes in the Bois de Boulogne.
1288. Brod and Kafka had the impression that Germans were met with "hatred and contempt," which was why they spoke Czech in public. "We're traveling as Czechs or Poles," Max Brod noted (BKR 119).
1289. "Luna Park, which derived its name from the English term 'lunatic,' . . . was opened in late June 1909." Among the main attractions was a large artificial waterfall (KP 198ff.).
1290. Kafka later called this description of a traffic accident observed on September 8, 1911, *my little automobile story.* See p. 115 and note 268.
1291. The members of the Czech gymnastics and sports organization Sokol (Czech for "falcon") were known as "Sokols." Under the headline "Zum Sokolkongreß," the *Prager Tagblatt* of June 29, 1912, reported: "Yesterday after 6 o'clock in the evening the delegation of the Paris city council and the French Gymnasium students arrived here with the Franz Josef Railroad." The guests were greeted by the Prague mayor as well as a "crowd counting in the thousands."
1292. Opels Hotel garni was a hotel "for the less demanding" and was located on Blücherstraße 9 near the main train station. Griebens Reiseführer, *Leipzig und Umgebung,* 6th ed., rev. and expanded (Berlin, 1913), pp. 8–9.
1293. The construction of the new Leipzig main train station began in 1902; it had been in service since May 1, 1912, but the construction work was completed only in 1915.

1294. The Renaissance building on Grimmaische Straße (at the corner of Universitätsstraße) had been known as the Fürstenhaus (Princes' House) since the seventeenth century, "because several Altenburg princes had lived here as students." Griebens Reiseführer, *Leipzig*, p. 56.
1295. In 1912 there was new construction on the site of the wine cellar made famous by Goethe's *Faust* (Grimmaische Straße 2), including an expansion of the tavern.
1296. Brothel.
1297. Ernst Rowohlt; see note 561. The publishing house was located on Königstraße 10.
1298. The Deutsches Buchgewerbemuseum (German Book Trade Museum), established in 1885 with its collection dedicated to the history of the book as well as an extensive library and collection of papers, was housed on the top floor of the Deutsches Buchgewerbehaus (German Book Trade House) on Dolzstraße.
1299. Kafka probably visited one of the two centrally located public reading rooms: either the one on Blücherplatz, in the building of the former Dauernde Gewerbeausstellung (Permanent Trade Exhibition) near the main train station and the hotel, or the one on Johannisplatz, not far from the book trade museum.
1300. A vegetarian restaurant in the center of Leipzig, Schulstraße 8.
1301. Probably Richard Brandeis (1865–1944), who in 1911 had taken over the Jüdische Universalbibliothek (Universal Jewish Library), the Prague publishing house and bookshop founded by his father, Jakob Brandeis.
1302. The bronze statue of the young Goethe by Carl Seffner was erected in 1903 in front of the Alte Börse on the Naschmarkt.
1303. Kurt Pinthus described the wine tavern Wilhelms Weinstube as the "Leipzig headquarters of young Expressionism, . . . where the authors of the rapidly flourishing Rowohlt Verlag, from 1913 onward of the Kurt Wolff Verlag: poets and writers from Berlin, Prague, Vienna, Munich and Leipzig itself gathered daily." *Das Kinobuch. Dokumentarische Neu-Ausgabe des "Kinobuchs" von* 1913/1914, ed. Kurt Pinthus (Zürich, 1963), p. 9.
1304. The tragedy *Judas* by Gerdt von Bassewitz (1878–1923) premiered in Leipzig in 1912 and was—like his other dramas—published by Ernst Rowohlt.
1305. The writer Walter Hasenclever (1890–1940), one of Ernst Rowohlt and Kurt Wolff's literary advisers, was involved in the founding of the book series "Der Jüngste Tag."
1306. Café Français was located on Augustusplatz 4.
1307. Kurt Pinthus (1886–1975) was then a part-time, later full-time literary adviser and editor for the Ernst Rowohlt and Kurt Wolff publishing houses.
1308. The daily newspaper *Berliner Tageblatt*, founded in 1872.
1309. The historical tragedy by Hanna Rademacher premiered on June 28, 1912, in the Neues Theater in Leipzig.
1310. Brothel.
1311. Max Brod wrote in his travel diary: "Rowohlt asks him seriously for a book" (BKR 225). See also note 561.
1312. The Hotel Chemnitius was located on Karlsplatz. It was among the hotels "for the less demanding." Griebens Reiseführer, *Weimar und Umgebung*, 3rd rev. ed. (Berlin, 1914), p. 6.
1313. This refers to the Städtische Badeanstalt on the Ilm. The street Am Kirschberg runs parallel to the river.
1314. This refers to the Schwansee ponds, adjacent to a bathhouse (Schwansee-Bad on Schwanseestraße 24).
1315. Kafka's notes on his visit to the rooms, converted into a museum, where Schiller lived from 1802 to 1805.
1316. Grand Duchess Maria Pavlovna, daughter of Czar Paul I, was the wife of Grand Duke Karl Friedrich. See p. 552.
1317. Schiller's oldest daughter, Karoline, was married to the mining official Franz Carl Emanuel Junot.

1318. Johann Kaspar Schiller, *Die Baumzucht im Großen nach zwanzigjähriger Erfahrung im Kleinen* (*The Cultivation of Trees on a Large Scale after Twenty Years of Experience on a Small Scale*) (Neustrelitz, 1795; new ed.: Gießen, 1806).

1319. At the Goethe House, Kafka became acquainted with Margarethe Kirchner (1896–1954; called Grete in the entries that follow). Brod noted in his travel diary: "Kafka flirts successfully with the beautiful daughter of the caretaker" (BKR 226). In his 1928 novel *Zauberreich der Liebe* (*Magic Kingdom of Love*), in which Brod endowed a character named Richard Garta with character traits of Kafka's, he wrote: "A little, quite tender relationship forms between him and the pretty daughter of the caretaker of the Goethe House on the Frauenplan. . . . As a result, Garta and with him Christof are invited to the caretaker's residence, then go in and out of Goethe's residence with the beautiful girl as if at home, are admitted into the otherwise inaccessible garden, may look around Goethe's rooms outside visiting hours, thus undisturbed by the patter of tourists."

1320. Max Brod noted in his travel diary: "Kafka takes an excursion to Tiefurt with the family of the caretaker" (BKR 226).

1321. The Gasthaus zum weißen Schwan on Goetheplatz.

1322. This refers to the Goethe-Nationalmuseum.

1323. The summer residence of the Duchess Anna Amalia in the village of Tiefurt, about four kilometers from Weimar.

1324. The lady-in-waiting Luise von Göchhausen.

1325. This street meets Goetheplatz.

1326. Today: Frauenplan; not identical with today's Goetheplatz.

1327. This refers to the small dead-end street Am Palais.

1328. See the facsimile of Kafka's surviving drawing on a notepad sheet (privately owned) in Kafka, *Tagebücher: Kommentarband*, p. 245.

1329. The inscription on the stone plaque, chiseled in capital letters and without punctuation marks, reads:

> HIER GEDACHTE STILL EIN LIEBENDER SEINER GELIEBTEN
> HEITER SPRACH ER ZU MIR WERDE MIR ZEUGE DU STEIN
> DOCH ERHEBE DICH NICHT DU HAST NOCH VIELE GESELLEN
> IEDEM FELSEN DER FLUR DIE MICH DEN GLYKLICHEN NAEHRT
> IEDEM BAUME DES WALDES UM DEN ICH WANDERND MICH SCHLINGE
> RUF ICH WEIHEND UND FROH BLEIBE MIR DENKMAL DES GLYKS
> DIR ALLEIN VERLEIH ICH DIE STIMME WIE UNTER DER MENGE
> EINEN DIE MUSE SICH WAEHLT FREUNDLICH DIE LIPPEN IHM KYSST

Goethe had it mounted in 1782 in memory of his encounter with Charlotte von Stein.

1330. Kafka means Erfurter Straße; due to its length, a distinction is made between inner (the part located in the city center area) and outer Erfurter Straße. See p. 551.

1331. Notes on a visit to Franz Liszt's villa, which had been converted into a museum.

1332. In the Liszt House, Kafka might have seen a picture of the singer Pauline Viardot-Garcia (1821–1910), who had taken piano lessons with Franz Liszt; she celebrated triumphant successes on all the great opera stages of Europe and later enjoyed a legendary reputation as a singing teacher.

1333. The high-class hotel Russischer Hof on Karlsplatz.

1334. Regarding their visit to the Cabaret Tivoli, Brod wrote: "2 ladies—blood-red stockings, black velvet skirts, with a red laced jacket—high German helmets—shako. . . . A magician, old lady contortionist. Kafka prays for her, applauds a great deal. He sighs and is sad" (BKR 228–229).

1335. See the picture in BKR 224.

1336. Wolfgang von Oettingen (1859–1943), then-director of the Goethe National Museum and the Goethe and Schiller archive.

1337. Between 1761 and 1766, the building on Fürstenplatz 1, erected by Duke Johann Wilhelm in the sixteenth century as a garden palace and known as the Grünes Schloß (Green Castle), was converted by Duchess Anna Amalia of Saxe-Weimar-Eisenach into a library. The second-floor Rococo Hall was the gem of the newly designed building. Today the collection bears the name of its patron: Duchess Anna Amalia Library.

1338. Bust of Goethe by Alexander Trippel; this refers to the second one, completed in 1790.

1339. Here and in the rest of the entry, this refers to Carl August of Saxe-Weimar-Eisenach.

1340. A marble bust completed in 1831 by Pierre-Jean David d'Angers.

1341. From 1797 until his death, Goethe had taken over the supervision of the grand ducal library. At his suggestion, an extension was built connecting the library with the old town tower (Stadtturm) from the year 1453. From 1821 to 1825, the tower itself was converted into book stacks, and a neo-Gothic front building was added. The construction work on the historic library building was not completed until 1849—Goethe's centennial.

1342. Franz Passow, a classical philologist acquainted with Goethe, taught from 1807 to 1810 at the Weimar Gymnasium.

1343. The poet and dramatist Zacharias Werner, in the course of his frequent and extensive travels, stayed for some time in Weimar, where he met Goethe.

1344. Among the busts displayed in the great hall and on the railings of the gallery of the grand ducal library in Weimar is that of the composer Christoph Willibald Ritter von Gluck (by Jean-Antoine Houdon).

1345. This refers to the spiral staircase installed in the old town tower (see above), originally from the Osterburg in Weida, the central supporting pillar of which is fashioned from a single oak trunk "by a prisoner." Griebens Reiseführer, *Weimar,* p. 38.

1346. Max Brod noted in his travel diary: "A boy, 11 years old, Fritz Wentzky joins us. . . . He wants to be a carpenter, his father is one too" (BKR 230).

1347. In the Park an der Ilm, designed by Grand Duke Carl August in collaboration with Goethe and modeled on the Wörlitzer Park, a building in the form of a Roman temple was erected in 1798.

1348. Goethe had this hermitage erected in the Park an der Ilm in 1778 in honor of the name day of Duchess Luise; it was also known as the Luisenkloster (Luise Monastery).

1349. In an artificial ruin near the Bark Hut (see note 1349) stands the marble William Shakespeare monument created by Otto Lessing and unveiled in 1904, the only monument to the English dramatist on the European continent.

1350. During his second stay in Paris, Kafka attended a performance of George Bizet's opera on September 8, 1911. See August-September 1911 Trip, pp. 534–535.

1351. The publisher Eugen Diederichs (1867–1930).

1352. The temple-like ducal vault built by Grand Duke Carl August in 1824 is located in the Weimar Cemetery on Amalienstraße, in the southern part of the city. It is the final resting place of the members of the grand ducal House of Saxe-Weimar-Eisenach; Goethe and Schiller too are interred here.

1353. The essayist Kurt Hiller (1885–1972), then a leading figure in the literary life of Berlin, had championed Max Brod's early work; his mother was named Ella, née Singer (1862–1936).

1354. The Weimar archive contains, among other holdings, the literary estates of Schiller, Goethe, Herder, and Freiligrath.

1355. The Goethe and Schiller Archive includes letters from Jakob Michael Reinhold Lenz from the period of May 1775 to November 1776 (fifteen to Herder, six to Sophie von La Roche, and one each to Goethe, Frau von Stein, and Hofrat von Kalb), as well as an April 1780 letter to F. J. Bertuch from St. Petersburg. Brod too studied the Lenz letters on view there: "Heated letter from Lenz to Herder" (BKR

233). When Kafka received the newly published two-volume edition of Lenz's correspondence from Kurt Wolff in early 1918, he wrote to him: *the book, which I wished for long before I knew of your intention to publish it, is thereby worth twice as much to me* (KWBr 47). See also p. 227 and note 576.

1356. From Goethe's poem "Generalbeichte" (1802), part of the "Gesellige Lieder" cycle.
1357. The manuscript of this poem shows the handwriting of the seven-year-old Goethe.
1358. Karl Wilhelm Jerusalem committed suicide on October 29, 1772, with the pistols borrowed from Johann Christian Kestner.
1359. The grand ducal Belvedere Castle, about four kilometers from Weimar, can be reached by the Belvedereallee, an alley lined with lindens. In the castle, there are ceiling paintings by Adam Friedrich Oeser. In the neighboring coach house is a collection of historic carriages. In the castle park, designed by Duchess Anna Amalia and further elaborated by Goethe, there's a nature theater designed by Goethe.
1360. The dramatist, writer, and essayist Paul Ernst (1866–1933), subsequently abbreviated P. E., lived with his second wife and his three children in a villa, Am Horn 45/47.
1361. The dramatist and writer Ernst von Wildenbruch, who died in 1909, had at times lived in Weimar.
1362. See note 1360.
1363. The Franciscan father Expeditus Schmidt (1868–1939; originally Hermann Schmidt).
1364. The writer Johannes Schlaf (1862–1941) was an early exponent of the naturalist literary movement in his collaborative work with Arno Holz.
1365. Johannes Schlaf lived at Lassenstraße 31. He occupied two attic rooms of a Jugendstil house built in 1904, one of which adjoined an unfinished garret.
1366. In later years Schlaf attempted to refute the heliocentric system and to reintroduce the geocentric system, contrary to the findings of the exact sciences. He espoused this conviction in numerous publications.
1367. The woodland known as the Webicht, northeast of Weimar.
1368. In the park (Gleimgarten) in Halberstadt. The notes from July 7, 1912, were written in Halberstadt, where Kafka spent the night.
1369. By personally addressing Max Brod, the travel diary in this passage explicitly becomes a diary letter. The diary pages written after their stay together in Weimar Kafka sent in installments to Brod in Prague.
1370. The novel *Ein Augenblick im Paradies* (*A Moment in Paradise*) by Ida Boy-Ed, published in 1912 by Ullstein.
1371. Streets in Halberstadt.
1372. At the time Halberstadt had one of the largest Orthodox Jewish communities in Germany.
1373. One of the "Lichtlufthäuschen" ("light-and-air huts") in Rudolf Just's Jungborn sanatorium in the Harz Mountains, at the foot of the Brocken, near Stapelburg and Ilsenburg.
1374. The members of this cultural reform movement oriented their lives according to the teachings of Zoroaster, with particular emphasis on his hygienic instructions in the broadest sense. Since 1908 the association had its own monthly journal, *Mazdaznan. Zeitschrift für Zarathustrische Philosophie, Körperpflege und Diätetik.*
1375. Judging by the context, the destination of this walk was the Landerziehungsheim Ilsenburg, a country boarding school established in 1898 by Hermann Lietz, founder of the German country boarding school movement, as the first in a series of such schools in Germany. Gustav Wyneken, who originally worked with Lietz, later parted ways with him and co-founded with Paul Geheeb the Freie Schulgemeinde (Free School Community) Wickersdorf. The conversation topics indicated by Kafka suggest a discussion of the tradition launched by Lietz.

1376. Hermann Cohen founded the Neo-Kantian School, with whose work Walter Kinkel (see p. 558 and note 1381) dealt extensively.
1377. Kafka later corresponded with the municipal official and recalled him on the occasion of a trip Felice Bauer took to Breslau. See pp. 228 and 229.
1378. Founder of the naturopathic sanatorium, which by then was run by his son Rudolf.
1379. Day on which paper flowers were handed out in exchange for charitable contributions. This custom, prevalent at the time, provoked sharp protest.
1380. Here and in the entries that follow, Dr. Schiller. See p. 556 and note 1377.
1381. This probably refers to the 1907 book *Aus Traum und Wirklichkeit der Seele. Stille Gedanken aus einsamen Stunden*, by the philosopher and poet Walter Kinkel.
1382. Refers to Eugen Kühnemann, *Schiller* (Munich, 1905).
1383. Kafka is referring to a German edition of Gustave Flaubert's letters on his work, *Briefe über seine Werke*, which he had read before setting out on his trip. See p. 222 and note 559. The passage he mentions begins with the words: "It may be a perverse taste, but I love prostitution."
1384. Kafka illustrates the "lack of a true common language" with the local girls by noting their varying levels of comprehension of different ways of asking in German whether they have eaten dinner yet, that is, whether they have genachtmahlt, had their Abendbrot, or gefuttert. The three words exhibit regional particularities and distinct registers of formality.
1385. The *Vorwärts* (*Forward*), the "Central Organ of the Social Democratic Party of Germany," had been published since 1876, first in Leipzig, later in Berlin.
1386. See note 1070.
1387. Kafka is referring to the poet (and anthroposophist) Christian Morgenstern, the painter Hans Baluschek (known for his depictions of Berlin urban life), the poet and author Hans Brandenburg, and the essayist Felix Poppenberg.
1388. Rudolf Hans Bartsch's 1911 novel *Zwölf aus der Steiermark.*
1389. In the Viennese parliament building, the Eleventh Zionist Congress was held from September 2 to 9, 1913, and the Second International Congress for Rescue Services and Accident Prevention from September 9 to 13.
1390. The director of the AUVA, Robert Marschner (see note 69), whom Kafka accompanied to the congress on Rescue Services and Accident Prevention.
1391. Regarding the stay with Otto Pick (see note 489) in Vienna, on September 16, 1913, Kafka wrote to Max Brod from Venice: *Literature, which has long shown me no favor, has again remembered me, by keeping P.* [Pick] *in Vienna. Judging by my previous experience, I can travel only with you, or, much worse, but still bearable, alone* (KKAB2 no. 611).
1392. Heiligenstadt was part of Vienna's nineteenth district.
1393. Theophil Hansen was the architect of the Viennese parliament.
1394. See note 1396.
1395. This could be the same person mentioned on p. 285 (see also note 673); but it is also conceivable that Kafka was referring to the name of the protagonist in Else Lasker-Schülers prose work *Der Malik. Eine Kaisergeschichte mit Bildern und Zeichnungen* (Berlin, 1919). In the form of letters to the "Blue Rider Franz Marc," an earlier version of the first part of this work was serialized in various magazines from 1913 to 1917, beginning with the piece "Briefe und Bilder," which appeared on September 6, 1913, in the magazine *Die Aktion. Wochenschrift für Politik, Literatur, Kunst.* There's reason to surmise that Kafka and Pick discussed this publication that day (*literary chatter with Pick*) and that Kafka's *repugnant dream* that night was connected with it. Pick was close with Else Lasker-Schüler and is even mentioned in the publication: *"my dear Prague comrades: Paul Leppin, Otto Pick and Franz Werfel"*; in February his efforts on her behalf had already provoked a strong reaction from Kafka: *Her prose too is bothersome to me . . . at work in it is the indiscriminately twitching brain of a high-strung city dweller. . . . I don't know exactly why, but I always just imagine her as a drunkard dragging herself through*

the coffeehouses at night (KKAB2 no. 431). In her contribution to *Die Aktion,* she wrote: "O, ich hatte einen boshaften Traum; allerdings mein sehnlichster Wunsch erfüllte sich—ich war plötzlich König, in Theben—trug einen goldenen Mantel, einen Stern in Falten um meine Schulter gelegt, auf dem Kopf die Krone des Malik. Ich war Malik" ("O, I had a wicked dream, although my most fervent wish came true—I was suddenly king, in Thebes—wore a golden coat, a star draped around my shoulders, on my head the crown of the Malik. I was Malik"). The name *Malik* corresponds to the Hebrew *Melech* and means roughly "king" or "leader."

1396. Heinrich Laube, *Franz Grillparzers Lebensgeschichte* (Stuttgart, 1884). The following day, in a card to Felice Bauer, Kafka referred to page 164 of this book: *Staying Hotel Matschakerhof, where Grillparzer ate lunch, as his biographer Laube says "simple but good"* (KKAB2 no. 603).

1397. See note 383.

1398. Albert Ehrenstein. See note 719.

1399. The vegetarian restaurant Thalysia on Oppolzergasse 4, near the Vienna Burgtheater. (The owner was Louise Lederer.)

1400. See the picture in WB 172.

1401. Theodor Weltsch. See note 383.

1402. The Hofburgtheater offered Maurice Maeterlinck's drama on September 7, 1913.

1403. Klara Thein, from the Zionist District Committee of Prague. See note 776.

Chronology

1883 Born July 3 in Prague to Hermann Kafka (1852–1931) and his wife, Julie, née Löwy (1856–1934).

1885 Birth of his brother Georg, who dies at the age of fifteen months.

1887 Birth of his brother Heinrich, who dies at the age of six months.

1889 Starts German-language elementary school. Birth of his sister Gabriele (Elli; d. 1941).

1890 Birth of his sister Valerie (Valli; d. 1942).

1892 Birth of his sister Ottilie (Ottla; d. 1943).

1893 Attends German-language secondary school (*Gymnasium*).

1896 Bar mitzvah.

1901 Graduation from *Gymnasium*. Matriculation at the German-language section of Charles University.

1902 Summer vacation at the home of his uncle Siegfried Löwy, a country doctor, in Triesch. Meets lifelong friend Max Brod (1884–1968).

1904 Begins writing "Description of a Struggle," his earliest surviving work.

1905 Love affair during a summer sanatorium stay in Zuckmantel.

1906 Doctorate in law. Begins a one-year legal internship in Prague's courts.

1907 Begins writing "Wedding Preparations in the Country." Employed at the Prague branch of the Italian insurance company Assicurazioni Generali.

1908 Enters the Workers' Accident Insurance Institute for the Kingdom of Bohemia. Publishes eight short prose pieces under the title *Contemplation* in the journal *Hyperion*.

1909 Earliest surviving diary entries. Meets Franz Werfel. Vacation with Max Brod and his brother Otto in Riva on Lake Garda. Publication of "The

Airplanes in Brescia" in the daily newspaper *Bohemia* and two dialogues from "Description of a Struggle" in *Hyperion*: "Conversation with the Praying Man" and "Conversation with the Drunken Man."

1910 Publication in *Bohemia* of five short prose pieces later included in the collection *Contemplation*. Promotion to the position of *Concipist* (a clerk responsible for drafting legal documents) at the institute. Trip to Paris with Max and Otto Brod (October). Trip to Berlin (December).

1911 Trip to Friedland and Reichenberg (January–February). Trip with Max Brod to Switzerland, northern Italy, and Paris, followed by a sanatorium stay in Erlenbach near Zurich (August–September). Attends performances of a Yiddish theater troupe in Prague and befriends the actor Jizchak Löwy (1887–1942). Founds an asbestos factory with his brother-in-law Karl Hermann.

1912 Delivers a public lecture on the Yiddish language. Publication of "First Chapter of the Book 'Richard and Samuel' by Max Brod and Franz Kafka: The First Long Train Trip (Prague-Zurich)" in the magazine *Herder-Blätter.* Trip to Leipzig and Weimar, followed by a stay at the Jungborn Sanatorium in the Harz Mountains (June–July). In Leipzig meets the publishers Ernst Rowohlt and Kurt Wolff, who encourage him to send them a manuscript. Meets Felice Bauer (1887–1960) and begins correspondence with her. Writes "The Judgment." Begins work on the novel *The Missing Person* (also known as *Amerika*). Writes "The Transformation" (also known in English as "The Metamorphosis"). Publication of *Contemplation* by Kurt Wolff (December).

1913 Abandons work on *The Missing Person.* Visits Felice Bauer in Berlin (March). Publication of *The Stoker,* the first chapter of *The Missing Person,* in book form by Kurt Wolff. Publication of "The Judgment" in the literary yearbook *Arkadia.* Befriends the writer Ernst Weiß (1882–1940). Trip to Vienna for a conference on accident prevention and a visit to the Eleventh Zionist Congress, followed by a trip via Trieste, Venice, Verona, and Desenzano to Riva (September–October). Relationship with "the Swiss girl" during a sanatorium stay in Riva. Meets Grete Bloch (1892–1944) and begins correspondence with her. Promotion to the position of vice-secretary at the institute.

1914 Official engagement to Felice Bauer in Berlin (June). Dissolution of the engagement (July). Trip via Lübeck to Marielyst. Begins work on the novel *The Trial.* Writes "In the Penal Colony" and the fragment "The Village Schoolteacher."

1915 Abandons work on *The Trial.* Reunion with Felice Bauer. Publication of *The Transformation* in book form by Kurt Wolff. Receives a donation from the German playwright Carl Sternheim of his winnings from the Fontane Prize for literature. Moves out of his parents' apartment and into a rented room.

1916 Vacation with Felice Bauer in Marienbad. Publication of *The Judgment* in book form by Kurt Wolff. Begins doing his writing in a house rented by his sister Ottla in the Castle District. Writes several of the pieces later collected in *A Country Doctor.* Public reading of "In the Penal Colony" in Munich.

1917 Second engagement to Felice Bauer (July). Begins to learn Hebrew. Diagnosis of tuberculosis (September). Takes leave from the institute and lives with his sister Ottla in the rural village of Zürau. Begins writing aphorisms. Dissolution of second engagement (December).

1918 Resumes work at the institute (May). Falls sick with the Spanish flu (October). Travels to Schelesen for a convalescent stay (November).

1919 Engagement to Julie Wohryzek (1891–1944). Publication of *In the Penal Colony* in book form by Kurt Wolff. Writes long, posthumously published letter to his father, never delivered to its addressee.

1920 Promotion to the position of secretary at the institute. Three-month convalescent stay in Meran. Begins correspondence with Czech journalist and translator Milena Pollak, née Jesenská. Publication of *A Country Doctor: Short Stories* by Kurt Wolff. Visits Milena Pollak in Vienna. End of the engagement to Julie Wohryzek. Begins eight-month sanatorium stay in Matliary in the High Tatras.

1921 Befriends the medical student Robert Klopstock (1899–1972). Resumes work at the institute (August). Takes leave again after eight weeks. Publication of "The Bucket Rider" in the *Prager Presse.*

1922 Travels to Spindelmühle in the Giant Mountains. Begins work on the novel *The Castle.* Writes "A Hunger Artist" and "Investigations of a Dog." Three-month stay with his sister Ottla in Planá in southern Bohemia. Granted "temporary" retirement by the institute (July). Publication of "A Hunger Artist" in the literary journal *Die neue Rundschau.*

1923 Last surviving diary entry. Meets Dora Diamant (1898–1952) while on vacation with his sister Elli in Müritz on the Baltic Sea (July). Moves to Berlin to live with Dora Diamant (September). Writes "A Little Woman" and "The Burrow."

1924 Writes "Josephine the Singer." Diagnosed with laryngeal tuberculosis. Accompanied by Dora Diamant and Robert Klopstock to a sanatorium in Kierling. Dies June 3. Buried June 11 in the New Jewish Cemetery in Prague. Publication of *A Hunger Artist: Four Stories* by Die Schmiede (August).

Index

Index of Kafka's Works

Entries in *italics* refer to illustrations.

General Index

Works are listed under author. Locations in Prague are listed under "Prague."

METAMORPHOSIS AND OTHER STORIES

Franz Kafka

'Gentlemen, esteemed academicians! You do me the honour of inviting me to submit a report to the academy on my previous life as an ape'

Kafka's masterpiece of unease and black humour, *Metamorphosis*, the story of an ordinary man transformed into an insect, is brought together in this collection with the rest of his works that he thought worthy of publication. It includes *Contemplation*, a collection of his earlier short studies; *The Judgement*, written in a single night of frenzied creativity; *The Stoker*, the first chapter of a novel set in America; and an eye witness account of an air display. Together, these stories, fragments and miniature gems reveal the breadth of his vision, his sense of the absurd, and above all his acute, uncanny wit.

Translated with an Introduction by Michael Hofmann

ISBN: 978 0 24 137 255 5

THE BURROW

Franz Kafka

'They come, you hear the scratch of their claws just below you in the ground, and already you are lost'

Strange beasts, night terrors, absurd bureaucrats and sinister places abound in this collection of stories by Franz Kafka. Some are less than a page long, others more substantial; all were unpublished in his lifetime. These matchless short works range from the gleeful miniature horror 'Little Fable' to the off-kilter humour of 'Investigations of a Dog', and from the elaborate waking nightmare of 'Building the Great Wall of China' to the creeping unease of 'The Burrow', where a nameless creature's labyrinthine hiding place turns into a trap of fear and paranoia.

Translated by Michael Hofmann

ISBN: 978 0 24 137 259 3

THE TRIAL

Franz Kafka

'Somebody must have laid false information against Josef K., for he was arrested one morning without having done anything wrong'

Josef K., an ordinary bank clerk, is accused of a crime he did not commit, whose nature is never revealed to him. As he tries to defend his innocence amid a labyrinthine world of anonymous bureaucrats, stifling courtrooms and casual brutality, he becomes increasingly uncertain of his fate and spirals towards destruction. Kafka's gripping, unnerving parable about the nature of terror and the futility of human life is at once nightmarish and chillingly real.

Translated and with an Introduction by Idris Parry

ISBN: 978 0 24 137 256 2

THE CASTLE

Franz Kafka

'K., he said, had taken the rousing from sleep, the interrogation, and the obligatory threat of expulsion from the country with a very bad grace'

The Castle is the story of K., the unwanted land surveyor who is never to be admitted to the Castle nor accepted in the village, and yet cannot go home. As he experiences certainty and doubt, hope and fear, and reason and nonsense, K.'s struggle in the absurd, labyrinthine world where he finds himself seem to reveal an inexplicable truth about existence. Kafka began *The Castle* in 1922 and it was never finished, yet this, the last of his great novels, feels strangely complete.

Translated by J. A. Underwood
With an Introduction by Idris Parry

ISBN: 978 0 24 137 257 9

AMERIKA

Franz Kafka

'He had almost forgotten he was in the uncertain hold of a ship moored to the coast of an unknown continent'

Karl Rossmann has been banished by his parents to America, following a family scandal. There, with unquenchable optimism, he throws himself into the strangest experiences that lie before him as he slowly makes his way into the interior of the great continent. Although Kafka's first novel can be read as a disturbing allegory of modern life in all its alienation, it is also a novel infused with blitheness and exuberance.

Translated with an Introduction by Michael Hofmann

ISBN: 978 0 24 137 258 6

THE NOTEBOOKS OF MALTE LAURIDS BRIGGE

Rainer Maria Rilke

'Now the heart had been pierced, our heart,
the heart of our family'

While his old furniture rots in storage, Malte Laurids Brigge lives in a cheap room in Paris, with little but a library reader's card to distinguish him from the city's untouchables. Every person he sees seems to carry their death with them, and he becomes obsessed by thoughts of mortality, ghosts and his aristocratic family, of which only he remains. The sole novel by one of the greatest writers of poetry in German, the semi-autobiographical *Notebooks* is a feverish meditation on being young and alone, full of existential disquiet, unsettling beauty and lyrical brilliance.

Translated with an Introduction by Michael Hulse

ISBN: 978 0 14 118 221 6

THE JOYOUS SCIENCE

Friedrich Nietzsche

'God is dead; but given the ways of men, perhaps for millennia to come there will be caves in which His shadow will be shown'

Friedrich Nietzsche described *The Joyous Science* as a book of 'exuberance, restlessness, contrariety and April showers'. A deeply personal and affirmative work, it straddles his middle and late periods and contains some of the most important ideas he would ever express in his writing. Moving from a critique of conventional morality, the arts and modernity to an exhilarating doctrine of self-emancipation, this playful combination of aphorisms, poetry and prose is a treasure trove of philosophical insights, brought to new life in R. Kevin Hill's clear, graceful translation.

Translated and edited with an Introduction and Notes by
R. Kevin Hill

ISBN: 978 0 14 119 539 1